Jane doing Penance.

JANE SHORE;

OR,

LONDON IN THE REIGN OF EDWARD THE FOURTH.

An Historical Romance.

BY THE AUTHOR OF "THE BLACK MONK," "VARNEY THE VAMPYRE," &c.

——— "And thou wert beautiful;
With all thy errors, thou wert yet beloved,
And gentle pity breathes a sigh o'er thy despair."

LONDON:
PUBLISHED BY E. LLOYD, 12, SALISBURY-SQUARE.

1846.

JANE SHORE;

OR,

LONDON IN THE REIGN OF EDWARD IV

An Historical Romance.

BY THE AUTHOR OF "ADA, THE BETRAYED," ETC.

CHAPTER I.

The Fete.

O, what a mansion have those vices got,
That for their habitation chose out thee!—SHAKSPERE.

LONDON, on the sixteenth of October, 1465, being the fourth year of the reign of Edward the Fourth, presented a scene of animation, gaiety, and splendour, which the extended resources and enormous wealth of the " first of cities" might even now in vain attempt to imitate. With our commercial prosperity we have grown sadder, some say wiser; but be that as it may, our ancestors certainly possessed a rare taste for " outward bravery," and were more luxurious in their fetes and public demonstrations than we, in our utmost pride of pomp and show, have ever attempted to be.

The narrow, ill-paved streets were thronged with passengers of all grades and conditions in life, " for the times had been out of joint," and much of the exclusive pride of

"Clear the way, clear the way!" cried a buxom dame, who was preceded by a diminutive, trembling piece of humanity, of about the fourth of her own girth; "clear the way, I tell thee, Mappletoft. Am I to be pushed here and there by every ragamuffin 'prentice and lawyer's boy?"

"No, my dear, no," said the small pioneer. "I pray ye, gentles, give way. I—I—dear heart! dear heart!"

"Ha, Master Mappletoft, art there, man?" cried a swaggering, broad-shouldered, roystering blade, attired in faded black; "art there, man? Ho! ho! ho!"

"Yes, Bully Bluster," screamed Mrs. Mappletoft, "and I'm here, too. Marry come up, and when am I to be paid for the slashed doublet and the ——"

"Devil!" muttered the faded gallant, as he bustled through the crowd amid a general laugh.

The loud braying of trumpets now sounded from far down the Chepe, and there was a denser pressure among the crowd.

"What now," cried one; "is it the king?"

"I trow," replied another, "it is the Duke of Norfolk, or my Lord Hastings, with his troop, coming to hold possession of the gallery that is even now finishing at the end of the Chepe: nay, perchance 'tis Vassa."

"Vassa, the cunning Italian, with his sleights of hand and his devilries; I like him not, friends, I like him not," said a little oily citizen, whose furred mantle bespoke him a warden of one of the incorporated trades.

Again the blast of the trumpets came full upon the air, and a small body of horsemen were seen pressing down the narrow way.

"By your good leave, gentles," said a low, mild voice, as its owner, a small man, with a pointed beard after the Flemish fashion, strove to push himself through the throng towards an opening leading to the southward of Chepesyde.

"Know ye him? know ye him?" whispered a clothier to those about him.

"Aye, truly," said one. "'Tis Master Caxton."

"Humph!" muttered the clothier, crossing himself. "'Tis said he has bad dealings."

"And is it not a shame and a disgrace," cried the little oily warden, putting himself into an oratorical attitude,—"a shame and a disgrace, I repeat ——"

"What's a shame, eh?" said a vintner. "Ale is eightpence a flagon, and wine, since the new half groates ——"

"A plague on thee and the groates too!" cried the little warden. "Here is this Caxton has a room in the blessed abbey of St. Peter's. Cross yourselves, gentles! cross yourselves! A room in the blessed abbey of St. Peter's! And why?—why?"

Caxton had glided on. The father of the art of printing in England was shrunk from in the crowd as a suspicious character.

The crowd now parted to admit a body of horse, under the command of the Duke of Norfolk, to pass onward.

The party was saluted by various cries, indicative of the disturbed political condition of the times.

"York—York!" cried some. "Long live King Henry!" was shouted by another. "A white rose! hurrah! Edward for ever! No rose nobles! Lancaster! York! Hurrah!" White and red roses were flung up in the air by partisans of the different factions.

"No York!—no York! King Henry!" shouted a man, just before the Duke of Norfolk's horse.

"No brawling, knaves!" cried the duke, as he struck the intruder to the earth with his heavy gilt baton.

"Hurrah!" shouted the crowd; and it was immediately evident that the York party were by far the most numerous. The soldiers pressed onwards, and took possession of the principal entrance to the immense gallery and stage, which had been erected at the end of Chepesyde, and which was capable of containing five thousand persons.

The king had only announced his intention of visiting the city on the day previous, and the workmen were still finishing the gallery when the guard arrived.

The whole structure was erected for the purpose of an entertainment, of a highly popular character at the period, by a celebrated posture-master and juggler, one Antonius Vassa, who, for the first time, was to exhibit before the young monarch.

CHAPTER II.

Jane.

Twin stars of Heaven were her eyes,
Her hair a golden sheen. HERRICK.

LONDON, in 1465, consisted principally but of one long straggling line of street, commencing on the river side of the Strand, and terminating a few hundred paces beyond the site of the present Mansion House. From this line of street, there were many off streets to the northward, into the open country; and to the south of Chepesyde, down to the bank of the Thames, was a mass of mean mud and thatched residences in such close proximity, and enjoying so truly a republic of dirt and filth, that Stowe might well grievously complain of the "noyous state of ye city," in which there was much danger—"pitfalles, and men of loose repute."

Chepesyde, as we have before mentioned, was the principal mart of trade, and that trade was to the greatest extent carried on with the court, the numerous gallants belonging to which were the principal consumers of costly stuffs and showy fabrics.

It is but comparatively in modern times that the different ranks in society have ceased to be distinguished the one from the other by dress and general appointments. At the period of which we speak in our tale, there was no difficulty in picking a lord from a mercer; and, in fact, we find that not only King Edward the Fourth, but several of the monarchs succeeding him, were in the habit of issuing what his celestial majesty would call a special edict for the suppression of vain bravery in costume, and "mortale vanitie in hose and doublet."

The parliament, which Edward in a rare fit of liberality called together, brought up an enactment regulating the length of the points of shoes, and fixing the extent of their elongation to a measure which we should think outrageously ridiculous.

If there existed a marked distinction between the different classes of society with regard to dress, there was as remarkable a difference between the habitations of the wealthy and noble, and those of the humbler classes. The houses, or rather hovels, of the poor, were composed of plaster and of timber, covered with thatch, while many really noble structures of solid masonry were to be found in and around the ancient city: these were, however, mingled indiscriminately with the meanest buildings. Henry, Earl of Northumberland, had a handsome mansion in Fenchurch-street. The Earl of Essex's palace, for a palace it was, was in Throgmorton-street; and both the bishops of London and Ely lived in Aldersgate-street.

There were straggling buildings from Lombarde-streate to the Tower, but not sufficient to be entitled to the name of a regular street. The Surrey side of the river was a swamp; and the traffic across London bridge was extremely limited.

There were few public buildings of any note; and of those that were, religious establishments formed the greater number.

The want of a regular system of national finance in the early periods of English history, was the prolific source of many of the civil wars which this country has been afflicted with. The nobility were proud, ambitious, and ignorant—ignorant of that fundamental principle which, for their own preservation, should have been their basis of action, namely, union among themselves. Their incessant petty jealousies, their eternal feuds, continued from generation to generation, would, with an intelligent and educated people, have ensured their extinction as a class. The early monarchs of England were mere puppets in the hands of some few score strong, wealthy, and violent men. Thus, "in the king's name," the most extraordinary and contradictory acts were committed, according as one party or another held the royal person in mock majesty, but in real durance.

These incessant broils of the nobility were unchecked even in the presence of the sovereign, and swords were several times drawn before the face of Henry the Sixth, by the turbulent men who professed to be his most dutiful subjects.

Well might these shadows of royalty—these kings that grasped but the phantom of a sceptre, exclaim,—

——————"Then happy low, lie down!
Uneasy lies the head that wears a crown."

There appear to have been some great difficulties in the way of direct taxation in early English history, for we continually find the monarch crippled for want of pecuniary resources, and placed at the mercy of those who could command money or credit. The greater part of the resources of the king were drawn from subsidies, or voluntary subscriptions on the parts of the nobility with whom he happened to be in favour, and the wealthier citizens. The common people gave nothing at all to the state; they merely filled up the streets, and looked on at the game of politics, and the struggles for power, being as ready to give

"Their sweet voices"

to one party as to another.

In fact, the whole of Europe was in an unhealthy and disturbed condition. The governments were generally weak, and lacked entirely the power of putting down commotions and broils between the overbearing and riotous patricians.

All who were rich enough kept, as it were, a little standing army, entirely independent of the state, and the barons declared war upon each other, and fought out their quarrels like so many petty sovereigns, without much interference from a government which was only maintained, as a small kingdom is frequently upheld, by the mutual jealousies of those who could at any time crush it.

One noble, for some real or fancied wrong, would assemble his followers, and lay siege to the castle of another in the open face of day, without troubling the state with the matter, and murder, rapine, and robbery stalked through Europe, unchecked by any one powerful authority.

Each castle or feudal dwelling thus became, as it were, a little kingdom; and so liable to change hands were these residences, that each was provided with numerous secret passages, and concealed modes of ingress and egress, as well for the purpose of concealing property of value, as in danger to admit of the worsted owner at the last extremity of his fortunes.

The continental barons took all their mutations of fortune in a very easy way, and the state took very little notice of the matter. The principal sufferers were the common people—the inhabitants of the surrounding villages, that were considered as much the individual property of the owner of the castle that frowned from a neighbouring eminence, as any of the cattle that fattened on the pastures.

It was ostensibly for the purpose of thanking the citizens for a liberal subsidy recently granted to him, that Edward had announced his intention of making a royal progress through the city, although it will be seen that gratitude for the past had not so much to do with the matter, as expectations of the future.

The throng of persons at the upper end of Chepesyde, where the gallery was erected, was now so great, that it was with considerable difficulty any one could proceed westward. Many petty squabbles among the *mobility* had already occurred, usually terminating in a few hard blows, and the spilling of what Froissart calls "*red puddle*," alias common blood.

Pressing gently, yet firmly through the dense throng, were two persons, who, although there was a similarity in their dresses, presented otherwise the most striking contrast.

The elder of the two presented to the eye that clear, candid, open countenance, which our Saxon ancestors have bequeathed to so many of the inhabitants of England, and which, if not peculiarly indicative of intellectual power, is always full of promise of homely virtues and generous feelings. There was the clear grey eye, which is not to be found except in England and the northern parts of Germany. The thin skin, through which could be traced the pure blood mantling in the cheek "in delicate tracerie."* This person was evidently past the prime of life; but age had rather been bountiful than otherwise, and had given more than he had taken. The step of the substantial citizen, for such he was, was firm, and his deportment easy. What he had lost in grace and activity, he had more than gained in dignity and ease. His companion was a much younger man; his complexion was sallow, his hair of the darkest hue. There was something, however, prepossessing about the face. The mouth and chin were decidedly handsome, and the brilliant black eyes were well calculated to command admiration. He did not appear to be of English origin; and, in fact, he had some drops of Venetian blood in his veins. This man was not popular, for no one liked the ever shifting glance of suspicion which was habitual to him. He seemed always on his guard, and to live in momentary expectation of the sudden appearance of an enemy.

The press of persons very much decreased as these two citizens proceeded westward; and, when they could with greater ease make their way, the elder of the two resumed a conversation which had been interrupted by the dense throng through which they had been forcing their way.

"Master Shore, Master Shore," he said, "believe me, you do not wisely in placing your rarest plate and jewels in the gaze of the court. These are but ticklish times, my friend; and beshrew me if I know which is best, to be poor or to seem rich. The court gallants, not to mention the king, are most marvellously easily tempted. I say, Master Shore, you act not wisely."

"In sooth, my good friend Wainstead," replied Shore, casting round him his habitual glance of caution and suspicion, "I have not perfect faith in the king's coming."

"Say you so?" whispered Wainstead. "Think you the young king would disappoint the citizens?"

"Humph!" answered Shore. "Danger is not the less dangerous because it is driven from the open field."

"True enough—true enough," said Wainstead, whom the reader will have recognised as the proprietor of the Lamb and Angel.

"The times," continued Shore, "are full of suspicion. There is not a brawling knave who to-day will throw up his cap, and cry, 'God save King Edward!' who would not—a-hem!"

"Wherefore do you pause?" said Wainstead.

"Methought yon knave in the livery of my Lord Hastings cast an eye this way. Humph! Caution—caution!"

"What?" cried Wainstead, "are we to stop the wagging of our tongues in Chepesyde for a lord's lacquey? Now, by the Holy Rood, I ——"

"Come on—come on!" said Shore. "Your blood is hot, good Master Wainstead."

"Nay, your's should be the hotter," answered Wainstead, "seeing that your mother, as I have heard you tell, was a Venetian, and nearer the sun than we of England ——"

"Yes, yes!" interrupted Shore, and his sallow cheek reddened as he spoke; "it may be hot blood that bubbles through my veins, but there is less of it than in your English system, and—and—but no matter. Come on—come on!"

"The king can hardly disappoint the city," muttered Wainstead.

Shore coughed, and whispered in Wainstead's ear,—

"The king has a great want."

"A want of what?"

"Money. Gold—gold."

"I'faith," answered Wainstead, "I wish that were news. Since I have held way in the city, I have heard of nothing but subsidies, royal letters of collection, and such like. The king, however, I understand, visits us now from gratitude."

"Yes—a-hem!" said Shore.

"It was a kinsman of my Lord Hastings that brought notice of the visit and honour intended us," continued Wainstead. "I heard him tell Master Knevett, that seeing Heaven in its justice had prospered the king, and a peace was made with France, the French troops in Scotland embarking this very day, the king would make a progress through the city to thank us for subsidies freely granted."

"Yes—oh, yes!" assented Shore. "Yes—a-hem!"

The speakers had now arrived within a few paces of the mercer's house, when Shore paused, saying,—

"I must now get home, Master Wainstead. My man Ritcher is a sore despoiler of goods."

"I wonder," said Wainstead, "you keep that Flemish varlet about you, Master Shore. 'Tis a huge knave, and grievously given to bad living."

"Yes—yes," said Shore. Then, after a slight pause, he added, "In sooth, your pretty Jane, Master Wainstead, would like the cunning tricks of Vassa. 'Tis a shrewd and wonderful man—a-hem! A Venetian, too."

"I have promised to take the child," answered Wainstead.

"Nay," said Shore, "Jane is now scarce a child. Her age is—a-hem!"

"Fourteen," answered Wainstead. "God bless her! A better, dearer, kinder heart——"

The mercer paused, and looked up to the balcony of his house with eyes beaming with joy and pride. Shore likewise fixed his eyes, which seemed to flash with redoubled fire, while a hectic tint suffused his sallow cheek, in the same direction.

"Jane—Jane!" he muttered.

There was a general pause on the part of the throng that was previously hurrying towards the upper end of the Chepe. Young and old seemed alike transfixed with pleasure. Leaning partially over the carved front of the heavy and blackened balcony, with her eyes fixed upon her father's face, was the mercer's daughter.

If ever in one person were united the graces of childhood—the rounded, soft, infantine beauty of early life, with the maturer charms which enchant all hearts in the season of happy girlhood, that person was the mercer's daughter. She looked like some heavenly visitant that had stooped for a space from its own ethereal home to smile upon mortality, and light with joy the hearts of those who were so far below its ærial nature. An exquisitely moulded arm—an arm which scarcely contrasted with the silvery tissue over which it hung, was thrown carelessly upon the hanging from the balcony. Her soft cheek, so delicately pure and white, rested nearly on the extremity of the carved projection; for she had been watching for her father, and tracing his form in the crowd as he wended his way down the Chepe. The light, roseate tint upon that cheek was like the faint colour on the damask rose when it first unfolds its trembling blossom to the sun, ere yet the light of Heaven hath lent it all its blushing sweetness. Her eyes were partially closed, for the lights all around were brilliant and dazzling; but the small glimpse that could be seen of those "twin orbs of beauty" was like the clear glow of heavenly blue we sometimes see in "the small crevice of a summer's cloud." The lashes that fringed those fair windows of the soul, hung upon her "moste daintie cheeke" like silken fringe: her hair fell like a flood of sunshine upon the balcony, and thence floated, in dancing ringlets—ringlets of nature's own creating, far down below the heavy grotesque carvings, mingling strangely with grinning faces, and floating airily across quaint devices cut in the gnarled oak of which the balcony was composed. If her hair could have been deprived of the glorious tint of golden sunlight that sparkled among the luxuriant tresses, it might have been, perchance, named some colour; but as it was shifting momentarily, as it appeared in different lights, from deep auburn to brilliant yellow, and then to some rare combination between the two, it defied nomination. And who shall describe the dear temptation of those pouting lips? who tell of the worlds of beauty in the rounded chin and ivory neck? what kingdoms could purchase the witchery and fascination that dwelt in every feature?

A buz of admiration arose from the crowd; the buz deepened to a cheer; the cheer to a ringing shout that would have been music even to the ears of King Edward, had it arisen to greet him.

"See—see!" cried several voices. "'Tis she! Jane Wainstead, the mercer's beautiful child!"

"God bless her!" cried one.

"Her hair!" said another; "look, friends; it is surely powdered with gold dust."

"Now," cried a young man, "she smiles. See—see! Those dimples are worth ——"

"Father!" said Jane.

Her voice was like the soft tinkle of a silver bell,—a voice to dream of, and sigh when we awake that the vision of so sweet a sound has passed away.

The mercer looked up at his beautiful child a moment, and then he turned to the throng, and gracefully lifted up his cap from his head. A tear—a tear of pride and pleasure—glistened in his eye, and then rolled gently down his cheek.

The crowd saw that the father's heart was full. It was an English crowd; and the cheer that burst from a thousand throats rang from one end of London to the other, and awakened many an echo in its crowded streets.

CHAPTER III.

The Assassins.

"Help! help! More lives than one
Hang on this chance."

Exactly opposite the mercer's house in Chepesyde was an ancient building, which had once belonged to the well known Lord Scroop: it was now, however, deserted, and dismantled of all its interior adornments, and it had assumed that peculiar appearance of utter desolation and cold gloom, which gathers so soon over a building deserted by human occupants. This house was built in a style prevalent at the period of its erection: it seemed as if some of the fragments of a destroyed city had been brought together, and heaped up in masses to make a habitation, without regard to order or regularity. The principal feature, however, with which we have to do, consisted in the peculiarly deep entrance, which was so dark and large, and, moreover, so overhung by a balcony above, that any person seeking admission to the mansion became quite lost to the sight of the passengers in the Chepe before he could reach the actual door.

This house was commonly called "Scroop's Castle," from the battlemented appearance of its balcony. The deep door-way we have mentioned was frequently used as a lurking-place for night robbers, and men who might well be classed among those mentioned in a succeeding reign by the Duke Humphrey of Gloster, as "grievously ill-minded varlets, and huggers of bad courses." Many a citizen, who perchance had tasted too freely of sack, or some other enemy to steadiness, was pounced upon without mercy from the doorway of Scroop's Castle, and robbed of money, cloak, hood, and, in fact, everything which could be made a few groats of. Nevertheless, Scroop's Castle remained a nuisance to the Chepe, until it shared the fate of the whole range of building, by falling a prey to the flames some years after the date of our tale.

In the present instance, the doorway of this house had stood some one apparently in good stead, for scarcely had the mercer entered his dwelling, when a figure emerged from the dusky entrance, and shading his eyes with his hand from the glare of light in the balcony of Wainstead's house, he took a long and curious look at the fair girl, who still remained there among the lamps and flowers.

"Now by the mass!" he muttered, "if I were not very busy indeed, methinks I could idle a pleasant hour in looking at those blue eyes. By my life, an angel!—a jewel for a noble!—a fit mate for a king!"

A flourish of trumpets at this moment came sounding up the Chepe from the direction of "Flete-streate." The man suddenly withdrew his eyes from the window, and drawing his cloak closer around his face, he darted down a narrow turning which led by many tortuous windings down to the banks of the Thames.

With hasty strides he pursued his way until he came to a low, thatched dwelling, at the door of which he knocked thrice.

The summons for admission was not immediately answered, and with an impatient gesture he again struck the door. In a moment more it was opened cautiously, and a voice from within asked,—

"Is it time?"

"Time and tide," was the answer. "Quick! quick!"

The door was immediately flung back upon its hinges, and two men appeared on the threshold.

"Lose not a moment," said the stranger in the cloak: "the Chepe is crowded. Run round by the back lanes. You know your man?"

The men nodded assent.

"Off—off, then! By heavens, this will be the best or the worst day's work you ever did. Off—off, I say!"

The men started from the spot, and were soon out of sight among the intricate windings of the lanes and alleys which crowded the back of Chepesyde. For a few moments the stranger stood by the threshold of the door; a smile of peculiar meaning played around his mouth, and he muttered between his clenched teeth,—

"In another hour! but an hour, and York is mingled with the dust! Yon knaves will do their duty. How dangerous it is for a goldsmith to plot with nobles!"

He drew his cloak again over his face, and hurrying down the narrow thoroughfare to the water's edge, sprung into a boat.

He spoke not, but the boatman seemed to know his duty; for, after respectfully touching his cap, he plied his oars steadily, and the boat glided along the dark, silent water in the direction of Westminster.

When Shore left the mercer at the door of his house in Chepesyde, he made every endeavour to push his way through the throng of persons, towards his own dwelling in Lombarde-streate. With gentle violence he insinuated himself through the dense mass of people that were now assembled at the end of the Chepe, and it might have been noticed, that as he did so, his right hand was buried deeply in the breast of his doublet, as if he there clutched at something which was too precious to be out of his grasp in so dense a crowd.

Thus urging his way, he arrived at the end of the Chepe, where the gallery was erected, and there he was compelled by the compact mass of persons that blocked the way, to pause until some portion of the living stream had obtained seats within the enclosure. Young and old—citizens and patricians, were alike anxious to obtain favourable stations in the gallery, in order to gratify themselves with a view of the expected pageant. The building was in the form of a horse-shoe; and, although the range of seats was nearly level with the ground, yet as the different tiers rose one above the other, the uppermost places were elevated some twenty feet or more from the level of the Chepe.

As nearly as possible in the very centre of the rough amphitheatre was a gorgeous chair of state for King Edward, standing upon a dais of cloth of gold. Immediately in front of the king's seat, a long strip of rare purple velvet was laid down from seat to seat until it reached the ground, and upon each seat stood a soldier, with his arms in readiness, the whole arrangement forming a well-guarded staircase for the young king to ascend to his station.

Shore was so wedged in the crowd, that perforce he became a spectator of all the preparations for the royal visit, although it was evident he was inwardly chafing at the delay.

Rapidly the gallery filled with curious spectators, and presented a sea of heads in tumultuous and excited emotion. The prentices fought and tussled with each other for places, and not unfrequently two of them, locked in an unfriendly embrace, would roll from seat to seat, tearing off hoods and caps in their way, amid oaths from the men, and screams from the women, until they arrived fairly in the open space at the foot of the seats, from whence they were unceremoniously ejected by the city guard.

The tender and delicate Mrs. Mapletoft was there, and had secured to herself and trembling spouse a choice seat, by seizing the caps of all who stood in her way, and casting them back in the throng, leaving the owners no resource but to push back for their recovery, or put up with the loss. As many, however, adopted the former alternative, Mrs. Mapletoft thinned the crowd before her amazingly.

In vain Shore intreated and begged for a passage; he could move but at the rate of an inch a minute, and his impatience to proceed became painful in the extreme. He still kept one hand concealed in his vest, and with the other only he strove to force his way. For a moment the clamour of the crowd ceased, as the sound of martial music came faintly from far down the Chepe. Then arose a general cry of "The king—the king!" and the confusion became "worse" confounded.

The perspiration stood upon the brow of the goldsmith as he muttered between his clenched teeth,—

"I must be home, or all is lost—lost for ever!" Drawing his hand from his vest, he made a desperate effort to force his way past the gallery in the direction of Lombarde-streate. His long black hair curled about his swarthy face like writhing snakes, and the warm blood that now gave a transient glow to his hollow cheeks, betrayed the fever of anxiety he was in from some hidden cause. Many shrunk from his path; for there was a look of savageness about him which few relished, and thus, with his teeth clenched, and panting with exertion of body, and anxiety of mind, the goldsmith tore through the crowd towards his own house.

Again, the sound of trumpets came sweetly upon the night air, and, at each flourish, there arose a prolonged shout from the joyous multitude, and a deep groan from Shore.

Time may roll onwards, and generations of men may fade away in the dim shadows of the past. Their hopes and fears may be forgotten; their manners and customs but remembered to point a tale, or raise the ready laugh from those who despise follies that belong not to themselves. Forests may spring up amid the ruins of huge cities, and the curling foliage may burst through the gilded fanes of our temples and our palaces. The ocean may change its limits, and that which was the pebbly bed of the surging waters, may be rendered up to man as a green place on which to rest, while the sweetest spots on which "the wild vine trails its boughs," may receive the rush of waters. Hoary-headed frosts may

"Fall in the fresh lap of the crimson rose."

But there is one thing that shall remain unchanging, unchangeable—the human heart. The same motives—the same hopes—the same fears—the same dark passions—and the same dear gushes of warm, happy feeling, are to be found in all ages, and under all disguises. Love—hate—joy—grief—remorse—tenderness, and all the passions "that of them are made," have been handed from generation to generation in unalloyed beauty or deformity. The outward man may change; but, within the breast, "nature will be nature still." Different sounds may express our feelings, and different associations may awaken them; but the feelings themselves, they are of Heaven, and for ever! Hearts beat equally devoted to bright eyes beneath embroidered doublets in "antient Londone," as they now do beneath satin waistcoats, the glory of a Stultz. The mob in the old Chepe, in 1465, was the same in thought and action as the mob in 1845. They only called things by different names, and dressed a little better than we do. There are Mrs. Mapletofts now in every throng, at every sight or pageant. There are timid Mr. Mapletofts, who sail in the wake of their more valorous convoys. The bluff young armourers are no more, but there are brawny smiths. There are still merry prentices in London, only now they smoke cigars, and cultivate long hair and imperials. Those who got seats in the gallery at the Chepe, exercised the same small wit in the same spirit against those who were still panting in the crowd, as one may hear now in modern days. The asseverations, however, only were different. The spirit was the same.

In a short time Shore succeeded in passing the balcony, and, having done so, he found the pressure of the crowd sensibly diminish, and he with less exertion made greater progress towards his home. Once more he thrust his hand into the breast of his garment and anxiously assured himself of the safety of some important trust.

"Safe! safe!" he exclaimed. "The game is in my hands—fortune within my clutch, I grasp the destiny of England's king."

A smile then crossed his sallow countenance as he muttered,—

"The worshipfulle Master Wainstead was not so sure as I that the royal Edward would visit our poor city; but my reasons were good—golden. Let me consider again the condition of the bond. I and Master Faithful, and my Lord Hastings, to be bound to the Flemish merchants for this loan, without which Edward falls, and the York rose is turned to crimson in the blood—aye, the hot, bubbling blood—of its defenders. Humph! 'tis a brave thing to hold the fate of a kingdom in one hand! The life, too, of the young king hangs upon the breath of the goldsmith of Lombarde-streate. I will save him. Yes, he shall live; but the information that covers these foolish plotting nobles with confusion, shall raise me to a height above the proudest. I *will* save the king—at the last hour, but not till then. So shall my service seem more weighty, as stepping betwixt him and visible treason. Yes, yes; 'tis well arranged. Fortune, thou art mine!—and then—then Jane!"

The goldsmith had now arrived at a lonely spot of ground, which is as nearly as possible the site of the present Mansion House. This open place was not above three hundred yards in extent; but it was very dark, for the houses at the extreme end of the Chepe were of mean structure, and not well illuminated, while the commencement of Lombarde-streate was in complete darkness, from the fact of several uninhabited houses being there situated.

Shore cast around him his habitual glance of suspicion; and burying his hand still deeper in his vest, hurried onwards over the uneven and dark space he was forced to traverse.

For an instant he paused, as the clangour of musical instruments, announcing King Edward's progress through the city, came upon his ears.

"He comes! he comes!" he muttered. "In another short hour the poor goldsmith will have a king for his guest; and a grateful king, too, if kings are ever grateful. Humph! We shall see—we shall see!"

A loud hurrah now shook the air, and the goldsmith quickened his pace.

" Take credit to thyself, Shore, he said, half aloud. " Thy Venetian blood has taught thee some craft."

Scarcely had these words passed his lips, when, with a cry of pain, he bounded forward like a wounded stag, and then fell heavily to the earth.

" Help! help! Murder!" he shrieked.

" Strike him to the heart, Win!" exclaimed one of the two men who stood by the prostrate goldsmith. " Strike, fool! By Heaven and the earl's head, he'll raise the Chepe!"

" Help—help!" again cried Shore.

" Stop his bawling, I tell you, Win," cried the man again, as he stooped over Shore.

" Stop it yourself," growled the other ruffian.

" Nay, I've lost my poniard. Curses on him! he bounded on with it in his back."

" The king—the king!" cried Shore, faintly. " Oh, help—help!"

" We waste time. Lend me your dagger," cried the first speaker.

The weapon glistened in the faint light, as it was handed over the prostrate form of the goldsmith. In the next moment it was plunged to the hilt in his breast.

A loud burst of trumpets at that instant startled the assassins, and, for a moment, they stood in attitudes to fly.

" Our work's not done," whispered one. " The papers—the papers!"

He tore open the vest of Shore, and, by the light of a small lantern which he produced, snatched at a packet, which was soaked in the goldsmith's blood.

" Off—off!" he then whispered. " I hear footsteps. To the river, Win—to the river!"

In another moment the assassins disappeared in the surrounding gloom, and their victim, he who so lately smiled upon the supposed dawning of his better fortune, was left to welter in the blood which slowly oozed from his wounds.

CHAPTER IV.

The Conspiracy.

" Ah! what an invocation is the name we love!"

It seemed to the wounded man that he had slept an age, when he was aroused to painful consciousness by some one endeavouring to raise him from the earth on which he lay, and which was saturated with his own blood.

With a deep groan, he unclosed his eyes, and tried to fix his dimmed vision upon the dusky form that was stooping over him.

" Mercy—mercy!" he cried, faintly.

" Nay, sir, are you hurt?" said the stranger. " I would befriend you. If you be choked by deep potations, why e'en lie here, an ye will; but if you be in pain ——"

" Pain—pain?" repeated Shore, in a tone of unutterable agony. " Oh, Heaven! such pain!"

" Do I hear aright? Are you Master Shore?"

" I—I was—but—Oh, God—oh, God!"

" Nay, sir, speak to me. Do you not know me? What sore mischance has befallen you?"

" Help—help!" groaned the writhing man. " Where—where am I? Help, I say! Murder—murder! There—there! See the king! how his blood spouts forth like wine from a conduit! Ay, blood, blood, blood!"

" Master Shore—Master Shore! what mean you? Are you hurt?"

The goldsmith only replied by a deep groan, which seemed to rend his very heart.

" Help! ho! help!" cried the stranger, rising to his full height from his bending position over the prostrate Shore.

A loud cheer from the mob in the Chepe, at some circumstance connected with the fete, came full upon the air, and completely drowned his cries. The noise seemed to arouse the wounded goldsmith from the lethargy into which he had fallen.

" Who calls?" he said, in a faint voice. " Who calls? I—I—I want water—water. God of heaven! I could scream for water."

" Do you not know me, Master Shore?" cried the stranger, whose voice betrayed his extreme youth. " I am Walter Fane. You know Walter Fane?"

" Walter Fane? Master Wainstead's apprentice?"

" The same."

" He who—who ——"

" Who what, Master Shore? What would you say? Tell me what to do to help you."

" Who loves Jane?" said Shore, in a hissing whisper.

The young man was silent; and the darkness covered the deep glow of colour which rose like love's own banner to his cheeks.

"Who loves Jane?" repeated Shore, still more faintly. "There, now, he is saved. Yes, sire, that scroll holds the names! Help—help! There is murder abroad. Who holds me down?"

"He wanders strangely in his speech," said Walter Fane.

Another flourish of trumpets, and a ringing shout, now came from the nearest end of the Chepe.

"Lost! lost!" shrieked Shore, in a voice that rung screaming on the night air.

"What is lost?" said Walter. "I fear to leave you here, Master Shore; yet, by staying, I see not how to help you. I will get assistance. In a short time ——"

Hold! hold!" said Shore. "Walter—good Walter! how long, how long have I lain here?"

"Nay, Master Shore, I know not; but even now the King is coming up the Chepe."

"Now, Walter?—Now say you?"

"Even now, sir."

A loud shout at this moment rung on the air, and "God save King Edward!" arose from many thousand throats, and died away in the distance, like the fitful murmuring of a passing gale.

"Hark!" cried Walter Fane; "the king has now reached the gallery."

"Oh, what an age of pain may be dreamt in a few brief moments!" said Shore.

"Now, again," said Walter, with enthusiasm, "hark to the trumpets! How featly they come on the night air. I will bring you help, Master Shore."

"Stay—stay! Yet a moment—one moment!"

"Nay, sir, I am at your bidding; for Master Wainstead sent me to your house to bid you to the Chepe to a cup of spiced canary and a simmering toast, when the fete should be over, and, missing you there, I was even thinking to see the fiery tricks of Vassa, and—and ——"

"Cease, cease," cried Shore, raising himself partially upon his elbow; "what sound is that?"

"The king has surely taken his seat. Hark! the trumpets sound again! The cunning Vassa begins. By the mass, what merry shouts!"

"Swear," cried Shore, with a momentary energy, "swear to do my bidding!"

"What would you, Master Shore?"

"I—I have been basely set upon, Walter; and—and—grievously wounded. I had a packet about me, Walter. Put—put thy hand into my vest, and tell me is it there. I cannot move. I seem held down by clasps of welded iron."

"There is no packet," said Walter Fane, withdrawing his hand soaked in blood from the goldsmith's breast.

Again a glad shout swept past them from the multitude, joined to the clangour of cymbals and the braying of trumpets.

"How glorious is a fete!" sighed Walter Fane.

"Lost—lost!" shrieked the goldsmith.

"There is no packet," said Walter.

"On that packet hangs the king's life."

"The king's life?"

"It has three seals, and is wound with green silk. The king's life—England's fortunes—all, all are encompassed, Walter, in that packet."

"You surprise me, Master Shore. He surely wanders in his brain. What shall I do?"

"Listen!" continued Shore, in a husky whisper, for his voice was failing; "listen, Walter Fane; you—you love Jane?"

"Love Jane!"

"Seek the king—tell him there is treason ——"

"Love Jane!" repeated Walter.

"Tell him his life is at a cast. Or—or seek the Lord Hastings. Quick—quick, Walter!—ah, quick!"

"Love Jane!" said Walter. "Dear, dear Jane!"

"By that love I urge you. Seek and warn King Edward. Shout treason in his ears."

"Treason? Hark! hark! there is no treason in that joyous shout. How pleasantly the trumpets speak."

"Madness—madness!" shrieked Shore. "Walter Fane, do my bidding, or all in the gallery at the Chepe are lost; a sea of blood will wrap them up as in a mantle."

"All lost?"

"Aye, lost. And—and ——"

"Say on, sir. I will go. I will do your bidding."

"Jane is there."

With a cry Walter Fane sprang to his feet.

"Jane! Jane in danger! My Jane! my beautiful—my—oh, Heaven protect her! I—I—God help you, Master Shore! I must leave you. Jane! Jane! Jane!"

He rushed from the spot, and, with a deep sigh, the wounded merchant relapsed into insensibility.

Antonius Vassa was a man of no mean celebrity in the fifteenth century. He was in the habit of travelling to the different courts of Europe, ostensibly for the purpose of exhibiting his skill in pyrotechnics at the fetes and pageants which were then so frequent; but he was more than suspected of being a secret agent of some political party upon all such occasions; for it was generally found that Vassa was the precursor of some plot or outbreak against the authorities that were, although he had always managed matters so adroitly, that no treasonable practices could ever be clearly brought home to him. There is no doubt, however, that he would have fallen a victim to the mere suspicions of rulers, had it not been that his talents, as far as deceit went, were of so high an order, that there was no political party who would not gladly make him their agent. He had confederates everywhere, and he had, in fact, reduced the subject of secret political agency quite to a science. He had many times narrowly escaped assassination; in fact, so many times, that his own assertion that he bore a charmed life, began to be credited. None knew for whom or what party Vassa was acting but his immediate employers, and those were generally of the highest rank; for, vicious as was the wily Italian, he fancied that by plotting only with royalty and nobility, he robbed vice of its infamy. Such as he was, however, Antonius Vassa was universally courted and treated with distinction, partly from dread of his power, and partly from admiration of his great talents as an intriguante.

Upon the occasion of King Edward's going to the city the day we have mentioned, Vassa had suddenly appeared in London, from whence no one knew, and had readily obtained leave to exhibit before the young king an entertainment, consisting of, as we are informed from ancient sources, "*Moste rare, quainte, and singular devices ye which was never yet seene.*"

King Edward, on this memorable occasion, entered the City of London accompanied by all the insignia of royalty, and with every circumstance of pomp and state, which could be gathered about the person of a king. He was surrounded by all the nobility who had made themselves conspicuous by their adherence to the house of York: and as the long and glittering procession entered Flete-streate, where were waiting the Mayor of London, and the principal officers of the city, the effect of the brilliant costumes, rich arms, sparkling jewels, and nodding plumes, was splendid and gorgeous in the extreme.

The young monarch was mounted on a coal black steed, the trappings and housings of which glittered with jewels. In person, Edward the Fourth was about the middle size, of graceful and well-proportioned figure. His hair was fair, and fell upon his shoulders in massive curls. The effeminate appearance which the colour and disposition of his hair would have given to many persons, was in him amply compensated for by his general manly grace, and the dignity with which he managed his prancing steed. A procession of the officers of state had preceded the king, after which, followed by a compact body of his guards, came the young monarch himself, surrounded by the elite of his nobility. On his right hand rode his chamberlain, Hastings, who fell a victim to the blood-thirsty Richard. The blandest of smiles played upon the king's face, and his graceful inclinations to the fair faces that greeted him from each window and balcony, were the themes of every tongue. Those, however, who watched the king's face narrowly, might well have suspected that the heart was not quite at ease. There was an occasional slight quiver of the lip, and a restless wandering of the eyes, which told that the young monarch was paying the dear penalty of high station in suspicion and doubt.

And yet the greeting that Edward met in the ancient city was deep and cordial. Flowers were strewn before his horses' feet—bright eyes rained down glances of admiration upon him—good wishes and blessings arose from many a devoted heart; and the mob, as mobs always do, cheered and shouted, filling the air with that rude clamour which is such music to the great. Youth and high station will always receive from the multitude a certain enthusiastic welcome, and even those who think before they give a greeting, cannot help feeling "the divinity that doth hedge a king." There were few who were churlish enough to refuse a cheer, or at least a smile, to the gallant young monarch, as in graceful majesty he passed through the winding streets of old London.

Just opposite St. Dunstane's church there was a slight pause, for the Mayor of London there met the king, and dismounting from his horse, he knelt in his way, crying,—

"God save King Edward!"

The king reined in his prancing steed, and scarcely controlling the smile that had crossed his face as the mayor dismounted, with some difficulty, from his horse, he presented him his hand, which was reverently kissed.

Then the portly head of the city (for even in those stirring times mayors sometimes grew round and bulky) besought his majesty to alight, and partake of a most delicate and choice collation, humbly prepared for his gracious service.

"By our Lady," said the king, "it doth rejoice me to see thee in such well-being, good Master Knevitt. On our return, with appetites sharpened by pleasure at the rare loyalty of our good citizens, we will drain a cup with thee to all friends."

So saying, the king drew his sword, and laying the flashing blade lightly on the shoulders of the mayor he cried,—

"Rise, Sir ——"

"Peter, my liege," whispered Hastings.

"Sir Peter Knevitt," continued the king; "and a better knight, beshrew me, if I have in merry England."

A cheer burst from the populace, and scarfs were waved from the windows, while the enlivening strains of music mingled in the joyous din. The king gracefully waved his shining blade, and with it still in his hand, pointed onwards.

"God save King Edward! long live the king!" was shouted by young and old; and the procession, now augmented by the civic guards, proceeded slowly along Flete-streate, towards the Chepe.

It needs not, in this narrative, which must hurry on to darker scenes, and the stormier passions of the heart, to say, how Sir Peter Knevitt wiped his eyes, and with many manly thumps on his capacious chest, vowed how he would live and die for "Goode Kinge Edwarde," although of the two he rather preferred the former alternative.

A company of torch-bearers was collected at the foot of Ludgate Hill, and at the king's approach these distributed themselves along the line of street, and made a lane the whole length of the Chepe. The effect of the procession when it entered the Chepe was imposing and dazzling. The street was one blaze of light; and a chance spectator might have doubted if one evil thought could find a place among so much beauty, brilliancy, and joy. Occasionally the trumpets blew a thrilling blast, drowning all lesser sounds in their loud, warlike clangour; and as the echoes died away on the night air, the tinkling sounds of lutes and viols from the balconies and casements came in sweet contrast upon the ears.

Now the Chepe was traversed, and the king arrived at an entrance to the gallery, which had been carefully guarded from all intrusion, and which led directly to the flight of steps we have before described as leading to the seat prepared for him. With a quick movement Edward dismounted from his horse, and strode hastily over the rich velvet that was laid down to do him honour. In a moment he was at the foot of the staircase, and then sheathing his sword, and casting around him one glance at the sea of heads in the building, he strode up the steps, and stood in another minute by the temporary throne.

A general clapping of hands commenced on the part of the occupants of the gallery. Edward stood for a moment; then slightly bowing, he took his seat; but it was observed that his hand wandered to his sword hilt, and that he sat so lightly, that at a thought he could spring to his feet.

There was now a moment's dead silence, and all eyes were bent upon the king in curious scrutiny, when a single voice rose loud and clear upon the air.

"Treason!" it said, in a tone that thrilled to the hearts of all.

The king sprung to his feet. For a moment a death-like paleness came across his face, but it was instantly succeeded by a flush of colour. It would seem as if the blood had at first retreated with a frightful gush to his heart at that dread word, treason, and then flown with indignation to his cheeks.

CHAPTER V.

The Lover.

"He saw but her, and struggled onwards
Like a bold swimmer nearly faint."

For a brief space after the mysterious voice had spoken, there was so hushed a silence, that the loud beating of some anxious heart might even have been heard. Then a few swords were drawn; and, as the multitude recovered from the first shock of surprise, a confused murmur of voices arose, and many quitted their seats to leave the place.

King Edward glanced around him for a moment, and then waving his hand impatiently to the trumpeters, they, at the signal, blew an inspiring blast, and the loud flourish was responded to by a deafening cheer on the part of the spectators. With a smile of affected contempt for the interruption that had taken place, Edward again seated himself, and communicated an order for the entertainment to commence.

Vassa presently appeared in the middle of the open space prepared for him. He was a small, slim man, and his complexion was as dark as his heart. From his countenance one might well fancy that every malignant passion incidental to humanity had found a place in his composition. His dress was peculiar It consisted of a closely-fitting black silk woven garment, which adhered to him as tightly as if it were his skin. This was the costume in which he usually exhibited: and by a process only known to himself, it was rendered fire proof.

Vassa never allowed his audiences long time to speculate upon his personal appearance; and, after a slight bow towards where the king sat, and a glance of mingled scorn and effrontery upon the mass of human beings about him, he placed one foot upon what appeared to be a small peg stuck in the ground, and commenced whirling round upon that slight support with great rapidity.

Faster and faster he flew round, until all trace of his person was lost in the frightfully rapid whirl. One by one the torches were now extinguished, and a black darkness enveloped the whole scene. Still, however, by the dim glare of a few flambeaux that were kept burning in the immediate vicinity of the king, the dusky form of Vassa might be seen still whirling on its centre. All gazed with wonder and admiration upon the reputed conjurer, and expectation was at its height to know what wonderful performance this was the prelude to: for they well guessed that the gradual darkening of the arena was for the purpose of rendering some fiery trick of Vassa's more startling. Nor were they kept long in suspense; for scarcely was the last torch extinguished, than innumerable little dazzling jets of blue flame burst, as if by magic, from every part of Vassa, and shed a sweet, chastened light over the whole space. Still he whirled round rapidly, and the constant intermingling of the little dazzling lights, gave him the appearance of being enveloped in a halo of blue flame of the most heavenly colour.

A round of plaudits burst from the multitude, when, suddenly, all was darkness again, and Vassa was not to be seen. The change from the brilliant lights whirling rapidly before the vision to darkness so momentarily, was perplexing in the extreme, and scarce a soul could see his fellow distinctly for the dancing spectre that remained upon his eyes.

"By the mass!" muttered the warden, who entertained so great a horror of Vassa, "here's witchery and fiends! Who can see his own hand? Marry, no one. I like not this, Vassa."

"Beshrew me," cried another, "if a legion of dancing devils do not appear wherever I look."

"Where is the Italian?" cried several. "Where is Vassa? Nay, an we are to see no more, it were scarce worth the trouble of crowding through the Chepe."

Two apprentices seized the happy moment to get up a sham quarrel in the immediate vicinity of Mrs. Mapletoft; and one, under pretence of pummelling the other, contrived to get hold of that exemplary lady's head-dress, and cast it into the arena.

"Dear heart! dear heart!" ejaculated Mr. Mapletoft, who was knocked down in the struggle.

Mrs. Mapletoft's indignation was too deep for utterance; but seizing upon some one by the cloak, who she imagined to be one of the assailants, she commenced so vigorous a fistic display, that he who was so attacked roared for mercy, and untying the strings of the cloak, allowed Mrs. Mapletoft to roll with it, clutched in her infuriated grasp, right into the stomach of the oratorial little oily warden, who gasped for breath for several minutes after the concussion.

The tumult reached the ears of the Lord Chamberlain, who, after a whisper from the king, commanded the trumpeters to blow a royal flourish as a signal for the entertainment to continue.

Still there was no re-appearance of Vassa; and a feeling of dread and anxiety began to come over the multitude. A murmur of impatience arose which each moment became deeper.

Some personal conflicts were taking place in the gallery, and, favoured by the darkness, hoods, caps, and ornaments, were changing hands momentarily. The confusion was becoming every moment more apparent and fearful.

"Lights! lights!" cried some.

"Help! murder! help!" was called by others.

The king's attendants drew their swords, and crowded each other up the steps leading

to the chair of state, calling loudly for lights. Louder and louder grew the tumult. Oaths, shrieks, and entreaties filled the air, when, in the midst of the confusion and uproar, the same voice that had before produced so great a sensation, called, in a tone that rose above all other sounds,—

"Treason!"

The word was taken up as by one accord, and "Treason! treason!" burst from every mouth.

"Lights—lights! Save the king!" cried the courtiers.

The clash of swords, and the groans of the wounded (for many personal conflicts were taking place in the darkness), added to the din; many were thrown from the elevated seats upon the heads of those below, and old scores of vengeance among neighbours were in several instances wiped off with blood. The yells of the men—the shrieks and screams of the women and children—the oaths of the guards, and the incessant cry of "Treason! treason!" that still rose fearfully distinct above all other sounds, created a scene of confusion and horror baffling description, and to which darkness added tenfold terrors.

Suddenly the tumult was partially lulled, and even pain forgot to scream, in intense curiosity, as a dull, red glare of light began to diffuse itself over the gallery, and imparted to each excited countenance an unearthly hue. Then one voice shrieked "Fire!" and, even as the dreadful cry arose, the crackling of the wood-work of the balcony, and the roar of the flames, proclaimed too distinctly that the cry was true.

For one moment no one stirred. It would seem as if all were transfixed by some spell, which bound alike voice and action. And there stood the young king, in the very centre of that throng of wild, excited faces. The red glare from the burning timbers of the gallery fell full upon his noble form. His attitude was that of dignified command. His face was firm, yet anxious; and, as the glimmering light fell upon his figure, and glanced in trembling beauty from every sparkling gem that adorned his apparel, playing, too, like an electric flash upon his gleaming sword, and lighting his eyes with more than mortal brilliancy, he looked like some pure spirit just lighted on a "heaven-kissing hill," to calm the hearts of all, and give assurance of a better fate than death in that fearful guise it wore to every breast. His head was bare, and it seemed as if there were a consciousness and pride of youth, beauty, and high power, as he there stood with his glowing hair, to which the colour of the light that sparkled among its tresses lent just the warm charm that made it dazzlingly beautiful, flowing upon his jewelled vest, and mingling in flashing beauty, with a carcanet of diamonds upon his breast. His form seemed to dilate as he looked around, and he was about to speak, when a shriek rose upon the still air, and a young girl, so lovely that she alone seemed fit to compare with that young monarch in the height of his earthly splendour and beauty, rushed forward, and, throwing herself at his feet, exclaimed, in shrieking accents,—

"Save! save! oh, save my father! You are the king. Oh, save him! save him!"

At the instant, with a loud crash, the raised gallery fell to the ground, engulphing thousands in its ruins.

CHAPTER VI.

The Young King.

In ye confusione of ane fire ye Lancastrians sought to take ye life of ye kinge.

MS. Letters.

For a few moments nothing was heard but the crackling and crashing of the wooden rafters of the gallery. No human voice mingled with those sounds of destruction. It would seem as if terror was gathering breath to scream. The most fevered pulse there could hardly, however, have numbered six throbbing beats when the multitude gave voice, and the screams of women, the groans of the injured, and the shouts of those who had escaped, arose in one wild tumult upon the night air.

It was evident that the gallery in Chepe had been set fire to from beneath, and the rude supports becoming partially consumed, had lacked the power to support the superincumbent pressure. A dense smoke arose from the mass of ruins, rendering danger more appalling, by adding to it darkness and uncertainty. Cries for help from those entangled in the ruins, loud shouts from the injured to friends and relatives, incessant inquiries for the king, mingled with the clashing of swords, and the shrill screams of children, produced a scene of horror and dismay that had rarely been equalled in the ancient city.

In the midst of the confusion, some one began ringing the bells of St. Saviour's church, and it mingled strangely with the sounds of strife and pain from the multitude in the Chepe. The peal from the bells was a merry one, and might have heralded a royal bridal; and, as the spirit-stirring sounds filled the night with echoing melody, the din of voices in the area of the fallen gallery gradually subsided. The wounded alone groaned, and cried feebly for help; the sounds of mortal strife ceased, and the silence of surprise crept over the people at the merry peals that at such a moment rang from St. Saviour's bells.

Whoever the ringer might be, it was evident he was some master of his craft, for a more gladdening succession of liquid sounds never at fete or festival rang through the streets of old London.

Far down the Cheape there might be now seen the glaring of torches, and the sight of them seemed to give a new impulse to the shouts of the people, for an universal cry arose for lights, to which in a moment was added a single voice, shouting,—

"Save the king! save the king!"

That voice was Walter Fane's, who was striving through the crowd with greater efforts to reach the centre of danger than the most fearful made to escape from it.

"The king! the king!" he shouted. "Jane!—murder!—the king!—the king!" and stalwart men shrunk before him, and gave him passage.

One lighted flambeau now appeared, and again the cry for lights rose from a thousand throats. Lamps were brought from the nearest houses; extinguished torches were picked from among the remains of the gallery, and re-lighted; added to which, flames began to burst from among the ruins of the fallen structure, so that in a few moments the darkness in which the whole scene had been shrouded gave way to a brilliancy of light that presented everything in its clearest colours.

The gallery, with the exception of some of its lower seats, was a mass of ruins; the velvet which had been laid down for the king was dragged from its place, and rent into fragments, while the chair of state in which the young monarch had sat, lay overturned in the middle of the arena. But few of the multitude seemed to have sustained serious injury, for the greater part were grouped among the fallen timbers, pale and dishevelled, glaring anxiously around them, as light after light added to the clearness of their vision. When the last torch was lighted and held high in the air, and each person's eyes were too much occupied to allow the tongue to speak, the first of a band of armed persons, who had been rapidly advancing up the Chepe, arrived at the scene of confusion, and, springing upon some of the ruins, so as to command a view of the whole space, he cried, to the surprise of all,—

"God save King Henry!"

Each man looked in his neighbour's face aghast; and the bold speaker, waving his arm, again cried,—

"Long live King Henry! Shout, my masters! Listen to the merry bells of St. Saviour's! Long live King Henry! Hurrah!"

"Long live King Henry!" was echoed by the armed band who had followed the bold speaker up the Chepe.

The cheer died away, and the bells of St. Saviour alone broke the stillness that reigned throughout the panic-stricken assemblage.

Each man looked at his neighbour with distrust, and the intruder was again upon the point of speaking, when some one from the crowd cried,—

"York for ever! Hurrah for King Edward!"

The spell which seemed to have bound the faculties of all was broken, and a tumult commenced, baffling all description.

"York!" "Lancaster!" "A White Rose!" "King Henry!" "Edward!" shouted the mob. The torches were used as weapons of offence and defence—swords were again crossed in mortal combat—the wounded were trampled upon without mercy, and oaths, blows, screams, and imprecations abounded. The man who had proclaimed King Henry was dressed in half-armour, and wore a barred visor from his helm. In vain he shouted to be heard; in vain he waved his sword, beseeching silence. The apple of discord had been cast among the throng, and human passions are not to be calmed as easily as they are raised. It was reserved for another to quell the wild tumult than he who had raised it.

From the Lombarde-streate side of the gallery there suddenly appeared the foremost men of a compact and large body of troops, who, in obedience to the command of their leaders, spread themselves into a line, and, advancing steadily over broken benches, prostrate combatants, and all the debris of the fire and the conflict, in an incredibly short space of time reduced the chaos to order, and took entire possession of the place.

When comparative silence was restored, the man in half-armour, who had still retained his position, cried loudly,—

"Now, friends and citizens, hear me. Edward, hear me. Lift up your voices, and cry with me, God save King Henry!"

Slowly the compact body of troops who had quelled the tumult opened, and, sitting calmly and unscathed upon his black steed, appeared King Edward, surrounded by his nobility and the civic authorities.

The man who had just spoken staggered at the sight, which, to him, was evidently a most unexpected one. He seemed perfectly unnerved; and, making a false step, fell heavily to the ground from the height he had clambered to.

"Long live King Edward!" cried Lord Hastings, lifting his plumed cap from his head.

The crowd echoed the cry, and the young monarch gracefully inclined his head, although those who were near him did not fail to observe the sarcastic smile that played around his mouth.

Hastings pointed to the bold proclaimer of King Henry, and he was immediately seized by the guards, and, at a signal, dragged to the front of the king's horse.

"Arch traitor!" exclaimed Edward, his eyes flashing with anger as he spoke, "name thy employers; for thou, knave, art of small account."

The man preserved a dogged silence.

"Unhelm the villain!" cried Edward.

The common iron casque that he wore was taken from his head, and disclosed the pale, haggard features of a man apparently past the prime of life.

"Thy name, condition, and employers," said the king.

The man looked around him with a terrified air, and the colour entirely left his lips, as he replied, in a husky voice,—

"I am called Kenelm Austin."

The king still looked him keenly in the face, and he continued,—

"For my condition, I am whatever men please to call me."

"Then let them call thee a foul and pestilent traitor. Hark thee, fellow! name to us all concerned in this plot against our life, which, by Heaven's mercy, has been foiled—and thou art free."

The man's lips quivered, and he drew his breath short and thick.

"The names!" cried the king.

His pale lips moved, but he spoke not.

"The names!" exclaimed Edward, impatiently.

The man shook his head.

"To the rack with him!" cried the king; "to the rack!"

Two guards laid their hands heavily upon the man's shoulder.

"Mercy! mercy!" he said, in low, choking accents.

"To the rack!" repeated Edward.

Still muttering the word "mercy," the trembling man was roughly dragged away.

There was an angry flush upon the king's brow, which mocked the courtly smile with which he said,—

"By our lady, we have had great mercies. This plot, sirs, was a most vile plot. Is the villain, Vassa, taken?"

"No one has seen him, my liege," replied one of the suite.

"By our crown," continued Edward, not heeding the answer, "it was a most pestilent plot—a plot, sirs, that would have soaked England's greenest spots with blood. I tell ye, sirs, but that the traitorous knave who aimed at our life stumbled over the dress of a young knave, and gave us time to slay him, we might, had Heaven so willed it, have fallen beneath a knave's poniard."

"'Twas a rare chance, my liege," said Hastings.

"A most rare chance, Hastings. I fear me that some of our good citizens have suffered in this night's mischance. See that restitution be made; and Norfolk, let your men look to those who are hurt. A most vile plot, by the Holy Rood!"

The various sounds of strife, pain, and rage, had gradually died away, after the sudden re-appearance of King Edward. The armed band that had accompanied the man who had so boldly, and, as it turned out in the sequel, so indiscreetly proclaimed King Henry, had dispersed, some of them crying, "Long live King Edward!" and others, casting down their arms, hurried from the spot in confusion, nor was there any attempt made to stay their flight. They were merely the tools of faction, and their arrest would have been far more troublesome than their escape.

The throng of persons who had escaped injury from the fall of the gallery, crowded round the king as closely as the guards would permit them; and so mysterious had been the whole of the circumstances of the night, that every ear was upon the stretch to catch anything that might be spoken of an explanatory nature. It happened, likewise, that the king lingered for some yet unaccomplished end, and he whispered repeatedly to those around him, and more particularly to Lord Hastings, who, standing high on his stirrups, cast looks of anxious inquiry among the throng of persons in the arena.

At this juncture Walter Fane had succeeded in pushing his way to the foremost circle of those who were kept back from too close proximity to the king by the city guards, and then, raising his voice, he cried,—

"I am charged with a message for the king's ear."

Edward turned his head quickly in the direction of the sound, and, looking keenly at the speaker for a moment, he said,—

"Say thy bidding. From whom is it?"

"Master Shore, an' it please ——"

"Ha!" cried Edward, interrupting him. "Come forward, boy."

Walter Fane was permitted to pass the military cordon that surrounded the king, and, according to custom, he would have knelt at the charger's feet, but Edward exclaimed impatiently—

"Quick, boy! quick! Thy errand."

"Master Shore, my liege, is sorely wounded by assassins."

"Assassins! Now, by our Lady, our good city is grievously beset with villains! Say on—say on."

"He charged me to seek your majesty, and say that a packet of precious value had been stolen from him, on which hung many lives."

"In sooth, a precious packet! And how fares the merchant?"

"So urgently he pressed me, with frantic cries and tears, to leave him and seek your highness, that even in his extremity and weltering in his gore, I quitted him."

"A packet!" muttered the king; "a packet! It must have been—Hastings." The king whispered to his chamberlain, who replied—

"It may have been the same traitor who assailed your sacred person. Your highness slew him."

"Even so," replied Edward. "The traitor's blood is now upon our sword blade. The body lies somewhere by the too dangerous seat our good citizens placed us in."

Suddenly Walter Fane darted forward; for at some distance behind the king he caught a glance of Jane Wainstead and her father. The action, however, was of too suspicious a character, in the neighbourhood of a king in the fifteenth century, not to create some alarm, and Edward reined up his horse, exclaiming,—

"Seize the traitor!"

Walter stopped short, or he would have been cut down by a dozen swords; and he cried,—

"No traitor, King Edward, am I. But I saw dear friends; and for the moment unheedful of where I was, I would have joined them."

"What friends, knave?" cried the Duke of Norfolk.

"No friend's knave, nor knave's friends," cried Walter, his cheek flushing with anger.

"Ha! you dare ——"

"Hold, Norfolk!" said the king. "Beshrew me, but you are over hasty. Who are you, boy?"

"There is one there can answer for me," said Walter, indicating the mercer.

The king wheeled round his horse, and as Wainstead dropped on one knee before him, and Jane stood timidly by his side, he said,—

"Sirs, this young maid is she who sought protection of her king; and, under Heaven, was the instrument of saving his life. Come hither, damsel."

Jane timidly advanced until she stood close to the king's stirrup.

"Thy name, pretty one?"

For one moment those sweet blue eyes were lifted from the ground, and rested on the young monarch's face; then, as a brightened colour spread slowly over her face, she dropped the long silken lashes, and gently answered,—

"Jane."

The king continued for a minute or more gazing on her blushing face, then taking her hand in his, and looking with wonder and admiration upon the small, delicate fingers, he said,—

"Thy father, pretty Jane, should be prouder than King Edward; and thy lover ——"

The king paused; and a smile crossed his face, as he saw that Jane le one glance in the direction where stood Walter Fane. He then stooped from his saddle until his sunny flowing locks mingled with those of the mercer's child, and imprinted upon her forehead a light kiss.

Jane's eyes were still cast to the ground; but in weal or in woe, in pain or sorrow, years afterwards, when persecuted by bigotry, and held up to public scorn and execration by those who, compared to her, were incarnate fiends—at times when her heart danced with joy, and the earth was to her a path of flowers, the sky an eternal sunshine—she never forgot that kiss from the young monarch, bestowed so gently, and received so purely.

Walter Fane alone trembled, and he felt as if a cold hand was laid upon his heart. A mystic shadow, as of some coming evil, seemed to creep across his soul, and he could almost have fancied that a voice rung in his ears, saying, "Woe—woe is coming."

There was now a slight movement among the nobles behind the king, and Lord Hastings, leaning forward, said,—

"My liege, the body of the assassin slain by your hand has been searched. Here is a packet ——"

"Ha!" cried Edward, snatching the small parchment scroll, and tearing it open. His eye wandered for a moment lightly over the words it contained, then suddenly a dark shade came over his face, and he compressed his lips till they became as white as death. With nervous energy he crumpled the parchment in his hand, and turning with flashing eyes to his nobles, he cried,—

"To the palace! to the palace! By God's Holy Word, there are high traitors even now revelling in our halls. To the palace! to the palace!"

Striking the golden spurs he wore deep into his horse's flanks, he dashed from the spot, and making a detour round the mouldering ruins of the gallery, he was soon, followed by his splendid retinue, galloping down the Chepe towards the palace at Westminster.

CHAPTER VII.

The Rivals.

"She was the worshipped of all hearts."

THE autumn of 1465 had passed away, and with it nearly the memory of the gay pageant of the sixteenth of October. An attempted deposition or assassination of a monarch excited in those "stirring times" but little attention after the first flush of excitement had passed away. The history of half a dozen attempted assassinations of King Edward the Fourth, during the first few years of his reign, were quaintly summed up by an early writer, who says:—"*Ye Kinge ledde a troublous life, and fulle of strategies and bloodfulle alarms, ye whiche kept him wakefulle alway.*"

That the attempt to assassinate the young king at the gallery of the Chepe was well matured, and that it was the emanation of a plot extensive in its ramifications, and important as regarded its contrivers, none could doubt; for numerous arrests had succeeded the affair, and the next public show that ye goode citizens flocked to see, consisted of divers grisly heads spiked on Tower-hill; after which a short season of calmness obtained, until "more iustie traitors" had gathered strength of heart.

The winter, too, had come and gone. The ancient thoroughfares of London had been blocked up by walls of snow. The cold east winds had swept over the land, and huge masses of ice had for weeks collected around the abutments and arches of London-bridge, rendering the river unnavigable. But all this had passed away, and time had brought back to the old city sunshine and warmth. It was spring—that balmy time,

"When the young air is full of joy,"

and the meanest habitations in London began to wear the rich, warm covering, which sunlight imparts to all things.

We will now beg the reader to enter with us the dwelling of Master Wainstead, the mercer.

In the room above the shop—that room from the window of which projected the heavy carved balcony which has been before described, sat the mercer and his daughter. The substantial citizen was seated upon a richly carved chair covered with pile velvet, and in his hand he held a paper, the perusal of which appeared to have brought a cloud upon his brow.

By his side, and resting one arm affectionately upon his shoulder, stood Jane. She was looking kindly and inquiringly in her father's face, and occasionally shifting her glance to the paper which he held in his hand, as if that had been the subject of discourse between them.

"This paper," said Wainstead, "is silly, my girl. Some idle prentice has stolen the verse. Avoid the balcony, Jane—avoid it, my Jane. A plague on the varlets tormenting thee. Did'st see what manner of man he was who threw this scroll at thee?"

"Scarcely, father," said Jane. "I was tending my flowers when the note fell at my feet, and Walter ——"

"Well, Jane, and Walter?"

"He would have begged it of me, but I feared to give it him, he was so chafed."

"Right," said Wainstead. "If this be anything but an idle jest, some older and calmer head than Walter Fane's should meet the knave. I prithee, Jane, bid Simon bring my hood and staff."

"Father, father," said Jane, throwing her arms round his neck: "you will not meet this man?"

"Fear not, Jane! fear not, my darling!" replied the mercer, kissing her cheek. "You know I love not brawls, and ——"

"And for my sake, dear, dear father," interrupted the fair girl, "you will be careful. Oh, do not go!"

"For thy sake, Jane? Heaven bless you! We are alone in the world, my child, and—and ——"

Again the father kissed the fair cheek of his beautiful child, then gently disengaging himself from her embrace, he rose, saying,—

"Nay, now, fret not thyself, Jane. I will be back anon."

His daughter looked after him as he left the room, and then throwing herself into his seat, with a sigh, she said,—

"I should have let Walter go; and yet—yet I know not what I should have done."

The mercer's shop was very dark, for the evening was rapidly approaching, and when Master Wainstead descended the narrow staircase leading from the upper room, it was only from habit, and an intimate acquaintance with the localities, that he was enabled to steer his bulky form clear of all impediments.

There were two persons in the mercer's shop. One of those was his serving man and porter, Simon ———, Simon what—nobody knew; for if that individual had ever luxuriated in a sirname, it had long since been forgotten. Simon's particular peculiarity consisted in a great economy of the parts of speech. The personal pronoun, I, he was never known to utter. In fact, he frequently passed whole days together without condescending to address any one. He was tall and thin; and a certain obliquity of vision gave him a peculiarity of appearance, by no means romantic. Beneath this singular exterior, however, he carried a heart entirely devoted to the mercer and his beautiful child, both of whom, when he thought proper, he would, in his laconic style, rate soundly for any proceedings of which he disapproved. Simon was a great grumbler, too, in his way; for, although he obeyed all his master's orders with diligence and alacrity, and would have risked his life to do him or Jane pleasure, he never by any accident received a command of which he did not disapprove in toto, and at once refuse to execute, at the very moment that he set about it.

Thus, when the mercer demanded of Simon his hood and staff, he was met by a decided negative, and a refusal to allow him to go forth at all just then. Nevertheless, the hood and staff were brought, and the former adjusted carefully over the mercer's shoulders.

Leaning his head upon his hands when Wainstead entered his shop, was Walter Fane, his prentice. The youth started at the noise of his master's approach; and, had there been light sufficient, Wainstead must have observed the mantling blush that spread over the young man's cheeks, and probably surmised that he (Walter) had been thinking upon something which he would not have his master know of.

"Walter," said Wainstead, "you saw a note thrown into the balcony?"

"In truth, sir, I did," answered Walter; "but before I could gain the street, the knave was gone."

"Of a surety, Walter, it was a knave; for see, my lad, the villain would beguile from me my child; I show you the note, Walter, to the end that should you see such another circumstance, you may take heed to foil it."

With a trembling hand Walter Fane took the note, and skipping some extravagant verses, he read the postscript, which ran thus:—

"To ye moste faire and exceedinge gentle.
"Ye moste true hearte yt loves thee lingers at ye gate of my Lorde Norfolke's house at sun sette."

"Let me beg—implore of you," cried Walter.

"What?"

"That you will let me go to this impertinent knave."

"No, Walter, no; you are young and rash. I will go; and, if needs be, the writer of this shall not find me either 'faire or exceedinge gentle.' My mind is troubled, Walter; for, of late, my house has been beset by gallants by day, and lurking spies by night. Remain thou here. I will return anon."

"The way is lonely," suggested Walter.

"But since the tall trees have been removed 'twixt here and Charing, Walter, we have heard of few misdeeds. Those trees were a rare shelter for evil-minded men. Be wary, Walter—be wary. Close the shop, Simon."

"Won't," said Simon, and forthwith commenced closing the heavy shutters.

The mercer smiled, and left his dwelling to go towards Norfolke House, which stood in the fields half way between Charing Cross and the city.

Scarcely had the mercer left his shop, when a man entered, with a swaggering air, exclaiming,—

"A sword-knot! a sword-knot! One of your choicest and most rare, ah!"

"A light, Simon," said Walter Fane. "Quick, Simon!"

"Sha'n't be quick," mumbled Simon, snatching up a lantern, and running over the road to a bowyer's opposite, who kept a light hanging at his door.

"A dainty sword-knot," continued the stranger. "One of spring colours. Ha!"

"We have them," said Walter, "of all kinds and qualities."

"Good. Ha!" cried the customer, stamping his foot with an air of great consequence and assumption. "I repeat, good. Ha!"

Simon now appeared with the light, and Walter Fane was enabled to obtain a sight of his vain-glorious customer. He was a tall, burly-looking man, attired in faded finery, no one article of which fitted him; and Walter knew, at a glance, that he was one of those devil-may-care, idle, disorderly fellows with which London abounded, who are generally said to "live by their wits," if there be any wit in robbery and violence.

The manners of the shopkeepers in those days were by no means so pliant and conciliating as they are now; and Walter Fane, disliking his customer, without a word, threw on the counter before him a collection of the articles he demanded.

"Ha!" cried the man. "These like me not—these like me not. Ha!"

"We have none other," said Walter.

"Fire and flames! none other! Say ye so much to a person of my quality? Ha!"

Walter made no reply, but looked invincibly cool, while Simon began packing up the sword-knots.

The man looked from Walter to Simon, and then back again to Walter, as if meditating some sanguinary stroke of vengeance; but, seeing that they were both unmoved, he thought proper to relax a little of his dignity, and, stroking his mustachios, he exclaimed,—

"We warriors are too easily chafed. Show me the knots again."

"Sha'n't," said Simon, unpacking them, and laying them once more before the stranger.

One after another he slowly examined the sword-knots, and placed each by the hilt of a long rapier he wore, to judge of the effect.

Walter Fane was, at length, growing out of all patience with the fastidiousness of the man, when a smothered cry broke upon his ear, and he started like one electrified.

"Help! father! Walter! help!" cried a voice. Too well Walter knew whose it was. It was Jane's.

With one bound the young man sprang over the counter, sweeping before him all the sword-knots, and upsetting the difficult customer; then, pushing past the amazed Simon, he rushed up the narrow staircase with a loud cry.

The first sight which presented itself to Walter Fane, when he entered the room above the shop, was Jane lying upon the floor apparently lifeless. The sight for a moment deprived him of all power of thought or action; then he rushed forward, and frantically calling her by name, he lifted her on a seat.

"God of Heaven!" he cried, "what is all this? Jane—Jane! Dear Jane, look up! 'Tis I—Walter—Walter Fane, who—who loves you!"

"Euh!" grunted Simon, at the door.

"Simon! Simon! she's dead. Jane, dear Jane is dead!"

"She ain't," said Simon.

"Call Mistress Martha, Simon. Oh, quick! quick! Jane, speak if you live! Oh, speak."

"Shan't," said Simon, and he immediately began shouting at the head of the stairs for the mercer's female domestic, an old woman whom he kept in his house, more from charity than for any utility she was of.

Before, however, Mistress Martha made her appearance, Jane opened her eyes, and looking imploringly in Walter's face, she said, with a shudder,—

"Walter! Walter! protect me from them!"

"Dear Jane," cried Walter, "say you are unhurt. Tell me you are well. What has happened?"

"The balcony," said Jane.

"There is no one there, Jane. Why do you look to the balcony with such alarm?"

"I was sitting at the open window, when, suddenly, a man appeared in the balcony, and throwing something over my head and face, strove to force me away. Oh, Walter, then I tried to cry for help."

"And, thank Heaven, I heard the cry, Jane."

"Old woman's out," said Simon, returning from the staircase.

"Simon," said Walter, "keep your watch below till Master Wainstead returns. Here has been some foul work in hand. I will remain here till your father returns, Jane."

"Shan't watch below," growled Simon, descending the stairs.

When he arrived in the shop, the important customer was gone, leaving the door wide open.

"Euh!" grumbled Simon. "Girls faint—trash."

Walter Fane closed the window leading into the balcony, for the night air began to blow coldly, and then trimming the lamp that stood upon the oaken table, he sat down opposite to Jane, to wait the return of the mercer.

Walter Fane had often sat with Jane Wainstead the better part of a summer's day, and although he had ever loved her with one of those pure, holy affections, which are so rare, and can only find a place in the hearts of the young and good, he had never thought to give his inmost feelings words. To see her—to speak to her—to hear her talk of flowers, and occasionally to be wrapt into forgetfulness of all but Heaven and her, by

listening to her voice, as she warbled some pastoral, had been his dearest joy. He felt, too, in his heart, that the mercer's beautiful child must know that he loved her. Could she misconstrue the devotion of his eyes? Ah, no! she must know how dear she was to Walter Fane: and the young lover had so accustomed himself to the idea, that he spoke and acted towards the mercer's beautiful child with all the delightful consciousness of accepted love.

But now, on this evening, as he sat gazing into the depths of those blue eyes, which were to him as glimpses of Heaven, a new feeling came across the mind of Walter Fane, and while his pulse quickened at the thought, and his heart beat wildly in his bosom, "like a new-caught bird," he whispered softly to himself, "I will tell Jane how I love her."

When once the determination was made, the difficulty of carrying it into execution increased momentarily, and, in five minutes, Walter Fane had worked himself into such a state of nervous excitement, that had his and Jane's life both depended upon his eloquence, they must have died the death.

Jane immediately saw the changing hues of his countenance, and she said, in a voice of alarm,—

"Walter, you are ill."

With a deep sigh, Walter Fane welcomed this breaking of the ominous silence, and he replied,—

"No, no, Jane; I—I was looking at my heart."

"Your heart, Walter?"

"Yes, dear—dear Jane; and there, just like as the glorious sunlight shines in noon-day majesty upon a fertile plain, there shone undiminished my sun. My heart, Jane, is filled alone with thee."

"Me, Walter?" faltered Jane, trembling excessively.

"Yes, dearest, ever best and dearest!" cried Walter, passionately, dropping on one knee at the feet of Jane. "My only love," he continued, "my beautiful Jane! you have known me long, and, long as you have known me, Jane, the knowledge of my fond heart's passion must have shown itself in many guises. Then say you knew I loved you. When first I became an inmate of this house, and you were a young, happy child, I loved you, Jane, and would hold you to my beating heart for hours of pure happiness. Ah, Jane, then, even then, you knew I loved you! This is no confession. The eyes, the voice, each trivial action, told the tale more eloquently than I can now find words to clothe it in. And forgive me, dear Jane, if I have sometimes doubted if you could love the poor, dependent Walter Fane. But, then, I thought you knew I loved you, and knowing that you still had a morning smile and an evening sigh for me. Let me hear from your own mouth, direct, that you have all along known my heart. Tell me you have whispered to yourself, 'Walter Fane loves me!' Tell me you have blamed, and yet excused my hopes. Could I quaff incessantly from a rich wine-cup, and not arise intoxicated with its fumes? Could I stand in the sunshine at day's decline, and not cry, 'How beautiful?' Could I be near thee—see thee—hear thee speak, and not adore thee? Ah, Jane, you knew I loved you, and this is but the weak comment on a foregone fact."

Jane could not speak for emotion, and Walter continued, in the same impassioned accents.

"Speak to me, Jane. One word ——"

"Don't," said Simon, popping his head into the room.

"Simon!" exclaimed Walter Fane, springing to his feet in confusion.

"T'aint," cried Simon, in his usual spirit of contradiction.

"Simon!" said Jane, imploringly

"My good Simon," continued Walter, "I—you—you know."

"Don't—can't—shan't," said Simon; then, pointing downwards, he ejaculated,—"Master!"

Jane immediately made her escape past Simon into another room, and, at the same moment, the tantalized Walter heard the heavy tread of the mercer upon the staircase.

"If I can translate blushes and sighs, she loves me," thought Walter; and, with this consolatory reflection, he waited the appearance of his master.

When Wainstead entered the room, Walter Fane, for the first time, became aware that some one was with him. Gliding in after the mercer, with the silent footfall of a cat, came Shore. His wounds on the night of the fete had been severe, but not mortal; and, after a tedious illness, he had crept out again, the shadow even of what he was before that eventful night. The goldsmith seemed never to have recovered the loss of blood from his wounds; for, whereas before he was dark and sallow, while the warm blood would occasionally show itself in his cheek, he had become, since his wounds, of a deadly paleness, and all the peculiarities of his suspicious character appeared to have come out in more bold relief.

"Master Shore, be seated," said Wainstead. "You are still weak. Beshrew me, but the knave's dagger robbed you of some life-blood, Master Shore. And here have I, too, been on a sleeveless errand."

Shore sat down with extreme care, after taking a furtive glance round the room. He seemed almost to fear that the chair would, with unexampled treachery, double up its legs, and let him down.

"Nay, friend Wainstead," he said, in hollow accents, "I am gaining strength. Good Walter, how fares it with thee? Hem!"

"Simon! Simon!" called Wainstead. "Go to Mistress Carnaby's, at The Morrice Dancers, and bid her send us some spiced canary."

Simon only tarried to call up the staircase that he would do no such thing, and then, with great alacrity, departed on his errand.

CHAPTER VIII.

The Court Masque.

And ye Lorde Hastings beinge more amorous yan juste,
dede wrongouslye essai to steal ye maide. *Ancient MSS.*

The mercer and Walter, when they came to converse upon the events of the evening, were not long in fully understanding the nature of the scheme for carrying off Jane. It was sufficiently evident that the note appointing an assignation by the Duke of Norfolk's house was merely a device to take the citizen from his home, and, as might be expected, he found no one on the spot indicated.

Walter Fane was frantic with himself for allowing the troublesome customer for the sword-knot to escape so easily; for he doubted not that he, too, was an agent in the business, whose duty it had been to keep him (Walter) occupied while the balcony of the mercer's house was scaled by those who would have robbed him of his child.

"Walter, Walter," said the mercer, "it is a grievous thing, now, in my declining years, that the very beauty and gentleness of my own dear child should bring sorrow to my heart. Alas, Walter! 'tis a sad thing. Here am I, haunted by gallants of all sorts and degrees. By day my door steps are crowded with flutterers in faded jerkins and broken plumes; and such a demand is there for small wares, such as cloak ties, hood snaps, sword-knots, loose points, and the like, never exceeding half a groate, or a sorry half of a crossed penny, that we are in constant cry and bustle for nought; and truly, there is the while such corkscrew glances sent up the dark staircase, and penetrating oglings into the oak parlour, that, by the mass! my patience is ofttimes well nigh spent. Ah, Walter! I have prided myself, and carried my head high for the beauty of my dear child, but now I wish—I wish, Walter, she was only beautiful to me. My heart is sore."

"My good, kind master," replied Walter, "give me but the word, and not a roystering gallant of them shall show his brazen front on this side of the Chepe."

"Then there's this masque, too," continued Wainstead. "Sir Peter Knevitt must needs have me go."

"The masque at the palace, sir?"

"Ay, Walter. The king, you see, is overflowing with gratitude to the citizens, and he gives this much talked-of masque on purpose, it is said, as a compliment to the wives and daughters of the citizens; although, 'twixt you and I, Walter, some of them may pay too high a price for it."

"And you must go, sir?"

"Nay, I can scarcely refuse. And I have promised Jane."

"Jane?"

"Yes, Walter. It troubles me much. But still, my boy, there may be less danger in taking her than in leaving her in the city unprotected. Now, by the Saints! Is it not a sad thing that an honest citizen dare not leave his child in his own house without dread of violence? Walter! Walter! we live in grievous times."

"Do not forget," said Walter, "that there is one who would stand between Jane and the boldest ruffian that ever projected a villany."

"No, no, Walter, I do not forget thee; but I should be unhappy at this court mummery alone. I will take Jane. We will wander for a short hour in the Royal Gardens, and then return. She shall not quit my side."

Walter was silent for a moment, and then he said,—

"The masque is on Wednesday?"

"It is."

"And this is Tuesday. Alas! that I may not go!"

"Nay, Walter, fret not thyself, boy. With diligence and industry you may one day wear a gold collar and a furred gown in London."

"Ah!" thought Walter, "I would rather live in some lone island in the far sea with Jane."

"Since last year," said Wainstead, after a pause, pursuing the same train of thought; "since last year, Walter, I have known no peace. The public notice of Jane by the king drew all eyes upon her."

Walter sighed.

"I am growing old," continued the mercer. "Jane is my only care; and before I leave the world I must see her the wife of some one who can protect her."

Walter Fane drew his breath short and thick, and his heart beat so tumultuously, that he involuntarily pressed his hand upon his breast.

"I must see Jane settled in life," continued Wainstead, "with some one who has the power and the will to throw a protecting arm around her helplessness."

"Yes, yes!" gasped Walter.

"Walter, you are a good and a kind lad, and, withal, sage beyond thy years ——"

"My—my kind—master!" stammered Walter, clasping his hands.

"I will confide to thee, Walter."

Walter Fane would have spoken, but his feelings nearly choked him; and the mercer, in his deliberate manner, continued,—

"You shall know, Walter, that it is my intention to wed Jane with one who has long loved her."

"Oh, so long!" cried Walter. "From the first moment ——"

"Eh?" said Wainstead, in surprise.

"I—I—I pray you, pardon me, sir. I will listen. Say on, my kind master; say on."

"Jane shall be the wife, I hope, of ——"

Walter, in his eagerness, laid his hand upon his master's arm, and the latter terminated the sentence with "Shore."

"Shore!" echoed Walter, while a deadly paleness came across his face, and every object in the room seemed to swim before him.

"Yes, Shore," repeated the mercer. "My old friend, Shore; a wise man, and a rich one. Dost see aught objectionable?"

"Objectionable!" gasped Walter.

"Yes. Why look you thus panic stricken?"

"Panic stricken!"

"Why, Walter, can'st do nothing but repeat my words?"

At this moment the voice of Simon called up the stairs,—

"Here's Master Druggett has sent back the taffety, and says 'tis short, and withal grievous faulty."

"Eh, Simon? What say you?" cried the mercer, rising. "Short and faulty! Nay, now, a better taffety never left the shop. Tell Master Druggett's man to come up."

"Sha'n't," cried Simon.

Walter Fane, with a deep sigh and a tottering step, rose and left the room. Slowly he descended the narrow staircase leading to the shop, and when there, he leant his head upon his hands, and for a few minutes thought he should go mad. The words, "Jane shall be the wife of Shore," seemed to dance upon his brain in letters of fire.

The remainder of that day hung heavily upon Walter's hands. In vain he endeavoured to get an opportunity of conversing with Jane alone. He only saw her at the regular meal times, and then in presence of her father. Once or twice the masque of the morrow was mentioned, and he listened abstractedly to the mercer's complaints of the trouble of going. He only started into full consciousness when he heard that Jane was to accompany Lady Knevitt, and be under her special care as long as she remained, which the mercer declared should only be so long as to take a walk through the palace garden, and then return.

The day at length was done, and Walter Fane sought his pillow, not to sleep, but to mourn. Towards morning he succeeded in calming his mind sufficiently to snatch an hour or two's brief repose, by forming the romantic resolution of constituting himself the protector of Jane at the court masque, whither he determined to repair in some guise which should procure him admission, after which he would propose to Jane to marry him secretly, then they would together throw themselves for forgiveness at the feet of the mercer, and all would end happily. With this dream of joy Walter slept, nor waked till Simon entered his little chamber, and shook him roughly.

The masque to which King Edward had invited the principal citizens of London was to commence at noon, and terminate at sunset; for two or three disagreeable adventures that had happened at some of the night fetes which had been recently given, had made the young monarch rather in love with daylight when he summoned a crowd of revellers around him.

These court masques, which were so frequent from the fifteenth to the eighteenth century, were most unmeaning and vapid in themselves, and had it not been for the intrigues which they gave rise to and favoured, and the general licentiousness of which they were the cloak, they would scarcely have met the extensive patronage they did.

The masque, on the present occasion, was to take place in the gardens of the old palace at Westminster, which was then the royal residence. Those gardens extended down to the water's edge, and there was a handsome flight of stone steps, at which embarkations and debarkations might be made, at the foot of a sloping lawn. The gardens were laid out in what some one has, not unhappily, called "the conundrum style;" for, when in, it was difficult to find the way out again.

At these masques there was no order or precedency. The garden and palace gates were thrown open to all possessing tickets, and the lower parts of the palace were converted into refreshment rooms principally. The king was never recognised, although it it was always presumed that he was mixing with his guests; and, in fact, it would have been a great breach of etiquette to affect to know him, even if his disguise were ever so flimsy.

A vague feeling of uneasiness had been creeping over the mind of Walter Fane the whole of the morning, and he could not but think that the same persons who had made the audacious attempt on the Monday evening to carry Jane off from even beneath her father's roof, would not neglect the opportunity, in the throng and confusion of the court masque, to repeat an attempt which most likely emanated from a quarter more specially at home on such occasions.

The young lover saw the mercer and his daughter depart with a sad heart. He had determined to make an attempt to follow them even into the precincts of the royal gardens, but the means he left to chance. Turning to Simon, he said,—

"Simon, I leave you in charge. Do your best. Although the city is too empty for business, I must away."

Without heeding the remonstrances of Simon, Walter then donned his prentice cap, and with rapid step hurried to Westminster.

It has been already mentioned, that the mercer's daughter accompanied the Lady Mayoress to the palace, and her father followed on horseback, along with the civic authorities.

There was much crowding and bustling at the garden entrance to the palace; and a circumstance occurred within the observation of Wainstead, which he was not near enough to resent, although it gave him much vexation.

As Jane, leaning on Lady Knevitt's arm, passed through the throng of pages and lacqueys at the gate, one of the number, with an air of insolent freedom, twitched the lower part of her mask in such a manner that it was pulled down low enough to disclose her eyes, after which he who had done so immediately disappeared in the throng. The mercer rightly considered this an unprovoked outrage, and would have immediately returned with Jane, but the crowd in the entrance was so great that Lady Knevitt and Jane had passed on out of his sight before he could present his ticket, and gain admission.

The scene presented in the royal gardens was curious in the extreme; crowds of persons were thronging the walks and green plots, attired in every variety of extravagant costume; and whether it was that the members of the court disliked the company of the citizens, or really cultivated an extraordinary bad taste of their own, the fact was, that there was much more of the grotesque than the elegant in the costumes and disguises adopted by the greater number. Many of the nobility had dressed themselves as city prentices, and with serio-comic masks paraded the gardens, to the great surprise of the wardens and heads of the various guilds who were present.

Some of the masques were enveloped in the skins of bears and tigers, and one personated an immense dragon or crocodile, running continually among the feet of the dancers, and dealing heavy blows with a long elastic tail, which he had some means of managing.

Jane was as anxious to keep in company with her father as he was not to lose sight of her; and when a masque in the garb of a city guard whispered in her ear, "Master Wainstead wishes to leave. If you will follow me, young mistress, I will conduct you to him," she immediately turned to the Lady Knevitt, and begged her permission to retire.

"Nay, Jane, your father cannot leave yet," said the lady, "for the crowd at the entrance is immense."

"There is the wicket by the river steps," said the guardsman. "Master Wainstead there waits with young Master Fane ——"

"Yes—yes," said Jane, "I will go. Lead on, sir."

"Take care of thyself," said Lady Knevitt, as Jane bounded after the man.

With a rapid step the masqued soldier led the way towards the river, and opening a small iron gate, which kept free from intrusion several private walks of the garden, he beckoned to Jane to follow; then proceeding still onwards, he struck into a path which was overhung with tall trees, and which terminated in a small open spot, covered with the most delicious short verdure.

The man now turned to Jane, and saying, " Tarry a moment, pretty one," plunged among the trees, and was lost to sight in a moment.

One pang of alarm shot across the mind of Jane, but before it could assume a tangible shape, she heard a footstep behind her, and immediately she beheld a cavalier richly dressed, standing within a few paces of her.

" My peerless beauty!" he exclaimed, " can it be possible that so much loveliness ——"

He paused; for Jane shrunk from his address, as he would have taken her hand.

" Where is my father?" she cried.

" By the river side, damsel. Allow me to conduct you to him."

" No, no," cried Jane, thoroughly alarmed by the man's manner; " I will return to Lady Knevitt."

She bounded forward as she spoke, but the stranger caught her in his arms, and, with a laugh, cried,—

" What a dear chance! Beautiful girl ——"

" Help, father! Walter!" cried Jane, disengaging herself with horror from the man's embrace.

" Hold, hold!" he cried. " No noise, maiden. What, ho! Ho! friends!"

Two men immediately darted from among the trees.

" To the boat!" cried the richly dressed cavalier. " Quick, to the boat!"

Jane screamed, and called loudly upon her father; but she was unrelentingly seized, and dragged from the spot.

Scarcely had the low branches of the trees closed behind her, when, breathless and heated, a young man reached the open space from which she had been dragged.

" Jane, Jane!" he cried. " It was her voice. God help her! Jane, Jane!"

In the next moment the mercer's daughter, pale and dishevelled, burst through the bushes. She gave but one glance at the new comer, and crying,—

" Walter, save me!" fell insensible upon his arm.

There was scarcely time for Walter Fane (for it was he) to utter an exclamation of delight, when he was assailed fiercely by the two men who had dragged Jane away at the command of their ruthless employer.

The short grass was exceedingly slippery, and, fortunately for Walter, the foremost of the ruffians fell close to his feet. Before the other could assault him, Walter had possessed himself with the fallen man's sword, and dealing him a blow with it which put him, for the time, *hors de combat*, he placed himself in an attitude of defence, with the insensible form of his beloved Jane hanging on his arm. His eyes flashed fire, and a thousand hearts seemed to animate his frame.

CHAPTER IX.

The Rescue.

" Ande some dide make unrighteous remerkes, sayeing—Trulie in these daies ye might is ye righte."

How differently he engages in contest, whose heart as well as hand is in the cause, to the hired ruffian, who measures his blows by his reward. From the moment that Walter Fane crossed swords with the ruffian in the palace garden, the latter was evidently more intent upon escape than active resistance. After a few thrusts and parries, he darted suddenly through the thickets, and left Walter in undisturbed possession of the field. Forgetting, then, everything in his solicitude for the recovery of Jane, Walter flung down the sword, and still supporting the insensible girl, he, despite the peril of his own situation, called loudly for help.

Hardly had his cries awakened the echoes of that silent spot of the gardens, when he found himself roughly seized, and immediately surrounded by the palace guard. Jane, with a shudder, unclosed her eyes, and gazing with inexpressible dismay around her upon the armed men, she clasped her hands, and, still clinging to Walter, she cried,—

" Father! father! They will kill him! they will kill him!"

The trampling of many feet was now distinctly heard, and Walter Fane casting his eyes in the direction from whence the sounds proceeded, saw through the interstices of the trees that a number of masquers were rapidly approaching.

" There is greater safety in a multitude," thought Walter, " than with these hired knaves," and he raised his voice, crying, " Help, help, citizens; help, help!"

A tall man, whose face was covered with a velvet mask, now dashed forward, and seizing Jane roughly by the arm, he cried,—

"Carry off the knave! A broiler in the king's garden! Away with him; away with the assassin!"

"Liar!" cried Walter, striking the man in the face with an energy that at once removed the velvet mask.

"'Tis he, Walter!" cried Jane.

"Hastings!" ejaculated Walter.

It was the Lord Hastings; and, purple with rage, he tore his sword from its scabbard, for the purpose of plunging it into the breast of the defenceless Walter, when his arm was arrested by some one clinging round him from behind, and a voice cried,—

"Nay, hold, friend. I can't very well spare my 'prentice, any more than my daughter."

A bitter oath burst from the lips of Hastings, as he writhed to disengage himself from the grasp of Master Wainstead.

A murmur now arose among the motley crowd that had assembled, and the gallants of the court were slowly separating themselves from the citizens, and drawing their swords, when a mask, in a dark cloak and a green velvet cap, stepped forward before Lord Hastings.

"Peace, Hastings!" he cried—"peace! And you, sir, unloose your hold. By the rood! is this a brawl or a merry-making?"

"Sire," stammered Hastings.

"The king!" exclaimed Walter.

"Yes, the king," said the mask, throwing off his cap and mask.

Immediately every head was uncovered, and a respectful silence ensued. There was an angry flush upon the king's brow, and a slight tremor of the upper lip, as he glanced round him upon the brilliant throng of persons.

"Well, my lords, and you, my good citizens, are ye all dumb?" he cried. "Our masque is over, I say, my lords."

Instantly every mask was removed, and the crowd looked inquiringly into each other's faces; but no one spoke, and the king resumed,—

"Can no one, simple or gentle, explain to King Edward why swords are drawn here, and blood spilt upon his threshold?"

"I, your Majesty," said Walter, "can say something."

"And I," interrupted Lord Hastings. "This person (indicating Walter) is here without licence. How he procured admission, let him declare. He, and he only, is the brawler. Your majesty's guard was most properly apprehending him; and his unseemly resistance, for which, of course, he stands in present jeopardy of death, has caused this much lamented tumult."

"That is not the truth," cried Walter.

"Ha! this to me?" exclaimed Hastings. "My good liege, you hear the hot-tongued villain? I—I ——"

"We do hear him," said Edward. "Young man, you have said too much or too little."

"May it please you, sire, I have more to say," replied Walter Fane.

"But not against the honour of a nobleman?" said Hastings.

"Against your honour," replied Walter, "were you ten times a noble."

Hastings was about to make some angry reply, when some one touched his arm, and whispered in his ear,—

"What hast thou been bent on, to stir the thick blood of the bourgeoise thus, Hastings?"

"Your grace?" said Hastings, turning.

"Bide time, bide time," said he who had spoken to the chafed chamberlain.

He was a tall man, but looked ungainly from the shortness of his neck. His eyes were small and deeply set, but black and sparkling.

"His grace of Gloster's advice," muttered Hastings, "is always valuable. I will—bide—my time."

This conversation passed in a moment, and King Edward continued to shift his glance from Walter to Jane, as he said,—

"We hear—we hear. Say on. Is not this the maiden who did us good chance service in our good city?"

"True, King Edward," cried Wainstead, advancing to his daughter's side; "and a better wench ——"

"Yes, yes," interrupted Edward. "We will hear from thy own lips, pretty one, if thou canst tell us the meaning of all this."

"And, in the meantime," suggested Hastings, "this fellow, who has intruded himself into the precincts of your majesty's palace, shall be seen to. Guards, take him off, and—"

"Great haste, Hastings, eh?" said the king, a small red spot growing on his cheek—a certain sign of anger.

"Since your majesty," replied Hastings, humbly, "was so gracious as to give your poor servant the order and regulation of the fete, I ——"

"Would carry the authority to the utmost," interrupted the king. "We absolve you, my lord, for the present, from the cares of authority."

Hastings bit his lip, and bowed.

"I came here," said Walter, boldly, "upon an errand, for the success of which King Edward would have thrown open every entrance of his palace to the meanest of his subjects."

"Ha!" cried the king, bending his brow upon Walter. "Say on—say on."

"I came to protect the innocent and weak against the machinations of the wicked and the strong."

"As how—as how, sir?"

"This maiden ——"

"My daughter," interrupted Wainstead.

"This maiden was set upon by ruffians, commanded by one more cowardly than they, for he had the head to plan what he lacked himself the courage to execute. I climbed the wall of your palace garden, my liege. Will yon ruffian lying there, as I verily believe, in a pretended swoon, explain as frankly how he obtained admittance?"

The king cast his eyes in the direction Walter indicated, and the throng moving on one side, discovered the ruffian whom Walter had overthrown, still lying upon the ground, to all appearance dead.

"Ha!" cried the king. "Have we such knaves about our palace?"

"Your majesty," exclaimed Hastings, "shall not want a loyal sword to rid your sacred person of such vile company."

So saying, he drew his sword, and suddenly advancing, would have effectually put an end to all evidence from the wounded ruffian, had he not been restrained by the Duke of Gloster, who interposed in a manner that raised a smile from the king.

"Beshrew me, my good lord," said Gloster, "but you are unmindful of your fair repute. Now, an you had slain the knave, evil-minded folks would have said 'twas well done of the crafty Hastings to silence a rude ——"

"My lord! your grace!" interrupted Hastings, reddening.

"Nay, nay," sneered Gloster, still holding him.

"I—I meant but—my lord—I ——"

"Sagely spoken, good Hastings. How like to conscious guilt is the mantling blush of innocence on the good chamberlain's face."

"My—my lood—your majesty ——"

"See, brother," continued Gloster, "what young blood dances through the veins of merry Hastings."

Hastings bit his lips, and dashed his sword into its scabbard with a loud clash, as he whispered ——"

"This is ungenerous, your grace. Have I deserved it at your hands?"

"Now he is calm," continued the duke, in the same provoking tone. "See, my lords, how fair words turn away wrath."

"Your majesty! my gracious liege!" cried Hastings, foaming with rage.

"Blessed are the peace-makers!" said Gloster, patting him gently on the back.

The king laughed outright; and, as royal mirth is always contagious, the gardens rang with laughter, while Hastings stood the picture of wild frenzy, and yet unable to resent anything, while the Duke of Gloster still gently and caressingly patted his back.

"Enough—enough!" said the king. "Gloster, cease. We will inquire into this matter at our greater leisure; but see if yon ruffian be dead or alive."

"It seemeth a sluggish beast," said Gloster; "and by your leave, brother, we will e'en try a goad."

As he spoke he advanced to the prostrate man, and, to the great amusement of the semi-barbarous court, commenced goading him with his spurs. The man, with a roar, sprung to his feet, and was immediately seized.

Lord Hastings turned pale, and striving to catch the heavy eye of the hired bravo, he gave him a significant look, which, however, did not pass unobserved by the mischief-loving Gloster, who cried,—

"'Tis a knave of small wit, my Lord Hastings—allow me;" and walking up to the man, he winked close to his face.

Another roar of laughter, in which the king joined, drove Hastings nearly frantic.

"Gloster, Gloster," said the king, "wilt thou never cease thy tricks? Friends, our masque is over."

"But, your majesty," interposed Wainstead, "my daughter Jane ——"

"Shall be seen safely to your home, friend," interrupted the king.

"But, my liege!" said Walter Fane, who did not approve of this mode of settling the affair.

"Our masque is over," said the king, sternly. "Hastings, attend us."

"And this good fellow with the unfortunate physiognomy?" said Gloster, pointing to the man, who was still held by the palace guards.

"Hang him, an you will; or scourge the knave well, and let him go."

"But be sure," said Gloster to the officer of the guard, "he take not his ears with him."

"Mercy!" cried the man, dropping on his knees; "mercy! I will tell all."

"Eh?" said Gloster, assuming a vacant look. "If thou wilt be hung, friend, e'en have thy way."

"Mercy, your grace, I said—not that."

"Indulge him, then, and hang him," said Gloster. "It's politic to please the people."

The man was roughly dragged away, and the court masque was over.

CHAPTER X.

Jane's New Lover.

"If ye younge god of love turn ane strange and lustie braine, ye sillie and fulle
Of smalle conceites will plaie ye moste strange mummeries an antick feats."

People had almost ceased to gossip about the court masque; for a fortnight had passed away since it happened, and the city had relapsed into its usual state.

No changes or occurrences of any importance had taken place at the mercer's; but in the immediate vicinity of the worshipfulle Master Wainstead's shop something was occurring, which, if not instructive, may be amusing to the reader.

As we have before stated, immediately opposite to the mercer's was the old building, called Scroop's Castle; and the house adjoining that suspicious edifice was in the occupation of a bowyer, who rejoiced in the name of Snafflings. Now, Master Snafflings was a widower; and he did not rejoice in an only daughter, Miss Bridget Snafflings, who, had it not been that she possessed a tongue which left the most exalted ideas of perpetual motion quite in the shade, a voice like a tin trumpet with a bad cold, and a long wiry-looking neck, at the summit of which her head kept up a perpetual jerking, as if it were moved about by some complex system of cords and pullies, might have been a most amible and loveable young person; but as it was, Master Snafflings frequently, with a grave shake of his head, implying a great deal more than words could express, would hint at the extraordinary and daily-increasing resemblance between Miss Bridget and her lamented mother, Mrs. Snafflings, whose sharp, screeching voice had been for many years familiar to the inhabitants of the Chepe.

For a long time Mr. Snafflings, who was a quiet, easy, let-well-alone, make-yourself-comfortable sort of a little man, sat by his own fire-side, and endured the lecturing and screaming of Mrs. Snafflings, until one eventful evening a resource against all sorts of domestic annoyances suggested itself to Mr. Snafflings; that resource was "The King's Head," an hostelrie, situated in a court leading from the Chepe to Aldersgate, "where ye moste rare entertainemente for man and beaste was to be had, with righte merrie companie and sportfule gentles." This house was well frequented; for in those ticklish times the sign was considered felicitous, for whatever king reigned, be it a Lancaster or a York, he must by necessity have a head of some sort, consequently the sign of "The King's Head" was always loyal and proper.

Thither, then, at sunset, would Master Snafflings repair; and after a time mine host inserted in the wall, by the side of the seat which the bowyer always occupied, a small wedge of wood with a piece of soft padding on the top, and Master Snafflings duly placed his elbow thereon, and gave up his mind to enjoyment.

The bowyer's household consisted but of his charming daughter, and a gaunt-looking lad, his 'prentice, whom everybody called Jacob, and nothing else; for what other name Jacob might have legally laid claim to was never known, since he had been picked up an infant in the streets, and in due time apprenticed by the parish to Master Snafflings. Jacob was one of those lads who look all "odds and ends." He was tall and sprawling; preternaturally thin, and not at all remarkable for any mental characteristic, excepting an intense enjoyment of things in which nobody else saw any joke. Jacob would laugh by the hour together at a man walking past the door, who to an ordinary observer presented no comic feature whatever; the slightest street occurrence, the entrance into the shop of a chance customer, anything and everything, was food for Jacob's mirth, and he roared with a sort of insane glee from morning till night. This excessive mirth first amused, and then annoyed the bowyer, and, finally, put him in a great passion, in the excess of which he sharply reprimanded the laughter-loving Jacob, who ever after carried about with him a small piece of blue cotton, which had once been a handkerchief, and when anything irrepressibly comical occurred, such as a man looking gravely in at the shop window, or one citizen touching his cap to another, Jacob would stuff the piece of blue cotton in his mouth to repress his mirth, and look with starting eyes and a distended visage at his master, until once or twice the bowyer was seriously alarmed, and tore the stopper out of Jacob's mouth for fear he should burst, when such an explosion of bottled-up mirth followed, that Master Snafflings was fain to rush into the street till Jacob was exhausted.

Now poor Jacob might have passed through life a laughing philosopher, had not Jane Wainstead persevered in the habit of tending her plants in the balcony every sunset, at or about the hour when Jacob usually closed the shutters of the bowyer's shop. Then Jacob would look wistfully across the way, and his laughs sensibly decreased both in intensity and frequency, and each evening he would be slower in putting up his master's shutters, until at length the last one had always to be thrust into its place after Jane had retired from the mercer's balcony, and closed the window. Then, with a deep sigh, Jacob would don his 'prentice cap, and walk up and down the Chepe with his hands behind him, indulging occasionally in visionary dreams of setting up a shop some day for himself, and having the mercer's daughter in the back parlour thereof.

By constantly brooding over the extreme felicity which would be his portion, could he by any means make a successful onslaught on the heart of the mercer's daughter, Jacob came at last to believe that he had some sort of right to Jane's affections; and whenever any gay gallant swaggered into the mercer's shop, Jacob's jealousy was aroused lest the said gallant should be actually making violent love to the beautiful Jane, or slipping billets into the hand of Simon, breathing all sorts of vows. So strangely had this notion taken possession of the limited mind of poor Jacob, that he was always on thorns when any one entered Master Wainstead's till he saw them come out again.

One day Jacob hit upon a notable scheme for disturbing any consultation inimical to his peace that might be going on in the mercer's shop, and that was, to take a gold noble from his master's till, and run over to the mercer's to get its change in silver groates.

This sagacious manœuvre of Jacob's passed unnoticed for some time, but at last his applications for change became so numerous, that Walter Fane lost all patience, and Simon unceremoniously turned Jacob out of the shop, with an intimation not to come any more. Jacob then grew desperate, and resolved upon taking some bold step to declare his passion to Jane herself, despite Walter Fane, Simon, and all the court gallants who thronged the mercer's shop; but the when, the where, and the how? There Jacob was puzzled; and there Jacob would have remained puzzled had not an unexpected circumstance raised him up an ally, who promised much, if he performed but little. It happened, as Jacob was reposing against the shutter of his master's shop, and gazing across the way at Jane, there slunk down the Chepe no other than the troublesome customer who had engaged Walter Fane's attention while the attempt at Jane's abduction was proceeded with. This ingenious individual, who was the same faded gallant who had been apostrophised by Mrs. Mapletoft as Bully Bluster on the day of the *fete*, was upon the present occasion a much more faded gallant than before. His hose were sadly creased, and his doublet was a curiosity.

For a few moments this more crafty than scrupulous individual watched the direction of Jacob's eyes, and then advancing with his usual swaggering gait, he exclaimed,—

"Hilloa, my Trojan!—my gallant bowyer! How fares it with thee? Ha!"

A few weeks previously Jacob would have laughed for a month at such an adventure; but, alas! now the spirit of mirth was dead within him, and he found "a charm in melancholy," so, surveying the very faded gallant with a rueful air, he merely shook his head, and commenced putting up the last shutter.

"Hilloa, friend! Ha!" repeated the gallant.

"Well, what is it?" said Jacob.

"Look at me—observe me—note me—ha!"

Jacob looked and muttered something about having nothing to give away.

"Look again—ha!" cried the faded gallant.

"Well, I do look. What then?" replied Jacob.

"You are no conjuror."

Jacob shook his head; and the ghost of one of his old smiles came across his face.

"I am, then. Ha!"

"A con—jur—or—?"

"Yes. A—a—kind—of—a conjuror in fact. Your name is ——"

"Why, Jacob, to be sure."

"I knew it. And you love ——"

"Jane, the mercer's daughter, to be sure."

"And shall wed her ——"

"You—you don't mean that?" stammered Jacob.

"You have a rival," continued the gallant—"a deadly rival."

Jacob cast up his eyes, exclaiming, "It must be Walter Fane, that accounts for ——"

"Yes, it accounts for everything. Don't you feel thirsty? Ha!"

"Thirsty? Why I can't say I do, exactly."

"If," said the faded gallant, laying his hand in a solemn manner upon Jacob's shoulder, "if you would wed the mercer's daughter, and in time step into that shop opposite as its master—listen!"

Jacob looked aghast, for he considered Master Wainstead so great a man, that his wildest dreams of ambition had never compassed the remote possibility of him, Jacob, ever approaching so much glory.

"A charm must be contrived," continued the faded gallant. "Ha!"

"Ye—yes," said Jacob. "What must I do?"

"Have—you—a gold florence?"

Jacob shook his head despairingly.

"A noble?"

Again, with a deep sigh, Jacob's head indicated the low state of his finances.

"Ha! nor a royal?"

"I—I think," said Jacob, hesitatingly, "I've got three silver groates. Will you walk in?"

The faded gallant peered in at the open door before he would accept of Jacob's invitation, for he feared the bowyer himself might not be of so complying a temperament as his 'prentice; seeing, however, that the shop was vacant (for Master Snafflings had retired to "The King's Head"), he ventured to cross the threshold, and Jacob having placed up his last shutter, joined his knowing guest, and, with open mouth and fixed attention, listened for a full half hour to the gallant's glowing description of his own extreme courage and cleverness. The three groates, too, were produced, and melted into foaming ale, which Jacob and the faded gallant again converted into brilliant sallies of imagination, and all sorts of anticipations. Then the faded gallant, looking ruefully into the empty flagon, gave utterance to a sentiment which sunk deep into the breast of the love-sick 'prentice.

"Jacob," he said, "you are a marvellously proper fellow; that is—a—hem! You are thin and tall, and may be made anything of, from a May-day morrice to a city warden—ha! Now listen: women are all the daughters of Eve—ha! Appearance does wonders. Now if you could manage a few gold pieces to dress bravely, and walk the street with a swagger, my life on't you'd captivate the mercer's daughter— ha!"

"I—I—believe you," said Jacob, whose weak head was far from being proof against the humming ale. "I—I believe you: a swag—swag—swagger is the thing. Ha! ha! Hurrah!

"The red rose, the red rose,
Is blushing, is blushing;
The warm blood, the warm blood,
Is gushing, is gushing;
For ——"

"What a voice, too," cried the faded gallant, giving Jacob a blow upon the back, which at once stopped his breath and the song.

"I—I believe you; I have a voice," hiccuped Jacob.

"The cuckoo sings, the cuckoo sings,
So ——"

"Now a couple of rose nobles," whispered the faded gallant, "would attire you like a courtier. Your points should be silver; your doublet a Genoese; your hose of rare fancies; and on such legs as yours—ha!"

"I—I—believe you," said Jacob; "I—I have legs—of—of great—that is—how the shop turns—turns round."

So saying, Jacob fell upon the floor, and gave up consciousness for a time. The faded gallant then rose, and looked cautiously around him for some article of value upon which to lay his hands; but before he could decide upon what depredation to commit, he was startled by a shrill female voice exclaiming,—

"Hoity-toity! marry come up! What's here? What Jack are you, I wonder? Jacob! Jacob! Here's a figure of mischief. Jog on, you mummer; jog on. Jacob! Jacob!"

The faded gallant rushed from the shop at the same moment that the bowyer's daughter stumbled and fell, with a loud scream, over the prostrate form of Jacob.

CHAPTER X.

Jacob's Misfortunes.

"Then spake ye raven, sayinge, ye fine feathers
make ye fine birdes."

As Jacob's unlucky stars would have it, the very next day was a city holiday, and the 'prentices had agreed to meet in "Bunhille Fieldes" for sport. Now Jacob had been accustomed, in his laughing days, to look forward with great glee to these periodical merry-makings. He would laugh a full month beforehand in anticipation; and, on the occasion itself, he would create mirth wherever he went; and then what food for future mirth did not such days produce? For months afterwards Jacob would roar again at some small conceit that had mightily tickled his strange fancy, but which everybody else had quite forgotten. On this morning, however, Jacob rose with an aching head and bewildered brain; that is to say, more bewildered than usual; and when Master Snafflings said,—

"Well, Jacob, here are six groates, boy; take thyself to thy fellows, and be merry," Jacob took the groates and wandered into the Chepe, without any very clear notion of what he was going to do. He walked over the way mechanically, and, flattening his nose against the mercer's window, he strove to catch a glimpse of the interior of the shop, with the vague hope that Jane might be there; whereupon Simon sallied out and demanded, in an extraordinary long speech for him, what he, Jacob, meant.

"I'd ruffle it with the best of you," said Jacob, with an abstracted air, "an I had but brave apparel."

"You wouldn't," said Simon.

At this moment, as Jacob's eyes were wandering about, he descried, from the deep entrance to Scroop's Castle, the tip of a human nose, against which was placed a finger. Now the nose was a very red and inflamed-looking nose, and Jacob could not help surmising that it belonged to his tempter of the preceding evening, and that the peculiar attitude of the finger was meant as a kind of telegraphic sign to him, Jacob; and he accordingly crossed the road, and stood in the entrance to Scroop's Castle.

"Hist! ha!" said some one from far in.

"'Tis he," muttered Jacob.

"Ha, my Trojan! my salamander!" said the faded gallant.

"Sally who?" inquired Jacob.

The faded gallant now emerged more fully from his place of concealment, and, taking Jacob by the arm, he hurried him down the Chepe.

"What's the matter?" said Jacob, in some alarm at the impetuosity of his companion.

"Fortune," said the faded gallant, "favours you. Ha! you have met me."

Jacob did not exactly perceive the logic of this speech, and he only looked a little more bewildered.

"Listen!" continued the faded gallant. "A few gold royals would fit you out like a noble. Have—you—any ——"

"No!" sighed Jacob, jinking the six groates Master Snafflings had given him.

"Hist!" cried the gallant. "Never make music in the streets of London with your money. Give it to me. I am your friend. Ha!"

Jacob reluctantly parted with the groates, and the faded gallant would most probably have immediately parted with Jacob, had he not thought there was more still to be made of him. Suddenly stopping, with a jerk that made Jacob give a sympathetic start, he said,—

"Attend! I have travelled east, west, north, and south."

As he spoke, he indicated with successive waves of his hands, the several points of the compass, and Jacob's eyes followed each movement with a stare of wonder.

"The mercer's daughter," continued the faded gallant, "is beautiful; the mercer is rich."

"Very!" sighed Jacob.

"If the mercer's daughter was Mistress Jacob ——— what's your name?"

"I don't know."

"Don't know?"

"No; some call me Jacob Chepe, because I was found in the Chepe."

"Ha! a mystery; but suffice it now, that the mercer's daughter loves, adores you!"

"Me!" screamed Jacob.

"Hush! Doats—idolises!"

"You—you don't mean Jane?"

"Hush! I do—Jane, the mercer's daughter—ha!"

Jacob sat down on the step of a door, and covering his face with his hands, he burst into tears, exclaiming,

"Does she love me? does she love poor Jacob? God bless her! everybody loves her! but—but I couldn't think she could love poor Jacob, the bowyer's 'prentice—I—I mustn't have her: she's too good for me. When—when I thought she didn't care about me, I—I—oh, dear! oh, dear!—oh, dear!"

Here Jacob's tears choked his utterance, and in the fulness of his heart he sobbed aloud. The faded gallant waited unmoved till the tide of feeling had passed away; and then taking Jacob by the arm, he wrenched him up from the door-step, and said,

"Come, come, be a man!—ha!—no snivelling. I tell you she loves you."

"Are—are you sure? quite sure?"

"Ha! you doubt my honour?"

"No, no; I will be her servant. I'll wait upon her always. Bless her! I ——"

"Bah!" said the faded gallant; "listen to me. I'll tell you what she said."

"Jane said?"

"Yes.—'That Jacob,' says she, 'has very thin legs.'"

"Dear heart! so I have," said Jacob.

"'His nose rather turns up ——'"

"It does! it does!"

"'And his hair looks as if it was always in a high wind.'"

"Dear me!" said Jacob.

"'But—yet—yet ——'"

"Yet—yet ——"

"'I love him.'"

"Is it really true?"

"Ha! doubt my honour?—ha!"

"No, no; but—really—oh, how good she is, to love poor Jacob!"

"Then she went on to say, if Jacob was dressed becomingly, he would be a marvellous proper man; his thin legs would look genteel; his nose would scorn the vulgar; and his hair—a—a—his hair—ha! That's what she said."

"Oh, if I had but a few nobles!" sighed Jacob.

Suddenly the faded gallant again stopped, and Jacob again gave a sympathetic start.

"Take a handful of nobles from old Snafflings," whispered the faded gallant.

Jacob looked aghast; and his companion continued,—

"When you marry the rich mercer's daughter, you can pay him back again. Where does he keep money?—ha!"

This question was put so rapidly, and accompanied by so vigorous a grasp of the arm, that Jacob by a sudden impulse answered,—

"In a little oak cabinet in the parlour."

"Locked?"

"Yes."

"And the key? Quick!"

"Hangs in a nook behind the clock."

"Ha!"

The faded gallant then fixed his eyes upon the face of Jacob, and assuming a great solemnity of tone and manner, he said,—

"Meet me half an hour hence with five gold pieces at Master Mapletoft's, the clothier's. You can repay them with six out of Jane Wainstead's fortune—ha!"

So saying, the faded gallant walked away with a swaggering gait, leaving what he had said to work its way on the simple mind of Jacob.

The half hour passed away, and Jacob, trembling and pale, with the gold pieces clutched in his hand, stood at the door of the clothier's with the faded gallant.

The bright nobles were soon transferred to the pockets of his tempter, and Jacob found himself dragged into the shop.

Mrs. Mapletoft actually for one brief moment lost the power of speech when she saw the faded gallant; then, with a full tide of eloquence, she burst forth with,—

"Wretch! knave! Do I dream? How dare you, scurvy thief, put your copper nose within my door? Pay for the jerkin, villain, and the loose points, and the hose, and the hood, and the ——"

In vain the faded gallant winked in deprecation of Mrs. Mapletoft's wrath; in vain he pointed over his shoulder at poor Jacob; the indignant lady would not be silenced; and it was not until he placed a gold piece against the end of his fiery nose, and full before Mrs. Mapletoft's eyes, that her voice decreased to a whine, and she finished with,—

"Ah, you are a sad man! a wild ruffler, I warrant: better pay late than never. It was but the other day I said to my poor wretch, that snivelling, sneaking, horrid little man, 'Mapletoft, says I ——'"

"Hush! hush!" whispered the faded gallant. "Good Mrs. Mapletoft, hush! there is a gold noble to be earned again and again, my charming and decidedly handsome Mrs. Mapletoft, by merely lending yon scare-crow boy a court suit; never mind its fashion, beautiful Mrs. Mapletoft, or its wear, most beautiful of women."

"Oh, dear!" sighed the bulky lady. "If that little, snivelling, wretched, abominable, sneaking ——"

"I know. Hush! A gold noble for half an hour's wear of an old court suit. Have you such, dear, delightful, bewitching, fascinating woman?"

"Y—e—s," simpered Mrs. Mapletoft, "to be sure. Oh, deary me!"

So saying, Mrs. Mapletoft pocketed the noble, and advancing towards Jacob, alarmed him very much, by turning him round and round by his head, to note his size.

"We have a suit," she then said; "a suit of great fashion. Lor, he's a atomy."

"Rather thin—ha!" said the gallant.

"Gracious!" said Mrs. Mapletoft, as she glanced against poor Jacob. "Well, well, we can pad the hose and the trunks."

Jacob looked bewildered from one to the other, and allowed all the preparations for his adornment to proceed without hindrance.

The dress was produced, and it was evident it had been used as a caricature of fashion at some court masque, so outrageous was it in all respects. It was not at all necessary to denude Jacob of any of his own apparel, for every article went over him with exceeding fullness and ease.

The gallant produced from his pocket a pair of formidable mock moustachios, which he stuck with a partial twist beneath Jacob's nose; then, when the long-pointed shoes were looped up with chains to the knees, and the doublet properly padded out, the faded gallant retreated a few paces, and affected to fall into a very paroxysm of intense admiration; and Mrs. Mapletoft, taking her cue from the faded gallant, exclaimed, that—"well, she never, goodness gracious!" &c.

"Do—do I really look tolerable?" said Jacob, beginning to be reconciled to himself.

"Tolerable?" cried the faded gallant. "Tolerable? You look like—like——tell him what he looks like, charming Mrs. Mapletoft."

"Dear heart!" replied the lady, "I really ——"

"You—you think I'm rather the thing?" said Jacob.

"The very thing," said the faded gallant solemnly.

"Ah, to be sure!" cried Mrs. Mapletoft. "Heigho! I wish I was single. If it wasn't for that sneaking, wretched, grovelling ——"

"Ha!" interrupted the gallant. "Good Master Jacob, go and prosper; walk opposite the mercer's house; give thyself an air, man; and here, take a groate, and should you see the charmer herself, boldly walk in, and buy a trifle. Ha!"

"If—if I should meet Master ——"

"Bah!"

"Or—or Mistress Bridgett."

"Bah!"

"But—but ——"

"Ha! Doubt my honour?"

"No—no—no, I hope she'll be pleased. Beautiful Jane! Bless her! She ——"

"Go—go," cried the gallant; and he pushed Jacob into the street.

"And be sure you come back in half an hour," screamed Mrs. Mapletoft.

CHAPTER XII.

The Chamberlain.

"Ye toe of ye citizen was gibing ye heel of ye courtier.'

We must leave Jacob to pursue his mixed career of gallantry and dread, while we conduct the reader to personages of a more exalted, although scarcely so innocent a class.

The Lord Hastings had "*ane statelie house*" at Westminster: the most superb hangings graced the walls, and the floors were strewed with the finest rushes, which an ancient writer says "kept a most musicale and pleasante sounde under ye feete." Massive carved oaken furniture graced the large, but, in most cases, low-roofed apartments; rare stained glass conducted the light into the rooms in streams of rainbow beauty, and everything which the genius of the age could produce, of taste or luxury, was assembled within the walls of that princely residence of the great chamberlain and favourite of the monarch.

In a small octagon chamber, the walls of which were hung with rich padded tapestry, sat Lord Hastings himself. He was engaged in earnest converse with another person, and by the energy of his manner, as well as the angry flush which was upon his brow, it was evident that the chamberlain's passions were much aroused by the subject of the conversation.

The person who was with him sat indolently listening to his impassioned speaking, nor did he betray by look or gesture the remotest sympathy with the excited feelings of the chamberlain. He was gaily attired, and wore a sword, the jewelled hilt of which was of great beauty and price. There was a half-suppressed sneer upon his lips as he listened, or seemed to listen, to Hastings; and, upon the whole, he seemed a person who might well be the depository of plots and dangerous contrivances.

"I tell you," said Hastings, rapidly, pursuing the theme of the discourse, "I tell you it is something new for us nobles to be thus bearded; the king is the king of the common people, and the tolerated head of the nobles. What attacks nobility attacks majesty. If the trunk fall, the head will reach the dust."

"You *are* indeed chafed, my lord," replied his companion, in indifferent tones.

"Chafed!" cried Hastings; "I may well be chafed. By my head, I have been fooled!"

"Yes," yawned the other.

"Yes!" echoed Hastings; "but that bespeaks something to come. This girl ——"

"Ay, the girl."

"You mock me, Retelier."

"I beg your grace, but I do not call myself Retelier now."

"What, then! By Heaven, you have as many aliases as you have faces!"

"True," replied the other; "I call myself now Sir Loyal."

"Call yourself the devil an you will; but see that this matter is done for me."

"Half I will do."

"Half?"

"Yes; the other matter you may manage yourself."

"The—the girl?"

"Yes; you may carry alarm into the houses of the burghers when and how you please. For this little piece of red and white humanity—this Jane, you may incur what risks, and be as ridiculous as it may please you; I have neither time nor inclination to dabble in low intrigues."

"Well, sir, well?"

"'Tis well or ill, as you please to take it, my lord."

"But the—the youth—the young lack-beard who dared to brave me to my face?"

"The rather to clear your mind for matters of graver import, than for any disposition to stoop to such small matters, I will see him disposed of."

"I thank you," cried Hastings; "I would have it so. 'Tis a small matter, as you say, but made large by the surrounding circumstances; a noble must battle with a citizen now-a-days for the right of the causeway."

"Then our conference is over, my lord?"

"It is."

Sir Loyal, as he chose to call himself, rose, and taking a small key from his vest, he drew aside the hangings between two of the windows, and opened a small door.

"Adieu," he said, and disappeared through the narrow opening.

Hastings remained silent for some moments, then he muttered,—

"Hem!—Sir Loyal! It strikes me you will come once too often to this chamber. The tools by which we hew the path to power are dangerous when thrown aside: they should be destroyed. Look to it, Sir Loyal; thy craft is almost superhuman, but cold steel will reach thy heart as well as an honester man's."

The chamberlain stepped to the door of the room, and called,—

"Ho, within, there!"

A page immediately appeared.

"Has the mercer brought the stuffs I ordered?" said Hastings, anxiously.

"In truth, my lord, no."

"No?"

"Even so, my lord."

"Who took the order?"

"Humphrey, and please your lordship."

"Well?"

"He met with strange treatment at the mercer's, my lord, such as I dare not tell your lordship."

"Ha! Send Humphrey hither."

"So," muttered Hastings, "the purse-proud citizen carries it with a high hand."

A tap at the door disturbed his reverie, and he cried in a husky voice—

"Come in."

A serving man in the gorgeous livery of the great chamberlain entered the room, and stood respectfully by the door.

"Well, Humphrey, you took my order to the mercer?"

"Yes, an it please your lordship, for my ears I dare not have lingered. Truly he was to bring a goodly pack—all new and curious morains, striped and not striped; Genoa velvets, cut and piled; silks with a variation, which means, as your lordship knows ——"

"Tush! tush!"

"Nay, I dare not have forgotten one for my ears. There were gauze tissues ——"

"Peace, knave! Did the mercer bring the goods?"

"Nay, my lord, there ends Humphrey. For my ears I dare not tell your lordship."

"Thou shalt make close acquaintance with the whipping-post, knave, if I do not hear from thee all that passed. Speak! quickly!"

"Ye—e—s, my lo—o—rd. The mercer is a—huge knave."

"Well?"

"He—he kicked me out of the shop."

"What?"

"Yes, my lord; and a marvellous ill-favoured varlet they call Simon, he—he kicked me down the Chepe."

"They dare not!" cried Hastings. "My meanest hind is sacred."

"Mer—cy, my lord. They did, indeed."

"Now, by the Holy Rood! was that all that passed?"

"Yes, my lord."

"What said they?"

"Nothing. It was all—kick—kick. Then says I to myself, says I ——."

"Begone!"

Humphrey darted out of the room, and Lord Hastings stood boiling with rage.

"I'll—I'll to the king," he cried: "this insult to a nobleman's retainer. By Heavens, had it been to my hound, it would have merited death! Am I noble or not? I'll to the king. They should have been honoured—yes, I'll get a warrant from the king; and yet—yet—did not Edward look with flashing eyes upon that peerless beauty? Love may conquer the favourite, Hastings. I must be cautious—one word from those rosy, pouting lips—one glance from the swimming eyes of the mercer's daughter would turn the feeble mind of Edward to any purpose I had prompted him to. I must be cautious. Curses on the greasy citizen!—kick a man of mine!—kick!—by my nobility I—but caution—caution."

He lifted his plumed cap from the table, and dashed from the room.

CHAPTER XIII.

Lovers' Vows.

"I saw one cherry weepe, and why?
Why wepte it but for shame
Because my lady's lips were by,
And did out redde ye same."

Long and seriously did Master Wainstead think over the events of the Royal Masque, and deep grief was in the father's heart as he thought of the dangers which threatened to surround the life and happiness of his beautiful child.

That the attempts which had already been made to deprive him of his daughter, were but the preludes to more desperate and audacious ones, he but too truly dreaded; for well he knew the haughty and turbulent disposition of the nobility who surrounded the young monarch. Then, as he reflected upon the situation in which he was placed, he became more and more convinced of the necessity of providing Jane with a protector in a husband, who had means and power to foil the efforts even of the haughtiest noble of Edward's court.

Who but Shore could accomplish so much?—the creditor of one half of the nobility—the secret agent of the king—a man of great wealth, and one, too, who the fond father believed really loved his child with a pure and disinterested affection.

By some wonderful fatuity of vision, Wainstead was completely blind to the mean selfishness of Shore's character. He had taken it into his head that Master Shore was an honest, pains-taking man, and nothing could dislodge the idea. It is true that Shore had committed no one overt act that persons could lay hold of, and say, "He did this;" but he was more than suspected of many.

The mercer likewise entertained an opinion, which is as common among persons who are past the meridian of existence as it is rare among the young, namely, that what are commonly called love matches, seldom turn out well, and that the best foundation for happiness in the marriage state was respectability of means.

Thus, with every feeling of affection for his daughter to excess, he would have consigned her to Shore, with a conviction that he was consulting her happiness, even if he were doing a little gentle violence to her inclination in matching with her one who certainly could not possess many attractions in the eyes of a young, beautiful, and enthusiastic girl.

Full of his determination, Master Wainstead summoned his daughter to him, and smoothing affectionately the thick masses of beautiful hair which hung in nature's freedom far down the neck of his darling, he said,—

"My beautiful child—no—that is, my good child, I mean."

Jane smiled, and Master Wainstead continued—

"My dear child, I am getting old."

"Old, father! Oh, no."

"Oh, yes, Jane! and when I am gone ——"

"Father!" sobbed Jane, as she threw herself on his breast.

"Tush! I am an old fool," muttered Wainstead; "how I've frightened the child."

"Father," murmured Jane, "you never said so unkind a thing before."

"Well, well, I—I didn't mean it—I only meant to say that I should be quite happy if I could see you protected by some one who might be better able to do so than your own father."

Jane would have given the world to have had courage to say, "There's Walter, father, who loves me; he will protect me, and honour you:" but she could not frame the words, and Wainstead continued—

"I want to see you some honest man's wife, my Jane."

"Wife, father?"

"Yes: your mother was a wife."

"Yes, father, but—I—I—you see, dear father ——"

"Oh, yes, I see. Well, I have chosen a husband for you."

"A husband?"

"Yes, Jane; one who has both will and power to protect you; a most respectable man."

"That can't be poor Walter," thought Jane, with a sigh.

"Master Shore loves you."

"Shore?" cried Jane, shrinking.

"Yes, my old friend ——"

"Oh! father! I cannot love him."

"Pho, pho, Jane! love is all nonsense. The dream of sixteen, the blush of five-and-twenty, and the shame of forty. People do more ridiculous things for love than their whole lives can make up for afterwards. Respect your husband, girl, that's enough—love grows cold—it's like over hot canary, very nice, but troublesome at first; wait till it gets cool, and it's as insipid as the—hem!"

"But, dear father," whispered Jane, "your simile supposes that there is nothing but the extremes of too hot and too cold."

"Why, you little jade, are you going to hold an argument with me?"

"No, father, no; but ——"

"But you only thought the old man had made a blunder. Now I'll tell you how it is if you drink the canary just when it becomes pleasant and palatable, why then it's gone and so with your love; the pleasanter it is, the sooner it's used up, my girl."

"But—but ——"

"But what?"

"Simon says love is our lost inheritance from heaven."

The mercer absolutely gasped as he repeated—

"Simon—says—Simon—Sim—Si—Oh! oh! oh!"

"It might, perhaps," whispered Jane, with a face of crimson, "have been—Walter—Fane."

"Ah!" cried Wainstead, drawing a long breath; "it might have been Walter Fane. So I think; but to father such a speech upon poor Simon—now that really was too bad. Simon say such a thing! Sim—Ho! ho! ho!"

"But, father, you will not ——"

"Will not what?"

"Force me."

"Force you, girl! No. If you can't please your poor old father, and let him go to his long rest with the reflection that he has properly provided for the—the darling of his heart—I—say no more. No, no, girl, I will not force you. Bless you, Jane!"

"Ah, father!" sobbed Jane, "this is force indeed."

For a few moments there was a deep silence; for the father's heart was full; and sore was the struggle in the breast of the young and beautiful girl between her long-cherished affection for her father and obedient duty to his lightest word, and her young heart's fond love for Walter Fane, who reigned in her breast the undisputed lord of her dearest love.

In these few moments of bitter feelings, there came hope; for she thought that if her father but knew how Walter loved her, he would, he must tell them to be happy. She would tell Walter all that had occurred, and together they would throw themselves at her father's feet, and tell him they would both be his children, and crave his blessing. Then what a radiant future opened to the glowing imagination of Jane!—she smiled through her tears, and, turning to her father, while the trembling drops danced in her eyes, and her voice shook with hope, fear, joy, and love, she said—

"Father, give me till to-morrow to—to ——"

"To think of what I have said, my child?"

"Yes, father."

"Freely, freely, Jane: now kiss me and leave me; for I would fain indulge in a little lonely thought, too."

Jane kissed her father, and then slowly descended the narrow, dark staircase, to see if Walter was in the shop.

A murmuring of voices met her ears as she reached the foot of the staircase, and while she paused for a moment to recover the agitation of her spirits, she heard the voice of Simon, contradicting everything, as usual. Then she heard Walter laugh, and the sound was as grateful music to the ears of the young girl. Gently she pushed open the narrow door which led to the shop.

"Jane?" cried Walter, springing forward.

Jane paused, and glanced at Simon.

"You would speak to me, Jane," said Walter; "dear, dear Jane!" he added, in an under tone.

"Yes," replied Jane.

"Simon," said Walter.

"Well," replied Simon, stiffening himself up as if with a determination to be more than usually contradictory.

"My good Simon, will you go to Master Lanklaster, the calenderer, and ask ——"

"No," said Simon.

"But, Simon ——"

"Sha'n't."

The doorway was at this moment darkened by a figure, which in a few minutes effectually arrested the attention of Simon, as well as astonishing, if not amusing, both Walter and Jane.

Peering in at the doorway of the mercer's shop, with an expression half of fright and half of exultation, was the singularly ornamented face of poor Jacob.

One of his formidable moustachios had taken leave of his lip, and the other turning up, as it did, nearly to the corner of his eye, imparted to his countenance a peculiarity of expression that had in it something both comic and alarming. His long rapier stuck ungainly across the doorway, and with one hand placed upon his heart, and the other grasping the doorpost, he strained his long, snake-like form into the shop, and fixed his eyes upon the mercer's daughter.

Jane shrunk back as Jacob, with a peculiar leer, nodded his head at her, and adjusted his cap and feather between each nod.

"This is some madman," said Walter.

"Get out!" cried Simon.

"I—I'll buy a trifle," said Jacob. "Hurrah! We are gallants—are gallants—ha!"

Poor Jacob thought he had perpetrated a most exquisite and remarkable imitation of the bold, blustering manner of the faded gallant by this speech, and he concluded by dragging the cap from off the bridge of his nose, whereon, being full large, it had a galling propensity, upon the slightest movement, to fall.

Walter laughed outright, and Jane could scarcely forbear a smile, which Jacob no sooner observed, than he considered it a tribute to his personal appearance, and a signal of the dawning of his hopes; and, with a mincing air, he stepped one foot down the step into the shop.

"Let him come in, Simon," said Walter.

"Sha'n't," cried Simon; and suddenly meeting Jacob, he clasped him in his arms, and rushed with him into the Chepe.

Walter ran to the door, and far down the street, he saw Simon and Jacob struggling together, and a crowd of admiring and delighted prentices and citizens who were returning from "Bunhille Fieldes," rapidly collecting round them.

Walter turned from the window, and to his surprise he saw Jane in tears. He was by her side in a moment. She laid her small hand upon his arm, and the delicate fingers played nervously with his sleeve, as she said,—

"Walter—I—have something to say—that—that ——"

"That what, dearest Jane? You alarm me. What has happened?"

"Hush, Walter! my father wishes me to marry Shore."

"I guessed it," cried Walter, clasping his hands; "my fears told me. Never, Jane, never! I will to your father: he shall know how truly, how long I have loved you; he is wont to be good and kind in ordinary matters—he cannot be so changed. Oh, Jane! Jane! what a weight is at my heart!"

"Walter!" she said, in a voice choked with emotion, "I have asked but for one day's delay."

"One day?"

"But one."

"'Tis ample—an hour—a moment would suffice. Now, even now, I ——"

The mercer at this moment entered the shop; he was attired for the street, and by the dim light he saw not the tears that stood upon his daughter's eyes.

"My child," he said, turning to her with his foot upon the door-step, "I have bethought me I was bidden out to meet a man of substance from Hambro'. I shall be back anon."

He passed from the shop. Walter spoke faintly,—

"He is gone," he said, "and I have not told him."

"To-morrow," whispered Jane.

"Yes, to-morrow," cried Walter. "I will throw myself on his kind heart ——"

"We," said Jane, "we will both ——"

"You, dearest!—you—and—will you speak for me? I should, I ought to be, and am the happiest lover in merry England. All will be well—so well—so delightful. I fancy even now I see the tear in your father's eye, as he will say, 'My children, go and be happy! bless you both!' Then, Jane, we will have but one heart—one undivided, incorruptible heart: we shall live in the perpetual sunshine of her own joy; time will glide on like a summer's streamlet; love our theme, and happiness our breath. Oh, Jane! Jane! how happy we shall be! My own! my beautiful!"

Jane looked in her lover's beaming eyes, and her own reflected the dancing joy which sparkled in his. Closer and still closer she crept to the heart that beat alone for her, until her long tresses mingled with his raven locks.

"My Walter!" she murmured.

A bright gleam of the setting sun streamed in at the narrow window, and fell upon the young lovers.

"Heaven smiles," said Walter; "but is there another heaven like this?"

CHAPTER XIV.

The Arrest.

"In ye damp prisone adjoieneinge ye Blacke Friares, were committede ye moste monstrous villanies. Hope dide not dwelle therein."

Grief and joy seem alike to produce an animal irritability, which involves the necessity of physical exertion. When we are afflicted, we find generally that to be still is as impossible as it is to be serene. When the heart is full of some new joy, and the imagination is radiant and happy, we fly to physical exertion to sober down our feelings into the rationality of a calmer enjoyment.

So it was with Walter Fane. He loved Jane so completely—the sum and substance of all his happiness in life was bound up with her; she was his ambition, his hope, his dream of joy; and now how sure he felt that she loved him. Should he ever forget that timid, sweet caress? Ah, no! in sickness and sorrow—in danger—aye, when the shadow of the valley of death was upon his heart, he still would cherish the dear remembrance, and pain would vanish—sorrow fly before the extacy of joy—the grave have no triumphs—death no sting.

"She is mine! mine!" he shouted, as he bounded along the fields to the north of Charing, in the dim light of the dying day. "She is mine—my heart's treasure! my beautiful and true!"

Master Wainstead had returned quickly to the shop, and Walter had been compelled to separate for a time from Jane, and it was to cry out in the exuberance of his delight to the twinkling stars and slowly climbing moon, that he had left the city behind him, and chosen so strange an hour for a country ramble.

"To-morrow! to-morrow!" he repeated, as he bounded to the brow of a small hillock; "to-morrow! what a long day will be to-morrow! The mercer loves his beautiful child—loves! he adores her, doats on her every glance. He will know to-morrow that she has given her young heart to poor Walter Fane. To-morrow he will hear that Walter Fane has loved even as well as he his Jane—the fair flower of ancient London. To-morrow he will tell us, between a smile and a tear, to make much of each other, and let him see how happy we can be. Oh, what a day! what an epoch in my life will be to-morrow!"

The last tints of the setting sun had now faded away in the far-off west, and the round yellow disc of a nearly full moon seemed to rest, as it were, upon the edge of a bank of massive black clouds, that were piling themselves up in the eastern sky.

How different are the aspects of nature to us under different circumstances connected solely with ourselves; the heart will make its own gloom as well as its own beauty.

To Walter Fane all was bliss and sublimity; the mild radiance of the moon never appeared to him before with such pure beauty; delicious perfumes seemed to be wafted to him upon every idle air that blew: he thought, too, of the great God

"Who made and loveth all,"

and a silent aspiration of the heart arose to Heaven for a continuance of such pure happiness; and even as his eyes were cast upwards to the blue ether above him, the black clouds swept onwards, and eclipsed the silver moon; a hollow wind moaned across the fields, and when Walter looked again around him, the face of nature was gloomy and chill.

An undefined sensation of dread came across his mind, and twice he looked behind him to assure himself he was alone.

"'Tis growing late," he said. "I will return. Where Jane is, there is joy and sunshine again."

He turned his face towards the city, and with rapid steps hastened from the open fields in the direction of the Strand.

As he neared the detached houses which stood by the river's brink, he heard a clock strike eight, and wishing, now that a revulsion of feeling had taken place in his breast, to be home as quickly as possible, he made for a little jetty by Arundel-street, wishing to take a boat to "ye stone steppes at Southwarke," which would bring him within a few moments walk of the mercer's.

He readily procured a wherry, and in five minutes more was rapidly gliding along on the bosom of the stream which has witnessed so many strange sights and changes in ancient London.

"The stone steppes at Southwarke," as they were called, consisted of a wide landing-place, not far from where the present bridge of that name now stands, and it was usual for the citizens to proceed by boat from Westminster to that point, especially at dusk, as they avoided the dangers of the Strand, which, being then quite a suburban locality, was the scene of many barefaced robberies.

The boat had reached "Blackfriars," and Walter Fane was in a deep reverie, when he was suddenly aroused by the waterman exclaiming,—

"Nay, now, what mean the knaves? Is this river craft? Hi—hi!"

Before Walter could fully comprehend what had occurred, or was about to occur, a long boat, with six rowers, dashed alongside the wherry, and he found himself seized, and forcibly dragged into the strange cutter before he could recover sufficiently from his surprise to resist.

One of the oars had been dashed from the waterman's hand by the strange boat, but he made good use of the other; for, shifting it from the rollocks to the side of the assailants, with a vigorous sweep of its long blade, he produced a temporary confusion, and a diversion in Walter's favour; and had it not been that Walter himself, in the melee, came in for rather a sharp crack on the head, he might have profited by the assault; as it was, however, it sealed his fate; for the lights by the river's bank danced for a moment like a thousand meteors in his eyes, and then he dropped, insensible from the blow, at the bottom of the boat.

A deep groan was then heard, and a heavy plunge in the black stream; the waterman had met his death, and his tenantless wherry floated idly down the river.

"Give way!" cried a hoarse voice; and the boat in which lay the ill-fated Walter Fane made for a low arched landing-place by Blackfriars.

CHAPTER XV.

The Marriage.

"An' she see [illegible] and [illegible]falle,
[illegible] lefte her father's home,
To weepe beside a stranger's hearth,
With manie a [illegible] moane."

Ye Rhyme of ye Lasse Maidene, 1471.

Simon sat up till the grey tints of morning began to peer in at the mercer's, to let in Walter Fane, but he came not; then the early sun gleamed upon the house-tops, but still he came not, and Simon was both vexed and uneasy, for, with all his contradictions and roughness, he had a kindly heart, and he loved Walter Fane, although he was wont to quarrel with him every hour in the day.

He opened the shop, and then stood anxiously on the door-step, straining his eyes down the Chepe, with the hope of catching a glance of Walter's light, agile figure approaching, in which case he, Simon, had determined to make a desperate quarrel with him; but as Walter did not come, and another hour elapsed, Simon got very melancholy and fidgetty, and began to hope "that no harm had happened to the poor lad, who was the best creature he (Simon) just then knew."

Then Master Wainstead came down from his breakfast, and he was told of Walter's disappearance, upon which he walked to the door, and looked up and down the Chepe just as Simon had done; after which he went up stairs again, prophesying that "the young dog would soon come home."

Home, however, he came not; and who can paint the agony of Jane when she was told of this sudden and critical disappearance of Walter? Oh! how drearily the hours passed as she sat watching by the casement where she was wont to tend her flowers.

Still he came not, although the morning brightened into noon, and the long shadows of the evening crept on apace; then the sun sank upon the city, and Jane dropped her head upon her hands, and wept bitterly.

Another night and another day passed away, and there were no tidings of Walter Fane. In vain the mercer made every inquiry; in vain did poor Simon visit every field, every copse in the vicinity, and every court and alley in the city. No tidings could be got, until at last a waterman said that a young man answering Walter's description was believed to have been drowned by Blackfriars, for the empty boat was found far down the river.

With this melancholy suggestion Simon came home, and wept like a child.

The mercer, too, grieved for Walter, for he loved him as if he had been a child of his own; and Jane, the heart-stricken Jane, while she clasped her hands, and strove to murmur that she was resigned to the will of Heaven, presented such a picture of consuming grief, that the mercer trembled for her life; and gloom was upon the once happy dwelling.

Shore then took occasion to possess Wainstead's mind with the notion that a change of scenes and occupation would arouse Jane from the lethargy into which she was fast sinking, and upon that plea again urged his suit for her hand.

The mercer then cautiously questioned his beautiful child as to her feelings upon the subject, and she threw herself with a burst of frantic grief into his arms, saying.—

"Father—father! do with me as you will. I *did* love poor Walter—but he is gone!"

Three more days past listlessly over the head of the heart-stricken girl, and on the morning of the fourth, a merry bridal peal sounded in sportive mockery from the steeple of a small church which stood in the Chepe, wedged in among houses and shops so completely, that any one seeing its steeple for the first time rising among the gable ends, thatched roofs, and chimney pots, might well wonder from whence it could possibly come.

The mercer led the way with his beautiful child hanging heavily upon his arm, and then followed many friends of the substantial citizen; a crowd, too, had collected; for carefully as the secret had been endeavoured to be kept, the bruit of the marriage of the lovely Jane Wainstead had spread far and wide over the city; and some had come with prayers, some with regrets, and some with tears, to see her on her way.

Jane heard not the blessings that were given to her by old and young, for her heart was oppressed with deep emotions; she saw not the tears of some who followed her and loved her, for her own eyes were dim with weeping.

"Jane, dearest, look up," said her father. "Do you not hear, my child, the merry bells? Hark, my darling! they tell you to be happy."

"Oh, father, father!" sobbed Jane, "how different to me is the strain they play."

"Nay, Jane, 'tis as merry a jingle as ever shook the ancient steeple. Hark! there again!"

"Oh, father, father!" said Jane, "I seem to hear another bell, and it is tolling for—for ——"

"For what?"

"The death even of hope. Walter! Walter! why am I not cold and still with thee?"

She burst into an agony of tears; and the people who were thronging round heard her sobs, and pressed closer on her path.

"Here's a bridal," cried one, "and the bride sobbing as if her heart was broken."

"Poor thing! poor thing!" said another; "I'll warrant me, now ——"

"You'll warrant, small wit," interrupted a woman of herculean dimensions; "ah! well-a-day! I recollect when I was bidden to church, I was a delicate young thing then, you must know."

"Ah, we know, mother!" cried a waggish 'prentice; "you washed the porch of St. Sepulchre's away with your tears, and cuffed the cunning clerk Magnes for lifting up his tongue, and crying ——"

"It's no matter to you, jackanapes, what he cried," said a young woman; "I know if I were going to be married, I should begin to cry the first thing in the morning, and go on cry, cry, crying, till I don't know when."

Now they had reached the church door, and Jane shuddered as she ascended the steps.

Her father clasped her arm closer within his, as he whispered,—

"Courage, courage, my child!"

They entered the church, and the people made rather an indecorous rush to be present at the ceremony. The bells sounded loudly and clearly,

"Filling with joy the sunny air:"

but such joy is only the joy of association. To Jane how mournful were those sounds.

The priest, clothed in his sacred habit, stood by the altar; and a little apart, stood Shore.

He was gorgeously attired in a closely fitting suit of purple velvet, and round his neck he wore a gold chain of the costly and esteemed workmanship of Venice. He seemed never to have recovered completely from his wound on the night of the *fete* in the city, and wore the same ghastly pale appearance which was noticed on his last introduction before the reader.

It was strange that such a man should stake his future life upon the smiles of a young girl. He had, before he saw Jane Wainstead, gone through life without one kindly emotion or feeling for his fellows: he had always looked upon himself as a being set apart from the rest of humanity; and while, in the lone bitterness of his heart, he could not help confessing at times that he missed some of the dear pleasures of name, kindred, and friends, he with sneering exultation vaunted his exemption from human weaknesses and sensibilities.

It was reserved for the master passion of humanity to conquer the stubborn heart of Shore; but even this passion of love, wilful and wayward as it is, took in his case a peculiarity of complexion from the dark and lonely tenor of his former life.

He did not intend that Jane Wainstead should draw him, by the soft influence of her many charms, into the busy vortex of common life. No; his object was to drag her into his solitude; to keep her as he would a costly gem, far, far removed from the fulsome gaze of vulgar admiration. He fancied that he would prowl among mankind as usual, with scorn and contempt at his heart; and that at home, in the penetralia of his own house, he would have a dear treasure, whose sweetness would be his, and his only—who, when she smiled, would smile only on him, and who he could set up in his lone heart as a great possession, a something that he had achieved and acquired by his own talent and deep cunning.

His lips would have trembled as he saw Jane approach the altar, but he compressed them too firmly. His hand might have betrayed the deep emotion of his mind upon the eve of the fruition of his hopes, but he clutched the gilt railings of the altar, and to outward show was as calm and still as a piece of sculpture.

The bride was led to the sacred fane—the friends crowded round—there was a deathlike stillness some minutes; then the deep tone of the priest, the faint response. At a signal the bells burst forth a merry peal—Jane was a wife!

Exultation sparkled in Shore's eyes; he took the hand of his young bride, and appeared to be about to say something, but his habitual caution left it unsaid; he merely turned to the throng of persons around, and cast on them a look of withering contempt.

A confusion of voices at the church door now attracted the attention of every one.

"Get out—get out!" cried out a voice. "By our Lady! is this a place for mummers?"

A scuffle ensued, and poor Jacob, who, hearing of Jane's marriage, had rushed with desperation to the church, was turned into the street.

"My child," said Wainstead, "'tis nothing. Jane, how pale you look! Stand back, my masters: air—air! Jane, speak to your father!—my child! my Jane!"

"JANE SHORE!" cried Shore, laying his cold hand on her wrist.

With a shudder Jane fainted in the arms of her father.

CHAPTER XVI.

The Prison of the Black Friars.

"And ye lighte of love made ye darksome place beautiful."

ALAS! alas! poor Walter Fane! No match were you for such a man as Shore. In your innocent heart you could not imagine such villany as his; and, therefore, you armed yourself with no weapons to meet it. Truly, a wonderful advantage had Shore over you, Walter Fane, for he could do more wickedness in a day, than it ever would have entered into your imagination to dream of the possibility of in a year—ay, an age.

Resistance to the men who had taken him prisoner would have been now madness; and yet, poor Walter Fane was almost maddened enough to attempt it. They were stout, stalwart, indifferent looking fellows, such as would just as soon get rid of the trouble of a living prisoner by knocking him on the head, and converting him into a dead one, as not. They were well armed, too; and Walter was not. Yet did he contemplate more than once having a struggle for liberty and for life.

The boat shot under a narrow archway, within which all was blackness and gloom. It looked like some fit entrance to the infernal regions, and no wonder that poor Walter's heart sank within him, as he found himself hurried to such a place.

"If," he cried, "my life is to be taken, do not bring me to such a place as this to die. Let me die in fair fighting with any one of your number. 'Tis cowardly so many of you to set upon one man. Help, help, help!"

"Aye, bawl away, youngster," said one. "They do say, though, that bawling provokes an appetite, and if it be so, then you are imprudent; for, in the prison of the Black Friars, they are not famous for gorging their prisoners with overfeeding."

"The prison of the Black Friars!" exclaimed Walter. "What have I done to be consigned to such a place?"

"Oh, my master," replied the man, with a brutal laugh, "that's your business, not ours."

"But I am innocent of all crime."

"Very likely."

"Then, wherefore should I be dragged here?"

"Ah! that's the question."

"Oh, there is some mistake—some grievous mistake. You take me for some one else. I have injured no one. I have committed no crime. I have outraged no law. There is some mistake."

"Psha, boy! be quiet," said another.

"Nay, I will not be quiet. I protest against this usage. To be quiet is to give a tacit consent to such a proceeding, as if I admitted its justice. I am innocent, and I will speak. I am innocently apprehended. I have done no wrong, and I protest against this wrong which is done to me."

"Go on—go on. Ha, ha, ha! Go on."

The boat was stopped at a narrow flight of stone steps, and two of the men seized Walter each by one arm, and lifted him on to his feet.

"No, no," he said, "I will not submit."

"Fool!" said one, "how can you resist? You may enforce us to more violence than we wish to take the trouble of using, or you may tumble into the water and be drowned if you like; but escape you cannot. Take a wiser thought of your situation, and learn patience."

"Yes," growled another, "be a what's its name?—a—a—d—n it! I forget. What did the worshipful Master Andrew Beauvois call himself when his gracious grace the Duke of Gloster had the hand-screws put upon him, eh?"

"A philosopher."

"Oh, ay; a philosopher. Be a philosopher, young fellow, and take things easy, can't you?"

Walter had reason enough left him to feel conscious that, although he might protest against the treatment to which he was subjected as much as he pleased, yet it would be madness indeed to enter into any physical contest with his captors; so he ascended the damp, slippery steps which terminated in a narrow passage, a short distance down which was a door, with a light above it.

"For Heaven's sake!" said Walter, "at least, some of you tell me of what I am accused."

"A good joke that," said one.

"Ha, ha, ha!" laughed another; and in that arched and tube-like passage the laughter sounded like that of some fiend exulting in human woe and misery.

Walter shuddered; and the words,—

"Ah, Jane—Jane," escaped from his lips, which seemed to afford his captors intense merriment, for they shouted again with laughter, which only ceased partially when the door, above which was a light, suddenly opened, and several persons made their appearance.

"How, now, knaves!" cried one, stepping forward with an angry flush upon his brow. "How, now, knaves! Take you this for a change-house, that you make such an unseemly tumult? By the mass, now ——"

"Pardon, Sir Godfrey, pardon," said one. "It was this young fellow here, for whose apprehension we have a special warrant, who made us laugh. We knew not, most worshipful Sir Godfrey, you were near at hand."

Sir Godfrey Knagworth was well known as the keeper of the prison of the Blackfriars. He was a ruffian of the first order, and had been convicted of several crimes. In the Duke of Gloster, however, for reasons only known to themselves, he always found a powerful protector, who stood between him and the consequences of his offences.

The appointment of keeper of the prison at Blackfriars was by no means one eagerly sought after. Indeed, something like the governorship of Sierra Leone now-a-days, it often went a begging; but the Duke of Gloster had persuaded Sir Godfrey to take it for many special reasons, one of which was that he would let him be hanged for the very next scrape he fell into, if he did not.

After he had his appointment, however, Sir Godfrey "took to it," and became well pleased with the numerous opportunities it gave him, not only of petty peculation, but of an exercise of arbitrary and brutal power over the unfortunates who were committed to his charge. He became, in all respects, the mere creature of the ambitious and rascally Duke of Gloster, and the dungeons of what was commonly called "The Damp Prison of Blackfriars," were filled with the victims of his private resentments.

It was a fact, although not known to Walter Fane, that persons brought to the prison upon the duke's warrants, were always conducted there by the water-gate, so that Sir Godfrey—who, by-the-bye, had about as much real right to be called "Sir" as Walter Fane had—always knew where such a class of prisoners were.

A man was always on duty in the narrow passage, at the door where was the light, and he had in this instance, as in all others, communicated the news of an arrival to the keeper.

The small slip of parchment on which the duke wrote his warrants, was handed to the governor. On it was merely written these words,—

"Fast bind, fast find.—GLOSTER."

At the back, in another hand, was the name, quality, and condition of the prisoner, so that there could be no likelihood of a mistake: nor could anybody be at all enlightened, by a perusal of the document, with respect to what the unhappy prisoner had done to be placed in such sad durance.

"Humph!" said the governor, if we may dignify him by such a title—"Humph! my master, you are a precious rogue, you are."

"You lie!" said Walter Fane.

"Ha! Blood and fury—destruction—death and the devil!"

"I said you lied," added Walter, "and so you do. I know you by common report, Sir Godfrey. 'Tis you who are a precious knave."

"God's blood! Thunder—the devil! Is this language for a prisoner? Here Slankey—Slankey, I say, Hugh Slankey."

"Here, here," said a man, coming forward. "What's all this bellowing about?"

"Here's a pestilent knave—a wonderfully pestilent knave, Slankey. He wants the common discretion of being civil to his keeper. Have you any nice damp place for him?"

"Eugh—eugh—eugh!" coughed the hideous-looking ruffian, whom the former named Slankey—"eugh—eugh—eugh! I have. By the ten toes of St. Peter! I have—I have!"

"Take him off, then—take him off. My lad, we shall bring you to your senses soon. We are about to confer an obligation on you, by bringing down that malapert spirit of yours to a level with your fortunes. Ha—ha—ha! We are famous for doing that. Ha—ha—ha!"

"Will any one here," cried Walter, as the great fellow Slankey laid hold of him by one of his arms—"will any one here confer the obligation upon me of telling me what is my crime?"

"Ah," said Sir Godfrey, "will anybody? Come, merry men all. Who will oblige this pleasant-spoken, beardless youngster, by telling him what he has done? Shall we be so explicit, or shall we leave him to consider of it at his own leisure in his dungeon?"

The men laughed, and looked at each other as much as to say, "A clever fellow is Sir Godfrey when he likes."

"I think we have had enough of this," added the governor; "so, Slankey, you may take him away."

"There will be a good reward," said Walter, "for any one who will take news of me to Master Wainstead, the mercer, at the sign of the Lamb and Angel, in the Chepe."

"You hear, all of you," said the governor. "There's an offer—a reward from a mercer in the Chepe. By my faith, it's brilliant!" Then suddenly altering his tone to one of the most brutal ferocity he added,—"Away with him—away with him! D—n him, away with him! and if you have any dungeon of a worse aspect than another, cast him in it. Away with him, I say!"

The man who held the light form of Walter Fane in his herculean grasp urged him forward, and Walter felt that in that powerful ruffian's hands, he was no more than an infant would have been in his own. Another man, too, followed with a light, so that if the noble-spirited youth had been inclined to risk the chances of a contest with Hugh Slankey, he could not have had the smallest chance with the two of them.

They conducted him along numerous intricate passages, and then they stopped and twirled him round and round several times, evidently for the purpose of effectually confusing any observations he might be possibly making as to the route he was taking. Such a precaution, however, was needless, for poor Walter's mind was in by far too great a state of excitement to enable him to pay any attention to his route, and they might have taken him a short distance or a long one, for all he knew.

Now they reached the top of a flight of rude stone steps, down which he was rather dragged than allowed to descend, and at the bottom of these he found, by the splashing sound that his feet made, that the place was extremely damp, and, indeed, in parts, pools of water had actually collected, upon which the light cast a dim and a sickly radiance for a fleeting moment as they passed.

Now the man who held him began to rummage in his pockets with the one hand he had at liberty, among a number of large keys, and at length he turned to his companion, saying,—

"Lay a hand on the youngster. Bother the keys, I never shall know one from another of them, that's flat. Oh, here they are. Now, my merry man, we shall soon have you as safe as any bird in a cage. Ha, ha, ha!"

"If you are men," said Walter, "I implore you to do me the poor grace of letting those know, who would be interested in my fate, what has befallen me. Surely you do not fill your present situation from choice. It is a work of inhumanity in which you are engaged, but which the pressure of stern necessity induces you to do. You are paid for this, and, therefore, if you can earn money by doing a good action, why not earn it as well, and far better than by taking part in a bad one?"

"Go on, go on."

"Then I implore you, if you have one spark of humanity in your natures, go to

Master Wainstead, the mercer, in the Chepe, and tell him that Walter Fane is in the prison of the Black Friars."

"Indeed!"

"Yes. You will get gold, I well know, for your pains. You will have the satisfaction of knowing that the gold you do get is nobly earned."

"Is that all?"

"And is it not enough? I am innocent of any crime—and even if I were guilty, why should not those who could see justice done me, and no more, know of my detention here? I have many times heard that unhappy persons have lingered years in this place without even knowing of what they were accused, without the mockery even of a judicial examination. Surely you will both acknowledge the injustice of that barbarous proceeding?"

"Quite an oracle,—quite an oracle," said one of the men to another. "Quite an oracle he is."

"Oh, very like a *curricle*," said the other.

"You will do it? You promise me?"

"Have you any money, my young spark, about you?"

"Alas, no; but ——"

"No buts for us. That won't do. It's of no use prating now. Come on, come on, I say. All this is moonshine—this way."

"Then am I lost indeed," said Walter, despairingly.

"Lost? Oh, nonsense. How can you be lost when you are safely locked up here? Lost, indeed. That's a good idea."

Walter felt convinced that the men were only intent upon mocking him, and he desisted from saying anything further to them. All was, he now felt positive, in vain. He was a doomed man. No aid could now reach him, and he seemed to himself like one bidding adieu to the world for ever. Still there was the pride of courage about him, and he would make no lamentation that could be made sport of by his ruffianly gaolers. He walked with a firm step and an erect carriage, although bitterness and despair were at his heart.

Suddenly now his conductors paused at a low arched door, and after trying several of the keys, he who had the principal custody of them found one which turned in the lock. Slowly the door opened, creaking on its hinges. Beyond it, all was blackness.

"Now, my man, walk in," said the ruffian, who was named Slankey. "Now, my man, walk in, will you?"

The villain shaded, as he spoke, the lamp with his hand, and Walter unsuspectingly walked forward, of course having no knowledge that he was at the head of a short flight of stone steps. The consequence of course was, that he fell from top to bottom of them; but he did not fall alone, for in the tremendous swing of the arms, and efforts he made to save himself, he caught hold of Slankey, and down they both went together.

By little short of a miracle, the lamp, although it turned over on one side, was not extinguished, and as the ground was soft and muddy, they neither of them sustained any serious injury, and least of all, Walter Fane, who was a very light weight indeed, compared to Hugh Slankey. Walter was first on his feet, as he exclaimed,—

"Villain! you have yourself, as Heaven would have it, fallen into the snare you laid for me."

Slankey was half stunned for the moment, but when he recovered, the torrent of invectives he uttered, baffled all description. His rage was perfectly demoniac, and but for the interposition of the other man, who ran down the steps and laid hold of him, doubtless he would have done Walter some serious injury.

"Come, come, Slankey," said the other, "you know it's dangerous work taking the life of a prisoner. Nobody knows here what's wanted of any one such, by such a warrant as we had. Leave him alone, leave him alone, man."

"Curses on him. I will be even with him yet."

"I winked at you not to do it," said the other. "You always serve prisoners so in these dungeons, but it's dangerous. Some of these days now, some one who is wanted will break his neck, and then you will be much blamed, you know."

"I wish he had. I've very nearly broken my back."

"A just retribution," said Walter, "for the contemptible trick you would have played me in my situation. Big and burly as you are, if ever it be my fate to see again the streets of London, and I meet you, I would have you beware."

"Beware of you," cried the ruffian. "Now, I've more than half a mind to brain you here."

"Come away," said the other, dragging him along. "Leave him alone, I tell you. Come away."

"Tell me at once," said Walter, as they began to ascend the steps, "am I to be starved to death here?"

"Yes," said Slankey, catching at the idea, as one which enabled him to torture the mind of Walter. "Yes, you've guessed it. How do you like it? Ha, ha, ha!"

"Villains! murderers! it would be more merciful to murder me at once."

"Yes it would; wouldn't it? It would be a great deal more merciful, of course, you know, but we don't mean to do it. If you can live upon dirty water you can, for loads of it will drop from the roof into your mouth as you lay on your back. You are under the bed of the Thames."

"You cannot," exclaimed Walter, "you dare not meditate such refinement of cruelty."

"Come along—come along," said Slankey. "Leave him alone. Ha, ha! A likely enough young gallant. What a skeleton he'll make. I make a vow now that I'll come and see how he looks in a month. What an odd figure he will cut to be sure. Ha, ha, ha! Upon my word it's droll. A morris dance or a pageant is nothing to it. Come along—come along."

"Hold—hold!" cried Walter.

"Hark at him! Hark at him! He wants us to stay and keep him company, for all he has abused so."

They reached the top of the steps; Walter rushed up after them, but the dungeon door was slammed in his face, and all was darkness. He heard the key turned in the lock, and he seemed completely shut out from the world. He groped his way down stairs, and then, with a deep groan, he threw himself on the damp floor. Tears, unbidden, gushed to his eyes. He could not stay them, and once again he exclaimed,—

"Jane—Jane. My beautiful Jane!"

CHAPTER XVII.

The Noble and the King.

"And so ane diamonde cut ane diamonde, and ye subtleste
Knave did trample on hime who was ye weaker."

The Lord Chamberlain was as good as his word. He did go post-haste to the king, whither, indeed, the duty of his office took him, and he on the way cooled down sufficiently to concoct a good story against the mercer; and, moreover, he made up his politic mind to be very careful as regarded the time at which he propounded the same, for my Lord Hastings was cunning in his way, and he felt that to make a move against Wainstead, and to fail therein, was but weakening himself.

"I will be cautious," he said; "I will be very cautious, and since by fair means this pragmatical citizen will not permit me to get an introduction to his house, I will by foul ones carry my purpose. Ay, and I will carry it boldly, too, yet surely. I will have revenge as well as love. By the mass it is something new in England to have these greasy knaves of citizens talking of kicking the meanest hind of a noble. Curses on him, why did he not kill the man I sent? That would have been something; but to kick him. To have it said that Wainstead, the mercer of the Chepe, kicked my Lord Hastings's serving-man. Oh, it is monstrous, indeed: most monstrous."

By such a style of reasoning as this his gracious lordship would work himself up into a tolerable passion, and then he would commence again impressing upon his mind the necessity of being quite cool again; so that the route from his own house to the old palace at Westminster, where was the king, became diversified by these hot and cold passions, which by turns held possession of him. Then again he muttered,—

"Retelier, or Loyala, or whatever he chooses to call himself, curses on him, becomes choice, and will not assist me in this matter further than merely disposing of that apprentice boy, who, forsooth, is my rival. The rival of the king's chamberlain! Things, truly, are come to a pretty pass, indeed. One's tools pick out what work they will perform, and what they will not, and a noble is bearded by an apprentice."

By this time he had reached the palace, and resigning his horse to the care of a royal page, he strode into the building as far as the ante-room, and then requested to be announced to the king. Of course the person of the chamberlain was well-known to the lounging attendants of the monarch's ante-chamber, and one proceeded with noiseless steps to let Edward know who was there.

"Is the king alone?" asked Hastings of another.

"I think my lord the Duke of Gloster is with him."

"Curses!" muttered Hastings.

At that moment a curtain was drawn aside, and Richard of Gloster made his appearance.

"Ah! my Lord Hastings," he said.

"Your grace's humble servant," said Hastings, bowing low.

"That is well. You wish to see the king?"

"I wish for that honour."

"Well, wish it. The king is chafed."

"Indeed, my lord."

"Ay, good Hastings, he is. It appears that the Lombards do not kindly respond to the exigencies of his majesty, and, notwithstanding the great honour done the city by the royal progress there, the fat rogues do not feel that they would like to part with their money."

"Really, your grace, the insolence of the citizens is getting alarming."

"It is alarming."

"It is, indeed. One of my men has actually been kicked down the Chepe to-day."

"Now, by St. Paul, that's too bad. What if it had been yourself, my lord. Indeed, you are kicked virtually in the person of your serving-man. You ought to feel the smart, my lord. Why, you will be called Hastings the kicked, now."

"Your grace is ever facetious."

"I facetious? Oh! what an error. I facetious? Look at me—do I look, now, a seemly person to be facetious? Just cast your eye upon me, most observant Hastings."

"I see but your grace's acknowledged wisdom and courage."

"Oh, indeed!"

"On my life, your grace, I see no more."

"Humph!"

Gloster folded his arms and walked away without another word, as was very frequently his odd mode of terminating a conversation, just when any one would have naturally supposed it had reached an interesting point, from which he would have been glad to continue it.

"As warped in mind as in body," muttered Hastings. "A man, too, of strong ability, but of yet stronger passions. If Richard Duke of Gloster lives, I prophecy he will not live quietly, but will earn for himself a higher name, or a tomb. Dark, subtle, scheming, dangerous ——"

"His majesty will see you, my lord," said the page who had been sent to announce the chamberlain.

Hastings started and turned round, for his back was towards the royal chamber; he glanced at the boy who spoke as if he would have read his very soul, and then he strode forward and passed into the smaller apartment, in which sat King Edward.

There was an air of thought upon the king's face. He was a shade paler than usual, and a slight knitting of the brows seemed to carry out fully the assertion of the Duke of Gloster, that the king was chafed.

"Well, Hastings," he said; "well, well?"

"I crave your majesty's pardon, if I intrude; I merely came to offer your majesty my humble duty."

"That will become of some value in our realm, methinks," said the king: "for it seems getting scarce when we had hoped to find it ample."

"Indeed, sire!"

"Aye, indeed, my lord. Now, by God's mercy, one would suppose that all men knew, and felt, and understood the king of England was not a cormorant, that he could eat and drink up all subsidies. What are we in our present position, but, by Heaven's behest, to fight the battles of the state—and have we ever shunned them? Personally have we exchanged blow for blow with the enemies of England, and yet, Hastings, the citizens, whose houses, baubles, wealth, wives and daughters we protect, tie up their money bags against us."

"Monstrous ingratitude, your majesty."

"Monstrous, indeed. We want money, Hastings: we want money most sadly."

"I grieve much that people are so misguided as not to supply your majesty most freely. By all the saints it doth surprise me much, for, by supplying you they supply themselves, and protect, without personal danger, all the remainder of their possessions."

"Truly spoken, my lord; most truly spoken. Have we not arranged matters with Flanders, so that our traders in stuffs and specie are more than on an equality with all the world? Have we not crippled France in most bloody engagements, and here we are a king with scarcely a denier in our purse—a puppet of royalty? By the mass, 'tis fearful to think upon, my lord."

"My liege, may I presume to speak my thoughts?"

"Certainly, Hastings. We accord you faithful; speak on. Richard would tell us the citizens don't like wars; but we do not think that, when the result of wars is to disembarrass trade."

"My liege, the citizens, as a mass, are well-thinking men, but I do believe that there are some among them—a very few—who are the causes of this apparent disaffection."

"Ah! indeed?"

"Yes, your majesty. It strikes me that if some were removed from among their fellows, and their goods confiscated, there would be better thoughts among the remainder, and they would not only see your majesty's honour, but their own interests, in a clearer light."

"You think so?"

"I do, so please your majesty. Now, there is one Wainstead—a mercer—a well-to-do man in the Chepe ——"

"Ha! he with the fair daughter?"

"Has he a fair daughter, your majesty?"

"Has he! Why, Richard says he has, and you know it, and sought to carry her off, and assassinate her lover, and ruin the merchant. That you were head and ears in love with her, whom they call 'the Rose of the City,' Jane Wainstead, and that the whole affair was the finest jest that ever was."

"Your majesty!"

"Nay, we had the news from Gloster."

Hastings bit his lip till the blood nearly came, as he said, confusedly,—

"Your majesty is aware that his grace of Gloster hath a merry vein."

"Ah, but he swore 'twas all true; and, by the mass, how he lauded the beauty of the maid."

"Indeed! my liege."

"Yes. My lord, honestly, do you speak of this mercer in the Chepe from private pique?"

"Oh, your majesty, can you fancy I would dare to bring the weaknesses of private passion to your royal footstool? Do not, I implore you, do not think so hardly of one of the most devoted of your subjects."

"We are not disposed, Hastings, to judge harshly; and, after all, Richard may have been indulging in that merry vein you mention, which, to say truth, he is too fond of in grave affairs. We will speak to him again."

"Nay, your majesty: in such a case he will but heap supposed fact on fact, and as I dare not too roundly dispute with one so high, I shall, I fear, suffer unworthily in your majesty's opinion. Let me rather pray that the subject should henceforth drop."

"As you please, Hastings—as you please; but turn over in your politic brain some plan for recruiting our nearly exhausted exchequer. We must have money, Hastings."

"Could not your majesty make extensive purchases in the city, and then part with the goods again for money?"

"Without paying for them?"

"Exactly, my liege."

"Perhaps it might be done. But still, I fear, they would resist even that, Hastings. If, however, the worst comes to the worst, we must issue a decree calling for a certain subsidies upon the value of all merchandise, and then enforce its collection the best way we may. We will give the subject patient investigation, and should aught occur to you which may seem available and wise, you can communicate with us, my lord."

The king rose for a moment and then sat down again, which was the understood signal that the interview was over. Hastings bowed low, saying,—

"I humbly take my leave of your majesty."

He backed himself out of the royal presence, and passed into the ante-chamber. The folds of the heavy curtain which concealed the entrance to the royal closet fell over it, and then Hastings, with a stamp of his foot, exclaimed bitterly, and with vehemence,—

"Foiled again—foiled again, and all because Richard of Gloster is devoured with mawkishness, and loves a jest. Foiled again!"

"As how?" said a voice close to him, and turning sharply, he beheld Sir Loyala, as he now chose to name himself, close to his elbow.

CHAPTER XVIII.

The Spy.

"What shalle availe 'gainst wickede mighte?
Alas! ye poore defence of righte.
Not in ye worlde of mortale lighte
Shall virtue seeme one goodlie sighte."

"You here?" exclaimed the surprised Hastings, as he saw who it was who had so coolly interrupted his meditations.

"As you see," was the reply.

"But how gained you admittance?"

"I said I came by your orders to meet you, and here I have met you. How nice and probable it will look now. Besides, it may serve my turn another time, you know."

"You are a bold man, Sir Loyala."

"I would need be, my lord. I play with too many edged tools to make it safe for me to be otherwise than bold in the handling them."

"Come with me. Although I had no notion of finding you here, yet am I not sorry to meet you. I have once more to urge you to do me further service in a matter which, however you may consider it far beneath your abilities, is yet very near to my heart."

"Indeed!"

"Yes; the girl—this Jane."

"Really now, my lord, I am surprised."

"Surprised at what?"

"That, with your lordship's large resources, you cannot find means of conducting this intrigue without me."

"I have tried to engage the king to assist me without knowing that he did so; but I am foiled."

"You foiled by Edward—you, the crafty, foreseeing Hastings—you, a man whose whole life has been a lie?"

"You are plain spoken."

"Oh, between friends, as the devil said to the last chamberlain he took possession of, plain speaking is best."

"You are wrong, however, for I was not foiled by Edward."

"By who, then?"

"By Richard of Gloster."

"Ah! then you had a worthy opponent. He is craft itself. Take my word for it, Hastings, Richard is born to be great. Tack your fortunes to his, and you will not repent it. Be not querulous and waspish with him. Why, my lord, he has towards you a kindly liking."

"Think you so?"

"Nay, I know so; and if occasion seemed to pleasure you he would do it, be assured."

"Well, it seems he knows as well as I do myself about this affair of the mercer's daughter; why does he not pleasure me in that?"

"He has commenced."

"Ah! say you so?"

"In truth do I, my Lord Hastings. By the Duke of Gloster's warrant will the mercer's apprentice, Walter Fane, find a home in the ancient prison of the Black Friars, and then he will surely die."

"I am beholden to his grace for so much courtesy, by Heavens! And you asked this of him, Loyala?"

"In truth no. He said to me that he knew that the youth was pestilent to you, and of his own free liking to do you a good turn he had him there placed. Doubt not but by this time you have no rival."

"That is some relief, Loyala—a great relief I may say. Much rather, of course, would I that the boy should find a living tomb in the old prison than that I should have the trouble and the cost of taking his life—much rather—ay, a hundred times."

"Then you will see how gracious and really kind the duke is disposed to be towards your lordship. He seems at times wayward; but, in fact, he has a constant soul—a very constant soul, and when he takes a liking, which, by the mass, he has to you ——"

"To me?"

"Ay, to you. It was but yesterday he said, 'Show me a man with judgment keen as Hastings has, and, by St. Paul, I'll bow to him.'"

"He does swear by St. Paul."

"Always, as you may have noticed, when most in earnest he does swear by St. Paul; but come with me, I have a humble lodging hard by, and can, if it so please you, entertain you with some of that rare vintage so new in England, which comes from the banks of the deep Rhine. If you have tasted it not it will enchant you."

"I am no drinker."

"And should not be. Look at me. Think you I am a drinker, Hastings? Psha! Now, because you sit down before some wine, it does not follow that you should give up all judgment."

"Men deem you an adept in reasoning," said Hastings.

"In truth, my lord, I have learnt something of an art which lifts me nearer to the

sweets of Heaven. Ah! if your honour goes that way, I care not if I show you some proofs of my skill in divination."

"Curiosity and prudence are at war."

"Then let the former obtain the victory, and indulge itself, while, at the same time, it adopts its adversary's laurels."

"I am much tempted to go with you, Loyala. You are a wonderful man—one among thousands. God only knows what are your objects, or to what party you belong; but still, be you who or what you may, you have great powers."

"Now, is this kind?" said Loyala. "I am, of course, a man who wishes to make kind friends by kind actions. If I can do you a service, I shall flatter myself I make a friend of Hastings, and so on. As for the great matter which you and I have spoken of, it is progressing, you may depend. I am not at all neglecting it."

"But you refuse to aid me as regards the girl?"

"Not absolutely refuse; but we will talk more largely of that anon, and now here we are by my humble home."

The singular being took a small key from his pocket and opened the door of a mean-looking house. All was quiet as the grave, and the place had an uninhabited, sepulchral appearance about it that made Hastings hesitate a little before he chose to enter it.

"Have you any doubts?" said Loyala.

"Doubts—no—no—but—but—this seems almost a fit place for murders."

"It is a very fit place for murders; but I am not such a bungler. My lord, when a man is dead he is but so much carrion, of which nothing can be made, and from which nothing can be got but danger; while, if he lives, if he have wealth at all, he has a purse into which I can always dip my hand. If powerful, he can do me services—if rich, give me money in return for services I can do him; but let him be dead, and what is he? My lord, what would a dead High Chamberlain be to Loyala in comparison with a living one?"

These words were spoken with so much real sincerity, that it would have been almost impossible for our suspicious friend Shore to have had any doubt of the good faith of Loyala, as far as personal safety was concerned.

"Do not imagine, for a moment," said Hastings, as if ashamed of his fears, "that I harboured the most distant thought that you meant any false play, Loyala."

"I do not, my dear lord."

"I beg you will not. I hung back merely as a man naturally will who sees a strange, dark place before him."

"Most true, my lord, and most natural. May I now hope for the light of your lordship's countenance to make my abode less gloomy for awhile?"

"I am at your service, Loyala; and the rather that you might have fancied that I doubted you."

"I am much honoured, my lord."

Hastings walked into the house, closely followed by Loyala. The moment he had done so, he heard a little sharp bell tingle loudly, and he turned an inquiring look at the conjuror, who said,—

"You hear a bell?"

"I do."

"In the next house. They are perpetually ringing that bell. Hark! there it is again."

Even as he spoke the bell tingled again, for it had left off; and, whether he was really so or not, Hastings appeared to be satisfied.

Loyala led the way up a dilapidated staircase, which creaked fearfully at every step they made, and which had as threatening an appearance of falling down as any staircase could well present. On the landing above were several doors, and one of them Loyala opened, saying,—

"Enter, my lord. Here you are in the poor lodgings of Loyala."

Hastings entered the room, which, although far from boasting of anything in the decorative way, was yet as far from being destitute of comfort. It was rather a large apartment, and the walls were hung with rough wove tapestry. The floor was clean, and, from here and there a stray one, it seemed at no distant period to have been well strewn with rushes. There were several articles of furniture, and on the hearth smouldered a wood fire, from which there came a strong odour, as if the wood that lay there gently gleaming, had been strongly scented. The room was warm to the feel as you entered it, but rather dark than otherwise.

"What think you, my lord," said Loyala, "of my humble home, after your lordship's princely one?"

"Why, Loyala, I do not know how you would have such a question answered," said Hastings. "My impression of your resources and abilities is, that you might have what sort of house you please."

"Indeed."

"And that if you reside in a dull, gloomy house, it is because you do not care for a sprightly and a cheerful one."

Loyala laughed, as he cried,—

"My Lord Hastings, perhaps the cunning duke was right when he set you down as a man of rare discernment, notwithstanding you modestly would say no to the panegyric. I pray you to be seated."

Hastings sat down on a richly-carved chair, and as his eyes became more accustomed to the dim light that was in the room, he was able more minutely to look at its various appointments. He saw that there were several doors from it; and once he fancied, that behind one of them he heard a slight noise, and he called Loyala's attention to that circumstance, who replied,—

"Yes, I often hear loud noises, my lord, as well as slight ones. Before I came here, the rats held possession of the house solely; and now and then they feel inclined to dispute my human right to a joint occupancy of the premises."

"Indeed."

"Aye, they gallop over me rarely if I chance to sleep here. 'Tis a creature, too, that loves warmth, and sometimes when I have come home suddenly and noiselessly, I have seen them crawling round the embers on the hearth with evident enjoyment."

"A loathsome animal."

"To many, my lord, it is. But taste ye of this, and you will soon find such a pleasant fillip given to the brain, that when imagination lags in its healthful moment, and you feel the want of some mental spur to goad ye on, ye will sigh for such an one as I here present to you."

He produced a curious bottle, partly covered with wicker-work, and poured from it two glasses of sparkling liquid. Raising his own then to his lips before Hastings drank, as if to assure him of the harmlessness of the liquid, he drank it off, saying,—

"Welcome, my lord, welcome."

Hastings carried the glass to his lips, and he did, indeed, find the wine of delicious flavour.

"This is fine," he said, when he had drank it all.

"It is, and pure as a mountain spring, my lord. It is the genial juice of the grape, mellowed by age. Such a vintage does not always succeed, but when it does, it is beyond all price."

"So, indeed, I should think. The royal goblets never held such wine."

"How should they? But touching the Duke of Gloster?"

"The Duke of Gloster?"

"Yes; we were awhile ago speaking of him. Nay, my lord, never fear the wine—drink! drink!"

Hastings took another glass of the really delicious wine, and then an odd, rumbling sort of noise sounded in the house.

"You hear him?" said Loyala.

"Who—what?"

"That noise."

"Is that your friends the rats?"

"Oh, no. Since I have been here I have tried some experiments on what is called the *oraculum tabulam.* I got the matter into such a shape that I thought I could name what names I chose, but it turned out I had made some error, and I ran home thinking nothing of any one but of the Duke of Gloster."

"You are speaking in riddles to me."

"Am I? Then I will explain. Hush—hush! Seeing is believing. They are coming!"

"Who—who are coming?"

"My—my lord, sit still. There is nothing—there can be nothing to fear while I am here. You will be gratified, and you will see a strange sight which I will explain to your lordship."

A sudden darkness came over the room, which increased to a pitchy intensity, and the Lord Hastings sat down again, for he had suddenly risen, and something like a wish that he had not trusted himself in the conjuror's house came across his mind. Perhaps that wish would have been stronger, but for the generous wine of which he had partaken.

CHAPTER XIX.

The Omen.

And from ye same countries there came one man, cunninge beyonde cunninge, and artfule alway, who did foretel strange things of this realme.—*Biber Chron.*

"WHAT is going to happen?" said Hastings.

He wanted to hear the voice of Loyala, that he might be assured he was not left alone.

"Nothing alarming," said Loyala, as he gave a kick to the embers that lay upon the hearth, and scattered them. "Nothing alarming. Keep your eyes fixed before you, and you will see an odd sight, which is presented to me almost every day, at all sorts of times."

Hastings did as he was directed, and he saw a dim light begin to appear, as if at an immense distance off. Gradually, then, it increased in intensity, and presently an oval piece of white light was distinctly visible; where it came from he could not form a guess. At one moment, he thought he was looking through such a shaped opening, and then at another, he was more induced to believe it was light upon the opposite wall; but then the odd thing was that it cast no reflection, no radiance about it; but there it remained, cold, wan, and sickly-looking.

"What means it?" he said.

"You will see. Look steadfastly upon it, but let me warn you not to say anything derogatory of what you do see, or to imply any doubts about its correctness—if you do, you will offend those who are not easily pacified. There are supernatural beings who have limited powers of mingling with humanity, and those powers require much assistance from man, to bring them at all into operation. But when once you get the key to their conduct and appearances, you never lose them, except by such doubting of them and their powers as shall awaken passions which threw all human ones into the shade."

"You surprise me."

"Yes, to one who has not seen such things——"

"Hush. There is something."

A confusion of images suddenly appeared upon the oval piece of light, which now became much larger, although Hastings could see that what it gained in size, it lost in brilliancy. On its surface he saw as if an immense number of images were passing with great rapidity, and he again addressed Loyala, saying in a subdued tone,—

"What does that mean?"

"In that space," said Loyala, "are depicted the future fortunes of hundreds and thousands of the human race."

"Is that possible?"

"It is. The difficulty is to find out the particular spells which enable me to stop the image of a particular person."

"It is very strange."

"It is, indeed. The only one I am enabled to stop, is that of the Duke of Gloster; but I am in hopes that ere long my art will extend to others."

"Then you can foretell his fate?"

"Oh, with certainty. I know the word which will stop his image when it comes round."

"Can you? Do you feel disposed to give me such a proof of your occult skill, Loyala?"

"Most certainly I will."

He spoke something in a language which Hastings did not understand, and as he did so, he threw something among the dimly consuming embers of the fire he had scattered, and a pleasant odour pervaded the apartment.

"It's astonishing," he said, "how fond of perfumes the supernatural agents are."

"I have heard as much."

"Look now."

Hastings saw that the confusion of passing images on the oval piece of light had ceased, and various disjointed things seemed to be arranging themselves into some regular form. There were some columns which placed themselves erect, and then a vaulted dome which seemed deliberately to place itself above them. He saw plainly the interior of a cathedral or a chapel, but it was not like any he knew.

"What place is that?" he said.

"Nothing in existence, but something that you may depend will be."

Suddenly then the lower part of the spectacle began to fill with a throng of figures, and more prominent than all the rest, was one whose form and countenance grew each moment that he gazed clearer and clearer. That one was seated on a chair, and suddenly Hastings exclaimed,—

"By Heaven! the Duke of Gloster."

"It is the Duke of Gloster."

"On his head he wears a crown. About him are the robes of the kingly office. He sits upon a throne. By Heavens, he is a king!"

"The King of England."

"Now this is strange, indeed. Why, why, it is a delusion. Let me consider—a delusion—a delusion."

A loud shriek almost cracked the drums of Hastings' ears, and in a moment all was darkness.

"I ordered you," cried Loyala, "to express no doubts. Why did you so? There is some danger here now."

Hastings found something come swinging through the air at this moment, and only narrowly missed his face.

"This way, this way," added Loyala, as he took hold of him. "Come this way, it will not be safe for you to stay just now."

He dragged him towards the door, and as he went, Hastings heard a low wailing sound, as of some one in deep affliction.

"Good God," he said, "what is the meaning of all this?"

"I'm glad to hear that sound," said Loyala. "You will be able to get comfortably out of the house now, before passion succeeds to grief. Come on. Here we are. You can see now."

Loyala had opened the door which conducted them to the landing of the staircase, and there was light enough for the bewildered Lord Chamberlain to see his way, and still urged by Loyala, he descended the stairs with rapidity, and was well pleased to find himself breathing the open air once again. Loyala pretended to draw a long breath, as he said,—

"Now God be praised we are safe."

"Was there much danger?"

"There was, indeed. You should not have expressed a doubt. Had one of the spirits of the tabulum fastened upon you, you would have ran a good chance of being strangled."

"The devil I should!"

"Yes. I wonder they did not send one at you."

"Why, something did pass my head."

"Did it?"

"Yes, most certainly; and nearly touched me."

"Then, my Lord Hastings, you have had a narrow escape. These beings are the most fidgetty beings to have aught to do with you can possibly imagine; but what think you of the vision?"

"It was very strange."

"Is that all?"

"Nay, I know not if 'twere true. If one could be convinced it were a true prophecy—if one could say now that one knew thoroughly from that, that Richard, Duke of Gloster, would one day be king of England, one might shape one's conduct so as—so as—humph!"

"And can you doubt?"

"How can I believe? I certainly have seen a strange sight, but beyond that, I have no demonstration."

"Well, it is not for me to attempt to convince you. Let each now lock up in his breast his own belief."

"And you believe it, Loyala?"

"Do I believe in my own existence? Do I believe that you are a living man, my lord?"

"Well, it is strange."

"And no less strange than true. Those subtle spirits cannot present aught but what really will be. They can invent nothing; they have no power to do so. What they do is as surely what will be, as that you and I, my Lord Hastings, are at this moment standing here."

"I will think of it."

"Do so. From the love I bear you, I have more than once felt inclined to show you the indication of what will be, that you might trim the sails of your conduct in such a manner as to work for higher honours than those you now enjoy. If, my Lord Hastings, you make good use of the certain knowledge you have over all other men, regarding who will eventually fill so high a place as England's throne, you may lay that individual under great obligations, and pave the way, quietly and imperceptibly, to being but second in the realm yourself."

"Ah!"

"'Tis true, my lord."

"And you say his grace of Gloster thinks well of me?"

"Nobly."

"Tell me one thing, Loyala—knows he, or guesses he at his high future destiny?"

"No. He is the last man to whom I would show what you have seen."

"Indeed! and wherefore?"

"It would goad him on to dangerous enterprise, and you, who know it, would lose the merit of attaching yourself to his interests. Besides, I may have some hopes and some views of my own, for I am human."

"True; most true, Vassa."

"Call me not Vassa."

"I forgot. You have so many names, you know, that when one speaks to you, one or the other may by chance come uppermost."

"Psha! Be careful—be careful. I do not wish to be recognized in the streets as the king was at the City fete."

"I will guard my tongue better, good Loyala; and now, you will assist me about this girl, Jane?"

"I have certainly half promised so to do; but I certainly feel a strong impression that you will be unsuccessful."

"Indeed!"

"Yes; I have a powerful presentiment that such will be the case, and would advise you to forego an intrigue which will, I think, bring mortification in its train."

"I love her; she is beautiful as an angel."

"Be it so; I will bring you some news of her, and advise you how it is best to act, at all events, so as to present to yourself the greatest chances of success. To-morrow I shall see your lordship."

"To-morrow be it, then; and as for the Duke of Gloster——"

"Aye."

"When next you see him, Loyala, it would not be amiss to take occasion to tell him in what high terms of admiration you heard the Lord Hastings speak of him."

"I understand."

"And what attachment he showed to him and his fortunes."

"It shall be done, my lord."

"Let it be done, and done, too, with all your wondrous tact. There must be a subsidy almost directly raised for the king's purposes, and when there is, Loyala, it shall be my special care that some of it reaches your pockets."

"I am much beholden to your lordship."

"Adieu,—adieu; and remember the duke."

"I will, my lord. Adieu."

They parted, and the chamberlain proceeded towards his own house, full of strange thoughts and surmises as to what he had seen; Loyala, with a glance of supreme contempt after him, muttered,—

"Indeed. So, my lord, you swim round the bait but a short time ere you nibble it. Well, well. Oh, what fools are these men who hold high places. Drawn aside from their purposes by a thread—puffed onwards by a breath. What puppets do I not make of them!"

He made his way down to the river side, and called for a boat. In a few moments he was in the middle of the stream, and in answer to the waterman's inquiry as to where he should take him, he said,—

"To the market steps, by the mayor's house, at the end of Lombarde-street. Give way, for I am in haste, and care not if I double your fare."

The waterman, thus urged, plied his oars rapidly, and that man, whose brain was one mass of intrigue, was rapidly wafted towards the city, where he landed at the place he had mentioned.

CHAPTER XX.

The Dungeon.

"No hope—no prayer—no joy—no smile,
To cheat the weary hour
Of bitterness, and hopeless woe,
And wild oppression's power."

And ye irone of ye chaines eat into theire limbs nce mo than ye irone of despaire dide eat into ye soules of ye poore prisoners.—Stowe.

As much called upon are we by inclination, as by the pressing events of our narrative, to return to a consideration of the mental sufferings of poor Jane, who had thus been sacrificed to a man whom her very soul abhorred, and we should do so at once in this present chapter, but that we lament to leave the high-spirited, noble, generous Walter Fane in such fearful straits as when last we parted with him in the dungeon of the prison at Blackfriars.

When the unhappy youth cast himself on the damp earth which formed the flooring of his dungeon, he gave himself up completely to death, for he fully believed he should be kept there to starve, and that, perhaps, more than a month might elapse before curiosity might tempt any of his gaolers to look after him.

Such a fate, and to one just upon the threshold of existence, was sure to present itself in a terrific aspect, and no wonder, then, that the feeling of despair that crept over him was of the most agonising nature.

"Ah, Jane! Jane! my beautiful Jane!" he cried; "never to see you more—never again to look upon your face!—to be immured here, the living tenant of a loathsome tomb! My Jane, could you but see him who loves you now, what pearly tears would fall like rain from those sweet eyes! And when I am gone who will protect you? Who will stand between you and harm? Oh, God! oh, God! if I had been but spared to guard her, I had been happy."

Pat, pat, pat came drops of moisture from the roof of the dungeon, as if mocking him by the calm regularity with which they fell. It was the only sound, except the echo of his own sighs, that disturbed the death-like stillness of that fearful and hopeless place.

Suddenly then he felt something soft touch his face, and he sprang aside—a long something, like the lash of a whip, dabbed across his mouth, and then he heard a splashing and a swamping, and he said,—

"Rats—rats—this place is infested with rats."

Lie down again he could not, not but the fact that there was some enemy to contend with rather diverted his gloomy thoughts, and, as he stamped to frighten the animals away, he found that he was not so disposed entirely to give way to despair.

"I have heard," he said, "of perseverance accomplishing wonders in the way of escape from prison. When my eyes get more accustomed to the darkness, I may perchance see, after all, some food for hope."

He commenced groping about the place, to ascertain its extent, and he found that it was divided into two compartments, by a row of stunted pillars, that, at regular intervals, went down the centre. The walls seemed to be merely of a clayey kind of earth, into which had been wedged large stones of a jagged shape; they were trickling with moisture, and, as he walked, he found that he occasionally trod in a complete pool.

By degrees, as he had then anticipated, he could see a little better, and, without much difficulty, he found the steps which led up to his dungeon-door. These he ascended, and tried the door, but it was as fast as a rock; and, had he not known it, he could hardly have believed that there was an opening there at all, so completely a part of the wall did it seem.

He remembered that the man had told him the dungeon was under the bed of the river, and he thought of how dreadful it would be for the tide to flow in upon him, and so drown him in that dark hole, without he being able to make the least effort to save himself.

"There is something horrible," he said, "in death creeping on in such ways: I am not afraid to die, but I would have some struggle for the life that God has given me; and fain would I, if I resign it yet awhile, do so beneath the canopy of Heaven only, and in the attempted accomplishment of some worthy object; but, to be tunnelled up thus to die, is indeed too horrible—too horrible to think of."

Oh! how his thoughts flew back to the happy years he had spent at the mercer's! How he pictured to himself Jane five years since, when she was little more than a child, coming down, on the clear summer's evening, to speak to him in the old shop, and bless him by her presence for a while. He could see the sweet contour of her face—he could see the sunny masses of her golden hair—he could hear her merry laugh—and now again he could feel how he had thought it would be worth an emperor's crown to fold her in his arms, and drown her with kisses.

And where was he now?' Oh! dreadful change—a prisoner in a dungeon—doomed to starvation; and, ere the breath of life had left him, to become the food of reptiles. The thought was horrible, and clasping his hands, Walter exclaimed,—

"Oh! is there indeed a God in Heaven, and so much wickedness on earth? Help me—help me, Heaven, in this hour of my utmost need! Let me not perish yet!—let me not die this death."

As he spoke a noise rent his ears. Was it the key in the lock of the dungeon-door? Was there hope yet? Yes—yes—it was—it was; he saw a glare of light: the dungeon door is opened; he rushes towards the steps—something is cast at his feet, and the door closes again. Hope has fled—he hears the key once more turned in the rusty lock—despair again takes possession of him, and he exclaims,—

"Lost! lost! lost! They do but mock me! It was but a mockery after all—I am still the doomed man."

But what is it that has been cast upon his dungeon floor? He suddenly remembers there was a something thrown in.

"What can it be?" he said; "what can it be?" All is darkness—worse darkness than before; because, for a few brief seconds, as the dungeon-door was opened, a light flashed in his eyes.

Suddenly, now, he heard a snuffling voice, and then such a splashing as convinced him the rats had come out in abundance.

"It must be food! it must be food!" he exclaimed, "which has been cast into my dungeon, and I must fight with these voracious animals for the possession of it."

As he spoke he stooped towards the spot where the object, whatever it was, had been cast, and he laid his hand upon nothing but rats.

Moved by despair, he clutched the animals one by one, and threw them, screaming and yelling, to the further end of the dungeon, with all his force, and, after a severe scramble, he found that it was a loaf of bread which had been thrown into the gloomy place.

Hunger blunts the sensibilities; and, although at any other time Walter Fane would have loathed that food he had been compelled to rescue from the very mouths of reptiles, yet now he eagerly devoured it, and felt a sensation of satisfaction, as he remarked,—

"It was but, after all, an idle threat; they do not mean to starve me here; I am rescued for something yet; while there is life there is hope."

A loaf of hard, dry, coarse bread was not the most invigorating meal in the world; but all those matters are merely comparative, and, balanced against nothing at all, it certainly became a treat. Poor Walter found it so, and he felt a new man after having partaken of it. He longed for something to drink; but it was some time before he could bring himself to partake of the drippings from the roof of his dungeon.

When, however, he was hard pressed by thirst, and found it absolutely necessary to have some drink, he thought he should have a better chance of getting it purer from off the flints that formed part of the walls; and, accordingly, he found a place where the water trickled down in quite a mimic stream, and slaked his thirst thereby.

"I will not," he then said, "even yet, give up to despair, knowing, as I do know, that, in this prison, unhappy persons are confined for years; yet I will not despair. If I had but some weapon, however slight and inefficient, I would yet have a chance of escape. I would yet fancy I might be free. Let me consider: of course, the direction of the door leads to the body of the prison. The other way would but take me further under the Thames. That would not do. Let me consider: I must think over all I have heard and read of prison escapes; how, under apparently the most impossible circumstances, prisoners have, to the consternation of their gaolers, freed themselves. I must call all that to mind, and, from a recollection of such narratives, gather what hope I may. For your sake, my own, my beautiful Jane, I will not despair."

He paced his dungeon for more than an hour in deep meditation. Sometimes the saddest feeling of gloom would begin to creep over him, and then the natural buoyancy of youth would induce him again to hope almost against probability.

Suddenly he made a determination to institute a much closer search in his dungeon than he had hitherto done, with the hope of finding something which might facilitate his escape.

"Others, no doubt, have been confined here," he said to himself, "as well as I; and I may discover some weapon which, perchance, may do me service. I fear I shall have ample time for search."

His eyes had now become more familiar with the darkness of the place by a great deal than they had been before the appearance of the light at the door had dazzled them, and he could distinguish now from the walls the range of low stunted-looking columns which supported the roof of the dungeon.

"I have heard," he said, "of prisoners whose eyes, from long acquaintanceship with the darkness of a dungeon, have become so accustomed to it, that they could see the smallest creeping thing upon the floor. I find, even already, that this place is not so gloomy to me."

Loneliness was a thing of which Walter Fane was not afraid, however he might naturally dislike such a state of things for a continuance; but his mind was too correct an one and had too many intellectual endowments for him to labour under those superstitious fears which would have attacked many persons if confined in such a gloomy place. Walter Fane was no sceptic. He took a more rational view than scepticism ever takes. He denied nothing. He believed all possible with Heaven, and what Heaven chose should be, he did not see why he should particularly fear.

If it was part of the design of creation that even the apparitions of the dead should at times visit the earth, he did not see why he should be terrified at that one natural phenomenon more than at any other. He very much doubted if such were the case, because he thought if it were, there would be more abundant evidence of the fact; but if it were, he would not alarm himself about it; therefore solitude had not so many terrors for Walter Fane as it would have had to hundreds and thousands of the people who were walking about in freedom so near to him, and yet as much separated from him, to all real purposes, as if he were in his grave, and they still bustling inhabitants of the great world above his lonely sepulchre.

With, then, a far stouter heart than, probably, his gaolers dreamt that he, so young, too, could possibly possess, he commenced an accurate search of every corner of his dungeon, with a sanguine hope of finding something to reward his labours.

CHAPTER XXI.

The Skeleton Prisoner.

"And he had died despairing, for there was no hope in Heaven nor on earth."

It was, in truth, a dreary, comfortless search that which poor Walter Fane made in his dungeon. He commenced close to the steps which led up to the door, and he examined as he went, most carefully, every nook and corner, but weapon found he none. There seemed no hope of any, and in the course of half an hour he had felt his way all round the gloomy place, finding nothing—laying his hands on nothing but the slippery rugged stones which were let into the wall, and from which the moisture that crept in by the roof kept so continually trickling.

"I cannot endure the pangs of thirst here," soliloquized Walter, "and that appears to be about the only consolation for a prisoner in this place, which the utmost ingenuity of the fiends who keep it cannot deprive them of, although, no doubt, if it were possible in any way to do so, it would most assuredly be done."

He felt wearied with his hopeless, profitless search, and he sat down on the lowest step of the flight which led up to the dungeon door, to try to think over the possibilities of bettering his condition. He felt that the term probabilities would be sadly out of place.

"Nothing—nothing but my hands," he moaned, "to work with! Oh, if I could but see a prospect, however dim, of achieving something towards my liberty, Heaven knows I would be thankful and not despairing."

He happened to cast his eyes towards the stunted pillars that supported the roof, and he thought that at the base of one of them there was a darker mass than was warranted by the shadow that the place was in. To go towards it, in a moment, was, of course, his first impulse, and as he stooped over the object, he became conscious that from it had proceeded a strange and horrible smell, that had at times crossed his senses since he had been in that place.

He could not see sufficiently distinctly to detect what it was, but he touched it with his foot, and then gathering more strength over his loathing from necessity, he placed his hand upon one part of the mass and took it up. Both by the feel and the slight sight he could get of it, he knew that he held in his hand a huge bone. He felt still further, and the result of that examination caused him to quail with horror. A dead body, half decomposed, and the bones yet in many cases hanging together by the cartilages, was there.

"Gracious God!" he cried, "and this has been the end of the last tenant of this dreadful place. Is this an intimation of what is to be my doom? Oh, Heaven! am I reserved to become such a hideous mass of cold corruption as this? Rather, oh, a thousand times, then, strike me dead at once, great God, than let me linger here in such horrible company!"

He sank to the damp ground at the foot of another of the columns, and resting his face upon his hands, he remained crouched up for more than an hour, while all the original despair which had taken possession of his mind when first he was brought to that dreary place, returned upon him with twofold force.

Suddenly, then, it struck him that he had assumed almost precisely the same position in which the dead body appeared, from the casual observation he was able to make of it, to occupy. There it was huddled up at the base of one of the columns. The thought of such a similarity, even of position, was hideous, and he at once sprang to his feet.

"No, no!" he cried, "I will not die thus—I will not die thus! No, no, by heavens, I will not!"

The sound of his own voice—for he had spoken in loud accents—startled him, as it echoed through the dreary place, and he felt almost induced to believe some voice had answered him.

"No, it was but an echo," he said, mournfully. "Oh, for any human companionship, rather than to be entombed alive in such a place as this along with the dead, too."

He walked slowly away from the column, at the base of which was so dreadful an object. He did not like to turn his back upon it; a strange, undefined fear began to creep over him, and he soon detected that it was laying hold of him in such a way.

To make such a discovery was to Walter Fane but as a signal to fight up against the feeling. At once he drew himself up to his full height as he said, in a voice bold, without being boastful,—

"What have I to fear from the dead? What harm can yon senseless mass of corruption do to me? It may be loathsome to the touch—it may offend the senses, but, beyond that, what is it? No more than any other heap of animal putrifaction. I will not now, at the outset of Heaven only knows how long a residence here, allow myself to be cowed and terrified by such an object. I am innocent, and have no fear."

At once he turned and approached the spot again, determined to see as much of it as he could, and to force himself by as close an inspection of the reality as he could possibly make, to discard all imaginary terrors upon the subject.

"The mind," he said, "would never rest, both sleeping and waking, upon such a theme as this, and were I to avoid it, each day it would be dressed up by my imagination with new terrors, and might ultimately drive me mad. I will face it boldly, while I have the strength to do so."

It did require great moral courage to do what Walter Fane now did. He stooped over the skeleton remains, and ascertained that it was fastened by a chain round the waist. The bones of the back had, in consequence of the great thickness and strength of the cartilaginous remains between them, not separated; but the body hung forward by the chain, and the head had, either before, or in consequence of his touching it, fallen off below the feet.

It was one of the thigh bones that Walter had at first picked up, and now, by forcing his eyes very intently upon the figure for awhile, he could distinguish its outline pretty well, and see how it was held up in so odd looking a crouching attitude. He could not exactly bring himself to touch the corpse, but he looked curiously at the stunted column to see how the chain was fastened to it. By dint of patient examination, he found that there was a tolerably stout upright bar of iron, about six feet in height; one end of this was buried in the ground close to the pillar, and then there was a strong band which fastened it at its upper end close to the shaft. Fastened to this bar was the iron chain that was round the body of the skeleton. The arrangement was simple enough. Doubtless, the material of the column would not hold a screw or nail, so the chain could not be absolutely fastened to it, and hence had the upright piece of iron been used, in order to give the requisite strength to the whole arrangement, and keep the prisoner effectually secured.

The moment Walter Fane ascertained these particulars, the thought occurred to him that if he could but get possession of that straight upright piece of iron, it would make for him, if not too much corroded by the damp of that place, a most powerful weapon.

Simultaneously, however, with such a thought, he much feared that he should find it thoroughly rotten and eaten through with rust; still it was a chance, and as it appeared to be the only one which that place afforded him, he was not disposed to waste time in melancholy conjectures that it might not prove available. He proceeded to the other side of the column, and carefully felt the iron band which held the upright piece of metal to the shaft. It was very strong, and appeared to have been rivetted, and yet, strong as it was, he could take the rust off it in huge flakes. With the thought of a moment, he went to one of the walls, and feeling for one of the jagged stones which were let into it, he commenced with his hands attempting to force it from its hold.

This was a work of more difficulty than he had anticipated, for he found that the part of the stone which was discernible outside was the smallest, and that it had a firm position, in consequence of its irregularity, and by far the greater part of it being embedded. Still to procure that stone could be but a question of time, and by degrees Walter succeeded in loosening it. Then he got his hand partly behind it, and with a powerful wrench, he drew it out from the wall. It fell at his feet, but instantly picking it up, he hurried to the column, and commenced hammering at the band that held the upright piece of iron with a vigour that threatened its very speedy and effectual demolition.

When the will goes with any work, the speed made in its execution is proportionably great; and this was an instance in point. In less than two minutes the staple, or band, which was clasped round the column, gave way, and the iron bar fell forward a short distance immediately.

Walter cast down the stone, and was round the column in an instant. But yet he had something to do to force the iron from the ghastly remains that clung to it. This he effected, however, although the task was a sickening one, and when he had done that, the chain still hung by it, and he felt that if he could not succeed in breaking it off, it would be a serious hindrance to him in any operation he might project with the weapon so rare a chance had thrown in his way.

The large stone he had procured with so much labour here aided him again, and two or three vigorous blows soon forced the chain from the bar of iron, which he found a weapon of great power, and one which, when he freed it from some of its superficial rust, was still thick enough to possess a great degree of strength.

"Now," he exclaimed, "I will hope; I am armed, and I will not give up myself to despair; but before I think of what can now be done for my own deliverance, I will perform a duty by those sad remains of the last occupant of this place."

With considerable toil, Walter succeeded in digging a hole with the iron bar in the dungeon floor. It was necessarily very superficial, but still it sufficed. He drew the ghastly skeleton into it with the end of the bar, and then he covered it up with the wet earth, and stamped the whole down as well as he could. It was a great relief to his mind to have done this; he felt as if the place now wore quite a different aspect; the bodily labour, too, that he had gone through had restored the circulation of his blood, and he felt much better than he had yet been in that place.

He sat down on the lowest of the stone steps, and he was glad there was such a seat for him, and holding the bar between his knees, he began to think upon what he should do with it.

While he thus thought, he heard the key placed in the lock of the door, and the thought of concealing the iron bar immediately occurred to him. He placed it behind one of the columns, and scarcely had he done so, when the dungeon door was thrown open, a light gleamed down the steps, and a voice said,—

"Prisoner, come hither; you are wanted."

Walter was half a mind to resist the mandate, but there was something hopeful and delicious in getting for even an instant out of that place; so he ascended the steps.

Immediately above were three persons—one was Sir Godfrey, the keeper of the prison; the other two were the men who had with so much brutality conducted him to his present place of confinement.

Sir Godfrey regarded him inquisitively for a few moments, as if he would fain discover what effect his imprisonment had had upon him. Walter regarded him with a stern gaze of defiance.

"Well, young sir," said Sir Godfrey, "you don't seem at all thankful for my great humanity and consideration."

"Humanity!"

"Yes, to be sure."

"Ruffian!"

"Didn't I send you a loaf of bread? Haven't I put bread into your mouth—oh, you ungrateful fellow!"

Slankey laughed outright, for which Sir Godfrey gave him a blow on the mouth, saying,—

"Now a murrain take you—how dare you laugh?"

"Oh, I—I—ha, ha, ha!"

"Am I to be set at liberty?" asked Walter. "Have you or your employer found out that I have committed no crime, or that I have been mistaken for some other person?"

"Not exactly, my lad, not exactly; don't be so hasty. You can write, I suppose, eh? Now-a-days, any 'prentice boy is learned."

"I can write."

"Very good. Now, Hugh Slankey, give him the pen, and hold the ink-horn ready for him."

"What do you wish me to write?" said Walter, in no small degree of surprise at these preparations.

"A mere trifle. You will write an invitation to Jane Wainstead, the mercer's daughter, of the Chepe, to meet you at eight o'clock this evening, by St. Saviour's church."

"Is that all?" said Walter, calmly.

"All for the present. I'm glad to find you so tractable."

"But you are mistaken."

"Mistaken! What do you mean, eh?"

"That I will not write as you desire,—that, had I fifty lives to lose, and you had sworn to take them all if I did not write these words, I would not. That the world's wealth should not induce me to do; no, nor the threats of any ruffian it contains."

"You will not? D——n! Boy, do you know who you are talking to?"

"Yes; to Godfrey, the infamous keeper of the Blackfriars prison."

"Now, by ——"

"Rant on, sir. You can kill me, I know, but I do begin to suspect you dare not. You have some infamous employer, who, through you, hopes to get me, by fear of a dread of death, to betray an angel. Oh, God! it is the worst pang of all to know, as now I do, the cause of my imprisonment; but it shall soothe me in my hour of bitterness and anguish, to feel that it is in vain they make me suffer, for not even death shall induce me to betray you, my beautiful Jane. Live on, dear one, in your beauty and in your innocence; Walter Fane can die for you, but he cannot purchase the world's sovereignty, were it the prize, as the price of one word or look which should bring danger upon thee."

"D———n!" said Sir Godfrey, "we want no heroes here. Do you mean to say you will not write the note?"

"I will not, so help me, Heaven!"

"Why, fool, we might have released you, for all you know."

"I am not the less worthy of release that I will not stoop to do a base, dishonourable action."

"It was you yourself that was to meet her."

"I need not do so. I can go to Master Wainstead's house; but this is idle lying. It was a plot to carry her off, because some noble has become enamoured of the beautiful girl. Oh, the trick is too transparent. You thought to find me terrified; you thought to find me enfeebled; and because I had been for some hours confined in the dark, that you could convert me from what I was, to a trembling wretch so abject that I could refuse you nothing. You see you are mistaken."

"Am I?"

"You know you are—I defy you."

"We will find some means to break down that stubborn spirit, be assured. We have tortures here."

"You may make me suffer pain—I grant you the brute's power, so far, but you cannot move my soul. That is constant to one object. The safety of her I love—I will not betray you, Jane!"

"Now, of all the brain-sick fools that we ever had here, Slankey, saw you ever one like this?"

"Never, my noble master, never! A boy—a mere love-sick boy, my noble master."

"And you," said Walter, "are a great coward, huge and bulky as you are."

"A coward!"

"Yes. If you had been half the time I have down below here, with a ghastly and rotted corpse as a companion, you would have gone distracted."

"A corpse!" said Godfrey.

"Yes, noble master; I shouldn't wonder," said Slankey. "I put him in when the ——"

He whispered something to Godfrey, who replied,—

"Indeed! I didn't know it. It's just as well, though; it serves him right. Ha, ha, ha! So you have a pleasant companion down below?"

"Yes, I have; will you come and see him? I have placed him close to the bottom step, as if looking up for liberty. Come and see him."

"Not I, by G—d!" cried Slankey, as he hastily retreated a step or two.

"Youngster," said Godfrey, "is this madness or courage?"

"Call it what you will, villain; your opinion is a matter of indifference to me. I know I have nothing to hope for at your hands."

"You are a fool. If you had written the note I spoke of, I dare say you would have been let out in a week or two. Slankey, go down into the dungeon, and see if you can contrive to chain up this youngster, since he carries matters with so high a hand."

"But, noble Master Godfrey," stammered Slankey, "there's the corpse—the dead man."

"And what of that?"

"He's a mere skeleton now," said Walter, "and scarcely hangs together."

"I'm d—d if I go!" said Slankey. "There now, that's flat. I can't go, and there's an end of it."

"You great coward," muttered Godfrey, "I've half a mind to go myself, only it ain't worth my while, that's all. Be off with you, youngster. Into your den again. It strikes me you won't see daylight in a hurry."

The door was shut so suddenly, that it was only with great dexterity that Walter avoided being struck by it. They thought they had struck him, no doubt, for he heard them laughing; but he descended the staircase, rather congratulating himself, than otherwise, that he had terrified his gaolers from coming into the dungeon and taking cognisance of any operation he might attempt for his release.

What with the work he had done, and the long time he had been in a state of excitement, without repose, and insufficient food besides, Walter began to feel a sense of weariness and exhaustion creeping over him. He sat down by one of the columns where the ground felt the driest, although that was damp enough, and soon he lay down completely, and, despite all the horrors and anxieties of his situation, he fell fast asleep.

CHAPTER XXII.

Jane, the Wife.

"And her young heart's hopes were blighted,
As early blooming flowers
That miss the sunshine of the skies,
The gentle summer showers."

In a handsome apartment in Shore's house, in Lombard-street, were two persons. The room was filled with costly plate, rare stuffs, and trinkets of rich design, and much intrinsic value. It would seem strange that such a man as Shore should decorate a room at all so showily, and at such a large cost; but when we shall state that every article there was for sale, and that, when he had a customer to whom it was prudent, as well as worth while, to show his choicest commodities, he introduced him there, we shall no longer feel any surprise at the profusion of magnificence that glittered in every direction one might chance to look in that handsome apartment.

It was an odd state of things at that time, but no less odd than true, that it was but a common measure of prudence on the part of the dealers in precious wares to keep the more valuable portion of their stock out of sight. The daring robberies that were committed when much booty was to be obtained, formed one good reason, and it was much suspected by the citizens that some of the more reckless and money-wanting of the nobles thought nothing of setting a gang of their idle retainers upon some burglarious enterprise to refill their exhausted purses.

There were good enough grounds for such a belief, for, somehow, it often happened, that when a robbery of great importance was committed, my lord somebody might be found to stifle inquiry, and thwart the ends of justice in the matter. Then, again, there was another class of the nobles who would have taken these valuable articles on credit, a credit which it would have been unsafe to refuse them, and yet which would have lasted till the day of judgment, and a little beyond, for payment of any debt from the turbulent nobility of the times was out of the question.

It was only, then, to a chosen few, who had money and character both, that such men as Shore chose to deal with, and to show what he really had in the way of articles of great worth and rarity. That his customers were consequently few, may be guessed; but still he was a rich man, for he took care that appended to what business he did do there should be immense profits; and, moreover, nothing came amiss to him that promised money, and there was no doubt that he had acted as a spy at different times to both the factions of York and Lancaster, although now all his predilections went one way only, namely, to uphold the Lancastrian faction.

We have said there were two people in this room. One of them was Shore himself. There was an angry spot upon his brow, and his manner betrayed excitement. He was very plainly attired in faded velvet, and looked inexpressibly mean and contemptible. He had never quite recovered the loss of blood from his wound. The additional sallowness which had been given to his cheeks seemed destined to remain there through life. He stood by the back of a chair, which he clutched with nervous energy, as if he would prevent the trembling of his whole frame from being apparent: but it was very apparent, notwithstanding.

The other person in the room was seated. The hands were over the face. Tears were gushing betwixt the small child-like fingers, and deep sobs came from the labouring heart. It was Jane—the beautiful Jane—beautiful as ever, though much paler; a short time had sufficed to rob her cheeks of their bloom—she was very, very unhappy. Her heart was a charnel-house of lost affections—she was wretched—she had told Shore as much, and hence the state of anger, fear, and general excitement in which we now find him. Alas! poor, poor Jane! The sun of your once happy heart has set for ever. Doomed are you to a turbulent and wild career; but the light of day shall never again shine in your bosom—a genuine smile of happiness never again light up those sweet eyes.

Shore spoke in hoarse, guttural accents.

"You love another," he growled—"you love another, Jane. Some other has your heart; do not deny it. Curses on him! I know it; your tears are not for me. You love another."

"Did I ever say I loved you?" remarked Jane.

"Yes, at the altar."

"Oh, God! forgive me."

Now, the reader will believe that this was sufficiently aggravating, and Shore was worked up to a pitch of frenzy, as he said,—

"Jane, you—you wish to kill me; but I will not die. You wish to drive me mad; but I will preserve my sanity, Jane. I love you—I adore you. I never in all my life loved anything human but you. I—I worship your face. I have toiled to get you. I have vowed to die, or you should be mine. You are my wife. I tell myself a thousand times a day that you are mine. If I am crossed in business, I say, 'what matters? Jane is mine.' If I am insulted, I still say, 'Jane is mine.' If I lose my money, I comfort myself with these words, 'Jane is mine.' Have you no return to make for so much devotion?"

These last words were spoken almost plaintively, and they seemed to touch the gentle-hearted girl a little.

"Master Shore ——" she sobbed.

"Oh, God—God!" he cried, interrupting her. "Master Shore! I have never heard yet from her lips a tenderer epithet than Master Shore."

"What would you have me call you?"

"No matter—no matter. Jane, I love you still. God! I love you still."

"All that a wife can be in duty to a husband," sobbed Jane, "that will I be to you; but no one, surely, no one can stop the sigh that will come from the anguish-laden heart. No one can say to the unbidden tear, 'begone,' for ere we know it is there."

"You do not love me."

"Take my duty—take my respect, Master Shore."

"There—there again. Master Shore. God! She never calls me anything but Master Shore."

"I will be obedient. I will be faithful. You shall always find me gentle to you. Alas! I know not how to be otherwise."

"And yet not love me."

"Why do you press that which of itself should spring up in the heart spontaneously, like some rare flower in a wilderness? If I give you duty, respect, fidelity, and gentle words ——"

"Pooh—pooh!"

"Surely they should suffice, good Master Shore."

"There—there. God! she does nothing but call me Master Shore. I shall think of nothing but being Master Shore. I shall dream I hear some one shouting in my ears, 'Master Shore.' She has never yet called me by a tenderer name than Master Shore."

"You would not have me play the hypocrite?"

"As I say—as I say, you do not love me."

"You know I wedded at my poor father's earnest wish. Perhaps I then doubted the wisdom of so much blind obedience; perhaps I doubt it more now than then; perhaps I may have cause to doubt it more hereafter than even I do now."

"Bravo! D——n! Well spoken. Oh, yes. H—ll!"

"Is this the way, Master Shore, to make me respect you, even if I cannot love you?"

"God! there she goes with her Master Shore again."

"It is your name. I cannot call you out of it."

"Go on—go on."

"Nay, I wish not to protract a dispute which can bring no happiness to either of us. Let me pray you to be content with my duty—to be satisfied with my fidelity—to know that you may make me respect you as a kind and indulgent friend—be satisfied with all this, and I shall be more cheerful. I shall not weep so often. I shall not speak so sadly. I—I will learn to forget, that is, I will try not to remember too keenly, the happy—happy past, which, like a dream ——"

Her tears flowed afresh, and she could say no more. Shore was silent for some few moments, and then he said,—

"Jane, you are my wife. I will have no divided empire in the soul of her I love. You have sworn to love me, to honour me, to obey me. The latter you promise to do."

"Which I can promise."

"Listen to me, and interrupt me not, Jane. People think me cold and passionless; they are wrong. My heart is a volcano—a volcano."

Jane shuddered.

"I have set my all upon your love; but you love another. You promise me duty, but I know how futile is the promise. Jane, beware—beware, I say. Some men have stated that I am revengeful; and those who have done so, are, to a certain extent, men of sagacity. You hear me?"

"Yes—yes."

"'Tis well; but they know not that I can carry vengeance to a length that would paralyze them with dread."

"God help me!"

"You swore to love me."

"And you knew," said Jane, gathering momentary strength in her own defence, "you knew I loved you not."

"I knew?"

"Yes, Master Shore."

"Ah! Bah!"

"You knew I did not love you. Can you lay your hand upon your heart, and say you believed you led a willing bride to the altar? I ask you, can you do that?"

"Can I?"

"Yes. You knew I loved you not. You know I wedded you in deference to my poor father's wish. You know you took me as your wife, with the avowed conviction that I loved you not. You knew all this, Master Shore, and wherefore do you now reproach me?"

Shore felt this to be unanswerable, so he caught at the part of it which he could, he thought, object to, and, as usual, he exclaimed,—

"There, she calls me Master Shore again."

"I will not belie my heart," she said, "by calling you by tender epithets I feel not. And oh, great Heaven, forgive me, that I swore at thy sacred altar to love this man."

Shore gave almost a howl of rage, as he cried,—

"You do well—you do well, minion, to turn it off thus. If I knew you did not love me—if I knew that I had to gain your affection after you were my wife, which I could have done—d——n, if I was aware how your heart was set upon Walter Fane, your master's idle 'prentice—a scapegrace—a good-for-nothing scamp—a ——"

"Peace, peace! Oh, would that you ——"

"Were like him, I suppose, to go ambling after you like a well-paced jennet—to grin at nothing, and pick up your fan—to listen to nonsense, and applaud it to the echo—to—to—d—n it, I thank Heaven that I am not like him."

"Enough, enough!"

"It is not enough."

"I am unable, I have not strength to support these discussions. They happen daily, and I am wretched enough without them. Say what you will, I am too spirit-broken to contradict you now."

"There may be still enough conscience left to make her stick in your throat."

Jane made no answer, and Shore, after waiting for a moment, exclaimed,—

"Let this Walter Fane beware, say I. A malapert youngster—a beardless boy. Let him beware how he cross my path—let him beware. His blood be upon his own head."

This roused Jane again, and she said, faintly,—

"After that threat, now listen to me. If any harm befal young Walter Fane, on your head be it. I will leave you."

"Leave me—leave me!"

"I swear it. If I have to beg my bread, I will leave you."

"Indeed! Be it then my care to prevent you. To your chamber—to your chamber! We will see what virtue is in a lock and key."

"A prisoner?"

"You threatened to leave me."

"Upon a contingency—yes; but I will not be made a prisoner of, Master Shore. I am weak, and unused to broils and contentions, but you may rouse a spirit you cannot quell again. You tell me to beware, but I tell you that there is a point of endurance beyond which it is dangerous to push the most timid, and apparently gentle and yielding. Do not force me to resist to the uttermost."

Shore looked, as indeed he was, a little frightened, and he replied,—

"Jane, you have yourself to thank for the threat. I met a threat by a threat."

"Nay, you contemplated murder. Yes, a murder. You talked of the death of Walter Fane, and although I know well he has nothing to dread from you personally, yet I know not what treachery might not achieve against him. He is of an unsuspecting nature. God help him, be he where he may."

"Perhaps you do not know where he is?" said Shore, suspiciously.

"I would I did—I would I did."

"It's strange to me you never yet firmly believed that he was drowned."

"I do not believe he is. Something whispers to me that we shall meet again."

"The hope dictates the whisper."

"Be content, Shore. If I do meet Walter Fane ever again in this world, it shall be but to take of him a last adieu. You have my duty."

"And he ——"

"I cannot—cannot deny it."

"He has your love?"

"He has—he has—he has!"

Shore threw up his arms in an agony, as he cried,—

"I knew it, I knew it. God, I knew it!"

"Then why wring the secret from me?"

"It was more damning when coming from your lips."

"Then hear me out. I own he has my love, but I will not forget what I have sworn, and can keep to. Shore, I repeat to you, I should be the happier for seeing Walter Fane, and bidding him farewell for ever."

"If ever I permit such an interview to ensue, may I be roasted in the lowest pit of ——"

"Hush, hush. I can believe you without such asseverations," said Jane. "Again I

tell you, I am too weak and ill, Master Shore, to hold these harassing dialogues. I pray you allow me to retire."

"Go, go, go."

Jane rose, and tottered from the room.

"She always calls me Master Shore," muttered Shore, when she was gone. "She does not love me; but that would not matter, it might be a negative evil; but she loves another, and so she will call me Master Shore, and that is positive. Death and the devil, she will not give me one word of endearment—she hates me. In my arms she shudders, and lies like a corpse. Yet she is beautiful. Great God, how beautiful. Master Shore—Master! d—n Master Shore!"

CHAPTER XXIII.

The Father.

"And when age maketh prudence a weaknesse, woe be to ye young and ye beautifulle, who with much virtue make obedience a religion."

WAINSTEAD, the mercer, had been a hale man;—we say had been with regret that we are compelled to speak of his heartiness in the past tense; but the fact was—as indeed is extremely common with such men—he had broken down suddenly, and within a few weeks he was no more the man we first presented to the reader, than poor Jacob could have been fat Master Lowestaff, the burly butcher.

With this sudden decay of his bodily energies, had also gone much of the strong, sturdy spirit, which had made "the worshipfulle Master Wainstead" so much looked up to among the citizens, and so great a man as he really was in the Chepe.

The reader cannot have failed to perceive some indications of this great falling off in the mercer in his conduct as regarded the marriage of his much-loved Jane with Shore —a match which, he could not but perceive, was much against her inclinations, but which he had, in a manner of speaking, forced on her.

When a man, too, like Wainstead the mercer falls off from his accuracy of judgment, and what may be called the boldness of his character, he does more mischief than an ordinary weak-minded, timid person possibly could, because, like a reputed honest man, who suddenly turns a rogue, he has all his former character to trade upon, and is some time in being found out.

Thus Jane had been so accustomed to know, and thoroughly to understand, that her father had a good judgment, and a strong sense of right and wrong in defiance of anybody, that she more easily gave in to his expressed wish for her to wed Shore than she otherwise would have done.

She had not detected the falling off in his mental characteristics, but Shore had; and, with the cunning of his disposition, he had taken the opportunity to press his suit, and to prey upon the mercer's fears in such a manner, that he had made him eager for a match that, under ordinary circumstances, he would never have pressed as he did upon his beloved Jane.

Poor Wainstead, however, thought he was counselling his daughter's happiness—a sort of presentiment, which often attacks men like himself, had come over him, that he was not long for this world, and hence he had become nervously fidgetty for Jane's establishment in life with some one who, at all events, had the means of protecting her from the dangers which had lately appeared to be thickening around her so tremendously.

He began to think that the beauty he had taken so much pride in—the improving charms he had watched with so much heartfelt satisfaction—were a fatal gift; and Shore persuaded him that the only chance Jane had of happiness, or of escaping from the snares and perils which would be sure to surround her more than ever when he, Wainstead, was gone, was in a marriage with one like himself, with ample means for her protection, and of an age to repel attacks, which a younger man would lack experience or might to do.

And so poor Jane was sacrificed, in order that she might be preserved; tortured, that she might be saved from possible anxiety; and made the true object of pity for fear she should not be happy.

Alas! short-sighted philosophy. Had Walter Fane been at liberty, surely he could have opened the merchant's eyes to his mistake; but he was virtually dead, and poor, weak, failing Wainstead became a mere tool in the hands of one of the most artful and designing men, in a small way, which the world ever produced.

Had fate cast Shore in a higher station, he would have become renowned—perhaps notorious would be a more proper term to apply to him—for his extreme craft and cunning. He would have done mischief to a whole nation instead of to families; but, as it was, his means of evil were restricted, but, to their extent, he was certainly a bold, bad man, and as unscrupulous a one as ever lived.

Wainstead used to call repeatedly at Shore's, now that his darling Jane was there, and it so happened that some short time after the rather strong interview which Jane and her husband had had, and which we have just recorded, old Wainstead made his appearance in Lombarde-street, on a visit to his child.

The disagreements between them he, as yet, knew nothing of. Jane would not vex him by a recital of them, because she felt that each word would unnecessarily sound like an implied reproach upon him for having induced her to make the match.

This was of a piece with the rare generosity of Jane's mind, than which at that time, a purer and a better could not have been found throughout all England.

Shore, of course, said nothing of it. It was not likely he would; but never had they had so many words as upon this occasion, and when the one serving man which Shore kept came into the room at the back of the shop, and said,—

"An it please you, Master Shore, the worshipfulle Master Wainstead is near the door," Shore started and turned pale.

"The mercer has money," he thought, "and if Jane, in the bitterness of her heart, should tell him she is unhappy, he may get angry, and make some sudden disposition of it to my great prejudice, which would, indeed, be dreadful."

After a moment's thought, he turned to the serving man, and said, in a hurried voice,—

"Keep Master Wainstead here in talk for a few minutes till I return. Just tell him I will be here anon."

"Yes, master, yes."

"Here he comes—here he comes."

Shore ran up stairs just as the mercer stopped at the threshold of his house, nor paused he until he reached Jane's chamber, at which he tapped loudly.

Jane herself opened the door, and he could see, by her swollen eyes, that she had been weeping bitterly.

"Jane," he said, in a mock voice of condolence, "Jane."

She looked at him with surprise, as the thought came across her mind of,—"Can he be relenting?"

"Jane—Jane, your father is below."

"My father? Oh, let me fly to him! My dear father! He never said an unkind word to me yet."

"Hark you, Jane, there is one matter which I think it is absolutely necessary you should now be made acquainted with."

"More sorrow."

"No—no; not that. But, in your anger or your grief, call it what you will, you might let your father know we quarrel—you and I, I mean. Now, if you do, he and I will quarrel, and the consequence of that will be, that I shall feel compelled to sell your father up, on account of monies lent to him. All he has in the world is mine. That would break the old man's heart—you understand? Jane, you hold the old man's life in your hands."

"Good God!" exclaimed Jane.

"It is of no moment if you are discreet. Mention it, and he is lost. I swear to you, that if you hint at a knowledge of this matter, I will execute my threat, and your father will be disgraced."

"Can this be true?"

"Try it, if you doubt it—try it."

"Oh, no—no—no!"

"'Tis well. You adopt the wisest course, Jane. Now, go to your father. I thought it best to be thus explicit with you at once. You hold his fate in your own hands."

"Oh, you will not harass him?"

"If you are discreet, I will not."

"Thanks—thanks, Master Shore."

"Master Shore again. Bah! Methinks I ought to have received a better title for my forbearance."

Jane shuddered; but she could not, even if her life had been at stake, bestow on that man one word of affection. In a low, tremulous voice, she said,—

"I will not mention anything that may displease you."

"Go, then. I have your promise, and you have mine. Concealment on your part, and immunity for your father while he lives, on mine. 'Tis a fair bargain, Jane."

She trembled, and passed down the staircase. Oh, what a heavy heart she carried in her bosom, and yet how much she strove to summon up one of her old smiles with which to welcome her poor, fond, weak, doting father.

She did not accuse him of the misery she suffered. Oh, no. She knew he loved her—she told herself how good were his motives for bringing on the match with Shore, although she trembled at the result of it, and the life of misery she could not fail to see before her, let her view it how she would.

"I can never be happy," she said; "but I will not make my poor father unhappy by telling him so much. Shore might have kept the secret, and spared his caution."

And, indeed, he might; for a far higher motive would have kept Jane silent—love for her father would have prompted her to hide her miseries in her own heart; but, then, Shore had no notion in the world of such feelings as found a home in Jane's gentle and truly affectionate and guileless heart.

The moment Jane was gone, he broke out into one of the short, hollow laughs, in which he so rarely indulged, and which he always stopped short in the middle of.

"Ha! ha! Humph! A lie is a very convenient thing, when well told; but it does require to be well done. Wainstead owe me money, indeed! How can she be so simple as to believe so much? Truly, he has plenty of money, I think, but owes none. He could lend me money, if I wanted it; and should any rare speculation offer, I would, of course, apply to him; but, as for owing me money, that is quite a different affair, though poor, simple Jane may believe it."

With a dubious, sinister look, now he slowly descended the staircase, having, as he considered, given Jane and her father time to converse a little together before he joined them, and necessarily turned the conversation into a more general channel.

Jane had not seen her father for some days, and now the moment she cast her eyes upon him she might, figuratively, be said to see the hand of death upon his head. It was not that he looked altogether so much worse than usual. It was not that any settled sickness was upon him, but there was a remarkable change in the aspect and the expression of his countenance, which induced the belief in her mind, that soon, too soon, would she be without the only human being to whom she could now look with eyes of real love and affection, with a certainty that those feelings were, to the fullest extent, reciprocated towards her. It was too much for her strength to bear the harrowing conviction that burst upon her—that he would soon pass away from her.

"Father—father," she cried, as she flung herself into his arms, "dear father."

She burst into tears, and the old man shook with emotion, as, in a tremulous voice, he said—

"Why—why! Jane—Jane! what mean this, dear heart? Jane, what has come over thee, girl? What mean these tears, Jane? My Jane—my beautiful child—are you not happy?"

"Happy!"

"Yes. Speak—speak, darling. Dear you know you are to your old father's heart. Confide in me, my Jane. Speak—speak freely, dear—dear Jane. Are you not happy?"

The caution which Shore had given her came with painful intensity across her heart, and Jane shuddered, as she fancied how much mischief to that dear parent, whom she loved so fondly, an incautious word might produce.

"Yes—yes.. Oh, yes! How can I be otherwise than happy—with such a father, how can I not be happy?"

"But you are no longer with me, my beautiful Jane. You are no longer with me, you know."

"No—no!"

"And are you happy here, dear one? Are you very happy, love?"

"Father—you—you are altered. It was that which forced the tears from my eyes so suddenly. You are altered, dear father. You are not looking well. Are you well?"

"I am much as usual, Jane. But you know, my darling, that I am not getting younger."

"No—no! But you are fretting about something. Your looks are anxious, dear father. What grieves you?"

"Nay, Jane, I am not anxious now. I own I was anxious, fearfully anxious, concerning you; but I cannot be so now, for you are united to one who hath both power and will to protect you—one who cannot be so easily overcome as even your poor old father, Jane."

"He calls himself poor," thought Jane, with a shudder. "It is true, then, what Shore has told me of his want of means. Oh, I must be very—very careful, or all is lost!"

"Yes, dear father, yes. You were saying that about me you felt anxious?"

"I did, my child, I did—but not now—not now. Let it please God to call me when he will, I shall lay down my head in peace, because I know that my dear, beautiful child is safe."

"And, father, has—has nothing yet been heard of poor Walter Fane? No news of him?"

"None—none. Jane, you will not believe that he is no more?"

"I cannot. Father, it may be wrong—it may be superstitious of me, but I cannot help feeling an inward conviction that Walter Fane is not dead, and that we shall some day meet again."

"Indeed!"

"Yes. The evidence of his death, father, is but suppositious. He is not dead—he is not dead."

"Jane, Jane, you—you thought kindly of poor Walter—a good lad—a noble lad—one full of high qualities—would have made a rare good citizen. He had good courage too—I loved him, Jane—I loved the lad."

"You loved him, father! Oh, if you loved him—what ——"

"Good day to you, worshipful Master Wainstead," said Shore, who had crept into the room unobserved. "Good day to you, worthy and excellent father-in-law—ahem! You are well, I hope?"

"Oh, Master Shore, I am passing well, as things go. Any news, good Master Shore?"

"None—none. I should think, Wainstead, you ought to bring news hitherwards. You are somewhat nearer the source of all uncomfortable tidings than I am. You are nearer to the court, if it be not by much."

"Truly am I, as you say; from thence generally come uncomfortable tidings; and now I bethink me, Master Snafflings, the bowyer, was saying something about a subsidy."

"Ah! subsidy—nothing but subsidy for the court. The citizens are fully expected to keep the host of lazy gallants who flutter about the regal state. One would really think we enjoyed some rare advantages from them. By the mass, Master Wainstead, a man's substance would soon become worn to nothing by such inroads."

"Ay, truly. They talk of a large subsidy."

"Do they! Then 'tis time I took care to place my most valuable possessions out of sight, for the king's commissioners will be some day, when least expected, popping in upon me to value what I have."

"'Tis a measure of good prudence, Master Shore. Don't you think our dear Jane looks pale?"

"Pale! Master Wainstead?"

"Yes; to my eyes she looks but pale."

"She never was a bright red, you know, Master Wainstead, nor should we desire her so to be."

"No, no; but she looks not so full of life and happiness."

"Indeed! Perhaps something has vexed the gentle good soul. Jane, are you unhappy?"

"No," said Jane, faintly.

"You have been very happy—she is. She could now, Master Wainstead, I warrant me, almost weep for joy. You are aware, good sir, that tears are alike indicative of excesses, either of joy or grief."

"Yes—yes—yes."

"And Jane, being so very happy, always looks as if she were about to cry, and thus you think her dull, perhaps, and pale, and not so well as she might be. Good Master Wainstead, you could not possibly make a greater mistake than in such a supposition."

"No doubt you are right, Master Shore; no doubt you are right; of course, you ought to know best. You have opportunities of watching her tenderly—eh, Master Shore? She is a delicate plant. Nurture her gently, and she will amply repay the culture you bestow upon her. For years, now, has she been the one great joy of my heart. I have toiled, and the thought that it has been for her has sweetened it. I have met with difficulties and disappointments, but one glance upon her sweet face has recompensed me a million-fold for them all. No one knew—I don't think that any can ever know how much I really loved her. How dearly, how darlingly, how fondly I love her still."

Jane crept closer to her father, but she could not speak. As Shore truly enough said, she could have wept; but her own feelings would have placed a very different interpretation on the cause of her tears.

"And, now, my darling," said Wainstead, "I—I think I will walk homewards again."

"Will you take no refreshment, good Master Wainstead?" said Shore. "They tell me a spring has gushed up somewhere by Aldgate, and that the water is very cool, and wonderfully wholesome."

"I don't drink water, Master Shore."

"No—no," said Jane. "You shall have wine, father—wine. Master Shore, you will give my father wine. The best—the finest. Such as I heard you praising to the courtier who called upon you yesterday."

"Humph!" said Shore, "of course. Wilt get it?"

"Yes, yes."

Jane left the room to procure the wine, and the moment she was gone Shore approached close to Wainstead, and, in a voice of suppressed passion, he said, in a hissing, spluttering voice,—

"God, sir, she always calls me Master Shore."

"Ah!"

"Master Shore, you understand; she always calls me Master Shore."

"Well, it's your name, ain't it?"

"Yes, it is," said Shore, with a hideous grin; "of course, it is my name—Master Shore. But one would have hoped—one would have expected that some more tender epithet might have been used. Were you wedded long, Master Wainstead?"

"Moderately long."

" Ah! and what did Mistress Wainstead call you?"

" Why, sometimes one thing, and sometimes another. I recollect once she called me a brute because I went as far as Oxford to see the merry-making on occasion of the ——"

" Bah! I mean in ordinary converse. Did she call you Master Wainstead—that's what I want to know?"

" Well, I don't think she did."

" Ah!"

" But what she did call me I really cannot call to mind now; but I know it wasn't that."

" Perhaps it was dear Wainstead. Eh? eh?"

" No—no—no."

" Perhaps it was—Hush! she comes."

" No, it wasn't that either, I'm sure."

" Bah! You are wonderfully dull. The wine—the wine. Now, good Master Wainstead, and most worshipful father-in-law, here is a cup of wine as rare as it is expensive; a little of it goes a long way, as you will find. You might not think so at first taking it; but in about half-an-hour afterwards you will find it warm your blood."

" Half-an-hour?"

" Yes; and, therefore, it is prudent not to take much of it, you see, at once; of course, I don't speak for the sake of the wine, or to save it; I only tell you, because I know you will put no misconstruction on my words, good, worshipful Master Wainstead."

The mercer shook his head, but he said nothing. Jane could guess what he thought, and she was proportionably vexed that anything costly, or otherwise, should be grudged in the house where she was now the nominal mistress.

" Dear father," she said, " the wine will do you good."

" In half-an-hour," said Wainstead, " it may. Is the effect very extraordinary, Master Shore, in half-an-hour?"

Before Shore could reply a noise was heard in the outer shop, or place of business, and such a voice as had never saluted the ears of Shore, but which Wainstead and his daughter knew at once, for to hear it was never to forget it, as there was nothing like it, exclaiming,—

" Five nobles reward, I say. Five nobles. Oh, the knave, an I had him but here I'd break his thin back across my knee, I would. The pestilent rascal—a thief. Get out of my way."

" But my master," said Shore's serving-man, " will not allow it."

" Your master, you villanous-looking scrub! I'll tear your master's eyes out, I will, if he says a word; and, as for you, take that."

There was heard such a swinging box on some one's ears, that it made every one else's tingle to think of it, and then Master Shore's man called out, loudly,—

" Murder—murder—murder! A she-devil—murder! I'm killed and stunned! Help—murder!"

" What can all that mean?" said Shore.

" It's Mistress Bridget Snafflings' voice," said Wainstead, " the bowyer's daughter. It's well known about the Chepe she is cursed."

" But what wants she here? Come with me, Master Wainstead, and let us see what has moved her to come here."

" By the mass, you are right," said Wainstead, " to have a care how you risk yourself within arm's length of such a termagant as the bowyer's daughter."

He and Shore then, followed by Jane, went into the shop, and there, sure enough, was Mistress Bridget Snafflings, presenting to their eyes the most extraordinary figure that could be well imagined.

She was attired for the streets; but around her neck was hung a small tin pot, and in one hand she held a number of small slips of paper, one of which, with some paste cleaned out of the tin pot with her fingers, she had just stuck up in a conspicuous place in Shore's shop.

" Marry come up," she muttered, as she patted down the slip of paper. " I'll have him yet. Ten groats have I given to the cunninge Master Mayedwell's boy, who can write—more betoken he won't live long, owing to being so clever—to get me out these bills. Ten groats, as I'm a sinner and a female; but I'll have the rascal yet."

" May I ask," said Shore, " what is the matter?"

" Matter enough. Hoity toity!—marry come up! Can you read?"

" I can."

" Then look there, and read it to me. Oh, the blessing of learning, I didn't ever hear before that you were such a conjuror, Master Shore."

Shore looked curiously at the bill, which, per force, had been stuck up in his shop, and found it to the following effect:—

"Ye worshipfulle Master Snafflings, bowyer, of ye Chepe, robbed by ane thin knave yclept Jacob, righte willinge is he to bestowe ye sume of ten marks on whoever shall yielde up ye same Jacob, and five nobles for ye vaine accomplice, ane faded gallante of much villanie.

"Wrote for ye lovelie Mistress Bridget Snafflings, God and ye Saints alway willinge."

"There," cried Mistress Snafflings—"I had what they call the last *pandagraph* put in myself. What do you think of that?"

"Do you mean to say," cried Wainstead, "that poor, silly Jacob has robbed you?"

"I do mean to say it, Master Wainstead," exclaimed the lady, placing herself in an attitude of defence—"I do mean to say it."

"Well, it seems to me very unlikely."

"Does it—does it?"

"Good Mistress Snafflings," said Shore, "can you oblige me by stating what you have done with my serving-man? I heard him crying murder. Have you swallowed him, madam?"

Shore took good care, before he made this irritating remark, to be some distance from the lady, or she might, upon the impulse of the moment, as she was rather an impulsive character, have made him repent the attempting a jest with her. As it was, she only screamed out,—

"I shouldn't like to swallow you, parchment and drumsticks as you are, you ill-looking brute!"

"Master Shore," said Wainstead, "take counsel from one who has some acquaintance with Mistress Bridget Snafflings' abilities, and leave her alone. You will get the worst of the encounter, whether it be with the tongue or the hands."

"A she-devil!" muttered Shore.

"A what do you call me?" shrieked the lady, as she seized a huge inkstand, and flung it like a cannon shot at Shore's head. "Just say that again, and if I don't throw something at you, I'm not a born female with delicate feelings."

Everybody retreated in a moment to the back apartment, leaving Mistress Bridget Snafflings in possession of the field of battle, and after an harangue in her peculiar style, which lasted about ten minutes, she condescended to go to stick up bills elsewhere, and then Shore slowly ventured to come out again to see what damage had been done.

He tore down the bill at once, and then called aloud for his serving-man, whose sudden disappearance was the most mysterious part of the whole affair, and appeared quite inexplicable.

After a few moments, however, that prudent individual slowly emerged from under the counter, where he had taken refuge after receiving the stunning salute on the ears from Mrs. Snafflings—a salute which had made such a singing in his head, that he was unable to hear what was going on, or to be aware for some time whether it was safe to emerge from his hiding-place or not.

"Oh, you are there?" said Shore.

"Ye—ye—yes, I think I'm here."

"You think?"

"Is—she gone? Oh, God, deliver us!—is she gone?"

"Gone—yes; and for all you know, she might have been a thief, and while you were under the counter, Heaven only knows what serious losses I might have had to endure."

"A she-dragon, sir—a she-dragon!"

"Be more mindful in future, knave, or to the streets you go again, from whence I took you."

"I shall never hear with this side of my head again," murmured the serving-man—"never. It sounded like the end of the world coming, exactly. I have lost my hearing on the left side of my head for ever and a day. It was so dreadfully sudden, too. Oh, Lord, deliver us from such a woman!"

"Anybody," said Wainstead, "may say amen to that wish—she is a desperate one. Adieu, my Jane, adieu. Master Shore, I bid you good day, and give me leave to congratulate you upon having so easily got rid of Mistress Bridget Snafflings."

"Easily?"

"Ay, easily. You don't know her so well as we do in the Chepe."

"Thank God, then, I do not."

"You may well thank God you do not."

"Adieu, dear father," said Jane.

"God bless you, my dear child; God bless you, my dear, dear Jane. Since you have been gone, the old place has been very dull; the rooms look deserted, and nothing seems right, my child. There's Simon, too, he's worse than ever, and he's got so crabbed now, that he contradicts himself from sheer ill-humour; and when I want him to do anything, I'm forced to beg that he will not do so on any account, and he says, 'I will,' and goes and does it on the moment."

"Indeed, father?"

"Yes, my child; you were the life—the soul of the whole house. By the mass, it's dismal now."

"But I will come and see you sometimes, father; and I will speak to Simon. He will attend to me."

"He will, if he attends to any one. He has taken the loss of poor Walter Fane much to heart."

"He loved him."

"Yes, if Simon loved anybody but you, it was poor Walter Fane; and now he has lost you both, poor fellow, he seems to wander about like one going mad by degrees."

"I will come and see him, father. Everybody—loved—Walter."

"A good youth—a good youth."

"Farewell, father; farewell."

Jane could not trust herself to say any more; she hurried away to the domestic apartments of the house, and then, with another brief adieu to Shore, the old mercer left the place.

CHAPTER XXIV.

The Gaoler's Daughter.

"Beneath ye Thamis flowinge tide,
Ye dungeons stout and stronge
Of old Friars Grisey prisone met
Blackfriars dreare and longe."

MAGNUS CPPALLI, 1730.

THE prison of the Blackfriars, in the dungeons of which Walter Fane was confined, was supposed to penetrate so far under the Thames, that some of the cells of the convent of Friars Grisey, or Grey Friars, which was on the opposite side of the stream, were popularly believed almost to meet them. More modern excavations proved, however, that such was very far indeed from being the case, and that only one or two damp, cellar-looking holes had given rise to the generally received belief—a belief, however, which, no doubt, was fostered by the authorities, who in no way wished to detract from the terrors of imprisonment in either of those unpleasant places.

Science at that time was not in so pleasant and prosperous a state as that secret results could be produced, but still it sufficed for popular belief, that when a wherry passed down even the very middle of the Thames, it crossed some of the dungeons of the Blackfriars prison.

We left Walter Fane sound asleep in his miserable place of confinement. Far more sound asleep, probably, than any one within the walls of that building; for he was young, and although there were many anxieties pressing upon his mind, yet that death to repose, an evil conscience, was far, very far, from haunting him.

There might be much that was painful and full of grief for him to think of—much that was calculated to give him acute pangs of wretchedness and sympathetic feeling, but upon no action of his whole life could Walter Fane look back with the blush of shame. He was innocent of all wrong, in word, or in deed, or in thought. He knew no duplicity. The worse passions and the mere sordid feelings of humanity belonged not to him. Ah, how happy would the beautiful and gentle Jane have been with such a partner through life, instead of the cold, suspicious, avaricious man the fates had assigned to her.

Many foolish people, who fancy that providence is always interfering in every little muddling concern of life, have a notion, from a long habit of fixing everything disagreeable upon the aforesaid providence, that marriages, in consequence of their turning out so dreadfully disagreeable in so many cases, must be made in Heaven.

We cannot, for our own parts, while we have the pleasure of referring the uncomfortable and the harassing to another place, not to be mentioned to ears polite, think of libelling Heaven in such a way; and, however convenient it may be to lay all our mistakes upon the expansive shoulders of a special providence, we won't do it; and, therefore, declaim against the often mooted opinion, that marriages are made in Heaven.

It's no such thing. We firmly believe—always provided we are called upon to believe

the one statement or the other—that they are "got up" in some office "down below," and that the most careful research is expended in ascertaining what incongruous tempers, habits, modes of thought, and general dispositions, can be yoked together in the noose matrimonial, so as to produce the greatest amount of jarring feelings and anti-religious reasoning, and all that sort of thing.

Truly, the course of true love ran no smoother in the days of Edward the Fourth, than they did in those of Elizabeth, which had he glory of a Shakspere cast upon them. Walter Fane ought to have been happy with Jane—Jane ought to have been happy with Walter Fane; and the old mercer, Wainstead, he, too, ought to have been happy in the happiness of those who were dear to him, and formed the only ties which bound him to existence.

But all this was not to be. Some malignant destiny chose that it should be otherwise. Jane had the dangerous, often fatal, gift of beauty. Alas! alas! that the rare endowment, which ought to be a source of much happiness, should almost invariably, in this world of jarring interests and evil passions, be productive of much mischief.

Whenever we see some fair young creature, with the bloom of youth, innocence, and beauty upon her cheeks; with that exquisite but undefinable charm in her countenance, which all the world calls beautiful, we look upon her with a smile and a sigh; we cannot help telling ourselves, as we do so, that there is fresh cause for discussion, anger, grief, crime, misery; perhaps, even some of the darker and more terrible crimes of humanity. It is very sad that such should be the case; but it is quite incompatible with human nature that it should be otherwise.

And it was this fatal, but glorious possession, beauty, which had wrecked all poor Jane Wainstead's hopes of happiness; it was her beauty that filled her doting father's mind with a world of anxieties—it was her beauty which made Shore, the cold-hearted unsympathetic Shore, covet her for his own. Alas! it was her beauty which evidently threw Walter Fane into the damp dungeon of the prison of Black Friars—it was her beauty which now thoroughly bewildered the few remaining wits of Jacob, the bowyer's man—it was her beauty which turned the wise and politic head of my Lord Hastings, the Lord High Chamberlain, and made such a confusion in his mind between his court intrigues for power, and his private affections, that he scarcely knew what to do—it was her beauty—but, hold, we will not anticipate. Much as Jane's beauty has already accomplished, it is as nothing compared with the important results which have still to ensue from those radiant charms.

And now let us return to poor Walter, who, at all events, as far as present appearances went, was the greatest sufferer, by that loveliness of the mercer's daughter, of all. He was sleeping in his dungeon—the rats and the mice were galloping over him and around him—a few old fat toads likewise crawled up to him, and glanced with their starry eyes upon him, as if they would have said, "What the devil brought you here?" There was a frog, likewise, who much disgusted the toads by his restlessness, and who might be compared to a Frenchman, while the toad, not inaptly, might represent a native of the land of dams and dykes. Other crawling reptiles, too, some with such magnificent shiny backs, that it seemed perfectly wonderful how they came by them, crept over the sleeping man.

Thus some hours passed away, and still he slumbered. He dreamt not—it was one of those deep dreamless sleeps, such as weariness, but not extreme exhaustion, only can know. It was not until the bodily vigour had returned with repose that the mind became more active, and the imagination began its phantasmagorial tricks upon the soul.

Then, indeed, he began to dream. With every vision, too, of his slumber, was mingled Jane, his own beautiful Jane. His own, he called her, as he murmured her name in his sleep. Alas, little knew he, that already had another a better claim to call her so. And well was it that poor Walter was spared the pang of knowing that Jane was wedded actually to Shore. The anxieties which were now, perhaps, just redeemable, might, and in all probability would, have deepened into such absolute misery, that dejection might have killed him in that gloomy place. But he knew it not; and if, in such an instance, ignorance could not be called bliss, yet was it much better that he should, while a prisoner there, know it not, than have all his lingering happier hopes at once blasted by so dreadful—so killing a piece of sad intelligence as that.

Then he dreamed that he was walking with her in a delicious garden, when suddenly he thought they were parted, and he found it impossible to approach her, or to move from the spot on which he was. Then there seemed to slowly rise around him black walls, which were enclosing him on all sides. He could not move to escape from them—he could not speak, although he strove to do so—he would fain have called out to Jane, but his tongue refused its office—he could only waive his hands despairingly, and allow the walls to close around him. They bent over, and formed a roof above his head. All was then darkness. He thought he heard a voice say,—

"Farewell for ever."

Then a light suddenly gleamed across his eyes, and he felt confused and dazzled by its brilliancy. A soft low voice said,—

"Prisoner, awake! awake!"

He opened his eyes, but for a moment he still fancied that he beheld the vision of his slumber. He was lying by the foot of one of the columns that supported the low roof of his dungeon, and some few paces from him was the light graceful figure of a young girl, who held in her hand a lamp, the rays from which, more than the soft voice in which she had spoken, had roused him from his slumbers. He looked at her without speaking for a few moments, and then his words showed the state of mental confusion he was in.

"Is this a dream?" he said.

"It is not," said the same soft, sweet voice that had spoken before. "It is real."

"Can this be possible? I surely am awake; and you,—you are some benign spirit, some pitying angel come to cheer the lonely prisoner in his dungeon. Oh, blessings—blessings on thee."

"No—I am mortal, like yourself," she said, in a tone of sympathy that had about it so musical a touch of sadness, that it was mournfully beautiful to hear. "I pity you as I have pitied others, but I think I pity you more than I have pitied any one."

"Are you really mortal?"

"I am. My name is Alice."

"But how came you here? Am I not still in the dungeon of the Black Friars?"

He covered his face with his hands, and in a wailing voice added,—

"Yes, yes, it is still a dream,—still but a vivid dream, assuming a nearer than usual likeness to reality."

"Do not think so," said the soft, gentle voice of the girl. "Do not think it a dream. Touch my hand. 'Tis life-like as your own."

She approached him, and placed a small, delicate hand upon his arm. The touch thrilled through him like magic.

"I am awake," he said; "I am awake—but to what rare chance owe I your presence here?"

"I saw you brought up the steps of the prison by the water-gate. I heard you refuse to betray some one, as the price of your liberty. I do not think that you can have done anything very bad to cause your being brought hither."

These words were uttered in a tone of inquiry, and Walter Fane immediately replied,—

"Heaven and my persecutors only know what my imputed crime is, I do not. What I am confined here for I can only guess."

"You can guess?"

"I can."

"And—and ——"

"It is that imprisonment, the fear of torture and of death, should so unnerve me, as to make me betray one who should be the care and joy of all, as the price of my liberty, and restoration to the light of day."

"And you will not?"

"Rather let me perish a thousand times, than for one moment cherish the thought of purchasing life and liberty upon such terms."

"And you are innocent?"

"I am—I am. I have done nothing. I have outraged no law, human or divine. I am innocent of an intention to do wrong."

"I did surmise so much, from what I overheard. It is very, very cruel to keep you here."

"Oh, can you aid me? You have come here by some mysterious means, perhaps to save me."

"I cannot, because I dare not. You do not know me. I am your gaoler's daughter."

"Sir Godfrey's daughter?"

"Yes," she said, with a deep sigh, and then hastily added, as if deprecating what might be said by Walter. "Of—of my father say nothing, young sir. He is my father, and—and—do not speak of him."

Walter understood the motive which prompted these words, and his was just the heart to respect it.

"Fear no harsh judgments from me," he said. "For your dear sake I will be trebly guarded. I would not give you one moment's pain to satisfy a world of rancour. Nay, for the sake of those dear pitying eyes I could forgive my worst of enemies."

He saw a tear steal down her cheek as she said,—

"It is very seldom that these dungeons are used—very seldom indeed now; but I have visited them all from time to time—visits which I was permitted to make, they being empty. This morning I was forbidden any longer to wander about the gloomy passages of the prison; but chance has favoured me with the means unobserved of coming hither. I am as much a prisoner in this gloomy building as you can be, although I am not confined to a dungeon; probably were my visit discovered I should be. I have a key which enabled me to unlock your dungeon door."

"A key?"

"Yes; I may ameliorate your condition, although, alas! I cannot set you free."

"But, fair one, you have the means of enabling me to leave this place. You surely ——"

"Could," she interrupted him by saying—"surely could facilitate your escape. I am very, very unhappy, and have sometimes thought that even the death which has been threatened me for such an act, I would brave, and be the means of restoring to the world and hope some persecuted being who was wearing out a life of sorrow in these dungeons."

"Death, say you?"

"Yes; I have been told that if, in the romantic fervour of my heart, I ever accomplish such a purpose, that I shall surely die."

"Oh, perish," cried Walter, "the thought that for a moment found a home in my breast. I will be a prisoner still, rather than purchase liberty at even the price of a harsh word to you."

"You—you would not take so precious a boon ——"

"I would not—I would not. Thankful, deeply thankful am I for this visitation; but ——"

"Hush!" said Alice—"hush!"

In an instant she extinguished the light she carried, and glided behind one of the columns, to the surprise of Walter.

CHAPTER XXV.

Love's Devotion.

"To love trulie is to love so welle that ye joy of ye loved one far surpasseth ye joy of ye loving one, and life itselfe weighs nothinge in ye balance, contrarie to suche passiones."

THE quick ears of the gaoler's daughter had detected the coming of some one to the dungeon, although the other had not, and the accuracy of her observation was verified almost immediately.

The dungeon door, after much rattling with a key, was cautiously opened a little way, and a strong stream of light shone down the stone staircase which descended from it.

"Hilloa—hilloa, there below!" cried the voice of Slankey.

Walter did not think it at all necessary for him to put himself out of the way by returning an answer.

"Hoi!" again shouted the fellow. "D——n! why don't you speak—eh? Hilloa there, my young spark! Eh—eh?"

Still Walter made no reply; and then he heard the fellow give a long whistle, as if he were in great perplexity, after which he heard him say a few words, which at once explained to him how the matter stood.

"The door unlocked," muttered Slankey, "and nobody answers. By G—d! he's gone; but how the devil he got out I don't know."

Walter at once understood that Alice had left the door unlocked when she descended to the dungeon, and that it was from such a circumstance that Slankey suspected he had made his escape. The necessity, however, for Alice's preservation, of making his appearance was soon made sufficiently manifest by Slankey saying,—

"I must go down and see, whether I like it or not. Sir Godfrey will brain me an I bring him not correct intelligence. I'd as soon go to the very devil as down these steps; but I must, I suppose, so here goes at once for it."

The ruffian carefully came down a step or two, and then Walter Fane thought it high time to make an appearance, so he sprung suddenly forward and up the steps, crying,—

"Hilloa! who comes here?"

Slankey was so terrified at this unexpected movement, that, with a shout of terror, he ran back again, and slammed the door shut in a moment. It was some minutes before he ventured again to open it an inch or two, and to say through the crevice,—

"Who are you?"

"Your prisoner, of course," said Walter. "What is the meaning of this strange conduct?"

"Oh, it is you, is it?"

"Do you not know my voice?"

"Well, I—I think I do. Why didn't you answer at once?"

"I have been sleeping."

"Curse you—have you? Sleeping, indeed!" Then he added, in a lower voice,—"I suppose he has, or he would have found out that the door was left open by some one on the last visit. So you've been sleeping, have you? Well, there's your loaf, my fine fellow; and the next time I come and ask if you are below there, I advise you to answer."

"I shall answer or not, as the humour suits me," said the other.

"You will?"

"Ay, will I. I regret I did not give you the trouble of coming all the way down. You would have been frightened to death. I could have waited at the foot of the stairs to throw the dead body I have below here in your face."

"Curse you!" growled the fellow,—"curse you!" and he slammed the door shut again with vehemence.

In an instant, Walter heard the key turn in the lock, and then the faint sound of the retiring footsteps of the man.

"He is gone," said Alice.

"He has; but tell me, can you, now that the door is locked, emerge from this place?"

"Yes. I have a key which opens the door on either side indifferently, and I have been too frequent an explorer of these dungeons, and the dark, damp passages which lead to them, not to have the means of replenishing my lamp."

With materials that she carried with her, Alice, in a few moments, relit her lamp, and then turning to Walter, she said,—

"I must leave you now, but expect me soon again. Your fare shall not be so bad as it has been."

"Oh, if you would do me a great mercy," said Walter, "provided it involve you in no danger, you will let Master Wainstead, the mercer of the Chepe, know that I am confined here. He has some friends at court who would assist him in obtaining my release. Nay, perchance he would be able to make some direct application to the king himself upon the subject, when an inquiry would be made."

"Understand me," said Alice. "I am as much a prisoner here as yourself, although I am not confined within the particular four walls of my dungeon. Why or wherefore I am kept in such strict seclusion, I know not; but it has now lasted some years. There was a time when I was very happy in a very different home, but a red glare one night proclaimed a fire—the home of my youth—my childhood—I should have said, was burnt to the ground. Weak and insensible, I was brought here, and Sir Godfrey declared to me that I was his child. Since then, I have been kept in this gloomy building in a strict seclusion."

"And do you believe you are his daughter?"

"Alas! what can I say? I know not. I cannot say it is not so. I cannot say it is. I am unhappy—very unhappy."

She wept bitterly, and Walter was much affected by the artless grief of that young creature whose age could not exceed fifteen.

"It is indeed," he said, "very sad and very wrong that one like you, in all the spring of youth, should be doomed to waste an hour in such a place as this; but it seems as if, by some inexorable decree of destiny, that those who could help the unfortunate, have not the inclination; and those who would, have not the power, and can do nought but pity."

"It is so—it is so," sobbed Alice. "Farewell, now. I will visit you again—I shall be pleased to visit you again; for, although I have shed more tears here than my eyes have known for many months, yet do I feel the calmer for them. I will come again, and bring you food."

"Blessings on you," he said, "for the promise. I shall dream of your coming again to rob, as you have done, for a time, this dungeon of its gloominess."

"Have I so robbed it?"

"You have, Alice. Let me call you dear Alice, for a human voice which speaks to me in kindly sympathy here is very—very dear."

"How strange to my ears," she said, sadly, "do words of endearment sound. I am unused to them now. There is no one here to love me—no one—no one!"

"I will love you, Alice. You shall be to me as some dear—dear sister; and the affection which has commenced here in the confines of a dungeon shall live under happier circumstances."

A smile broke through the sadness of her tears, and as she placed her hand in Walter's, she said,—

"I do not know your name."

"My name is Walter Fane," he said.

"Walter Fane. I shall not forget it—I shall never forget it. Adieu, Walter, adieu, for a time. I shall think of you until we meet again, Walter."

"Heaven's blessings on you."

She waived her hand, and slowly she ascended the steps. Twice she paused, and looked back; once she reached the door, and then, when she had opened it, she spoke again, saying,—

"Walter, hope for happier days."

"I will—I will," he cried.

"And if it be possible to communicate in any way with those without who love you, it shall be done."

"I shall owe you, dear Alice, more than a life of active gratitude can ever hope to repay."

She smiled again, and then the door was closed; darkness fell upon the heart of the lonely prisoner, and with a deep sigh, he leaned against one of the ancient columns of his dungeon.

"When will she come again—when will she come again?" was the question he asked of himself now through many hours of his weary solitude.

And Alice, too, she, when she found her way unobserved to her own room, sat down and wept for a long time. The first words she spoke when she could in some measure restrain her tears were,—

"He called me dear Alice—he called me dear Alice."

Our readers, perchance, may surmise what was passing in the heart of the gaoler's daughter. Alas—alas! Walter could find no second place in his heart even for her. It was wholly Jane's; and be she his or not, he told himself that no new idol could usurp her throne—no new passion ever warm his heart.

He was one of those dispositions that love once and love for ever. Alas! poor Alice. More misery from the best and holiest of human feelings. Ah! why are we not all compassionate, or all selfish?

CHAPTER XXVI.

Shore's Jealousy of Jacob.

" Trifles light as air, are to the jealous confirmation strong
As proof of Holy Writ."

Alas, poor Jacob! what has become of thee? Where hast thou conveyed thy sorrows, thy bitterness, thy disappointment? We left thee at the church porch, battling with that dreadfully stout " bedel," who would not let thee catch even one glimpse of thy beloved, but now lost Jane.

That was a desperate bad fellow, the faded gallant. We could almost have forgiven him for his sins against Mrs. Mapletoft. We could have only gravely shaken our heads had he himself robbed the stronghold of the bowyer; but to drag poor, witless, innocent Jacob—poor, childlike Jacob into such a snare,—there was the villany.

But it is upon the witless and the ignorant that rogues thrive, and there is no morality in roguery, any more than there is conscience in lawyers. What mattered it to that desperate rascal, the faded gallant, if he acquired a few coins, at the sacrifice of such a simple heart as Jacob's, or in any other way? It was the acquisition he looked to, and not the means of acquiring.

When Jacob, then, had been turned away from the church porch, he had not the poor consolation of being permitted to wait there, even in the open street, until Jane should come forth. There was an idle mob outside the sacred edifice, and Jacob's first appearance in the very original costume he wore, was sufficient food for mirth; but when he was turned out so promptly by the fat " bedel," the mirth knew no bounds, and, upon the popular principle of " down with him, he don't seem to have any friends," poor Jacob was considered fair sport for the multitude thus assembled.

Mobs have not altered a bit since the beginning of the world. Man, in his individual capacity, may become more honest, more refined, and more conscientious; but in his collective one, he is still the same brute he ever was. It would appear as if people, when they get together in a crowd, not only for the time give up all idea of exercising any judgment, but they likewise sink to the condition of downright savages. A London mob now would be quite as ready to persecute some poor, half-witted creature to death, as it was in the time of Edward the Fourth.

" Look at his jerkin," said one. " And his feather," shouted another. " There's a ruff," suggested a third; and then one dealt him a blow on his back, and another twitched the feather from his cap, which had really been such an annoyance to his eyes.

Poor Jacob turned and said, in grieffal accents,—

" What have I done to any of you?"

The question was hailed with a shout of merriment, and he soon found that, unless he made good a retreat, he would meet with some very rough usage indeed from the free and enlightened citizens of London; for then, as now, they were called free and enlightened, whenever they were wanted to succumb to tyranny of any kind, or to stultify what little judgment any of them, by the bounty of nature, might really possess.

Luckily for him, there was too much expectation on account of the coming forth of the small bridal party from the church, to induce the mob to follow Jacob, so he did get away, and, after traversing a few streets, he sat himself down, very sorrowfully, upon a step, and wept like a child.

" She didn't love me," he said, wretchedly—" she didn't love me! It was not true. She never loved poor Jacob! How could I ever believe for a moment that she did? She does not love me. Alas! alas! alas! Why did he tell me she loved me?"

Jacob's tears fell faster. The faded gallant had deserted him, and where was he to go now? What was to become of him? His dream of joy had faded away for ever—all was lost. A more desolate heart than poor Jacob's could not have been found in all London, always excepting Jane's. Yes, we must except Jane Shore's, and she was very desolate indeed.

" She does not love me a bit," commenced Jacob again—" she does not love me a bit!

Alas! alas! alas! Of course, she was too beautiful to love me, and—and—I suppose I was too thin."

Some who passed by looked earnestly at Jacob. Some laughed, for there was a something odd even about his grief, while others looked more compassionately at him, and one woman stopped and said to him,—

"What art crying at, eh?"

"She don't love me," said Jacob.

"Well, I don't wonder at it," said the woman. "You are no more than the shaving of a man."

"I don't wonder at it neither," said Jacob.

"Well, then, why dost thou sit there?"

"Because I've got nowhere else to sit, good lack! I wish I was dead!"

"Dead?"

"Yes, extremely dead. I should like to be very dead indeed, and then Jane, when she heard of it, might say 'poor Jacob!'"

"A poor consolation, i'faith," said the woman, as she walked on, considering Jacob unworthy of any further sympathy.

"Yes, I do wish I was dead!" added Jacob. "How cruel it was of them not to let me see her before she married him. I'm sure he's ugly too, and yet she loves him. Shore,—he's ugly, very, and he is rich they say. But would my Jane ever marry anybody for money? Oh, no! dear—dear Jane!—Jane Shore now. What a fool I am! Let me see. Oh, what can I say to Master Snafflings? what can I say to Mrs. Bridget Snafflings? That's the worst—oh, a great deal the worst! I can't say anything to her, for I wouldn't go home for King Edward's crown. Home—home? What home has poor Jacob to go to? None—none—none! Deceived—thin—dreadfully thin and broken-hearted—quite—quite broken-hearted."

"Jog—jog," cried a voice behind him; "jog with you. How dare you sit on my door-step?"

Jacob rose, and looked at the speaker. He was the very antithesis of Jacob's figure—short and fat as a butter firkin.

"Jog!" he cried. "An it was not that I am given to be short-breathed, I'd lay an oaken staff over thy back."

"Oh!" said Jacob; "I'm going—I'm going."

"You had better. The impertinence of a merry Andrew sitting down on the step of a respectable citizen! What will the world come to next? What shall we find next?"

The inquiry was not an interesting one to poor Jacob, and he walked away slowly, neither angry nor otherwise, at the man who had turned him from his door-step so suddenly. Poor Jacob's life had not been one of unmingled sweets. During his career at Master Snafflings', he had been well taught that might was right; and, so little consideration had Mistress Bridget Snafflings ever bestowed upon him, except in the way of a hearty cuff now and then, that he might be said to be thoroughly inured to ill-usage.

He walked on, scarcely knowing whither he went. He was both weary and hungry, and much he longed to meet with even the faded gallant by whose pernicious counsel he had been so much led astray. But that individual was not likely further to cultivate the acquaintance of poor Jacob. He had made of him as much as he could. That Jacob could again successfully rob the bowyer was now out of the question, for Mrs. Bridget Snafflings had made the city ring again with the news of her loss. For all he, the faded gallant, therefore, cared, Jacob might starve in the streets, or drown himself in the river; indeed, once or twice the thought of doing the latter did cross the mind of the poor destitute fellow. He dared not pass down the Chepe, for there he was well known; and, notwithstanding the disguise he was in, would have been at once recognised and handed over to the tender mercies of Mrs. Bridget Snafflings, when Heaven only, in its prescience, knows what would have been his fearful fate. So he took his route by some of the more intricate and back streets of the city, although, where he was going, he knew no more than any one else; all he felt was, that he must go to that comprehensive place called "somewhere;" but, where it was to be, was still in the womb of futurity. By mere chance he found himself in the open fields, where now Finsbury-square stands, and he sat down on a green, sloping bank to try to think. How long he had been there he knew not; but he was suddenly and alarmingly aroused by some one laying a heavy hand upon his shoulders, and pronouncing his name.

"Jacob," said a voice; and Jacob sprang to his feet, crying,—"Oh!—no—no—no—don't. I'm going to drown myself, so you wouldn't take me to prison, good master. I shall take a long while drowning, too, on account of my being so thin, you know; so leave me alone, good master."

"Why, you idiot, don't you know me?"

"Know you? I—I—you must be somebody who knows me, for that's what I am always called."

"Look again."

"What—no—yes. Can it—eh? No—yes—it is not. Ah! ah! ah! it is Simon—ah, Simon, she does not love me, after all. She never loved poor, poor foolish Jacob."

He sat down again, and wept as before, occasionally sobbing out,—

"No; she never could have loved me. Never—never—never!"

It was Simon, the mercer's man, who knew Jacob so well, and who had been across the fields on an errand, when, on his return, he had seen Jacob sitting so disconsolately on the grassy bank, in his odd costume. Simon waited until Jacob's fresh flood of grief had a little subsided, and then he gave him a pat on the top of the head with the knob end of a stick he had with him, as he said,—

"Look up."

"Lord have mercy upon me!" said Jacob; "what's that?"

"Me."

"Oh! Simon, have compassion on me."

"Sha'n't."

"Oh, do! Pity me, good Simon! I know I was a great worry to you when I wanted change so often, Simon; but you will pity me now."

"Won't," said Simon.

"I am hungry, Simon—I am weary. I have nowhere to lay my head. I have no one but yourself who will bestow upon me a mouthful of food, Simon—not one—not one."

"Sha'n't feed you; so get up, and come and have something to eat. Sha'n't get you a bed; so, come along to my acquaintance, Morgay Steelworthy, at Aldgate. Do you think I'm going to give you anything? You'll find yourself much mistaken. There's a few groats, stupid. Are you coming?"

Thus, contradicting himself at every other word almost, Simon slipped four groats into Jacob's hand, and then, taking him by the arm, forced him on to his feet, and dragged him along, whether he would or not.

"Oh! good Simon," said Jacob; "I—I am such a wretch."

"Oh!"

"Yes, I am. Dear, dear, beautiful Jane; you don't know, Simon, how I loved her, you don't."

"You loved her? Jane—our Jane do you mean? Our own Jane—the Rose of the Chepe? Ah!"

"Yes, Simon. Jane Wainstead, God bless her. I love her, Simon—I would die to do Jane any service—God bless her, Simon!"

"Humph!"

"And it's because I—I loved her so, you see, Simon, that I have become what I am. I was always an idiot, you know, Simon—at least Mistress Bridget Snafflings always said so; but I did see that Jane was beautiful—I thought often she was some angel, Simon."

Simon whistled a very elaborate tune, and quickened his pace.

"And then you see, good Simon, there came one to me who told me Jane did affect me a little, and persuaded me to put on brave apparel, and to take five gold pieces out of Master Snaffling's strong box, you see ——"

"What?"

"Five—pieces—out—of ——"

"You robbed him?"

"Ah, Simon, Simon—I loved Jane—and I was mad—mad—mad, and I knew not what I did. My head was running round and round. I knew nothing but that I loved Jane. I saw no one but Jane—I was mad!"

Simon stopped short, and looked Jacob in the face.

"Poor devil!" he said, and then he commenced the tune again at the exact note he had left off whistling it.

"Yes," groaned Jacob, "ain't I a poor devil?"

"You are."

For once in a way, even Simon was so much impressed with the truth of a proposition that he did not dispute it.

"Ah, well a day, I thought I was."

"Hold your row, will you—I will get you a lodging for to-night and some food. Now to-morrow you must take a staff and leave London—beg your way into the country, and the first place you reach, where you find any compassionate person, stay as long as you can."

"Yes, Simon, yes. And Jane—dear, dear Jane!"

"What have you to do with Jane?"

"I—I should so like to look upon her sweet face before I go to put me in mind of heaven, and all that is good and beautiful!"

"Not such a fool as I thought him," growled Jacob.

"Then I think I could go more peacefully, Simon. Oh, saw you ever one so truly

beautiful?—knew you, Simon, ever one so good? Her voice was like some swee bird's, and sometimes I heard her laugh—oh, Jane, Jane, Jane! Beautiful Jane, why have you given yourself to such a man as Shore? He cannot love you as you ought to loved. He will not worship you—and fancy all you say, and all you do, so beautiful and good. Jane, Jane, Jane—poor Jacob loves you better than Shore."

"Hold your row," said Simon, "will you," and then he added in an under tone, all to himself—"He does love her—he does love her—poor fellow! He shall not perish without a helping hand to save him. He loves Jane. That shows he is something worth, and how true, too, what he says about that vagabond, Shore. He loves her—poor, poor Jacob!"

"Can I not see her, Simon, before I go?"

"No."

"But I must look upon her once again. Oh, Simon, you cannot tell how I love Jane!"

"Can."

"Then if you can, you will know, Simon, that I will go to death rather than not see her once again."

"The deuce you would?"

"I would—I would, Simon. She is life to me. There is no one like her in the whole world—nor was there ever—nor will there ever be, Simon."

"Right again," said Simon. "Jacob, listen to me. You shall see her once again before you go. I've got a message to deliver from Master Wainstead to Jane, and I will go with you as far as Shore's door, and wait for you while you deliver it, and so shall you see Jane again."

"You will?" said Jacob. "You really will, Simon?"

"I will."

"Oh, how shall I be grateful to you, Simon? and I used to worry you so for change, too."

"Never mind that, come along. What sort of a man was he who got you to take the gold pieces from Master Snafflings?"

Jacob began explaining to Simon all about the faded gallant, and as poor Jacob was not the most concise in his explanation, it fairly lasted until they reached Lombarde-street, and paused at the door of Shore's shop.

CHAPTER XXVII.

Jane's Compassion.

"Ye brighteste gem in beauty's diadem is pure compassione,
Outshininge all in wondrous lustre."

"Be discreet," said Simon. "Here we are."

"Hush," said Jacob, "hush!" as if by so saying he impressed upon himself the necessity of extreme caution. "Hush! hush!"

"Yes, hush, indeed," said Simon. "Now, look ye here, Jacob—here is a book."

"A book—a book?"

"Yes, I don't expect you to read it. It is choicely written by one of the most cunning clerks in London. They do say that one Caxton will make books in plenty—but it won't do to believe all we hear. This book has been bought by Master Wainstead as a present for Jane, you understand, and I was to take it to her, but you can do so, and its great value can be your excuse for refusing to deliver it into any hands but her own."

"Yes, Simon, yes."

"Well, now walk boldly in. Say you come from Master Wainstead, and insist upon seeing her. Be bold and resolute, Jacob."

"I will—I will. Anything to see Jane. They can but kill me, you know, Simon."

"Pshaw! I will wait for you here. Now be off with you, and mind when you do see her you say nothing to make Shore jealous."

"Jealous?"

"Ah, he'd be jealous of a scarecrow—off with you; there is no time to lose."

Simon handed to Jacob a volume bound in vellum, such as were then only to be found in the houses of the very wealthy. The owner had bought it of a Circestian friar, for a good sum, as a present to Jane; and what made it the more rare was, that it was a work of some literary merit, instead of being, as almost all the works then were, a paraphrase of some religious disquisition.

Jacob received the book with due reverence. He had never had such a costly article in his hand before, and then he stepped into Shore's shop, where was the serving-man who had to receive such treatment from Mistress Bridget Snafflings on Jacob's account. Jacob looked at him for a moment without speaking, and then he said,—

"I—I want to see our Jane."

"Our who?"

Jacob then felt the necessity of naming Jane by her own name, however dreadfully obnoxious it was to do so, and he added,—

"I mean Mistress—Shore."

"Well, you needn't say Shore as if it stuck in your throat. Where do you come from, stupid?"

"From Master Wainstead, with a book which I am to give to no one but herself."

"And who are you?" said Shore, as he crept out from the back apartment, and bent a curious gaze on Jacob. "And who are you, I say? Give me the book."

"Worshipful sir, I dare not."

"You dare not refuse it, you mean."

"Yes," said Jacob, plucking up courage, "Master Wainstead charged me not to give it to any one but his daughter, and so, if I cannot do that, I must e'en take it back to him again."

"Bah!" cried Shore, "go call your mistress, fellow. Master Wainstead, methinks, is mighty particular."

"Yes," said Jacob.

"Peace, fellow, who gave you permission to speak? By the bye, I never saw you in Master Wainstead's service."

"Likely not, worshipful sire."

"Well? well?"

"I am very well, thank you, though I look so thin."

"Idiot—an idiot," muttered Shore.

"Ah, everybody knows I'm an idiot," thought poor Jacob.

The serving-man had summoned Jane, who now made her appearance, anxious to hear any message from her father. The moment he caught sight of her, Jacob could act a part no longer; he dropped on his knees, and holding out the book to her, he exclaimed,—

"I don't care what becomes of me now, as I have seen you once again, dear dear, Jane. God bless you, you are paler than you were. I love you; I never told you, you know, but I love you, beautiful Jane; I love you better than I love life. Oh, let me once only for a moment hear your voice. Say what you will, dear, dear beautiful Jane, but let me hear you speak a word or two to me."

"What is the meaning of all this?" said Jane.

"Yes—yes, she speaks," said Jacob, "she speaks. God bless her; I—I am going, now, God bless her."

Shore at this moment made a rush from the back apartment, where surprise had for a few moments paralysed him, and with a drawn sword in his hand he made a savage cut at poor Jacob's head, as he knelt before the bewildered Jane. A stout stick, however, was suddenly placed so as to receive the blow, and Simon, who had seen what was intended, and just rushed into the shop in time to save Jacob's life, cried,—

"For shame, Master Shaw, for shame; would you kill a poor creature for no other fault than that he hopelessly loved Jane Wainstead? For shame, sir; and thank me, in your soberer judgment, for preventing the crime."

"Let him kill me," cried Jacob.

"Oh, Simon, save him," said Jane.

"Death and fury," shouted Shore, "she says 'save him!' D———n! I will have the blood of some of you."

"Don't attempt it," said Simon, "I'm an ugly customer. Come along, Jacob, you have seen Jane, and achieved your object; now come away."

Jane laid her hands upon Shore's arm, and held him. Jacob stretched out his own for a moment, and then, from excitement of feeling, coupled with the exhaustion he felt from want of food, he fainted into the arms of Simon, who dragged him at once out of the shop.

If pity could have done poor Jacob any good, he might have had a world of it from Jane; but, alas! it was all she had to bestow. She was compelled to permit Simon to remove him from the shop, without daring to utter one word indicative of consideration or compassion for one who had, through her beauty, come to such ruin.

Shore stood by with the sword in his hand ready, at the smallest possible provocation, to strike any one with it who might not be strong enough to resist him. He never yet had got into such a passion as to blind his judgment to the chances of a strikingly unequal encounter. Hence he would have been quite ready furiously to have assailed poor Jacob, but when Simon joined the fray it was quite another thing altogether, and not to be thought of.

He must, however, vent his spite and ill-humour upon some one. There was poor Jane, with none to stand up in her behalf, what was to hinder him from abusing her—what was to hinder him striking her if he chose? Nothing, nobody; and, therefore, he manfully resolved upon, at all events, abusing her. Turning upon her suddenly, he cried,—

"So, madam, I am to be tormented, even here, in my own house, by fellows who come to make love to you before my eyes. Pretty doings, Jane. D——n, do you think me a stick or a stone, that I am to put up with such matters quietly? By the holy rood I will be revenged."

"Master Shore," said Jane, "you must have seen that the poor fellow who came here was witless."

"Must I?"

"Did you not mark his looks, and hear the words which came so innocently from his lips? I know him well."

"Do you?"

"I do. He was in the service of Master Snafflings, the bowyer, opposite my father's, where I was so happy."

"Eugh!" growled Shore, "which, of course, is to say, by implication, that you are not happy here."

"Happy," said Jane.

"Yes, happy. Mistress Jane, hear me once, and for all, I will have no visiters here; cold steel shall reach the heart of any one who may show himself in this house on pretended messages to you. You are my wife, Jane, and by the heavens above us, and the h—ll beneath, I will look to you."

If it were possible for such a countenance as Jane's to express contempt for anybody, it did express it then for Shore. She disdained to make any answer to what he had said; but, with a deep sigh, a sigh for the happy past, she turned, and commenced ascending the staircase to the upper rooms of the house.

"Hold!" cried Shore, in such a furious voice, that she involuntarily paused to know what new accession of anger had come over him. "Hold! that book. How do I know what it contains? By the mass, it may be stuffed with love letters for aught I can tell. Hand it to me."

"I will not," said Jane. "I will not."

"You will not?"

"My father sent it to me, and I will not part with it. Master Shore, I am young and timid, but you may hunt a hare until it turns upon the fiercest of its pursuers, and, forgetting its nature, struggles for its life. I will not give up the book my father has sent to me. I will not let you have it, Master Shore."

Shore was petrified at so much boldness, and Jane had disappeared up the staircase before he recovered himself sufficiently to make any reply to it. Then his first impulse was to go after her, but he did not do so. He contented himself by muttering,—

"Wait a bit—wait a bit. Wait till old Wainstead is dead, and then, Mistress Jane, you shall break my heart, or I will break yours. Wait a bit—wait a bit. She goes on calling me Master Shore, too, as if she thought I liked it. Yet, no, I am wrong there. If she thought I liked it, she would be the last in the world to address me by such a name."

Shore put on his hat, and slunk out, hoping that he should see Simon and Jacob lurking somewhere in the neighbourhood. Shore was jealous; yes, actually jealous of poor Jacob; but a straw is sufficient for the jealous mind to seize upon as food for its strange imaginings. He was actually jealous of Jacob, and considered in his own mind that some desperate plot was going on which was calculated to end greatly to his dishonour, unless by extreme artfulness he succeeded in circumventing it.

Jane crept up stairs to her own room. She locked the door, and then flinging herself into a chair, she wept the most bitter tears that had ever yet come from her eyes. Had Shore been but ordinarily kind to her, she could have, from a strong sense of duty, endured the deep-seated anguish of feeling that she was for ever separated from him she could have loved; but harshness and abuse were so new to her, that she trembled and wept fearfully to think that she might be while she lived now subject to them.

"My father, too, he in the power of this man," she said, mournfully. "But for that I might still have flown to him for protection; but Shore can ruin him, and well I know that such a step would bow him down with sorrow to the grave."

Poor Jane implicitly believed what Shore had told her of her father's pecuniary obligation to him.

"Alas! alas!" she sobbed, "what will become of me? Can I really endure the life of wretchedness which appears opening before me? I dare not think it, or I shall surely go mad—quite mad. Oh, Walter Fane—Walter Fane, what has become of thee? Art thou living, and I the wife of another? Art thou dead, and I so unhappy as not to be in the grave with thee? Oh, Walter, Walter."

Her tears flowed more freely. They fell upon the vellum binding of the book her father had sent to her, with a melancholy sound like the dull splashing of a thunderstorm. In fancy she saw pass before her all her past life—so full of joy—so replete with tenderness—spoilt by her dear father, who never, in the waywardness of infancy, could be brought to believe that his dear child, Jane, could possibly be wrong,—idolised by her old nurse, who seemed to consider that what she was specially sent into this world for, was to tend upon the mercer's daughter,—beloved by Walter—spoken gently to by all,—ah, what a contrast did the past present to the present. No wonder that Jane wept anew, as all these thoughts and feelings passed rapidly through her mind. Suddenly then, she exclaimed,—

"Just Heaven, I am punished for making the false vow at thy altar. I swore to love this man, when God knows my heart was another's. I swore to obey him, when, alas, I shrink from his commands."

She let her face drop upon her hands, and remained for many minutes silent—then suddenly she arose, saying, with a shudder,—

"I shall go mad—I'm sure I shall go mad, if I give way further to these dreadful thoughts—I shall go completely mad. I must not think thus. Oh, Heaven grant me patience and resignation to bear with the evils of this life, that I may not miss the joys of that which is to come."

She sank on her knees, and remained for some time engaged in prayer. Her mind became more soothed—her imagination calmer, and when she rose again, she succeeded in stemming the current of her tears, and to a great degree in overcoming the emotions which had found a home in her heart.

"And this is from my dear father," she said, as she gazed upon the book. "This is from him, to show that although she is away from him, he does not forget his child."

Jane had been taught the then rare accomplishment of reading. The affection of her fond father had induced him to take that extraordinary step in her education, and to give her an extent of learning which the wives and daughters of many of the highest of the nobility did not aspire to. It was quite a phenomenon for a boy to be able to read in these "fine old times," but as for a girl having such a wonderful heap of scholarship, it was really enough to make a show of. But Jane was one of the very few females of the period who could peruse a manuscript book, and now she opened the one which had been sent to her by her father, and found it was a collection of little romances, with a prayer at the commencement of each.

"I may find some solace here," she said, "from my own absorbing cares. How rare now-a-days is it to find a book which is not of a direct religious tendency—perhaps in some of these pages I may find recounted circumstances of as great unhappiness as my own, and I may learn with what fortitude others bore grievous trials, and through what chances they perhaps emerged to joy again. I will search for such a story, if it may be found here in these pages."

She opened the book at the commencement of a tale, which was entitled,—"Ye Two Guestes;" but we will put it into modern English, and our readers will suppose Jane then reading.

The house of Master Grimstead, the vintner, was situated in the East Cheap, and was very well known to the citizens about that quarter, especially to such of the visitors as came to London for a limited period, as the Golden Lion was famed for its good cheer, and reasonable charges. Master Grimstead, too, was much respected by his brethren, and had more than once done favours in the way of screening from the law such as were pursued for opinion sake, for men in those times fell and died for the colour of a rose. For this reason Master Grimstead was respected by his military guests, of whom he had not a few, but none ever knew of his having done so; and the few who had been gainers by his extending a helping hand to them in a time of need, ever respected his secret, and he never was questioned respecting it.

There were several reasons why Grimstead was respected, and also why he was now and then an object of curiosity and speculation. No one knew anything of him—none knew who were his parents, his birth-place, or profession. He seemed perfectly at home in his calling; but his conversation, information, and manners, spoke of something higher than a mere citizen innkeeper. However that might be, no one could form the remotest notion. He had now been there many years master of the Golden Lion. He came there one winter—he and his daughter, Margaret, and after remaining there as guests some months, purchased the business, which was relinquished by the former, he having grown old and rich by his trade.

Master Grimstead purchased his freedom, and all was satisfactory so far, and he stepped into the business with all the confidence of a man who felt himself capable of succeeding, and of deserving success. His house soon became frequented, and his daughter was the only one who appeared to be about him that knew anything of him, or bore any relation to him. This was singular, for though when he came there Margaret was scarce eight years old, yet she was a remarkably well educated and quick child of her age, yet no one, not even those who did not scruple to make inquiries of the child they would not have made of the father, learned nothing from her save her mother had been dead some time, she could not tell how long.

Margaret was now nearly twenty—a beautiful and bewitching maiden, such as would ravish the heart of a bachelor at first sight; yet she was modest and unassuming; not pretending that she was a perfect fright, yet never paying more than momentary attention to those who chose to flatter, and whose compliments were lost upon her as quickly as the words died away. She was kind and courteous to all. She was well skilled in many things—far beyond her station; and yet she neither went from home to a school, nor yet received any governess at home; but it was all attributable to her father.

At this time there came two gentlemen to lodge at the Golden Lion; they were men of some quality and of noble connexions. The one was Sir John Warrenne, and the other Captain Mowbray. The former was by far the best furnished with means, though they both held the same rank in the army at the period. They were also friends, and had come to London to transact some matters entrusted severally to their cares.

Here they remained for some days, and were much pleased with the attention and accommodation they met with, at the same time they could but express their surprise and admiration at the beauty and innocence of Mistress Margaret, as she was called.

They both often conversed together about her in a light and jesting strain; yet, whenever Sir John spoke thus, it grated harshly upon the ears of Captain Mowbray, but he could not complain. They both had a feeling lurking at their hearts respecting the vintner's daughter—a citizen's daughter—it was absurd!

However, matters went on till they both conceived a violent passion for Margaret, which neither chose to avow; and each seized every opportunity that occurred of conversing with her; and when both were present, there was a difficulty scarce to be imagined. Both were anxious to conceal his passion from his friend, at the same time he felt annoyed if the other were but for a moment to engage her in conversation.

As it was impossible they could remain in this state very long, Captain Mowbray determined to converse with her seriously, and ascertain what she really was, and for that purpose chose an opportunity when his friend was engaged at court.

This interview lasted long enough to disarm the captain of any dishonourable intentions, if he had any, for he was so struck with her mental accomplishments, that he was fain to confess his passion there and then, and found it not ill-received, though cautiously.

Sir John Warrenne returned that night; he had been engaged late, and had taken a little more wine than usual, and was somewhat heated by the same; and unfortunately meeting with Mistress Margaret, he felt emboldened, and began to speak in a warmer strain than usual.

"Pretty Mistress Margaret," he said, "you would grace a court better than an inn, though none so fair as thou art ever did so before."

"You have been to court, Sir John, to-night, I perceive," said Margaret; "will you walk up stairs?"

"I would sooner stay here, were it the whole night, and converse with thee, thou goddess of the city, whose very lips are ——"

"Nay, Sir John, if you go on at that rate, I must leave you."

"Not without the penalty."

"The penalty! Sir John."

"Yes, that is the word."

"I do not understand you, sir."

"A kiss, sweet Mistress Margaret, is the penalty I mean to exact."

"Sir John, you forget that I am under the protection of my father's roof, and—and ——"

"And what, pretty one?"

"You are a gentleman."

"Well said, and therefore thou shalt be rewarded; thy lips were never intended for any less than a knight to kiss, as sure as I wear spurs."

"'Tis well my father hears you not."

"Fathers are cross-grained animals," said the knight, "and not over welcome at times."

"Let me pass, Sir John; you do quality an injustice in thus annoying a poor maiden."

"By my quality I do it no such thing; thou art an honour to it, and a jewel in any man's cap. Come, come, pretty one, a kiss, a kiss."

"Sir John, I pray you let me pass."

"No, by Heavens, not without the penalty; come, prepare, and be as kind as you are good and beautiful."

"Have I no one to protect me at hand?" she exclaimed, in a pettish, but sincere tone of grief.

"Yes, you have," said a voice from above; and in another moment, Captain Mowbray descended the stairs, and then stepping by Sir John Warrenne, he gave his hand to Mistress Margaret, who immediately accepted it, and stepped by her tormentor.

"Now, by Heavens!" exclaimed Sir John, "this shall not be. I will have the forfeit, if blood be shed to win it."

So saying, he made a dart after Margaret, but he was met by Captain Mowbray, who impeded his passage, and enabled Margaret to escape from the scene.

"Stand on one side, Mowbray."

"If you want to go to your chamber, I will," replied Mowbray; "but Mistress Margaret is under my protection for this night."

"Ha! ha! ha! sir self-styled protector, you shall pay an ample penalty for such insolence."

"Insolence!"

"Yes, insolence, in standing between a gentleman and his pleasure. What greater insolence could be imagined, I would know?"

"Such insolence I would repeat again. I protected the wench against your brutality."

"So, then, you have turned conservator of the vintner's daughter have you, Captain Mowbray. Perhaps you'll marry her, and present her to the regiment; she'll make a good property."

"Sir John Warrenne, your conduct is not that of a gentleman; but this matter cannot now be settled by words. My sword shall pay you the penalty you are desirous of having, to-morrow morning."

"Very good—very good. I will grace you so far, and condescend so much."

"Your condescension is nothing, but your insolence much. You have insulted me, and dare you refuse me satisfaction, I will post you and your knighthood cowards."

"You shall hear different to-morrow. You shall learn how to escape the chastisement that awaits you."

"If I may judge by the present outrage, you are more apt with the bowl than the sword; but you had better betake yourself to sleep than stand brawling here; you will need a clearer head than you have now to help you."

"Well, Sir Conservator, it may be so; but I sleep not here."

"Your hour?"

"At seven."

"And place?"

"In the fields at the end of the lane leading from Holborn Bars."

"I know it, and will be there."

So saying, Sir John Warrenne turned from the Golden Lion, and sought for some friend, to whom he communicated the cause of the quarrel, the time and place. All being arranged, there was no necessity for bearing messages backwards and forwards; but Sir John was advised to sleep upon it.

After the departure of Sir John Warrenne, Captain Mowbray proceeded to his own apartment, which he had scarce reached ere the light and graceful form of Mistress Margaret followed him. She hesitated as she stood at the door to enter, but being resolved, she did enter a short way, saying,—

"Captain Mowbray, I fear I have been the cause of an unhappy quarrel between you and your friend."

"No—no, Mistress Margaret, do not think that, nor disturb yourself about our relations."

"Will you promise me that you will not go to this meeting to-morrow?"

"Ha! did you overhear us?"

"I must confess I did; for being the cause of your altercation, I felt interested and concerned in it. Let me beg of you to keep away. I shall never knew happiness if anything should happen through me."

"But, my pretty Margaret, it is not through you; but you must know that I am a soldier, and my honour is not my own only. I must protect it at any cost, and while I wear a sword I must use it. But do not let this trouble you, since you know the meeting is to take place. You may be assured it is more for the purpose of affording explanation than ought else. There will be no harm done."

"God grant there may not; but I know not how to act in this business."

"Think nothing about it, and say nothing to any third person whatever, for it may do much mischief. But now farewell, Mistress Margaret; good night to you, and may you be happy."

"Good night, Captain Mowbray; I could have wished that this affair had never happened."

"But, having happened, it must be brought to a conclusion. Good night."

As the captain uttered these words, he led her to the door, and gently kissed her hand. There was a respectful demeanour about the captain, and the near approach of danger, that gave him a great advantage over the mind of Margaret, and a tear stood in her eye as she left the place.

* * * * * * * *

The next morning, Captain Mowbray was accompanied back to his lodgings by his friend, who had attended him in the duel; his arm was in a sling; they had been both wounded, Sir John Warrenne severely; indeed, his life was despaired of for some days; but he eventually recovered.

Margaret was an attentive nurse to Captain Mowbray, during the few days that he was detained in doors; we need hardly say that this affair gave him an additional interest in her eyes, and that before another week had elapsed, her heart was irrevocably the captain's. He was no less pleased with her, and he had made up his mind that he would act with decision and uprightness at once. There was but one bar to their union, and that was the captain was poor; he was well connected, but, like a great many more, he was poor.

However, he determined to speak to Master Grimstead about the matter, and endeavour to make some arrangement respecting Mistress Margaret. He called Master Grimstead on one side, and plainly told him the love he bore his daughter, at the same time he informed him of his own situation; his commission was his only wealth.

"Since you have behaved so honourably, Captain Mowbray, I will tell you my daughter's happiness is all I seek, and I have wealth enough to place you beyond the reach of want, or of using a sword to earn a living by cutting and hacking men's bodies. I, too, bore a commission, till I lost my wife, and became disgusted with the trade of blood. But you must consent to relinquish the sword, which you can do with honour, seeing there is no immediate call for service."

After much conversation, this was all agreed to by Captain Mowbray, and two months after the marriage took place, and Master Grimstead quitted the East Cheap, with his daughter and son-in-law, to take possession of a small estate that had been purchased for them, when they all lived in happiness and harmony.

A sudden knock at the chamber door caused Jane to start from a perusal of the volume she held in her hand, and the voice of Shore cried aloud,—

"Jane—Jane! you must go to your father directly. The old man is dying!"

CHAPTER XXVIII.

The Death of the Mercer.

"And deathe has sealed ye eye which once
Beamed with the lighte of love;
Ye spirite of ye aged man
Is with its God above."

SUCH a summons as this was calculated to produce upon Jane an effect which obliterated every other feeling. The words, "The old man is dying!" rang upon her ears as if they had announced the world's dissolution, and the end of all things that inhabit it. For a moment, she could hardly believe her senses, and, springing to her feet, she cried, in terrified accents,—

"Speak again—speak again! What sound was that, what dreadful sound was that? Speak again, I charge you, speak again!"

"Jane, Jane, Jane!" cried Shore, as he rattled at the door. "Open the door! I tell you, your father is dying!"

Jane sprung to the door, and flung it open in a moment.

Shore, pale and agitated, stood on the landing of the stairs. He trembled to such a degree that he had to support himself against the side of the door, as he gasped out,—

"The—the old man is dying at last, Jane; Simon—has come—to—to say that he is dying, Jane—dying!"

"No—no! not my father?"

"Yes, yes—he!"

Jane rushed down the staircase in an instant, without pausing to hear another word or to make any preparation for the streets. To gain the outer shop was the work of a

moment, and there she saw Simon. Seizing him by the arm, she looked in his face with terrible earnestness, as she said,—

"Simon—Simon, is it true—is it true?"

"Your father—your father is ill."

"Dying?"

"They say so."

"I go—I go! Oh, would that it were me instead! I must be with him. Oh, God—oh, God! And I called myself unhappy before this!"

Simon held her by the arm, as he said,—

"Put something on you, Jane, for Heaven's sake!"

"No!" she screamed. "He is my worst enemy who now detains me on any pretence even for a moment."

"Very good," said Simon; and he left Shore's house with her just as she was. He would not let her run on by herself, though; he placed her arm beneath his, and perseveringly kept it there.

"No, Jane," he said, "no; you sha'n't scamper along and kill yourself. There's time enough. It won't make three minutes' difference one way or the other. Come quick, but there's no occasion to run."

"But Simon—oh, Simon, if he should be gone before I see him."

"He won't."

"You cannot tell, Simon—you cannot tell. Let us go quicker. Quicker still, good Simon. I know you mean well, but how can you feel as I feel in this matter?"

"Quick enough," said Simon, obstinately. "Here we are almost—don't you see the old sign swinging about, Jane, eh?"

"Yes—yes. As we are so near we will go a little quicker. Simon, tell me how my dear father was taken ill?"

"Why, Jane, he was sitting in his chair, and I saw him breathe hard, and when I spoke to him he could not answer me, but only moved his head, so then I knew he was ill, and sent for the cunning leech, Master Anthony Slade, who shook his head when he saw him, and when Master Anthony shakes his head, it's well known what's going to happen."

"Does he give no hope, Simon?"

"None—none."

"Oh, Heaven, yet preserve my dear, dear father," sobbed Jane.

"Stop!" cried a voice suddenly behind Jane, and she felt herself seized by the shoulder. "Stop! stop!" It was a voice Jane knew too well—the voice of her evil genius, Shore. "Stop!" he cried again, "fellow," to Simon, "pass on. Jane, I must speak to you."

"Sha'n't," said Simon.

"Not now—not now," cried Jane, hysterically, "I can speak to no one now, Shore. Let me go to my dying father—I cannot now be stayed."

"You shall. You must listen to me for a moment, Jane. Go on, fellow, go on."

Simon snapped his fingers in Shore's face as he said—

"Go on yourself, will you. Will you go on yourself?"

Shore finding that he could not get rid of Simon, or stop the speed with which he and Jane were proceeding, ran on by her side saying—

"Jane—Jane. Mind, Jane; you can get your father to leave me anything, you know, and that will be to your own advantage, Jane. Mind that—mind that!"

"Peace—peace!" said Jane, "I know nothing. I mind nothing but that my dear father is in danger. Peace—peace, I say."

"But people must die sometimes, Jane," persisted Shore, "and if the old did not go off, there would be no room in the world for the young."

"A good thing if you would go off," said Simon. "Some one else might occupy your place in the world that would look better."

"You scoundrel," said Shore, "I will find a means of repaying you yet for this insult."

"I defy you," said Simon, "I defy you."

They had now reached the mercer's door, and by a sudden and adroit movement Simon permitted Jane to enter, but completely blocked up the doorway to Shore.

"Let me in, villain. Let me in," he cried.

"Wait a bit," said Simon. "You wouldn't surely interfere now between the father and his child. Say you won't go up stairs unless you are asked for, and you may go into the shop. I don't mean to trust your word, you know, but if you give it I shall make you keep it honestly, whether you like or not."

"I—I don't want to go up stairs," Shore cried, thinking that he might have a chance of so doing in spite of Simon's precautions, and that it was better to get into the shop than to be kept in the street.

"Very good," said Simon, "walk in."

Shore did so, but to his great mortification Simon sat down upon the bottom one of the flight of stairs leading to the upper rooms, so that there was no chance whatever of his, Shore's, being able, as he had hoped, to dash up suddenly and reach Wainstead's chamber, from whence, if once he got there, it would make too much noise and confusion to attempt to remove him.

And now let us follow Jane to the chamber of her father, in which, in addition to the dying man, was Anthony, the leech, and the old nurse who had been in the family so many years.

Any spot of that house was, of course, familiar to Jane, and she reached the room where she felt sure her father would be taken in a very few minutes. She paused a moment at the door, and pressed her hands upon her heart, as if by such means she could still its wild, tumultuous beating.

"Calm—calm," she said, "I will try to be calm."

She heard the faint murmur of voices in the chamber, and then she gently opened the door and entered it.

The nurse saw her, and uttered an exclamation of satisfaction, which caused Master Anthony, the learned leech, to look up, and when he saw Jane, he bowed, and said—

"You are welcome, young damsel. You are in time."

He pointed to the bed on which Jane saw her father—but, oh! how altered was he! The hue of death was upon his face—its expression even was completely altered. He was sensible; but there was an anxious look about his eyes that was extremely painful.

He spoke, but it was in a thick, hurried voice, as if he felt he had not much time in this world to say what he wanted to have said before he left it for ever.

"Jane—Jane—Jane," he said, "my own, my beautiful child, Jane! Come to me, my darling Jane."

Jane flew towards him and buried her face in his breast. Her long beautiful hair streamed around upon the bed, some of the tresses almost touching the floor as she stooped over that pallid frame of him whom she loved best of all.

"My Jane," resumed the mercer, "my beautiful child!"

He smoothed with a trembling hand her hair as he spoke, and then a gush of tears came to his eyes, and he wept bitterly.

"Father—father," half screamed Jane, in the anguish of her heart. "Father, I will die with you!"

"Hush!" said Master Anthony, "hush! Be calm—be calm. This must not be; maiden, learn to respect God's wishes better. Be calm—be calm. Death is but a change from uncertainty to certainty. I pray you add not to the grief he has in leaving you for a time, by such loud lamentations."

"You are right," said Jane. "Forgive me—you are right. Dear father, speak to me again."

Slowly the sobs of the mercer died away, and then he said, in a calmer and clearer tone than he had before spoken in,—

"Jane, I know that I am going from you, and when I am gone I must leave you to God. I see things clearer now, when the hand of death is upon my heart, than I did some time since. Jane, I have been your greatest enemy."

"You, father—you!"

"Yes, Jane—yes."

"Oh, no—no—no!"

"Unwittingly I have. Motive may excuse me; but, Jane, I feel, now, that it was affection for me that made you wed Shore. I know, now, that you are not happy."

Jane could not contradict these words, and she only wept.

"I know it, my darling," continued the mercer. "I know it now, my Jane—now that it is too late, as is commonly the case with human judgment. I made a great mistake, Jane."

"Think not of it now, dear father."

"I can think of nothing else. Oh, my child! can you forgive your poor, old, doting father, that he went the wrong way about to make you, as he thought, happy?"

"Forgive—oh, I have nothing to forgive."

"Alas! you have, and I have much to lament. Oh, Jane, there was one who should have called you his. There was one with whom you should have been happy."

"Father, forbear!" said Jane.

Too well she knew—too well, for her peace and happiness, she knew to whom her father alluded. Oh, what pen shall describe the pangs that rent her heart at that sad moment?

"Walter—Walter Fane," gasped Wainstead. "Poor Walter!"

"Father! father!" sobbed Jane, "do not—oh, do not speak of him now. I pray you do not!"

The mercer gave a deep sigh, and then turning restlessly, he said,—

"Shore—Shore! I must see that man."

"Hush! hush! Do not see him now," said Jane. "Do not see him, father—I—I would not wish him here at such a time as this."

"Shore—Shore! I must see Shore," said Wainstead. "I have, before I die, something to say to Shore. Where is he? I will rise and go to him. Shore—Shore! Fetch him to me—drag him here. I must and will see him before I die—drag him here—where—where is Shore?"

"Let him have his will," said Master Anthony. "If Shore, who I suppose is the cunning goldsmith of Lombarde-street, be near at hand, let him come."

"Let him come, then," said Jane. "God forbid that at such a moment as this I should say nay to anything that my father can request. Let him come if it be his wish. I believe he will be found below."

"Indeed!" said Master Anthony. "Is it true that you have married him?"

" It is—true."

Jane shuddered as she spoke, and Master Anthony elevated his eyebrows, as he nodded his head, as much as to say,—" Oh, I perfectly understand—an unhappy marriage. Heaven help you!"

The nurse, understanding that Shore might be produced, if possible, left the room to see if he was below, and if not, to send some one for him instantly.

CHAPTER XXIX.

The Curse.

" And about ye dyinge there be those who believe subtile sprites linger, whisperinge to them strange things, ye which in life they would know nothinge."

THE above extract is from an old black-letter volume, known as " Ye Maximes and Rare Sayinges of Richard Staples, some time of Londone." There would seem to be a certain amount of truth in it, for we often find that those who are upon the point of death, seem gifted with an accuracy of judgment and a felicity of illustrating what they mean, to which in health they had no sort of pretension.

It was odd that, all at once, the mercer should appear to have awakened to the fact that his child's happiness was sacrificed to a mistaken policy, and that her marriage with Shore was much to be deplored; but certainly such was the case. He had, as it were, suddenly awakened to such a consciousness, and hence appeared to arise his great eagerness to see the husband of his child.

Perhaps if Shore had been aware of what had passed in the chamber above, he would not have jumped up so readily as he did from the mercer's counter, on which he had seated himself facing Simon, when the nurse appeared, and said, in a voice shrill from grief,—

" Is Master Shore at hand, Simon?"

" Here—here—I am here," cried Shore.

" My poor master would fain see you."

" Are you sure of that?" said Simon.

" Am I sure!" said the old nurse. " Why, is he not now calling for him? Get thee out of the way, Simon, wilt thee."

" Very good," said Simon. " You may go up now, Master Shore, since it is my poor master's wish."

Shore scowled at him as he passed, but he would not waste precious time, for all he knew, just then, in an altercation with Simon, so he followed the old nurse up the stairs, saying to her as he went,—

" Is he worse or better, good Margaret?"

" He will be worse before he be better," said the old woman. " He will have to pass through death to glory."

"Indeed!" said Shore. "Humph! Glory! Fudge!"

The old nurse did not catch this irreligious sentiment, or, doubtless, she would have got up a private quarrel with Shore on its account; but she went on, adding,—

" Oh, we must all go the same way some day. When my poor husband was killed in the wars, 'Peace be to him,' said I, for once in a way. A quarrelsome man he was, surely."

"D—n him and you, too!" muttered Shore.

"What say you, worshipful sir?"

"Nothing—nothing."

" Walk in, sir. Here you will find Master Wainstead, bless his soul! and if he be long for this world, I am much mistaken, which will be a rare thing, for it's seldom I'm mistaken about anything."

Even as he entered the room, Shore heard Wainstead calling for him in an excited tone of voice,—

"Where is Master Shore?" he cried. "'Tis Shore I want. Send for him. If he shrink from coming, drag him hither. I say I must see Master Shore now, or I cannot die in peace."

"Here I am, good Master Wainstead," said Shore, who expected, from the eagerness with which the mercer spoke, that he was going to be honoured with some signal mark of favour. " Here he is, good sir. I have been below waiting your pleasure, Master Wainstead. God bless you, and grant you a happy end, and a gracious deliverance. Amen!"

" Oh, you are here," said Wainstead.

"Even so. Ah, Master Wainstead, we must all die at last. And if our ends be peace, what matters?"

"What—matters," repeated Wainstead, mechanically,—"what matters? Shore—Master Shore, I say."

"I am here."

"You are the husband of my Jane. The best—the kindest—the most beautiful being in the world."

"Ah—hem! Yes," said Shore.

"She is young," he continued, "and has probably a long life before her. You will die first."

"Who, I?"

"Yes, in all human likelihood. In fact, I feel assured you will die first, Shore, as you ought."

"I am much obliged," said Shore, with a ghastly grin.

"But while you do live, the happiness of my child is in your keeping."

"Most assuredly, good Master Wainstead. May I presume to ask if you have settled your worldly affairs?"

"I have."

"And, no doubt, properly. As you say, the happiness of Jane is in my keeping; and as a man of the world, you know as well as I do that happiness depends a good deal upon money."

"I have found that such is a prevalent opinion; but it is not of money that I sent for you to speak."

"Indeed!"

"No, Shore, no. A higher object claims my consideration. You are aware that I am dying?"

"Why, I—I hope not."

"Tell him, Master Anthony, that I am dying; and that my capacity to speak as I am now speaking is but the last faint flush of the expiring flame of life."

"It is true," said the leech.

"Hush, my darling. Jane, do not weep."

"Will you have a priest?" said the nurse.

"No," said Wainstead. "God's own spirit is in this room. I want no priest to translate my heart to my Creator, or my Creator's goodness to me."

"Very good," said Anthony, the leech,—"very good."

Shore fidgeted about uneasily, and then, after a brief pause, Wainstead slowly lifted up his hands above his head, and said, in a solemn and deep voice, that sounded fearfully ominous,—

"The curse of Heaven light upon the man who, with unkindness, blights the heart of my beautiful child! Awake or asleep, dreaming or thinking, in all his various pursuits in life, may the bitterest curse of God cling to him. May his heart be seared with evil thoughts. May disease rack his limbs, and death come not as a solace, but with agony, as an anticipation of the terror that is beyond the grave. A curse—a curse for ever on the head of him who is to my child cruel and unkind!"

He let his hands slowly drop, and there was an awful silence for the space of about a minute. Then Shore sprang to his feet, exclaiming,—

"He is mad—oh, he is mad—quite mad. I saw it when I first came in. What a sad thing that, before his death, Master Wainstead, the rich mercer of the Chepe, should go mad—raving mad."

"I do not see the madness," said Anthony, the leech.

"Not see it? Did you not hear him even now. 'Twas me he meant by that curse—'twas me."

Wainstead raised himself partially up in his bed, and he pointed in the face of Shore, as he said, slowly,—

"Thou art the man!"

Then, with a deep sigh, he sank back again.

The leech hurried forward, and laid his hand upon the heart. Jane saw the suspicious movement, and, with a shriek, she threw herself upon the bed.

"Father—father, speak again—oh, speak again to me," she cried, frantically. "Father—father, speak again."

"He will never speak again," said Anthony.

Jane fell heavily to the floor—she had fainted with the shock of that piece of dreadful intelligence, which, however it may be expected, is always, when it does come, a fearful shock to those who loved, and would fain have had the departed spirit linger yet awhile with them.

"Is he dead?" whispered Shore.

"Dead," said the leech.

"Mad—mad. Oh, most decidedly mad."

Jane was lifted from the floor by Anthony and the nurse, and carried from the room. As for Shore, he trembled too much to be able to render any assistance. Besides, he seemed to have a superstitious horror of turning his back upon the corpse, so he backed out of the room, looking to the full as pale and as death-like as those sad remains of what was once the kind-hearted, noble-spirited, well-known mercer of the Chepe.

Jane's swoon was a protracted one, and almost alarmed Master Anthony by its long continuance. At length, however, by dint of very stringent applications, he succeeded in restoring her to animation, when she burst into tears, which he was well satisfied to see, as by frequent experience in such scenes he knew how effectually they would relieve the overcharged heart.

"She will soon be well enough to go home," he said, to the nurse, "and I should advise you to go with her."

"Bless you, sir. I was to have gone, but Master Shore would not have it."

"Indeed!"

"No, sir; he said he would have no useless old grubs eating him out of house and home."

"Humph! well, I cannot, of course, interfere in any one's family arrangements; but I can see enough to form my own opinion usually. I pity Jane. I do sincerely pity her."

The old woman shook her head sorrowfully, as she replied,—

"As do I—as do I. God help her, Master Anthony."

"Amen!" said the leech, as he walked slowly down the staircase into the shop of the mercer, where he found Simon and Shore, who seemed to be very much on the snarl about something.

CHAPTER XXX.

The Disappointment.

"And he would have left ye ancient serviter to starve, but that Jane forbade ye same."

MS. Letter.

When Shore came down stairs from the chamber of death, in his usual stealthy, uncomfortable manner, it was with very different feelings to those which had found a home in his bad heart as he ascended them previous to the dissolution of Wainstead, whom he most heartily wished dead before that event happened.

"I am now master here," he muttered to himself. "I am now master here, and those who have braved me and set at nought the authority I ought to have, and the authority I will have in this house, shall soon find that I am master indeed."

It was Simon of course against whom he was so very inveterate, and if he, Shore, hated any one more than another, he did certainly hate Simon with an enduring hatred which knew no bounds of mercy or even common justice.

Shore was what may be termed a general hater of humanity, but Simon was most particularly obnoxious.

He paused, did Shore, just before he set foot in the shop from the staircase, and it was to prepare himself to assume an air of intense arrogance that he did so. Then he walked in, and knitting his brows, he cast a withering look at Simon, who returned the gaze with all the indifference as if he had been looking at one of the quaintly carved monstrosities that adorned the door-posts.

"So!" said Shore.

This was a speech to which Simon did not think it necessary to make the least reply, so he left it in Shore's hands to do the best he could with it.

"So, sir," added Shore, still louder, and in the tone of a man who has made up his mind for a quarrel, whether the other party like it or not.

"Won't!" said Simon.

"Won't what?"

"Nothing and everything."

"Indeed! I can tell you what you will, though."

"What?"

"You will sleep somewhere else than here to-night, if you sleep at all, my friend."

"Ain't your friend—never was," said Simon,—"never mean to be."

"Too well I know that, you most insolent and ill-mannered varlet," said Shore, his rage carrying him almost beyond the bounds of prudence. "Too well I know that. You have been my active enemy. Think I was blind—besotted—so that I saw not the artfulness of your ways while your old fool of a master lived; but now your reign is over. Troop—troop, I say; get out!"

"Out?"

"Yes; get out, or by the mass you shall find that Shore, the rich goldsmith, is not without the power to crush such as you are. Get out, I say!"

"Out where?"

"Out of this place. Curses on you! the very sight of you here is hateful to me!"

"Very like," said Simon; "I hope it will make you ill."

"Will you go?"

"No."

"You—you refuse?"

"Most decidedly."

"Then must I, which will be wonderfully the worse for you, inasmuch as the whipping-post will teach you better manners, appeal to his worship the mayor, who will send his men to convince you with the argument contained in a quarter stave that you are wrong and must e'en troop."

"You sent for me, Simon," said a voice at the doorway, and it was additionally darkened by the shadow of a man. "You sent for me, Simon?"

"Yes."

"In good truth, I was at the King's Head."

"Knew it."

"Who are you?" roared Shore. "What do you want?"

"Who am I?" said the stranger. "Why, as you must know, I am Master Snafflings the bowyer."

"Snafflings—Snafflings! oh, I recollect you. Simon will, after to-night, oblige you with his private address; he remains not here."

"I am open to reason, Master Shore, and yet——"

"Dare you contend with me as to what I shall do in my own house?"

"Your house?"

"Aye, whose else?"

"Truly Master Wainstead named it not your house in his will."

Shore staggered back a pace or two as he gasped,—

"His—his will?"

"Yes, Master Shore, which I have in my keeping."

"And which I sent for you to produce," said Simon, making an unusually long and connected speech, for him.

"I am quite ready."

"His will?" again repeated Shore. "Do I hear aright? His will. Oh, it—it matters not. Of course his daughter's husband is duly honoured. Well, well—his will. Let us, then, have this will, Master Snafflings, if it so please you."

"Truly, I am wonderfully willing. You have heard of Master Cope, I'll warrant me?"

"Yes—yes; a political fellow, who can write and read. A friend of Caxton's, who, to my mind, is made by far too much of."

"Be that as it may; the will, I was going to tell you, was drawn by Master Cope, and lies in wonderfully small compass."

"Yes, yes—small compass. It leaves all to me."

"Nay—nay."

"Not so—not so? D——n!"

"It states that, as his dear daughter Jane is well and worthily wedded to one able and willing to support her as a gentlewoman, and one who loves her right well, he, Wainstead, leaves all that he dies possessed of to Walter Fane."

A howl of rage came from Shore's lips, and, after a slight pause, Master Snafflings, who, out of his own house, was a very proper sort of man, continued,—

"And in my care all is left for Walter Fane, in case he should appear again; and if he should not, I am to do what I like in my discretion with the substance of my friend."

"A will!" screamed Shore. "Call you this a will? The scroll of a morris-dance pageant. A will, indeed!"

"It is Wainstead's will, and I shall act upon it as best may suit with what I know his wishes were."

"You will?"

"Ay, most truly—no detriment to you, Master Shore."

"And—and—pray," said Shore, trembling with passion, "what do you propose to do?"

"To allow Jane to choose whatever she pleases from the house, in the first place; and in the second, to let Simon carry on the business as it is."

"Simon?"

"Yes, truly. He is trustworthy—he is honest as the day."

"Now, by the—but no matter. Ha! ha! no matter. Laugh while you can, both of you. There will be a different tune played here ere long. Laugh away. Ha! ha! I will alter all this, or my name is not Shore. Think you that in such a manner I am to be bereft of that which is mine own?"

"'Tain't yours, and never was," said Simon.

"Peace, villain!"

"Villain yourself."

"Now, I could find in my heart to brain you as you stand."

"I know it; but you are afraid. That's the only thing that at all prevents you doing it."

"Afraid!"

"Yes."

"Nay, nay—let us have no brawling," interposed Master Snafflings. "Pray remember, both of you, what is up stairs."

"No danger," said Simon—"no danger. He won't do anything, and never had any intention of doing anything. All's right. He's a great coward; I know him well."

Simon fixed his eyes upon Shore in a manner which induced that worthy individual to quail a little, and then he thought that it would be far better for him to go, but he was resolved not to go before he had spoken again to Jane, so he went to the foot of the staircase, and in a loud, angry voice, he called,—

"Jane—Jane—Jane."

There was no answer, and again, louder than before, he shouted,—

"Jane—Jane—Jane."

Then the old woman who had been so long in Wainstead's service came hobbling down, and while her head shook, partly from palsy and partly from indignation, she said,

"The Lord knows, Master Shore, an' it is a shame and a sin, with death in the house, to hear such a brawling and shouting. Some judgment will come over you, truly. Really a great judgment is wanted, for the times are sinful. Alack and well-a-day! Jane cannot come to you; the poor child is ill."

"Ill?"

"Ay, sick at heart—sick at heart."

"Tell her, if she come not, that I will drag her down stairs by the hair of her head."

"Will you?" said Simon.

"Yes, I will."

"If you so much as hurt a hair of her head, I'll knock your own head off your shoulders."

"Here's times—here's pretty times we live in," said Shore, looking towards the street, as Simon, with a hostile look, advanced a step upon him. "Here's rare times, when a varlet threatens to knock a citizen's head off."

"With the greatest pleasure in life," said Simon.

"Good—good," added Shore, as he nearly stumbled over the step, to which he did not think he was so near—"very good. We shall see what we can do."

"Hold, Master Shore," said Snafflings; "do not let passion govern you wholly. You must recollect you have called Simon some hard names; and you must make allowance for some natural feelings as regards Jane, who so tenderly loved her father, as to be a pattern to the whole city, although I grieve to say (and here Master Snafflings groaned) it was not followed in all cases."

"I will have my revenge," said Shore, and shaking his clenched fist for a moment above his head, he dashed from the mercer's shop in as great a rage as ever he was in in all his life.

Alas, poor, poor Jane, what a wretched prospect is opening for thee! What will become of thee? Sad, sad indeed were those words which bound you to the will of such a man as he, who, with thy poor father's corpse even in the house, would play the braggart and the bully.

And Jane was insensible—she had fainted, and the old nurse, when she told Shore that she was ill, had by no means exaggerated, for when her father was no more, the sense of utter desolation that came over Jane's heart, was enough almost to kill her at once. No kindred—no friend—no one who loved her—no one to whom she could turn with a look of affection, and be sure of an answering look in return. Alas, alas!

and she so full of all the better, finer feelings of human nature. She so gentle, so affectionate—with a heart overflowing with kindly feelings—surely she ought to have been happy, since Heaven had so profusely in her nature scattered the seeds of joy. When Shore had left, Simon shook his head, and then Master Snafflings shook his head, and they looked at each other ruefully.

"Jane is to be pitied," said Snafflings.

Simon made a wry face, as he muttered,—

"I know what it will come to. Sure of it—sure of it."

"What, Simon?"

"Some o' these days I shall take hold of Shore by the head, and wring his neck."

"Hush, Simon, hush, be careful what you say. Were one unfriendly to you to hear you, or one with lack of discretion, who was in the way of prating of what he heard, you might fall into much mischief, and evil to you might result."

"Can't help it."

"Well, well, Simon, have a care—have a care. And now I will leave you here in authority. Simon, remember that poor Master Wainstead seemed to have a notion that Walter Fane would come back to him again. How he loved the lad."

Simon could not trust himself to speak, now that Walter Fane was spoken of in words of kindness, so he looked up at the ceiling, and whistled.

"How he loved him," added Master Snafflings; "and no wonder, too, for a more likely lad lived not, nor one more full of gallant, noble bearing."

"Be quiet," said Simon. "Hold your row."

"Well, well, well."

"Be quiet."

"I am, Simon, I am. But you know everybody loved him. Even poor half-witted Jacob, who ——"

"Stop—about Jacob—he's robbed you. Forgive him."

"Forgive him?"

"Yes, Master Snafflings. I'll give you back the money, but forgive him. He was led astray, poor fellow, by his love for Jane. He ain't right, you know, quite in his head, but he is in his heart, poor fellow. You will not persecute him?"

"It is not I, Simon, but Miss Bridget."

"I know, I know; but if you see poor Jacob you will forgive him?"

"Yes, yes, poor fellow. He has been misled, I am sure, by some evil-minded varlet."

"Ha, ha!" cried a voice at the door at this moment. "Ha, ha! my rollicking blades—my Trojans. Thunder and war. Ha!"

"That's the villain," cried Simon, and he made a rush to the door, but somehow or another Master Snafflings was in his way in such a complicated manner, that the faded gallant who had perpetrated this piece of insolence had ample time to escape down the Chepe, which he did with great speed.

CHAPTER XXXI.

Shore's Strange Visitor.

"And Master Shore could verily have believed ye devil himselfe had come to counsello him."

SHORE made the best of his way home. He was never comfortable at home or abroad. When at home, he always fancied he might be in some way missing some advantages that might be gained abroad, and when away from home, the idea that some piece of wasteful extravagance might be going on in his absence, was always sufficient to keep him on the fidget.

But now rage and bitter disappointment were the predominant feelings of his heart, and he set his teeth, and growled at anybody he met in such an odd manner, that several quietly disposed people crossed to the other side of the way, verily believing that he was some one who wished to pick a quarrel in the public streets for some sinister purpose.

As he ran for the most part of the way, he very soon reached Lombarde-street, and then, as was his custom, he paused a moment to peer into the place before he entered it, in order that, if anything contrary to his wishes was going on, he might become aware of it, and so be down upon their serving man.

Shore looked and looked, and he thought he saw somebody seated on a high stool in the middle of the shop, but he was not quite sure. The figure, if it were one, had a very odd, dingy sort of look; and, moreover, it seemed perfectly motionless, and the place being rather dark, tended to confuse the vision.

"Humph!" he muttered, "I will go in very suddenly, and then I shall confound whoever it is."

Acting upon this idea, he did go in rather suddenly; but as for, by so doing, confounding anybody, he was quite wrong, for the thin serving man was confounded to the full extent which he could be already, and the stranger, for there was one there, did not seem of the class of persons who were easy to confound.

Seated on a stool, as if waiting the coming of Shore, was a man completely attired in grey. His doublet was grey, his breeches were grey; his cloak, his hat, and his very face had a grey, odd ashy sort of look about it, which was far from pleasant and agreeable. When he saw Shore he fixed his keen eyes upon him for a moment, and then he said,—

"Welcome!"

"Wel—come," stammered Shore. "I—I suppose I am in my own house. I do not know you."

"Yes you do. Tell him who I am."

These latter words were addressed to the thin serving man, who, with his eyes and mouth wide open, and his hair very nearly on end, with terror, was glaring at the stranger.

"An it please you, worshipfulle master," he said to Shore, "this is the—the—devil."

Shore stepped back a pace, and the stranger said,—

"Complimentary, but wrong. I am not."

As he spoke he struck his hand upon his knee, and a shower of red-hot sparks immediately flew all around.

"Mercy upon us!" cried the serving man, and he made a sudden spring past Shore, and ran into the street.

"Shut the door," said the stranger. "I must have some talk with you, Master Shore."

Shore's knees knocked against each other, and his tongue clove to the roof of his mouth. A cold perspiration broke out upon his brow, and he could neither run away nor speak.

"Now, really," said the stranger, "I thought you were a different sort of man, Master Shore."

"I—I. The Lord preserve me," Shore managed to stammer out, after a few moments' pause.

"Oh, stuff and nonsense," said the stranger. "The Lord has something better to do than trouble his head about you, you may depend. What do you think of a white rose in a cloudless sky?"

Shore drew a long breath as he replied,—

"Are you human?"

"Feel my hand."

"I—I dare not, just yet. I do not know you, and as for a white rose, all I have to say is, long live King Edward."

"Mighty prudent," said the stranger; "but not called for between friends, you know. I repeat, what do you think of a white rose in a cloudless sky?"

Shore was silent for some moments, and then, in a low voice, after a glance of caution round him, he said,—

"Be you man or devil, I can only say that, pray Heaven, the only red it knows is with the blood of its enemies."

"Ah! now we understand each other."

"Who are you?"

"I am one whom to know is not to know—one whom not to know, perchance, is to know best—one whose good report is of more value than the good he reports. I am one who knows you well, and for the future you would do wise to trust me, and when difficulties arise the man in grey will be your friend. How do you mean to manage now about the death of old Wainstead?"

"Manage?"

"Yes. Being disappointed of his money, which is considerable, although not so much as many thought, what do you mean to do?"

"I will have it," said Shore, firmly.

"You may, with my help, Shore; but be quiet for awhile. The white rose will do for you what the red rose never will."

"I know it," said Shore, eagerly. "I know it. And at the last progress through the city, but that strange circumstances happened, there would have been a little change."

"True. Vasso did his best."

"He did; and as you seem to know everything, perhaps you can tell me where he is."

"I can; but am not at liberty just at present. There will be another royal progress through the city."

"I have heard as much."

"To collect a subsidy. All articles of gold or silver will be weighed, and one-fifth of their value must be paid into the hands of the king's treasurer."

"Now, that is too bad."

"Of course it is; but ——"

"You pause. Can you tell me of any politic mode of escaping the impost?"

"Yes."

"Name it—name it."

"Shore, you are a cunning man, and an unscrupulous one. During your residence in Lombardy some years back, you took care to make yourself acquainted with the properties of poisons."

"How know you that?" said Shore, suspiciously.

"Suffice it that I do know it."

"Well—well—well."

"I say you took care to make yourself acquainted with the properties of poison, and being so acquainted, you can use them well. Now, what if a deputation of all the dealers in gold and silver was to meet the king—say in the Chepe."

"Yes—yes."

"And then and there present him with such a loving cup of rare beauty and workmanship as should tend to put the monarch in a happy humour. Then would he drink to you all, and in that drink ——"

"I understand."

"I knew you would. You are quick-witted, Shore."

"I will consider; but tell me who you are."

"You know me not. A name can give you no information, unless you can attach some foreknowledge to it. I say you know me not; but you will know me. I am your friend, and finding you apt on this occasion, shall call on you again."

"With such caution as my personal safety warrants," said Shore, "I am willing to contend for a party which has promised me some advantages."

"Just so. Imprimis, you were to have the place of grand almoner of the household."

"I was—I was."

"Which would enable you to pocket for yourself what was intended for the poor."

"A-hem!"

"Secundus, you were to have the keepership of the crown plate and jewels."

"I was—I was."

"Which would enable you to take out the real stones from their setting, and replace them with false."

"No—no—no. Really ——"

"Unless that process has been already gone through by your predecessor."

"Now may all the plagues of hell torment him if he has," cried Shore. "My malediction light upon his head."

"Good. And you were to have some little annuities and privileges besides, Master Shore."

"I was, and since I find you know so well what was the agreement, I feel convinced that I may trust, and therefore convey to those for whom you act my assurance that what man may in prudence do for the white rose, that will I."

"Enough. I was charged to break this matter to you, and I can now say I find you sufficiently apt and loyal."

"Do say for me as much."

"I will. And as for your own concerns, let me advise you not to treat her whom you have wedded with so much austerity. She is young, and loves the spirited bustle of existence."

"But she does not love me."

"And did you ever expect she would?"

Shore gave a groan.

"You could not entertain so extravagant a proposition; but I can tell you, Master Shore, that you will lose her entirely an you be not more discreet than you have been latterly."

"I will lock her in her chamber—I ——"

"Pshaw! bolts and bars are the clumsiest and most inartificial modes of confining a woman. Depend upon it, she will find assistance to escape all those."

"What can I do?"

"Let her mingle more with society; allow her the company and the companionship of some discreet person of her own sex."

"Indeed. You think that a good plan?"

"In this case."

"Humph! I have always found that one woman was troublesome enough; but when two got together, they were a match for the very devil himself."

"You have heard aright. But let me, as one feeling an interest in your welfare, advise you to find some discreet female, as a companion to your wife, who will be in your confidence as well as hers, and let you know almost every thought she has."

"I should like that."

"Do you know such an one?"

"I do not, indeed. My acquaintance among women is limited."

"Leave it to me, then, and I will arrange all that for you. By the time we meet again, I shall have been able to make some inquiries, and, perchance, to have found one who will suit you well. Be assured, Shore, I will make it my special care."

"I am much your debtor, worshipfull sir. And about Wainstead's money ——"

"You must have patience. When the white rose is in the ascendant, the will can be put aside, and no one will be permitted to hinder you taking possession of all that was the mercer's."

"I will take your advice, inasmuch as one part of it appears to me to tell in well with another."

"You will find it so, Master Shore. And now good even to you; for I have still much to do."

The stranger dismounted from the stool, and strode towards the door, while Shore followed him closely with his eyes, as if he expected him to disappear in some remarkable manner; but he was disappointed, for no particular phenomena marked the exit of the mysterious visitor.

He passed out of the shop, and Shore was alone, for the thin serving man had not yet again made his appearance.

CHAPTER XXXII.

Walter Fane's Projected Escape from Prison.

" And hope, ye happieste delusione
Man can presse unto his hearte,
Will not till lateste breathe we draw
From out ye soule departe."

ALONE—alone now for many, many hours had Walter Fane been in his gloomy dungeon. No voice to cheer him—no friendly eyes to beam upon him.

"She does not come again," he groaned; "she does not come again. The visit of the gaoler's daughter was surely but one of curiosity, and she will not come again."

He threw himself down at the base of one of the stunted columns, and there he lay for nearly an hour in great sadness of mind. But as it frequently happens that an exaltation of spirits is followed by an undue depression, it now in the contrary way occurred that his undue depression was followed by a greater energy of mind, and a more urgent clinging to hope.

"Away, gloomy, unearthly thoughts," he said. "I will not despair—I will not even yet despair."

He sprang to his feet, but, alas! it was not with the buoyant elasticity of yore. Short as had been his stay in that dungeon, it had been long enough to produce considerable effect even upon his young frame. Bad air, no exercise, and deficient food, are not favourable circumstances, and poor Walter felt that already half his strength was gone. A sudden trembling, too, seized him, and for the moment produced an alarm in his mind that he was dying; but it passed off again, and he attributed it, no doubt correctly enough, to the damp of the dungeon.

"They would not be my executioners," he said, mournfully. "A long stay here in this wretched place of confinement will soon number me with the dead."

He paced to and fro for some time, and stamped on the soft earthen floor to recover the wonted circulation of his blood, and then, as he felt his physical energies a little revived, his mind became in better order, and he exclaimed,—

"If I am getting here day by day weaker, and wasting away in this tomb-like place, the more reason is there that I should, while I have strength sufficient, endeavour to make my escape from it. By Heaven's aid, and this stout bar of iron, surely I can try to do a something."

He took the bar in his hand, and stood in the middle of the dungeon, quite undecided where or how to commence operations.

"To work on under the river," he said, "is worse than madness. In the other direction, I may reach some other dungeon, which possibly being untenanted, the door may be open, and so I may find myself in the passages of the prison. Better to die there fighting with those who may attempt to stop my progress, than hour by hour feel weakness creeping over me in such a place as this dungeon."

Although the walls of the dungeon appeared so roughly constructed, time seemed to have consolidated them; and, notwithstanding Walter worked with vigour, he was some time before he succeeded in getting out a few of the large flint stones, which were there so firmly embedded. When, however, he got some out, he obtained a kind of leverage, and he soon cleared a tolerably large space.

There appeared to be nothing behind these stones but earth of a clayey texture, and Walter worked away at it manfully. Suddenly, however, he found his iron bar strike against something hard, and then the conviction came across him that those walls must consist of more than mere flint stones embedded in clay.

"There is stone regularly built, no doubt," he reasoned, "and if so, I am foiled."

Scarcely had these words passed his lips, when he heard a slight noise at the dungeon door, and, hastily concealing the iron bar, he fixed his eyes in that direction. The door was opened—a stream of light came from a lamp, and he saw the gaoler's daughter commence slowly descending the steps.

As the light gleamed upon her countenance, he saw that it was very sad, and as she came nearer, he could perceive tears streaming from her eyes, and every now and then a deep sob came from her breast, as if her very heart was breaking under the pressure of some terrible affliction.

So intent was Walter in looking at her, and so full of pitying conjecture of what could be the cause of so much more affliction than she had before exhibited, that he did not speak, and his silence appeared to alarm her, for suddenly she paused, and, shading the lamp she carried with her hand, she said,—

"Gone—gone? or sleeping?"

"No, no," cried Walter. "Welcome—thrice welcome are you. I began to fear I should never be blessed with a sight of you again."

He approached her and assisted her down the last three steps, and then, as she leaned upon his arm, she wept freely and bitterly.

"Some fresh affliction has come over you," said Walter, tenderly,—"oh! tell me—what has happened?"

"I—I thought," she sobbed, "that I should never see you again. Never—never!"

"Indeed! You have been ill?"

"Very—ill."

"And yet you have ventured here to cheer me. Oh, how can I ever hope to repay you for so much kindness to me, a perfect stranger to you?"

"Not strange, although a stranger," she said, gently.

"How mean you?"

"I know not what I mean—it was a foolish speech."

"But do you think we have ever met before?"

"Never; and yet I do not seem to look upon you as a stranger. It seems to me as if I had known you long."

"Indeed!"

"Yes. Sometimes I think that when in my imagination I have fancied one possessed of noble qualities and gentle carriage, I must have unconsciously pictured such as thou art, and so, when I came to see you and to speak to you, you were not strange to me, but the embodiment of many a dream."

There was an exquisite artlessness about the manner in which these words were spoken.

"God bless you," said Walter, "for thinking of me at all. God bless you, always!"

"And you too! If I could get your release, he might kill me then if he chose!"

"Who—who?"

"My father!"

She shuddered, and a gush of tears came from her eyes.

"Some new cruelty," said Walter, with a flashing eye and a burning cheek,—"some new act of oppression has been practised against you, I am certain."

"Not very new. He struck me."

"Hurt you?"

"Yes; and I lay insensible for a time, they tell me, from the blow. Oh, God—oh, God! what had I done to deserve such a father? Oh, that I were dead."

Walter could not find words in which to give utterance to the indignation he felt.

"Oh!" he cried, "if I were but free—if I were but free for one minute, to let him feel ——"

"Nay, nay," sobbed the beautiful girl, "say not so. It was because I was found to have wandered about the passages of the prison, contrary to the express orders I had had not to do so, that he struck me."

"And yet you have come again."

"It is to bid you an eternal farewell, unless ——"

"Unless what?"

"Unless," she added, hysterically, as she threw herself on Walter Fane's bosom,—"unless I stay here and die with you."

She clung to him with a frantic eagerness that shewed to what a sad state the cruelty of him who should have screened her from all harm had reduced her mind; and Walter, scarcely able as he was to control his own tears, clasped her fragile form on the impulse of the moment to his heart, as he exclaimed,—

"We will—we will live and die together."

A cry of joy came from her lips, as she said,—

"Yes—yes. Oh! joy—joy—joy!"

Reason came back like a rushing tide to Walter's brain, and he immediately added,—

"God of Heaven! what was I saying? Perish the selfish thought. No, no, no!"

"Oh, unsay it not. Rather again let me drink in those words of hope and joy."

"Hear me—hear me, calmly," he said, in a tone of deep emotion.

"I will—I will. I could listen to you the live-long day, and yet feel no touch of weariness."

"You must not be sacrificed for me."

"It is no sacrifice."

"Yes, yes—and a cruel one too. Let me advise you. I cannot now, situated as I am, help myself, but I can advise you what to do."

"I attend."

"Go from the prison on the first opportunity you have of making your escape from its dismal walls. If no such opportunity offers, you have another chance: claim the protection of the first visitor of rank you see. Declare the cruelty of your father, and get a safe conduct to the streets; then fly to Wainstead, the mercer of the Chepe—for my sake, he will make you welcome."

Alas! how little did Walter Fane suspect the desolation that now reigned in the mercer's house.

"Fly, and leave you here!" said the girl, as if incredulous that she could have heard aright.

"Yes, yes, yes."

"Never!"

"Oh, think again. I am doomed."

"And then am I doomed."

"This is madness. You may, too, aid me, if you yourself escape. If you could get to the mercer's and saw once Jane, the mercer's daughter, she would listen to all you had to say of me."

"She loves you."

"Oh, blissful words, even here in a dungeon's gloom! I love her as I love light, joy, liberty, and Heaven."

He felt the light form of the gaoler's daughter tremble in his arms, from which now she gently withdrew herself, saying,—

"Yes, you love Jane Wainstead. I knew you loved her; but had, in a moment of delirium, forgotten. Oh, would that that moment had been my last!"

"And you, too," said Walter, "such tender love as a brother might bestow upon some dear sister, shall I always feel for you."

"Yes; thank God, I am dying!"

"Dying? Oh, no, no."

"Do not try to make me desolate and wretched, without a hope. What else but a consciousness of coming death could support me now? I will bring you food, Walter; I will tend upon you while I can. When I come not, give a tear to my memory, for I shall be no more."

"Why not—oh, why not adopt the plan I have pointed out to you of escape?"

"I cannot—I cannot."

"Nay, but ——"

"I mean, I have not the heart to do it. Life has no charms to me. As well die here as elsewhere; yet fain would I save you, so that when you were happy with her you loved, and her arms encircled you, you could say there was another who—who ——"

Tears choked her utterance, and she appeared ready to sink into the floor.

"Oh, pride, pride!" she continued, as she wrung her hands, "where are you now?"

Walter knew not what to say. That unwittingly he had lit up a flame of love in the heart of that gentle and confiding creature, he could not be ignorant; but his whole heart was Jane's, and he was too truthful to affect feelings which he really had no pretensions to.

"Be comforted," he said—"be comforted. How many are there who would think that such a heart as yours was, indeed, the dearest possession the world could offer them."

"Hush, hush!" she said. "Talk not to me in such a strain as that. Hush, hush!"

"I will talk in no strain but such as you shall approve," he said, tenderly. "Heaven knows how deep and truly heartfelt is my gratitude towards you."

"Gratitude?"

"Yes; surely 'tis a noble feeling."

"It is. Oh, if I could think now of some plan."

"Plan of what?"

"Self-sacrifice that would save you."

"And can you imagine I should ever be happy in feeling that I owed my own safety to a sacrifice of you?"

"I should die happy."

" And I live wretched."

" No, no, no!"

" Yes, most assuredly so. This dungeon may be my tomb—in all likelihood it will—but much rather would I feel the certainty of such a fate, than owe emancipation from it by inflicting upon you even a passing pang."

" Oh, say no more—say no more."

She turned towards the staircase to leave the dungeon. Walter saw that her steps faltered, and he placed his arm around her to support her as she ascended. Bitterly she wept as she went, and when they reached nearly the top of the stairs, he said,—

" Think you there would be any chance of my liberating myself from the intricate passages of this prison, could I free myself from the dungeon?"

" None—none," she said. " Oh, do not attempt it; they would kill you. Let me think of some means of action that may free you. If that would suffice, you were free now, for see, I could allow you to pass from your dungeon."

" You could?"

" But do not ask you so to do, because I know they would, even before my very eyes, kill you."

" I will take your advice," said Walter, sadly. " God help me!"

" He will—he will."

" Farewell—farewell!"

" Farewell! and yet soon will I come to you again—be assured that I will come to you again. And food, too—alas! alas! I must have been sadly bewildered not to bring you food. I ought to have done so."

" Do not think of that. I have had my allowance from the hands, I presume, of the ruffian Slankey."

They had now reached the dungeon door, and Walter pushed it open for the gaoler's daughter to pass out. Another moment and she was in the passage; she turned and looked in his face, as she said,—

" Heaven knows only if it will be so, but something seems to whisper me that it will be long, if ever, we meet again."

Walter could have told her he had the same sort of presentiment, as, in truth, he had; but he felt that that was not a time to press such a feeling, and he assumed a cheerfulness he was far from feeling, as he said,—

" Nay, do not think so. We shall perhaps meet again in happier circumstances still."

" Pray God we may!" she said. " It is not willingly I close the door upon you."

" Well I believe it; and yet, close it, and may heavenly blessings attend you. If it be but a second place in my heart that I can give you, believe me, it is a sincere one."

She waved her hand, and then closed the door.

CHAPTER XXXIII.

Walter's Fight with the Brutal Governor.

" And his very heart was stricken; and madness seized upon his brain, endowing him with great might."

WALTER lingered for a moment. He had no expectation of hearing the least sound even of the retreating footsteps of the gaoler's daughter, through the thickness of that massive door; but yet he lingered a moment or two, ere, with a deep sigh, he turned to descend the staircase again to the floor of his dungeon. He had taken three steps only, when, with sudden and awful distinctness, he heard a piercing scream, and something fell heavily against the dungeon door.

So utterly unexpected was the alarming sound, that Walter staggered and very nearly fell down the staircase; but quickly recovering himself, he retraced his steps, and, with a bound, gained the door. The scream was instantly repeated, and then he heard the sound as of a heavy blow being struck, and the voice of the brutal governor of the prison said,—

" D——n you! I'll teach you to go to the dungeons of the prisoners. You little thought I was lying in wait for you, when you came here to your young gallant. May all the curses in hell stick to me, if I don't cure you!"

" Oh! mercy—mercy," shrieked the girl.

Then came a bumping against the door, as if the ruffian was, as indeed really was the case, knocking her head against it.

" Villain! monster!" shrieked Walter, in a voice of thunder.

"Ha! ha! ha!" laughed the former; "you don't like it. Oh! oh! oh! I didn't calculate upon this. It's a pleasing addition. Hilloa! my young goldfinch. Hearken again! I'm bumping her head against the dungeon-door. There it goes. Ha! ha! ha!"

"Help—help!" shrieked the girl. "Oh, Walter, Walter, save me!"

Stung to desperation, Walter flung himself against the door with almost superhuman

force, but it resisted him. He tore the nails from his fingers in a vain attempt to grapple it. He shouted—he stormed—and he prayed.

"Villain—villain—monster—unnatural monster! Hold! hold! There is surely a God in Heaven! Mercy! mercy! mercy! I shall go mad—mad—mad!"

"Do you hear it again?" said the former.

There was a loud shriek from the girl, and then bump! bump! again went her head which ought to have been pillowed on the breast of affection, against the dungeon-door.

"Help!—oh, God!—Walter—Walter—help me!" she cried again, and, in her agony, she added, "You have deserted me, Walter, you have deserted me!"

"I shall become a raving lunatic," he said, as for a moment he clasped his head in his hands.

Then, summoning all his energies into one terrific effort, he threw himself recklessly and furiously against the door. The only result was that, in the rebound, he was flung down the stairs on to his dungeon floor, where he lay for a few moments half stunned from the shock of the severe fall. Still the shrieks of the gaoler's daughter rung in his ears, and tended more than aught else to restore him to consciousness. He scrambled to his feet, and seized the iron bar; but, by the time he had done so, all was still. Walter said not a word; but he ascended the steps, and then, with both hands holding the bar in an attitude to strike, he said, in too low a voice for any one to hear outside,—

"Let him beware who next visits me!"

His feelings were wrought up to the highest pitch of agony. No one could, by any possibility, have recognised his voice, so altered was it by the dreadful ordeal he had gone through, and there he stood as still as a statue, and apparently as calm as one waiting what should next ensue without the dungeon. He felt convinced that the young girl who had met with such savage treatment, in consequence of having come to visit him, had been knocked on the head until insensible. It was a dreadful thought; and to have heard her calling upon him for help, too, in such frantic tones, and he so utterly unable to render it to her. Oh! it was enough to produce an accession of madness in such a mind as his. Suddenly now he heard the sound of voices without the dungeon, and by listening attentively he could hear the words that were spoken between the parties.

"Have you killed her?" he heard somebody say.

"What's that to you, if I have?" was the reply of the governor.

"Nothing—nothing."

"Then you needn't have asked. I only bumped her head against the dungeon-door."

"Oh!"

"That was all; just to cure her of visiting the young spark who is here any more."

"To my mind, master, she's took a fancy to him."

"Oh, d—n her, like enough."

"Well, I've brought him his loaf."

"Give it to me."

"Oh, very good."

"I want to speak to him, so I'll cast it down myself. You should have heard him raving just now, Slankey, it would have amused you for a month. Ha! ha! ha!"

"I heard the girl screaming."

"Ah, but you should have heard him; he nearly choked himself, he got into such a rage, and at last I heard him fall down the steps. Ha! ha! ha! I shouldn't wonder but he's lying below now, stunned by his fall, for it was not a trifling one."

"Indeed!"

"No; he tried to burst the door open, Slankey."

"Ah! that won't do at any price; here's the key."

Walter heard the key turned in the lock; and still, with his purpose as fixed as ever, he strained every muscle to give effect to the blow he was about to deal upon the first one who came within his reach upon the opening of the dungeon-door. The bar of iron was of sufficient weight still, notwithstanding so much of it had been eaten away by corrosion in the damp place it had been in so long, to be a formidable weapon in determined hands; moreover, it had length enough to give it a powerful purchase, and death would most probably be the portion of him on whose head it fell. Slowly the key turned in the lock, and now the door began to yield.

"I don't hear anything of him," said the governor.

"No; he's stunned, you may make up your mind to that," observed Slankey.

"I should not be at all surprised, for I heard him go down the steps myself, and, as it was just after one of his drives against the door, I dare say it half killed him."

Slankey laughed, and so did the governor; and then the latter, as he opened the door about six inches, and placed himself in the gap, called out,—

"Hilloa there!"

Scarcely were the words out of his mouth when down came the bar of iron with a hissing sound.

Somehow it struck against the side of the door slightly, which, although it did not diminish its force much, yet directed it off the head of the governor, which, had it struck, it would have smashed directly, and produced instant death. As it was, it came upon his shoulder, breaking the bones it came in contact with, and sinking to the extent of its own depth actually through them. The yell which the cowardly governor gave was heard all over the prison, and he tumbled backwards, to the great astonishment and dismay of Slankey, who was so thoroughly bewildered that he could not, for the life of him, imagine what was going to happen, or what had happened. Then out sprung Walter over the prostrate body of the governor, and, with a shout of defiance, he whirled the iron bar round his head, bringing the flat side of it, with a ringing sound, against the head of Slankey, that it made him see a thousand lights, and he toppled over on to the prostrate form of the screaming governor, as if he were diving into deep water. Walter Fane seemed to be thoroughly maddened. He had vanquished both his foes, and yet he whirled the iron bar about as if it had been a mere straw.

"Come on, villains!" he cried, "come on. Fiends—monsters—who would strike a weak, defenceless girl. Come on, and fight a man, if you dare!"

But there was nobody to come on. Slankey was nearly insensible, and was shaking his head in a very odd manner, while the governor was screaming. Then Walter saw, lying by the door, the insensible form of the girl who loved him, and who, for him, had suffered so much. A pang of agony shot across his heart. To stoop and lift her in his arms was the work of a moment. Then, holding her fragile, light form on his left arm, while, with his right, he held the iron bar, he rushed along the dreary passage, not knowing whither he was going, but shouting as he went in a loud voice,—

"A rescue—a rescue! Help—help! A rescue—a rescue!"

The outcries of the governor upon receiving the frightful wound which Walter had given him were quite sufficient of themselves to alarm the whole prison; and as he went on without any pause howling and screaming, the locality of the disturbance, whatever it was, soon became known.

Hence when Walter, with the insensible form of the gaoler's daughter in his arms, commenced scampering along the long passages which led from the dungeons to the upper light of day, he soon became conscious that footsteps were approaching him in the other direction. But he heeded them not; escape he could not think to lie within any reasonable possibility; and the only object he could now have was to sell his life as dearly as he could.

Some lights flashed upon the darkness, and he saw five or six men approaching him. Then he gently laid down the still inanimate form of the young girl, and, with the iron bar in both hands, he sprung among the advancing men before they could be aware of him, and commenced dealing death and destruction around him.

So sudden, so utterly unexpected, and so terrific was the onslaught, that had he chosen, which he would not, to abandon the gaoler's daughter, there can very little question but he would have broken his way through them all, and perhaps actually made his escape from the prison.

As it was, though, he did not attempt to accomplish that, but continued fighting with the same awful, desperate energy as at first, until his foot slipped, and he fell, upon which the only two who were sufficiently uninjured to do so pounced upon him and held him down to the ground. One of them produced a small chain and an iron clasp, with which he secured Walter's hands together, and then drawing a long breath, the man rose and said,—

"What's it all about?"

"Hang me if I know," said the other. "A very pretty tustle we have had for it, to be sure."

"Kill me," cried Walter—"kill me, cowards; why do you not kill me now you have conquered me?"

"Wait a bit," said one of the men; "we don't do things that way, my fine fellow."

"What's the matter with the governor?" said the other.

"I don't know. Hurt his finger, perhaps, and making all that brawling about it."

"Vincent's killed. I saw the side part of his head go in with one of the pats this fellow gave it."

"Did you?"

"Oh, yes."

"You are afraid to kill me," said Walter.

"Yes, we are," said the man. "Just fancy so, if you like. That won't do with us."

Walter said no more. He was conscious now that the men would not take his life, and he lay with a feeling of such utter despair at his heart, that he would almost have thanked the hand that would have been so kind as to bestow what would have been the boon of death upon him.

"Help! oh—oh—oh—help!" roared the governor. "Help! murder—murder—murder!"

His tones were weaker than before, for he had lost much blood, and his continued bawling since he had received the hurt he had tended not to make his voice any clearer.

"Come along," said one of the men to the other. "This young fellow is safe enough. Let's see what's the matter with the governor."

"Ah, it's amusing hearing him a bellowing," remarked the other, as he followed his companion.

It needed but a very trifling inspection to convince the man that the hurt the governor had received was no trifle; so a plank was brought, and he was placed upon it, and carried past where Walter lay, followed by Slankey, who, although he had sufficiently recovered to get up and walk, kept on shaking his head, as if something very uneasy was the matter with it indeed.

"Oh—oh—oh!" groaned the governor; "I'm a dead man—a dead man. Gently, there, gently, will you, for God's sake! My shoulder is all smashed to pieces."

"Is it?" said Slankey. "The side of my head feels uncommonly odd somehow, I can tell you."

"Curse your head! Oh, dear—oh, dear! That ever I should come to this! Oh—oh—oh—oh!"

"Was it him?" said one of the men, pointing to Walter—"was it him who did it?"

"Yes—yes. Oh, my arm—stop a bit. Have you sent for a leech?"

"We have."

"Then before he comes, I—I will see you do something to him. Get a hot iron and poke his eyes out—a red-hot iron, and do it gently. I want to hear him howl with pain, and then I shall be easier."

Walter Fane disdained to make any reply to this, but he fixed his eyes upon the savage governor with a sweet satisfaction that, at all events, he had succeeded in showing him that, even at a moment when, doubtless, he considered himself free from all mortal retribution, he had been made to suffer much pain and misery.

"Do something to him," again groaned the governor. "I cannot be carried past him in this way and nothing done to him at all. Kill him in some slow way, so that in dying he may suffer much agony."

"We can't," said Slankey—"we can't do it, governor. Don't ask us; you know we can't."

"You shall—you shall."

"Come on."

"No—no—no—I will not. If I were in ten times the agony I am, I will not be carried past him unless some one inflicts a hurt upon him."

"Do it yourself, then," said Slankey.

"I cannot—I cannot. My arm—my arm. I think the iron reached to my very heart. I grow fainter, and am dying. D—n everybody and all the world."

At this moment a new accession of numbers was made to the party, and a man advancing, said,—

"An it please you, here is the leech."

Then came forward a small, neat-looking man, in black, and he looked curiously around him from one to the other of the parties who were present.

"Who is hurt here besides this man?" he said, pointing to the governor, whose face had turned quite livid, and who seemed to be fast sinking into a swoon.

"I am hurt," cried Walter Fane—"hurt in all the feelings that become a man—badly hurt. As for that ruffian, although I deprecate not the exercise of your skill to save him, he richly deserves all the punishment he has received at my hands."

"Indeed!"

"Yes, yes. That hand of his that struck a weak, defenceless girl, I feel assured will never again be raised."

The governor groaned deeply.

"Who may you be?" said the leech, as he glanced at Walter, in passing him to reach the temporary litter on which was placed the wounded governor.

"My name is Walter Fane. If you have the feelings of a Christian man you will seek out Master Wainstead, of the Chepe, and tell him I am wrongfully confined here."

"Oh, pho—pho—pho!" said the leech. "I never carry messages—you need entrust me with nothing of the sort. My sole duty here is to attend to those who want my aid. When here, I see nothing, and hear nothing."

"A discreet leech," said Slankey.

"Oh, a leech of marvellous discretion," remarked another.

"You wretch!" said a third, to Walter; "so you would really try to create a dissension, would you?"

"To all of you," said Walter, "I disdain to reply. As for you, sir leech, I despise you, too, for your want of feeling."

"Very good," said the leech; and he proceeded to make a cursory examination of the governor's arm.

"A bad hurt," he added, "a very bad hurt. These bones will not unite again."

"Oh—oh—oh!" groaned the governor.

"They are too much smashed and splintered. Your arm is lost."

Another series of groans was the response.

"Take him to-bed," said the leech, "and I will do the utmost that my skill suggests for him; but, as I say, it is a bad case, and, for my own part, I would rather the blow that had inflicted so much complicated injury had fallen on the head, and been instantly fatal."

The governor looked upon this as a sentence of death, and he burst forth into such a torrent of invective that it was fearful to hear him. He blasphemed, he swore—he railed against Walter. He called down the curses of the Heaven he the next moment denied the existence of, upon his head, until, exhausted again by the sudden gust of passion, he did actually faint, and then, by the orders of the leech, he was at once conveyed to his chamber.

Walter, after his unsuccessful attempt to excite the compassionate feeling of the leech, had not spoken; he gave up in despair every idea of bettering his condition. He sat upon the floor, and only seemed to all appearance an indifferent spectator of what was going forward before him.

The leech lingered behind when the insensible form of the governor was carried away. He kept speaking to the attendants, and yet he seemed to Walter's perception to be lingering for some purpose, so marked did his wish to be last appear.

Suddenly then he dropped his gold-headed cane close to Walter, and as he stooped to raise it, he said, in a whisper,—

"Be of good heart, I will do what I can for you."

"You will? Oh, a thousand thanks! I ——"

"Hush!"

The leech walked on, and Walter was silent; but, oh, what a gush of new hope had come across his heart.

CHAPTER XXXIV.

The Daught r's Love.

"And he who loved her best of a l,
Was torn by death away;
Her heart's best treasure wrapped in gloom,
Amid the grave's decay."

THE worshipfulle Master Wainstead had been dead two hours, before, by the unremitting attention of the old nurse, who loved her so well, and who had so often tended her with a mother's care, Jane recovered from her swoon into which grief and despair had thrown her. When she did awaken, that shuddering, strange feeling came over her which besets one on awakening from a sleep which has been full of painful dreams.

"Oh, God!" she said, "I am awake again."

Then she glanced around her, and upon finding herself in her old and well-known chamber at her father's, she covered her face with her hands, and bursting into tears, she exclaimed,—

"Is it—is it all a dream?"

"My dear child," said the old nurse, "now don't you be taking on now—it's the will cf Heaven."

"What—what?"

With a full tide came memory to her aid, and instantly she knew all that she had lost, and how much death had bereaved her of, in taking from her the father she so dearly, fondly loved, and who was all the world to her, since poor Walter had so mysteriously disappeared.

There was something dreadful in the style of grief that now beset her. She did not weep for some minutes, but she looked in the face of her old nurse with such an expression of woe, that the old woman wept more to see her in so much grief than she did for him who had gone to the tomb.

To the old, death must seem so much a matter-of-course event, that, let them shrink personally from it as much as they may, they cannot much sympathise with the grief of those who mourn the departed.

But, in this case, the old nurse so loved Jane, that her warmest sympathies were excited to see her unhappy, without any reference whatever to the cause of it.

"Oh, my dear child," she sobbed, "do not look at me in that way, do not, my dear, beautiful Jane, I implore you, or you will break my heart."

"My own is breaking," said Jane.

"No, no, my darling Jane, do not say that—do not say that, or you will kill me."

"Father! father!"

"Alas! alas! he has gone—gone for ever, my dear; but we must all go when our time comes, and at the best, we are not far behind each other."

"Oh, if I were but sure I was dying!" sobbed Jane.

"Don't you speak of dying"

"It is the only theme that now would form to me a grateful one upon which to discourse."

"And you so young, too!"

"Old in sorrow."

"And so beautiful!"

"Fatal beauty! since it has united me to one my very soul abhors. Oh, fatal beauty!"

"Ah, well-a-day, I never was taken with that match with Master Shore. No, no. My opinion was not asked, and when I gave it unasked, I was grievously snubbed by him who is now among the blessed, let us hope. I always endeavour to hope for the best. Oh, now, if the good Lord had been pleased to take Master Shore instead of Master Wainstead, what a blessed release that would have been, to be sure."

"I cannot go home with that man," said Jane.

"But, my darling ——"

"Do not attempt to reason with me, I am desperate now. Before I spoke those vows which now I consider to be wicked ones, inasmuch as in uttering them I falsified my heart before Heaven, I knew the man was selfish and cruel; but now I have found how much more selfish and more cruel he is than ever my imagination painted him."

"Ah!" sighed the old nurse, "I have always heard that husbands don't improve upon acquaintance."

"Has he gone?"

"Oh, deary me, yes, peace go with him—we must all go some day."

"I—I mean, has Shore left the house?"

"I don't know. He made a most marvellous disturbance, but I chid him for it soundly, aye, marry did I most soundly. I dare to say now he is gone."

"Oh, if he would let me be here—if never more he would come near me, I could forgive him the past."

"I will go and ask Simon what he said."

"Do—do, good nurse, ask Simon if he thinks Shore will come back again. Simon is honest, and will tell the truth. Go to him, nurse, go."

"I'm going, but I cannot move my old limbs quite so fast as you can yours, you know; but it's always the way with the young. They think the aged are to fly here and there, and skip about like May-day queens, marry come up."

Jane knew, by experience, that her old nurse meant no unkindness by such speeches as these, and that the best plan was not to answer them, in which case they reached a natural climax and then went out of themselves.

The old woman slowly went down the staircase to speak to Simon, while Jane laid her head upon her hands, and in silence took a painful and sad survey of her position.

"What! oh, what is to become of me now?" she thought. "Walter lost to me—dead! and now my father—all gone, and I left to the mercy of such a man as Shore. Oh, horror, horror! How wearily will my days creep onward. How sadly will each morn break—how dismally will each evening come. I shall never—never again know a moment's joy. I can but sigh for the oblivion of the grave, which will soon, I hope, close over me and my sorrows."

Suddenly she felt a hand gently touch her arm; she looked up, and by the dim light she could see a tall, thin figure standing before her. Surprise prevented the alarm which it gave rise to from breaking into a scream, and before she opened her lips the stranger spoke.

His accents were low, and soft, and musical; eminently persuasive too were they, and it would have been something outrageous to have screamed after he had spoken, however impulsively she might have done so beforehand.

"Lady," he said, "be not alarmed that I am here, and that you know me not. That mystery surrounds my coming I admit, but, oh, believe me, I come as a sincere friend to you in your deep distress—a friend devoid of selfishness, except so far as he felt the pleasure of seeing the good, the young, and the beautiful. If you refuse my proffered aid, refuse it gently, and I shall find so much grace in that refusal as shall take from it the sting of rejection."

"Who are you?" said Jane; for a thought come over her that this being might not be mortal.

"My name is Grandola. It is, doubtless, one utterly unknown to you—but I knew well your noble, kind, generous, gifted father, who, alas! is now no more."

"He was noble, kind, and generous," said Jane. "Ah, you must have known him well."

"You find I did by the description I give you of him. You are unhappy! and, oh! fain would I make one effort to alter the prospect of your existence,—to pluck from your heart the thorns that now rankle there, and plant in their stead love's dearest flowers! I would be your good genius."

The air of romance which was thrown around these words was well calculated to subdue the prudence of Jane, and to interest her much in the conversation of the mysterious stranger. She forgot at the moment that she knew him not—she forgot that his being there was an intrusion, and that how he got there was a very great mystery indeed, and she bent forward listening to him with an interest she paused not to scrutinize.

"Yes," he exclaimed, "that is the glorious position to which I would fain elect myself—I would be your good genius!"

"My good genius?"

"Aye, and save you from all ill—stand between you and all evil. I would watch over you even as some young mother, with throbbing heart, plays the part of sentinel over her slumbering babe."

"Are you human?"

"Ask me not, but let me paint to you in speech of human texture what I would fain do to rescue you from the deep sadness of the present prospect of such affairs that lies before you."

"Go on, go on."

"The man who, taking the advantage of a good man's weakness, had you dragged to the altar to become his unwilling bride is so much ingrained in selfishness, that he will never, of his own mind's suggestion, leave you free."

"Never—never."

"There are some spirits who would scorn to keep in trammels the heart that loves them not."

"Yes—yes."

"But his is not one of those. He would see you drop into the grave, worn out with grief, ere he would say to you, Jane, leave me, for I see you cannot love me."

A kind of strange awe crept over Jane as the man spoke, for he seemed to be able to read her very heart.

After a slight pause he continued—

"And thus it is that you yourself, repenting you of the rash vows you have spoken, must break asunder the bonds that hold you to a man you cannot love. You do not hate him even, for such a feeling belongs not to you."

"No—no. I hate no one."

"But would free yourself from him you cannot love?"

"Alas, alas! What power have I to do so?"

"What power?"

"Yes. I am helpless. How can I burst asunder bonds that have been formed strong enough to hold the strongest? Bonds forged in life, and only with death to be unrivetted."

"Nay, you reckon hastily."

"Indeed!"

"Yes. You have a power common to all, of resistance to such a state—you have an alternative."

"Name it to me."

"Flight!"

"Flight, flight! Ah, no! Without friends, without means, I am helpless, and have no such power surely. Whence could I fly to? Impossible—quite impossible!"

"You are wrong."

"No, no. My fate is to remain and suffer. Heaven has cast upon me its wrath, and my existence must now be summed up in the one word—endurance."

"So would not I be trampled on by a fellow creature."

"I am powerless!"

"There are those full of power who will lend you strength. There are those who have wealth at command who will tell you to take freely. I tell you, Jane, I hear that your one great possession is more than sufficient to raise you up hosts of defenders."

"Possession?"

"Yes. Your marvellous beauty!"

Jane shrank back.

"Your most marvellous beauty," added the stranger. "The shield of a protection would be thrown over you which Shore might spend a life time in battling at in vain.

Power you would have to silence such a clamourer. Riches would be your sport. Flashing diamonds, only equalled by your eyes. Troops of willing slaves, who, but for a passing glance, would peril life to make around you a perpetual summer of delight!"

"And have I listened for this?" cried Jane. "I see my heart's weakness—I have listened thus far to the tempter."

"Tempter?"

"Yes, tempter. Now I know your purpose. I am unhappy—I am full of grief, but I am not the wretch that you would make me. Help—help!"

"Peace, Jane. You know not what you say."

"Help—help! Simon—Simon!"

"Ha, ha! As you please."

"Simon—Simon—Simon!"

"Here," said Simon, popping his head into the room.

The stranger was gone. How he had disappeared, or where he had gone to, Jane could have no idea. All she could be aware of was, that a moment before he stood on the opposite side of a small table which had been between them during the dialogue, and now he was not there.

CHAPTER XXXV.

Simon takes Vengeance on the Faded Gallant.

"And in those days he who had a strong hand found it advisable to settle his own quarrels and leave his adversary to the law, if he chose, rather than do so himself."

Simon was silent for some moments after he had announced his presence in the chamber where Jane had just had so mysterious an interview with the stranger whose disappearance was as odd as his appearance there. In truth, Simon had not seen him at all, for, however he contrived to get away with such great speed, it was done the moment before Simon popped his head into the room. And now that lusty personage looked at Jane scrutinisingly, as he said, in much of his usual tone,—

"You called 'help!'"

"I did Simon, I did; there was some one here."

Simon strode into the room, and fastened the door on the inside in a moment.

"Some one here?" he said.

"Yes, Simon, there was. What are you going to do?"

"Find him."

With this extremely brief explanation, Simon made a rapid, but very clear and systematic search of the room; and when he had quite satisfied himself that no one was there, he turned to Jane, and said,—

"Been asleep"

"No—no."

"Yes, you have dreamt it."

"But there is the window, Simon."

"Couldn't do it."

"Then he who was here could not have been mortal."

"Humph! All fancy, Jane; all fancy."

"Could it be possible imagination could paint so vivid a picture? I could almost repeat every word he said. My heart, though, is so full of grief, Simon, that it may be I am mad."

"Mad? Pho!—rubbish—no!"

"I might be happier."

"Ah!"

"If I were dead, though. Then, indeed, Simon, I should know peace. Alas! my poor, poor father."

"Dead—gone. No use grieving—all gone. Ha! don't mean to grieve myself. Leave it off—don't care for anybody."

"Oh Simon—Simon!"

"Don't want anybody to care for me—never did. Ain't sorry a bit. Won't—shan't."

Simon looked up at the ceiling, now satisfied that he had been as contradictory as circumstances would permit him to be with his present opportunities.

"Then it must have been a waking dream," murmured Jane.

"Told you it was."

"Simon, has Shore gone?"

"Yes."

"Long ago, Simon?"

"Yes. Told the old woman to come and let you know. Would stay down stairs gossiping—old fool. Sat down in the middle of the shop when she heard you call out for help. Nearly tumbled over her. Old women no use—ought to be suppressed."

Simon seldom hazarded an opinion. He generally kept them all profound secrets, but this was one which he had before, upon more than one occasion, given utterance to,

and therefore, the seal of secrecy as regarded it being once broken, he had no hesitation in propounding it when necessary. It was a very ungallant opinion, but then Simon was more candid than gallant, by a great deal; and as he really thought what he said, why, he had no hesitation at all in saying it.

"And he has gone, Simon?" said Jane.

"Hem!"

"Do you think he will come back again?"

"No."

"He will not—he will not! Oh, Simon, do you think—can you flatter me by a hope that Shore will not want me to go to his house again, now?"

"Of course he will."

"Ah me! The new-born hope has vanished."

"He won't come here, though, for we don't agree somehow. Depend upon it, he will send for you. I wouldn't go; stay here, if you like; it's all yours."

"But force would drag me hence."

"Humph! Should like to see 'em try it. Quite willing to play at cracked crowns with any of them."

"Alas! Simon, I have spoken vows which keep I must. There is no hope for me on this side of the grave."

Simon whistled a tune, and walked down the stairs. The moment he got into the shop some one ran out of it, and, from the glance he caught of the figure, he thought it was the faded gallant, and for a second time Simon made a rush after that individual, and for the second time was foiled in catching him, by a similar circumstance, viz., tumbling over somebody on his rush to the door; for whereas he fell over Shore on a previous occasion, he now tumbled over the old nurse, who, as he had reported, had sat down plump in the middle of the shop, upon hearing Jane's cries for help.

"D—n it!" said Simon; "you are always in the way."

"Murder!" said the old nurse.

"What the deuce do you sit there for?"

"What's the matter?"

"Why you occupy all the floor."

"But our dear Jane?"

"Might have been murdered for all the good you would have been to prevent it."

"Murdered!"

"Yes, to be sure, while you were sitting down there. Ah, you do well to scramble up now that the danger is over."

"The Lord have mercy upon us all, Simon!"

"Ah!"

"I have had another fright."

"That man—what did he say?"

"Why, Simon, all he said was 'ah!'"

"Oh!"

"No, he didn't say 'oh!' it was 'ah!' and he knocked a number of the things about in the shop, and terrified me."

"Why didn't you call me?"

"Oh, I was too frightened."

"Humph! What's the good of old women? Providence overlooked the fact that women had a propensity to get old, and consequently made no provision against it. Ah!"

Simon went to the door, and looked right and left, but nothing could be seen of the faded gallant. Then he thought there might be a small chance of his coming a third to the shop, since he had had the audacity to come twice, and escaped with impunity.

There was, next door to the mercer's, a very deep door-way, indeed, and into this did Simon get, resolved to keep one eye on his own door, so that if a customer came in he could serve him, and then pop out again; or, if the faded gallant should make his appearance, he should be able at once to lay hold of him, which was what he, Simon, had been wishing for some time most devoutly to do.

Simon, when once he took a thing into his head, was not one to give it up readily; therefore he waited with the most exemplary patience for nearly half an hour before the reward of his perseverance appeared in the shape of the faded gallant coming down the Chepe, with that unsteady gait which shewed that he had been sacrificing at the shrine of Bacchus.

There was a half cowardly, half blustering appearance about him, which showed that although he had taken enough to endow him with a little false courage, yet it had not entirely obliterated his real character of cowardice. What on earth he could want by coming so repeatedly to the mercer's on that evening was a mystery. That he had some project on hand was quite clear, or he would not have been so persevering in his visits. Probably between each he had applied himself to the wine cup or to the ale flagon for assistance, and hence arose his present condition.

There was scarcely any one but himself in the Chepe, so that as he came along Simon had a good view of him, and he saw him pause every now and then, and wink with tipsy gravity, as if he were the cleverest person on the face of the earth, and at that moment was perpetrating some splendid and complicated piece of chicanery.

"Confound him! what does he mean?" muttered Simon.

The faded gallant now, as he neared the mercer's shop, slackened his pace, and placed his finger knowingly against the side of his fiery nose, and then he shook his head waggishly, as though he would say,—"Who but me? Ah!" Then he came on a little further, after which he looked all around, and seeing nobody, he gathered fresh courage, and assuming a lofty air and swaggering braggadocia, he moved on a step or two further, and then suddenly he turned round, and went back a little. His courage had failed him from sudden mental suggestions concerning the possible danger he was running into. Then again he paused, and slowly turned round towards the mercer's shop, as if some new impulse had revived him a little.

"What is he at?" muttered Simon. "An' he don't come on, I shall be off after him."

But the faded gallant, as his evil stars would have it, did come on now, until he got quite close to the half-door. He ran past, then, in order as he did so, no doubt, to catch, from the passing glance he got, the useful information of whether Simon was within or not. He appeared to be abundantly satisfied with the scrutiny, for now and again he laid his finger by the side of his nose, and wagged his head, and laughed.

"I'll make you laugh on the other side of your mouth," said Simon, in a low tone, to himself.

Now the faded gallant went to the door, and, as with one hand he grasped one of the door-posts for support, he looked in, and even where he was, Simon could hear him say,—

"Ah!"

Simon, however, was not likely to remain long where he was. He walked as demurely out from his hiding-place as if he were not quite delighted, and he stood behind the faded gallant, who was dreadfully frightening the old nurse.

"Ancient friend, ah!" said the faded gallant. "Elderly old crone, on your life's sake, answer what I shall condescend to propound unto thee—ah!"

"Yes, worshipful sir," said the nurse.

"Is the fair Mistress Shore here?"

"Yes, worshipful sir."

"Oh! Now, my piece of feminine antiquity, tremble for your life, if you do not answer me truly my next question. Tremble, I say; for, by my valour, I'll take a hundred lives if I am deceived."

"Oh, be merciful, noble sir! We are an afflicted family."

"Oh! ah!"

"Have mercy upon us!"

"Ah! Well, I will take that into my gracious consideration; but what I do desire to know truly is, where a knave they call Simon is. Where is he, ancient woman?" continued the faded gallant.

"Out, noble sir."

"Out—oh, out?"

"Yes, worshipful sir."

"Then I am sorry, for I wanted to thrash the pestilent knave; and, perhaps, I would have taken his life. His life—ha! ha!"

"The Lord be good to us, sir! I believe that we are only two lone females now in the house, noble sir."

"Really! Then I'll come in."

The faded gallant's faded head was about three inches from the outer door-post against which he supported himself, and at this juncture Simon, who was unable to exert any more patience, doubled his fist, and gave the head such a whack on the other side, that it went against the door-post with an alarming sound, and made the faded gallant fancy that the end of the world was come, and chaos had commenced with his head. Before, then, he could in the smallest degree recover, Simon up with his foot and shot him into the shop with a vengeance that sent him to the further end of it in a moment. Simon closed the door, saying,—

"Don't brawl here, we won't have it;" and then he looked at the faded gallant, who lay huddled up in a corner, and probably never, in all his life, had looked so entirely done for or faded as he now looked. He was completely bewildered. The drink he had had, the stunning blow on one side of the head and the concussion on the other, and then the kick, had altogether formed a combination of disagreeables that were amply sufficient to distract any one's animal economy, and no wonder, therefore, that when Simon said to him,—"What brought you here, my friend?" he only glared at him, like a man bereft of sense, in answer.

"How came you here?" cried Simon.

A confused response, of which nothing intelligible could be made, was all the faded gallant could execute.

"Oh, dear—oh, dear!" said the nurse; "whenever will my feelings get the better of all this, I wonder?"

"Be off with you up stairs," said Simon. "A nice article you are, to tell the first bully that chooses to ask you, that Jane is up stairs, and nobody to defend her."

"Oh, but ——"

"Be off with you, old fool." Then turning again to the faded gallant, he said,—"How came you here?"

"I—I—oh!" gasped the rascal. "I was kicked in. What's all the bells ringing for? Oh, my head!"

"What do you want here?"

"Nothing—oh, nothing. Oh, great sir, nothing."

"And yet this is the third time this evening you have come here."

"I didn't want to come, really. Some dreadful person kicked me behind, and I came right in whether I would or no."

"You have some object in coming here, and if you wish to save your life, you will tell me what that object was. You know best, though, whether your life is worth saving or not."

"Oh, yes—yes, to me, worthy sir."

"Don't call me worthy sir. What did you want here?"

"There's a hundred church bells ringing in my head."

"Serves you right. As you don't seem disposed to answer, here goes."

Simon took a large clasped knife from his pocket of very rough workmanship, but it looked a formidable article, and the moment the faded gallant saw it he cried out,—

"Mercy! mercy! Great, illustrious individual, I will tell all."

"Do, or I shall cut your throat."

"Imprimis, then, I was to have ten crowns for delivering a letter this night to Mistress Shore."

"Where is it?"

"Now, on my word and honour, I ——"

Simon unclasped the knife, and laid hold of the faded gallant by the hair of his head.

"Murder!" he cried; "here it is;" and he produced a folded paper tied round with green silk.

"Very good," said Simon. "Now, who employed you?"

"One Peter."

"Peter Who?"

"Strangeways, a man of my Lord Hastings; and now I have told you all, great sir, let me go."

"Hold; you don't go yet. It's near to nine o'clock, and the mayor will be round with his men."

"What have I done, oh! worshipful Master Simon? I am, in innocence, strongly resembling a new-born baby."

"Very likely. Do you know one Jacob, a poor 'prentice to Master Snafflings, the bowyer, opposite?"

The faded gallant pretended to be trying to recollect, and then, with a well-acted air of candour, he said,—

"No—no—no; oh, no."

"Indeed!"

"Oh! no—no—no; never heard of him."

"Well, some people have short memories, and he must be brought to your mind somehow or another. You induced that poor half-witted fellow to rob his master."

"I—I?"

"Yes, you. Hark! here comes the mayor's men, going their rounds. I hear them now."

The faded gallant's fiery nose took a blueish hue, as he now began to fear there was no hope for him. In a whining, hypocritical tone, he said,—

"Oh! good sir, kick me—knock me on the head—have me ducked somewhere, but don't give me to the mayor's men."

"I will."

"Nay, think again; have mercy, kind Christian; I was not always the odd sort of fellow I am."

"We must all have a beginning," said Simon.

"Yes, yes—as you say. Oh! what a powerful wit, and an accurate judgment you have; really, it's astounding."

"Ain't it?"

"It is, indeed; I am bewildered at it quite; and, go where I will, be in what company I may, I shall always raise my voice, and say, Gentles, all of you, if you want a man of extraordinary judgment—if you want a man of powerful and overwhelming wit, you must go to Master Wainstead's, the mercer, in the Chepe, and see Simon, his man."

"Eugh!" said Simon.

"Good night—God bless you!" said the faded gallant; "it's affecting to part with you so soon. Will you have a cup of canary? You won't. Well—well—another time. Farewell! angels guard you!"

The faded gallant crawled to the door; but, ere he did so, Simon went out and called to the mayor's men, who soon came up with the cry of,—

"Evil doers—evil doers!"

"One," said Simon, as he pitched the faded gallant among them. "He's a robber, and, I believe, something worse."

The faded gallant gave a loud groan, and laid himself flat upon the pavement.

"What has he done?" asked one of the mayor's men.

"Worse than all wrong himself," said Simon, "for he has induced a poor fellow, named Jacob, who had not wit enough to know what he was about, to rob his master."

"We'll take him, and lodge him in the new sanctuary, by the bridge," said one; "come along."

"I'm dead," said the faded gallant. "Ah! but I feel very ill, and, if left here, shall satisfy everybody and every one by dying very soon, you may depend."

"Come along; get up."

"Ah!" said the faded gallant, as he assumed a sitting posture; "does your malice really extend beyond the grave? Don't I tell you I'm a dying man?"

"No nonsense," said one of the mayor's men, as he gave the faded gallant a poke with the end of a stout halbert; "no nonsense—get up at once, my friend."

"Now, save me from such friends," said the faded gallant, as he scrambled to his feet upon finding there was really no other resource. "Simon What's-your-name, you are sending to prison the man who could tell you something you very much want to know, but who, of course, will now keep it all to himself."

Simon advanced a step, and looked anxious; then he suddenly turned back, saying,—

"Psha! knows nothing."

"Don't I!" said the gallant; "don't I! You are a fool, Simon; you are sending to prison the only man in London who could really tell you what you would give one of those long ears of yours to be made acquainted with."

"We cannot stay here while you are prating," said one of the mayor's men.

"Hold a moment," said Simon; "what is the subject of your news, bully?"

"Ah—that's it!"

"Then I can come to no judgment upon it; take him away; I will bring Master Snafflings, the bowyer, against him in the morning, and satisfy Sir Peter Knivett that I have had him arrested on no weak grounds."

"As you please—ha! as you please," said the faded gallant. "I know what I know. Bully in all your teeth! I am a soldier, and have fought on the same field with King Edward."

"And yet you will sleep to-night in the New Sanctuary," said the chief of the mayor's men; "and, if you do not come on at once, you will have the chance of a broken head along with you."

"Simon—Simon."

"What now?"

"You want to know if Walter Fane ——"

"Yes—yes. Hold a moment!" cried Simon, as he rushed forward, and seized the faded gallant by the arm. "Tell me that—tell me—go on!"

"You want to know—ha! ha! I thought I should bring you to your senses—you want to know if Walter Fane is alive or dead? Ha! ha! ha!"

"I do—I do."

"Don't you think I will tell you? Ha! ha! ha! Really, now, the extreme modesty of some people! Why, now, I came to tell you, but you must needs kick me into the shop, and then you must needs give me to the mayor's men."

Simon made a gesture of impatience, as he said,—

"I don't believe a word of that; you may know what has become of poor Walter Fane, but you did not come to tell me. Another errand brought you here; and now, only the present jeopardy you are in induces you to endeavour to buy yourself off, by offering to tell me."

"We cannot wait here, Master Simon," said the chief of the mayor's men, "or we shall get into trouble."

"One moment," said Simon; "if you can tell me where Walter Fane is, you shall be free. Now, take him away."

"Hold!" cried the faded gallant; "I will tell you; he is in the prison of the Black-friars."

"He lives?"

"I suppose so; he was arrested, and taken there."

Simon looked in the face of the faded gallant, as he said,—

"I think you are speaking the truth; if a lie, you shall be found out and punished, if you were to hide in the bowels of the earth. Let him go; I will undertake that Master Snafflings shall not press the charge against him."

"And we have been detained here for nothing?"

"No," said Simon; "here are two groats; get yourself a cup of something, but let him go."

The mayor's men released their hold of the faded gallant, who once again assumed a swaggering air of importance, and said, "Ah!" as he stretched himself up. The mayor's men passed on, and then Simon beckoned to the faded gallant, saying,—

"Come here; I want to talk to you."

"Another time, my friend, when you catch me," exclaimed that individual, and he ran down the Chepe as fast as his legs would carry him.

CHAPTER XXXVI.

The Chamberlain's Secret Visit to the City.

And, with a perseverance worthy of a better cause, did my Lord Hastings pursue Jane, even to her husband's house.

HASTINGS had that sort of passion for Jane which seemed to increase as obstacles sprung up to thwart him. Day by day he was becoming more angry at his failure, and more resolved, if possible, upon converting it into success. Engaged as he was in political intrigues, he found what Loyala had said to be true—namely, that this passion for the mercer's daughter would absorb all his faculties, and deprive him of that steadiness of purpose, and real power of action in other affairs, which were so essential to their success. Instead, however, of considering such a conviction as an argument for quitting the prosecution of an intrigue, in which he had hitherto been unsuccessful, he took a strange view of it in quite another way, and said to himself,—

"I must now, for a brief space, bend all the energies I possess upon this point, so that I may either thoroughly convince myself of the impossibility of making Jane mine, or actually succeed in conveying her off, despite all resistance."

Having, then, made up his mind thus far, he debated seriously within himself what immediate steps he could take, and the result of his cogitations was, that he determined to make a secret expedition into the city himself, to try to deliver a note to Jane, a measure in the accomplishment of which several emissaries he had employed had signally failed. He accordingly attired himself in a plain sort of apparel, such as might become some respectable citizen, and he took care to rid himself of every insignia of his rank at court. Wrapping then round him a mantle of sombre hue, he started into the city. Perhaps my Lord Hastings had not laid down for himself any particular plan of operations by which he hoped to deliver his note—probably he resolved to be only guided by circumstances; but he made his way first of all direct to Shore's house. It was the evening time, just at that period when the last rays of the daylight are fading away in the obscurity of the coming night, and when objects seem more confused from the small quantity of light that is thrown around them than they would be in the utter darkness. He walked down the Chepe, and, as he did so, he cast a passing glance at the mercer's house.

"Were she still there," he muttered, "I should have a better chance; but that husband of hers is dreadfully vigilant. Nevertheless the letter I have written will, I think, produce some effect."

This letter to which Lord Hastings alluded, we may as well state, purported to come from some one who knew where Walter Fane was confined, but who durst not put such into writing, for fear of a miscarriage of the note, but who would, providing she, Jane, would come unattended to a place named, give her every information, not only with regard to his arrest, but the manner in which his release could be effected.

He intended, if this should so far succeed, to meet her himself alone, and to tell her that Walter Fane had been by mistake imprisoned, but that his release would be immediately obtained, by an explanation to the Duke of Gloster personally by some one who could declare to Walter's identity. He then meant to offer to escort her to the Duke of Gloster, and by such a piece of trickery get her to his own house, after which, in those lawless times, all attempts to rescue her, even if it were known where she was, would be abortive.

Thus was poor Jane to be betrayed through her best affections, and we generally find that those are the weapons which knaves usually turn against the breasts of the honest, the confiding, and the honourable. The great difficulty was now to get the note delivered into Jane's own hands, and how to do that my Lord Hastings knew not, except it was to be done boldly by walking into Shore's house and asking to see her. Of all plans, this was the most likely to be effectual. It was simple and straightforward, and, the more Hastings thought of it, the better he really liked its appearance.

"Yes," he said, "I will do that boldly; and if even Shore meets me and questions me, it is but a failure, and I can trust to the impulse of the moment to get myself out of the scrape the best way I can."

Hurrying on, Hastings reached Lombard-street, and paused at the door of Shore's shop and house. All seemed dark and dreary within the house, except at one window, from which a small twinkling light gleamed.

"What if Shore be out," thought Hastings, "and that one light comes from Jane's chamber? That would be fortunate. Well, well, be it so or not, here goes for a chance, at all risks."

As he spoke, he entered the shop. At first he thought there was no one there, but he was quickly, as well as disagreeably convinced, by hearing a man's voice say,—

"What business, worshipful sir?"

"Oh, business! I—I—who are you, my friend?"

"What should I be but the master of the house? Whom did you expect else to question you?" said Shore, advancing a pace or two towards his visitor.

"Oh, you are Master Shore?"

"I am."

"Then—a—a—you sell gold and silver plate?"

"Ay, truly."

"Well, some other time—a—when it is lighter, I will come and look at some ——"

"It is lighter," said Shore, suddenly uncovering a screen from before a light, and allowing its full glare to fall upon the face of the high chamberlain.

Shore certainly had seen Hastings several times, but then he had been surrounded by all the trappings and appointments of his office, which made him look a very different man, indeed, from what he now appeared, so that, although he thought he had some recollection of the face before him, Shore could not name the owner of it on the moment.

Not knowing how far Shore's knowledge of his face might extend, Hastings was at first disposed to shrink from the light which cast so full a glare upon him, but when he heard no word of recognition, and saw that Shore really knew him not, he assumed a bolder aspect, and said,—

"Well, Master Shore, do you know me?"

"I do not."

"But it is not necessary to know a man who comes with such an introduction as this."

Hastings, as he spoke, produced a small bag of gold nobles, the musical sound of which, as he gave it a slight shake, came sweetly and pleasantly to the ears of Shore, who said immediately,—

"Shall I show you, worshipful sir, my poor stock of goods?"

"Not now—not now," said Hastings; "I only wished to-night to be certain that you lived here. Another time I will call, and hope to suit myself with what I want."

Shore began to get suspicious, and when Hastings added, "You were recently married," he got doubly so.

"Well?" he said.

"Oh, nothing; only so was I."

"Indeed!"

"Yes, and to too pretty a wife. Oh, Master Shore, Master Shore, I am beset by court gallants."

"By the saints, and so am I, good sir."

"Are you really. Is your wife handsome?"

"You must be a stranger in London, friend."

"I am from Westminster, and know London scarcely more than by common repute."

"From Westminster?—a goodly city."

"True—true. I promised to bring home something to my wife, and hearing a fair report of you as a dealer, I have made bold to call upon you."

"Not more bold than welcome," said Shore, who always had an eye to business in the midst of all his anxieties.

"I thank you, worshipful sir. Will it please you to step to a neighbouring tavern, and taste some canary?"

"I cannot," said Shore. "My wife is at her father's house, and I have sent my only serving-man with a message to her to come home; therefore am I, being alone, compelled to keep house."

"I'm sorry for it," said Hastings, "and wish you a good even, sir."

"Good even."

Hastings muttered a curse as he left the shop.

"At her father's house, is she, in the Chepe," he muttered. "Well, I will go there and see what luck will befall me. I can but fail. Let me consider. I can buy something there. I wonder now an the knave who kicked my serving-man be there?"

Hastings had a suspicion that it would not be the pleasantest thing in the world to come across that same knave, and be recognised by him; but he comforted himself with the idea that he could not be known; so on he walked to the mercer's house in the Chepe, quite ignorant of the fact of Wainstead's death, which Loyala, although he knew it, had omitted to inform him of. It was very provoking, but when Hastings reached the Chepe again, he found the mercer's shop shut up.

"Curses on them all!" he cried, impatiently. "They seem intent upon thwarting me, somehow."

He paused a few moments to consider, and then, nodding his head after the manner of a man who has made up his mind to do something desperate and abide by the consequences, he knocked heavily at the mercer's door.

Now, Simon could not be always at home, and it happened unluckily that this was one of the times that he was out. In point of fact, he had gone to make inquiries concerning Walter Fane, for whom he entertained so great an affection, although he expressed it in so odd a way.

Had my Lord Hastings been aware of this fact, and that there was no one in the house besides Jane and the old nurse, the former having resolved to remain there until her father's funeral should be over, he would have made some more vigorous demonstration than a mere knock upon the old oaken panels of the door.

The knock produced no effect, and it was not until he had repeated it thrice, and the last time with very great vehemence, that the old nurse came out upon the balcony, and said,—

"Is that you?"

"Yes, it's I," said Hastings.

"And not Simon? Go away, jackanapes—go away."

"My good woman ——"

"Go away. There are no good women here. Marry come up, indeed! Good woman, quotha!"

"I don't mean to offend you."

"Then what do you want? Hoity toity, indeed! Good woman!—marry come up! Good woman, quotha!"

"Confound the old fool!" muttered Hastings. "If ever you happen to utter a stray word that is offensive to an old woman, she never will let you hear the last of it."

"Ah—ah!" continued the old nurse; "a nice time of the day, the saints be good to us! an we are to be knocked up to be called good women! The saints preserve us from devils and conjurors say I. Marry come up!"

"Why, mother, what is the matter?"

"Mother yourself, good man Jack—mother yourself! An I stay here to be made a show of, I am past thinking!"

So saying, the old nurse, thinking, doubtless, it was advisable to have the last word, hobbled from the balcony into the house again to tell Jane how grievously she had been insulted by being called a good woman.

"Now, what am I to do?" thought Hastings. "Something strikes me there is no man in the place. Ha! who is this slinking along as if he had just cut a throat or a purse?"

Hastings placed his hand upon the hilt of a long two-edged dagger with which he was provided, and fixed his eyes intently upon the figure of a man which was coming crawling along by the houses, as if extremely desirous of escaping from observation.

This figure that thus came creeping along was no other than the faded gallant. If the imperious and haughty chamberlain knew him, it was, at all events, not very likely that he would, under existing circumstances, do him the honour of a recognition. With an imprecation, Hastings withdrew into a doorway, and then kept an eye on the faded gallant and his movements. That he was bound for the mercer's house appeared now but too apparent, for he walked stealthily towards its door, and placed his ear flat against it, as if to listen to any sounds of life that might come from within.

"What on earth," thought Hastings, "can he want there, the villain and fool to boot!"

Truly the faded gallant was a mysterious personage, for he now walked over to the other side of the way, and took a careful survey of the house. Then he nodded to himself several times, as if he had come to some very accurate and most important conclusion; after which he crossed over again to the mercer's, and taking from the roadway

as he went several very minute stones, he cast one of them up at the latticed window of the first floor.

The moment he had done this he seemed to consider it was necessary to get out of the way, and, as his evil fortune would have it, he popped, with great precipitation, into the very doorway which was occupied by Lord Hastings. So unexpected was this movement on the part of the faded gallant, and so suddenly was it executed, that the chamberlain had no time to get out of the way, or to signify that the doorway was already occupied. The faded gallant not only trod on his illustrious toes, but gave him such a hard punch in the stomach, that for a moment he had neither breath nor strength to enable him to speak or resist. As soon, however—and that was in a very few moments—as the violence of the shock had subsided, Hastings grappled the faded gallant by the throat, and with such a string of anathemas as might well have made any one's hair stand on end, he shook him to and fro as if he had been a reed.

"Now, beshrew me!" he shouted; "what villain's trick is this? By the holy rood, I'll have your life!"

"Murder!" cried the faded gallant. "As I am a nobleman, I knew not any one was here. Spare me, gentle sir—spare me! You don't know who I am. You—really, and this old doublet, that I have put on by way of a disguise, will not bear rough handling."

"Who are you, rascal?" cried Hastings.

"Truly, you do not ask the question in the kindest of tones; but if you must really know who I am, my good friend, I am my Lord Hastings, the lord high chamberlain of his majesty, in disguise."

"Curses on the fellow!" muttered Hastings; "he must know me by my voice, even in this dark place."

Even as he spoke, he dragged the faded gallant out of the dense shadow of the doorway, nor stopped until he brought him to a corner where a miserable oil lamp was shedding a wretched ray of light around it.

"Now," he said, "look at me."

The faded gallant did so, and then he knew the chamberlain in a moment. Fear took possession of him, for he really had not the least idea precisely of who it was he had encountered, and had only attempted to pass himself off as Lord Hastings, because that name came uppermost to his thoughts, and it was popularly rumoured that he was in the habit of going about and mixing among the people in disguises.

Now, however, the faded gallant considered that he had indeed fallen into the lion's den, and so impressed was he with a sense of his danger, that he made a desperate effort to escape from the grasp of the chamberlain. Hastings, however, was by no means willing to quit his hold of his prisoner, and rather a fierce struggle, for a few moments, took place between them. Getting one of his hands at liberty, Hastings drew the poniard which he had before taken from its sheath but returned again. The moment the faded gallant saw the glittering blade of the weapon he surrendered, and, slipping down to the ground, he cried,—

"Have mercy on me, noble sir! I am your prisoner, and will obey you in anything. Don't kill me, for the sake of my wife and fifteen small children, all under the age of nine!"

"Now by the king's life!" said Hastings, "it would be well to rid society of such as you at once."

"No—no, I assure your lordship—no. I am useful sometimes, and always ornamental, my lord."

"How dared you attempt to pass yourself off as Lord Hastings?"

"Oh, my lord—my lord, don't consider for a moment that I deserve anything like very severe reprehension for such an act."

"And why not?"

"I beg your lordship to consider it in its proper light, namely, as a delicate compliment to your greatness, your valour, and your virtues. I did, I own, want to pass myself off as somebody whose very name was sufficient to strike everybody dumb, and at once secure me the most wonderful respect. I said to myself, then 'Who is the greatest, the wisest, and the most admirable of the nobility?' and my heart answered the question at once in your lordship's favour, and therefore was it that I made so bold as to call myself by your most honourable name."

"Do you mean to say you knew me not, villain?"

"As Heaven and all the saints are my judges, I did not till I saw your noble and highly honourable face."

"I think I have seen you before."

"Doubtless, my lord. I have had the honour twice or thrice to attempt to do some service to one Antonio Vassa."

"Ah, indeed!"

"Yes, noble sir; and once, nearly twelve months since, your lordship was pleased to speak to me concerning one Brandies, a Jew, who ——"

"Enough—enough," said Hastings; "I do remember you now."

The faded gallant had by this time got upon his legs again; and as Lord Hastings put up his poniard he considered his danger over. He gave his moustachios a ferocious curl, and, as he stamped with his foot, he said, in something of his old strain, which his danger had for a time subdued,—

"Oh, I am a soldier of fortune; one whom the jade has oftener kicked than favoured. Oh, I love rosy wine, bright eyes, bright gold pieces—ah!"

"And what was your errand here?"

"Oh—ah, my errand here--why, my lord, the real fact is, that I have not had the treatment of a soldier."

"Indeed."

"No. I have been made to endure blows: actual blows I have felt fall on my back; that back which a foe never saw. Oh, I have been beaten by a most pestilent knave they call Simon."

"I have heard of the fellow."

"And I have not only heard of him, but, to my grief and indignation, he has made me acquainted with a cudgel he has."

"Then your errand was one of revenge?"

"It was."

"By what means did you propose to accomplish your object?"

"That, my gracious master, I had not decided. My first wish was to find out if the pestilent and ungodly knave they call Simon was in the house or not. Your lordship will understand I do not wish by any means to kill him—far from it, my lord; and therefore it is that I, as a humane man—for a soldier should only kill the enemies of his country—keep out of his way, and when I do come across him, rather than take his life, I allow him to strike me divers knocks—ah!"

"I admire your discretion."

"Oh, what's a soldier without temper? True valour consists in not fighting, I have become convinced of that."

"It is not a popular opinion," said Hastings; "but since you have now taken the pains to come here and commence ascertaining if this said Simon be in the mercer's house, go on with your investigation, for I wish to know that fact likewise."

"I will, my lord. I am now, then, to consider myself as in your noble service—ah?"

"If you like."

"Ah—ah—ah!"

"What now?"

The faded gallant held out his hand, as he said,—

"The gallant soldier is worthy of receiving the largess of the noble. It is a curious and an amazing fact how the chink of gold sharpeneth the wits of man. Ah!"

"Take these gold pieces," said Hastings, placing several in his hand; "I have no more about me. But if you do me good service I am not one who is likely to forget you."

"I am a happy man," said the faded gallant; "my star is in the ascendant, and I am a happy man. What service shall I shrink from in the cause of the most illustrious of the nobles of Edward's court? What danger shall appal me? Beelzebub himself shall not stop me."

Hastings wisely ensconced himself again in the doorway in which he had so roughly encountered the faded gallant, while that individual proceeded again to make divers experiments to ascertain who was at the mercer's house.

He cast up another of the small pebbles he had taken from the roadway, and then another and then another, after which, and just as the patience of Lord Hastings was beginning to get exhausted, the latticed window was opened, and Jane's old nurse inquired, in shrill accents,—

"Hoity-toity! are we to have no peace here—what brawling knaves now disturb us?"

"Elderly female," commenced the faded gallant, "I have a very great desire to know—the devil!"

The old woman, before she opened the window, had taken good care to supply herself with some defence, or mode of aggression. The moment she heard the voice of the faded gallant, she threw a large jug full of hot water, which she had at hand, in his face, and as he was naturally looking upwards, he got a full share of it. Hence the sudden exclamation with which he finished his speech; and with a great spluttering and a number of oaths, he sought the doorway where was the chamberlain.

"What's the matter?" said Hastings, who heard that something was amiss, but did not know very well what it was.

"The matter? I have literally gone through fire and water for your noble lordship, now. The skin is coming off my nose whole like the finger of a glove."

"What do you mean?"

"They have thrown some dreadful hot liquid over me. Oh, for a sea of ice to put my head in."

"And that was the reception you got?" said Hastings, as he bit his lips, angrily. "By the mass, difficulties in this matter seem but to accumulate the more they are endeavoured to be overcome; but I will not be foiled—I swear it—I will not be foiled. She shall be mine by fair means or by foul. She is beautiful—do I say beautiful? Oh, too weak a word by far to express such heavenly charms! I will not lightly give up this pursuit—she shall be mine—I swear it—she shall be mine!"

"I dare say," said the faded gallant, mournfully, "that they have got some more water boiling by this time. You had better go and try your own good fortune, my lord."

"Psha!"

"Oh, it's very easy for anybody whose nose is not hurt at all to say psha! to one who don't know if his is left on his face."

"Go again, and demand to know who is in the house."

The faded gallant was silent for a moment, and then, with anger swelling at his bosom, he went into the roadway, and with the heel of his boot loosened a large, heavy stone.

"Since a little gentle note of inquiry does not suit them," he muttered, "we will try something of a stronger quality. Let me consider. Here I have four gold nobles from my Lord Hastings, and they are all I shall get, to a certainty. Humph! ha! I am decided."

He took up the heavy stone, and after poising it in his hand for a moment or two, he flung it with all the force he was master of against the latticed window of the mercer's house. With a loud crash it went into the room, carrying with it several of the small diamond-shaped panes of glass, as well as part of the framework of the window.

The moment he heard the crash he set off at full speed in the contrary direction to that where Hastings was hidden, and he was soon clear of the city, and among the fields and gardens lying by the banks of the river, towards Westminster.

Hastings was thus left to do the best he could alone, and he felt that the faded gallant had by no means bettered his condition or prospects by the outrageous manner in which he had acted previous to his taking to flight. Could the chamberlain at that moment by a wish have sheathed his poniard in the heart of the faded gallant, there is no doubt he would have done so, to the great detriment of this veritable history; but as he could not accomplish that, he was fain to content himself with growling a resolution that he would have him put out of the world somehow, and by somebody, at the very first opportunity.

As to now seeking any information at the mercer's house, after what had passed, he felt that it would be perfectly futile. Indeed, to hazard it would have been a dangerous experiment, for the old nurse had provided herself, as the faded gallant had prognosticated, with more hot water, a jugfull of which she kept throwing out at a venture. Hastings gathered his cloak around him, and took his route towards Westminster, much fretted at the want of success that had attended upon his night's exertions, and yet as much resolved as ever to persevere in the pursuit of the beautiful Jane, who, like all lovers, he thought more of the more obstacles were placed in the way of his getting access to her presence.

He had not got very far on his way when he became conscious of a footstep behind, which he fancied adapted itself rather too closely to his own pace to be at all agreeable in those ticklish times.

In order, however, thoroughly to ascertain if such was the case, Hastings quickened his rate of walking considerably, and he found still that the footstep was close behind him. Then he stopped short, and faced about with his hand upon the hilt of his sword, and confronted the individual who with such troublesome pertinacity seemed intent upon following him. It was a man enveloped in a cloak very much resembling the one which he, Hastings, himself wore. This man stopped immediately that Hastings thus turned upon him, and the two were silent for a few moments.

"Well," said Hastings, at length, "did you wish to speak to me?"

"No," said the man.

"You followed me."

"Because you went before."

"But you adapted your pace to mine."

"No; you did so as regards myself; but I was not at all offended at such a circumstance, my Lord Hastings."

"You know me?"

"Well."

"Indeed! who are you? Your voice is perfectly strange to me."

"I wonder at that. You have had no success to-night, in your attempt to see the mercer's daughter, and you were not likely to have any. How could you be so foolish as to employ so mean and despicable a tool in a matter requiring some discretion and tact, as that lump of cowardice and rascality with whom you were conversing in the Chepe?"

"Who are you?" said Hastings, impatiently. "You are a stranger to me, and yet you talk as confidently as if you knew my affairs."

"Have I then really deceived you?"

"Ha! you alter your tone. I know you, Loyala. It is you. Why play off these pranks of disguise upon me?"

"Because," said Vassa, for it was indeed himself, "I cannot form any judgment of them otherwise. It is people who know us that we want to deceive by disguises. This one is good, I presume, as you knew me not."

"You have a wonderful facility of altering your voice."

"Yes, from long practice, I have."

"And now you look taller."

"I can sink several inches when I please. But what could induce you to go on such an errand as this? You have no chance of success by such means."

"It was partly by your own advice."

"Nay, nay."

"Indeed it was so. I sought Shore's house to make a pretended purchase, but Jane was not there."

"And that made you impatient? Why, man, it was the best thing that could be, for it was a circumstance which would have disarmed Shore's suspicions. It was the very time at which you should have striven most to make his good acquaintance."

"I see—I understand."

"Without awakening any suspicion you could have done so, and again and again you might then have called, until you got to be a familiar visitor."

"When I found that she whom I sought was not there, I own I got foolishly impatient."

"Most foolishly. I tell you, Hastings, I much wish, for your own sake as well as for the sake of much more important matters, that you would give up this mad intrigue; but if you must and will carry it on, do so well and at once, I pray you."

"You positively refused me your assistance."

"I removed your rival."

"True; but you did no more."

"Well, well—you shall not have cause to complain. I will do more; you shall have an interview with Jane."

"When—oh, when?"

"Very shortly; but you must promise ——"

"Promise what?"

"That, if you find your cause hopeless, you will, like a sensible man, at once give it up. If you find her so much disinclined to listen to your suit that you can have no hope, you must promise to dismiss the matter from your mind, in favour of more important projects."

"It is hard to promise that."

"Upon no other terms will I assist you further."

"I do promise then."

"Good. You shall, you may depend, have an uninterrupted interview with Jane Shore, of half-an-hour. I undertake to procure it for you; but, mark me, I shall hold you to your word, and any attempted violence will be by me considered as a forfeiture of it."

"I consent to your terms. Let me but have the felicity of half-an-hour with her, and I consent to anything."

"You are more infatuated than I thought."

"I love the girl, because she is the most beautiful my eyes ever beheld! Even you cannot but admit her wondrous charms."

"I admit she is beautiful."

"Then can you wonder that I love her? Can you wonder that, even in the midst of affairs of state that would seem to demand my whole attention, I am still not insensible to the charms of one who stands unsullied?"

"Let me wonder how I may, or as much as I may," said Vassa, "it can make but little difference in a fact. I have seen so much that is strange and inexplicable, that you will excuse me wondering at anything now. I wish to bring this intrigue to a termination, one way or the other. I have no feeling for or against your success; but let me implore you not to waste time in any useless pursuit. You may depend that a woman is always won at once, or never won."

"You think so?"

"Think so! I am sure."

"Will not sometimes devotion and perseverance do wonders?"

"Never!"

"Indeed! Most persons hold a contrary opinion."

"Most persons are wrong, then. Woman's favour generally depends on some little circumstance unknown to any but themselves. He whom they fancy they fancy at once apart from any earthly consideration of who he is or what he is. Nothing moves them. If they like you, you cannot make them dislike you, do what you will. If they dislike you, you cannot make them like you, were you to spend the devotion of a life upon them, and discourse with the wit of an angel."

"By Heavens! there sounds a truth in what you say!" said Hastings. "And now I promise you, Vassa, that if you procure me this interview, and I find Jane Shore repugnant to me, I will give up the vain pursuit wholly."

"'Tis well."

"And I will turn my attention to matters of graver import, such as you would have me study."

"Do so. And besides, self-preservation is a great law of universal nature, which you should ever bear in mind now."

"Why now? You place a marked emphasis upon that word."

"Are you not aware that in Lancasterian intrigues you have gone already far enough to endanger something which you might, from old acquaintance, wish to preserve."

"What do you mean?"

"Can you not guess?"

"No, truly. My wealth, mean you? My house—my grounds—my title, do you mean?"

"No; a more personal possession."

"What—what?"

"Your head!"

Hastings staggered a step or two, and then, in moody silence, continued his walk.

CHAPTER XXXVII.

The Storm.

"And ye wrath of Heavene showed itselfe in ye red glare of ye lightninge, warninge all men that much evil was in ye land."

Master Snafflings, the good-tempered bowyer, was himself willing enough to pardon poor, deceived, heart-broken Jacob for his share in the robbery at his shop; but he happened to know well that it required two people to come to one conclusion on that point before Jacob could be at all considered as free from the consequences of his indiscretion. And although one of these people was himself, yet he was not much forwarder in getting the consent of the other party, by the mere fact of having his own, than was the Irishman who got his own consent to marry an heiress.

Mistress Bridget Snafflings, that most intractable piece of womanhood, had to be consulted, and from the partizanship she had shown against poor Jacob, in actually going to the hideous expense of having bills written, offering a reward for his apprehension, it was not at all likely she would readily accord a full and free pardon to such a culprit.

"Truly," thought Master Snafflings, with a sigh, "I must now speak to Bridget about it, or my saying that Jacob shall go free will be of but little avail."

With this melancholy determination, for it was indeed melancholy to be compelled into a conversation on any subject whatever with his daughter, Master Snafflings went homewards with something of the feeling of a man who has made up his mind to have a tooth out; and, therefore, thinks, wisely enough, that the sooner he gets over the infliction of the necessary amount of pain attendant upon the operation the better.

And yet Master Snafflings even, made up as was his mind, walked twice down the whole length of the Chepe, and back again, passing his own door four times during the course of those peregrinations, before he could gather sufficient courage to venture in. At length, with a sort of desperate resolution, he did, and made his appearance on his own premises.

He was quite amazed at the stillness that pervaded them, for he fully expected, the moment he showed his face, to receive some salute from Mistress Bridget, in the shape of the commencement of a torrent of invective, which he had intended first of all to let blow over before he ventured to proclaim the object of his errand. All, however, was still, and at length he found a boy lying asleep among the stock.

"Hilloa!" he cried, as he shook the youngster. "Hilloa! where is Mistress Bridget, boy?"

"Anan!" said the boy.

"Where is Mistress Bridget?"

"Oh, gone to stick up bills of the thief they call Jacob, and I'm minding the shop."

"Nicely you are minding it, too; whither has she gone?"

"To Mistress Moore, good sir, the midwife who has set up hair-dressing close to the Conduit."

"Oh, very well."

And away walked the bowyer; but now he found, much to his discomfort, that a great change for the worse had taken place in the weather.

The winds rose that evening, and a storm came on that had seldom been equalled in strength and violence. Men were seen hurrying to and fro, traversing the streets, and the citizens who had been called from whatever motive beyond the limits of the city, were seen hurrying back with all the speed they could make, lest they should be caught in the coming storm. The wind blew and howled round the gable ends of the old-fashioned houses, now moaning, and now screaming in the chimneys, as if in defiance of all the efforts made to keep the enemy without. Doors banged and blew together with a terrible crash, and the rain began to fall with great violence in the streets.

The mud and water, where there was any stoppage in the streets, and these were frequent, formed large pools, and made it difficult for men to cross through, without wading deep into the annoyance. The loud thunder crashed and re-echoed in the heavens, as though the elements were at war with each other. The very houses shook in the shock, and the lightning played round the old churches, as if it had been familiar with the places for ages. At one moment the good citizens were almost deafened by one tremendous peal of thunder, that seemed to leap and roll about as if it would never cease, and with it came such a flash of lightning, that made its way into the deepest and most carefully guarded apartments, causing the timid to shrink and to scream.

That flash had not descended on the good city harmless. This was a remark made by many, and it was true, for the steeple of one of the churches was thrown down in consequence. The rain fell in heavy torrents, and the streets were wholly deserted, the citizens either keeping to their own firesides, or that of some favourite tavern.

"I must see her though," thought Snafflings, as he breasted his way. "I must see her, or otherwise if she should fall in with this poor fellow Jacob, I doubt not but it would be the death of him."

With this feeling uppermost in his mind, he passed on till he reached the place mentioned by the boy, when the first object that struck his eyes was one of the eternal bills which Bridget Snafflings had had written, and which seemed to have taken so firm a hold of her imagination, that it was likely she would go on now posting them wherever she could obtain leave so to do for the remainder of her earthly career, and she was one who, of all others, was likely to obtain leave to do anything, however inconvenient, with the greatest facility, for well known was she in "ye anciente citie," and her oratorical powers were wonderfully respected.

There was a dim light burning in the deeply sombre window of Mrs. Moore's shop, and by applying his eyes as close as possibly he could to the dingy panes, Snafflings could see his daughter within, in an attitude which convinced him she had been giving one of her graphic descriptions of the robbery, and calling down all sorts of grievous denunciations on the head of the unfortunate Jacob. This did not seem a likely time to speak to her of mercy, but he had promised Simon, and he had wished not that any circumstances should make him seem even to have gone back from his word.

"Who knows," thought Snafflings, "she may be a little milder than usual from fatigue; I will even step in now and speak to her."

"Well, Bridget," he said, as he walked into the little shop.

"And well," cried Bridget, "Mr. Snafflings, well?"

"I'm glad to see you have amused yourself by taking a little turn."

"If I was not," she exclaimed, in her own peculiar screaming voice; "if I was not to take a few turns about the business, it would take one turn, I can tell you, and that would be to turn us out of doors, and out of bread."

"Indeed?"

"Yes; and out of everything, I can tell you. While you are idling about with one Morrice Joggs and another, and drinking your spiced canary at somebody's head or another, the house is robbed."

"Well, well, Bridget, you have told me of the robbery before."

"And I'll tell you of it before and behind, too, and as often as I like."

"Well, well."

"It is not well, well. Will well, well, put five nobles in a bureau? Will well, well, enable me to keep a house over your head? Will well, well, pay the subsidies, and God only knows what imposts besides? Mercy on us! a man thinks he has nothing to do but to say well, well, and he has done all that can be expected of him now-a-days."

"It is hopeless," thought Master Snafflings to himself, but still he would make the trial; so, gathering up what courage he could, he said,—

"Now, hearken to me, Bridget; it is some time since poor Jacob was deluded into committing this robbery, which you have done nothing but talk about ever since."

"I talk!"

"Now, do listen to me for a moment; I will not have him prosecuted. From now, mind, I forgive him."

"You forgive him?"

"Yes; it was my money."

"Is the world at an end? Now, all the saints look at us! was ever anything like that heard in all the universe! Your money?"

"Yes; as you know."

Mistress Bridget placed her arms akimbo, and commenced giving her head that tremulous movement from side to side, which ladies of her description indulge in previous to some more than common effort of eloquence. Master Snafflings saw the coming storm, in comparison with which the storm without was as nothing, and he at once fled from the shop, satisfied that, at all events, he had made a beginning, by declaring his intention of pardoning Jacob. He was some distance from the King's Head, where he usually spent his evenings; and, as the rain continued to fall, he betook himself to the Boar's Head, in East Chepe, then a small place, and procured a shelter from both the storms—that of the weather, and that of his daughter's eloquence.

As Master Snapplings took his seat in the house, a tallish, good-looking man, with thin, black mustachios, was apparently endeavouring to excuse himself from some task which was sought to be imposed upon him by the assembled company.

"Nay, now," he said, "I pray you excuse me, friends—some other time."

"That is Master Hans Trebbet," said a man who sat next to Snafflings, and saw him gazing with curiosity. "He is the celebrated story-teller, who goes from court to court and amuses even monarchy by the rare manner in which he adapts his conversation to the taste of his hearers. I warrant you, now, he will relate something to the citizens that will chime in well with their humours."

It turned out as the stranger predicted, for Trebbet, who was a man of no mean importance in his day, suffered himself to be prevailed upon, as no doubt he had intended all along, and in a fine, clear voice, he spoke as follows,—

There was a group of substantial-looking citizens standing on the outside of the Boar's Head, East Chepe, and they all appeared to be engaged in conversation, and, as may be imagined, it related to the troubles of those unquiet times, when the kingdom, from one end to the other, was filled with many and various reports, and the good citizens were every now and then alarmed at the news that was brought and spread among them by some tarnished captain, or dissolute companion of the warlike leaders of the factions. Many of the more aged citizens were anxious for peace, to which they owed so much, and the younger cared not for war. Indeed, the citizens of London were often of importance, and could occasionally throw great weight into the scale of either party. They were, indeed, both wealthy and turbulent, and those who stood by the Boar's Head were men who loved to talk of the dangers that had been evaded, rather than any which they might yet run the risk of.

Indeed, they loved to talk of unquiet times in the Boar's Head, while sitting round the large fire that cheered the heart and gladdened the eyes as much as the tankard of mulled claret that a citizen might indulge in.

"What you say, Master Oldshaw, is very just; but trust me, notwithstanding all that has been said or done, a king is a king."

"Ay, marry he is."

"Well, then, when did you ever hear of one that did not promise fairly enough?"

"That's very true ——"

"And," continued the citizen, with increased energy, as he waxed warm in his argument, "did you ever see one who did not want his subsidies, his grants, and his taxes?"

"Ay, ay," said one.

"What Master Beltboro says is quite just, and I will wager a quart of good claret to a glassfull of cold water, that we shall have these very monies to raise."

"And the winner shall be compelled to drink the wager."

"Ay, that I would, little as my constitution can abide the application of cold water internally."

"You don't often indulge in that, I'll be sworn," said another.

"Indeed I do not, neighbour, for you may depend upon it, it goes so much against the grain that it nearly produces hydrophobia."

"Ha! ha! ha!"

"But touching King Edward," resumed the pertinacious speaker; "my opinion is,

decidedly, that we shall be called upon to grant fresh subsidies, and the go od city will called upon, as usual, to pay."

"I doubt, friend Beltboro, that proposition; we have been very fairly mulcted of late."

"Very unfairly, I say."

"That's good."

"Yes; but too much of it to other ears but our own would bring us into jeopardy."

"Well, but I am convinced, by past experience, that the good city is considered of no consequence to the state, save so far as the state can open and dip its hands pretty deep into the purse of our fair city."

"There's no disputing that."

"No, marry, it is the truth."

"Well, let us see; how long is it since the last subsidy was granted for the serv ce and emergencies of the state?"

"Scarce six months."

"Ay, an is it so long since even as that?" inquired the speaker, incredulously.

"Yes; six months."

"I think you are mistaken, neighbour."

"No."

" Four months is about the time."

" Six, I say, and a few days over."

" I will not dispute your authority, but I think it cannot be four months."

" Six."

" Well, then, be it six; but I think it's only four. However, say six; is that a proper time to come again to drain the citizens of their cash? If so, they had better shut up their shops and cease to trade at all, for surely ruin will stare them in the face at this rate."

" And if they do they will be immediately supplanted by others, who will weather the storms of state," said a younger man.

" I suppose, if the citizens prove treacherous to themselves ——"

" Trust me, gentles, these are unquiet times," said another, whose face betrayed some white looks, " and the less men embark in them the better, and the safer will be their throats and their money; that's my notion."

" And a very good one too."

" Good even, gentles," said a tall, square-built man, in tarnished lace and military appointments, as he walked up.

The group looked round as the man of war stalked up, for the sound of his heavy heeled boots, spurs, and the clank of a heavy cut-and-thrust sword was somewhat formidable.

" Ah, Captain Stanmore, good even."

" Good even, gentles all," said the captain, as he lifted his helmet, with military parade. " Fine evening this."

" But cold."

" Yes, cold; but that is bracing to the nerves."

" Ay. However, if you stay too long standing in the cold, you may be sure it will strike a chill to the heart."

" Then warm it with canary or sack," replied the doughty soldier.

" A very good plan. Shall we adjourn, gentles?"

The citizens looked doubtful, and seemed to hesitate to accept of the company of the military man, as if they feared him.

" It is over early yet," said one who looked on all sides for an excuse.

" Not a whit. Good citizens should keep good hours, you know, and my friend Captain Stanmore has been a man of action and seen some service; a most worthy and companionable officer."

" My friend here does me much honour. But my poor services in the Low Countries, they had their reward at the time," and he pointed to a small medal he wore on his breast. " Not that it makes me any richer; it is almost a shame for a soldier to be rich, for it deprives him of half his courage and his valour."

" Indeed! How do you prove that?"

" Because a man who has so much to live for becomes more careful of his safety than he who is needy."

" But, then, you ought to derive riches from your courage and valour, captain."

" I ought; but I found that a little fame and honour were all that came to my share, and a few hard blows."

" Well, captain, will you go in and spend a pleasant hour? It grows cold; and if you will, we will have the pleasure of your company."

" With all my heart," replied the captain. " But stay—do you see yonder man coming?"

" Ay; him with the downcast look."

" Some studious man, who spends his days in dreaming over musty volumes."

" No, no; not so. But mark him well, gentles, for he's worth seeing; but hush! he is at hand."

The individual, a spare man, dressed in black, hurried past them, paying little or no attention to them. Indeed, he passed as though he saw them not, and they gazed after him. When he was out of sight, and, perhaps, out of hearing, the captain said,—

" That is Caxton."

" The man who has introduced some strange device for making books!"

" The same."

" He is a strange innovator."

" And a strange man. Why, you would hardly believe it, but they say that he never sleeps."

" Never sleeps!"

" No. Men have seen him at work at all hours of the night."

"Where?"

"He has a room near St. Paul's, where he has a small press, and works at it, composing books and printing them."

"He has more knowledge of this world than we have, you may depend upon it."

"And the other one too, if all be true that I have heard," said the captain.

"Indeed!" said one citizen. "Let us go in; it is cold here, and there may be too many ears listening out here."

"With all my heart," said the captain, following his friend into the house. "Master Caxton is a strange character, I assure you."

They now entered a large room, in which there were plenty of seats, and a large fire at one end of the place. There was some noise in dragging such of the seats as were moveable near the fire, and then calling to the drawer, each ordered what he chose. The captain was gratified with a tankard of sherry sack, burnt, and taking his steel cap off, and placing it beside him, seemed much at home and at ease.

"Regarding this Caxton," said the citizen who had before spoken; "I have seen him on another occasion, but I scarce knew him until you pointed him out."

"I have seen him on several occasions, both in this country and abroad."

"Indeed!"

"Yes; and his habits were always the same. Now, I have been by his house on many occasions, from all hours of midnight till daybreak, and yet there has always been a light burning in his window. I never went by but what there was one of some kind or other. Sometimes it burned dimmer than at others."

"Ay, so I have heard; and I had it pointed out to me exactly as you describe it, captain."

"No doubt. Any one who was passing through the neighbourhood would see the light, for it reminds me of a watch-tower, such a one as was well termed by a facetious friend of mine, who served with me in the wars, as 'The Devil's Watch-tower.' No offence, gentlemen, to Master Caxton, but I could not help saying at the moment, a good jest was often a good truth. However, that may be a matter of opinion; I have my doubts."

"And many more, too, captain."

"Well, as I said, the light has been seen of various colours; sometimes dimmer, sometimes stronger and brighter, and sometimes there has been a shadow at the window."

"Aye, aye."

"'Yes, gentlemen citizens, I assure you I have heard it doubted, too, whether the shadow came from the inside, or was thrown upon the outside; it's quite uncertain."

"And equally doubtful," added another.

"You may say that. Well, you know, the matter of printing, as they call it, is a devilish invention, and will so multiply books, that the common people will know as much as a clerk."

"Ay, marry!"

"And there will be such a wagging of tongues, that there will be no peace for an honest man; for he who has read most will always be accounted to know the most; though that is not our way of doing matters in the army."

"No, I should opine not," coincided one of the citizens.

"No, experience does the matter there; though it is not every man of action and experience that is properly rewarded for his services."

"That's a common occurrence."

"A great deal too common; and yet it is natural enough, because there are plenty of good men, and there is not employment for all, and those who have fewest friends go to the wall."

"Ay, ay."

"I don't complain of this so much in my own case, because I have the promises of certain great men that my present commission shall be but the step to one considerably better."

"Success to your friends, Captain Stanmore," said Beltboro, "and may they be good men and true."

"I believe they are, from my soul," replied the captain. "But a soldier's life, you know, is an uncertain one; to-day we are here, and to-morrow, if we ain't in the same place, we are somewhere else—there's no saying."

"Marry, an that's true."

"But, touching Master Caxton."

"Oh, ay; he is a strange man, and I have heard that he will cause a great revolution in the world."

"Aye, aye."

"Yes. I wonder that he is allowed to come; in some parts of the countries where I served they would have burned him."

"Well, I am free to say there is much that is fearful, not to say strange, about him; if there was not, what should be the reason why one of his rank should receive protection of great people—that's what I want to know."

"There's more in it than we think for, gentles. The man has the power, perhaps, of doing great mischief, and, to further their own views in certain mysterious particulars, they give him that countenance he could not otherwise obtain."

"He is a strange man."

"Why, gentles, I could tell you how they served, some ten years ago, when I was in the Low Countries, a printer, or philosopher, or astrologer—they are all pretty well of a kidney, you know."

"Yes; different names for the same thing, like labels in a doctor's shop,—a very few samples make up the number."

"They do; on my faith they do."

"But, touching this philosopher, or whatever he was; what of him?"

"I will tell you—it's a strange tale, and I dare say you will be surprised; but that is too weak a word—you'll be amazed, astonished, ay, thunder-struck."

There was an evident eagerness on the part of the good citizens to hear what strange fate befel the philosopher. It was a marvellous thing, no doubt, else the captain would not have said so, for he was a man of action, and of truth too.

This was a subject upon which they could converse and listen without danger, for there could be no spies, and exciting their wonder gave them sufficient and pleasant mental employment, and the time flew rapidly by.

"Well, Theodore Splutgen was a citizen born of the good city of Cologne, though he had gone, and was residing, at the time of his death, near the forest of Rheims.

"However, to begin at the beginning—for as you, being in a siege, commence at a distance, until you get closer and closer, and then you take the place by storm, and you get to the very centre, the very penetration of the enemy's quarters; and so with my tale, you will know as much as I know myself."

"And that is as much as anybody can desire, and more cannot be had."

"Certainly, there's no having more than there is, I suppose."

"No, marry! he that would take more, and do it, must be a clever wight."

"There's none, save me, who can do that," said the captain.

"Ay, marry, and if he can do that, he might be satisfied with doing so, without interfering with the world."

"Well, gentlemen, to proceed," said the captain, giving his moustache a twirl with his finger, after a deep draught of the sack.

"Theodore Splutgen was born in Cologne, the son of a respectable, but an uncommon fortunate tradesman. There were several rumours respecting the rapid way in which he got money, and there were many strange visitors who came to his shop. It was said that there was other business carried on there by which he made more money than he could otherwise have had.

"However, Theodore had, or was supposed to have, no knowledge of this; and his father, it was supposed, by way of penance, or making a kind of compromise between Heaven and his own conscience, determined to devote his son to the service of the church. The more and more so did this resolution appear to him reasonable and just, because young Theodore was of a very quiet and studious habit and of a bookish turn.

"In this, he thought he saw the hand of Providence, and was the more rejoiced at it. According to his intentions, he sent Theodore to a neighbouring convent to be educated, and, knowing the intentions of the father, the monks spared no pains to instil into the mind of their scholar the pleasures and benefits arising from such a life.

"Young Theodore was very studious, but it seemed he soon outran his instructors in the score of knowledge. He then turned about, and sought from among the different branches of study, and seemed taken towards the occult sciences; but here he had no instructors. The books which treated upon such subjects were carefully kept out of the monastery; not one of them could have entered through the holy gates, for it was supposed that the earth would have opened, and swallowed them up, and those who bore the burden of them."

"I shouldn't have been surprised if it had," said one of the citizens.

"Well, be that as it may," resumed the captain, "one day, as he was sitting in his cell, musing upon the hard fate of a man who had learned so much that he could learn no more, when he began to think that he might obtain some of the desired knowledge at another place and in a different quarter. The mind suffers jointly with the body, and the imprisonment of the one is only felt through the medium of the other; and this is no doubt the fact, notwithstanding the many assertions to the contrary of divines and wrong-headed men.

"The bird in the cage leads an active, merry life, and his imagined attempts at escape are merely the effects of its instinct, and not from sorrow; for habit domesticates it, and renders it perfectly satisfied with its fate, as indeed the song alone would indicate; but wonderfully clever people, who have listened to the learned discourses of the clergy, are suddenly become abstruse metaphysicians, and attribute to instinct all the faculties of the mind, and forgetting that joy and sorrow are not identical with pleasure and pain.

"However, Theodore sat musing and wishing he had the power of unlocking the arcana of nature, and discovering all the many secrets there hidden, as he would use them for the benefit of the whole of his species.

"Suddenly he thought he heard some one breathing beside him. He turned, and to his surprise saw a strange being in the dress of a monk. However, his cowl was off, and a pair of black sharp eyes were fixed on his features with reat intensity of expression. Theodore, though surprised at this intrusion, was by no means fearful, but he turned his gaze upon his visitor.

"It was a moment or two before either of them spoke. The stranger's cast of countenance was that f a man of the world, and a philosopher; but there was also a strange, undefinable, sinister expression in the face and brightness of the eyes, that was superhuman.

"'Brother,' said the philosopher, speaking the language he usually spoke among the monks.

"'Brother,' repeated the stranger; and he held out his hand to Theodore.

"Theodore grasped the proffered hand, and the —— grasped his so tight that it brought the blood to his face.

"'Are you the spirit of philosophy?'

"'I am.'

"'And why comest thou?'

"'To tell thee what thou wouldst know.'

"'Well?'

"'Say what it is, and I will tell you how you shall obtain the knowledge you so ardently desire.'

"'Then I would know something of the means of communicating with those spirits of the invisible world that rule the elements, and stand sentinels over the secrets of nature. Do this, and I am your debtor.'

"'The search is long and arduous; have you strength of purpose sufficient to enable you to attempt so great an achievement?'

"'I have, undoubtedly.'

"'Then listen to me.'

"Theodore pushed a seat towards the stranger, who whipped a long appendage out of his way before he sat down, and then placed one leg across the other—leg, I say, but it was a mere apology, for there was nothing but the shin bone. However, when seated, he turned to Theodore, and said, in a confidential tone,—

"'I see you are just the man to know all that is, and wield the power that is given you with strength and boldness.'

"'It were useless to have it if it were not used,' remarked Theodore.

"'Exactly; but you cannot have it while you continue in these walls.'

"'Wherefore?'

"'That is of no consequence. You must quit the convent and the cowl; you must eschew such a life.'

"'Indeed.'

"'Yes; and, moreover, the pretty daughter of Von Rockenbrock is yours in heart, only you have not been sufficiently urgent in your suit.'

"'Ah! you know that?'

"'I do.'

"'Then you are the ——'

"'I am.'

"There was a pause.

"'Now,' said the visitor, 'there are two things I would advise you to do preparatory to your possession of the great secrets of which I have been speaking about.'

"'Indeed; what are they?'

"'Simply, that you should marry this girl, and quit the cloister.'

"'And do you recommend a philosopher to marry?' inquired Theodore.

"'Undoubtedly,' was the reply; 'for two reasons.'

"'And what are they?'

"'Why, the first is, I know you love this girl very passionately, and your day-dreams respecting happiness and felicity will always be returning with greater force to your mind, destroying your equanimity, and interrupting the progress of those studies you so much wish to complete.'

"'And the second is ——"

"'The second is a very rapid dissipation of all these day-dreams in the actual possession of the much-coveted being.'

"'A dangerous remedy.'

"'For a dangerous disease.'

"'Well?'

"'Then there is an ancient tower at Rheims, in the forest.'

"'Well?'

"'You must go there, and reside there; for the tower is high, and you can study the stars, if you will; and, moreover, it is strong, and in the vaults you will find a large coffin; in that coffin you will find books that were the instructors of the once celebrated Alarovandus Spikaletta.'

"'If I can obtain such a name as his,' said Theodore, in a rapture, 'I shall be well repaid for all my trouble and denial.'

"'You will; and, until you get to the tower in the forest of Rheims, farewell!'

"'Farewell!' said Theodore, as he looked round to let his visitor out, but he was gone.

"Theodore paused, and thought over the past. He thought over what the stranger had said, and he was determined that he would follow the advice he had given him.

"The next day he quitted the monastery, and went home to his father, who was somewhat annoyed at seeing him.

"'What brings you home, Theodore?'

"'I am tired of the monastery and the monks,' said Theodore.

"'Tired! Good heavens!'

"'Say no more, father; I am tired, and shall not go there any more.'

"Old Theodore was thunderstruck, and could not say anything. He sent for the fathers at the monastery, and inquired the reason of such a change of sentiment in his son. They could not understand it, but were completely at fault, and then they sought an interview with young Theodore, during which every topic was urged to induce him to take the vows, but without avail. Theodore was resolute, and refused wholly and absolutely to go back into the bosom of the church, as the priest affectionately called it.

"Immediately after this, he went to Von Rockenbrock, and, being fortunate enough to see the daughter, he besieged her so strongly, that she yielded to his entreaties, and they were both quietly and privately wedded, to the amazement of their parents, who thought they were going mad; Theodore especially, because there would have been no objection to the marriage on either side.

"The young couple, in a few months, took a tour, and Theodore, going to Rheims, saw the tower, and expressed his desire to live there, and, to prevent any objection on the part of his young wife, he went and hired it. Here he lived, and passed away years of his life, and had one daughter, who grew up the image of her mother. His wife died in the second year of her marriage. It did not appear that Theodore grieved much, and yet he was fond of his daughter, who lived with him.

"The search in the vaults was supposed to be successful, for the philosopher was constantly at his books; he studied day and night, and grew in knowledge, and it was believed, as, indeed, there are no reasons to doubt it, that he grew in the knowledge of unlawful things. One night in particular, the whole castle appeared in various and party-coloured fires, and sparks flew around, and formed all sorts of shapes and devices.

"This much alarmed the good people, and many went to put the fire out; but they saw the philosopher walking about in the midst of it, in a very unconcerned manner; but he was all colours, first one, and then another, which gave him a very fearful aspect. They gazed upon him for some time, and, absolutely terrified, they fled the spot. Well, his place was watched; and this occurred more than once, and the poor of the neighbourhood were terrified at the temerity of the wizard, for he was known as the Wizard of Rheims.

"A very terrible calamity had occurred to the inhabitants of the country about, a kind of pestilence, of which many died, and cold as well, yet the philosopher or wizard did not suffer, neither he, nor anybody about him. This settled the matter, and, terrified before, they now became exasperated, and determined to be revenged upon the object of their hatred, the cause of all their woes. One night they came and surrounded his tower, and piled up brushwood and huge logs round it; there was a light in the philosopher's room, and a shadow on the window. They immediately set light to the pile, and then rushed from the spot. The fire was seen afar off, but no one durst go near, and, when it was entirely out, two days after, the people went to look at the tower. The walls were standing, but they were blackened and charred; but no vestige of the wizard or his daughter—nothing but a blackness of ashes lay all around.

"Thus, you see, gentles," added the captain, "it is a fearful thing to possess a bad reputation, and I much doubt if Master Caxton would fare better than the wizard himself did, if he were in some countries I could name."

Very great applause followed this story, and, the hour now waxing late, Master Snafflings thought it time to wend his way homewards, which he did with a faint hope that Mistress Bridget had already retired to rest, and that, consequently, he should escape for that night, at least, any more of her vivid remonstrances and reproaches.

CHAPTER XXXVIII.

The Visit.

"Small is ye sympathy of knavery, and ye band that holds together ye wicked is made of sand."

The above saying of a writer, who was cotemporary with the celebrated Marcus Aurelius, is one which we imagine very few will be inclined to dispute. It contains, in a few words, one of those pieces of practical wisdom which belong not to a race of men, or to an age, but to all time, and to all human nature. Never, perhaps, was the truth of such a matter more fully developed than on the morning after the meeting we have described as taking place in the streets between Lord Hastings and Loyala, when the latter individual repaired to the prison of the Blackfriars. Generally speaking, the rogues of an age know something of each other, and have a tolerably just appreciation of each other's abilities. Like the lawyers of our own day, they take pains to discover what each other are capable of doing, and then, when they happen to be ranged, by the force of interest, on opposite sides of any question, they know fully well what to do as regards each other. And thus it was with many of the paid partisans of the rival houses of York and Lancaster. Some were on one side of the question, and some on the other, and it is not going too far to say that many, among whom might be classed Loyala, were on both. That is to say, as occasion served, they espoused the cause of either for a consideration. As regards this Antonio Vassa, which is asserted by writers of the period to have been his real name, there can be very little doubt that, from some dark congeniality of spirit, he had, even thus early, attached himself to the fortunes of Richard, Duke of Gloucester. Vassa probably thought that the man who was totally unscrupulous as to the means by which he accomplished his wishes, had a good chance of success. That he had not miscalculated with regard to this particular, the results of that individual's future career, which are so well known, abundantly testify.

Vassa even then saw the malignant blood-thirsty spirit of the Duke of Gloucester, and he, no doubt, augured that his future career would partake of a character that would have a constant tendency to crush opposition in the grave. It will be understood, then, that Vassa, at the time we now introduce him, may be considered as affecting to belong to the York faction—as acting in the capacity of a spy for the Lancastrians, and as having a private engagement with Richard, Duke of Gloucester, to act in any way for the advancement of his general interest. Whether to the extent which he afterwards carried them, the dark and hideous crimes that makes Richard the Third's reign a black page in English history, were then even dimly shadowed forth in his mind, it is hard to say. Perhaps there was no occasion at all that they should be so, he being a man who was guided by circumstances, and who committed the most heinous crimes quite as a natur part of his conduct, without any more pre-arrangement concerning them than was just sufficient to enable them to be carried out with proper effect.

But be all that as it may, he and Vassa were certainly just the sort of persons to get on together. There was not one solitary ray of principle, of religion, of virtue, humanity, or common justice in either of their dispositions to interfere with their arrangements or consultations. And then Vassa was so strict and so exact in all he did. He was so punctual a man, and such a man of his word as regarded distinct promises to do distinct things. What he said he would do he always did, and he always, unless circumstances fairly beat him, did it at the time he promised it.

It is very singular, and really a great anomaly in human nature, that some of its greatest social excellencies are most commonly only to be found in some of its worst specimens. Why cannot well-meaning, candid, virtuous people be as clever and acute in their virtue as rogues are in their roguery? That they are not is well known; and the bitter taunt of Voltaire, that people are virtuous from mental incapacity to be vicious, and truthful from lack of inventive genius, is true in very many cases. Of course we do not, for one moment, pass so sweeping a condemnation upon human nature as the above quotation would imply; but it would be well if the good members of society were to endeavour to rescue themselves from the taunt, by trying to be as ingenious in their virtues as the bad are in their vices. But to return to Antonio Vassa, whom probably we had better most commonly call by that name, as being the one to which there can be no doubt he was best entitled.

Early, then, on the morning after his meeting with the disappointed and angry chamberlain, he repaired to the prison of the Blackfriars, where poor Walter Fane had gone through so many distressing adventures. Having promised Hastings so particularly an interview with Jane Shore, he set about accomplishing that result, and one of his means of doing so consisted in something he wished to consult the brutal Sir Godfrey about. He knew nothing of the tremendous uproar which had taken place at the prison, during which Sir Godfrey had met with so serious a wound from the half maddened Walter Fane. All that was news to him, and when he reached the prison and rang the summons bell, he little imagined the tale he was about to be told. In a few moments he was answered by one of the officials of the prison, to whom he said,—

"I would see Sir Godfrey. You know me, my friend?"

"Yes, an it please you, worshipful sir," said the man, who knew Antonio Vassa by sight very well as a visitor of Sir Godfrey; "will you be pleased to walk in and hear grievous news."

Vassa looked inquiringly at the man, as he said,—

"Grievous news, my friend. To what do you allude?"

"Sir Godfrey, sir, is hurt almost to death."

"Indeed?"

"Ay, marry. There has been a desperate attempt made by a prisoner to escape, and Sir Godfrey is likely to lose his life through it."

"Who was the prisoner?"

"A youth, really from whom one would not have expected so much; one Fane by name, as I understand."

"Ah, say you so?"

"I grieve to say so, sir. You cannot see Sir Godfrey, I think. The leech gave orders to keep him quiet."

"I must see him. He will see me, you may depend, if he have life in him at all."

"Say you so. Then, good sir, I will send to his chamber, for well I know he values your worshipful company highly, as I have heard him express more than once."

"I thank you. Tell him Master Loyala is here."

"It shall be done."

When the man went to execute this errand, Vassa laughed in a strange manner, but without making any noise. It was a muscular laugh merely. It had nothing hilarious or hearty about it.

"Indeed," he muttered; "Walter Fane has nearly killed him, has he. Well, well, be it so,—be it so. I have no particular objection to the deed, had he done so completely. I long now to hear how this affair could have happened. Sir Godfrey has ever boasted of how wonderfully well he kept the prison."

In a few moments the man returned, and as he had found it no doubt necessary to whisper in the sick chamber, he now whispered when he was out of it, and he said to Vassa,—

"Yes, he's awake. You can see him. You won't mind his swearing a bit. It's dreadful to hear him. They have got a nurse from the monastery of St. Olave attending upon him, and she says she is horrified, and forced to keep her beads in one hand, while she hands him anything he may want with the other."

" Ah, indeed."

" I will show you the way, Master Loyala, an you please to follow me to the chamber."

Vassa followed him to that part of the prison in which were situated the governor's apartments, and in one of these, which was darkened, was the wretched governor lying

on a couch, and apparently nearly at death's door, from the effects of the desperat wound he had received from Walter Fane. The nurse approached Vassa, and said,—

" It's a mortal charity, good sir, to come here, that there may be another Christian soul in the room besides my own."

" How is your patient?"

" Worse and worse."

" Curses, curses. Oh, for some worse damnation than man ever yet thought of, for him," groaned Sir Godfrey.

Vassa approached the bedside, and bending over the suffering man, he said, in oily, soft, low accents,—

" You have met with a little misfortune, have you?"

" What's that to you?" said Sir Godfrey; " what's that to anybody? Oh, if I could scorch him to death slowly—slowly as I am suffering."

" Methinks now," remonstrated Vassa, " this is an unkindly reception to an old friend."

Sir Godfrey was silent for a moment, and then in a groaning tone he replied,—

" Suffer one-half what I do, and you will feel as I do. I am dying even now."

" Oh, you are mistaken, I dare say. What is the nature of your hurt?"

" A smash."

" Indeed. A smash, did you say?"

" I did. I am dying—Vassa, hear me. I have come by my death at the hands of him who was placed here by you know who, for reasons that I know nothing about. Will you do me a favour that none here like to venture upon?"

" It depends a little upon what it is," said Vassa. " Propound to me your wishes."

" I want you to have the prisoner Fane, who has maimed me, brought to my bedside."

"Well?"

"And then I want you to hold him, while I, with what strength is left me, plunge a knife in his heart."

"Well, it's a trifle, and I am very sorry I cannot oblige you in it."

"You cannot?"

"Oh, dear no, it is quite out of the question, and not at all in accordance with my mode of doing things. There would be a world too much publicity in the act. You do not consider, my good kind patient, Sir Godfrey, that what you ask is rather outrageous."

"You will not do it?"

"You will excuse me."

"Curses on you—curses on you. You are like everybody else. Curses loud and deep upon you, say I. May you come by a worse end than I have, although that is needless—that is needless."

"Nay, now," said Vassa, "I really never saw you so unamiable in all my life, good Sir Godfrey."

"Away, away. Leave me."

"Soon I will; but as I am here, tell me, will you, have you succeeded in getting from the prisoner a note to her who was the idol of his heart?"

"No."

"You have not. Really, now, you wanted tact, Sir Godfrey, or you could not have failed in such a small matter as that. I am really sorry to find you not half the man of genius I took you to be. You have got, too, a hurt from one who was your prisoner, and upon whose movements you had it in your power to place what restraint might suit your fancy. Oh, fie, fie, Sir Godfrey. I really thought much better of you. You had better die as soon as you possibly can, my good friend, and then you bespeak a certain amount of charitable consideration you can never know while you live."

"I ought to have expected this," said the wounded man. "I ought to have been prepared for this from you. I am dying, and perhaps you have heard that dying men have the gift of prophesy?"

"Humph! I have heard a wonderful number more things than I ever believed," said Vassa.

"Believe this one, though," added Sir Godfrey. "Believe that my curse will stick to you, and believe, as you will believe, that your death shall be a far worse one than this. I suffer, but you shall suffer much more. My end is one of pain and misery, and I lie here mangled and bleeding, but yours shall be ten times more horrible, Antonio Vassa."

"Is that all you have to say, my good friend?"

"Is it not enough? Is it not enough?"

"That is quite a matter for your consideration, if you think it enough I am satisfied."

"Then be satisfied that what I say shall surely come to pass. Where is the woman who was here? I want drink—a perpetual thirst now preys upon me. Drink—drink!"

"She has left the room, and we are alone," said Vassa, in a low, hissing tone.

"Call her—call her. I have no power to do so. Call her for me. Do not, oh, do not touch the couch. The slightest tremble of the room, from even a footstep crossing it, is a pang to me. My bones lie crushed and shapeless. I am dying."

"And do you mean to say," cried Vassa, "that you are so ticklish you don't like the very couch touched?"

As he spoke he gave one of the legs of the bedstead a heavy kick, which gave the wounded man such a shake that a moan of pain burst from his lips.

"Bless me," added Vassa, "did that hurt you?"

"Fiend—monster!" roared Sir Godfrey; "leave me."

"But really you know it will never do for you to be so excitable, my friend."

Another kick followed, and another shriek from the wounded prison-keeper resounded through the room.

Vassa laughed as he said,—

"You cursed me, and I am none the worse. It was imprudent of you. Now I don't curse you, you see; but I have a practical mode of making you suffer. You have prophesied that my end will be worse than yours. I tell you that if I was suffering from one half of the amount of injury that tortures your frame, I would put an end to it with my own hand. Do you think that I would lie at the mercy of any acquaintance who might come in and kick the leg of the couch on which I lay? Most certainly not."

Another kick followed this speech, and Sir Godfrey cried,—

"Mercy—mercy! Vassa. Have mercy upon me!"

" Oh, indeed. You no longer curse."

" Have some mercy upon me. Surely I suffer enough."

" You are a fool, and deserve to suffer."

" I—I am dying, and would now have a confessor."

" What! do I hear aright? Do you intend to patronise one of the holy cheats you have so often scoffed at?"

" I am not the man I was. I am dying, and would seek for mercy."

" Indeed! You know some things which I would not have told."

Sir Godfrey was silent, and, after a slight pause, Vassa continued,—

" Do you hear me? Would they form a part of your confession?"

" I cannot, at such a time as this, tamper with my soul."

" Pho—pho! I thought you upon the whole rather thought you had not got one."

" Vassa—Vassa, those are fearful words. I must have a priest and confess my sins."

" You would confess all?"

" All—all. I am repentant now."

" Yes, like most scoundrels, when they find their career in this world over, and that in another, as they suppose, about to begin. By a lip repentance they think to cheat the Heaven they, with the same breath, declare to be omniscient."

As he spoke, Vassa took from a secret pocket, which was only just large enough to hold it, a very minute viol, and held it up between him and the light for a moment.

" I feel faint," said Sir Godfrey.

" Do you really?"

" What—what have you there?"

" A restorative which will all the better enable you to make your confession. It quickens the perceptions, and arouses the dormant powers of the memory. 'Tis a most rare medicament."

" It is poison!"

" What an ungenerous supposition. Hold your head still while I place upon your lips one drop of this. You were complaining of thirst. Take one drop from this viol and you will complain no more."

" No—no—no. Help—help!"

" Wherefore this outcry?"

" It is poison. I know it is poison. Spare me. Oh, spare me, Vassa!"

" Nay, an you will be so obstinate, I must even force you, for your own good, to swallow it."

He seized the governor by a handful of the hair of his head, and held him down, for, notwithstanding the agony of his wound, the terrified man was making an effort to rise. With a grasp of iron, however, Vassa clutched him with one hand, while with the other, which held the viol, he poured a drop or two from its slender neck upon his lips.

There was one half stifled shriek, and then the form of Sir Godfrey was most fearfully convulsed for a moment or two, after which all was still. Vassa, who had until now kept his hold of the miserable wretch's hair, now let him go. The head swung on one side, and the glazed eyes made no movement. He was dead.

Carefully avoiding the very odour of the liquid that was in the bottle, Vassa placed the stopper in it, and replaced it in the pocket from whence he had taken it.

" Now, there's no knowing," he said, " when a little matter of this sort comes in usefully; I always have it with me, and now it has done good service, for yon lump of clay did, when in life, know some things of his highness the duke that were as well unspoken to any confessor."

At this moment the nurse returned, and she said to Vassa,—

" Is he in a better spirit, good sir? Have you exhorted him to a better state of mind?"

" I have. He is now in a deep sleep. It is questionable when he will awaken; but I would not attempt to disturb him."

" Disturb him. Oh, dear no. I wish he would sleep till doomsday, and I should not disturb him! The dreadful things he says I shall never forget."

" Ah! I am afraid he is a bad man."

" There's no doubt, good sir. There can be no doubt. We are all sinners; but some are worse than others."

" That is a melancholy fact, my dear madam—a most melancholy fact; but it cannot be helped. Pray, remember me in your prayers, as I shall you in mine."

" You are very good, sir. I will, most assuredly. I don't know your worshipful name."

" Master Stephen."

"Thank you—thank you. This bead on my rosary with the crack in it shall be yours for the whole of to-day."

"Good mistress, I thank you; I feel much beholden to you. Fare you well."

"Farewell, noble sir. Farewell."

The nurse sank into a chair, and Vassa left the room.

"Pray for him," she muttered, when he was gone. "Indeed, I shall do no such a thing. A murrain take him. I fully expected a rose noble, at the least, and here he has not even so much as said, 'Mistress, here is a silver groat.' Pray for him, indeed. I think I see me. Anathemas upon him, say I—anathemas upon him."

Vassa took his way to the vestibule of the prison, and when he reached there, the man whom he had first seen said,—

"How do you find Sir Godfrey, noble sir?"

"Better. I left him sleeping."

"Then he must be better, for he has not slept yet since his hurt, and I heard him say that he should never sleep again."

"Indeed! You would find now that he was precisely of the reverse opinion to that."

"Should I, sir?"

"Yes. Good-day, friend—for now," muttered Vassa to himself, as he left the prison, "he will never wake again. But I must now see about keeping my promise to my Lord Hastings. He is infatuated with this girl, Jane, the cunning goldsmith's wife, and he must either have her, or he must be sickened of the intrigue in some way. I will consider of that how it may be accomplished, for my Lord Hastings is gradually becoming, as I would wish him, more and more impressed with the necessity of attending to the interests of the Duke of Gloster, who will, most assuredly, be one day England's master, though he wade through blood the course."

CHAPTER XXXIX.

Jane and the Chamberlain.

"Ye errand of sweete mercy moved her to much riske."

Vassa went to Hastings, and procured from him an understanding that a few days, in consequence of various occurrences, must elapse before he could fulfil his promise as regarded giving him an interview with Jane Shore. This the chamberlain consented to, although not with the best grace in the world.

"You know well, Vassa," he said, "my extreme anxiety on this subject—an anxiety which increases each moment of my existence, and materially tends to withdraw my mind from other and more important matters."

"For that last reason," said Vassa, "you may depend upon my being as brief and expeditious as I can."

"Be so, then, and I shall be satisfied."

"Your lordship, I hope, will remember the conditions under which this meeting is to take place."

"I do."

"If you find Jane Shore repugnant to your suit, you consent to give it up wholly and completely as hopeless?"

"I do, as hopeless," said Hastings, rather despondingly.

"'Tis well. Upon those terms, then, you shall assuredly have the interview you seek; nor should you have experienced any delay at all in the matter, but that Wainstead, the mercer, the father of this girl, lies now dead in his own house, and Jane is too overwhelmed with grief to attend to anything but what concerns his obsequies."

"Be it so. I will wait."

"For about three days," said Vassa, as he rose and left the house of the chamberlain, in which this brief dialogue took place.

Vassa was right indeed when he said that, in consequence of her father's death, Jane was too much absorbed in grief to attend to anything but the mournful duties which she considered devolved upon her on account of that most sad event.

She adhered to her resolution of remaining in her father's house while the body was above ground, notwithstanding all that Shore could urge to the contrary. And now the evening before the day on which the funeral of the mercer was to take place had arrived, when the leech, who had attended upon Wainstead in his mortal illness, for the third time sent up his name to Jane, with an intimation that he wished to see her.

On the two former occasions that he had induced Simon to go and ask Jane to see him, she had begged to be excused, on the plea of great affliction; but he now told Simon to say to her that he much wished her to see him, as he had something really of importance to communicate to her.

Simon, at first, had been rather averse to taking the message to Jane, for he had a strange aversion to doctors, imagining, perhaps truly enough,

"That in the main the worst diseases
Stop, or go on, as God Almighty pleases."

After saying most positively that he would take no such message to Jane, once or twice, he did take it, especially when the leech said,—

"Master Simon, what I have to say I feel certain will bring some sort of contentment to the heart of Mistress Shore, and if, after I have been with her and told her my errand, she say not so, I will give you leave to rail at me as a pretender."

"Sh'an't do any such thing," said Simon, as he walked out of the dingy shop to go and tell Jane what the leech said.

"Admit him, then, Simon," said Jane. "I will see him, since he says so much, for Heaven knows I have need of some good means to content me now. Tell him to come up here to me."

"Sha'n't," said Simon; and down stairs he went and told the man of physic to go to the room above, where he would find Jane.

The leech immediately ascended, and, being used to the house, he soon reached the room indicated, although the staircase was ingeniously built so as not to have the least light upon it of any kind or description, direct or borrowed. The room was darkened, but the greater darkness of the staircase was a very great preparation to the eyes for its subdued light, so that when the medical man arrived he found himself in comparative lightness. Jane rose to receive him, but he said,—

"Continue seated, I pray you, and believe that it is from no idle wish to make myself busy or important that I now intrude upon you."

"I did not for one moment imagine so," said Jane, "when I declined seeing you; it was because I feared my grief of mind would prevent me from showing to any visiter proper courtesy."

"You need have been under no apprehension of misconstruction from me," said the leech. "My profession unhappily makes me much acquainted with scenes of sorrow."

"Alas! it must."

"But I will not revert to the past," he added. "I know that the very sight of me must awaken painful remembrances, so I will at once proceed to what brought me hither. Am I right or wrong in supposing that you feel a great interest in the fate of one Walter Fane, a young man was an apprentice to your father?"

This was touching upon a chord which awakened all Jane's sorrows anew, and she burst into tears, as she exclaimed,—

"Oh, why come to me with his name on your lips, and yet speak to me of consolation? It is cruel—it is very cruel. He is gone, and lost to me for ever—for ever! Oh, Walter—Walter!"

"Calm yourself," said the leech. "Believe me I have not mentioned his name with any view of awakening sad recollections, but rather to banish them by present hopes."

"Hopes, said you?"

"Yes, Mistress Shore. Why should you banish hope—that last fond solace of the unfortunate? Surely you cannot so much doubt the goodness and the wisdom of Providence as to believe that it has left you without any hope?"

"Hope of what?" said Jane—"hope of what? Oh, do not keep me in suspense. If you would have me indulge in any hope concerning Walter Fane, give me at once, I pray you, reason for it, and I will bless the words you utter."

"It is of him I came to speak."

"Of him—of Walter? Oh, he lives—he lives! You say you came to speak of him? Were he no more, you would not mock me by mention of him. Only tell me that he lives."

"I pray you to be calm. This agitation will do you serious injury."

"My question—oh, answer me that. Does Walter Fane live? Tell me he lives, and you shall see that I can then be calm."

"He does, as far as my opinion and judgment will carry me."

"Thank Heaven—thank Heaven!" cried Jane, as she clasped her hands; "he lives—he lives—Walter lives!"

"It was to tell you of that much, and more, that I came here," said the leech.

"And I sent you from me, and would not see you the while you had such news as that to tell me. Oh, if you had but hinted at your message—if you had but used one word to indicate it was of him you came to speak, you had not solicited to see me in vain."

"I feared to agitate you too much, and therefore went my way when I found you were not disposed to see any one."

"You know that in me it was no mere excuse."

"That I felt assured of, and so left and came again the more readily. I saw him in whose fate you feel so great an interest some days since."

"Where?—how?—under what circumstances? Tell me all, leech—oh, quick—tell me all!"

"There, now, you said you would be calm."

"And I am calm. Oh, if you knew how much I have suffered on this head—how much I feel on it, you would tell me, with what haste you could, all that I can wish to know."

"Beyond," said the leech, "the fact that he lives, of which I have already informed you, my news is sad. Had it all been of a joyous character, you had had it quickly. He lives in the prison at Blackfriars."

"The prison!"

"Yes; in that gloomy abode where it is said the innocent as often lead a weary life as the guilty."

"In prison!—Walter Fane in prison! He, the soul of honour—he, who never by word or deed wronged mortal man! Walter Fane in prison—oh, it cannot be!"

"I can but assure you that it is so. I was hastily sent for to attend some persons who had received hurts in the prison, and then I saw him. With frantic and imploring accents, he begged of me to carry news of his condition to Master Wainstead, the mercer of the Chepe, who he said he knew would use his influence to learn of what he was accused, and rescue him from that most dismal of all abodes."

"And he knows not that death has been busy among those who loved him?" said Jane.

"Certainly not."

"And you promised him—you gave him hope? You told him that he should be rescued?"

"I did not. That prison is looked upon with jealous eyes of scrutiny. If it were known that any visitor to it had disclosed the name of any victim within its walls, not only would that visitor never be again admitted, but some evil would be done to him before long, not openly, but by some secret agency."

"Blessings on you, that you have run this danger for poor Walter's sake!"

"I do not consider that I am in much danger. To you, and to you only, I entrust the secret. Make what use you can of the information you now have, without naming your informant."

"Betray? Never—never!"

"I know I can trust you, and therefore I did so without exacting any promise of you of secrecy."

"You may indeed rely upon me. Oh, Walter—Walter! upon what pretext have you been treated thus!"

"Probably upon no pretext at all," said the leech. "Many who are cast into prison now-a-days have no excuse made to them for the most iniquitous act."

"Can there be so much wickedness in the world?"

"Your notions of the world, Mistress Shore, cannot be founded upon much experience, if you think there is such bounds to the amount of villany which may possibly be acted up to."

"What can be done to save him?"

"There I am a bad adviser, and know not what to say to you. If you have any influence with any member of the court, I pray you to use it, and it may be effectual. If you have none, I fear the case is hopeless."

"Hopeless—hopeless! Oh, no—no—no!"

"I cannot stir in the matter, without at once pointing suspicion—nay, almost certainty—at me, as the person giving you the information. I have those dependant upon me whom I cannot bring myself to sacrifice."

"God forbid you should," said Jane. "I, for one, would not hear of such a step. There is misery enough, without spreading it still farther. Make no sacrifice, I pray you!"

"For myself," said the leech, with feeling, "I am an old man, and care not much now what rubs and slights fortune may give me, but I have those dependant on me whom I love."

"Then are you happy—for I am alone in the wide world, and have none to love me! Forgive me, Walter—you love me!"

"And you have a husband."

Jane shuddered, as she said,—

"Yes; I—have—a husband!"

"Who ought to love you, and ——"

"I understand you, sir. Whom, you would say, I ought to love. But I cannot dissemble."

"Well, well—I will not take advantage of this little service I have done you, by obtruding upon your affairs with either my advice or my questions. I pray you pardon me for having said so much as I have said."

"It needs no pardon. We cannot take offence with those whom we know wish us well. I am unhappy. My history is a painful one, and too well known. I have been weak and foolish, to an amount of criminality, and I am surely now suffering a just retribution for my perjured soul."

"Perjured, say you?"

"Yes. I swore, in God's holy temple, to love one whom I loved not. I was then perjured."

"I think you take too harsh a view of that matter. But can you think of no one who in this affair of Walter has power, and would likewise have the will, to aid you?"

"Yes," suddenly cried Jane, with animation in her looks,—"yes—yes! Oh, how could I forget? Yes—there is one."

"Who is he?"

"The king!"

"Indeed!"

"Yes—King Edward will aid me. He knows who I am. He said as much once as he would aid me."

"If so, then you get to the fountain head of power at once. His simple word restores to you Walter Fane."

"To me! No—no, not to me. I must never look upon his face again. He—he shall be free, but we must never in this world meet again."

"Indeed."

"I cannot repine. I did myself pronounce that sentence, when, at the altar's foot, I consented to become the wife of Shore. We must never, never meet again!"

"It were well to pursue the determination. Rescue him if you will, and see him not."

"I will attempt to move the king in his behalf. I may succeed; and, if I do so, Walter shall be free, knowing not from whom came the intercession that made him so. Oh, it will be glorious to feel that I have saved him, and yet he knows it not. I pray you to secrecy."

"For all reasons, I shall be secret as the grave."

"'Tis well. I will to the king."

"Have you weighed well the difficulties in the way of getting access to the monarch?"

"Difficulties!"

"Yes. You know kings are not to be called upon at their homes, like your lawyers, and asked questions. You will require some interest ere you can reach the person of a monarch, surrounded by many precautions, to guard him against concealed enemies, who would gladly take his life if opportunity offered."

"You have discouraged but not daunted me. I will attempt the task, let the difficulties be what they may."

"There may occur some opportunity of attempting it with me. Should such come to my knowledge, you may rely upon hearing so much from me, together with as much information as I can possibly give you in furtherance of your design."

"I owe you many thanks."

The leech then rose to go; and, after exhorting Jane to be of better cheer, and most of all to do nothing hastily, he left the place.

Jane wished much to be enabled to tell Simon that Walter lived, and she was on the point of calling to him, but a sudden thought crossed her mind that, by doing so immediately after the departure of the leech, she should be clearly pointing him out as the party from whom she had her information.

"No—no; I must wait awhile before I tell him," she said. "I cannot break my promise to the leech; for, although I know I can rely upon Simon, yet, from one to another, that is the way secrets of vital importance soon become known."

This was a very just and proper resolution of Jane's, and one which reflected equal honour on her head and heart. But with her to feel convinced of the justice of anything was at once to make up her mind to it, so she did not call to Simon; and she was earnestly considering how she might best obtain an audience of the king, when Simon again popped his head into the room, saying,—

"Somebody else."

"Who, Simon?"

"Don't know. Says he wants to see you, and has got something to tell you"

"Do you know him, Simon?"

"No."

"I cannot see a stranger. Go to him, Simon, and say so."

"I have. Did the leech say anything worth hearing?"

"Yes—that is—no, Simon—oh, certainly."

"Humph! don't understand that."

Simon went down stairs again, but he returned in a few moments, and said, wonderfully harshly for him,—

"You must see this man. He says he comes to say something about somebody we all think lost, but would be glad to find again. Who can he mean but Walter?"

"I will see him, Simon, on such a plea as that. But, as he is a stranger, you must remain within call."

"You need not tell me that," said Simon. "Just you raise your voice a little, and I will hear you, when he had better be in anybody else's skin than his own."

Simon again departed, and in a few moments Jane heard a footstep ascending the stairs deliberately. The door was opened, and an elderly-looking man presented himself. He was tall and thin, but seemed much enfeebled by age, for his limbs trembled, and his head had a continual slight palsied shake. Jane rose and said,—

"I pray you be seated, sir."

"Do I speak to good Mistress Shore," he said, "sometime daughter of the right worshipful Master Wainstead?"

"Yes, sir," said Jane, "I am that unhappy—I mean I am she whom you have named."

"You said unhappy ——"

"Let the word pass; I should not have uttered it."

"Ah, well-a-day—ah, well-a-day! when unhappy is the word uppermost in a young heart. It should not be so."

"We cannot help our destiny."

"No, no, we cannot. I am unhappy; but, lady, let that pass too. We have not here met to talk of our unhappiness or our joy. I am very old; I am over four-score, lady."

"Are you, indeed, so old?"

"Ay, truly; I have outlived all I loved—all, all I loved."

The old man bowed his head upon his hands and shook more than before, as if the memory of a thousand buried affections were arising up before his mental vision. Jane pitied him sincerely, and in a softened voice, she said,—

"Bear yet awhile with this mortal pilgrimage. I were happier than I am, could I look forward to a nearer approach to the grave."

"Well, well," said the old man, suddenly rousing himself; "I ought not to give way thus. I am a stranger to you, but I have come to tell you that one whom you thought dead lives—one Walter Fane."

"Then you confirm what I have already heard," said Jane.

"Already heard?" said the old man.

"Yes—that is, already fancied. Tell me all you know."

"It amounts not to much, lady. It is this. There is a young man of a well-favoured aspect now in the ancient prison of the Blackfriars, who, I was told by one of the official persons of the prison, mentioned you and your father as his dearest and best friends."

"Yes—yes."

"I inquired further, without seeming too curious, and I learnt that he was placed in prison by some great personage, I could not learn who, for some real or supposed offence. I thought this a hard case, and now I am here to tell you so much."

"I thank you from my heart."

"Lady, you are welcome. Alas! I had a son once, a poor fellow, who gave some sort of offence to the Earl Marshall, and he was cast into that very prison of the Blackfriars."

"Indeed!

"Yes; but I made a friend, who got me an interview with King Edward, and so he was rescued. You are aware, now, that the chiefest favourite of the monarch, and the man who can do anything, is the lord high chamberlain, whose interest I have obtained."

"Hastings?"

"Ay, the Lord Hastings. That is the man. The Lord Hastings has the king's ear, and can do wonders."

"The Lord Hastings?" said Jane, with a shudder, for she had been warned of him by her father.

"Yes," added the old man. "A nobleman generous and just, although hasty, and a

little given to ostentation. From the mere pride of showing that he could do so much, he would rescue the young man I speak of from the prison of the Blackfriars. But——"

"But, what?"

"From the same reason he would oppose his liberation, if it were sought through any quarter but by his own mediation."

"You think he would?"

"I am certain Edward refers such matters confidentially to him; therefore it is that I strenuously advise you to seek him, and what is more, let your period of seeking him be at three of the clock, at his new house in Westminster. I speak from mature reflection. Farewell, lady. God speed you, and save you from suffering."

"I thank you. To whom am I so much indebted?"

"Heed not that—heed not. I am the last of my race. I have outlived, as I said to you, all whom I loved, and I am willing now to go down to the tomb unknown."

He tottered from the room with a deep sigh, and left the house, Simon kindly assisting him over the door-step; but when he had turned the first corner, he drew himself up, and said,—

"She will visit him. I could stake my head upon it, she will now visit him."

It was Antonio Vassa himself.

CHAPTER XL.

The Interview with the Chamberlain.

"Jane sought ye lord highe chamberlaine in his newe house at Westminster, to gaine much intercession with ye kinge."

JANE pondered over the words of her visitor, and much as she had reason to dread Lord Hastings, inasmuch as her father had warned her that he was one of those who, under the pretence of admiration for her beauty and virtue, would have done her as much evil as possible, she each moment became more and more inclined to go to him, and see what could be done in the way of intercession for poor Walter Fane.

It was a sad thing now that Jane had no wiser or more experienced counsellor than her own heart. The only two persons on whom she had been for years accustomed to rely for counsel and assistance in everything, were now gone from her—one dead, and the other a prisoner. But, oh, what a new and pure delight it was to Jane, to find that Walter, after all, was not among the dead. As she repeated to herself these blissful words, "He lives, he lives!" she almost forgot that he lived not for her, and that perchance he had still to feel the pang of knowing that she was now another's. But these thoughts were sure to come, and after the first excitement of joy that he was not actually among the dead had subsided, such a gush of exquisite misery came across the heart of poor Jane, that she was nearly fainting from its excess.

"Oh, what have I done? what have I done?" she exclaimed. "Upon the faintest, poorest report of Walter's death, I have matched myself with another, and that, too, without the excuse that he occupied a place either in my affections or my respect. Oh, Walter, Walter, what will you think of me?"

This was indeed a dreadful question, and Jane found now more and more, as circumstances developed themselves, what a fearfully erroneous step she had taken, when, contrary to her own feeling and her own judgment, she had wedded Shore. She wished that she could rescue Walter, and then that before he could learn she was another's, she could die, so that his sorrow for her death might in some measure obliterate his despair at her faithlessness.

That he was in ignorance of what had occurred, she felt was far more than probable, for how was he likely, immured in one of those gloomy dungeons of the well-known prison which had been named to her, to obtain any information of what was passing in the great world without?

"And how he would smile incredulously," now moaned Jane, "were any one to tell him I was now the wife of Shore. He would not believe it, though an angel were to vouch its truth. I know he would not believe it from any lips but mine; and shall I have the horror, the despair of having to assure him of the hideous fact? Oh, no—no, no. I can die with a less, a far less pang than that would cost me to utter."

But these feelings and reasonings, however much they tended to inflict upon her heart the severest pangs, in no way went towards any thought of escaping them by leaving Walter Fane to his fate in the miserable prison of the Blackfriars. No; Jane was by far too generous for that. She foresaw her own misery when he should be rescued; but yet she resolved upon hazarding all in her power to rescue him.

"I will, come of it what may," she said, "seek this Lord Hastings, who, I am told, alone has the power to aid me in my fixed purpose. I go to him on an errand of mercy. He is a nobleman, and surely a man of honour. He must respect me for the errand on which I seek him, and which can admit of no misconstruction."

Alas, poor Jane! unversed in the world and its vicious, tortuous usages wert thou. A nobleman was no more a man of honour in the days of Edward the Fourth than he is now; and then, as now, the world was quite ready always to place the worst possible construction on the most innocent actions.

There was one view of the subject, too, which the urgency of the case seemed completely to shut out from Jane's remembrance, and that regarded Shore. She quite forgot to ask herself what line of conduct she was to pursue towards him in the matter. Whether she was to attempt to keep a secret from him the fact of her visit to Lord Hastings, or avow it and its object—what would be the consequence? Already angry enough at all thought or mention of Walter Fane, such an act as this which Jane now contemplated was enough to drive him to positive madness. But she thought not of that; she only saw a dismal picture of Walter Fane in a dungeon; she only remembered that she had been told that to go to the lord chamberlain, and beseech his interference, was the only means of saving him; and, therefore, with scarce a passing thought of Shore, or of the consequences to herself which might result from the visit, she made up her mind to go, at the hour mentioned, to the house of Lord Hastings.

There was one circumstance which ought to have made Jane pause, and ask herself if her own judgment really approved of the course she was about to adopt. That circumstance was one, too, of her own motion, and showed that at the bottom of her heart there must be some lingering doubt with regard to the prudence of the step she was about to take,—it was that she dreaded to tell Simon of it.

Now she could only have such a dread from a consciousness that the project would meet with Simon's instant disapproval. Had she been quite clear about the wisdom and propriety of the step she was about to take, she would not have hesitated for a moment in making Simon her confidant. But she did not feel quite clear on these points. There was a latent suspicion in her mind that she was allowing herself to be hurried away by feeling and excitement, and yet that feeling and that excitement came with too strong and rushing a tide for her to attempt to resist.

"No," she said, "I will not tell Simon. It will but make Simon unhappy. I will not tell Simon anything of it until I return, and then, perhaps, I shall be able to tell him that I have been successful, which must silence all objections."

Thus did Jane, in this most unhappy transaction, isolate herself from all but her enemies. The hour of his visit had been well and artfully chosen by Antonio Vassa, for it only by a little preceded that at which he had told Jane the chamberlain was most accessible. He calculated then upon her not having time for calm reflection, or to take counsel of any one whose feelings might not be so deeply interested as her own, and who, consequently, would be enabled to bring a cooler judgment to bear upon the circumstances.

"She will make the visit," he thought, "in the first excitement of her feelings; for the time will come for her to make it in the midst of that excitement."

He reasoned correctly. The time did come; and giving herself scarcely a sufficient number of minutes in which to accomplish the walk, Jane, to the surprise of Simon, came down the staircase ready attired for the street.

"Going out?" said Simon.

"Yes," replied Jane—"yes; a short distance."

"Go with you?"

"No, Simon—no. There is no occasion. You need not do so. I am not going very far."

"Where to?"

"Merely to make a call; but I wish, Simon, to go alone."

Jane said this because she knew that Simon would follow her, unless she said something very stringent on that head to prevent him. Her wish to go alone, of course, did so; but it was with anxiety that Simon saw her walk out.

He shook his head gravely, and muttered,—

"Where's she going now, I wonder? I don't like her to go alone; but if she will, she will. A deal too pretty and too good to go out alone in such times as these. Well, well, I can't help it if people will do all sorts of foolish things."

This remark, although it sounded like a consolation, was far from being one in reality to Simon, for he was too much attached to Jane to feel satisfied if any evil should befal her, merely because he might have warned her of it, and she had brought it on herself by her own imprudence. Under ordinary circumstances, and with any one to whom he felt indifferent, it would have been all very well, but, with Jane, who stood so first and foremost in his best affection, such rules of action held no contest at all with feeling.

He watched her from the shop-door down the Chepe, and his anxiety visibly increased. He shook his head a great number of times, and then, taking a sudden resolution in his head, he ran over the way to Master Snafflings, and said to him,—

"Give an eye to our house, Master Snafflings."

Then, without waiting for any answer, he walked with a rapid pace after Jane.

Not at all expecting she was followed, Jane proceeded as quickly as she could walk towards Westminster. She drew her hood close down over her face, so as to avoid the recognition of any one who might chance to meet her whom she knew, for she wanted not now to be stayed by any one on her errand.

As she went, she strove to arrange in her own mind what she should say to the lord chamberlain when she should see him, and so intent was she upon her own thoughts and the subject that engrossed them, that she was not at all aware that a tall man, in a rich scarlet cloak, was following her closely.

It was Vassa, who had lingered in the neighbourhood of the mercer's house at a little before the time when, if Jane went at all to seek the house of Lord Hastings, she must start from home to do so. And he was not at all disappointed.

As she got clear of the houses, and was walking hurriedly down the side of the street which was not built upon, he passed her; for he wished to get to the chamberlain's house first, in order that not the least obstruction should be thrown in her way, or any violence offered her by the lacqueys. With rapid strides he left her a considerable distance behind, and was himself at once admitted to an audience of Hastings, to whom he merely said,—

"She comes now. Give orders that she be admitted at once, and most respectfully treated. A stray word or look from any of your domestics might even now awaken her to a sense of her own imprudence, and send her back."

"Most true—most true!" cried Hastings. "By Heaven and all its saints, I will be the death of any one who shall so foil me."

"Give instant orders."

"I will—I will."

Hastings summoned a page, to whom he gave the necessary directions, charging him to be at the outer gate, and bring at once to an apartment which he named, the young female who in a few minutes would ask to see him.

These orders were received by the page with all the gravity of profound respect, and when he had bowed himself out, Vassa said,—

"And now, my lord, all I again implore of you is to reconsider your solemn promise made to me upon this subject."

"I do—I will; but, Vassa ——"

"What now?"

"I shall be puzzled to know what answer to give to her request about this lad who is in prison."

"Puzzled?"

"Yes; I have not yet pre-arranged what I shall say to her."

"Most certainly, tell her you will intercede with the king to obtain his instant liberation."

"Yes, yes, and ——"

"And then call upon her gratitude to aid your suit."

"I will; and if she yet refuse me—if she yet scorn me, Vassa, what then?"

"You must let her depart in honour as she came. I tell you, Hastings, as I have told you before, that the position of affairs at present will not allow of your making your name so fearfully obnoxious to the citizens as it would become, were you to offer any outrage to Jane Shore."

"What you say is true."

"You cannot but feel its truth; curtail your passions as best you may. In honour as she came, so must she go, if such be her own will. Use what arts of persuasion you please, but if you find her obstinately virtuous, rather assume yourself to be convinced and reproved by her, than show the extent of your disappointment by word or even by a look."

"'Tis a hard part to play."

"Psha! not for a courtier, and a man who looks forward to being the greatest but one in this realm. What would the Duke of Gloster say if he thought Hastings could not so far dissemble?"

"Enough—enough. You shall not be able, from any conduct of mine, to go and tell the duke that I am so foolish a man, Vassa. As this girl comes so shall she go, if she wish it."

"Enough—enough."

At this moment a page opened the door. It was the same to whom the urgent and particular commands had been given; and now he stood in a respectful attitude just a pace or so within the room, waiting until by an inquiry from his master, he should be permitted to speak.

"Well?" said Hastings.

"My lord, the lady your lordship mentioned has come."

"And in the apartment I mentioned?"

"She is, my lord."

"Gave she any message to you?"

"None, further than that on urgent business she would see your lordship, if that your leisure served."

"'Tis well; say I will be with her anon."

The page returned, and Hastings walked to the door of the room, as he said to Vassa,—

"Will you wait for me here?"

"As you please."

"Do so, then. The domestics will bring you what refreshments you please to order. Wish me success, Vassa, for, by Heaven! I love her as I never yet loved woman."

Hastings left the room, and Vassa looked after him with a meaning smile.

"Wish you success!" he muttered, "wish you success! Indeed! you will find that all the wishes of all the world would not give you success. You must know but little, my good lord chamberlain, of her upon whom you have now fixed your desires, if you fancy aught that you can urge can give you even a hope. Ha, ha! Her heart is already too much possessed. No, my good Lord Hastings, you will find that you have not a chance, and that you will be met with scorn; but I must hold you to the very letter of your agreement; and, that I may do so securely, I had better overhear what passes."

Vassa glided from the room, and, crossing a corridor, he took a small key from his pocket, and opened a door in the wall, which was hidden by some coarse tapestry. This door led to a narrow passage that ran in the thickness of the wall for some distance, and then took a sudden turn at a right angle. This he pursued for about a dozen paces, and then he paused, and, folding his arms across his breast, he stood in an attitude of listening, while the murmur of voices came each moment plainer upon his ears.

Jane had taken no notice of the cavalier with the red cloak, more particularly as he had passed her, and made no attempt to look back. She hastened on, and reached the gate of the chamberlain's splendid mansion, just about the same time as the page who had received his instructions from Lord Hastings reached the porter, and was communicating them to him.

"By the mass, and here she is," said the latter personage.

"Yes, indeed," remarked the page, "and from what I can see of her, although that is not much, beshrew me, if I don't think our lord has a good taste."

"Hush!—she's here—a charming pair of eyes."

"Ay, and look, there is a wandering lock of her hair. How beautiful—how very ——"

"Hold your tongue, master page."

This brief confabulation was carried on at a little wicket which opened in the great gate, and at which now Jane arrived.

"Is the Lord Hastings within?" she said, timidly.

"Yes, mistress."

"I would speak with him on urgent business."

"Well and good," chimed in the page. "This happens to be an hour of the day when his lordship is much at leisure. Will it please you to walk in?"

Thus encouraged, Jane entered the court-yard, and she was pleased to hear so ready a confirmation of what had been told her by what she thought the benevolent old man, who had visited her.

The page conducted her with the greatest respect to the apartment which Hastings had mentioned, and when there, he said,—

"What shall I say to my noble master?"

"Tell him," said Jane, "that there is one here who would fain see him on most urgent business, and on an errand of mercy."

"I will so report to him."

"You have my thanks."

The page left her, and Jane, who felt a little more assured, in consequence of the courteous reception she had received, had leisure to look around her at the room in which she was. It was small, but according to the fashion of the times; and, as far as the means and appliances of art then suffered, a very elegant one, notwithstanding, as some one has said of tapestry, "that our ancestors were so careful of their carpets, that they hung them on the walls." Certainly, tapestried chambers had a most magnificent appearance, and this one was adorned with some of the most chaste specimens of that fabric which the age could produce.

The floor was thickly strewn with fine rushes mingled with some fragrant herbs, so that there was an agreeable odour in the apartment, which otherwise had not much furnishing, being merely supplied with some very low-seated carved chairs, and a table made octagonally, the wood of which was of the walnut tree.

Jane was a little fatigued by her hurried walk, and she sat down on one of the chairs, and threw back her hood from her beautiful face, which, from the exercise she had taken, had more of the glow of health upon it than it had exhibited at all since the disappearance of Walter Fane, and the presumption that he was no more.

"Surely," she thought, "when the domestics are so courteous, the master must be so, or they would borrow rudeness from him. I gather new hope even from the manner of my reception. Oh, Walter—Walter! if I can but save you, I shall at least be enabled to lay up in my heart one most gratifying reflection against the sea of troubles that has so lately so much oppressed me."

The moments now passed to Jane with leaden wings, and she fixed her eyes anxiously towards the door in expectation of the coming of him to whom she wished to make so urgent an appeal.

"I will beg of him," she thought, "not to let Walter know to whose intercession with him he owes his release. He shall not be encumbered with a supposed debt of gratitude to me, and so, when he comes, which perchance he may, to reproach me with my falseness to him, I shall know that I have saved him, though he will not."

Tears nearly started to her eyes as these reflections occurred to her, but she felt the necessity of calming herself, and she stemmed successfully the current of her feelings, that she might retain strength and courage to plead for him whom she loved, but who, alas! could never more be other than a stranger to her.

She heard a footstep, and she rose hastily, with a flush of colour upon her face. The door of the room was opened by the page, who stood respectfully on one side of the entrance, and Lord Hastings, with as much grace as he could command, and as amiable a countenance as he could put on, made his appearance.

CHAPTER XLI.

The Temptation.

It was said that my Lord Hastings had a severe illness, from the agony of his disappointed love for some one who scorned him; others averred he was poisoned.

MARCUS's *Chronicles.*

So entranced for a moment was Hastings by the really transcendant beauty of Jane, that the complimentary and kind speech he had conceived as he came along, and had intended to utter, died upon his lips.

And she, too, notwithstanding all her resolution--all her wish to say something which should propitiate the man whom she was assured could alone save Walter, Jane felt all her courage desert her now that she was in his presence, and the magnitude of the stake for which she preyed came across her mind in such strength, that she feared much that she should be totally unequal to the task she had so suddenly, and with so very little calmness or consideration, assigned to herself.

Hastings, whose temporary confusion solely arose from his delight at looking upon so much loveliness, was the first to recover to some degree his wonted composure. Advancing with a gallant air, he took her by the hand, saying, with as much affected deference as if he had been addressing a queen,—

"Madam, since you have done me the honour of visiting my poor home, I pray you be seated."

"My lord ——"

Jane paused, for she had not breath to proceed.

"Pray compose yourself," said Hastings; "I shall be happy in waiting your leisure, and in the reflection that my house will be honoured perchance by your longer stay."

Jane was glad to be seated, for her limbs trembled under her; and could she, at that moment, have given creditable utterance to her most candid thoughts, her words would have consisted of a passionate regret that she had adventured on a task she now found herself so utterly unable to accomplish.

But this was a feeling which was likely soon to pass away. She thought of Walter Fane in a dungeon, and that nerved her. She clasped her hands, and, turning to Lord Hastings, she said,—

"My errand here is—the only one which could—which ought to have made me bold enough to seek your lordship."

"Indeed, fair one."

There was a something in the tone of admiration with which the chamberlain spoke to her, from which Jane instinctively shrunk, and she wished her errand over now when she had scarce commenced to state its purport.

"I am all attention," said Hastings. "Need I say that you can ask nothing in vain of me, fairest of the fair?"

"Do you know me, my lord?" said Jane.

"To see you once is never to forget you. You are she who is called the Rose of the City. The fairest maid in London."

"I am a wife, my lord. As I say, I came here on an errand of mercy. You are pleased to say, that ere I utter it my request is granted. Heaven send it may be so. I will hope so, because it cannot but be a small matter to you to liberate from bondage one who is innocent."

"Pray explain your meaning, lady."

"My poor father, who is now no more, had a 'prentice, named Walter Fane, one who did his duty faithfully and honestly."

"No doubt—no doubt. Residing in the same house with so much beauty as you possess would dazzle anybody into honesty."

Jane did not stop to analyse this speech of the chamberlain's, which had in it so much more gallantry than common sense; but she proceeded rather more hastily than before.

"For some offence—I know not what, but of which I could stake my life he is innocent—he is confined in the prison of Blackfriars. It is to release him that I come to pray you."

"He must have done something?"

"No—no. He could not. He is incapable of doing aught that is incompatible with the strictest code of honour."

"You take a warm interest in the youth."

"I do. He is now my only friend."

"Indeed! Are you a widow, and so young?"

"No—no—no."

"Well, lady, it does not become me to question you of your own concerns; but you must be aware that the king only can command the release of a prisoner?"

"Yes, I am so told; but I have been likewise told how difficult, nay, how utterly impossible it would be for a suppliant to reach the presence of the monarch, and that you, who can do so with ease, in consequence of your high station, might be induced to this act of justice."

"You are right."

"You will—you will? Oh, may Heaven shower its choicest blessings on you. You will save him?"

"I said that it would be hard to refuse so fair a pleader as yourself."

"Nay; but on the high ground of his own innocence I would have you rescue him from prison. Believe me, he has done no wrong. We thought him dead, because he came not to us. Alas! alas! he could not come. Who knows what horrors he may have gone through in that dreadful place of most evil repute."

"Was ever cause of mortal man pleaded with such silvery accents?" said Hastings, admiringly. "Was ever so much eloquence tasked to save aught human? Oh, happy, happy prisoner, with such an advocate. Who would not languish for an age in chains to provoke such sympathy from such a soul as yours, in such a casket of wondrous beauty?"

Jane was a little alarmed, and would gladly have left the house, for, as he gave utterance to those sentiments of admiration, Hastings approached closer to her, and would have taken her hand. She drew back, and wrapped her cloak closer around her as, in faltering accents, she said,—

"My lord, I will believe that you will plead to the king the cause of the prisoner."

"For your beauty's sake, I will."

"Nay, for common justice sake. In the holy name of right I ask of you to rescue this innocent man from bondage."

"I swear to you, by your own radiant charms, that I will see the king this very day, and your request shall become to him one from me, which I will urge as far as a subject may dare to urge a king."

"Thanks, my lord—thanks. My prayers and deepest gratitude shall be for ever yours. The king will listen to your suit?"

"I think he will. It is a small matter, and, innocent or guilty, I do not see why such unparalleled beauty as yours should not have the prerogative to save any one."

"My lord, you have a far higher motive for action in this matter in the justice of the cause you espouse," said Jane, coldly.

"But you will not quarrel with my motive, fair saint?" said Hastings. "Let me save him whose safety is so dear to you, from what motive I may, so that I do save him."

"I—I have no more to say," said Jane. "You have promised me."

"On the word of a noble."

"Then I am satisfied. Farewell, my lord. You have the thanks of one who will do you more justice than you seem inclined to do yourself."

"Nay, why so hasty? You talked of gratitude even now."

"I did. I feel it ever glowing in my heart to those who have called forth the sentiment."

"But gratitude should be a practical virtue."

"What means your lordship?"

"You are not happy?"

"Happy?"

"No. You are not happy. Your husband, Shore, is not a man to mate with one of nature's fairest flowers. Oh, it is most monstrous that one so cold, so full of unappreciating qualities, should possess a jewel which he knows not the value of, and the lustre of which has no becoming loveliness in his eyes. Jane Shore, you are not happy."

Jane felt ready to sink as Hastings uttered these words. A swelling sensation came up in her throat; but she could not weep, although tears, just then, would have been, indeed, a luxury.

The chamberlain fancied he was getting on famously, and, in his softest tones, he continued,—

"I have before seen and admired your beauty. In common with many more, I have regretted the cruel fate which united you to one who will be a blight to your young existence, and who will cloud the best, most, beautiful, and what ought to be the happiest portion of your life, with sadness and sorrows."

There was truth in every word he spoke, even although it came from such tainted lips as those of the dishonourable, reckless chamberlain. Jane felt there was truth in what he said, but she roused herself from the state of despair into which she was falling, and, in firmer accents than she had yet spoken in, she said,—

"Enough of this, my lord. If all this be true, you do but repeat a tale which my own heart can tell me best. If false, I ought not for a moment to listen to it."

"My fair one, it was not to pain you I spoke."

"Indeed!"

"No. The cunning leech, if he take pains to describe the malady of a patient, concludes with proposing a remedy for the disease."

"There is none for me," said Jane, passionately; "there is none for me. I pray you let me go."

"Nay; you go too hastily, by far, to a despairing conclusion. There is a remedy for all the ills you suffer."

"No, no, no."

"Yes, I say, yes. Why, in the name of all that is joyous, bright, and beautiful, should you waste youth and beauty upon one who cannot appreciate either, but who, in fact, uses the existence of both as if they were reproaches to you, wherewith to feed his mad jealousy? Why should you remain the slave of such a man as Shore?"

"This is language I may not hear," said Jane; "I am his wife!"

"A foolish agreement, I own, which the fine sense with which you are gifted will soon enable you to scatter to the winds. If it was an error to become his wife,—as you seem to confess it was,—why perpetuate the error by continuing to be so? Leave him."

"No! no!"

"I repeat, leave him. Wherefore remain with the man who would make your life a misery to you?"

"There are two answers to what you say, my lord. In the first place, I took the marriage vow to that man of my own free will, and I must keep it. In the second, I have no father now to fly to."

"We will consider the first reason," said Hastings, "as completely disposed of by my former argument; and, as for the second, there are hearts which will receive you as fondly as ever a father's could; there are arms which would shield you far more powerfully from all harm than ever he could hope to do."

"Not one."

"Jane, I love you! I adore you!"

Jane shrunk towards the door, and Hastings continued, in a tone of passionate pleading, now that he had once fairly broken the ice, to plead his mad, frantic, hopeless suit.

"Jane, I love you. You are the one sole object of my fondest idolatry. You, and you alone, have awakened in my breast those sentiments of adoration I had heard and read of, but never believed the full existence of till I saw you. Never—never did man love woman as I love you, Jane. With me, your whole life shall be one dream of never-ending joy and luxury. My power will protect you—my wealth, which is greater than

men think, shall be wholly at your disposal. Do not, I pray you, hastily reject an offer made so honestly and so sincerely."

Jane was thunderstricken when first he began to speak, and she had let him go on so far, not because she wished to hear his criminal addresses, but because she had not power to interpose. But now indignation aroused her, and she replied to him,—

"Shame upon you, sir, to take advantage of the cause that brought me beneath your own roof to heap upon me the greatest insult that could be uttered to my ears! Shame upon you, that some more fitting place than your own house could not be found in which to insult me! Here you know there are none to aid me."

"Jane—Jane ——"

"With such scorn as my nature makes me to feel—with such contempt, and with such abhorrence as I can summon to my aid, I leave you."

"Nay, reflect."

"Reflect? Reflect on infamy?"

"But, think again."

"The thought is the sin, for when thought of, it is more than half committed. I leave you, sir."

Hastings stepped between her and the door, as he exclaimed,—

"Jane—Jane, will you drive me mad?"

"You are mad to imagine for one moment I was formed for listening to such words."

"I cannot brook denial. Give me a hope."

"Not one."

"Jane, I am a desperate man. I have staked my whole earthly happiness upon this cast, and I must win or die. Jane—Jane Shore, you are my divinity! For your sake I will discard even Heaven from my thoughts, and own none but that which is in your sweet eyes."

"My lord, allow me to pass."

"Not yet, not yet. Have some pity on one who loves you as I love. Your own beauty is to blame, and partial nature, that made you such a glorious piece of workmanship. Jane, you cannot blame me that Heaven, having made you loveable, I should obey its high behests, and love you as I do."

"This is horrible!" said Jane. "Let me pass, my lord, or my cries shall summon your own servants as witnesses to this scene."

"They dare not come."

"Does it befit your valour to detain a woman? You a noble, too—one to whom the common herd are told to look for an example of what is high and honourable! Oh, shame, sir, shame upon you. Let me pass, I say, and ask of Heaven pardon for your fault."

"I ask no pardon—I ask nothing but your love. That will content me if placed against all other possessions."

"Stand from my way, my lord, I would pass out."

"Yet a moment hear me. You cannot tell how much I love. You have yet some doubts."

"Let me pass."

"I tell you I must live for you, or die."

"Then die; for, as my hope is in Heaven, you have now obliterated even any sentiment of respect you might have made me feel for you, and there remains nothing in my heart associated with your name but absolute detestation."

"No, no,—no, Jane, you do not—you cannot mean ——"

"You are answered, my lord."

"And yet I adore the lips that move to the utterance of such harsh sounds. Jane, such love as mine cannot be quenched by coldness. Like some fierce flame sought to be quenched by its very opposite element, it burns the brighter."

"I will hear no more."

"Yes, yes—hear me tell you of the state, the regal state, to which I would raise you—to which, indeed, I can raise you. There may be a queen in England, but in all but the actual name you shall be her peer."

"Not for a crown itself would I listen to such wickedness as this. My lord, save yourself from the scandal of detaining here a weak and unprotected female until she was compelled to call for the assistance of your own servants against you."

"You will drive me mad!"

"And yet not so mad as you were, to imagine I could listen to such infamy."

"Have you forgotten him for whom you have come to plead?"

"I have not."

"He shall die ——"

"Heaven's will be done!"

"Unless you consent to be mine. Now, in plain language, you have my fixed resolution. Be mine, remain here, and he shall be saved. You shall be assured of his safety with your own eyes; you shall see him at liberty, and he will owe his life to you. Ay, within this very hour he shall be free, were he, as doubtless he is, in the deepest dungeon that hate can place him in."

"Walter—Walter!" exclaimed Jane, as she clasped her hands despairingly, "to the great God of Heaven I commit thee!"

"Consent to be mine, and to be mistress of all my wealth," continued Hastings, "and he is free. Refuse, and I will send you as a present his head."

"Monster!"

"I swear it. He shall die the death."

"A greater power than yours to kill may yet preserve him."

"You mean the king; but I can arrange that. If by the court good fortune you reached Edward, not the voice of an angel should suffice to save that prisoner for whom you plead from the worst doom that can befal him."

"There cannot, just Heaven, be so much wickedness," said Jane.

"There is much revenge," said Hastings. "Do you know what the rack is, girl? This young spark of yours shall, if you do not, and such suffering as I would not have inflicted upon you shall all be heaped on him. For your scorn he shall pay the full penalty."

"Jane wrung her hands, crying,—

"Mercy—merey—mercy!"

"Nay," said Hastings, in a more softened tone, "let me be the suppliant. Consent to be mine, and then blot out from your memory the last ten minutes of time for ever."

"Never!"

"You have pronounced his doom."

"I'll not believe it. Even you cannot be so doubly, trebly base. Reflection must and will come to your aid, and save you from the commission of a sin which, on your death-bed, would appal your startled conscience. I tell you, Lord Hastings, you dare not, for your own sake hereafter, be the villain you profess to be."

"Indeed you little know me. I look upon priestcraft as a juggle. I have no faith in it, so there you miscalculate, if you imagine I am to be awed by this superstition, repeated even by your sweet lips at second hand. I believe in nothing, and so fear nothing."

"Wretched man!"

"Nay, forbear your pity. I can spare it."

"You cannot—you cannot. Well may you need the pity of all who have the heart to pity. Let me pass, I say. You have said all you can say to move me, and you see it is in vain. Now, let me pass, and leave you to the stings of that conscience which, say what you will, I know cannot be dead even within such a breast as yours. A day of retribution will come for this."

"Let it come. If I am to have accusers, they shall not say that Hastings threatened what he dared not perform. By fair persuasion you will not be mine. You have got to learn that I have power of a harsher character."

He seized her by the arm; a shriek burst from her lips; and in an instant a secret door was opened in the tapestry, and Antonio Vassa stepped into the apartment.

"Hold!" he cried, "my Lord Hastings. Is this your promise?"

"Help—help! save me!" cried Jane.

"It will be perilous!" shouted Hastings, as he tore his sword from its scabbard. "Keep off, Vassa, as you value life."

"Oh, pho—pho!" said Vassa, as he drew an amazingly long, glittering rapier he wore. "You can leave now, madam."

"No!" cried Hastings, furiously, as he crossed swords with Vassa, "not while I am armed. Vassa, beware, for I am now a desperate man. Beware, I say! I am goaded to madness."

"Exactly," said Vassa, "and, therefore, a much easier conquest. Leave the house madam, with what expedition you may, and leave me to manage your mad-headed wooer."

Jane waited not for another bidding, but, rushing from the room, she made across the court-yard for the outer gate, and gained the open streets in the course of a very few moments. The gate porter, and the few retainers of the chamberlain who were lounging at the gate, were amazed at her speed, and the look of agitation she wore; but they had no orders to impede her in leaving the house, therefore they allowed her to pass on uninterruptedly.

With a feeling of great relief, when she was once clear of that detestable mansion, Jane turned her steps towards the Strand. A new alarm, however, suddenly came across her. Some one was evidently pursuing her. She quickened her pace; but she felt she was being overtaken. There was no open house, or passenger close at hand to whom she could call for protection, and her pursuer at last caught her by the cloak. She turned in an agony of alarm, and then what a revulsion of feeling on the instant took place, when she saw that her pursuer, from whom she had tried her utmost to escape, and of whom she had had so much dread, was no other than her best and undoubted friend, Simon.

CHAPTER XLII.

The Fight.

"This same Antonio Vassa was upheld to be so skilled in fence, that none could hope to cope with him."

We left the lord high chamberlain in an extremely ticklish position. Had his antagonist been as intent upon mischief as he was, there would, without a doubt, have been bloodshed; but it was no part of the scheme of Vassa to rid the world, as yet, of the chamberlain. That he could conquer him, and conquer him easily too, he had no manner of doubt in the world; nor had Lord Hastings any doubt upon that head after he had made a few unsuccessful lunges at his opponent, which were parried with an ease, a self-possession, and a skill which set him at complete defiance altogether.

"How, my Lord Hastings," said Vassa—"how can a man of your profound sagacity and great acquirements, be so foolish as to stand tilting at me in this manner? You know well what will be the end of this."

"What?" foamed the chamberlain—"what?"

"I shall feel compelled to create a vacancy in his most gracious majesty's household."

These words were rather too significant to be lightly passed over, so Hastings threw down his sword, and sinking on to a chair, he said aloud,—

"Why did you run yourself into danger from my sword at such a moment, Vassa? What could it matter to you that a pretty woman chose to squall?"

"Nothing," said Vassa, "if it had been part of the plan; but it was not, as your lordship happens to know well. Thrice I took occasion to call your attention to the agreement which you had entered into."

"But I was maddened," said Hastings.

"So I thought."

"Then it was I used my sword as readily as I would against a foe. Excuse me, Vassa: I am now more myself; but, by Heaven! I knew not what I did. I was mad, desperate, infuriated."

"It is of little importance," said Vassa. "Had I been a worse swordsman than I am, I might have thought it necessary, in case of accidents, to spill a little noble blood; but a man who carries death, whenever he please, at his sword's point, may well afford to be generous."

"No one has a chance with that long rapier of yours," remarked Hastings.

"Nor do I intend they should," said Vassa, with some degree of bitterness; "it is jesting to fence with me."

"Jesting, and how can it be that, and you such a master of your weapon?"

"Simply because those whom I desire to kill, I kill at once. If I fence, it is for my own protection, not aggressively. You had the refusal of your cold beauty, why persevere then in the face of all hope?"

"I have had a refusal," said Hastings, angrily; "and my impression is, that you knew it beforehand."

"Your impression is marvellously correct. I did know it beforehand, not from any knowledge of the precise fact, for that could only follow upon the temptation; but there are a thousand things we know will happen, under certain circumstances, from the knowledge of what has happened before. You can never hope for success with Jane Shore."

"You spoke not so correctly before."

"It is ill arguing with a man possessed by his own passions. You would still have tried the experiment, with the additional bitterness on your mind of a prophecy against its success. You have now tried it fairly, and have failed—think no more of it; and now turn your attention to noble and more lofty projects. I meet the duke to-night."

"I will have revenge," said Hastings, clenching his hand, and shaking it above his head. "I will have revenge."

"Ay, oceans of revenge," said Vassa, "but it will keep. Revenge is one of those sweet commodities that turns not sour upon the hands of him who loves it. At present I crave your attention to better things. Again, I say, I meet the duke to-night."

"Perdition seize the duke!"

"With all my heart, but not yet awhile. He is a marvellous useful man, one of your bright spirits far in advance of the age in which they are born—a man who, having discovered that circumstances master other men, makes himself the lord of circumstances, and so knows himself the lord of other men."

"He is one who creates for himself motives, and then avows them for his rules of action."

"The duke is a great man, but he will be greater still, and he will not pause in his upward ascent because others may cling to him."

"Yet he perchance may kick them off," said Hastings.

"Nay, if we forbade ourselves the acceptance of all that is gratifying, because something might follow of a different complexion, we should be slaves of a most abject fear that would know no end but in the grave."

"How beautiful she is!" said Hastings, abstractedly.

"Cannot you forget this wench? Console yourself in the arms of others more complying. What is she to you, that her image should stand before you, and a thousand impulses of glorious action? When first I knew you, you possessed a mind above such petty trammels; but now the love-sick Hastings is no more like the man I knew, than I unto a saint—and there is difference enough, although I yet live in hopes of canonization."

"I know you make a jest, Vassa, at all that other men revere, but let it be so. You have taught me to believe we are the creatures of the moment, and with the disorganization of the earthly material which compose our forms, we become extinct in that long sleep which men call death."

Vassa turned a look of contempt upon him, as he exclaimed through his clenched teeth,—

"Why do you not free yourself from the cant of priestly phrases? You still speak of death as of a long sleep. Sleep, I tell you, is a thing from which we may awaken. Death is annihilation—a disruption of the arrangement of that matter which made the man, and then the man is no more."

"I am aware that such are your feelings, Vassa, and have heard you express them; but a truce to such a subject, it is all conjecture, at the best."

"Pardon me," said Vassa; "he who theorises may be lost in conjecture; but he who thinks it unnecessary to set up any doctrine at all, walks brain free of such chimera. The great mistake of mankind is, that they must have some kind of religion, and so get perplexed between the rival schemes of fanatics, of thieves, and fools; but I, who cannot see the sheer necessity of such a choice, discard the whole, and, taking nature as it is, will know no more than what I see, and, perhaps, scarce half of that."

"You are a man of strong mould, Vassa; your peer I never saw."

"By Heaven, 'tis monstrous that there should be in the material world so many things mocking the senses; but the man who has gone through life with common observation must perceive them ere he believes that which he thinks he sees; and yet, that same man of observation must be called upon to yield his belief to such abstractions as mock the commonest of his senses! But, as you say, a truce to this—and, for the third time, I say, I meet the duke to-night."

"Does that imply an invitation to the meeting?" said Hastings.

"As you may please to take it. I think you may be welcome; 'tis at my own humble lodgings, by the abbey."

"On what errand do you meet the duke?"

"He wishes to consult his horoscope."

"And yet Holy Writ falls dead upon his ear. Oh, inconsistency, thy name is infidelity!"

"Not at all," said Vassa; "I don't see why people should not get up a few superstitions of their own for their domestic use, if they please; there may, at least, be the merit of a little invention in the business, and any man of originality of idea likes not to follow in the beaten track of ancient sayings."

"I have ever heard that the Duke of Gloucester, with all his reckless doings, had a vein of superstition running through his mind. As we all have said, Vassa, 'tis a love of the marvellous, hidden to human nature."

"I would not intrude upon his grace's privacy."

"Nay; 'twould be no intrusion. Say you will come, and leave me to ensure your welcome."

"Then I will be there. At what time will it suit your leisure?"

"His grace is to be there at sound of curfew."

"I will be punctual; by the way, Vassa, I knew not that you were a listener to my interview with Jane Shore."

"Do you not know that it is said, one's evil or one's good genius is always at hand?"

"I have heard as much; and so, when I least expected it, I found the former here."

"Nay; the latter rather. I saved you from yourself."

"Well, well—as you will—as you will. I will be with you at the time you mentioned. Till then, farewell!"

Vassa merely nodded, and then passed out of the room, leaving Lord Hastings alone, with a mass of stormy emotions struggling in his breast, which he had only contrived during the presence of the Italian to control. Now, however, that he was alone his anger burst out afresh, the more intently that it had been for a time smothered; he paced his room with rapid strides, while his brows were knit, and his whole aspect was indicative of the angriest emotions.

"I will have revenge," he said; "nothing shall turn me from my revenge. She spurns my love; she affects to scorn me; but she shall find my vengeance far from despicable. I'll make her feel through the heart of another; but I will await a little; she shall endure for a time the agony of some suspense, and then, when she is beginning to hope again that all is well, I will swoop upon that object of her affections, for whom she is willing to do so much, and yet sacrifice so little, and let her see that the promised revenge has been delayed, not forgotten.

"Curses on the mock virtue that would have yielded to one whom she would have admired, but assumes all the heroism of virtue to another, for whom she feels no particular predilection. Had this boy—this Walter D———n, or whatever his name may be—been the wooer, instead of myself, we should have a different result; then virtue would have succumbed to inclination, and all its lofty, high-souled attributes, would have melted in the lover's arm. Curses on him—fiends devour him!"

My Lord Hastings, in his anger, gave so many stamps upon the floor, that an attendant at length came, thinking that surely he wanted something, and had adopted that means of summoning some one to his presence.

"What now?" cried Hastings, in a voice of such passion that the serving-man stopped not to give an answer, but, shutting the door again, he rushed down stairs with all the speed and precipitation in his power, for he expected something thrown at his head if he delayed any longer.

It was now getting near the time that it would be necessary that the chamberlain should think of keeping his appointment with Vassa. He made a few essential alterations in his dress, and then wrapping a cloak about him, he left his house to walk the short distance towards what Vassa chose to call his humble lodging, although there can be no doubt that the tolerably-sized rambling old house that he occupied was taken by him as being specially adapted to his necromantic tricks. There can be no doubt, likewise, but that it was inhabited by confederates.

In those days there were always one or two men who were acknowledged conjurors and fortune-tellers—readers of the mysteries of the stars, propounders of nativities, and compounders of horoscopes; and so much was to be done by confederacy, that the minor conjuring fry generally went into the cabalistic great guns, for the time being, finding it more to their account to work with them than independently.

So it was with Vassa when he took up his abode in London, and became known to those who could pay well for a peep into futurity; there was a sudden disappearance of several little conjurors from the metropolitan horizon, and no doubt they consented to play second fiddle for a time to the great man.

Such men as these were generally the most unscrupulous in the whole community, and among them, no doubt, if he wanted it, Vassa could find spies and assistants enough. He himself too, was, for the period in which he lived, a good chemist, and no doubt possessed the secret of some of those Italian poisons which, in an after age, produced so much alarm, and filled the whole of the courts of Europe with terror.

That Richard of Gloster should be eager to employ a man of such great abilities as Vassa, can excite very little surprise, considering that even then, in all human probability, the shadows of some of his dark, desperate, and bloody plans, were working upon his imagination. That he should in reality, or affectedly, give way to any of the superstitions which had such weight with the unthinking multitude, appears strange in such a man, but anomalies of this description are common enough in human nature; we shall often find that he who has power of mind to discard the dogmas of doctrinarians, because they were repugnant to his calm reasoning powers, should take to some of their most obvious superstitions instead. That such things are, however, is one of the great facts in the history of the human mind, which no one can dispute, and comment upon it, however curious, can be but useless.

And, as regards Richard of Gloster, we cannot take refuge in the belief that he affected such feelings merely for the purpose of effecting some imposition, for he did not make them public, and Vassa was the very last person he would have taken trouble to impose upon, so that there can be no doubt that it was a genuine feeling.

Of course, we must make every allowance for the state of knowledge of the ages in which he lived, and at a time like that, when a proper understanding and an appreciation of the phenomena of the material world had scarcely begun to dawn even upon those who called themselves philosophers, so much of the wonderful and the inexplicable must have appeared to everybody that the mind, if it rejected revelation, could scarcely take refuge in anything but superstition.

The curfew was sounding in the old abbey turret, when Lord Hastings reached the door of the mysterious-looking house, occupied by Antonio Vassa. As he was upon the point of demanding admittance, another figure, in a cloak, came briskly up to the door, and at a glance Lord Hastings recognized the Duke of Gloster.

Richard appeared to be in one of his devil-may-care, merry humours—humours which he frequently put on to cloak his darker and more mysterious designs. Laying his hand upon the chamberlain's arm, he laughed curiously in his face, as he said,—

"Well met, good Hastings. Have ye a star above, think ye?"

"A star, your grace?" said Hastings, inquiringly.

"Yes, I have. By mutual consent, Antonio Vassa and myself have picked out one of the flitting host to represent me and my fortunes. A good thought, is it not, cunning Hastings?"

"If your grace think it cunning, doubtless it is so?" said Hastings.

"Humph! spoken like a courtier. Were you about to visit Vassa?"

"I was, but hesitate now to intrude upon your grace."

"Tush, man, tush! by St. Paul, 'tis no intrusion. We will in together, and we will hear what this wonderful Italian has to say to-night. In truth, he is a man of no mean acquirements."

CHAPTER XLIII.

The Conjuror.

"The Duke of Gloster's superstition was well known to be great in early life."

TURNING towards the door at the conclusion of his speech, Gloster rapped sharply, and in an instant it was opened wide by a domestic of a very strange and doubtful appearance. His features were none of those which men love to admire, and there was an expression in his sharp, active eye, that seemed as though it ever sparkled more when mischief was astir than at any other.

"Is Vassa within?" said Gloster, looking at this familiar with an air as though he would have made some remark upon his peculiarity of appearance; but, for some reason, he forbore.

"Will your grace be pleased to follow me?" said the man; "my master waits your presence."

"Lead on, then, thou doubtful being, and we will follow thee and trust to thy guidance. Trust me, Hastings, yon fellow has most marvellous eyes for mischief; he must be surely Vassa's familiar and kindred spirit of darkness."

"Your grace truly remarks that he is no ordinary personage in his vocation. I can see little in such an one to recommend him for a door-poster; his countenance would beget suspicion and fear in an ordinary mind."

"And yours, Hastings, is no ordinary mind; and, as for myself, seeing there are more evils in imagination to contend with than any that can be found in life or death, I fear nothing from this evil prognosticating countenance."

"Your grace is merry," said Hastings. "I would I could laugh and forget all."

"Forget all, and then what are we? Why, good Hastings, we may not forget the evil, we may not forget the past, without we are prepared to stand alone in the world, without hope or ambition, and that, you see, would be a poor solitary life, a mere existence."

"It would in that light," said Hastings; "that is why one might wish to remember all the evil one might do."

"You are in a strange mood; what evil men do, their destiny leads them on. We have done nothing that we could not, and only what was possible to humanity, and then we could not do more, eh, good Hastings?"

"It is as your grace says."

"Humph! here we are at Vassa's room. I suppose he is minutely examining the immensity of space, and then calculating combinations of influences and asterial probabilities."

The door was now opened by Vassa himself, who seemed somewhat abstracted at first, and then said,—

"Your grace is welcome. My Lord Hastings, your presence will serve to pass the time."

"Ah, Hastings! you are a very good pastime itself, and will scarce be equalled; albeit you will not mar by your gaiety the influence of the unknown powers."

"Your grace is marvellously facetious, and I marvel that your spirits should be so high, while so grave an individual as Antonio Vassa is the host."

"And yet," said Vassa, "I know no reason why his grace should not be merry while I am thoughtful, or your lordship reflective."

"How marvellously we are pourtrayed, good Hastings. Are your reflections grave or otherwise? Aye, there's the rub; I see you are not light of heart. Come, Vassa, to your work. My horoscope is not complete; I would know something of the future."

"Your grace must know I cannot so construct a scheme that may exactly tally with your wishes."

"Nay, I do not desire that my future course should be directed or made. Should the stars read ill, never let that disturb thee. I can look on with equanimity."

"Such only should be the feelings of the heart, directed as they might be by the superior powers of the mind."

"Dost not believe I am capable of being directed by our sleek-pated bishops; dost thou, Vassa? I think I see the swine, as they break their bread in silver salvers; but something more savoury than primitive feeding suits them; they are ambitious, most laudably ambitious, and the crook and the crosier, as time goes on, are good and powerful weapons."

"And yet the sword," said Vassa, "will one day be one of the great arbiters of the destiny of men in this nation."

"The prediction is bold," said Gloster. "What says our good Hastings?"

"As your grace says 'tis a bold prediction, and yet it may come to pass."

"It may; and now, Vassa, let us see what your starry host proclaim of the destiny of Richard of Gloster."

Vassa now turned towards a window that looked towards the east, and opening it, he said,—

"Behold, your grace, the starry host; they are brilliant, though far off, like the glory of departed heroes, whose halo shines in the minds of men."

"'Tis something when the departed spirit leaves behind it the dying glory of a warrior or a statesman. Such a thing is worth living for, though one died to obtain it."

"Your grace is inspired."

"By what?"

"The ambition of a prince."

"What thinkest thou of Vassa for a courtier, good Hastings?" said Gloster, gaily. "He surely has been studying the stars, and found which way they tend."

"There is your own star, your grace; see, 'tis a bright and fiery planet, one that will light your grace's noble career."

"Well, if its course be like that of meteors, bright and short, why, 'tis more pleasing, and better worth living through than any other to my mind."

"There is much philosophy in that. 'Tis not the length of course that marks the race, but the spirit with which 'tis run. The comet in its fiery course causes more sensation than the sun's diurnal motion."

"And the life may be measured more by the acts than the long, listless existence of the mind in abeyance; then, you know, we exist, and enjoy life with that brisk spirit, the very essence of our brief career."

"It is so. Does your grace see yon star?"

"I do."

"Then behold it through this instrument; it will bring it nearer to you, and you can see it better."

So saying, he pointed to a night telescope, or reflector, to which Gloster immediately stepped, and gazed intently upon the star.

Hastings was yet moody; his recent repulse had not been forgotten, and he gazed around him, and saw little in the apartment to induce the same flighty spirits that seemed at that moment to possess the Duke of Gloster.

The room was sombre and spacious. There were dark hangings fitted up about, but there was no lack of apparatus. There were shelves with books, and a furnace; many little bottles and boxes, and many curious specimens of nature, either natural, or such as she sometimes takes delight in producing to the amazement of men.

Rare and costly were many of the articles that he had procured from various climes, and instruments, the use of which were quite a mystery to all save himself.

"'Tis a glorious star, and one that shines most brilliantly. Look, Hastings. What thinkest thou of my indicator?" And as he said this, he pulled Hastings by the arm and placed him before the glass. "Say, what thinkest thou of that brilliant orb for my destiny?"

" 'Tis not destiny itself, your grace," said Vassa, "that is made up by the events that have been, or are to be; but yet the influence exerted by strange influences may be brought to bear upon the destiny of man, and by those who know how to read them they may be read, and the future in part known."

" 'Tis that I wish to know."

" Your grace is destined to a high and glorious career—none higher I know of in the life of man."

" Sayest thou so ?"

" I do but tell you what is told to me. Would your grace look for yourself ?"

" Aye; but how ?"

" It will be but a word. The mirror of your future greatness stands before you."

Gloster turned as Vassa spoke, and the latter pulled on one side a portion of the hangings that projected over a large instrument. This he struck with his bare hand; a mask that covered it, on which was pourtrayed the features of a negro with horrible grimace, fell from off it. Beneath was a mirror, the glass of which was pure and clear. There were lights, and a long vista could be distinguished, but how it was formed, or its extent, no one could judge. Suddenly, and before Gloster could well make any remark, there were several shadowy figures seen flitting about when Vassa interposed, and said,—

" What would your grace desire to see? What action, or part of your career would you have pourtrayed to your sight ?"

" Vassa," said the duke, " could'st show me those things we are told will happen—the marvels of the future ?"

" Your grace must command my services on something that is, or may be, and not on that which is not. That which is nothing, casts no shadow before it."

" What sayest thou, Hastings ?"

Hastings quitted the glass through which he was gazing at the star which had been chosen to represent the fate of Gloster, and believing he referred to that, he replied,—

"'Tis a brilliant one, but methinks every now and then a reddish tinge seems cast over it—that may portend blood."

"But not my own. Had it been so, my star had been extinguished."

"His grace is right," said Vassa. "The blood, if blood it portends, must be that shed on the battle-field—such as well befits the life of a warrior or a general."

"And such you think I ought to be?"

"Has your grace no knowledge in, or longing for, the battle-field—the shout of triumph, and the crown?"

"Of laurels?"

"Ay, as you will; and yet," said Vassa, gloomily, "there were times when the successful general accepted the regal crown; are those days past, and are the spirits which were once animated, quenched for ever?"

"Well, well, then to the portrature of the future of Gloster."

"'Tis well," said Vassa; "will your grace step here, and I will do my part."

So saying, he placed the duke and Hastings behind a portion of the curtain, and then setting light to some fragrant pastiles, which burned with different coloured forms, and was succeeded by an explosion; instantly the room was darkened, and the mirror was illuminated with a blaze of light so dazzling, that it was painful to gaze upon.

This soon subsided, and then the first thing that could be seen was a battle-field, in which men on horse and foot were furiously engaged, and men were falling on all sides. The contest was continued with spirit, and one party gave way while another was gaining ground. Then a fresh impetus was given and the losing combatants turned retreat into flight—and at the head of the victorious veterans charged the Duke of Gloster himself. Then all became confused, and the whole became shrouded in vapour.

"Truly, Vassa, thine art is great at pictures, and would they were true—that they were infallible."

"Your grace will find more truth in this than you may even in courtesy feel inclined to admit; but the time will come when, even in the midst of the busy scenes of a victorious life, you will look back upon the past and yet remember this night."

"Well, well, now show me, if you have not done so, the highest point in which my fortune may place me, though I doubt if there is anything more that could be desired than to be a successful general."

"It is a glorious position, but there yet steps in human ambition that will carry the daring and high-souled man yet farther."

"Let me see if I am destined to be one such as you describe. I would we were sure of the truth of the prediction."

"And why should your grace not be so? Has your grace not heard and seen enough already to know that there is much truth in the picture that has been shadowed up for you?"

Again they looked on the mirror—all was indistinct, but by degrees the mist cleared off and many figures were seen which soon began to reveal themselves. There was a regal chair—and round that there stood many smiling faces. The chair was occupied by one whose brows were encircled by a victorious wreath, and this was surmounted by a regal crown.

Gloster and Hastings both stared, for they both at once recognized the features, they were Richard's own, and he said,—

"By my faith, but there is no step beyond that save to the scaffold."

"And that will never be your grace's fate," said Vassa; "yours will be a death of glory."

"That is one I would desire—no, I could never die the death of a slave—it must be that of a soldier, fighting before my own troops, hacking and hewing with my good sword until my body, no longer capable of fighting, might then fall honourably under a multitude of wounds."

"The time for such considerations has not yet come—death, we know, ends every career; wherefore should we be solicitous to know the moment or the manner? It gives but marvellous little joy to the present moment—when we are ripe, like the fruit of the trees, we must fall and become what we were before."

"Aye, and there's the secret."

"The secret?" said Vassa.

"Aye, of the grave."

"'Tis only a secret to such as fear and hope; these two classes tremble on the brink of the fulness of time, and desire to linger on the stage that has no charms for them, and yet they fear to go."

"Men do not usually like the step that lets them fall into an abyss."

"And wherefore not, good Hastings?—for in such a fall they would not have to fear the bottom."

"And yet, your grace, men fear they know not what, and though there be nothing but the end of all things to be encountered, yet they do not willingly encounter that."

"Encounter nothing is the end, and who should fear such a meeting?" said Gloster, laughing.

CHAPTER XLIV.

The Assassin.

THE mirror in which Gloster had seen two important events blazoned forth became darkness, and no more was to be distinguished—all was a blank, and the curtain fell down before it without aid.

"Well," said Gloster, "time flies, and I must be gone. Do you go, my Hastings, or do you stay with our merry friend, Vassa?"

"Vassa, your grace, is not the most lively companion in the world; but I will go with your grace, if it be meant as an invitation to do so."

"If you will, it shall be so; Vassa, we meet again. See that my star be looked to; and, should it resolve aught eccentric, note it, good Vassa, and let me hear. I would not lose any of the asterial influences, lest I should escape some pleasing dream."

"The star that shines so brightly is a fixed star, and all its motions known; it will not, like a debtor, be glad to escape from the sky, lest we should impress its services until it resolves itself to its ultimate atoms; then we will say it is gone."

"And may say so most truly; it needs no conjuror for that. By-the-by, you have no lights."

"Would your grace like lights?"

"I confess I should."

Vassa seized a small instrument which lay on his table; and, gently scratching it across a strong, rough instrument, a sharp report, and a bright flame, were simultaneously produced, and in a minute the room was brilliantly lighted up.

"Upon my word you have a convenient way of producing a blaze of light. I would some other things could be done as well."

"There are many things that, in the fulness of time, will be common enough, but which now would not be believed. I could at this moment do that which your grace would scarcely believe possible."

"If it takes not too long 'twill confirm our good Hastings in his amazement and silence."

"Your grace sees that iron chain that hangs along the walls?"

"I do."

"And you, my Lord Hastings?"

"I do."

"What if I cause a stream of fire to run along each link, and illumine the whole—it shall appear as a pure flame, and, at the same time, no trace shall be left."

"Well, we shall see, then, some of your miracles, Vassa. I shall be better pleased if your marvel takes no time in executing—time flies, and I have other matters on hand."

"Then, see," said Vassa, "it will be some three seconds in performing."

"'Tis well."

While he spoke, he stepped across the room, and, turning a wheel a few turns, a vivid stream of fire ran along the chains, causing each separate link to become illumined, and show distinctly in the room—the lights having been extinguished first, the whole room, though darkened, was illumined by this mysterious light. The chain looked like links of pure flame, and ten thousand little explosions that resembled the snapping of sticks, or the crackling of burning materials, were heard. This continued for near a minute, and then Vassa ceased, and the whole was quiet—the flame suddenly disappeared.

"Go forward and touch the links, Hastings," said Vassa.

"It were scarce wise, when they emitted flames but so few moments ago."

"They are as cold as your own sword-blade," returned Vassa, as he held one end of the chain in his hand.

Hastings touched the chain gently, and then took it in his hand. Gloster did the same, and exclaimed,—

"They are as cool as though they had been drawn from the bed of the Thames. Ha, ha, it were indeed a joke worth recounting if you could have passed yon mysterious flame through the bodies of a regiment of men, or through the armour they wear, without heating their corslets; they would affright the enemy, who would think they had just been let loose from hell, to scatter death and destruction to them all."

"That fire, so subtle and powerful, and yet so mysterious in its effects, if supplied in a quantity sufficient to do what your grace proposes, would destroy the bodies contained within their corslets, and do the work the enemy would most desire to be done for them."

"It is strange, indeed," said Hastings. "I never saw the like; but Vassa possesses many secrets that astonish men in these days."

"In truth," said Gloster, "it would seem that he could call fire down from the skies, and play gambols on the earth."

"Your grace is jesting on what can be done and has been done; but in this worthy community it would be looked upon as tempting Heaven to destroy the city, and emulate the fate of the two cities in the plain, and I should run the risk of meeting with the fate of St. Stephen."

"And be stoned to death."

"In truth I might, Men—the mass of men—cannot bear to look upon that which is wondrous and strange, and for any one to exhibit these hidden mysteries of nature is a clear tempting of those powers they believe to exist, and so terrified are they at what they know not, that they will sacrifice any man to their thirst for vengeance to appease their own fears."

"That is casting oil upon troubled waters," said Gloster.

"Ay, your grace; but the mode of obtaining the oil is not philosophic or just, and such as ill suits with the appetite of the sufferer."

"That may be. And now farewell."

"Farewell," said Vassa.

The lights were relit, and Vassa signed to an attendant, who immediately bore a light before, and then descended the stairs, and in a few moments they stood outside the door.

"And now," said Gloster, "we have had an hour's entertainment with Vassa, what think you of him?"

"He is a strange man, your grace, and has great arguments. His studies and travels have made him master of many things, scarce possible to any one else besides himself."

"That is just. His arguments, added to his own genius, make him matchless. But come, we may not linger in these dark places."

They were about to remove from the door, when Gloster heard a scuffle, and the sound of feet behind him.

"Hey day!" he said, turning round. "What, have we company?"

Just as he turned, he saw a man rush forward and aim a blow with his uplifted arm at his breast, with a long and sharp poniard. Gloster had no time to save himself by any movement whatever; he could not raise his hands in time to save the blow; but ere it could descend, another figure rushed forward and seized the arm of the assassin, and thus saved the duke.

"Ha! ha! good fellow," exclaimed Gloster; "thou shalt not go unrewarded for thy timely assistance; but as for thee, assassin, why, thou shalt be rewarded, too, but thy reward shall be of a different complexion."

As he said this, he rushed, tiger-like, upon the man, whom he seized by the throat, and soon dragged him to the earth.

"Mercy—mercy!" shouted the ruffian.

"What now, sir!" said Gloster. "Ha! ha! think of the mercy you would have shown me. Ha! ha! it is a strange, merry moment to find such subjects for mirth and mercy."

"Mercy—mercy!"

"Who set thee on to this work?"

The man was silent.

"I did wrong to ask," said Gloster, "such a tongue as thine could but have slandered some gentleman. Here, good fellow, lend me thy gauntlet?"

The soldier, who was in half-armour, gave him his right hand gauntlet—that was heavily covered with iron.

"Now for the punishment, Hastings; didst ever see man tremble so before? he deserves to die by some less noble hand."

"Give him to this fellow, he saved you, and let him perform the office."

"Nay, he has performed a worthier one; and, besides, I think I will, for once, become the impersonation of justice, and do my own work—execute my own decrees."

" 'Tis well," said Hastings.

During this time Gloster had been putting the glove on his hand, while, with the other, he held the man.

"Mercy! mercy!"

" Oh, yes—mercy, quotha—mercy you shall have. Justice to the criminal is mercy to the community, and it is upon that argument I shall proceed."

" Oh, your grace, have mercy upon a poor fellow; I will serve you with my whole life."

" I need no such service. I have enough to command a thousand lives, and thine, assassin, would be no use to me."

So saying, he struck the man with all his force on the head and face, several desperate blows; the man staggered, and the blood flowed in quantities, and covered his face.

" In good truth," said Gloster, " this reminds me of the ancient art of war, when walls were beaten in with battering rams, and this fellow serves for a wall and my hand is the ram."

And again he struck the man another blow on the head, which brought him upon his knees, and a fresh gush of blood followed.

" Mercy! mercy! have mercy upon me," shouted the man, struggling.

" You shall have mercy, with a vengeance. Such mercy as shall send you to heaven —that's what the saints term a crowning mercy, and such you shall have."

He again struck him with his glove, and the man begged for mercy and struggled to get free, but his cries and struggles became less and less, until they entirely ceased, then taking the man up in his arms, he flung him down on the ground with great force and violence. Then all was still, and not a motion followed—he lay still, an inanimate mass.

" There," said Gloster, " he has perished—he was an assassin, and met an assassin's death."

" Yes, your grace will have no more trouble there," said Hastings; " his care is over, and to a pretty goal he has come at last."

" Ha! ha! ha! he has—he has—and to such a death may all come who use such means. I have brained him with a vengeance."

" Your grace is right."

" And now, good fellow, stand forward."

The man did so; he was a stout, stalwart man, a trooper in half armour.

" I see," said Gloster, "thou art a proper man of thy quarters—there is thy glove, take care of it, and use it well in fight, for it has been worn by the Duke of Gloster."

" I will do so," said the man.

" And, here, take this as a slight recompense for the service you have done."

" I thank your grace," said the man, who took the purse that the duke offered to him, filled with gold pieces.

" And now, good Hastings, let us see if we can pursue our walk, unmolested by any more of these kind reminiscences of our friends."

The duke and Lord Hastings then quitted the place, leaving the soldier standing alone, admiring the contents of his purse, and, as he heard fresh footsteps, he hastily hid the purse beneath his corslet.

CHAPTER XLV.

Jacob's New Situation.

And such was ye evil repute in which Master Caxton lived, that he durst scarcely stir abroade alone.—*Caxton's MS. Edited by Cox.*

When Jane found that he who had pursued her from the lord chamberlain's house, was indeed no other than Simon, she felt ready to drop from a sudden accession of delight, and she leant heavily upon his arm to support herself.

" Ah, Simon, Simon," she said, " is this indeed really you?"

" No," said Simon, with his usual love of a negative, and then he as quickly added, " of course it's me."

" And you have followed me?"

This was a question which, upon the principle of no one being required or expected to criminate himself, Simon might have felt justified in not answering, but as the following her had been from the first a contradictory step, he at once avowed it.

" Yes," he said; " I did follow you. You told me not, but I did."

" And in telling you not to do so, Simon, I was my own enemy."

"Oh," said Simon.

"I ought, and had I consulted my own safety and interest, I should have done so, to have consulted you before I went on the desperate errand from which I am now returning."

"Humph!"

"But I feared, Simon, that you would disapprove of my going, and there was so dear a hope to be gathered from the attempt, that I could not forego it."

"Stuff," said Simon; "what was it?"

"You will feel as I feel, Simon, when you hear what my motive was in seeking the house of Lord Hastings."

"Sha'n't do any such thing," said Simon.

"Indeed you will. I feel assured you will. Simon, it concerned the fate of one who I know is dear to you."

Simon turned abruptly, and looked in her face, as he said,—

"You mean yourself?"

"No, no. I know I am dear to you, Simon, but I do not mean myself."

For once in his life, Simon did not contradict what was said to him. His affectionate feelings for Jane got the better of all bad habits. He felt so much reverence and tenderness for her, that he could not utter the contradiction which sprung to his tongue's end.

"I am well aware of your devotion and your goodness to me, Simon," answered Jane. "I know there were but three people towards whom you felt an unbounded affection, that sufficed to cover even their faults. You loved my father, you love me, and you loved poor, poor Walter Fane."

"Don't want anybody to speak of him," said Simon, as he involuntarily quickened his pace, so that Jane could scarcely at all keep up with him.

"Well, but Simon."

"Don't say any more. Don't want to hear it."

"I know what you think, Simon. You have made up your mind, I believe completely, that poor Walter is no more, and therefore do not want those wounds of sensibility opened afresh, by your being compelled to hear any mournful complaints of mine concerning him. But, Simon, he is not dead."

They had now arrived at the commencement of the Chepe, and when Jane uttered these words, Simon turned upon her so abruptly, that she started back half terrified at the vehemence of his manner.

"Walter not dead!" he exclaimed. "Not dead?"

"No, Simon. I was assured he was among the living, and it was to make an attempt to restore him to us, that I took my present expedition to the house of the wicked chamberlain."

"And this, Jane," said Simon, "was what you would not tell to me?"

"It was, Simon; but I feared you would oppose so strenuously my going to Lord Hastings, that I dreaded to tell you."

Simon walked on in silence for some moments, and then he said,—

"There's more of it. There's more of it. Tell me all!"

"I will now, Simon. The man who visited me—the old man—told me that Walter Fane lived, and was even now in the dungeon of the prison of the Blackfriars. He added, that the only person who could release him, was the king, and that the only one who could or would induce the king to do so, was the lord high chamberlain."

"Indeed!"

"Yes; I believed the story, and went to crave mercy and justice through his exertions."

"Well?"

"He received me courteously, and then insulted me."

"Of course."

"I have left him now with no hope for poor Walter. Oh, Simon, what can be done? I much fear that by this course that I have now most unsuccessfully pursued, I have made his condition worse, instead of bettering it. Advise me, Simon, what I am to do?"

"Insulted you," muttered Susan. "Walter Fane in the prison of the Blackfriars, you insulted, and my poor old master dead."

Any one would have thought by his manner, that it was quite a pleasure to Simon to reckon up all his miseries, for he spoke in rather an indifferent tone of voice.

"What is to be done, Simon?" added Jane.

"Don't know. Come home."

"Yes," cried a voice, suddenly. "Yes. D——n! she shall come home, although she would fain, I know, forget which is her home. Come, mistress—home, home to my house, which is yours, say I. Curses on you all, and everybody."

It was Shore who uttered these words. His face was so pale and ghastly from passion, that it might have been compared to a piece of old parchment. He trembled in every limb, and there was a small stream of blood bubbling from his lip, where, in his intense excitement, he had bitten it himself.

Truly, Master Shore was in a most unenviable state of mind. Had it not been that scarcely any amount of passion would wholly obliterate the natural cowardice of his disposition, it is very likely he would have made an attack upon Simon, but that he did not dare to do while he preserved his senses about him.

Jane shrunk closer to Simon's side, and looked the terror she could not utter.

"Come, come," said Simon, "Master Shore, who has trodden on your corns to-day, that you are so waspish?"

"How dare you speak to me, knave?" said Shore. "D——n! I addressed no words to you."

"You did."

"Liar!"

"Hold," said Simon. "It is not always a feeling that we are certain of what we can do that keeps us from doing it. Say that word again in relation to me, and I will smash you."

"The city laws," said Shore, testily, "have most especial punishment for serving-men or parties who use threats and abuse to masters of crafts. Look out for your ears."

"The man who touches my ears," said Simon, "had better look out for his own head."

"Jane, come with me. Come with me," said Shore, passionately. "Home, home, I say. What do you in the public streets at such a time as this? I shall demand, and I will have an account of where you have been."

"I am not desirous of making a secret of where I have been," said Jane; "but I will not return to your house until my poor father is laid in the quiet grave."

"You will not?"

"Heaven hears me say I will not."

"Know you not that I could force you—the city's laws give me power."

"I suppose," said Simon, "you have been looking up the city laws lately, to see what you can do."

This speech was the more annoying, because it was exactly the truth; for that was just what Shore had been doing. He looked at Simon as if he were about to make some angry reply, but some feeling restrained him. He merely gave a hideous smile, and muttered,

"Very good—very good—it will not last long. Very good."

Jane heard him, and she said faintly,

"Master Shore, I here solemnly swear to heaven, that if you attempt any evil against this, my father's old servant and friend, I will never again cross your threshold."

"Pho, pho, never mind him," said Simon.

"He's beneath my resentment," said Shore, "but some one else may take some exception to him, for which do not blame me."

"I will blame you," said Jane. "Any evil that happens to Simon I will lay to your charge. He has no other enemy."

"Mighty liberal, truly," said Shore. "Are you coming home?"

"Not until to-morrow," said Jane, mournfully; "not until to-morrow. I have the last and most sacred duty to perform to my poor father. It will be all over to-morrow, and then I will return."

"To-morrow," he muttered; "then to-morrow be it. I will not exert the authority I possess, to force you. To-morrow be it; but methinks, Jane, it ill accords with your other notions of your sacred duties, for you to be in the streets at such a time as this."

"I am, I know, open to that reproach," said Jane, "but I have been on an errand of mercy."

"An errand of nonsense. What have you to do with errands of mercy?" He drew his scanty cloak closely around him, so that his thin, gaunt figure was visible, and he scowled upon her with his small piercing eyes as if he would read her very soul.

"We ain't all alike," said Simon; "some people may go upon errands of mercy, and others not. It's just as it happens. There would be very little time wasted on such matters if we were all like you."

Shore had evidently made up his mind that he would not answer Simon now, let him say what he would, and that was a grievous thing rather to Simon, who, in his heart, certainly did enjoy a little contention with anybody; but, most of all, with anybody for whom he had such an inherent dislike as Shore.

Had Shore been the cunningest of mortals, and exercised the most profound discretion in the world, as to the best mode of aggravating Simon, certainly he could not have adopted a better one than that of appearing not to hear what Simon had to say.

But Simon was an old hand at controlling his feelings to those he disliked, and although, unquestionably, he was very much provoked at Shore's conduct, he gave no verbal utterance to such a feeling.

"To-morrow," added Shore to Jane, "to-morrow, then, and I shall exact an account of how the time has been passed."

Jane made no reply, but walked close to Simon down the Chepe, while Shore preceded them by a few paces only.

When they reached the mercer's house Shore paused, and turned again, as he said in low hissing tones,

"To-morrow, at mid-day."

"No," said Jane, "later than that—later than that."

"Wherefore later?"

"To-morrow at sunset," was all she replied, and then she accompanied Simon into the house.

She went up stairs to the room where she had had her interview with the leech, and the stranger, who had succeeded him with the same piece of intelligence, and then her pent up feelings found vent in a gush of tears.

The old nurse evidently looked upon this sudden accession of grief as arising from the usual cause—namely, the death of Wainstead; and she uttered the same sort of condolence which every day, and several times a day, she had used since death had bereaved Jane of her father.

"You know, my dear, we must all die some day, and when our turn comes we must go. It's the will of Heaven, and we ought not to repine. There is another and a better world," &c., &c.

Jane heard this as though she heard it not; but, as her tears ceased, and she in the course of half an hour recovered her composure, the old nurse was satisfied that her arguments and exhortations had been wonderfully effective nd admirable.

"Now you are better, my dear," she said.

"Yes, yes."

"Well, I thought you would be, so you had better now lie down and take a rest, for you do exert yourself too much."

Jane did lie down, but it was not to rest. It was to reflect, long and painfully, upon the position of poor Walter, and to endeavour to devise some means yet of saving him.

But what could she do? Alas, the more she thought, the more she became convinced how powerless she was.

"Could I but reach the king," she said, "surely he would rescue him."

This was true enough, perhaps. The novelty of the application, and the beauty of the petitioner, would most likely have prevailed, and Jane would have had her suit granted by the young and chivalrous monarch.

But kings have always been difficult of access, and that difficulty was not at all likely to be decreased at such a period of civil strife as that in which our king is cast. The dread of assassination surrounded the person of the monarch with safeguards; and the more strongly expressed wish to see him was almost of itself enough to point the finger of suspicion at any one. To be sure, a young and beautiful female such as Jane, could hardly be said to be the sort of person who would come to assassinate a king; but yet, the difficulties which were thrown in the way of access to the monarch were established ones, and so not likely to melt before her presence.

She felt this the more fully the more she considered of the subject, and she could not invent any method by which such obstacles in the way of doing anything for Walter could be overcome. She knew that Shore had court connexions which very likely would have sufficed to accomplish the object she had in view; but the mere mention of the name of Walter Fane she well knew was at any time quite sufficient to produce in him an accession of rage, so that any attempt to interest him in the matter, like the fruitless one she had already made to move Lord Hastings to some consideration, could but tend to make Walter's position worse.

And thus she passed some of the bitterest hours of her existence, at one moment blaming herself for having gone to Lord Hastings at all, and at another, feeling that she should do so again under similar circumstances to those which had occurred.

While Jane was in this painful state of thought, Simon, although his mind was most painfully fixed upon what he had heard from her regarding the position of Walter Fane, was not neglecting a matter which that night he had promised to see to. That was concerning poor Jacob. The fact was, that Mistress Bridget Snafflings had made the whole

city so ring again with an account of Jacob's misdeeds, that it was quite out of the question for him to procure any sort of employment with any of the citizens.

Indeed, had a strong opinion in favour of Jacob induced any one to employ him, it would have been checked by the dread of a visitation from Mistress Bridget Snafflings, who was held in terror by every one who possessed the faculty of hearing what floods of eloquence came from her lips.

It was strange how, from sheer dread of her abuse, she was received everywhere—with very few exceptions—with much affected cordiality; so that she fancied, or pretended to fancy, that, notwithstanding the ill-will of some bad-tempered people, she was really a very popular character in the good City of London.

The forgiveness of Snafflings, since the gold pieces which poor Jacob, in a moment almost of insanity, for the love of Jane, had been induced by the faded gallant to steal, were his, of course prevented the possibility of Mistress Bridget taking legal vengeance against Jacob. But what could any amount of legal vengeance be in comparison to the bitter eloquence which she was capable of bringing to bear upon the character of any one whom she disliked?

Jacob was as much an outcast as if, by common consent of everybody in the city, he had been declared to be one for the greatest enormities that man had ever committed. The poor fellow might truly be said to have but one friend in the whole world now, and that was Simon. In a small chamber at the top of the mercer's house, which had been unoccupied for a considerable time, he had given Jacob a refuge from his enemies.

Among Simon's acquaintance was a man named Peter Short, and this same Peter Short was in the employ of Master Caxton, the printer, concerning whom so many vague stories were afloat, and who had created such an enormous amount of scandal, by having had given to him a room in the abbey of Westminster, in which to pursue his supposed conjuring experiments, for he was looked upon as no better than a necromancer, and one who dabbled in unholy services, at the best.

To this Peter Short, Simon had explained poor Jacob's desperate social condition, and at once Peter had said,—

"I can get him into the service of Master Caxton."

Jacob was not a man troubled with many foolish scruples, so he gladly acceded to the proposal.

"If you can do so," he said, "do so at once, and I will undertake to say, that a more willing fellow Master Caxton never had, always excepting yourself, master Peter Short."

"Well," said Peter Short, stroking his chin, "we get on very well together, but if the lad is simple-minded and honest and willing, he will suit Master Caxton, who he will find a kind master."

"He is honest," said Jacob, "notwithstanding the stoiy of the gold pieces which, in a moment of frenzy, he was induced to take at the instigation of a villain with whom I hope to be able to balance a little account some of these odd days, Master Short."

This than, was agreed upon; Master Caxton accepted Jacob on the recommendation of Peter Short, as an assistant; and it is probable that the poor half-witted fellow worked at the first printing press that ever was constructed in England.

It was on this same evening on which Jane had met with so very unpleasant and really perilous an adventure at the house of the lord chamberlain, that Jacob was to go to his situation. When he, Simon, returned, his first business was to go to Jacob's attic and tell him to make ready.

"Yes, yes," said Jacob, "I am glad you have altered your plans concerning me, Simon, and let me come here instead of remaining at the lodging you got for me. Moreover, most specially glad, good Simon, am I that I am to remain near to London, for who knows but I may, some time or another, see dear Jane."

"Come along," said Simon, "it's a short walk to the abbey, and being dark, you will get out of the Chepe without being seen by Mistress Snafflings."

"Dear, dear, if she should see me."

"Well, if she should?"

"She'd run after me."

"Surely you can run faster than she, with those long thin legs of yours, Jacob, can you not?"

"But I should fall down from fear."

"Then you would deserve to be caught, Jacob; but mind you, there is one thing which I am told Master Caxton insists upon."

"What is that, good Simon?"

"Absolute secresy as regards all you do for him, and all you see him do. If you tattle in the least concerning him you will be at once discharged, and perhaps have some cause to rue the day you entered into his service at all."

"Oh, I will be wonderfully discreet, Simon, you may depend; I mean to be a model of discretion."

"Good; then go along."

"But—but, Simon——"

"Well, what now?"

"Is not dear Jane here, good Simon?"

"Well, what if she is here, stupid, what's that to you, eh?"

"Oh, Simon, it is all the world to me; I am sure she would let me bid her adieu—I am sure she would."

"Why, you have once."

"But I should not be sorry of doing so a thousand times. If she would let me look upon her face but for a moment, good Master Simon; if she would but just say, 'Good bye, Jacob,' you know, Simon, it would be something for me to think of—something for me to dream of, good Simon."

"Stuff."

"Nay, nay, you will not refuse me; I know, Simon, that after all you are really tender-hearted."

"I ain't, I tell you."

"You know better now, good Simon; if you were not, you would never have been so good to me as you now are; and you will not refuse to let me see Jane for a moment—dear, dear Jane?"

"You are a dreadful fool," said Simon.

"Yes, I know—I know."

"I will ask her. She don't know you are here at all; but as you are going, I will ask her; but Jane has enough troubles of her own. You must promise me, Jacob, that you will not torment her, but that when she bids you good bye, you will go at once."

"Oh, yes, yes, Simon, I promise."

"Very well; mind, if you forget I shall push you down stairs."

"Yes, yes."

Simon spoke to the old nurse, and the old nurse spoke to Jane, who rose, and at once consented to see Jacob; and then the poor fellow came trembling into her presence, and, dropping on his knees, he pressed the hand she allowed him to take to his lips—Jacob was happy then.

"God bless you—God bless you," he said.

"Good bye, Jacob," said Jane, "and Heaven prosper you."

Simon gave a wrench by the doublet, which brought him to his feet, as he said,—

"Come on."

"Yes, yes. Angels guard you, dear, dear Jane—God bless you."

Simon dragged him away, and then, with a heavy heart, the poor fellow went towards the abbey where Master Caxton had his rooms, and where he was kindly received by the father of English printing, whom he found a very different personage to what common report made him, and no conjuror at all, but only a man of great talent and research.

CHAPTER XLVI.

The Chamberlain and the King.

"And the chamberlain, finding his own suit hopeless, stirred up the young monarch to seek Jane."

Lord Hastings could not forget the scene he had gone through with Jane Shore. It absolutely maddened him to think how completely he had been foiled, and how absolutely and entirely hopeless were any chances of success. Notwithstanding he had affected, in pursuance of the promise he had made to Vassa, to throw from his mind any further pursuit of an intrigue in which, as far as he had attempted to go, he had been so signally unsuccessful, the subject was for ever present to his mind.

As soon could he be expected to forget his own being as his deep disappointment regarding the beautiful Jane Shore. And he had, too, the additional mortification of knowing that, if before he was indifferent to her, he had now, by the unblushing effrontery of his conduct, placed an insurmountable barrier between them.

This was making the case worse with a vengeance. The reader will recollect with what a debasement of all common honour and principle he had offered to Jane Walter Fane's liberation as the actual price of her own dishonour; and now that the excitement of the time was past, and my Lord Hastings came more calmly to consider of what he had said during that interview, he could not but feel that it was the last he was ever likely to have with Jane.

To many minds the hopelessness of love is an incitement to revenge, and we shall find that an earnest desire to do what mischief is possible to the object which has scorned their affections becomes a leading principle with many minds. And in the mad excitement of rejection and disappointed hopes we have many instances of the greatest crimes being committed.

This feeling came over Hastings, who, now finding that his passion was a thoroughly hopeless one, and that any idea of bringing Jane to consent to become his could not be entertained for a moment, began to cast about for some mode of making her feel his resentment. Smarting under a sense of the bitterest disappointment he had ever in all his life experienced, he felt that he should not assuage the feelings of anger that filled his heart unless he succeeded in doing something which should let Jane see that by rejecting him she had involved herself in disaster and trouble. Like almost all men, he thought that the virtue of her whom he had attempted in vain to seduce was completely inaccessible.

The vanity of human nature generally enables people to get up such an idea, and my Lord Hastings was no exception to the general rule; for he believed fully that Jane Shore now was such a piece of discretion and virtue that nothing possibly could be to her a greater punishment than the salutation of a lover.

Then, as regarded Walter Fane, although he had threatened Jane that he would have some signal vengeance upon him, he dreaded to execute that threat. The fact was that the times were almost too unsettled for any one to do more deeds of violence than were absolutely necessary to the safety of their position; and Heaven knows they were enough.

What connexions this young man, who was languishing in the prison of Blackfriars, might have, and to whom the news might get that he, Lord Hastings, had compassed his death, he could not tell. Therefore was it, and for another reason, which only dimly, and with not much appearance of probability, came across his imagination, that he decided upon, for the present, leaving Walter Fane alone. He felt that at any time he chose he could crush him, and, therefore, was it that he told himself he could afford to spare him.

And now came the dark and insidious scheme of his revenge against poor Jane Shore.

That she would not be content after her interview with him, but would seek some means yet of preferring her suit to the king, was a natural idea, and one which, the more he, Hastings, pondered over the circumstances of the case, grew more upon him with the force of a settled fact.

"She will be sure to adopt yet some desperate project which may succeed," he thought. "She may see the king, and if she should do so, then out comes the story of her visit to me and its result."

This was an uncomfortable thought—uncomfortable in every way; for well he, Lord Hastings, knew the chivalrous temper of the young king in matters where his own immediate feelings and passions were not concerned.

"The result of such an application to Edward," he considered, "will be the liberation of the prisoner, and a censure upon me."

These were both of them contingencies which presented themselves to his mind in anything but pleasant colours, and the proposition he set about working out was how to get over them.

My Lord Hastings was not without a certain amount of ingenuity, and, after a time, he considered that he had matured a scheme which gave him a very fair chance of defeating Jane should she apply to the king.

The scheme was this. Being thoroughly convinced his own success was hopeless, he proposed to himself to seek an interview with Edward, and insidiously, as if without any particular design, to turn the conversation upon female beauty, when he did not despair of being able to paint the charms of Jane Shore in such glowing colours to the young monarch, as to induce in him a desire to become better acquainted with such a paragon of beauty as he, Hastings, would take care to make her out, and which, indeed, she really was; so, as regards that point, it was impossible for him to exaggerate, since no language could adequately do justice to the beauty of Jane.

If, then, he should succeed, as he doubted not he should, in awakening a strong feeling of admiration for Jane in the young monarch's heart, he well knew that Edward was not the sort of man exactly to smother such a feeling.

"He will wish to see her," reasoned Hastings, "and so there will be some facilities thrown in the way of her reaching the royal presence. Again, she will prefer her suit for the liberation of this Walter Fane; and again she will be met by the same offer as she received from me."

By this means, Hastings considered he should avoid the censure of the king, who would, by adopting a similar course, be prevented from blaming him. And he was likewise of opinion that Jane's refusal of the addresses of the monarch would subject her to so much annoyance and persecution, that he should be amply revenged upon her for her rejection of him.

"Edward is a man," he said, "who becomes furious from opposition; he is not at all used to it, and he cannot brook it. Let her treat him with one-half the sauce with which she treated me, and he will be desperate."

Such was the rascally plan which the chamberlain formed for revenge upon one whose only fault was not listening to his criminal address. Alas! poor Jane, what a sad gift was thy wondrous beauty to thee in such an age of turbulence and vice. Had you not been the creature of rare and exquisite endowments that you were by Heaven created, you might have been, as the wife of Walter Fane, happy; but you were beautiful, and you were mentally gifted, and therefore you became the sport of cruel and relentless fortune, who, as if envious of such transcendant charms, changed them to a curse, instead of to a blessing, as they ought to have been.

The chamberlain took some time to mature his plan, to consider well of it in all its bearings; and the more he thought of it, the safer he thought it as regarded himself, and the more he liked it. There was just a possible result—but to his mind only a possible one—which, perhaps, was, almost without his being himself thoroughly aware of it, the real reason why he spared the life of Walter Fane; that was, that Jane might yield to a young and handsome monarch what she withheld from a not over good-looking chamberlain. It was even to his mind just possible that Edward might dazzle her senses sufficiently to induce her to yield to him; and, should that be the case, it would not be exactly safe for him, Hastings, to be known, as he might be by her, to be the cause of the death of the prisoner in the prison of the Blackfriars.

This was a more potent argument than he allowed himself to believe. He happened to know a case in a preceding reign, where a nobleman's head was the price of a great favour granted to a monarch by a fair lady, and he considered, with abundant philosophy, that what had happened might happen again.

Our readers are well enough aware that Jane's was not the disposition to commit such an act; and whatever might be her influence with a monarch, it would never be exerted unworthily or vindictively; but my Lord Hastings was a cautious man, and had his suspicions, so he left Walter Fane alone, and in comparative safety. Then, having given as much consideration to the matter as quite assured him he was doing nothing hastily, he contrived to see the king upon another slight affair connected with public business, at a time when he knew Edward was disengaged, and with full leisure to enter into any extraneous matter.

It happened that the majesty of England was in a very gracious mood, possibly on account of its being after dinner, and that good digestion had waited upon appetite, and possibly because that morning a Lancastrian spy had been caught and hung up in the close vicinity of the palace.

The king wore a loose gown, composed of a mixed tissue of gold threads and silk, and his long fair hair hanging luxuriantly down his shoulders, according to the fashion in which he always wore it. He had been abroad riding, and a very light chain mail of silver links covered his legs. The room in which he sat was a small and costly one, it being adorned with the richest tapestries that could be procured. The roof was composed of the rarest and most beautiful carvings that the skill of the age could produce, and the whole appointments of the room showed that nothing had been spared in its decoration that was costly, unique, or magnificent.

Edward had a very small silken cap on the top of his head, and he sat on a chair the seat of which was not above eight or ten inches from the ground, while the back of it went up to a height of nearly six feet, and then spread out into a slight, but most exquisitely covered canopy.

The king was playing with a young greyhound that crouched at his feet, and seemed wonderfully pleased by the caresses that were bestowed upon it by its royal master.

Hastings had been announced and ordered to be admitted. He was preceded by two pages to the apartment, who opened the door of it, and then stood on either side to allow him to pass in. The chamberlain, according to custom, knelt on the threshold until the king should bid him rise and enter, which Edward immediately did with an air of the profoundest respect. Then the door was closed by the pages, who remained on the other side of it conversing together in whispers about their own affairs, and such little matters of court scandal as happened just then to be upon the tapis; although, by all accounts, there was nothing like the amount of intrigue and general villainy of one sort and another at court as there is now, when we have centuries of enlightenment added to our history, and a queen who, of course, is everything great and beautiful, and who lives, of course, in the hearts of her people, and all that sort of thing.

CHAPTER XLVII.

The King's Resolution.

"It is said that Edward always had a lively sense of Jane Wainstead's beauty, having seen her in a royal progress, and afterwards, at the instigation of my Lord Hastings, he again sought her."

"I CRAVE your majesty's gracious pardon," said Hastings, "if I have intruded on your gracious privacy."

"No," said the king. "You are welcome, my Lord Hastings. We have leisure ever at the command of those whom we know to be our good servants ever."

"My liege, such words fall like dew upon my heart. Never did faithful servant serve so generous a master."

The king slightly inclined his head. It might have been in acknowledgment of the compliment, or it might have been that he considered enough had been said upon that subject. Hastings chose to attach the latter meaning, and, as he stood some few paces from the king's chair, he said,—

"My liege have you reconsidered concerning the new subsidy?"

"In truth I have not, Hastings."

"It waits your gracious leisure."

"Gloster thinks it unwise."

"His grace of Gloster's opinion always weighs heavily with me."

"And with ourselves."

"Does his grace suggest a plan to raise those same supplies of which your royal state stands so much now in need?"

"He suggests a plan, but whether it be a better one or not I am not prepared on the moment to say."

Hastings was silent, and, after a slight pause, the king resumed,—

"Gloster thinks a subsidy would produce a number of malcontents, and he suggests that we borrow of some of the wealthier merchants on interest, raising only the interest of the sum so borrowed by a general subsidy, so that the sum wanted would be insignificant."

"The plan has plausibility about it."

"It has."

"But your majesty will see that when the amount so borrowed is spent, a subsidy then will have to be raised as usual."

"No, Gloster says we can borrow more, and still the interest of all we borrow for years to come will be felt but lightly by the people."

"But there must come a day, my liege, when the interest will amount to as large a sum as the most liberal subsidy now is."

"True; but Gloster says that such a time is so far distant that it is folly to heed it, and that a thousand circumstances may come in the interim to make what now appears an uncomfortable contingency, of no moment at all."

"If your majesty think well of this scheme I shall have great hopes of its entire success."

"Nay, Hastings, what think you?"

"It does look just and proper, and highly expedient. Moreover, I should feel disposed to lean heavily upon the judgment of his grace of Gloster."

"If you and others, on whose love I know I may depend, object not to the scheme, I have an inclination to try it."

"'Twere well to try it. But the Lombards, of whom, of course, this money must be borrowed, are accustomed to demand security."

"Our royal word," said Edward, "we will give them."

Hastings gave a short cough, and the king smiled as he added,—

"You think that will not be considered sufficient. I admire your candour, Hastings."

"Pardon me, your majesty. No one in this realm, and, I think, no one who knows aught of your majesty out of it, would for one moment hesitate to take your royal word for anything; but all men know the valour of your majesty, and how the enemies of England ever find your majesty at the head of your own brave soldiers. It is the dread that the fortune of war, and the will of Heaven might, to the deep affliction of this nation, carry your majesty to an early tomb, that would make the merchants hostile."

"Oh, indeed!"

"Yes, folks say that we, having a king so brave, so just, and so noble, is a good argument against our being so blessed again for some time."

"You have stated an objection, Hastings."

"It is a hasty one, my liege, and, after all, may exist only in my own imagination; but I am accustomed to speak candidly to your majesty."

"We wish all would do so."

Hastings bowed, and then the king added,—

"We will consider further of this more at our leisure; or, rather, at some time when we are not so disposed, good Hastings, as now to throw off the cares of state."

"None is more worthy of kingly leisure than your majesty," said Hastings; "and, oh, if you had seen what I have seen to-day ——"

"Ah, what do you mean?"

"So fair a sight my eyes were never blessed with. It is an image that will haunt me while I live."

"Be more explicit, Hastings. You rave."

"Pardon me, my liege, that, with the thought of so much beauty, I am scarce myself."

"Beauty, said you?"

"Ay, a very paragon of charms. I saw one to-day so exquisitely formed, so delicately and gently framed by nature, that my heart groaned to look upon her for the live long day."

"Indeed, where saw you this miracle of perfection?"

"Ah, most aptly named," said Hastings, evading the king's direct question. "She is indeed a miracle of perfection; I never saw such beauty and never shall again; I never could have imagined such exquisite charms as all belonging to one favoured mortal."

"You are smitten, Hastings."

"Not I, my liege; affairs of state, the anxieties of the troubled times and duty to my sovereign fill up my mind wholly; I can admire and reverence the charms and covet not the possession."

"You are more discreet, Hastings, or colder than I thought you. But who is the maid?"

"Nay, my liege, she is a wife."

"A wife?"

"Yes, of a citizen."

The king laughed outright as he said,—

"Hast been among the bourgeois, good Hastings, to find there a Venus?"

"I have seen her, my liege; she is the wife of one Matthew Shore, a goldsmith, of Lombard-street."

"Indeed! Matthew Shore! We have heard of that man."

"He likes not subsidies, and some have had suspicion that he likes not the Red Rose."

"Ah!"

"Even so, my liege, a morose man, one of no mark or likelihood whatever; and this creature of such heavenly charms but a girl in age, and with the true-hearted simplicity of an angel, has been by her father, since dead, sacrificed like some mercantile commodity to this Shore. Oh, how she hates him!"

"Hates him, does she?"

"She cannot but do so; and she is such a piece of metal as never yet shone upon the world. She wastes her time in tears, that heaven has not mated her with one whom she can love."

"'Tis a pity."

"It is, and he, Shore, is jealous—aye, to fury. They say he strikes her."

"Unmanly ruffian."

"Your Majesty's honest indignation well becomes you. As the sad tale was told to me, this paragon of gentleness and beauty sighs for some kindred soul to love—some heart on which she could devote a world of tenderness Shore can never know. Oh, your majesty should see her eyes—diamonds shrink before them. Then her mouth, so formed for lisping words of love and woman's kisses—her cheeks—her hair! Gods! she is something more than human."

A little of this enthusiasm was assumed and a little of it was real. The king looked amazed.

"Why, Hastings," he said, "you love her?"

"No—no, my liege, no."

"You speak in raptures of her."

"I speak but as speaks the general tongue of fame concerning her. The beautiful Jane is well known. They call her the Rose of London. Oh, well does she deserve the title."

"Has she been long wedded?"

"Far from long; but a short time, only sufficient to feel that she is made wretched."

"Who was she?"

"Her name was Wainstead; she was the only child of the rich mercer in the Chepe, of whom your majesty may have heard."

"Heard! By Heaven, I know her."

"And is she not ——?"

"An angel?"

"Aye, is she. Have I overrated her charms?"

"You have not. I do remember—twice has her beauty dawned upon my sight, and, since, her soft bewitching face has haunted me like the spirit of some sweet dream. I do, indeed, well remember her."

"I joy in that fact;" said Hastings; "for else your majesty might have thought me romancing when I praised her so."

"You cannot praise her beauty too much. I marked it well. And she who looked like some beautiful, angelic child so short a time ago, is now a wife?"

"An unhappy one."

"And an unhappy one?"

"Most miserable, your majesty. Ah, she should have had some happier destiny than that with all her beauty."

"She should indeed," said the king, musingly, as his eyes were cast on the floor, and he played with the ear of the hound that crouched at his feet. "So she should—she should indeed."

"He catches at the bait," thought Hastings.

"Married to a man she cannot love?"

"To one whom she must hate."

"Aye! What a fate."

"Fancy him lifting his hand to strike her—fancy the second blow given—then her shriek."

"No, no," cried the king. "The villain, he dared not! By my crown I'd hang him higher than ever traitor swung."

"Fitting reward, my liege, for a traitor to beauty."

"A flush of colour came over the king's face, and after a long pause he said, in a low tone,—

"Hastings!"

"My generous liege."

"Mention this to no one."

"My lips are sealed."

"'Tis well. By the holy rood it would be no evil act to rescue this fair creature from such a fate."

"Oh, a most saintly act, my liege."

"You think so, Hastings?"

"I am certain."

"Well, well, we will think. It is a scandalous thing that so much beauty should be compelled to endure the harshness of a ruffian."

"Most monstrous!"

"I fain would, which we cannot, in such a case, interfere."

"Humph!"

"Why do say 'Humph!' Hastings? What road to interference is there in such a case as this? She is his wife."

"Yes—a forced marriage."

"Indeed."

"So I am told. Forced by her insane father, who, not a doubt, was mad in the last few months of his existence, although she, in her blind affection, would never see what to any one else was so self-evident."

"You seem to know a great deal about the affair, Hastings?"

"Oh, my liege, beauty in distress affects the sympathies. Does not your majesty, even from what I have stated, feel that you could willingly dash aside the tear of affliction from those sweet eyes, and bid her smile again?"

"And Shore an enemy of the state?" said Edward.

"Yes; and she a warm friend to your majesty's cause and family."

"I am sure she is."

"Those who know her, say that her heart is possessed with some image of ideal or real beauty, which she sighs for; that she has at some time seen some one who forms to her young imagination her only dream of perfection."

"Indeed."

"Yes; one who knows her well told me, that sometimes she would sigh in the very midst of her affliction, and say,—'Oh, could I hope to reach so high, one smile of his would well repay me for all I have suffered.'"

"So high, did she say?"

"Those are the words as reported to me."

"It's very strange!"

"And those who know her are lost in wonder as to whom it is she thus cherishes in her heart."

"Most strange!"

"It is, my liege. I questioned my informant, a gossipping dame, closely, and she said, she believed that the beautiful Jane—for even women own her beautiful, which your majesty will acknowledge is wonderful—was languishing for love of some one whom she would never name."

"Hastings!"

"My liege."

"I would that I could see her"

"It may be done."

"How, good Hastings, how? For myself I do not see the way to do it. How might it be done?"

"If your majesty will give me till to-morrow ——"

"Pshaw! To-morrow?"

"But till to-morrow; I can then mature some plan which shall enable your majesty to look upon that face, which, even now in affliction, is so marvellously beautiful."

"Well, well, be it so. You will not fail me?"

"On my head be it, my liege. By heavens! a sudden thought ——"

"What thought, Hastings?"

"Her concealed love—her talk of some one too high for her to reach—her enthusiastic cherishing of some hopeless passion ——"

"Well—well?"

"What if she love your majesty?"

"Go to—go to."

"Nay; how the thought grows upon me. Already it has become gigantic! It may be—it must be so!"

"Perhaps some noble of the court ——"

"Oh, no. Is there one of such fair parts as to command such a creature's admiration? Look at me!"

The king smiled, as he said,—

"You are wonderfully modest, Hastings. I certainly did not suspect it was you she loved."

"Oh, of course not, my liege," said Hastings, not over well pleased, and finding it extremely difficult to conceal his vexation. "It can be no other than your majesty, I am convinced."

"On your soul, do you think so?"

"Whenever I have the honour to address your majesty, I always utter my truest and holiest sentiments."

"Well, well, I have found you faithful, Hastings."

"And will so find me ever, my liege."

"I am content to believe so."

"To-morrow, then, rest assured, when I am admitted to the honour of an interview with your majesty, I shall be prepared with some scheme by which this paragon of loveliness shall be submitted to your eyes."

"And myself unknown?"

"Most certainly."

"If, Hastings, you can do that, it will be an hour well spent, believe me, and one for the pleasure of which I shall think myself much indebted to your love."

"I am more than repaid, my liege."

The king glanced towards the door, and Hastings knew that was a signal to be gone. He moved backwards from the royal presence, and knocked at the panel of the door.

The page immediately opened it, and in another moment Edward was alone.

The king continued to muse for some seconds. Then a slight smile crossed his face, as he said,—

"Yes, I do remember her; I saw her amid the rout, and riot, and confusion in the city on that occasion, when well I know the Lancastrian faction made an attempt upon my life. I remember her well. I saw her, too, once since. Now, beshrew me, but I do much wonder at myself that I never felt a flame of passion for so much and such rare beauty."

He rose, and let the hound's head, which was resting on his knee, tumble off, as he continued talking to himself—

"She loves some one in a high station secretly, and Hastings thinks it is myself she loves. Humph!—I have some suspicion that he knows it is myself she loves—that some one has told him so, and that he is not unwilling to earn my thanks by helping me to such a conquest."

He paced the room to and fro for many minutes in silence. The hound followed him and whined to him, but his noble master's mind was too much occupied now to pay him any attention.

In the midst of affairs of state he might, perhaps, have paused to caress the dog, but what now occupied his thoughts was of a far more all-engrossing character, and took up his whole attention.

"Yes, she loves me, surely," he said. "Who else, as cunning Hastings says, can it be?"

This was a mode of settling the question highly favourable to the personal vanity of the young king, at any rate.

"Who else," he repeated, "can it be?"

He thought over all the different gallants of his court, and then he laughed, as he said,—

"It so happens I have a marvellously ill-favoured set of courtiers at present. Surely Jane Shore loves me. Heaven forbid, now, I should condemn her to a life of tears and blighted affection—I can love any pretty woman, and if she turns out but one-half what she is reported to be, my affection, commenced by an acknowledgment of her most rare beauty, will become fixed by her many virtues."

It was quite clear that the king did not think of connecting chastity among those virtues.

The more he reflected now, the more eager he became to make the acquaintance of the beautiful Jane Shore.

He wished he had insisted upon Hastings coming to him earlier than on the morrow, and once or twice he was on the point of sending for him, but he checked the impulse, because he felt a little ashamed to let the chamberlain know how deep an impression he had made upon his mind.

"I will resist," he said. "Yes, I will resist, since it has been arranged, until to-morrow. Already I feel that the vague sentiment of admiration I have had for this beautiful girl has ripened into love; she shall be mine, if kingly eloquence can move her. I love her, and she shall be mine. She shall weep no more, if she will allow me to dry her tears, and as for Shore, her husband—why, as for him—I—I will think of some means of stopping his mouth, somehow. He shall not complain—oh, no, he shall not complain."

How Shore's mouth was to be stopped the royal Edward did not at that moment stop to inquire, or to settle whether he was to have a pension stuffed down his throat as a recompense, or a pike ; but he satisfied his kingly conscience with the passing reflection that Shore's mouth must be stopped. Kingly consciences are generally very easily satisfied ; but, after all, Edward the Fourth was not the worst monarch that ever ascended the throne of these realms.

As for Hastings, when he left the royal presence, he knew not whether to congratulate himself upon his success or otherwise. He certainly had, with considerable tact, eloquence, and judgment, fully succeeded in awakening the king to a full sense of all the beauties of Jane Shore. But now he felt for the first time how this mode of revenge cut both ways ; and, if it was calculated to wound Jane in the shape of persecution, it touched him nearly that another should stand a far better chance of engaging her affections than he. And, in addition to this feeling, whatever might be the result, he had the full conviction in his mind, that, but for him, Edward would never have thought of endeavouring to make Jane his ; so that, if she should yield, and now Hastings, in his own mind, turned his former possibility into a probability, he had himself to thank for it. Where would be his revenge then ?

These reflections were absolute torture to him, and, when he reached his own house, he was in the most unenviable state of mind that it is possible to conceive.

"After all," he exclaimed, "what may I not have done ? She may yield to the king, and then, instead of revenge upon her, I shall have been the instrument of raising her to a height of power and greatness where she can look down upon me with scorn, and achieve what revenge she pleases against me for what I said to her, and the violence I was so near offering to her in my own house."

My Lord Hastings began to have a strong and uncommonly disagreeable suspicion that he had overreached himself. This, of all feelings, probably is the most provoking, and no wonder that, under its infliction, the chamberlain should fret and fume, and get into such a state of nervous excitement as to be totally unable to turn his thoughts towards fulfilling the promise he had made to the king for introducing him to Jane, or Jane to him, on the morrow. In the midst of all this turbulence of his feelings, Antonio Vassa was announced to him.

CHAPTER XLVIII.

A Friend.

"Ye kinge and ye chamberlaine went disguised to purchase ane gold cup of Master Shore."

Notwithstanding the state of agitation he was in, Lord Hastings was extremely glad to see Antonio Vassa. He had promised that to the king which he knew well he could not now perform without assistance ; and that it must be performed, let the consequences to himself and his own feelings be what they might, he likewise felt well assured of.

His appearance at once intimated to Vassa the turbulent state of his mind ; the cunning eye of the Italian soon saw that something seriously was amiss with the chamberlain. Assuming an air of surprise, he exclaimed,—

"Hey-day, my Lord Hastings, what has occurred to give that angry flush to your brow ? You appear in a most unenviable condition. Whence is it that I see you thus ?"

"Be seated, Vassa," said Hastings, "and learn that which I have to tell you. I am still sorely perplexed on account of Jane Shore. By Heavens, I think her beauty was created on purpose to be my bane."

"Say you so ? Then, have you broken your promise to me ?"

"Partially, Vassa, I admit, but only partially ; but, as a recompense, I will now give you my entire confidence."

"Recompense !" said Vassa, sneeringly ; "in truth I see not the value of such a recompense. Your entire confidence may be the result of some difficulties in which you find yourself, rather than any desire to be confidential with me. But say on, Hastings —I am content to hear you."

"No, not a difficulty exactly," said Hastings; "but, the truth is, I found a difficulty to chase the remembrance of the wondrous beauty of Jane Shore from my mind. I felt your arguments against further interference with her rather too keenly, and, smarting under the consciousness of having attempted something upon which I had set my mind, and of having utterly failed, I set about bethinking me of some means of revenge. I dared not myself persecute her, for her obstinate virtue—I presume I must call it, and yet I wished her persecuted."

"I regret to hear your mind is yet fixed upon such trivialities. Surely, surely, Hastings, you have much more important matters with which to engage your attention."

"It may be so," said Hastings, "I cannot say but it is so; but what I have now done I cannot undo, and it is idle to waste time in vain regrets."

"True enough—true enough; but, tell me, now, what is this that you have done, to get out of which again you require my aid and assistance?"

"Nay, I said not that."

"But I guessed it. The confidence of the politic Hastings might have been withheld had all gone smoothly. What is it now that works unevenly in the transaction, and which makes the confidence with me a matter to be desired?"

"Nothing works unevenly," said Hastings, "all is well; I only quarrel with my own arrangements—not their want of success."

"Say you so?"

"Yes; to tell a secret to you, Vassa, I have been but too successful in that which I have endeavoured to accomplish—I knew not that its accomplishment was detrimental to my peace till 'twas done."

Vassa laughed, as he said,—

"Such errors of the judgment are common; but let us have the particulars of this most oppressive state; perchance, even now, it may not be too late to mend it."

The chamberlain then related to him all that had passed between him and the king, concluding by saying,—

"And thus, as you perceive, I have pledged myself to a course of action which is likely to give me a world of uneasiness. I might have got over the fact of Jane Shore refusing to leave her husband for my arms, but, for the king to be her lover strikes me with dismay."

"And yet, you yourself, most consistent Hastings, have taken the greatest pains to bring about such a state of things."

"'Tis true, I have, and hence I am fretted."

"It cannot now be helped; you must keep your word with Edward, or you are lost. You have inflamed his passion, and it must be gratified."

"But tell me, Vassa—you know something of this same Shore—you overheard her conversation with me, which now I am glad of, inasmuch as it enables you the better to advise me; think you Edward will prove a successful lover?"

"In truth, I do; he is young, handsome, and a king—what more would she have? She must, indeed, be a very paragon of virtue if she withstand such dire temptations. She is his, and you, my Lord Hastings, have placed her in his arms."

"'Tis as I feared," said Hastings, as he dropped into a seat. "Your judgment tallies with my own, and I have thus not only defrauded myself of my revenge, but have, as if in return for the coldness with which she treated me, and the contumely she heaped upon me, done my best to place her at a height far above the wildest dream of ambition she may have fostered in her soul. By Heaven! I could kill myself of very spite, to think I have so trifled with my mind's fear as I have done in this instance."

"'Tis but the echo of your own words," said Vassa, "to tell you that what is done may not be undone. By what means do you propose to introduce her to the king?"

"I have not thought of that."

"Indeed!—then that is the point for which I am indebted for your confidence; you would devise some ready plan to meet the wishes of the king, whose passion you have inflamed, that in your state of mental distraction and disappointment you cannot do so."

"Do not torture me," said Hastings; "if it must be done, it must."

"If it must," said Vassa, laying emphasis on the monosyllable. "Is it with you a doubtful point whether you will sacrifice a love-sick fancy for a smooth-faced girl, or your position in the grand political arena in which you are an actor?—but why do I ask this question, when it is out of your power to decide? The king would woo and win Jane Shore, now that he is inclined so to do, were a thousand chamberlains to say nay."

"Alas, it is too true."

"And hence you better not yourself by a vain resistance to the royal will; you have now evoked a spirit which you cannot quell—resist it while you may."

"You are right—I feel that you are right," said Hastings; "but when did passion ever yet with judgment hold a fair contention?"

"Often; and in this case shall it. Smothering all passion beneath a subtle, calm, and courtly smile, you now, although you may not woo the wondrous beauty for your self, can play, with cunning art, the pander to the king—a nice and pious office, one upon which many great men have thriven, could we but look behind the curtain of their greatness, to see what made them great. You have assumed it, Hastings, I wish you joy of it."

Whatever rage or indignation Hastings might feel at this cutting speech, he did his best, and succeeded in smothering such feelings; the only reply he made was,—

"Vassa, this is ill talking, and can do neither you nor I a benefit. I may be hurt, I may be much angered, but I do not feel disposed to sacrifice that political existence that you mention for such a cause. I certainly cannot but feel some uneasy sensations at the possibility of Jane Shore becoming the mistress of the king."

"I think you may dismiss them."

"Indeed! May there not be much danger?"

"I scarcely think so. If she be as wise as reputed, she will think it good policy not to know you, and the past will be forgotten. The cause, too, of the angry altercation is in your favour."

"In my favour!" exclaimed Hastings, with surprise.

"Yes, in your favour. Whence arose it? From excess of admiration—a fault soonest of all excused by a woman; they will forgive a lover an insult in his enthusiastic pursuit of her affections, when their deadliest hatred would follow a slight thrown upon their personal charms; a rude and uncourteous salute is more readily excused than a fancied slight."

"Alike to you, Vassa, come all subjects; from the highest political questions to the merest detail of ordinary passion."

"I have studied human nature in all its phases; it is that which you call the merest detail of ordinary passions, which I find often dictates to the higher impulses. A woman's smile has lost and won kingdoms."

"I believe that you are correct. The king will see Jane Shore."

"Yes, and he must see her—wherefore not? What hinders you from facilitating her interview with the king to petition for the release of the young spark in the prison yonder at the Blackfriars?"

"No," said Hastings, "I have a decided objection to that. Confound him, I believe 'twas he who stood in my way before I raised up for myself this new evil, in the person of the king."

"My good friend," said Vassa, with a careless air, as he kicked some of the embers that smouldered on the hearth further into the flame, "one of two things must happen—Jane must come to the king, or the king must go to Jane."

"I thank you," said Hastings, "for the self-evident proposition; the latter course I should prefer."

"And is your brain not fertile enough in expedients? Now, if you were to persuade the king to go disguised to Master Shore's, and there boldly woo her; she knowing him not, the royal lover might meet with as ignominious rejection as yourself."

"Ah! now, if I could be sure of that," said Hastings.

"It might be so; you could accompany him, and so make yourself more sure."

"I!" exclaimed Hastings; "I should be known at once—unhappily I am too well known."

"That need be no objection," said Vassa. "You know my powers of disguise; I would transform you so the king himself should know you not."

"Say you so? By heavens I would like to venture with him, on such an errand."

"You shall if so you wish it. And now, since your own mind is so much engrossed by other matters, leave all this to me, and ere you see the king to-morrow, I will bethink me of some plan to carry out your wishes to the utmost."

"Then upon you, Vassa, I rely; you have given me a new hope, that after all the king may not succeed."

"We shall see, we shall see," said Vassa, laughingly. "At what hour to-morrow must I be with you?"

"The king dines late—at half past two; if you are with me at three of the clock, that hour will suffice; and let your greatest genius, Vassa, tell you what to do. It seems to me now more terrible that King Edward should become the favoured lover of Jane Shore, than that I myself should even be rejected."

"I have no doubt of that," said Vassa. "What daily opportunities you would have of witnessing her daily triumphs, in the court; at what a host of fetes and pageants would you see her, hanging upon the king's arm, smiling in his face with all the consciousness of love, and forgetting her past life in that new and splendid alliance of the heart. Methinks I see her now, attired in costly robes of state that might become a queen, with beauty so far outshining those, that she to them shall be an ornament, and lend new grace, not they to her."

"Enough, enough," said Hastings; "if you would not drive me mad."

"You have enough already to do that in your own breast to render that needless on my part," said Vassa; "see to what end so gentle a passion as love comes—such emotions must be pleasing and sweet, since their cause is so eagerly sought; but farewell, Lord Hastings, until three of the clock."

"Farewell," said Hastings; "I trust to you implicitly in this affair, and shall rely on your assistance."

"You may."

CHAPTER XLIX.

The Meeting at Scroop's Castle.

For some time after the departure of Richard of Gloster and Lord Hastings, Antonio Vassa paced his room in silence; he gazed out upon the starry host, and then he paused before an instrument composed of a glass tube, with various degrees marked upon a plate to which it was attached. There was, too, some dark fluid matter, that sometimes rose and fell. He looked at this carefully, and then again went to the window.

The stars shone brightly, and there was scarce a breath of air stirring; but there was a mournful sound came upon the night air and died away, and then again returned.

"Ay," muttered Vassa, "it will come, and that before it be very late. Before the night be two hours older, yon starry host will be invisible, and the cloudless sky will be veiled by a murky vapour. Strong winds shall blow, and heavy rains descend. A strange and fierce storm is at hand."

He paced his room in silence, and seemed to be meditating upon deep schemes within his own breast, to which he would not give utterance; and even his very thoughts appeared to be silently passing his brain, and occupying his mind, to the exclusion of all other feelings and emotions. He was a strange man, and one whom none could fathom; his purposes were hidden—not even suspected. The clock of the abbey struck eleven.

"'Tis time," he muttered; and then closing the window that stood open, he took a large cloak that hung on a chair, and wrapping himself up in it, and placing his sword so that it was within his grasp in a moment, and free for instant use, should occasion occur, he then quitted the house he resided in and walked slowly towards the city.

However, before he had gone far, he altered his mind, and walked to the nearest stairs, and desired one of the watermen to row him down the river. This the waterman did, and, as he sat in the boat, he cast his eyes up towards the heavens, where but lately he had seen so many brilliantly lighted stars, but there was not one now to be seen by him. The heavens were dark, and he could now feel the cold and strong wind that blew over the surface of the water. The waterman saw his gaze, and thinking he was making some observation on the weather, said,—

"There's been a great change in this last half hour, your honour."

"There has."

"And there will be yet more before the next half hour passes."

"There will be."

The waterman did not know what to make of his customer, but pulled away in silence for some minutes, and then determined again to try the effect of speech, and said,—

"I'm thinking there'll be a great storm to-night, sir; and the river won't be the safest place in London."

"Humph!"

"There it begins, now," added the waterman; and before he could well say another word, there came such a dreadful peal of thunder, that the very welkin rocked with the sound.

The rain now fell fast, and the boatman ran the boat into a creek near Somerset House, but Antonio Vassa insisted that the man should take the boat on further.

"Where to, sir?" said the boatman, "this is a night not fit for a dog to be out in."

"That may be, but Christians are; however, go on and land me somewhere near White-friars—do you mind me?"

"Yes. I have my boat to mind too, else we shall both go to the bottom."

They proceeded along until they came to a stairs at the bottom of the gardens, near the Temple, and at the bottom of that was some wharfing line. Vassa desired the boat to pull alongside, and having paid the boatman, he jumped out and proceeded on his journey.

The storm abated not, but Antonio Vassa heeded it not; the deluging rain and the loud claps of thunder scarce disturbed the current of his thoughts; even the vivid lightning scarcely caused him to close one eye for an instant. Once, and only once, did he stop beneath the doorway of a house. At that moment the rain fell in such torrents that the street seemed to be filled with aqueous particles; they fell so fast and heavily that they seemed to smoke, and large puddles and pools were formed by the water running off the eves and collecting in masses.

"By Heavens!" muttered Antonio Vassa, "a more propitious night could not have happened for my undertaking. I'll warrant that there are few playing the spy on such an occasion as this—'twould be a pretty office, and if pursued, the ardour which cannot be cooled by such a night deserves a reward. But as for me, there are none to watch me—none to suspect me; but what if they do? Antonio Vassa can baffle them all and lead them astray."

The rain now held up partially, and Vassa again made towards the residence of the Lombards, in whose vicinity lay Scroop's castle. On, on, he went, and nought, save his own shadow, was near him; no human being saw the dark figure of Antonio Vassa crossing their doorways—had they done so they would have shrunk from contact with that dark, mysterious man. At length he stopped before Scroop's castle, and then, giving a signal, as agreed upon, he entered the small postern door, at which stood two stalwart porters, whose heavy swords and partizans would have repelled any intruder who should have ventured to such a place.

Threading his way through several passages and stairs, he came to a door, before which was a sentinel, who, on a sign from Vassa, caused a small bell to ring on the inside, and then opened the door, and Vassa pushed open the second himself, and found himself in the midst of the conspirators, who had assembled there. There were several lamps distributed about, rather for the purpose of dispelling the darkness than to illumine the place.

Here were assembled several lords and leaders of the Lancastrian party—all well known to each other, and yet they addressed not each other by name, leaving that to be imagined; and they were careful not to speak over loud, lest they should be overheard by the sentinel, who, however, could not hear; but had he done so, there was little doubt that it was safe, as even he was a true tried man in battle for the party who were now in secret conclave. There was a suppressed murmur when Vassa entered, and all eyes were turned to him when he stepped into the throng.

"Welcome, Antonio Vassa," said one, a tall, burly man, whose sunburnt features and numerous scars showed that he had seen long and active service—"welcome, Antonio Vassa, our cunning Italian—what hast thy fertile brain devised now?"

"Little," said Vassa, "that other men could not do as well had they the wit to do it. And how does your lordship; have you stormed a castle single-handed and taken it?"

"No, by my faith, that is an exploit only such as thou canst accomplish. I am a man of mortal mould and means."

"And so am I, my lord."

"You are—but you seem to have means that none can understand or direct but thyself, good Vassa. What news hast thou?"

"But little, my lord; but that you shall hear presently, in good time:—but first, as I am last arrived, how goes the good cause?"

"The good cause goes as slowly forward as one could well desire it; men of inaction rule the day, and a rough old warrior, like myself, cannot find wherewithal to whet his sword."

"Your lordship's appetite is not destroyed, though; I see you bear the marks of the last fete upon your features."

"Tush! man, I am dying—heart-sick to return the service they rendered me. I never loved to be under obligation to any man; I wish the Yorkists were all concentrated into one person, then what a glorious revenge would I carve out for myself!"

"There may yet be an opportunity, and nearer than you can imagine; the time may come when your sword may do better service than even it has done yet."

"Then, out sword! cry I; and Mars once more is the deity I follow."

"A truce to your lordship's heroics," said a tall, thin man, whose eagle eye seemed to rest impatiently while the first was speaking, "and let us hear what Vassa has to say."

"I came to inquire what was doing," said Vassa; "how go on our friends in the north?"

"They are quiet yet; but, like the hounds in the leash, they wait the moment they are to be let loose, and then 'twill once more be 'a white rose for ever, and down with the flower that blushes for itself. Lancaster for ever!'"

"'Tis well."

"'Tis well, as you say, Vassa; and we are not without friends in other parts, who can bring a goodly body of men to the field. A good general will not allow himself to be destroyed by defeat; a battle may be lost, but yet the victors may not be sure of their conquest."

"I can imagine as much."

"And Edward sits upon a trembling throne."

"Why, so he does."

"And, moreover, 'he may once again be driven from that post the fortune of war may have given him.'"

"And so he may!"

"But yet we have determined upon no specific course; but propose in lieu, for a short time, to wait the turn of events, the growing confidence and fancied security of Edward and his party, and the increase of our own strength, and the consolidation of such strength, and then in a short time we may resume action."

"'Tis well, and wisely resolved, if no better course appear; but each day gives strength to those in power, and men's minds become accustomed to regard him in the post he has usurped, and to consider it's but right he should hold it."

"That is my argument," said he of the sunburnt and scarred countenance. "What gives us strength, gives them strength too."

"And yet how could it be avoided?"

"By drawing to a head, and gathering our faction to a point, and from that point rush boldly to attack the usurper."

"But he is a conqueror too."

"Granted."

"But——"

"Cease!" said Antonio Vassa, in an imperious tone, as though he cared for none, and would be heard at all events. "Cease! and listen to me."

"Speak on, Vassa."

"You all, at least, many of you," he continued, "may know Master Shore, the rich mercer?"

"Ay, ay."

"Well; he has a beauteous daughter, one well calculated to captivate the man whose passions are active; she has captivated the heart of Lord Hastings, who has been ignominiously repulsed."

"Ah! ah!"

"Hastings, finding he could gain nothing on his own account, like the child that would destroy because he cannot get the toy, he, in revenge, informed Edward of her beauty, and highly inflamed the mind of the king."

"The usurper!"

"Be he who or what he may, the word serves my purpose to describe who he is, and whom I mean."

"Well, well, go on."

"Edward desires to see this beauty, and has become desperately enamoured of her from the descriptions of Hastings, who is now equally mad at having procured such a rival to himself, especially as the king has destined him to fill the royal office of pander to himself."

"Hastings will be disgusted at being the minister of those pleasures that he once destined for himself."

"That may, or may not be true," said Vassa; "and it is of no moment in comparison to what is to follow from this."

"Ay, ay."

"No; listen. Hastings was compelled to promise to obtain the interview the king desired, though he knew not how it was to be done, or how the interview was to be effected. To me, therefore, he came, and I have the sole arrangement."

"And what will you do?" said the first speaker; "play deputy pander to Hastings' first?"

Antonio Vassa only replied to this by a look of so much scorn and contempt, that it would have produced an angry rejoinder from the stout bluff old soldier, who would bear no ill looks from friend or foe, but for what followed.

"Go on, Antonio. Go on, Vassa, and tell us to what all this tends?"

"To this," said Vassa; "as Hastings relies upon me to procure the interview, it can be done only thus, that he and the king must seek her in disguise, and then Edward will woo her thus."

"But will she come?"

"Hastings will not have her brought to him, lest she should demand the release of that young spark that he desired to see at the end of a rope."

"Well, well."

"Then he must go to her, and Edward must enter the city alone, save that Hastings will be by his side. Can your brains devise anything further, or what ought to follow?"

"By my good sword, you are a treasure, Antonio, and if you place the king thus within the reach of our swords, we deserve to lose our cause if he ever get out again, save to lay in state at Westminster Abbey."

"That is the exact thing to be done. Now then, you see, my lord, you will have yet good and speedy use for your sword."

"And by all the saints in the calendar, that ever were, or ever will be, my sword shall do good service, and help to place the crown on a better head than the one it now adorns.

"At what hour to-morrow does he come?"

"I know not yet," said Vassa. "I am to be at the court to arrange the appointment, means, and disguises, and until that is done, I am unable to give you any precise information."

"And at what hour are you to learn this, to us, most important news?"

"I shall be at the court by three of the clock, and then I shall learn what is so essential to be known. I will let you know, but be in readiness at a moment's notice to take to the Chepe."

"We will, we will."

"And now, good night."

"Good night."

Scarcely had these words escaped their lips, when a most astounding noise took place, such as clanging, and clashing, and thumping, and all tumbling about, and the whole place shook again. The conspirators glared in each others' faces for some moments in silence. They could not have heard each other speak had they tried to do so. Loud and deafening was the noise, but when it somewhat subsided, then each man drew his sword, and wrapping his cloak round his left arm, rushed forth from the room; but they found the place contained no foe.

" What is the meaning of all this ?" eagerly inquired one of the conspirators.

" It is the fall of some part of the roof, or a stack of chimnies, and nothing else, my lord," said the sentinel.

" What, was that all ?"

" Yes, save the thunder. The lightning struck the chimnies, and threw them down. I could scarcely tell whether the world was at an end or not," said the man.

" More noise would be unnecessary," said Antonio Vassa; " more important events have been done than that, I am sure—but, farewell."

" Farewell."

" Farewell, and speed you fairly," said the warrior; " we shall wait with impatience for the news."

" And it will come in its good time."

" 'Tis well."

Antonio Vassa wrapped his cloak around him, and making his way across the rubbish that had fallen down, he proceeded towards the door where he had entered, and where the two sentinels were very much scared by the noise that had been made in the castle.

He passed into the streets; the storm was yet hovering over the city, but it had evidently expended its utmost strength, and was gradually becoming less intense.

CHAPTER L.

The Spy.

When Antonio Vassa had once again passed out of the old building he began to walk rapidly through the streets without looking behind him; he was, in fact, deeply engaged in his own meditations, and noticed not that he was followed. At length, however, he turned sharp round, and saw that a man, enveloped in a large cloak, was dogging his footsteps.

In a moment his resolution was made, and he doubled on his course; but yet he found he was followed by the stranger, who, however, kept at a most respectful distance, and would by no means come near him. What was to be done? He had, no doubt, been seen come out of Scroop's Castle, and to Scroop's Castle he was determined to return.

This determination he soon put in force, and once more made for the rendezvous of the conspirators, and he again tapped at the small postern, which, though it bore the appearance of being ruinous, was yet capable of keeping men out who had not proper means for opening the place, and, with the two soldiers on the inside, the conspirators were not at all under any apprehension of being set upon.

" Are they gone ?" inquired Antonio Vassa.

" No, sir," was the reply.

" 'Tis well," he muttered, and immediately walked towards the apartment where he had held his late conversation with them.

" Ah, Antonio Vassa !" they exclaimed, " come back again; what's amiss ?"

" Nothing, but we are watched."

" Watched !"

" Ay—what—eh ?"

" What, an espial ! How knew you that, Vassa ?"

" By my own eyes. The man followed me, and I doubled on my course, and he followed; go which way I would, yet he followed."

" We are betrayed."

" Not yet."

" And why did you not poniard him, or run him through with that long rapier of thine. I know thou canst use it."

" I can; but this fellow seemed to think so, and carefully remained at a distance, and to have attempted a chase would have been to expose myself to greater risks than I would care about incurring, to no purpose."

" We had better all go out and secure him, and prevent his telling tales."

" It will be wise," said Vassa; " do you all part, and shake hands, and go all in different directions; but yet have some one near at hand, for that man must not escape to tell the tale, unless you are prepared to have your heads placed on London-bridge, or grace the gates of the tower."

" It is agreed—it is agreed," said a dozen voices; " he shall be killed."

" And you had better separate at once, and all together, since he will then suspect nothing, and will fall an easy prey."

They all now broke up, and looked towards the postern door, when the sentinels said that a man had been walking up and down before the door, and had endeavoured to open it; but finding it secure, he had gone and stationed himself on the other side of the way in a safe spot.

"Why did you not cut him down at once, and then there would have been an end to the traitor?" said the old warrior.

"We could not, my lord."

"Could not. How?'

"The door was secured, and any noise would have been a hint to him, which he would quietly have carried away with him, and then he would, perhaps, have caused an alarm."

"'Tis well," said Antonio Vassa; "if it can be done out of the city the better. It will not be so likely to scare the game you wot of."

"It shall be so."

They now all passed out of the postern door, and stood before the castle of Scroop. They could see the form of a man who was standing in the shadow of a door-way. The storm had passed over the city; but the rain had ceased, and it grew somewhat lighter. The conspirators stood for a few moments in anxious consultation, and then, having agreed among themselves, they at once parted, and moved from the spot in different directions, without taking any notice of the stranger, who remained in his place of concealment until the conspirators had got to some distance from the place where he was.

No sooner, however, had he moved away from the place where he had sheltered himself, than three of the conspirators came from out of Scroop's Castle, where they had remained on purpose to watch and follow him; and, in case he should not leave the city, they were resolved that they would assassinate him there.

The spy was perfectly unconscious of the fact that he himself was not only discovered, but that he was in turn watched; far from it; he believed he was safe on that score.

Believing he was engaged on a desperate and dangerous enterprise, and that he was by no means safe, he went forward with much caution and care, but at the same time believed that the danger he had to face lay in front—he might meet it; but it could not come suddenly upon him from the rear.

Antonio Vassa had taken the same boat he before took, and the conspirators mostly took to boats they had placed in readiness, while some few deemed it safer to remain in the city, at some of the hotels and taverns.

The spy hurried on until he came to the river side. This was not very easily accomplished, but it was so managed that he got clear of all kinds of impediments, and was soon on board a small skiff, which he rowed himself with great address and speed. The direction he took was upwards, and he seemed to be in great haste, and exerted himself to the utmost. At the same time he put off from the shore, the conspirators ran down to the boats, and immediately got into a large one, and three of them pushed off, followed by several others at short intervals. At one moment they were anxious of running him down, and thus swamping the boat and drowning the rower. This, however, was objected to, because an accident might occur to their own boat, and because they could not, in that case, examine the body and discover who their enemy was, and whether he had any papers about him. In consequence it was agreed, therefore, to defer his death until he should land, and also that they should, in case there was any prospect of his escape upon the water, without hesitation, sink him.

The river was very rough; indeed, it was somewhat dangerous for the small skiff that the spy occupied to be on the river; but yet he seemed to heed this but little, and pulled on with a strong arm over the raging surface of the Thames after midnight. The night was yet dark, and it was only by the sound of the oars that they could tell where they were, or their vicinity to their enemy. But having many oars—six to the other's two—they could in a very short time come up with him; but fearful lest they should give him any alarm or disquiet, they pulled in along the shore, and by this means, as the wind blew from him, they escaped detection.

They soon passed the extreme limits of the city, and now they were very cautious, for now they were passed this they had but little to shelter them, and they were liable to be discovered; and then the spy might put back, and reach the city, give an alarm, and he would be secured from all danger.

They could just see the boat on some way ahead, and it was drawing towards the shore, and, seeing this the case, they dropped astern a little, and there remained for a time. They laid down in their boat, and one of the party, taking off his hat, placed himself in such a position in the boat that he could observe what went on without exposing himself to observation in return. He could see the boat ran into a creek below Somerset House, and, when he had landed, they drew closer towards the place, and the moon, shining out at this moment, enabled them to see what course he took. Seeing that he was making for Westminster fields, they rowed smartly for that part, and before they got there they steered the boat in a favourable spot, and jumped ashore.

" I am glad I am once more on terra firma," said one of the conspirators.

" It was rough, it is true ; but there was no danger there whatever."

" I was not thinking of danger—save the danger of becoming so stiffened in joint, and so cold at heart, that I think it scarcely beats ; a good fight will warm me—at least, I hope it will."

" But hasten onward and cease talking. See how he walks on. He is making speed, as if he feared pursuit!"

" Onward, ho !"

They all three now walked rapidly forward, and for some time they concealed themselves beneath the shadows of some stunted willows and bushes which, grew about on parts of the swamps and barren places that were so abundant about that neighbourhood ; indeed it was almost one entire swamp—the whole district now a flourishing suburban city.

They pressed onwards with great speed, but their intended victim walked very fast too, and they gained but little on him, when one of their party, knowing the ground well, conducted the whole of the conspirators to a place that he must pass.

" Here," said one, " we'll wait his coming ; and then I'll warrant we will soon stop his prating."

" Do you think he can have spoken to any one on the road, and thus defeated our main object in view, that of preventing any suspicion of our meetings at Scroop's Castle ?"

" No chance of it—he could not have done so ; and, besides, if he had, it would be but policy to put him to death as a spy."

" It will."

" Agreed !"

" It will put an end to all the civil broils if we can once put Edward beyond the power of carrying on the war against us."

" It will put Henry on the throne, and end the civil wars."

" You forget, there may yet be another competitor arise, and one, too, as troublesome and bold as any other I can think of."

" Whom do you mean ?"

" I mean the duke."

" Richard ?"

" Of Gloster."

" Ay, ay—but there are no signs yet of such a stir, and his party yet reigns. If it be suddenly deprived of its head, then we can overpower Richard, or any other of the York faction leaders."

" There is much to be done in a case like that, and, I think ——"

" Hush ! hush !"

" He comes."

Two of the conspirators stood beneath the shade of a tree, while the third crept along, so as to get in the rear of the stranger, and prevent his retreating. A few moments sufficed to bring all parties in collision, and the doomed man stepped up close to the tree before he saw the conspirators.

" Stand !" said one.

The stranger paused, and, seeing his opponents, said, in a determined tone,—

" Say, what is't you want ? Money ? take it !—but lay not your hands on me. I wear a sword."

" And so do we. We want not your money, but the life of the spy all men may take who have any interest ——"

" Ha ! ha ! spy—dare ——"

" You were near Scroop's Castle not an hour since ; therefore, prepare to die."

As these words were uttered, the two conspirators stepped across the road, and, unsheathing their swords, they were preparing to attack him, when, seeing no escape that way, he turned with the intention of flying to the boat, but that was barred too, and he drew his sword, rushing headlong upon the man who barred his retreat.

After a desperate conflict of a few minutes, he was slain by a sword thrust through the body, and he fell dead on the road.

"There is one enemy the less," said one of the conspirators. "I would we could meet them all in detail, and cut them up like this."

"Has he any papers, now?"

"There, let's away, and return to the city, where we can enter, and we shall run no risk of being suspected of this."

They drew the murdered man on one side, and covered the body over as well as they could among the rank weeds and grass that grew in abundance.

CHAPTER LI.

Alice and the Leech.

"Oh, freedom, art thou little worth?
Ask of the moaning slave;
Ask of the warrior bold and free,
From chains he'll seek the grave."

Again did the leech present himself at the door of the prison to inquire concerning the governor's health, and to exert his skill towards restoring him to health and vigour. But this was a task he knew beyond his skill, yet the maxim, "that while there is life there is hope," was in those days as well known as at present, and men acted even against conviction in such cases, and then admitted the consequences.

The door was opened by the usual gaoler, and the leech entered. He looked around him at the features of those who were in the little vestibule, or room, and thought he could read in their features the tale he had to hear.

Slankey was not present, but he heard the man's voice, and as soon as the leech appeared, he came forward, saying, in a tone less loud than usual, but with the same insolence of manner, and the same brutality,—

"So, sir leech, you would see Sir Godfrey."

"I would," was the reply.

"You can do so, and yet I think you'll find he has benefitted little by your skill."

"His case is desperate, altogether desperate, but yet we must not neglect our patients because they are at the last, or because we think human means of no avail; we yet hope on, and do those offices which are so much required. Besides, it does happen that when we think a man beyond hope, he sometimes rallies and recovers."

"Do you think it will happen so in this case?" inquired Slankey, in a peculiar tone.

"We never can predict in any case, because if we could there would yet be hope, and that would take it out of the catalogue of hopeless cases. How is Sir Godfrey?"

"Well enough."

"For his state."

"Yes, surely, for *his* state," said Slankey, emphasising the pronoun strongly.

"His state—what mean you?"

"The state of a corpse."

"Sir Godfrey died of his wounds then?"

"I suppose so."

"Has he been dead long?"

"Some hours."

"I will see him."

"Oh, yes, certainly; you know your way, sir leech, only you must go in, as Sir Godfrey can neither desire you to go in or stop out."

"There is no one there?"

"None, unless Mistress Alice be there, and she is as likely as not; but there's no accounting for taste, you know, sir leech. However, the tough old knight sha'n't die unavenged anyhow; I have that matter on my mind, and sha'n't let it sleep."

The leech made no reply, but departed towards the room in which lay the body of the dead man. He paused and listened at the door, to ascertain if there were any sound that would indicate the presence of any one in the chamber of the dead—he heard none.

Entering the apartment, he saw that they had drawn the curtains, the room was darkened, and the hangings round the bed were drawn close. The leech drew them aside, and then gazed on the dead man. He stood looking on the corpse some moments with the air of one who was well used to such scenes as that before him.

"Well," muttered the leech, "his hour is run, and it might have been distant many years; but he died in his vocation. To shorten life was no consideration to him, and see, his own is shortened. There are those who say this man's fate was as it were wove when he first breathed the breath of life; but yet it seems the blow could not have been anything but the result of a combination of circumstances that might or might not take place."

"But men build up theories to suit the fancy, and not deduce their theories from the facts; that would require too independent an exercise of reason, and one requiring a greater degree of cultivation than the rude unquiet spirits of this barbarous age can well be conceived to possess."

"Well, Sir Godfrey is no more—a mere shape, a form that will quickly decay and become resolved into its original elements, to supply the waste that is going on elsewhere, or rather, the consumption, for nature, like a manufacturer, requires a replenishing, else her stock becomes low and runs out; reproduction can only be managed where the means are at hand. Farewell, thou remains of a strong man—passion, feeling, are alike dead, and thou art now at least calm."

He closed the hangings and the curtains that hung before the windows. He had scarce done this, when the room door opened, and Alice walked in, and when she observed the mediciner, she said,—

"Ah, my unfortunate father, sir leech, is beyond the aid of man; his time has come, and he is no longer one of us, but a tenant of the cold, deary tomb, where good and evil are alike."

"Yes, mistress Alice, he is beyond the reach of mortal aid; he has indeed quitted this world for an unknown journey. But still this is not all loss—there is even sweet amid the bitter."

"Indeed!"

"Yes."

"I cannot see what you could extract of a satisfactory nature," said Alice.

"Yes, mistress Alice, the evils he might have inflicted upon others, and those he may have suffered from others."

"You may be right, sir; but 'tis a subject that I cannot so well converse on as you can, neither can I do so unmoved."

"Pardon me, mistress Alice; I did not mean to allude to any unfortunate circumstances, but merely as I would have spoken of any one else. But what other news have you?"

"I wished to consult you, worthy and learned leech; and I must thank you, as a child, for what you did for my parent."

"I regret that that was useless; but what said he before he died?"

"He said something to Slankey, the gaoler, about Walter Fane, who lies yet in the dungeon."

"What said he?"

"He left some stern injunctions respecting the vengeance he was to take upon him."

"And has he obeyed them?"

"No; I believe that he is turning the matter over in his mind."

"How know you this?"

"The abominable wretch told me seriously that he was employed in considering in what manner he could torture him, so as to produce the greatest pain, and said my father made him swear that he would not fail to do so."

"Which the fellow has every inclination to keep?"

"He has."

"Then he must be liberated as quickly as can be. There is no time to lose, for caprice may at any one moment place him beyond my power."

"But how?"

"That we must see about. Where is the key?"

"Slankey has it."

"Cannot you demand it?"

"That would create suspicion."

"It must be had."

"He goes to sleep every morning, and he may be asleep now; it is past noon, and he may be asleep after his dinner and strong ale."

"Do not spare any pains if you wish to succeed. It must be had somehow, or else the youth's fate is sealed."

"I will go at once. Wait here, sir leech, and if I succeed, I will be with you immediately."

She left the room, and did not return for many minutes, for when she came to the room in which Slankey reclined, dozing, he awoke more than once while she was awaiting with great anxiety to seize the key, which was attached to some others.

To get this, without awakening the gaoler, was the great difficulty, for he slept so lightly that he would awaken at the slightest sound, open his heavy eyes, and look round.

However, Alice did succeed in detaching it from his girdle, and then she hastened back to the leech, whom she left in the room where her father lay dead.

"Have you got it?" inquired the leech.

"I have," was the reply; "and here it is. He will not miss it for several hours, I believe, unless he hits upon some plan of vengeance, and then he will go to do it at any moment."

"Do you know of any way by which we can reach the dungeon without passing through the room in which Slankey sleeps?"

"Yes, there is a way, and, if you will follow me, I will lead you to the dismal place into which he is thrust."

They had now quitted the apartment, and sought to reach the desired spot by a circuitous route, but one in which they were unlikely to meet with interruption. By the aid of a torch, for it was very dark in the passages they passed through, they succeeded in reaching the door which led into his dungeon in security.

"This is the dungeon," said Alice, "and this is the door; and you will, if you do not take care, fall below, as there are several steps down into the dungeon, as it lies low."

"I will be cautious," said the leech; "is there any one within hearing?"

"Not within hearing," said Alice, "but Slankey is above; and of him we must be cautious; shoot the lock, and take the key out when you have opened the door, and it cannot be then closed upon us, should we be surprised."

"That I will do," said the leech; "but hark! what sounds are those?"

"Hist! speak not," said Alice; "'tis Slankey."

They both stood in perfect silence, and uttered not a word; they could hear the sound of feet moving to and fro, and each moment they anticipated would be the last they should remain undiscovered where they were.

"Should he come," said Alice, "he would probably kill him from revenge; he is capable of anything, and he has received some blows himself, and is, therefore, burning with hatred and revenge."

"I see," said the leech; "and this is the more probable, as, when your father died, he mistook me for this Slankey, and gave orders for my death."

"Alas! alas!"

"By a slow and lingering death; and gave me directions where to find the keys, and pointed it out for that purpose."

"Thank Heaven that man heard not his purpose, or it would have been done by this time. Slankey would not have allowed such an opportunity to pass unseized."

They paused for some moments, and listened intently, and, to their joy, they found the sounds decreased, and at length died away in the distance, to the joy of Alice, who trembled lest they should be discovered, and Walter Fane's life be the sacrifice.

"Now," she said, "now is the time; there is no one near—we are alone—open the door."

The leech obeyed, and the lock slowly turned in the wards—the door was open.

CHAPTER LII.

Slankey the Gaoler, and the Dead Man's Orders.

THE light that trembled in the hands of Alice cast a gloomy radiance below, and disclosed the interior of the dungeon in which Walter Fane lay sore and wounded. Beneath them was a steep flight of steps, and down which the leech, having first taken the precaution to shoot the lock again, so as the door could not, with aid or by accident, close on them again, carefully and cautiously descended, immediately followed by Alice, and they both stood on the dungeon floor.

Walter Fane lay on the floor of the dungeon, and when he heard the whispered voices outside his dungeon door, and could see the rays of light shine faintly through the chinks in the door, he thought that there was to be an attempt upon his life. He was himself too weak to make any resistance, and he knew he must fall an easy prey to the strength of his assassin, whom he imagined could be no other than the brutal gaoler. Great was his surprise, therefore, when his dungeon door was thrown open, and he perceived, after the dazzling effect of the light had ceased to confuse his sight, the form of the leech followed by that of Alice.

" It is no messenger of death yet," he thought, and he endeavoured to support himself against an angle of the wall.

" Young sir," said the leech, " how fares it with you? are you able to use the necessary exertion to escape, if your friends have the means?"

" I am sore and weak," said Walter, " and of myself I fear I shall be unable to do so; but I will make the trial, if I fail."

" You must rouse yourself, Walter Fane," said Alice; " you will not have long to live, if you remain here, and there is no knowing the torture and pain that ferocious man Slankey will put you to, if he be much longer your gaoler."

" I will do all man can do," said Walter; " and I thank you both most heartily, and feel most grateful for this kindness; to me it is most welcome, and in the moment of my greatest need."

" Do not waste time in talking here," said the leech; " we all stand in danger of discovery. But how," he added, turning to Alice, " how are we to escape from this place?"

" There is a man and a boat in readiness in the basin, by the water-gate. If we can get there we shall be safe."

" I see," said the leech; " but how is the way between this and the water-gate guarded? Do you know the dangers between this place and that—what are they? Before we encounter them we ought to know them, and be the better prepared to guard against them."

" Slankey is the only difficulty—the only one whose vigilance I fear."

" And we must pass him."

" We must."

" Then the attempt had better soon be made, because we should be unable to make the attempt, the young man's strength not being sufficient to enable him to second our efforts, and make a struggle for his escape."

" We can return to the room whence we came," said Alice, " and conceal him there for a time."

" A good thought," said the leech, " a good thought. We can consult more at leisure there, and determine better what to do, with less chance of discovery, than in this place."

Alice placed the light upon the floor, and directed the leech to lift Walter from the ground, and place him on the lower step for a moment or two.

" Now," said the leech, " you must exert yourself a little; you have no bones broken, and are therefore not materially injured. You may be very sore and bruised, and are so, no doubt, and in great pain also, but you will do no mischief in attempting to walk a little."

Thus urged, and having the prospect of making an escape before his eyes, he, with their assistance, contrived to get out of the dungeon, and stood leaning against the wall, in the passage from which the dungeon opened.

" Wait a moment," said Alice, as she descended the steps, " while I get the light."

The leech waited by Walter Fane, and Alice soon returned with the light, which was very necessary, as the passage was quite dark.

" We can go on now," he said.

" No," said Alice, " wait a moment; secure the dungeon door, else all will be lost, for Slankey will no doubt walk about and ascertain if all be right and safe, and if the dungeon be locked, while we have the key, he cannot ascertain the truth of the case."

" You are right, you are right," said the leech; " we had better secure the door;" at the same time he relocked the door, and taking the arm of Walter Fane, he said,—

" Now, let us push our way back to Sir Godfrey's room."

" Sir Godfrey's room!" echoed Walter.

" Yes; he is dead."

" Dead!"

" Yes; he died but a few minutes since. No one knows of it yet, save ourselves, and on this hangs your safety."

They slowly and cautiously retraced their steps, until they reached the room in which Sir Godfrey lay a corpse. Alice walked by his side; she was anxious and agitated—she watched his pale face, and every expression of pain marked thereon was reflected in her own, for it seemed to her that she could feel every pang that tortured him.

" Here we are safe for awhile," said Alice. " Here is a chair—sit down on this."

Grateful indeed was the seat to Walter Fane; and the soft cushion on which he fell when he attempted to sit, appeared to him, after the hard floor of the dungeon, like heaven; it was with a feeling—a shudder, of mixed pleasure and pain that he reclined in that chair.

"We must guard against the appearance of Slankey," said Alice; "he comes to learn what was my father's will relative to prisoners, and it is uncertain how soon he may come."

"Where can we conceal him?" inquired the leech; "he must be concealed."

"Slankey, as soon as he knows my father is dead, will be sure to seek for his prisoner and wreak his vengeance upon him."

"We must provide against that too," said the leech, "or we might as well have not stirred in this matter."

"How can it be done?"

"He must be concealed in the bed of Sir Godfrey," said the leech.

"In the bed?"

"Yes."

"What, with the corpse?" inquired Alice? with some emotion of horror, and looking at Walter, as if she thought he would object to such an arrangement, especially as that corpse was the corpse of his enemy.

"We do not view with the same feelings that you do the inanimate remains of those who have quitted life; it is mere matter, and can do us no mischief; but come," he added, turning to Walter Fane, "you will not, for your life's sake, mind being concealed in the same bed with the body of Sir Godfrey?"

"No," said Walter," I am obedient to all you can wish—I am passive."

"There are no other means."

"There is a closet."

"But he could not bear being bent and cooped up in that space—his bruises and hurts would be by far too painful."

"Well," said Alice, "it can't be helped; the sooner the better now, for he will be here shortly."

"I hear steps now."

"Hasten, Walter Fane," said Alice, "and get into the only place of concealment that remains open to you—hasten."

"Yes," said the leech; "the counsel is good—be quick—be quick."

Thus urged, Walter Fane crept to the bed, and, by the aid of the leech, he was placed in the bed, and the bed-clothes were drawn tightly over him, and then the curtains were drawn around and tucked tightly in.

Walter Fane felt some disagreeable sensations creep over him as he found himself in such proximity to a corpse, and that corpse, too, his enemy, and a man who had died from wounds inflicted by himself; but there was so much of necessity in the arrangement that he could not either object or feel so much as is possible he would have felt of repugnance had it been otherwise.

"There," said the leech, as he had finished the arrangements connected with the concealment, "it is as well done as possible, and he is as comfortable as he can be."

A slight shudder ran through Walter's frame as he heard him talk about comfort.

"Hush! he comes," said Alice, and she sat down in the chair Walter had left.

With barely any intimation of his approach, save such as his heavy foot fall indicated, the brutal Slankey entered the room.

"Is it thus you enter the room of a wounded man?" said the leech, holding up his hand and exhibiting a stern look; "do you know the mischief you might ——"

"That's all very well, sir leech, with most of your patients; but I know Sir Godfrey ain't such a painted lady patient as all that, the old knight is one of my sort."

"But sleep is necessary to the strongest—a giant would sink for want of it."

"Giants, indeed; yes, wooden ones would, if one didn't prop 'em up."

"Be silent."

"I can't and I sha'n't unless I have Sir Godfrey's orders to do so."

"What do you want?"

"A word with Sir Godfrey."

"You cannot have it just now—bye-and-bye he may be better and will be able to speak to you about your duty."

"And in the mean time, sir medicine, he may die. Oh, no, that won't do for old Slankey, and I'm sure it won't do for Sir Godfrey; the good, tough old knight would laugh and swear at me if he thought I believed in such stuff."

"What would you desire to know?"

"I'll put my question myself."

"Well, if you must, it must be so, but speak low, and I will repeat the question to him. A short time of silence would be of great use to him now," said the leech.

"Ah, you always make a great mystery of your profession; but now, sir, I want to know what's to be done about the young spark below—ain't his time come yet?"

The leech drew aside the bed-curtain, and repeated the words slowly and distinctly, though in a low tone, so that Slankey, who stood near the bed, could hear them. An indistinct reply followed.

"What does he say?" inquired Slankey.

"That he is to be left alone for the present."

"To be left alone? Heaven's curses!"

"Hush, he speaks again."

Another sound came,

"What's that?" said Slankey.

"He says," said the leech, "that he will attend to that himself, and settle his own affairs, in his own way—he waits to see that done before his own eyes; he says," continued the leech, after another pause, as if he listened attentively, "he says he mustn't die until he is able to see him."

"Now, that's what I call d—d selfish," said Slankey, in a great rage. "I can't see why I shouldn't have my revenge as well as anybody else. I can't see why I shouldn't have the pleasure of wringing his neck after my own fashion. I'll warrant I can make him feel as much as ever Sir Godfrey can, and you may be sure I don't care about repairs, and I do call it a d—d shame. The young son of the city spawn, has knocked me about. I have got bruises and knocks—it won't do for old Slankey—slashing Slankey hasn't come here to be treated in this way; but mark me, Sir Godfrey, the young spark don't escape, if I swamp him in the dungeon, by pouring pailsful of water down the dungeon steps, and make it go through any small hole I can get it to run. I'm cursed if I like this. I thought Sir Godfrey had been a better man than that—I didn't think he'd ever take my revenge away from me."

A low mumbling now attracted Slankey's attention, and he exclaimed again,—

"What does he say?"

"He's swearing," said the leech, "and says he wishes he was well enough to get up and put an end to your insolence, and desires you to leave the room, and not come in again till he sends for you, or he'll teach you to question his orders."

"That's d—d queer salve to a man who has been knocked about by another, and only wants his revenge; but as long as the young spark does die, it's all one to Slankey."

So saying, he left the room, growling and cursing as he went out. They watched some time until they were assured that he was gone, and then the leech said,—

"'Tis well he has gone—his audacity made me fear more than once all would have been discovered."

"I feared greatly he would not have taken the answers you gave him second hand. I thought he would have come to the bed himself, and looked in."

"I expected so, too; but it has succeeded to admiration, and now what remains to be done must be done immediately."

"The sooner the better."

"I think Walter had better come out of his concealment now, and rest in the chair; it will be better that he sit up a bit."

Walter Fane was by no means sorry to hear this, and with the leech's aid he got out, and again sat in the chair. The short time he had lain on softer materials than the dungeon floor seemed to have had a beneficial effect, and no doubt proper care and attention would have done him much good.

"The only thing I can think of will be for him to dress himself in some of my father's things, and thus have a chance of passing the people unknown, and getting out of the prison, and trust to chance if found out. It cannot be worse than it is now," said Alice, thoughtfully.

"Let it be done;" said the leech, "and I will give him a cordial that will aid him for awhile, by giving him a little strength."

"I will watch on the outside," said Alice, "while Walter dresses himself; you will find all that you require yonder."

"It will do," said the leech.

Alice rose, and casting an agitated look upon Walter Fane, she left the room, and the leech began to aid in the task of arraying him in the garb of Sir Godfrey.

CHAPTER LIII.

Walter Fane's Escape from the Prison.

While Walter Fane was aided in dressing himself in such of Sir Godfrey's garments as would disguise his appearance, and cause him at first to pass unobserved among those who should only catch a transient view of his person,—and it was hoped that by these means even Slankey might be deceived by the appearance,—Alice stood on the outside of the apartment ready to give an alarm on the approach of any one who might, from either design or chance, approach. The leech tapped at the door to intimate that all was in readiness to make the attempt to descend and escape.

"Have you given the cordial?" she inquired; "he will have to exert himself, and will much need everything that can be done for him."

"He shall have it—bring me a glass with some water in it," said the leech, as he took from his pocket a phial filled with some amber-coloured liquid.

The glass was brought, and having poured out the greater part of the water, he emptied the phial into it, and then presenting it to Walter, he said,—

"Drink this, Walter Fane; it will do much towards enabling you to undergo the necessary fatigue to make the attempt, and also to go through with it if it should succeed."

Walter Fane took the draught, and putting it to his lips, he drank it off at once. There was an aromatic odour that pervaded the apartment after he had drunk it, and he felt himself much refreshed in a very short space of time.

"And now," said the leech, "we may as well make the best use of our time. Must we go through the apartment, or watch-room, in which that ruffianly gaoler is posted—or is there any other way by which we can leave the prison?"

"The only way we can hope to escape by," said Alice, "is the water-gate, and to get there, we must pass this man. Do not, however, despair—he can have no idea of the escape. He cannot suspect, and will, therefore, when he sees us, be led to take very little notice of us, unless, indeed, he thinks proper to be insolent."

"We must chance that," said the leech, "and the best thing to be done, will be to surround him as well as we can. Come, good youth, try how you can walk now, and then we will leave. Take this cloak and bonnet, they will be more useful than all the rest of the garments, being more capable of concealment."

Alice said nothing, but waited anxiously while this addition was being made to the toilet of Walter Fane by the leech, who seemed to understand the art of disguise very well.

"And now," said he, "we will proceed;" at the same time he took Walter Fane's arm, and led him to the door of the room.

"Before I go," said Walter, "and as there may be an adverse termination to this attempt, let me express my thanks and gratitude for this kind and active interest you have taken."

"Speak not of it," said the sage.

"I may never be able to say as much again, and I would not be thought ungrateful, and to die without thanks or gratitude, poor as they may be."

"Hush," said Alice; "do not waste your strength in words. When we are safe outside the prison, we may then congratulate ourselves upon the event, but not before."

They now moved towards the stairs, and slowly one by one did they descend them, and after some time they arrived near the place where Slankey lay. They could hear the ruffianly goaler talking to some of his fellows, and swearing in a round tone, while some of them were laughing.

"I'm cursed," he said; "but if I don't have my revenge, I'll give up the office. What's the use of a man's doing as I have done, and then be persuaded to wait? What's the use of waiting? But I'll not give him any food. Yes, a little starvation will do him good."

"Well, he's safe now at any rate."

"Safe! ay, safe enough. Safe as strong walls and locks can make him, and I warrant he's in no condition to get out."

"Do you think Sir Godfrey will be about again?" inquired one of his companions.

"I don't know, but I shouldn't be surprised—he's a tough old blade, and may disappoint the leech—he began to swear when I was in the room last, and that's a good sign, you know."

"Very good; and my opinion is, he'll be about before long."

The party now entered the place, and came within sight of the men. Alice and the leech, however, so placed themselves, that while they aided him, yet they concealed him from the eyes of Slankey. In this they succeeded, and actually passed out of their presence without exciting more than a passing gaze, for Slankey felt himself too indignant to pretend to see any of his superiors, and the whole party escaped detection.

This was purely accidental; for if Slankey had not been engaged with some strong ale, and venting his displeasure at the same time, he would have been curious and insolent, or officious, as the humour took him, and a discovery would have been the result. They soon found themselves on the stairs leading to the little basin, where a man and boat were always in waiting to convey any of the officials who belonged to the prison to and fro, whenever it was requisite so to do.

By the aid of this man they fully anticipated being able to make their escape. Alice had provided herself with a long, sharp dagger, and, if all other means failed, she thought she should be able to use it, and thus force the man with the boat into a compliance with her wishes; but then she scarce expected there would be any prospect of his suspecting anything without some previous circumstances occurring. When they came to the head of the steps they could hear the water plash against them, and she paused a moment or two, and then they heard the boatman singing some ditty.

"We are safe as yet, and I hope there is no other unlucky accident likely to happen, I will run down first, and beckon the boatman, and do you follow but when you are in the boat, do you—should anything unforeseen happen—can you use the dagger, should there be occasion?"

"Yes," said the leech. "I know the use of it, for I have often cured wounds inflicted by such weapons. I will use it."

"Hush, what noise is that?"

They listened a moment, and could hear voices shouting, and steps that seemed to come nearer and nearer.

"It is a pursuit," said the leech.

" Slankey suspects us—hasten down," she said; " follow quickly—life and death depends upon your speed—follow me!"

Alice rushed down the steps with a precipitation dangerous to herself, but she thought only of the danger of pursuit, and the mischief that would befal Walter Fane if he were detected.

" That villain would not hesitate to kill him," she muttered. "Oh, God! grant us strength and speed to get away. He comes! Where's the boatman? Here!" she exclaimed aloud, "boatman! boatman!—here, instantly."

" Yes, mistress Alice," said a coarse, gruff voice, that sounded unearthly; for the place was arched and bricked on all sides, and gave any voice a peculiarity, much more such a one as the boatman's. " Yes, mistress Alice; I'm here, and at your service. What do you want?"

" The boat instantly; my father cannot wait; he's too weak to be kept standing."

" Sir Godfry! I'm glad he's about again; 'twas more than I expected; but I'm with you in less than no time."

" The leech declares the air on the river to be necessary for his recovery, so be quick."

" There's nothing like the breeze on the river for anybody, in my opinion. I know very well that I thrive on it, and I know many more who would die elsewhere; but here I am."

As he said this, he rowed alongside the steps, and Alice seized the head of the boat firmly in her hands, saying,—

" Hasten, sir leech, my father cannot stand; he has already walked too much, and feels weak."

" Let me help Sir Godfrey in," said the boatman, rising in the boat.

" No, no," said the leech; "sit down, and have your oars ready; this place is cold, and like a well. There, never mind me, I'm right. Push off the head of the boat; Sir Godfrey is seated; we can jump in any how."

The boat's head was pushed off, leaving the stern grating against the steps, and the leech had just got in, while the boatman was looking very suspiciously at the supposed Sir Godfrey—not that he suspected anything, yet there was something so strange that he could not help looking at them all—when Slankey's voice was heard calling loudly, but they could not distinguish what he said. Alice was preparing to step into the boat, and when she heard this, she said,—

" Push off the boat—push off!"

" Get in, Miss Alice."

" I will," said Alice. " Now—now, use your oars; the air is very cold here."

" Yes," said the leech; " I told you so. Put off, boatman—put off at once."

" Well, I am; but what a hurry you are all in," said the boatman, in a suppressed voice. " It's d——d odd to me, but Sir Godfrey don't look the same man he did; but I suppose illness has pulled him down. What can be the matter with old Slankey?—what's he hollering about?"

" Hilloa! hilloa!" shouted Slankey. " Stop them there. I must see who that is—that's not Sir Godfrey, I'm d——d. Hilloa there! Treason! There's foul play of some sort going on."

" Push off!" said the leech to the boatman.

The boat was now three or four boat's lengths, and was turning into the archway, when these words were heard, and therefore beyond the reach of any one on the steps.

" Stop!" exclaimed Slankey to the boatman, beckoning him back with his hand. " Stop, and come back—come back!"

" Pull off!"

" What's the matter?" called out the boatman.

" Treachery! treachery! That's not Sir Godfrey. Come back. An escape!—an escape!"

The man was about to back water with the oars, when Alice whispered to the leech,—

" The dagger—the dagger! or we are lost."

" I have it ready," said the leech; and then, placing himself close to the boatman, he said,—

" You are a dead man, unless you pull out of this place. See this dagger—it is long and sharp, and, moreover, it has qualities you know not of—that you never can recover from."

" Put back—put back!" exclaimed Slankey, furiously; "put back."

"Pull out of this place," said the leech. "One prick of this—nay, a scratch with its poisoned edge, is enough to destroy life in one hour."

The boatman was alarmed, and looked at the dagger, and then at Slankey.

"Pull out."

"Pull back—pull back!"

"Pull out!" exclaimed the leech, as he placed the point of the dagger close to his heart, and then giving it a slight push, the man felt the keen cold edge of the blade through his clothes, and then shrunk from it.

"I shall thrust it between your ribs," said the leech; "and I know whereabouts to prick for the heart, and will not torture you, but put you out of your misery in as short a time as possible."

The man, seeing there was no help for it, gave a couple of strokes with the oar, which carried them very nearly out of the archway.

"Come back!" shouted Slankey. "Treason—treason! You are aiding a traitor!—the man's a prisoner. Come back—come back."

Slankey, however, spoke to a man in momentary fear of his life, and, therefore, he could expect nothing from it. The leech, in the meanwhile, kept thrusting the edge of his dagger into the person of the boatman, who, although thus urged, pulled but languidly; but they were now in the river.

"If he cannot pull faster," said Alice, "he will cause us to be overtaken, for a pursuit will be commenced by Slankey on the river."

"Come, sirrah," said Walter Fane, "if you do not row, you will be thrown into the river. If you do your best, you shall be rewarded."

"After a fashion!"

"Come, come," said the leech, "I have been in other countries. Will you row or not, or I will serve you as they serve the boatmen at Constantinople—I will fling you in, after I have stabbed you with this weapon—do you feel it?"

As he spoke, he thrust it actually into him for a considerable way.

"Oh!" exclaimed the boatman, "have mercy, learned sir; I am rowing."

"Put out your speed. I know well what such an arm as yours can do. Row as if you were rowing for a wager; you can row, I warrant, and, if you do not, I will try the efficacy of the dagger. Pull lustily."

The oarsman rowed, and they made their way on the bosom of the Thames. The banks of the river were not in those days studded with wharfs and jetties as they are now. Indeed, there was scarce a building by the waterside at all in those days. Trees, and tall rank grass, and sedges, were to be seen on every side; and wild fowl were plentiful where there are now bridges, wharfs, and houses. The banks of the Thames then by no means pretended anything analagous to what they now appear—the reverse was the fact, for now the river is confined to its ordinary channel by the encroachments upon its banks of bricks and mortar; then it expanded at high water over various places that now are covered by houses and streets, and formed pools and muddy places, and small creeks, which sometimes ran on such occasions a considerable way inland.

It was towards one of these places the leech wished to direct their course, and he then wished to make his way towards the city, the gates of which he could easily pass.

"Hasten," he said to the boatman, "or the dagger shall do its work; you have made no way at all these five minutes."

"The tide is against me, learned leech," said the boatman, "and I defy any man to run against tide as easy and as quietly as he can with it. I am doing my utmost."

"The tide scarcely runs against you at all," said the leech; "'tis just upon the turn in your favour."

"There is yet a current," said the man; "I can feel it against my boat."

"Pull on, then."

The leech saw there was nothing to be gained by urging the boatman, who, as long as he did pull, was doing all that the former desired, for he did not care about exciting any suspicion on the river.

They made very slow way, and they were all equally impatient; and it was evident the man, if he had not feared the dagger the leech kept in his hand, would have returned; and it is very doubtful if he would not have resisted them all, and would himself have thought there was no very great danger in doing so. Indeed, but for the steady watchfulness of the leech, a *coup-de-main* might have been attempted by the sturdy rower, and the whole party might have been immersed in the Thames. The leech, however, who seemed to be well aware that his own life, as well as that of Walter Fane, was in danger, and that a single mistake, or momentary neglect, would be fatal to them both, kept a vigilant watch upon the boatman's motions, and the long, sharp dagger, was an impediment he could not very well get over. To be sure, the leech was more accustomed to study than to fight, but a child might thrust that formidable weapon quite through the body of a strong man; and he appeared so watchful, and at every movement the waterman made, the leech always made a corresponding one, that in no case could he seize him at an advantage, and so gave up the hope.

CHAPTER LIV.

The Chase on the Thames, and the Escape.

WHILE the leech was thus continually urging the unwilling boatman on, the scene at the prison became animated, and all was bustle and confusion. It was all in vain that Slankey hilloaed and swore till he was hoarse after the boatman to come back; he was heard plainly enough, but the love of life did not permit him to obey the injunction of the infuriated gaoler.

"Come back," he shouted, "come back! Hell and furies! do you not hear? You shall suffer for this—I'll have vengeance!"

He stormed and raved on the steps; he would have rushed into the water, but it was useless; and, moreover, it was deep, and he would have been drowned in any attempt to approach the boat, which was leaving him fast.

"He'll not go faster than he's obliged," he muttered; "I'll chase them upon the Thames—we'll have them now—hurrah!"

He quitted the steps, and returned to the guard room, in which were some of his companions, and he rushed in, saying,—

"There's treachery afloat; I thought it couldn't be Sir Godfrey."

"Who is it?"

"I can't tell."

"Then how do you know it isn't?"

"Because they made off, and would return no answer, and got away in a great hurry; and you may be sure that there was somebody there as shouldn't be there, else they never would have made off in that manner."

"What's to be done?"

"Get a boat as quickly as you can, and we will follow them; they won't go very fast, and, at all events, we shall be able to keep them in view, and trace them to their concealment; when we can, at all events, pounce upon them. Come, stir about and get a boat—a boat! Who's good at the oars? it will be a long chase; and yet, I don't know, an unwilling rower is no good hand at escaping from his friends."

Slankey knew that the boatman must have either been in the plot, or he must have been forced to act his part, and the latter he believed to be the most likely, and concluded most justly that he would be very easily overtaken by any one who might be in pursuit.

There was another boat locked up in a boat-house, or place where there were a great many odd matters locked up, but, at the moment, he knew not where the key was placed. He could not go to Sir Godfrey for it, that would occupy too much time, and a shorter method was wanted; and Slankey, at all times ready of action, seized a crow-bar and wrenched the lock off in a moment.

"There, lads," he said, "now you can set to work; put your shoulders to her and bear her out; she'll carry more than yonder boat, and we shall be able to stow them in her easy enough. Come, boys, out with her; stab my vitals, what are ye afraid of—work?"

The men were hard at their work, but the boat was much larger than the other, and it required both strength and management to enable them to get her from its place, and then they had to carry her some distance before they could launch her on the Thames.

"Push along, boys," said the brutal Slankey, "and we'll have satisfaction from them, any how."

They now got the boat on the Thames.

"Now," said Slankey, "we want two oars—at least, four would be better. Come, jump in, lads, four hands besides myself."

So they all jumped in; and they were all ready for starting in less than ten minutes after Walter Fane and Alice, with the leech, had left the water-gate.

"Before we push off," said one of the men, "had you not better inquire which way they went? else we may be going one way and they another."

"Which way did they go? Why, up stream—where else? But we will ask of the fisherman, yonder, he will have seen them."

"Pull up the river, then."

"Yes."

The men then pulled towards a fisherman who was engaged in his vocation, and when they arrived near him, Slankey inquired if he had seen a boat with two men and a female in it, about ten minutes before.

"Yes," said the man; "they are a queer set. I didn't understand them at all."

"They were suspicious."

"I thought so."

"Why didn't you stop them?"

"That were a fool's errand," said the fisherman, "and I left it for them as followed."

"D——n you!" muttered Slankey; "which way did they go, eh? You can tell that, I suppose?"

"Oh, yes; I can tell that."

"Which way did they go?"

"Up the stream."

"Pull away, lads; we shall be on their track in no time."

The men did pull away—the fact was that the information given was all random, for the fisherman had no idea of another boat drawing up by his own and scaring the fish away, and he sent them up the stream because it was harder work in rowing in that direction. However, they had taken this direction, and the fisherman engaged in his occupation had failed to notice them.

"Push on, boys, push on; pull a strong oar; pull all together, and as one man; we shall soon be alongside of them."

The boat, with four strong oars, soon made its way over the bosom of the Thames, and they rowed at a steady and rapid rate. In about two minutes more they came to a bend of the river, and, on turning, they saw at some distance ahead the boat they were in chase of.

"Pull, pull for your lives! we have gained upon them, and they are now within sight; now or never they must be ours—they go along slow—we must pull for them—that's it—they may threaten him and he must row, but we shall have the advantage of his slowness and his blunders, of which he'll make plenty."

They pulled on afresh, and urged the boat through the water at great speed, and threw the water off at the head of the boat.

* * * * * * *

The boat which contained the fugitives was passing over the surface of the Thames, as fast as the circumstances of the case permitted; for, repeatedly as the leech urged the boatman onward, yet he could not, by promises or threats, urge the rower to exert himself in the affair. He evidently anticipated that a chase would be got up, and then came his turn, when he could revenge himself upon those who caused him to exert himself out of his proper course, and who had, moreover, threatened him and poked more of the sharp end of a dagger into his flesh than he liked.

"Hilloa—boat ahoy--boat ahoy!" shouted Slankey. "Hold hard—hold hard!"

The man rested on his oars a moment, but the next he felt the sharp edge of the dagger making a hole in his side.

"Pull a strong oar," said the leech; "you hear your companion, doubtless; but mind, if you allow him to come up, you are thrown into the water a bleeding corpse."

The man pulled, but looked sulky and sullen, and evidently only sought some opportunity to throw his persecutor overboard.

"Pull on!"

"I am pulling as hard as a man can pull. Would you like to pull yourself?"

"Boat ahead—boat ahead, ahoy—the gaoler—stop her—stop her!"

"Pull on, or the dagger," said the leech, as, indeed, he did say after every signal given by Slankey, and this had the effect of urging him onwards for a time; but an unwilling man can never contend successfully against the united exertions of stout men rowing manfully and *con amore* in the pursuit of the first. There was a secret sympathy between the rowers, but none between the pursuers and pursued, and Alice watched the boat chasing them containing the brutal Slankey, and saw with sorrow and terror that it gained fast upon them. She clasped her hands and uttered a prayer for their safety, and then watched the progress their own boat was making.

There were but few boats upon the Thames in those days, and on this occasion there was scarcely one about, and they were far from exciting any attention for that very reason; however, the distance was fast diminishing between, them and the adverse party kept gaining upon them.

"Oh, God! we shall be overtaken!" she exclaimed; "they will overtake us in a very few minutes now. What can we do?"

Walter Fane looked back and saw the boat containing his enemy close upon them. He saw that unless something desperate was done they would be taken back again, and he had rather die there than be taken back to that place, and he said,—

"We must do something else—we must try another scheme. I will take the oars,

and this boat, which is lighter than the other, ought to beat the other; at all events we must try it. Can you take one oar if I take the other?" he said to the leech.

"I can take it, and will do my best, but I fear I should scarce be able to second you."

"I will take them by myself."

"Since you can't or won't row, give the oars to me," said Walter Fane to the boatman, and moving towards him.

"Boat ahoy! a—ho—o—y!" Sang out Slankey, in a prolonged tone.

This sounded so plain and so close that the man gathered courage and refused to give up the oars to Walter.

"Give them to me."

"You can't row."

"I'll try."

"Not you."

"I will."

"You are in a hurry," said the man, who had left off rowing.

Walter made no reply, but seized the oars and was about to push the man out of his seat and sit down in his place, but the man resisted, saying at the same time,—

"Come, come; the game's up."

"In a moment," said Walter.

"With you," added the man, "so over you go."

And seizing Walter, by a sudden push and giving the boat a lurch at the same time he nearly threw him into the water, but he was saved by Alice and the leech, who seized him, and held him in the boat.

Driven to desperation, Walter Fane struggled stoutly with the boatman, who was a strong man, and had secured himself firmly in the boat, but the leech, seeing the desperate situation of affairs, gave him a sudden stab, which caused him to let go his hold for a moment, and before he could regain it, the two lifted him over the side of the boat, bodily, and cast him into the Thames.

"Now," said the leech, "that will give us time, we may yet escape! Pull for yonder creek, if we can gain that unobserved, we are safe. I will take an oar upon such an emergency, and for so short a distance I can do much."

So saying, they both sat down and rowed in a very different manner to that in which the boatman had done.

Slankey, who was at no great distance from them while the struggle was going on, shouted when he saw it, and encouraged his own man, and cheered his rowers on, saying,—

"Pull away, lads; they have stopped—one of them will be in the water. Make haste, or our man will have to contend with them all. Lash on, lads—pull away. They have left off rowing and turned to fighting. We are nearly there; a few more dozen hearty strokes, and all is well."

He paused a moment and stood up; he was much interested in the struggle, and when he saw his own man lifted up and thrown into the Thames, he exclaimed,—

"Hell and furies! they have thrown our own man into the river. Pull away, lads—pull away, lads, for life's sake, or he'll be drowned. We mustn't let him die like a dog."

Thus appealed to, the men pulled with fresh vigour, and they soon after reached the spot just as the man sank.

"He's gone, by G—d!" said Slankey.

"He'll be up again soon—wait for him. Curse them, whoever they are, that did it."

"Ay, curse them indeed! This will give them time to get away; but we will follow them yet. Here he is."

The man came up again, but at some distance from the boat; however, they held out one of their oars to him, and he contrived to seize it.

"Hold hard, lad, for a minute, and then you will gain your breath and strength. Hold quiet a minute, we'll pull you in. You hold on and keep quiet."

"I'm all right," said the man, tightening his grasp on the oar.

Then slowly and cautiously they drew him towards them, by drawing the oar athwart the boat, and when he was close enough three men seized him by the clothes and held him.

"All right," said the man.

"Trim the boat, lads," said Slankey, "and do you on that side hoist him in."

This was done, and the man, like a drowned rat, was lifted into the boat, and when they saw all was right, they began to joke him upon his ducking, which was a capital and funny occurrence among them.

"Well, William," said one, "how does Thames water taste—is it good?"

"I could have told you the flavour of it afore this time," said the boatman.

"You go in for amusement, then, now and then?"

"Yes, but only now and then. A ducking would do you good, if it only washed you."

"Pull away, lads—pull away," said Slankey; "there is no time to lose."

The men pulled heartily enough, but the boat was deeper laden now than it was, and this was against them, though the tide began to turn a little in their favour.

"I suppose," said one man, "the girl threw you in; though I should have tackled them all three myself."

"So would I; but then a stab is another affair, you know."

"Have you been stabbed?"

"I have. Lend me something to bind over the place to prevent it bleeding."

Something was given him, and he bound the wound up for the time.

"Where have they gone—where have they gone?" exclaimed Slankey, furiously.

Nobody could tell; they were to be seen nowhere. There was no such boat in sight, and they were at a loss to proceed.

"Perhaps he's doubled."

"Perhaps—but no; they have gone a-head, and taken shelter in some of the creeks.

Pull a-head, boys, and we will have them yet. Keep a good look out on both sides, lads, and pull heartily and cheerily."

Slankey was nearly maddened with rage at the escape of Walter, but after a time he had reflection enough to convince him that his best plan was to get back to the prison as quickly as possible. He accordingly directed the rowers to return, and, with gloomy anticipations of what Sir Godfrey would say, he entered the dismal gaol. It was an amazing relief to him to find Sir Godfrey dead—a fact of which he was not previously aware—and he drew a long breath, as he wiped the perspiration from his brow, and said,—

" This has been the strangest day's work I have known for one while!"

During this time, the boat which contained the fugitives turned into a small creek, that, when the tide was up, was filled with water, and ran round a small hillock and some tall sedges. Up this creek the boat ran, and round the sedges and hillock, and when once out, the leech and Walter Fane sank the boat amongst some sedges, where it could not be readily found.

CHAPTER LV.

Gloster's Visit to the Prison.

" The Duke was fierce in anger, and feared not the judgemente of goode men."

WALTER FANE had not been very long gone from that dismal and wretched prison where he had endured so much misery, and which it seemed so very unlikely he should ever leave alive, ere a large boat, manned by four rowers, shot under the gloomy archway from the river, towards the small basin, the water in which touched the prison steps. In the boat, beside the rowers, were seated two persons, closely wrapped up in mantles, the collars of which were so elevated as to prevent any but a very small portion of the wearers' faces to be seen. Yet there was quite sufficient in the quality of the garments to impress upon any one the fact, these two men were personages of distinction. In those days it was not as now, so easy for a man of inconsiderable rank, to ape the clothing and outward appearance of a noble. There were then what were called " sumptuary laws," which regulated the apparel of different classes of the community, and which made it a serious offence for any one of low rank to bedizen himself in garments which might have led any one into error, as regarded his condition in life.

We know perfectly well that the distinctions of society at the present day are clearly marked, without any legislative interference. He who supposes, or affects to suppose now that a blackguard, let him be dressed how he may, could, by any human possibility, be mistaken for a gentleman, must either be a person of small powers of observation and very weak perceptions, or a wilful perverter of what he knows to be the truth.

The manner of the rowers in the boat, too, in which were seated the two passengers who have led us into making these remarks, was quite sufficient to impress anybody with a notion that they knew they carried an important freight. The two cloaked passengers now and then conversed in whispers, but the manner of one of them was much more eager and agitated than that of the other, who appeared to take whatever his companion said very coolly and calmly indeed.

When the boat's head touched the lowest step of that stone flight which led up to the door of the prison, one of the underlings of the establishment came down the steps slowly and with a rueful countenance; for he well knew who the visitor was, although he had but a dim notion of the amount of anger he might display upon finding what was the state of affairs now in the establishment.

The fact was, that this prison at Blackfriars, from the hold which Richard of Gloster had contrived to get of it, and all its arrangements, might be said really to belong to him. A creature of his own had always been its governor. He was, in the habit of paying it regular visits, and his movements were most commonly the means by which its dungeons were occupied. This was so well understood among the dissolute and rascally portion of the nobility, that if they would get rid of any person who had become particularly obnoxious, they always knew that if they took him "in the vein," the Duke of Gloster would oblige them by sending the offender to the prison of Blackfriars, where, without a crime being alleged—without the least charge being brought against him—without a chance of succour or exculpation, the unhappy victim of private revenge or caprice, might linger out a weary life of horror, ending probably in insanity.

But what cared the bloody-minded Richard of Gloster? Already had he commenced treading that dreadful path which eventually led him to the crown, and then to a death far more honourable than he deserved. Alas! for Richard the Third there was no retribution. He waded through blood to the sceptre of England, and he grasped it. The death he died was a far easier and pleasanter one than many of England's monarchs,—who would have shrunk appalled from what he did—were compelled to suffer.

Our readers are, we think, aware that Richard of Gloster was one of the personages in the boat, and we may as well at once state that the other was the wily, but hasty and wrong-headed as well as wrong-hearted, Lord High Chamberlain Hastings. As they both ascended the steps conducting to the water-entrance of the prison, Hastings began to be rather profuse in his expressions of gratitude for some favour which had been done him, or was in progress of being done.

"Your grace," he said, "was ever kind and considerate, and no wonder that so many feel so much bound to your fortunes, and so anxious to do you good service upon all and every occasion."

"Think you it is so?" said Gloster, peering in the face of Hastings from beneath his angry brows.

"Conviction, goes far beyond a thought. I am certain it is so. I am quite certain."

"Ah! good Hastings, you speak for yourself, possibly; but there are not many like unto you."

"Your grace knows, that so greatly do I pride myself upon my devotion to your service, that I feel it rather as a compliment I should cherish highly the fact, that there are not many in that particular like unto myself. I believe, though, that there are many who would fly to do your highness good service; although, let me have the pleasure of thinking, none can rival Hastings in esteem for you."

"Ah! you are a true friend."

"And your highness has shown yourself a true friend to me by this day coming here at, I know, personal inconvenience, to do me a service."

"Think nothing of that," said Richard. "I only fear, from what I have seen and heard, that you will find the materials you have to work with more obstinate and unpliable than you imagine."

"Indeed! but ——"

"Ah, you don't know how mad-headed this fellow is. He talks and acts as if he had a dozen lives, and could well afford, for the sake of a little repairing, to lose three or four of them."

"I know he is headstrong—one can see it in his looks."

"Well, well, being so impressed with what I consider a just impression of his character, you must not wonder if you fail in this attempt to make him subservient to your wishes."

"At least I shall feel, as deeply as if I succeeded, indebted to your highness for the opportunity of trying."

"Well said—well said."

They had now reached the level space at the top of the steps, and Slankey, who was there, longed to say something; but, until he was spoken to, he knew it was as much as his ears were worth to interrupt the conversation that was being carried on in low tones, too low for him to catch, between the duke and the chamberlain.

"Your plan, then, as I understand it," said Richard, "is to give this young spark his immediate liberty."

"Precisely, on condition that he promises that which I desire."

"Which is?"

"That he will seek Mistress Jane Shore, and do his best to induce her to leave her husband and elope with him. In this I mean to incite him by a fear, that if he do not get off with her as quickly as he can, the king will."

"Ah! truly," growled Richard.

"If he do not entertain the project I have done with him. But if he will listen to it I will provide him with means to carry it, and then, when he has succeeded in the most troublesome part of the business, which seems to be the inducing of Mistress Shore to leave the city, it will be easy to waylay them, and take her by force from him."

"Be sure you knock his brains out," said Richard. "If you do not there is no knowing what trouble he may give you."

"It would, certainly, when affairs come to that juncture," said Hastings, "be the best way to put him out of mischief."

"Precisely."

"And your highness sees how promptly all this requires to be done, after I have been so indiscreet as to awaken the king's passions, and induce him to make so stern a resolve of seeking the goldsmith's wife for himself."

"Ah, good Hastings, that was indiscreet."

"It was, indeed, but is now irreparable, except in the way I propose now, unless your highness thinks again of my plan of taking a strong force into the city at night, and doing with a strong hand that which *finesse*, as yet, has failed to accomplish."

The Duke of Gloster shook his head as he said,—

"No, Hastings, no. That must not be. You will clearly understand me, that the measure, as a measure, I have no sort of objection to; but there are various and mighty reasons why it cannot be carried out."

"Of course, I bow to your better judgment."

"But your own judgment, Hastings, will suffice. In the present aspect of affairs such an occurrence would at once bring the court into collision with the city, which cannot be risked; and, moreover, as regards myself, I could not very well be off from interfering, to some extent, in the matter, and if I interfered at all, it would be absolutely necessary that it should be against you, which, of course, would place us both in a painful position."

"Your highness is right, and I, of course, abandon all idea of accomplishing my object by such means."

"'Tis well. And now I wonder what has become of Godfrey, that he shows not his unhandsome face to us."

Gloster turned, and bent his scowling glance upon Slankey, who, understanding from that that he was at liberty to say something, exclaimed, at once, in a gruff voice, that sounded like the sharpening of a saw,—

"He's dead."

"Who is dead, amiable fellow?" said Gloster.

"The governor."

"Oh, indeed! and so Godfrey is dead? Ah! You hear, my good Hastings, that Godfrey is dead. Ah, well, we are all mortal. I must send some one else here to assume his authority. What may be your name, my amiable friend?"

"Slankey."

"Indeed! Well, Slankey, until some one shall come here, armed with authority from me, you will please to consider yourself answerable with your ears, and, possibly, your head likewise, for everything within these walls proceeding with due regularity."

"Yes; but ——"

"Peace, now. Darest thou parley with me?"

"Yes."

"Ah! By St. Paul!"

The duke half drew his sword from its scabbard; but Hastings restrained him, saying,—

"Your highness, pray, excuse him. He speaks, I am sure, not from disrespect; but from a native roughness which he cannot divest himself of."

"I ain't afraid," said Slankey.

"Indeed!" said Richard, suddenly altering his tone, as he let the sword slide back into the sheath. "Indeed! You are bold if you have no other quality—speak freely—what were you about to say?"

"Why," said Slankey, "that before I took any 'sponsibility you ought to know what's just happened."

"Well?"

"There's been an escape. A young knave we had here has killed Godfrey, and got away himself. Bother the particulars, he's off, that's coming to the point at once, so, my masters, I ain't going to be 'sponsible for him."

"An escape from here!" said Richard, incredulously, as his face grew of a strange yellow colour from anger.

"Yes."

"And, Godfrey—hark ye, knave, if you deceive me for a moment, you are a dead man—is Godfrey really dead, or only, in dread of my vengeance, instructing you to say so?"

"Come and see him," roared Slankey, in a bullying tone. "If you don't believe me, come and see him."

"We will."

Slankey strode on before, and the duke and Hastings followed him closely to the chamber, where lay the mutilated corpse of the late brutal governor of the prison. There was that about the manner of Slankey which was sure to be pleasing to such a man as Richard of Gloster. First, there was the herculean frame, and the large amount of physical strength, which he always admired; and then there was the brutality of manner, and the utter absence of all fear, which latter was a quality he, Richard, considered as the greatest that could appertain to humanity.

He quite admired Slankey, and hence was it that he put up with from him a familiarity of speaking, and a kind of insolence of tone, which, probably, in any one else, would have excited his anger to a most dangerous and a terrific extent.

"If it be true," he muttered to himself, "that Godfrey is dead, I will make this fellow governor of the prison. He has all Godfrey's qualities, without any of his damnable cowardice."

Slankey knew little, and cared less about etiquette, and he marched on before the Duke of Gloster with all the indifference in the world until he came to the door of Sir Godfrey's chamber, which he flung open, saying,—

"There. He's dead enough: go and satisfy yourself."

"On the bed, is he?" said Richard, as he walked into the darkened room, and approached the couch.

"Yes, to be sure."

Richard had a great suspicion that this was a trick of Godfrey's to escape his anger for letting a prisoner escape. It seemed to his mind just one of those things that the wily governor would do, and he made up his mind that if it were a trick, it was one which should cost him, Sir Godfrey, dear. The curtains of the bed were just a little down on one side, and as Richard came up to that side, he quietly drew his sword from its scabbard, and said, in a bland tone of voice,—

"Sir Godfrey, are you really dead?"

All was still, and then the duke gave the body such a precious cut across the face with his sword, that if the governor had been shamming death it would have been quickly connected with a reality.

"Humph!" said Gloster, when he heard no sound except the crash with which the sword entered the head of the dead man. "It is true Sir Godfrey has really gone. Well, well, there is nothing like being perfectly sure about these things. He is really dead."

"And," said Hastings, in a voice of much anxiety, "the name of the prisoner who has escaped?"

"Ah, the name, my excellent Slankey," said the duke. "Who was it who escaped?"

"A young man—one Walter Fane."

"Ah! Hastings, we have come on a fool's errand, you see."

"Fate is against me," said Hastings. "I see now how useles to contend against one's destiny. I shall give up the matter in despair."

"As you please. And now, good Master Slankey, since the prison wants a governor, do you officiate in that capacity until I displace you. Do you comprehend?"

"To be sure."

"Amiable creature. How thankful he seems, Hastings, for his promotion."

"They won't believe it down below unless you tell 'em," said Slankey, "and I shall have to smash two or three of them before they submit."

"Oh, never fear, I will make known the fact of the new authority which is vested in you before I leave the prison. Come now, Hastings, do not look so dull."

"Your highness cannot wonder that I look dull, when I come to consider how your highness's condescension and goodness in coming here has been thrown away."

"Just now never mind that. Such a thing as an escape from here has not occurred within my memory. We shall soon pounce upon this young enterprising spark again, and be of good cheer, Hastings. Who knows but he may now carry out the very plan to which you have come here with the hope of circling him?"

"He has not the means."

"But we will find him out, and he shall have the means."

"How can I ever hope to repay this great kindness of your highness?" said Hastings.

"I will tell you when the time shall come that I want it repaid. Hastings, I can see in the dim future what a career you and I shall run. Vassa, do you know, has prophesied that you will be the second greatest man in England."

"Pray Heaven that your highness is the first."

"Go to, go to. I cannot, as yet, look quite so high without winking; but the time may come when I may; but no more of this now, good Hastings. Come away—come away. You know you are my bosom counsellor, and always will be."

Richard took care, before he left the prison, to mention the fact that he had invested Slankey with authority, and then he and Hastings re-entered the boat which had waited for them, and gave directions to be taken towards the palace at Westminster, from whence they had come.

CHAPTER LVI.

The Return of the Fugitives to the City.

Now that they had got out of the boat, and stood on the bank, and there was not the same urgent fear of a pursuit, Walter Fane felt his strength decline, and he tottered.

"Thank God!" exclaimed Alice, "that we have so far escaped that villain, Slankey."

"If he have not observed the creek we have run into, we shall be safe," said the leech, who wiped the reeking perspiration from his face, for rowing was an exercise he was unused to, and unseemly for his profession; however, the help was most opportune.

"We had better not wait here," said Alice, "for he will, when he finds he has missed us, turn back and examine every creek and inlet; we had better move on towards the city."

"Yes," replied the leech, "we had so; but we must not be seen from the river yet, else we shall serve as a beacon for the gaoler to direct his pursuit after us, and my patient here will scarce hold up much longer."

"I am well enough," said Walter Fane; "confinement and weakness have made me appear worse than I am, and I now tremble after the slightest exertion."

"Ay," said the leech, "such symptoms as those are always the sign of present weakness, be the cause what it may; however, we must just walk round this little inlet or bay, and then proceed direct towards the main road from Westminster to the gate at Temple-bar."

They now turned a little to the left to enable them to pass round the inlet, and then crossing a low and swampy place, they took a pathway that led to the road, in a diagonal direction, and this carried them round a rising ground, which stood between them and the river, intercepting all view on that side.

"By the time we get to the gates," said the leech, "it will be nearly dark."

"We shall have some difficulty in getting through them, I fear," said Walter Fane.

"None," replied the leech. "I can at all times go in and out; I am known to all, and my profession is a very good reason why I and those who are with me are out after sunset."

"They have grown particular about the gates of late," said Alice.

"They always close the gates, and keep a sufficient guard at them, and the city bands are always in readiness in case of an attack, and the citizens themselves would soon be ready to defend their ramparts, if they saw any necessity to do so."

The sun was now setting, and the scene was extremely beautiful for a short time; the clouds that had gathered in the skies were beautifully illuminated, and a thousand tints rendered the contemplation of them—when excitement and fear could for the time be drawn away and forgotten—an amusement the most engrossing. The gorgeous tints, varying in depth and intensity, lit up the heavens with a splendour not often seen, and the sun itself was sinking behind the hills by which the vale of the Thames is surrounded near London. The heights of Highgate and Hampstead could be plainly discerned, and their woody sides presented a deep and dark mass of foliage, that seemed to frown in the rays of the setting sun.

The scenery was altogether of a sombre hue below, and contrasted so strongly with the beauty of that above, that even in their present state both Walter and Alice observed it.

"I never saw a more beautiful sunset," he remarked, as they were walking along.

"Nor I," said Alice; "'tis beautiful and calm. Ah, such a moment as this is surely far better than all the tumult and noise of pageants."

"It is—it is," said Walter, "and nothing can compensate those for the loss they incur who prefer a life in the city to that they may enjoy in the country, undisturbed by the noise of state, and the circumstances of war."

"I would to God that our country was likely to be free from the scourge of war, which destroys the fair fields, disfigures the smiling and bountiful face of nature, and annihilates thousands of human beings."

"Such scenes," said the leech, "are likely to continue with greater or less intermissions only, while one set of men are allowed to possess superior privileges to another, and are considered to have a kind of native or inward nobility bred with them. While these men's passions are the only motives of their actions, and they can raise parties in a state, there will always be bloodshed and battle."

There was a short silence, and they emerged from behind high grounds that lay between them and the river, and turning towards it, they looked to ascertain, if possible how they stood with regard to the chase. Nothing was to be seen but a few boats, yet there were none within sight that at all answered the description of the one which Slankey and his companions were in.

"We are not observed," said Alice. "He must have gone up the river further after us, and will no doubt return as soon as he thinks we must have turned back again."

"And that will not be long first," replied the leech, "because the time he stopped could be but short, and with four men to pull them along, they would soon have overtaken us. After he got to the next bend, he would not fail to see we had gone away, and then he would pull back again, and examine all the creeks.

"No, doubt," said Walter; "but he will have the tide now against him, and that is the only reason, in my opinion, why he hasn't been back before."

"Well, they are not in sight, and we have nothing more to fear from them. Yonder is the city gate, and, once within that, we are safe."

"But they will stir the city through in search of us, no doubt."

"They will, no doubt," said the leech; "but we must contrive some means of taking care of you for some days, for you are, indeed, not yet able to do so yourself."

"I am only weak."

"And very weak," added the leech, as he took hold of him by the arm to support him, for he tottered and reeled about.

Alice, too, supported him on the other side, and then they walked towards the city gate. The sun had now sunk, and the shadows were long, and lost in the distance, and darkness was creeping on apace. Things looked sombre, and a melancholy hue overspread every object around, and those objects at a greater distance than their immediate vicinity could not be distinguished.

At length they arrived at the city gate, and were challenged by the sentinels who were on duty at the gate, and the captain of the guard was called, by whom they were examined; but the leech's profession and person being well known, he was immediately to depart, and his explanations for his companions were taken. When they left the guard-house, they proceeded along as fast as they could, and the leech said,—

"That difficulty is well got over."

"It is."

"But I know not if there be not others; there is more danger in the city at night, than there is on the high road—many robberies and disorders taking place, and passengers are robbed and maltreated by the robbers."

Walter Fane was very weak, and could scarce totter along.

"I am very faint," he said; "very faint."

"Keep up a short time," said the leech, "and we shall presently be at my home."

"I cannot walk, I shall sink."

"What can be done?" inquired Alice.

"Let me rest—I would rest awhile. I shall be better after that."

"He must rest awhile," said the leech; "but rest is not enough, he must have something more—a little cordial, or something, will be necessary. We must go into the first change house we can meet."

Alice said nothing, but exerted herself to bear up the weight of Walter, who leaned heavily, and was scarce able to walk.

"Here is a quiet place," said the leech, as he stopped opposite to an antique-looking house. There were two or three steps down, and then they entered the passage which led to a bar, and a room ran out to the right.

Into this room they all entered, and found the room lighted up by the flames of a large fire, which burned brightly. There were several people in the room when they entered, and their appearance seemed to excite a good deal of surprise amongst those who were present, and who gazed on them with much earnestness, and they were much annoyed at it.

"Sit down here," said the leech; "we can rest awhile until your strength has been somewhat recruited by repose."

"I shall be better very soon," said Walter.

"A small drop of wine will not hurt you now, and help you onwards."

"I think I could take it."

The leech having ordered the wine, he then turned his attention to Alice, and said,—

"We will not wait here longer than we are obliged, for I see our appearance here excites surprise among these people. At this I am not surprised; on the contrary, it was to be expected; however, no evil can result from their looks, and they may look on til[1] we leave this house."

The wine was brought and paid for; the leech poured out accurately the quantity he intended for the consumption of Walter, and then offered some to Alice, saying, as he did so,—

"Take a little of this, mistress Alice; it will do you good."

"No, thank you," said Alice, "I need nothing of the kind; I am well enough."

"But you do need it," said the leech; "I can tell you that you do need it, and that it

will do you a great deal of good; the time you have been out in the open air, and the hour of the night, excitement and all, make it highly proper for you at this moment."

"I will take a small quantity, since you so earnestly urge me," said Alice, and at the same time she placed the liquor to her lips.

During all this time, there was much conversation among the guests, and many stray glances were cast at them, which they scarce observed.

"I think," said one of the guests, "that there are strange travellers about."

"And suspicious, too," said another worthy, by way of reply.

"There are many reasons why such should be stopped by the guard."

"There are."

"These are stirring times, and no man can tell how long he may peaceably enjoy his own head on his shoulders above a night or two."

"No, while Margaret of Anjou lives, and can raise men to fight on her side."

"'Tis a shame that men should be so arranged against each other and made to fight battles and destroy each other, because others are more ambitious to egg them on."

"And yet I have heard good men say that Queen Margaret exerts herself most royally, and shows great prudence and foresight, and that her misfortunes are no bar to the justice of her cause."

"I am for the king that reigns," said another, sententiously, "and let him reign. What's the use of killing God's created, and for such a matter?"

"The use! You would not fight for your king then?" said another.

"I am a citizen," said the merchant, "and I will do my part by the good city. She has stood by me, and I gain my bread by her. I was born here, and bred here, and I will stand or fall by the prosperity of the city."

"Well said," remarked another; "a most sensible speech, and one that does a citizen credit. The city made me, and let us stand by our patroness—she is a good mother to us, and we will be good children to her. I honour the city."

"And there ain't a better rank, in my opinion, than that of my Lord Mayor."

"Nor better orders of nobility than the aldermen and common councilmen."

"The peers and the commons of the city."

"The same."

"But there are many who would undermine them, and pretend to cast contempt upon them; and moreover, spies are about;—they tread at all times and in all places."

"So they do."

"They travel under a hood, or under the garb of a leech, or anything that will serve as a disguise; and if they could set our citizens by the ears, their object would be attained."

"No—no; union is strength, and then we may defy the world."

"So we can; but we must sedulously keep out all suspicious people."

"And send for the guard."

"One is already gone for it, and then we shall see what they are."

"Truly," said a fat-looking man, "we must stand by ourselves. I can't run well, you see, but I could stand and fence on the city walls, or point an arrow at an enemy."

"And so could I, brother. I could draw my sword anywhere;—have you trained?"

"Yes, often, in St. John's fields—beyond St. John's gate; and have done duty occasionally."

"Oh, it keeps a man from rusting, and makes him a good man when he is wanted to fight in the defence of the good city. But we are all used to arms—'tis our safeguard."

"So it is."

"I wish there were means of accustoming the young men to the use of the military engines."

"Ay; and there are new ones invented, that are of such strange fashion and power, that it requires men to be well used to them before they can be said to understand them."

"But relating to those spies," said another, whispering; "when will the guard come?"

"Very soon,"

"It seems to me," said Walter Fane, "we are not very well regarded here; what shall we do?—are we not in some danger here?"

"I should think not; I can easily call the guard and raise a hue and cry if there be any necessity—but these are honest citizens."

"But I should not like to see the guard at all," said Walter Fane.

"It is some wounded rebel, no doubt, and treacherous designs are afloat."

"Yes; but hark! here comes the city guard."

The tramp of men was now heard, and the word to halt was given, the door was flung open, and the captain of the guard entered the apartment, followed by the band, armed with halberts and swords, steel plates and caps.

CHAPTER LVII.

A Night Scene in London, and the Leech's House.

THE captain of the guard, when he entered the room, looked round with a scrutinizing glance, and paused several moments. At length he fixed his eyes upon the leech, Alice, and Walter Fane, and the latter certainly did merit some attention.

He was very ill and weak; he wore clothes that did not belong to him, and which did not well fit him, but caused him to look as if he were desirous of concealing himself. These circumstances, the company of the leech and Alice, were not things that made the affair any better, and the captain of the guard stepped forward, saying,—

"I am sorry to disturb good company, but I must trouble you to come to the guard-house."

"Indeed!" said the leech; "and wherefore, I pray you, should I be so compelled, who have lived in the good city so many years?"

"You must explain who and what you are, and, if all is right, you will suffer but little from this interruption."

"This is my patient, and if I must follow you, you must carry him, for he will be too weak to walk by himself."

"We will give him what aid we can, and that's all I can promise you: if you are a leech, and certify to me the man is either incapable of coming, or that it would be dangerous to remove him hence, I will not do so, and that is doing the utmost I can for you."

"I cannot conscientiously say so much," said the leech, "and yet I must tell you he has already taken more exercise than his health permits, and he has to return, which will yet be more than he can bear."

"'Tis well," said the captain. "I will place him between two halberdiers, and they will help him along, and he shall not complain of our usage. It must be done, however, and I am compelled to do my duty—the times are unquiet."

"They are so," said the leech; "and yet one would think that sick men and maidens are not the most likely persons to make them more so."

The commander of the party made no reply, but proceeded at once to put them all in the custody of the guard. They soon quitted the house, and were conducted to the nearest guard-house, when they were conducted before the commanding officer by the subaltern who brought them there.

"What have you brought now, Wingfield?"

"Some persons whom I could not see much harm in certainly, but information was brought me that they were suspicious, and it was believed they must be Lancastrian spies, that they affected concealment, and were considered proper subjects for examination, if not detention."

"Bring them forward."

Accordingly they were marshalled forward by the same individual who had taken them into custody, and who was merely the captain acting for the night.

"Here they stand, and can say what they will in their own defence."

"I have no defence to make," said the leech, gravely. "I live in this good city, and expect to enjoy the usual privilege of going about in the lawful exercise of my art."

"Ah, my learned leech!" said the officer; "is it indeed you? could they bring no one more mischievous or fearful than you, who heal the sick and the wounded?"

"It would indeed seem so," replied the leech; "but here I am, and I hope you have found my calling is not a pretence."

"No, indeed," said the officer; "you cured me of a bad wound when I was not expected to live: I can never forget that wonderful cure."

"I am not in danger, I presume, of being detained as a suspicious person and a spy?"

"No, friend; you are free."

"And my patients?"

"Yes; are they your patients?"

"Yes; the young man has suffered from some dreadful bruises, and I am about to take him to my own house there to remain until he is cured."

"Ah, there he can be attended to in a manner much more conducive to his health."

"Yes; that is the truth."

"Then I will neither trouble you nor them with any other question."

"Thanks, most worthy sir; your consideration is most welcome under the circumstances, for my patient's strength has been unduly tried already."

"You are free."

"Farewell, courtly sir."

The whole party now quitted the guard-house, and continued their journey towards the leech's residence, which was yet at some distance.

"I feared there was a detention," said Walter Fane, "when the guard had us."

"I had not much fear," said the leech, "because I am well known, and have been in more than once before; and I well remembered the officer, having saved his life once"

"It was fortunate indeed."

"So it was; but I expected to have been obliged to give an account of myself."

"And I of myself," said Alice.

"Fortunately it's otherwise," said the leech. "And now we may hope to reach my house before we have any further interruption."

"I hope so, too."

The streets were all dark: there was scarce a light to be seen, save from some change house, and then only when a door or window was opened, and then a stream of light was thrown across the road, which enabled them to trace their way along without coming to any mischief.

They had succeeded in reaching about two-thirds of the distance, when they were disturbed by some shouts and cries, and the clashing of swords.

"Help!—Guard!—Guard!"

"There's more disturbances at hand," said the leech; "there will be blood spilt."

The swords clashed, and voices mingled, and a terrible uproar was created.

The next moment, the heavy tread of the trained band came along at a rapid pace; the clank of the swords, and the jingle of the arms as they passed along, and the glare of their torches enabled them to see who and what they were, and where they were going to.

The occurrence, which was purely personal, soon became popular, and cries of all sorts were uttered by those who took part with either one or the other of the parties; for all adopted the quarrel of one or the other without caring anything about the merits of their respective sides.

Thus they went on, till there were a few score combatants, which formed rather a desperate fray, in which wounds were given and received and no attention was paid to the guard.

The soldiers, however, soon rushed in between them, and they parted them, and plied the wooden end of their halberts to them, giving them many hard prognes, so that they were glad to desist, and cry for quarter, and get away from the spot the best way they could.

Walter Fane, Alice, and the leech, were surrounded on all sides, and were compelled again to pause on their journey, and for nearly half an hour they were compelled to stay where they were, and then, after some difficulty, they succeeded in getting clear off, and proceeded on their way.

"Once more free," said the mediciner. "How much longer shall we be kept from our journey's end? Men surely must be mad, or they never would commit the wild, lawless deeds they daily commit; the results of their acts are so glaring and so apparent that it is past belief. It would, indeed, seem that society is but composed of violence, rapine, and murder; any act of violence and injustice that can be committed is enacted by the great, without remorse, upon the commoners, who have to bear the loss of all."

"The time will come," replied the leech, "when all this will be changed—when great names will be no longer of any efficacy—when, indeed, they will be but remembered as historical recollections, and that have since ceased to be aught save as a thing that was once and no longer as any use in the economy of the world."

There was something that lay in their way, and which they could not at all distinguish, but which the leech stooped down to examine: it was the dead body of a man.

"Is he dead?" inquired Alice.

"Yes, quite," said the leech.

"Long?"

"No; he is yet warm."

"Killed in the affray?"

"No doubt either his friends or his enemies have left him there."

"His friends?"

"Ay, his friends," replied the leech.

"And why his friends?" inquired Alice. "Surely they, at least, would have borne him off?"

"In a battle they would probably have risked their lives to have brought him off, but in these street quarrels they all fly at the approach of the guard, and no one knows what may be the consequence of being found with a dead man."

"I see."

"He has not been dead many minutes, for, as I said, he is warm. However, we can do no good, and had better take no further notice of the affair."

With a shudder almost amounting to a perfect horror, Alice stepped over the prostrate form, and nothing but the absolute necessity of doing so alone enabled her to summon courage enough to do so. They all passed on, and happy were they when they heard the leech say,—

"A few yards more, and I am at home."

"Thank God," exclaimed Alice. "This has been a most eventful and perilous day."

"So it has, and the conclusion in quiet and safety is the more welcome. This is the door."

It was a large old-fashioned house, built, however, in the taste of the times, and capable of resisting much violence, for the houses were not always safe, as attacks had been made with impunity upon some citizens by large bodies of men, who were sufficiently numerous to overpower the guard, and defy all the efforts of the inmates. The door was strong, and bound with iron, and the staples enormously strong. The upper part overhung the lower, and appeared cumbersome and heavy. The windows were numerous, and secured by iron bars even in those apartments which were destined for the reception of guests and the use of the family; thus it could scarcely be supposed that, where they had seen so much turmoil and trouble and riot, such precautions were absolutely unnecessary.

The leech struck the door impatiently, and he seemed to think that they were a long while in answering his summons, and when they heard the sounds of footsteps, they could also hear the sound of a female's voice, complaining and mumbling to herself at the same time.

The door was opened by an aged but active-looking housekeeper, who, when she saw those who were with her master, opened her eyes to the fullest extent, and when she saw them enter supporting Walter Fane, her indignation had reached its limits, and she exclaimed,—

"Here's a pretty affair! Who would have thought of our learned leech returning home with a sick man, and a piece of painted goods! Alack, well-a-day. Oh, the days when I was young! things were very different then."

"Each age has its own peculiar customs, Margery," said the leech, "these are guests of mine."

"Ay, guests, forsooth; nobody comes now-a-days but there's plenty of trouble, and to attend upon such people, I won't do it. What would people say if I were to do it? something else would next be desired, and then it would be, I did this and I did the other, and I should be laughed at."

"Very well, do as you please, but you must attend; while you are with me, you must do as I bid you."

The door was closed, and iron bars and chains were drawn across to prevent any forcible attempt at making an entrance. They were shown into a small room, where they all entered, and the leech led Walter Fane to the couch that was in one corner of the apartment, and he had scarcely reached it ere he fell into it, and fainted off.

"'Tis no more than I expected," said the leech; "nature is quite exhausted; his pulse is low and feeble; he must have restoratives; he will be quite laid up after this."

"Do you think there will be much danger?" inquired Alice, anxiously.

"Not if proper care be used. He must, however, lay up to recover from his cuts and bruises, and to recover from the effects of the starvation he suffered while in prison; his frame is wholly exhausted, and generous but moderate diet is what he requires most now."

The leech arose, and going to a cupboard, he took a small phial, which he uncorked, and held it under the nose of Walter, and then he placed some of its contents on his temples and forehead. He quickly came to—he was very weak, and scarce able to speak. Then he gave him a cordial, which, in some measure, restored his health.

"Now," said the leech, "you must remain in bed for a few days, and then you may be well enough to get up; but you are far too weak and prostrated just now, to allow of your remaining as a convalescent."

"Indeed I am better now—better now," said Walter. "I need not remain in a sick chamber."

"You must; you are unable to continue up, and the fancied strength you possess is only that caused by the cordial, which is given as a restorative, and will be but temporary in its effects."

Walter Fane was placed in bed, and there kept for some days. Alice was domiciled in the house of the leech, and waited constantly upon Walter. The time passed over, and yet there were no inquiries made after him. The leech informed Walter that no search was made for him, which was a strange and singular affair.

During this time Walter grew better, although he found himself absolutely compelled to take the advice of the leech, who told him truly enough that he would not be able to sit up. However, towards the end of the fifth day he felt so much better, that he arose, and declared his intention of going out, although Alice persuaded him not.

He had been informed of the marriage of Jane, and yet he had taken no notice of this. He thought a walk would do him good, and he determined to go. The day after he came to the leech's house, he had been so prostrated and so ill, that he had not the least idea or desire to rise, but lay scarcely without motion for nearly four-and-twenty hours; but when they could get him to take food that was offered him, he gradually grew better each day, until now he felt able to walk out alone. He was not entirely recovered, for his bruises were, many of them, painful yet, and discoloured.

What most amazed him and all of them was, that as far as they had as yet learned, there had been no pursuit—no search—no attempt made to retake him. It was strange, very strange, but it was true. This was one motive why he did not fear going out, because there appeared to be no probable or immediate danger in doing so.

He completed his dress, and entered a small room where they used to sit in when the leech had leisure to converse with them.

CHAPTER LVIII.

The Suicide.

"And for ye love of one who could not love her, she soughte heaven's barred gates; but ye chrystale boltes moved not for the self-murtherer."

THE sun was just setting, and Walter Fane was better than he had been. He could be dressed now, and sit up, and he hoped, by the exhibition he could make to the leech, that he might induce him to take off at least some portion of the stern sentence which prohibited him from seeking her who was his heart's best and only treasure—his beautiful Jane. And yet if poor Walter Fane had asked himself seriously, what good to her or to himself he proposed to effect from an interview with Jane, he would have been much puzzled to make a rational answer.

That she was another's now, alas, he knew too well. That she now never could be his was a conviction that had sunk to the bottom of his heart, and life had consequently lost its value, and yet he wished to see her. He longed once again to look upon that face, which to him was heaven itself. He thought if he could but see her for a short time, and hear her tell him that it was because she thought that he was dead she had sacrificed herself to such a man as Shore, he should be content, and thankful to die.

After the first terrible feelings which had swept across his soul when he heard of Jane's marriage, he was able, from his intimate knowledge of her character, and that of the old mercer, to easily understand how she had been led an unwilling bride to the altar. He could easily imagine how the strong affection she always entertained for her father had induced her—believing at the same time, as doubtless she did, that he, Walter, was no more, to yield to the mercer's solicitations and commands and wed the goldsmith, who could certainly, from his wealth, protect her.

"God help her, though," moaned Walter. "Too well has she now, I am sure, found out how sad a mistake she has made. If there be one man more than another in the city of London, who was more calculated to make Jane unhappy, Shore is that man."

That he should eventually recover from the state of illness he was in, Walter Fane, notwithstanding all the natural clinging to life which is inherent in human nature, could hardly be said to wish. He only now hoped to be well enough to seek an interview with Jane—a last farewell interview—and then how gladly would he have wished the world and all its cares, all its anxieties and all its joys, good night.

But the physician had been so very peremptory that until now Walter had had no hope that he would let him leave the house.

"I am stronger," said Walter to himself on this particular sunset. "I am much stronger than I was yesterday. It is true that I look, I dare say, dreadfully pale, and I can find, now that I am dressed, how loosely my clothing sits upon me. Yet I am surely now strong enough to go out, and the cool fresh air of the streets will revive me instead of making me worse."

Even as he spoke he felt a sensation of dreadful exhaustion creeping over him. The mere effort he had made to dress himself had been sufficient to produce this, and with a pang he felt compelled to admit that it was just possible he might not have strength enough to go to seek Jane. As ill luck would have it, too—at least Walter Fane considered it ill luck—the leech came into the room at that moment, and it was not likely that his keen and practised eye would fail to detect the symptoms of weakness under which Walter was labouring.

"How do you feel now?" he said; "and yet I see I need scarcely ask. You find yourself not strong enough to sit up."

"Yes—yes," said Walter, "I am strong enough to sit up."

"But not—as no doubt you have been endeavouring to please your imagination by fancying—strong enough to go out into the air."

With a deep sigh Walter was compelled to admit that he feared not; and he showed so much depression on that head, that the kind-tempered physician sought to cheer him by saying,—

"Come, come, you but retard your recovery by this mental uneasiness. I can tell you, that what remains of your illness is but weakness, and as this day I shall make an important change in your diet, you will soon gather strength, and be able to go about."

"A thousand thanks, sir; and yet I ought not to attempt to thank you at all, since I can have no hope of doing so adequately, and thanks sink into such insignificance in comparison with the services you have rendered me, that I feel ashamed to utter them."

"Be quite easy, my young friend, upon that head. I want no thanks at all. What I have done, I have done of my own free will, or I would not have done it at all; and what a man does in that way, of course pleases him; therefore do not fancy you are under any obligation."

"Oh," said Walter, "this kind and generous sophistry cannot make me otherwise than so deeply your debtor, that were I to devote my whole future life to you, I could not repay you."

"Well, well, well—we will talk of something else, my young friend, if you please."

"Have you any more news for me, good sir?" said Walter, after a slight pause, during which the leech was counting the pulsations at his wrist.

"Nothing but mere detail," was the answer. "The mercer has been buried, and Jane is at Lombarde-street now."

"Yes, yes. Oh, Jane, Jane!"

"Your old friend, Simon, carries on the shop, and keeps on defying Shore. When he closes for the night, he always goes to Shore's and insists upon knowing how Jane is."

"He is right. Shore is a rank coward, and fear of Simon will be some check upon him."

"Then there has been quite a riot throughout the city, on account of a poor fellow they name Jacob, but Jacob what, nobody seems to know, or to have the least idea."

"Poor fellow, he does not know himself, He was with Master Snafflings, the honest bowyer, opposite Wainstead's, in the Chepe."

"Well, he has been in some trouble, and Mistress Bridget Snafflings, whom you may know ——"

"Know? Who in London knows her not?"

"Well, she has been raising such a hue and cry about this same Jacob, poor fellow, that people have been wishing her and Jacob both in the Red Sea."

"I do not wonder at it."

"No; nor I."

"What a strange fatality has attended all who loved Jane sincerely!" added Walter, after another pause, for he found conversation almost too much for him.

"Indeed. Did he love her?"

"Oh, yes; and I used to laugh at him, poor fellow, and his pretensions. He may now return the laugh, for what am I, and where are my pretensions now? Poor Jacob, I do believe he loved Jane sincerely, and it is that passion which in its despair has led him astray."

"Very like—very like."

"To-morrow, think you, Master Nicholas, I shall be able to move out from the house?"

"No, no. Were your situation a different one to what it is, I should not object; but when you do go out, you wish to attempt to procure an interview with Jane Shore. Is it not so?"

"It is."

"You cannot then suppose that such an attempt can be wholly unattended with risk, and how easy a prey to any one who might seek to do you an injury, would you become in your present debilitated state. I have no wish to keep you a prisoner here—none in the world. The ardour of pursuit for you, if there was any, has abated, and all seems now perfectly quiet. The trouble and the difficulty which I fully looked forward to as certain, when your escape was discovered, have not taken place; but let me beg of you to wait some days yet."

"Nay, command me," said Walter Fane. "You humiliate me too much, by fancying that it is at all necessary for you to beg anything of me. You know I will obey your commands."

"Then, my young friend, if it must be so, I will command that you wait at least until the third day from now, and then I have a sanguine hope that you may go abroad into the open air without doing yourself an injury."

"And how is the gentle Alice, who was so kind to me in prison?"

The leech shook his head, as he replied,—

"The gentle Alice, indeed. She is too gentle. It is mournful to see her. Some deep depression is upon her, which she will not reveal the cause of. Poor girl, she will not be long for this world."

"Think you not?"

"She cannot. Her voice is like music heard from afar off, and she glides hither and thither, as if she belonged not to this world."

"This is very sad."

"It is; for a better-hearted, kinder, gentler creature never drew the breath of life. I would gladly offer her an asylum for life, and I told her so; but she thanked me with a sigh that convinced me she knew the end of all earthly things to her was too near to require any assistance of mine."

Walter was much affected at this description of poor Alice's condition. Although the honest leech did not appear to do so, he, Walter, fully suspected the cause of her melancholy. It was not vanity which made him think so, for he was free from that common failing; but he had seen quite enough to convince him that Alice loved him, and he more than suspected that the cause of her depressed spirits was because she knew that his heart was another's.

This was a sad, a very sad conviction; for if ever brother loved sister with a holy and a tender affection, Walter Fane had such a feeling for Alice. Had she been as nearly as a sister to a brother related to him, he could not have felt a greater pang than he now did at the description of her melancholy state, as given to him by the leech.

After a little more conversation of a more desultory character, Walter was left alone, and he lay down, dressed as he was, for some minutes, to rest himself, as he really felt fatigued.

He had closed his eyes, but he was not sleeping, although to all appearance such was the case. He heard the door of the room softly open, and a light footstep upon the floor. Some unknown feeling induced him to lie still as he was, and presently he became aware that some one had crept up to his bedside and was weeping.

It was Alice—he knew that it was Alice, although he saw her not.

There was a pause of several minutes' duration, and then Alice, apparently having overcome her emotion, spoke in low, sweet tones, but with a world of sadness in them, that it was with the greatest difficulty Walter Fane could control his tears.

"He sleeps," she said, "he sleeps! Oh, may God's blessing lend a charm to sleep! May angels guard him. He sleeps, and 'tis better it should be so, now that I have come to take a last farewell!"

Walter did not intend to persevere in his sham sleep, but when he heard these words, he feared that Alice, in the despair of her heart, had made up her mind to some desperate step, which those who loved her and felt interested in her welfare would do well to frustrate. Therefore, he continued as he was, anxious to know what she meant to do contingent upon bidding him a last farewell.

For some few moments emotion seemed to choke her utterance, and when she spoke again, it was in a more painful voice.

"Time was," she said, "that I should have shrunk from uttering the words—'I love him;' but now they have grown familiar to my lips. Yes, I love him—I do love him! but not by my hopeless passion shall a pang be brought home to his heart—not by seeing me day by day sinking into the tomb, shall he be made wretched from sympathy with me. No; I will not be so wicked and so ungenerous as that. I will take myself and my afflictions away from his sight, with a hope that God will forgive me that I rush into his presence unsummoned. The river—yes, the river will roll over me and my sorrows."

When Walter Fane heard these words pass the lips of Alice, he congratulated himself upon the prudent silence he had kept, while a feeling of horror came over him at the idea of one so young, and beautiful, and full of virtue, committing, or even so much as contemplating, the commission of suicide.

She wept bitterly for several minutes, and at the same time she appeared to be attempting to control her tears lest she should awaken him.

"How sound he sleeps!" she said; "he shall never know how much I love him—never—never; he shall never know that! Along with my life shall the secret of my affection pass away from this world for ever. But we may meet again in another and a better world, if Heaven can pardon me my grievous sin of self-murder, and then, oh, what joy it will be to love him again even as I love him now."

Walter considered with himself, as well as the disordered state of his mind would let him, whether it would be better to lie still, and wait for an opportunity of telling the leech what were Alice's intentions, or to rise and reason her out of them.

More than once he felt inclined to think the latter alternative the wiser one; but he

dreaded the interview which must ensue, and he shrunk from seeming to awaken on that account.

"No," he thought, "no. I will let her leave the room, and then I will call the leech."

"Farewell—farewell, for ever farewell," said Alice. "Oh, that some more ready means would now at such a moment as this present themselves to me of accomplishing my dreadful purpose. Is it from some greater degree of pain that I shrink than my imagination pictures drowning to be? — why am I so foolish? The pang of death must come, come it in what shape it may—under the rolling waters, by steel, or by poison."

She knelt down by the bedside, and uttered a fervent prayer for forgiveness for herself, on account of the crime she meditated, and a blessing on Walter Fane—indeed, that he might be happy—he who knew that he could never be happy, formed the burthen, principally, of her prayer.

What her intentions were when she had finished this appeal to Heaven Walter could have no precise idea. She had left off in her cogitations concerning the mode of death she was likely to fix upon too suddenly for him to be able to come to a conclusion as to whether she had determined upon anything or not. Therefore it was, that when the prayer was finished, and she rose from her knees, Walter felt that he dared not let her eave the room, but as she reached the door he sprang from his couch, as he cried aloud n tones of earnest entreaty,—

"Alice, Alice, come back; oh, come back, Alice, and speak to me. We cannot—we ought not to part thus. Alice, Alice, do you not hear me, or do you not heed me?"

She turned instantly at the sound of his voice, and a cry of surprise escaped her lips.

"Alice," he added, "do not kill me by a perseverance in such dreadful words as those you have now uttered. Come back to me, dear Alice, dear as a sister to me; come back, and let me reason with you on the mad resolve you appear to have made. Alice, Alice, is it kind or generous of you to act towards me thus?"

Alice clasped her hands, and seemed for the time so much affected at the idea of what she had said being overheard by Walter, that she could neither move nor speak; when she did utter a word, it was the first of reproach that had ever passed her lips to him.

"Walter," she said "you love another. Was it generous of you to seem to sleep, and then act the spy upon me?"

"Forgive me, Alice."

"I do, from my soul. God forbid that we should part in any other feeling; and now farewell for ever."

Before Walter could say a word upon the subject, or interpose in any way to stop her flight, she rushed from the room and closed the door after her. His first impulse was to spring from the couch on which he was lying, and pursue her; but, to his mortification, he found that when she had closed the door, she had likewise, probably in contemplation of his pursuit, shot to a bolt which was on the outside, so that most unexpectedly he found himself a prisoner.

With all the power he was master of, he flung himself against the door, but it was a thick and massive one, and there was not the least chance of his succeeding, with the feeble force he could apply to it, in bursting it open. Of course, this was time lost, so that before he began to shout for assistance, Alice had ample time to leave the house.

The loud outcries of Walter Fane soon brought the leech himself to the room, and much he feared that the reason of his patient had given way, when he saw him, Walter, in such a fearful state of manifest excitement.

"Good heavens!" he said, as he stood in the way of the impetuous young man, as he attempted to leave the room, "stay where you are. What has come over you?"

"Alice—Alice!" cried Walter, "she threatens suicide. Let me follow her. She has been here. You found the door bolted?"

"I did, indeed."

"Then, for the love of Heaven, do not parley with me, but let me go at once to save her."

By a sudden effort, Walter got past the leech, and then, forgetting, in the intense excitement of the moment, all the debility of illness, he rushed down the staircase and into the street, on his fruitless errand of following Alice, when he could have no means of knowing whether she had turned to the right or to the left.

CHAPTER LIX.

The Body Rescued from the Thames.

"But ye finger of Heaven interposed, and ye rolling streame gave up its victim."

WHEN Alice so precipitately left the chamber where she had taken so strange a farewell of Walter Fane, she fled she knew not in what direction. Fear of pursuit from him now became uppermost in her mind, notwithstanding the precaution she had taken of fastening him in the room. That he should only have been pretending to sleep, and have overheard her utter those sentiments of affection for him which she would much rather have carried to death with her than have breathed them to his ears, was, to a sensitive mind like Alice's, calculated to be a source of deep mortification.

Had Walter Fane ever bore affection for, and able to say to her, "I love you for the love you bear to me," it would not have been the sort of affection she would have wished. The affection of gratitude would not have pleased her. He loved her not—she knew he loved her not—that his whole heart and soul were concentrated in another, and hence her despair. Hence her anxious desire to leave the house of the physician without the pain of a scene with him, Walter, in which she should have to play the sad part of one who loved and was not beloved.

It was only on the supposition that Walter slept, that she had spoken so freely as she had. Her object in seeking him was to bid him, in her own mind, adieu; and to feel the consciousness that he was the last person she had spoken to in that house. She would have uttered no words of farewell had he shewn himself awake, for such words would have provoked inquiry and remonstrance. She only wished to see him—to assure herself that he was getting better, and then to go to the death she had promised herself as a release from all worldly sorrow.

Now she hurried on, in such a confusion of mind, that if any one had stopped her to ask her what was her destination, she had not the least means of informing them, nor could she have told in what part of the City she was. It was chance or destiny, call it which we will, which led her to the Strand, and then down a narrow turning between two garden-walls towards the river, which flowed at that time in a much more even stream, and less polluted by the seriously deteriorating compounds that flow into it than it can possibly do now.

She was not conscious that she was in the immediate neighbourhood of the stream until she heard the wash of the water against the lowest portion of a flight of old wooden steps, that served as a landing-place for wherries, and the pleasure-barges of persons who had not houses in the Strand, and, consequently, no water-gate belonging to their own premises, as all the mansions which then lined the banks of the stream, and had gardens stretching down to its margin, had. She clasped her hands when she found that she was close to the river, and exclaimed,—

"It is to be—it is to be; I knew not where I was coming, and Providence has sent me here to do the deed. I accept the blind guidance which has conducted my footsteps to this place, as an indication that I shall be pardoned by Heaven for the act I am about to commit."

The evening had now fairly set in, and the twinkling stars were beginning to shew themselves in the world above. A cold wind came off the surface of the river, and Alice shuddered as it met her cheek. Tears fell fast from her eyes upon her clasped hands, and now, in more mournful accents than she had yet spoken in, she said,—

"I have no friend—I have no one to love me—not one! not one! My father was unkind, harsh, and cruel, but even he was something of a tie to bind me to life; now, I have none—not one! I am alone and desolate; oh, so very desolate!"

Sobs choked her utterance, and she could not, for several moments, command her voice sufficiently to speak. When she did again utter audible sounds, it would seem, from the general tenour of what she said, that some doubt had crossed her mind about the propriety, and even the necessity of the act she contemplated. She seemed as if she were holding an argument with herself upon the subject.

"Why should I live," she said; "of what use now can I be in this world? None—none. What can such a wounded, crushed spirit as mine accomplish? Nothing. I am utterly desolate—desolate in myself and desolate in my affections. If I live,—if I consent to live, what would become of me? No, no, I am a fit subject for death, and I will die. Let me die. Oh! let me die."

She slowly descended some of the old slippery wooden stairs. It was strange how even at such a moment natural instinct caused her to hold firmly by the frail balustrade for fear she should slip.

When she reached to within a few steps of that one to which the tide came, she paused and glanced around, as if taking a last farewell look of the world she was about to leave for ever.

Lights from stately houses—the homes of nobility—glimmered from various windows on to the cold stream, and from the squalid habitations too of meaner specimens of humanity gleamed similar tokens of habitation, while the bridge of London, which some distance upon her left, she could just see piercing the flood beneath, looking like an arch of dim lights, as from the windows of the strangely built low houses upon it came glimpses of all kinds of lights.

No one was near her, but she heard the dip of oars now and then as some wherry came slowly along the stream.

"Farewell," she said, "a last, long farewell to the world and all that is human. Great God! forgive me, and receive my soul."

She descended another step, and now the water laved her feet; a strange kind of frenzy seemed to come over her, and she waved her arms above her head frantically.

"Walter—Walter! oh, Walter!" she shrieked, in a voice that must have been heard a considerable distance from the spot on which she stood, and then she threw herself forward headlong into the river.

The tide was running down with some rapidity, although it was too soon after the hour for it to have acquired its greatest force. When the water received her it bore her on its surface for a few moments, until her clothing began to get saturated, and then she half sunk, and then rose again. A strong eddy of the tide seized her, and now she was whirled down the river with great swiftness, as if she had been some floating weed.

* * * * * * *

"What was that?" said a man, as he ran down the steps, with such rapidity, that in consequence of their slippery condition, he had a great deal of difficulty to keep himself from falling into the stream,—"What was that?"

There was no one to answer him, or indeed to hear his questions; but he was convinced he had heard some cry of alarm, and he now called in a loud voice,—

"Boat—boat, a-hoi! boat!"

From the other side of the stream he got an answer in a loud, prolonged tone of,—

"A wherry, my master?—ay, ay."

Then he could perceive a boat shoot out from the opposite stairs, which, urged by the arms of a powerful rower, was not many minutes in reaching the wooden steps on which the stranger stood.

"Hilloa! master waterman. Heard you nothing?" said the stranger.

"Ay, marry, sir, did I."

"A cry of distress?"

"Truly, I was taking my flagon at the Morris Dancer, the new change-house over yonder, when I heard it; and I had just came down to the water's edge when I heard you call, master."

"Some one, I fear, has fallen into the river."

"An if they have, there's no saving them. The tide will carry them now down too quick to afford a chance."

"Nevertheless," said the stranger, as he stepped on board the wherry, the head of which touched the wooden steps—"nevertheless, we will try what we can do. Row me down the stream. It seemed to me to be a female voice I heard, and if we can rescue any poor creature, we shall lay up some store in Heaven yet."

The boatman assented to this proposition, and turned his boat's head down the stream, which each moment was running quicker. It took but little exertion now with the tide to make great speed, and the wherry shot along at a good rate, while the stranger looked anxiously ahead to see if any object resembling a person in the water could be observed. After some time, during which a perfect silence had been maintained between him and the waterman, he said,—

"There! I see another person leaning from a boat, and endeavouring to take something from the water. Pull away; we may be of some assistance to them."

The boatman glanced over his shoulder, and gave a nod, as much as to say, "I see them;" and then he did pull away, with might and main, as hard as he could, to the spot where the people in another boat, which had evidently been coming up slowly against the stream, were endeavouring to lift some heavy object from the water.

As they came near, there could be no doubt but that the heavy object was a human body; and when the boat which the benevolent stranger had hired came close to the other, he bent over the side and gave such efficient assistance, that the body was at once got into his wherry.

"It is a young girl," he said. "Now, for the love of Heaven! pull towards Westminster as hard as you may."

"Westminster! against the tide?"

"Yes; we must get there as quickly as we can. There may be a chance of my being able to save her life if I get to my own place quick. I have seen in Flanders and Holland drowned persons recovered."

"Marry, good sir," said the waterman, "my best plan is to land you at London-bridge now, and let you get some land conveyance, which will take you much quicker to Westminster."

"No, no—I don't want to go into the City. Be quick—pull away."

There were two men in the other boat, and one of them now volunteered his assistance to help to row in the wherry which the stranger had hired, and which had now to go against the stream all the way.

This offer was at once and thankfully accepted, and at a steady but somewhat laborious rate, the wherry rowed through the water, while the stranger held the apparently dead form of her he had rescued from the water on his arm, with her head as high as possible.

Alas! poor Alice. Has thy pure spirit really fled, or art thou in that seeming trance of death merely, when the imprisoned spirit, traversing on the confines of its earthly tenement, may yet be caught, and again fettered in the bands of mortality? Strange state—most reflective condition—what a world of argument, and wild and vain conjecture, can be built upon such circumstances.

But this is a subject it is neither within our province nor our inclination to be discursive upon. Such matters of disputation may suit well the hours of recreation, when the mind misleads itself from sterner realities, and can afford to go into the notions of theological argument.

It was a long way to Westminster; but to do the two watermen justice, they did go to their work with wonderful vigour, and they never slackened at it. They got the boat into a good pace, and they then kept it. From experience, if not from science, they knew that they lightened their own labour considerably by keeping the wherry at the same rate of going, because then it lost nothing of its original speed, and a much less amount of impulse would suffice to keep it going.

Then they knew the river well, and they avoided eddies and currents, which, to persons less experienced than they, would have afforded obstacles, and materially retarded the progress of the boat.

The stranger felt satisfied that the men were doing their duty, and as they now neared the ancient landing-place, near to where the bridge now commences on the Middlesex side, he said,—

"You shall not go unrewarded for this extra toil. I have both the will and the power to let you feel that you have not worked for nothing on this night."

The men could not pause from their strenuous labour to make any acknowledgment to the benevolent stranger for this promise; but they heard it, and no doubt it still further nerved them to the task.

The boat shot with a quicker impetus through the waters, and in a few more minutes, the landing-place was reached.

"Now," said the stranger, as he sprang upon the shore; "hand me out the girl one of you, and come with me to my house, where I will give you a gold piece."

Alice was placed in the arms of the stranger, and while one of the men remained in the boat, the other followed him as he rapidly walked onwards, carrying Alice with all the ease as if she were a mere child, and no weight at all to signify.

"Is it far, master?" said the waterman.

"No; my house is yon white one with the low gable. You may see it now, even amid the darkness. Come on, we shall soon be there."

Perhaps when he uttered those words, the stranger expected they would have some more than usual effect, for he glanced round at the man as he spoke, to see what he did.

The waterman did more than pause, for he recoiled a step as the stranger pointed out his house, and then in terrified accents he said,—

"Why that's master Regandi's, the conjuror."

"Yes."

"And—and you?"

"I am the Signor Regandi, the alchemist."

The man turned upon his heel in a moment, and, at a sharp run, he took his way to his boat again, muttering as he went,—

"The devil! Who would have supposed it was he?—The necromancer!—The conjuror!—Saints preserve us!—what a wonder it was we did not go to the bottom of the river, boat and all!"

Regandi, the celebrated alchemist of the period—for it was indeed he who had rescued Alice from the river, and at all events intended to do his best to save her from death,—did not relax in the speed with which he bore her to his house, because the waterman went the other way, instead of following him for the reward he would have given him. He merely said,—

"Ah, I expected as much!" and he said it with the air and manner of a man who was used to being repudiated by his fellows.

In a few minutes, he reached his own house, where, with an arm which was disengaged, he struck against the door, which was immediately opened by a man who was fearfully deformed, and who, poor discarded wretch, had found a home with the alchemist when all the world had turned its back upon him.

"Aymer, tell mistress March to get lights and hot water, immediately, in large quantities. I have with me one who, I hope I may say, is only apparently drowned. Be quick, Aymer!—be quick!"

"Yes, honoured master, yes," said the deformed man, and he spoke in a high-treble voice, like some child, only that there was none of the happy, pleasant music of a child's voice in his.

The alchemist strode on, and carried Alice at once into a small chamber where there was a bed, upon which he gently laid her, and then he went himself to hurry forward and to superintend the remedies he knew well how to apply for the restoration of animation, if any spark of vitality yet remained in the seeming dead female.

The waterman who had so abruptly left the alchemist, when he discovered who he was, managed to get himself into a towering rage by the time he got back to his companion, to whom he said,—

"What think you? By the mass we are deceived and ruined. The boat will now have ill-luck with it, and the next gale that comes above bridge will send it to the bottom, unless we get some saintly relic such as would cost us more than we are both worth to preserve it."

"Why, what's the matter?" said the other.

"The matter!—Matter enough, i'faith: who, think you, was he whom we have rowed against tide so far?"

"Marry, then, I cannot say."

"But who, think you?"

"The saints be good to us, I don't know. Was it the evil one himself, think you?"

"No; but it's one of his acquaintance. It is no other than Regandi the conjurer"

Both the watermen crossed themselves as they spoke, and looked as scared as men might be supposed to do who were suddenly convinced they had been in company with some one who was not mortal.

"But are we to put up with this?" said he who had accompanied Regandi some distance. "Are we to be made the slaves of a conjurer? Are we to row him against tide in this way for nothing? Heaven forbid, certainly, that we should touch gold of his, but are we to put up with this?"

"What can we do?"

"Kick up a row."

"Oh, certainly, we may do that; the end of which might be the whipping-post, and possibly the loss of one ear. It's very easy to make a row, the great difficulty is to get out of it when it is made."

"Hark you, mate. You are a Christian man, and had a mother."

"Well, I shouldn't wonder but I had."

"Good."

"No, no; she was rather bad, between you and me."

"Well, well, no matter—be it so. But my opinion is, that Regandi, the conjurer, has got hold of the body of that young woman to try some of his devilish experiments upon her, and that she will never have Christian burial."

"Think you so?"

"Marry do I; and more, mate—much more than that."

"What?—eh?—What?"

"Why, it's far more than likely he pushed her into the river himself, just on purpose."

"What?"

"I say, pushed her in on purpose."

"Gracious Heaven!—St. Paul and all the saints, what a determined rascal!"

"Yes; he wants a young Christian maiden's blood, you may depend, for one of his charms, of some sort or another; and are we, as Christian men, to put up with it? No, no, we won't."

"But what can we do?"

"A great deal. Let us alarm the neighbourhood. Who knows but we may get enough resolute fellows together to pull down his house and him in it. Such a thing will be most acceptable to the saints, you may depend; and we shall feel the full benefit of it. What say you now, comrade, to mooring the boat and coming to arouse the people against Regandi?"

"I am with you," said the other, who had taken for granted the vague surmise of the other, that the alchemist had pushed the young girl into the water, and then got her out again, because he wanted a Christian maid's blood for some experiment he had to perform. "I am with you—it's too horrible. Come on, come on, and we will see what we can do."

"The dead body shall have Christian burial!"

"It shall—it shall!"

"Come then, you are, after all, just the man I took you for. Come on, comrade—now, come on."

Inflamed by the worst passions of bigotry, intolerance, and superstition, these men hastened from house to house of the low and closely populated district they were now in, and soon succeeded in getting together minds for the accomplishment of the object they had in view. They scrupled not, after repeating the tale a time or two, actually to affirm what had at first been only a supposition, so that in the course of about half an hour, an infuriated, reckless, brutally-ignorant mob of some thirty or forty persons, was making its way towards the house of Signior Regandi, the alchemist, and supposed conjuror.

The old proverb of give a dog an ill name and hang him, holds good in all states of society, whether barbarous or civilised, or holding a position between the two; but in the good old days, the fine old days, and all that sort of thing of our ancestors, the partial exemplification of the proverb was by no means rare, and if a dog had a bad name, he was hung.

Living as they did under a furious and arbitrary government, it was not to be wondered at that the people were brutalised and violent. They often took the law into their own hands, and took summary vengeance upon somebody, for something which the real authorities would never have interfered with.

When some popular commotion of this kind did occur, the government not unfrequently, after ascertaining that it had no political object, just let it take its course. Somebody would get hanged, or stoned, or torn to pieces by the enraged populace, and the king had too much on his mind concerning his own affairs, to bother himself much about what he considered other people's. The science of government, as a government, did not seem to be at all understood, or if understood, it was blinked completely for personal consideration.

There was no efficient police. Indeed, such as there was at all, only consisted of the men left as a sort of body-guard to the Lord Mayor, and little parties for mutual protection, got up in the different city districts by the inhabitants themselves, who might or might not do so, just as they pleased. Under such a loose, disorganised system of things, it was no wonder that almost any outrage could be committed, always provided the citizens let the court alone. If it was merely a riot in the city, the court authorities paid very little attention to it. Indeed, the sort of interest they might be supposed to feel in it, was not much more than is felt by one householder in the fate of another's chimney, which he may hear is on fire. Of course he would rather it was put out, because it might extend to his house, but he by no means thinks of going on the roof to knock in the chimney-pot, or to poke wet blankets into the flue. Regandi, the alchemist, was therefore in very great danger indeed, and all in consequence of his attempting an act of humanity, which hardly any one but himself in the city of London, or its suburbs, had the power of attempting at all with the least prospect of success.

We need not go at length into the means which Regandi used in order to restore animation to the insensible frame of the beautiful girl he had brought to his house. Suffice it to say that, with the active assistance of his housekeeper, an old woman, who had been with him many years, and of the poor, deformed Aymer, he had the intense satisfaction of seeing a slight movement in the hitherto deathlike limbs of Alice, and then, after a spasmodic quiver, the eyelids opened, and there was no fear of actual death.

The alchemist had the room immediately darkened, and taking some warmed wine, which he had ready prepared in a small silver cup, he held it to the lips of his patient, saying,—

"Drink of this; it will induce sleep, and when you awaken, you will find yourself nearly recovered."

It was at this moment, and while Alice was too bewildered to reply, or to have any idea of where she was, that a loud and prolonged shout from many voices outside the house came upon the ears of its inhabitants with a stunning effect, and first made them aware, at all events, that something was the matter.

CHAPTER LX.

The Riot.

THE sounds that disturbed the alchemist in his humane and kindly offices, little accorded with the scene within the house of Regandi. He had succeeded in restoring the life of Alice, and was filled with good and kind intentions towards her; his spirit, at that moment, differed widely from those without. Anger, roused by ignorance, and guided by a mistaken zeal to a mistaken object—revenge and turbulence, all contrasted strangely with the calm within.

Regandi listened, and again rose the shouts of the angry multitude, who were becoming more and more impatient and infuriated than before, though the same amount of cause existed at the beginning as at this later moment; but when popular wrath rises it goes on like a house on fire, until it reaches a climax, and when it has burned itself out, it still shows the ravages its fury has made and left behind it.

The sage could not understand the meaning of all this, and he listened in surprise, and wondered in his own mind the cause of so unexpected a disturbance as that he heard. He gazed upon Alice, and seemed inclined to leave her, and hasten to see what was the cause of all the disturbance, and the reason why a mob of men should be shouting and calling on the outside of his house.

"Maiden," said he, "thou hast been preserved from death, and I have restored thee thus far. Art thou better?"

"I can see and breathe," said Alice, with a deep convulsive sigh; "and yet life has no prospect for me that I care to live for."

"Thou hast nearly lost the most precious gift that the Creator has given to man. Take this cordial, 'twill restore thee and comfort thee, after such an accident."

Alice took the cup that was presented to her, and drank the contents off.

"Well," said the sage, "that will do thee great good, and in a short time thou wilt feel the comfort it will do thee."

Again the din rose to a deafening height, and the shouts and yells of human beings were distinctly heard and understood.

"What—what means all that noise?" inquired Alice. "Wherefore have such a mass of people collected together?"

"I know not, but I will go and see what is the cause of the tumult, and why they have collected here; but I dare say they bawl and tear their hearts out about something they do not even understand. The ignorance of the multitude is deplorable, and the evils that result from it are as lamentable. When will men become wise, and learn that reason is their best guide, and that knowledge is the best friend they can have?"

"Ay; see, some new misfortune and tumult has arisen, I dare say. When will all these deeds of violence and bloodshed have an end?"

"Time will do much," said the alchemist; "and now the art of printing—what may be effected by that is as yet hidden in the womb of time; but it must and will be great."

He turned from the room, and sought from the balcony to ascertain what it was that was going on below.

When the mob had delivered themselves of their first shout, there was a great feeling of triumph and of power. A shout does a great deal; it gives the individuals at either end of the mob a feeling of security; they think they are so many, and so many must be an overwhelming force, and they exult accordingly.

In those days mobs of men were formidable and powerful; they were difficult to contend with, and in some cases bands of armed and disciplined men have shrunk before them. Indeed, the citizens of London have at all times been formidable in mobs, and especially, as, formerly, when every man, whatever his condition might be, understood the use of the sword and the spear; nor were they deficient in archers—they were powerful and turbulent.

The first pause lasted some time, when another shout rose on the air, and made the welkin ring again with its sound, so full and distinct that it could have been heard to any distance. There were now many numbers, and among them every one's voice could be heard, but what was said was often lost in the indistinct murmur which arose from the mingled sounds of so many people.

"Bring her out—bring her out; no incantations—no experiments—no jugglery; down with the wizard, and down with the black art!"

Such were the cries that were called out from time to time, and which showed the feeling of men who were ignorant, and, therefore, capable of any absurdity and enormity.

"Neighbour," said one man, with a woollen doublet, "what is the cause of all this, and wherefore do you cry out?"

"That, neighbour, is more than I can tell thee; it is about something I suppose."

"But didn't I see thee shout and hilloa, as well as they?"

"You did, if you looked, certainly," said the man; "but, then, I didn't understand why it was done; I did it because others did it, and you know that is a sufficient reason."

"What has he done with the young maiden?" said another.

"A young maiden?" said the first. "Did you see her, sir? Is she pretty?"

"I know not; but I asked what she was to be done with."

"Oh, get her out of the enchanter's hands."

"Enchanter!"

"Ay,—an ogre."

"But what can he do with her?"

"There's no knowing the fearful rites these mysterious people perform."

"Why, I have heard," said another, "they feast upon their blood, and thus become young again."

"I have heard they take out the heart, and roast it before a fire, and make a drink of the blood; and they go through certain ceremonies, and raise the evil one, who comes to sup with them, and who rejoices in such a hellish feast, and then renews the bond with those who have anything to do with the spirits of darkness."

"Then we'll have her out, or else he shall swing for it, unless the devil saves his favourite; and that's not likely."

"No; and yet I have heard say you might hang such a man by the law, and it will have no effect; for he will come to life again, and live out his term."

"Ay—will he?"

"He will, indeed."

Another shout now rose on the air, and the screams and hootings of the multitude again filled the air.

"Pull down the house," cried one.

"Beat in his doors," said another.

"Set fire to his house, and burn him out—we must and will have him out."

"Burn out the wizard."

"Burn the sorcerer out; he wants to destroy the life of the young lady."

"No vampyre feast," said one.

"No incantations over the dead body."

A variety of cries and oaths were uttered, and the mob was becoming savage and unruly; blows and stones were used to assail the doors, and the din was truly terrific; not a sound could be heard but the confused noises of a hundred voices, and the noise of the sticks and stones used to assail the doors.

Presently this din was stilled for a few moments, and the man they had called upon so loudly to come forward threw open the window, and stood looking upon them with coolness, mixed with surprise.

All was stilled—not a sound escaped from any human being, and it seemed as though it were by an act of enchantment, that the din and noise of such a multitude of rampant human beings was hushed into a calm.

It was not of long continuance; for, as he seemed to pause before speaking, a prolonged yell arose from the multitude simultaneously, which merged into a roar, before it was concluded—so loud, so long, and so deafening that it was perfectly awful.

Still the alchemist stood and gazed upon the men below, as if he were musing deeply upon the extraordinary scene.

The noise continued to increase, and then began the attack upon the doors; but they were strong, and resisted their attempts.

"Fire the house of the sorcerer," said one man, and in another moment a considerable quantity of material was collected, and piled against the door of the house.

The lighted brand was applied to it.

"We'll smoke the wizard out, and see if the spirit can save him."

The alchemist leaned forward, and appeared to be desirous of speaking to the assembled multitude; he stretched forth his arm, but he was assailed by the loudest and wildest shouts that human beings could utter.

At length, after the storm had somewhat subsided, one man, in a stentorian voice, shouted,—

"Hear him—hear him, or you may burn the young girl, too."

"Hear him—hear him," cried several other voices in different parts of the mob.

When there was silence enough to permit him to speak, he said,—

"My good friends, what is it you desire, and wherefore do you assail me in this manner? I have done no evil to deserve it."

"The maiden—where is she?—the young girl whom you brought into the house with you?"

"She is better."

"Is she?"

"Yes."

"Is she living?"

"She is."

"Bring her out."

"She ought not to come out now. What can you desire to see her for? She is perfectly safe; and if you allow her rest and quiet, she will be well in a short time."

"She is not living!"

"You have killed her!"

"You want to feed upon her body!"

"No hellish rites!"

"Burn—burn him out!"

"Break open the door, and go in."

"Hold for a few moments," said the alchemist; "I will do all that you require. Have but a moment or two's patience and I will bring her to you alive and well."

"Be quick, then," said a man below, "else the flames will communicate with the wood-work, and you'll be all in a blaze."

"Do not commit injustice. I have done a good deed, do not requite me with a bad one."

"Hold," said a voice; "pull the faggot away, let him have five minutes' time."

"Be quick," shouted the multitude.

The sorcerer or the alchemist soon retreated from the window, and returned to the room where Alice was waiting his return.

"Ah! tell me," she said, "the meaning of all that dreadful noise I have heard,—there must be some dreadful tumult."

"There is a tumult," said the alchemist, "and one you have conjured up."

"Who—I?"

"Yes," replied the sage; "it is for you they make all this noise."

"I cannot understand it; but save me from them—save me from them!"

"Nay, I cannot do that."

"Oh, God! what will become of me? Why was I not left to my fate? I know of nothing that I have done to deserve injury at their hands."

"That is of no consequence," said the sage; "what the mob wills they will, and there is the beginning and end of it. But come, you stand in no danger now, 'tis I who stand in danger."

"You?"

"Yes; and you can save me from destruction if you will come and face the mob, and tell them that I have restored you to your present state, and have done you no evil, or intend to do so, as far as you can judge."

"That will I do," said Alice, "though life were to be forfeited for so doing. I owe you a life, and, though I value it but slightly, I cannot be ungrateful."

"Come this way," said the alchemist, "and you will soon see the mass of people awaiting impatiently enough."

"And wherefore should they doubt your care of me?" inquired Alice.

"Because the ignorant cannot understand the ways, habits, and tastes of the wise, my child; and yet they have more evil thoughts respecting us, than we have against them."

He led her to the balcony from which he had spoken to the people below. As soon as she saw the mass of people below she shrank a little, and when they set up a simultaneous shout that caused the place to rock again, she shrank yet more; but the alchemist said to her,—

"You must go forward, maiden, and speak to them, else they will believe it to be some juggle of mine, and that you are not a living and breathing creature."

Thus urged, Alice went forward and looked out of the balcony upon the angry multitude below. She was very pale, and they gazed upon her with something like awe.

"She lives!" said some of those who were nearer to her, and could see she breathed and moved her eyes.

"What does she say?"

"You must speak to them," said the sage.

"Good people," said Alice, "I am much indebted to all you for the interest you have shown in me. I thank you all; and this good man, who stands beside me, who has behaved with so much kindness, and to whom I am alone indebted for my restoration to life, has acted like a father to me."

"You are satisfied, then," inquired one of the mob, "that he means you no evil; that, in fact, he has done you none?"

"None whatever."

"Will you remain, then, or shall we see you away, if you wish to go anywhere else?"

"I am perfectly satisfied, for the present. I am very grateful to you for the interest you have taken in my safety. I thank you again, and also the person who has so actively engaged himself in being purely the cause of my recovery."

Alice went in, and the sage leaned out, and was about to speak, but they waved their hats, and gave a loud shout, and at the same time, by degrees, they began to disperse themselves, while some few others began to repair the damage that was committed by the intemperate zeal of the populace. There was much damage done to the house; however, all was left safe, and, when they were all gone. Regandi said,—

"Such are the wild, ungovernable spirits that animate the populace of any great and rich city, though I think I have seen worse mobs—men who would not wait or permit themselves to be satisfied; but once hurried on, in the tumult of passion, nothing is thought of, and they hurry on to all kinds of excesses, committing all the crimes that man can think of."

He led Alice back to the room, and seated her on a couch to rest and recover herself.

CHAPTER LXI.

The Unavailing Search after Alice.

The feelings of Walter Fane, when he found himself once more in the streets of London, were of a mixed and novel character. He felt some pleasure in treading the pathways he had so often trod, and in looking upon so many houses that were well known to him; it breathed a new vigour into his frame, but the pleasure was mixed with much pain. There were many recollections that came busy to his mind, and brought with them a pang that he could not stifle, but which seemed to balance the pleasures of convalescence, and the feeling that he was once more at liberty. The thought that he might be again seized was yet strong in his mind, and he looked suspiciously upon every one who approached him; this he could not avoid, for such might be an enemy. The marriage of Jane, too, was a thing he could not forget, and all the hopes he once entertained, now blasted and blighted, came back to him, but only in review before him with the stinging reflection that he had tried in vain to win one who could never be his; he had faced danger of every kind, but it had been without its effect.

"Well, well," he muttered, "time alone can soften affliction, and wear down the rough asperities of grief. I would they had never occurred; but no matter—no matter, the heart may grieve in secret for the past, and yet the world be none the wiser. I may run my allotted span yet in peace."

He looked around him and saw the old houses nodding to each other, as it were, across the streets, and overhanging considerably the lowermost story. The old houses were quaint and curious, but they were common in those days, and excited no emotion whatever in those who were daily in the habit of seeing them and living in them.

Walter Fane walked along listlessly, scarce knowing whither he was going, and he more than once asked himself the question "whither shall I go?" and yet he found no answer at all to the question. He was seeking Alice.

"Alas, poor Alice!" he sighed; "we are much alike in our position—loving; but the course of true love never did run smooth with the simple or the gentle, mercer or 'prentice, the noble or the plebeian; all are alike subject to life's chance, and the chapter of accidents of which that life is made up; though for some the toys may be gilded, while others have them presented rough enough. I scarce know which is preferable; the passions and prejudices of men disfigure the fair world, and make it a mere theatre of contention."

He walked along for some distance in silence, and with his eyes on the ground, he seemed lost in reverie, when he was roused from this state of semi-somnambulism by the exclamation of—

"Ha!"

This was uttered in a very peculiar tone and manner, and Walter Fane started and looked round to see who the individual was who uttered it, and when he did so, he at once saw the faded gallant.

"Ha!" he exclaimed, as he strutted up to the side of Walter Fane, and gazed on him in a peculiar manner, that he could scarce understand what he meant.

"He is," he muttered to himself, "aware of my condition and escape, no doubt, I must now endeavour to get out of his sight."

"Fine day this to be out, ah!" said the faded gallant.

Walter Fane made no reply.

"'Tis pleasant," resumed the faded man; "'tis pleasant, I say, to be able to pace along the streets with no occupation to detract from one's ease and comfort, ah! one can contemplate, you know."

"I dare say you can, friend."

"Ah! truly we can, and have no calls to destroy the illusory happiness that one may enjoy in such an ethereal occupation. Ah! yes, that is what I mean, ah!"

"That may be all true," said Walter Fane, "illusion must give place to realities."

"Ah! I find that; the calls of nature alone, however, disturb my reflections; ah!"

"Indeed!"

"Yes; one must attend to them, you know; they are imperative."

"Granted."

"Then he who seeks to gratify—ah! I should say, satisfy these is doing no more than is required of him, ah!"

"What does all this lead to—what do you mean by this? I would be alone; which way do you choose?"

"I am not particular," said the faded gallant. "I will yield precedence to you in this affair, ah! by Jupiter I am fond of company, and company I must have."

"But I am at liberty to refuse to give my company to any one, surely?"

"Have you a purse, ah?" exclaimed the faded gallant, suddenly.

"A purse!" echoed Walter Fane, looking at his companion for a few moments, and believing him to be a common cut-purse.

"Ay, a purse, ah! a purse, I said; but if you are unprovided with such an appendage I can countenance you, since I have none either."

"You?"

"Ay, me, ah! that is I, ah! have you a few rose nobles?"

" Wherefore do you ask these questions of me? I tell you I would be alone," said Walter Fane, who was scarcely in a condition to make good any sudden quarrel against a man who might have courage enough to attack a man almost incapable of defence, and sufficient strength to enable him to overcome a much stronger man than Walter Fane was at that moment.

" Why, you see," said the faded gallant, looking at Walter Fane very hard, and then up and down the street, and finally he gazed at the sky, "ah! you see liberty is a valuable thing in a free country, is it not,—ah? That is an undeniable proposition—ah! I conceive now, that is truth without being treason. Resolve me that,—ah!"

There was a sinister cast on the man's countenance, that made Walter Fane doubt him, and have some misgiving as to the result of this rencontre with the faded gallant.

" I cannot understand," said Walter, " what you mean, neither do I feel inclined to resolve riddles—I would be alone."

" Truly you would, and you might—but do you know of no circumstance in which it might be advisable to make a friend at court, one who could keep your secret, and would do so provided there was a consideration? "

" Eh!"

" Isn't liberty worth a purchase?" said the faded gallant; "can you compare liberty and a few rose-nobles, and, weighing each in your hand, say these are heavier than that? The rose-nobles are more to some than liberty. I say such may be said by some people, but you have only to inquire of some one who has escaped the cell, or the dungeon, and they will tell you better. Say I not right?—ah!

" If you wish to ascertain the truth of all these, you had better go to some one who has more experience and knowledge in these affairs, and let me alone to enjoy my thoughts."

" Ah!" exclaimed the faded gallant, as he marched by the side of Walter Fane, who saw that he had some design upon him, though he could not tell the nature of it; but he strongly suspected he was aware of his escape from the prison of Blackfriars.

" Are we to quarrel?" he said, suddenly turning upon the faded gallant, who took a step or two on one side, and placed his hand upon the scabbard of his sword.

" I think not," said the faded gallant, " if it depend upon me. I merely wish for the loan of a few rose-nobles."

" I have none to lend."

" Well, then, it seems to me I must satisfy the wants of nature, or I must go without; would it be prudent to do the latter when I have it in my power to do so?"

" Well, what is all this to me? Begone, before you get into any serious difficulty. I am not likely to suffer extortion, because you would make the attempt."

" Well, well, we shall see,—ah! we shall see. I would the guard were at hand."

" They may be nearer than you desire, for I will have you whipped as a common extortioner, you base, cowardly loon."

" Ah!" exclaimed the faded gallant, with a show of anger; "but no—a man of action is not to be urged into a fray with a mere boy—ah! and one, too, whom the law desires—no—ah! When you have purged your iniquity against the law and the state, I can conscientiously answer with the point of my rapier to any charge you may make against me; but come, have you a few rose-nobles?"

" I have none."

" Ay, I see, perversity; now it strikes me that you set a very light price upon liberty."

" I do not think it necessary to purchase that which I have."

" But you might purchase impunity for the future, you know."

" I know nothing of the kind."

" Ah!"

" What is done at one time, may be done at another," said Walter.

" Ah!" exclaimed the faded gallant, who resumed his walk by the side of Walter Fane, as he seemed to make no demonstration of immediate hostility; " I see, we do not understand each other; you want liberty, and I want money; you have the means of giving me some."

" I have not; but no matter; and had I, you have no equivalent for it."

" Yes, I have the right of calling on you to resign the liberty you now possess."

" The right!" exclaimed Walter Fane; " you must be mad; you can have no such right."

" I have such right—am I not called upon to see the laws put in force?"

" What has that to do with me?" inquired Walter Fane.

" This much: it may cost you that liberty you are so unwilling to purchase. I am sure you cannot hold the same opinion now you held a few minutes ago, and that you will find a few rose-nobles at the bottom of the purse."

It is doubtful but what Walter Fane would have given the money to have got rid of his tormentor; but he had not the sum, and, therefore, whatever might have been the necessity for quitting the troublesome individual whose cowardice and treachery were written on his countenance, yet he had not the power of satisfying him then; and all he could do was to face this matter out, and escape the best way he could; so he said—

"You waste your breath upon me, and had better try the same experiment somewhere else, where you may be feared; for myself, I feel more inclined to seize you by the throat, and secure you till you are lodged in the city prison, there to await the gaol delivery."

"Oh! we shall see—we shall see!" said the faded gallant, with a malignant glance; and just at that moment, some persons were seen coming in at the other end of the street. "You see those people yonder?"

"I do."

"They shall aid me in taking you back to the Blackfriar's prison, there to return to the same dungeon you came out of, unless you choose to give me the money I ask—ah! that is the way to put it. Now look you, Master Fane, something or nothing must come of this."

"Granted."

"Well, the something in either case will be of your own choosing; and it may be pleasant or unpleasant—liberty or imprisonment."

"And those people will lodge you in the same place as a shameless extortioner."

"Ah!" exclaimed the faded gallant.

At this moment, the people who were coming towards them were within ear shot, and the faded gallant stepped out, saying—

"Gentles, this man has broken prison, and I call upon you in the king's name to secure him, and lodge him with the guard at the nearest guard-house, or prison."

"This fellow," replied Walter Fane, "has attempted to extort money from me, and now prefers a false accusation against me because I will not submit to his demands."

"It is not true, I assure you, gentles: had I been so minded, I, a man of action,—I could have easily taken whatever I might choose from him; I wear a sword."

"Which you did not use."

"I do not condescend to bandy words with such a one as you are."

"I think I know you, good friend," said one of the individuals who had been charged to take Walter Fane into safe keeping.

"Know me," said the faded gallant; "ah! many people know me, and are proud of their knowledge too.

"And so am I."

"Doubtless—ah!"

On this occasion I must beg a closer acquaintance than I have hitherto had."

"That depends upon circumstances," said he: "but I dare say we shall be mutually proud of the acquaintanceship."

"No doubt—no doubt."

"Oh! none at all."

"You are the man who was found lurking in the Rose and Crown the other night, and purloined a gentleman's purse."

"I purloined a purse! Oh! false as false can be; I defy you."

"If you did not steal a purse, you stole the contents, and that to the owner was the worse evil of the two; but come, you did not pay your reckoning; you shall come back with me now, and when I get you to the inn yard, I'll have the reckoning out of your bones."

So saying, he who spoke, being a stout hostel-keeper, rushed upon the faded gallant and seized him by the throat, and, despite, all his swagger and denials, he dragged him back towards the hostel, aided by those who were with him.

Walter Fane seized the opportunity, and quitted a scene which was dangerous to him, and arrived at the leech's house without effecting his object.

CHAPTER LXII.

The False Friend.

One woman named Blague was ye bad companion of ye swete and beauteous Jane.—*Old MS.*

WHILE these affairs were thus proceeding, Master Shore was casting about for the means of allaying the melancholy of his wife and of winning her affection, and indeed for the carrying into practice the advice he had received to procure his wife such companions as would both enliven and please her.

There was still a great deal of caution to exercised in the choice of companions and friends for his wife; so thought Shore, and, indeed, he could not prevent his suspicions from forming a part of the motives that led to his choice.

It is strange that when a man once lets the green-eyed monster enter, there is no shutting him from any thought or plan that may be formed in the mind; and, do what he will, it binds or influences more or less every action, word, or thought, that he hears or does. Shore believed, that by giving his wife opportunities to visit acquaintances afar off he should have her less under his own eye than he would should she only be in the immediate neighbourhood. This, to a man like Master Shore, was a matter of much importance, and he bethought himself of Mrs. Blague, of whom he had before been thinking, and to whom he was no stranger.

Now Mrs. Blague passed for what might be termed a discreet woman, possessed of matronly excellencies, and just such a one as would be the most fitting companion for his wife.

"She will give her good advice," said Shore to himself, as he canvassed the matter over in his own mind; "she will learn her duty towards her husband, doubtless, for Mrs. Blague has always been a discreet woman, and at the same time she can be mirthful and pleasant. Moreover, Mrs. Blague has pleasant companions; ay, visitors who may not be so unexceptionable as herself; but then I cannot choose and limit her friends, and they will but give a change to the scene, at the same time they will not be constant friends. Their counsels cannot be very bad, since they will be scarce familiar enough; and yet what can be said of women? There's no knowing or saying what they may do or say when they are not under the correction of their husbands. They are so easily influenced—the younger and prettier—and there is more danger of their going astray; not but others are equally so. Oh, yes, women are all alike, and be they ugly or not, they will find some one who will go astray. Mrs. Blague, then," muttered Shore, "it must be, notwithstanding I could well do without her aid; it's very singular that Jane wants so much looking after; but there it is, she was always so treated by her father—a spoiled child—a spoiled child!"

As Shore uttered these words, he gave a suspicious glance around, and waved his hand in deprecation, as though he thought, or meant to imply that old Wainstead had been a very bad manager in his affairs to have had so self-willed a child, but that now he must be compelled to follow in a course of treatment that he could not help blaming; and yet it was necessary, because it had been so originally. It was exposing her to much temptation and danger, he thought, but then, as things were, the danger must be encountered, to prevent certain and positive evils that seemed about to arise from another cause.

Shore was deep in thought; this part of the affair constantly conflicting in his own breast between his desire to keep Mrs. Shore constantly under lock and key, and allowing some scope for amusement in society to dispel melancholy and relieve the tedium of her existence. He would have adopted the former plan, had it not been against the usage of the day, and perhaps it would have deprived him altogether of her society if he had lost her love. Necessity alone moved Shore, and, as may be imagined, his was not a happy and contented mind; he constantly fretted and fumed, and examined everything and everybody with an eye of suspicion.

Now it so happened that Mrs. Blague was a very close neighbour to Master Shore, living within a stone's throw. She was a pleasant, serviceable woman, of matronly habits and age; was well to do in the world, and was much respected and sought by her neighbours and acquaintances, many of whom were scarce such as would have been found under all circumstances. She was lace-woman to the court, and her neighbours, knowing that she was often there, and in the company of the great personages of the day, would come to hear her converse of them, and of many other diverting matters.

Now Mrs. Blague's occupation of lace-woman was her ostensible and creditable living, and one that throve; but it so happened that it was not the only one; there was a less praiseworthy source of gain carried on secretly under cover of the other. This, of course, was known only to those high personages who were, in fact, the occasional employers of this woman. They were well acquainted with her two-fold character of "lace-woman" and "procuress."

Ages and men have passed away—a change, a vast change has come over the world—the very physical features of the world are in many places changed; but there is no change in human nature, and we doubt much if there will be any for ages to come. The pleasing dreams of philanthropists, indeed, would urge us to think different; but we cannot. Wealth and luxury will always produce such fruits; the passions are fostered by the means they possess, and the means of sensual gratification will never be wanting while there are the means of procuring it. Wealth will do much, and will always do more than its legitimate object.

Mrs. Blague well knew that much of her usefulness to those about the court depended upon her keeping up her fair fame with her neighbours, and her ostensible occupation allowed her to conceal the object of many great personages who visited her house, which they did, but usually in disguise; but they could be sometimes recognised; but then there could be no difficulty in accounting for their presence, or their desire not to be known—they did not choose to come with a retinue to purchase lace, or give her orders, they rather chose to come and purchase by themselves. This patronage of the nobility was by no means useless in her trade, and she frequently killed two birds at one throw.

Master Shore little knew the character of the cunning Mrs. Blague, who, in her own mind, thought him a very silly man, and a fit object to be duped and imposed upon. Shore determined upon taking Jane to Mrs. Blague's, and show her some rich laces Mrs. Blague had recently procured, and he even thought he would purchase some for her.

"She will learn some of the usages of court from Mrs. Blague," he muttered to himself; "not that they are extremely beneficial and praiseworthy, indeed they are often the reverse; but she will hear some of those petty pieces of scandal about the court that women all like, and will tend to amuse her, and draw her attention from the past."

This was accordingly resolved upon, and Shore sought his wife, and informed her he would take her that evening to Mrs. Blague, where she would see several things that would amuse her—that she had some rare things there that were well worth her examination.

Jane was somewhat surprised at this speech of her husband's, but she did not seem overjoyed with it, but answered lispingly,—

"I will be ready to attend you to this Mrs. Blague's. When do you go?"

"This evening, after I have closed the shop," said Shore; "for I expect those to be here who will go away if they see not me."

"Very well."

"She does not seem much relieved by the announcement," thought Shore. "What if the experiment fails? I shall then have induced her to habituate herself to the society of others, and she will then go out when I know nothing about it, and then all my fears may be realized. Curses! what a thing it is to keep a woman from the presence of those whose very touch is pollution. Such people ought to be shot; they ought to have some peculiar means of torturing them both mentally and bodily. Here am I, a citizen of London forsooth! a member of a guild, and one of the Worshipful Company of Goldsmiths! Here am I, living in the city, to be continually in fear, either from my wife or from others! A citizen ought to have more power—ay, more power—not only over his wife, but—he—he should have more power to punish any such as should invade his dwelling, or to look at his wife. I would have them beaten!"

While Shore was thus employed in meditating, he cast many an anxious and suspicious glance at his wife, although he could not bear the idea that another should even look upon her, and believed women so frail that they were likely to be contaminated by a look.

The hours passed on, and the evening came round, and he looked at the hours with some impatience—why, he could not tell; but there was to be a new epoch—he was to carry his wife out, and that to him was something to think of.

No doubt Shore loved Jane then; but the love of such a one was a selfish love, and one that gave no credit to the object loved, and, indeed, said plainly, that those very qualities which had won him was the reason why he deemed her more than usually frail.

Shore was also well aware of the character of the times and the court, even to the king

himself; and it was very dangerous to have a handsome wife, since it oftentimes brought evils upon her husband, unforeseen in the earlier stages of their love.

Shore had this knowledge from good authority, and not from mere common report; he himself often disposed of articles in his way of business that were intended as presents from nobles to courtezans, and individuals whose birth and station placed them above suspicion, and whose real characters could only have been known or guessed at, by those in his situation.

However, the evening came, and Master Shore, having seen his shop shut up and carefully secured, took Jane out with him to the house of Mrs. Blague, that was scarcely a stone's throw from her own.

When he arrived there, Mrs. Blague was at home, and busily employed in arranging some costly boxes and valuable matters that were to be sent to the court the following day.

"Good even, good Mistress Blague," said Shore, when he found himself with Jane before her; "I have brought Mistress Shore with me, to see some of your fine things, and to hear your gossip of the court."

"Oh, there's little doing there, Master Shore, that I know of—true, now and then, we are amazed or frightened, as the case may be."

"Ah, you are happy in having such customers to deal with, they always order without hesitation."

"So they do," said Mrs. Blague, "but then they often hesitate when payment is demanded, and that makes up for it. Do you not, good Master Shore, find that great folks require time?"

"Yes," said Shore, "they are great people, I believe, at other times, but when they come to my place, it is good Master Shore this, and my friend Master Shore that, and so they go on till they get the money, and when payment or interest is spoken of they seem to imagine that one ought to be grateful for these honeyed words, and accept them instead of gold."

"That," said Mrs. Blague, "does not suit the inclinations or the wants of a goldsmith."

"Certainly not; how would you desire to be flattered out of your stock?"

"Not at all."

"Well, they would try it. There are many things to be avoided among these people."

"So there are—so there are," said Mrs. Blague, desirous to change the subject; "but we must not quarrel too closely with our customers. See, mistress Shore—see, what think you of that?"

As she spoke she held out a beautiful specimen of lace, that formed an entire dress, and was such a piece of workmanship as they had never before seen.

"Ay, that is very beautiful," said Jane. "I have seen many things at my father's, poor man, but at the same time I never saw anything equal to that—it is superb."

"Yes," said the goldsmith, "these things are very beautiful in their way, really excellent, but they are more fit for show than wear."

"They are only intended for those who can afford to buy them," replied Mrs. Blague; "but they are beautiful. I say they—I mean all such things—though I believe there never was such another."

"Indeed, and who may that be for?" inquired Jane; "it is surely for some very great beauty."

"The lady it is intended for is indeed very beautiful, but not more beautiful than yourself, I assure you, and for that reason, I believe, she is to have this given her. She has been beloved by some gallant, and that will be a marriage dress. Is it not a beautiful dress, one you must admit to be a fit present for such an occasion?"

"Indeed it is, and shews a liberal and generous lover," said Jane. "I don't know which to admire the most, the beauty of the present, or the generosity of the giver."

"What is your opinion?" inquired Mrs. Blague, as she turned to Shore, who was looking on very unconcerned by the remarks.

"Oh!" said Shore, "I was thinking it was very handsome, and of course would fetch a good sum, which ought to admit of a very fair profit to the shopkeeper."

"Oh! you are a man of trade, I see?" Master Shore, "and you will have a prosperous life, I am sure, you are careful of business."

"I thank Heaven, I am," said Shore; "it needs one to be both provident and careful of what one obtains by way of gain, to enable one to hope at a future day to do as every honest citizen hopes to do, and which I hope I may yet do."

"Yet do, Master Shore—why it's well known that you are as wealthy a man as any about here."

"Oh, Mistress Blague, but see how I attend to my business."

"And do I not attend to mine?" inquired Mrs. Blague; "have I not been to the court to-day, and have I not been home in my shop all the rest of the day? You are not more industrious and persevering in your track than I in mine."

"You are, certainly, I must do you justice on that head, and so does every body else."

"Well, I have now done here, come with me into the next room, and then we can talk this matter over, and have a pleasant half-hour's chat,—you seldom come and see me now, friend Shore."

"I have business to attend to, and you see I have not very long been settled."

"Aye, aye, that accounts for it, but you must come and visit me; I shall be very glad to see such near neighbours."

"I dare say Mrs. Shore will now and then see you, but for myself I am sometimes much occupied, though I will come whenever I can,—and you, Mistress Blague, must not be a stranger to our poor house."

Thus it was arranged, and Jane, much surprised at all she saw and heard, was soon led into conversation by the artful woman, with whom she felt much pleased.

CHAPTER LXIII.

The Appointment.

Vassa was punctual, and at the appointed hour he was at the palace, and as Hastings had given him directions, he sent up word to him that there was one waiting to speak with him.

The lord chamberlain was at that moment attending in person upon the king, and for some minutes he was rather at a loss what to do, being engaged in conversation with his majesty, and unable to quit the royal presence.

Vassa, in the meanwhile, was conducted to an ante-room, where he awaited the coming of Hastings. He strode up and down the apartment, and looked upon the different articles of furniture and ornament with a careless air.

"So this is Edward's palace, is it?" he said; "aye, 'tis his while it lasts, and then it goes to his successor, as it has done to others. I am here; aye, I would I had with me the same hands that I had last night, it would make the work clear, and then—but no matter—no matter, time will shew more and more the full workings of minds that are of no common order."

Hastings was all this while with the king, the monarch was employed in conversing with some of his nobles, and Hastings was taking his part, and, thus detained, he could not quit the royal presence; however, seizing an opportunity, he slipped from the presence chamber, and at once proceeded to the place where Antonio Vassa awaited him.

"Ha!" he exclaimed, as he opened the door of the apartment in which Vassa was waiting, "I have been detained, Vassa, and could not come; but are you prepared with your plan by which Edward can be introduced to Mrs. Shore? Bah! I hate the name; but what can be done?"

"I will tell you," said Vassa—"I will tell you. Forget yourself, Lord Hastings, and remember only the king. You must be well aware that you have but one course left which you can pursue with safety or with credit."

"I know it—I know it."

"Then why hanker about the possession of a piece of painted beauty, that you have wooed, and have been rejected, contemptuously rejected by her? What more would you have? Is your love like that of the slave, who blesses the hand that administers the blow?"

"No, no. I will persevere."

"You cannot do otherwise. What would you do with the king if he came to inquire concerning the beauty that has so far fascinated him? You know that Edward is not the most likely monarch to allow an affront of this nature to pass unpunished."

"I know—I know," said Hastings. "You need not remind me of what I know so well—of what I, of all men, must know better than any other."

"Then you, of all men, have least room to hesitate," said Vassa.

"But tell me, Vassa," said Hastings, "how have you managed that matter of obtaining the king an interview with Jane Shore?"

"Thus," said Vassa. "You must be disguised, and the king also."

"Aye!"

"Yes."

"But how, Vassa—but how?"

"It will be easy for Edward to ——"

"Hush!"

"You do not think," said Vassa, "the walls will fall in at the sound of that name? Wherefore should it not be uttered?"

"No reason, Vassa; but here, at least, a king's name ought not to be uttered, save as a king's name should. It is not safe."

"Well, well, be it so; but I thought that none would have dared play the evesdropper, or have walls ears here?"

"They may."

"'Tis strange!"

"But speak your errand, Vassa. You had one to me by promise, you recollect."

"I do."

"Then, how am I to manage this matter for the king's interview with Jane Shore?"

"As I told you before, you must both of you go to Jane's husband, and then, disguised as merchants, you can gain access to the house. Edward will know how to be liberal enough in his purchases and orders, and he will even gain upon the simple citizen, for his passion of avarice will be gratified, and he can tell him some tale of an intended voyage, so that his jealousy in this case would not be excited, and then you would have opportunities of gaining access to the jewel he guards with so much care and caution."

"'Tis well," said Hastings, musing; "and yet I thought that you would have had some better plan to bring forth on such an occasion."

"Better plan?"

"Yes."

"And what could be a better?"

Hastings paused and bit his lip. He saw no other plan open, and, moreover, this had the great merit in it of being secret, and breaking through no particular law, and there could be no such outcry raised against the deed.

"Does it not present a thousand pleasant aspects?" said Vassa. "What more could you have? what could offer fairer advantages than such a plan; for you cannot make an onslaught on the house, and carry her off; and what medium course could there be?"

"I know not—I know not," said Hastings; "but I must make the best of this matter with the king, and then we must put it in practice. I know, however, that Edward will but ill relish the idea of going into the city alone."

"You will be with him."

"Yes, yes, I understand all that; but you cannot make that palatable."

"The object must make it so; and I think he will see at once he will have some opportunity of doing something to advantage himself with Jane, or, at least, he can then propound some other scheme, should it ever become necessary to do so."

"Then, at what hour?"

"Say sunset."

"Sunset be it, then," replied Hastings. "There will be but a short time to attend to this matter, and get all things arranged."

"There can be nothing to arrange," said Vassa, "save your disguises. I have already left such things within your reach, whenever you require them. You know I am able to do you service in this affair, and, therefore, you can rely on me."

"I will, Vassa, I will," said Hastings; "and now farewell, for I must to the king, and, on the first opportunity, draw him on one side, and inform him of the plan."

"Do as you will. I have done my part, and have performed my promise; but there is one thing you must take especial care to remember, that it is the king with you."

"Could I forget?"

"I know not; you recollect you forgot your promise to me on one occasion, and a false step will spoil all."

"I will demean myself so that Jane shall not know me, and I have determined to give up all hope; she shall be the king's. I cannot succeed, and, when I cannot do that, I will have something in the shape of revenge."

"Let that be your object, and to-morrow I shall hear how you have prospered in your undertaking. I wish you may have it in your power to tell me much of your interview."

"I will; but I cannot conceive we shall be able to succeed entirely in the goldsmith's house; he himself will always be a stumbling-block in my way."

"But he may be removed, but not forcibly; it would cost your king his life or his crown, for these citizens have been, as you know, great supporters of his party."

"They have. No, no; he would not do aught that would cause any tumult in the city; it must be managed, and then, until to-morrow, farewell."

Hastings quitted the chamber, and returned to the presence of the king, filled with the project that had been broken to him by Antonio Vassa. The latter remained in this apartment for some time after, and sat musing.

"Yes, yes," thought Vassa, "he will be there, they will fall into the snare that has been laid for them; little do they imagine the net that has been spread for them; they will tread on it, and they are safe, and then Duke Richard will not be the man he is now."

Then, after some short time spent in reflection, Vassa also left the room; he, too, had plotted and planned, and now, like Hastings, he thought he had caught the fluttering bird; it could not escape him; and he was not like others—he played with dangerous tools, but natural ones, and set on fierce spirits to contend with and exhaust one another. It was easy to see what party would be the gainer by the other.

Hastings returned to the king, who was as yet engaged in conversation, as he left him, but he looked towards Hastings as he entered the apartment again, in a very significant manner.

It was some time, however, before he could get an audience of the king—a secret one —and then he was obliged to take an opportunity of conveying his wish by gesture rather than otherwise.

"Well," exclaimed the king, "our good Hastings seems disturbed, and this last hour he has scarcely been himself."

"Your majesty forgets that I had an affair to plan for your majesty, one that concerned your pleasure. Do you please, yet, to see Mistress Shore, the goldsmith's wife?"

"Ay, we do, surely; but the details of this we have entrusted our good chamberlain with, as being better acquainted with the necessary means of obtaining the desired interview."

"I have thought of means which will give your majesty the opportunity of seeing and even conversing with this beauty."

"'Tis well; relate the plan."

"We must go in disguise."

"Aye!"

"In disguise, surely, unless your majesty would wish to be recognised; and that would make the affair so public, that the citizens would all band together, and there would be such a noise all over the kingdom, that would give the Lancastrians new hopes and expectations."

"Certainly; it must be managed with discretion and surety. I would, however, under no circumstance, omit seeing her."

"Then, disguised as a merchant and his servant, we can make our way to old Shore's shop, and there see and converse with him, and his wife also."

"But she may not be at home; or, if at home, at liberty to see and speak with any one privately."

"Of that, little can be said till the venture is made," said Hastings; "and, if it please your your majesty to make the attempt, I will immediately procure the necessary disguises."

"Let it be done."

Hastings was about to quit the king, when the latter suddenly called him back, saying,—

"At what hour, Hastings, will all this be ready?"

"At sunset."

"Then sunset we will be ready," said the king, "and you and I, Hastings, will enter the city, and go to Lombard-street."

Hastings departed, and made the best of his way to his own house, where he found the articles he needed, they having been sent thither, by Vassa, for that purpose.

"This Vassa," mused Hastings, "is a strange being; he has rare qualities, such as would, were he better born, have brought him either to a crown or a sceptre—he is a strange man. So perfect a master of himself, I never saw; and seeing, cannot understand him; he is an enigna."

Hastings was now between contending emotions and feelings; his passion for Jane Shore had in no will abated, but yet he saw the utter hopelessness of the case; he could expect no abatement of her contempt for his suit, and revenge for those slights was the feeling that urged him to bring such a suitor for those smiles that he would have purchased at any price, were that possible.

He would have carried her off by main force, but there were reasons, cogent and strong, that induced him to abstain from that, though such was the strength of his passion, that he would hardly have abstained from doing that; but he did so, by a violent effort, and succeeded in subduing what appeared almost impossible, the frantic love for Jane Shore.

And now that he had surrendered all hope and prospect, it was astonishing to see how great the clinging after what he could never hope for—Jane's love. His own friendship and fidelity to his king and friend were too great to be shaken, and their feelings produced a contrary effect at different times.

He would at one time be resigned, then again he would be furious, passion maddening him, and causing him to be no longer the same man he was, and at such times he ceased to be so completely master of himself as it was necessary.

However, he saw that there was no means of securing Jane to himself; on the contrary, every reason and motive why he should not attempt it, and he saw plainly enough that his whole course of ambition and future greatness entirely depended upon his conduct and his self-control.

So many opposing emotions might well exhibit themselves in the person and actions of Hastings. While in the royal presence he was too great a courtier to allow emotions that he felt to be seen; he schooled himself down, so that he was not even suspected of feeling what he felt.

But when he ceased to be any longer in the immediate presence of the king, his pent up feelings then burst forth in a paroxysm of anger and rage, and it was sometimes dangerous for those about to come in contact with him.

There was, however, no cure, and he resolved in his own mind that he would act no further than was necessary to introduce the king to Jane, and now that matters had gone thus far it was really necessary he should do so much.

The day was on the decline when Hastings walked to his abode, and as he looked about him saw that the day was on the decline, and the sun's rays shed a golden light, tinting the very clouds with those shades of grandeur and magnificence that can only be seen at such times.

" Ah!" exclaimed Hastings, " the sun sets upon me, I shall see it rise upon Edward's success; but no matter; 'tis but a woman, and I cannot afford to lose such prospects for her, and yet there are moments when I would have sacrificed life in the eager pursuit of her favours."

Thus thought Hastings as he strode along, and vexing little thoughts came across his mind while he was thus proceeding from the palace.

When he arrived at his abode he found that Vassa had kept his word; there were the disguises he had spoken of, and admirably well adapted they were to the occasion and scene they were required for.

" It would almost be imagined," said Hastings to himself,—" it would almost be imagined that this man had been an actor, and that he was well acquainted with the part of dissimulation to a degree unparalleled; but no matter, these things will serve the purpose I require, and is all that need at this moment be thought of."

CHAPTER LXIV.

The Two Strangers in the City.

THE evening was growing dusky, and the sun had sunk some time in the west, when two strangers were seen to enter the city gates. They were both tall and courtly, though they were habited as merchants, and they had wrapped ample cloaks about them, as though they either sought to hide their features, or desired not to be recognised.

They walked leisurely, and they gazed about them from side to side; they examined most things with the eyes of curiosity. They passed through the gate of the Temple, and they walked through Fleet-street and looked at the shops.

" These London citizens," quoth one, " are men of rare wealth; the churls possess nearly half the riches of the whole kingdom."

" Half!" replied the other; " the knaves have two-thirds of it, I believe, and, moreover, could raise the other third in cash upon credit, if they chose. See how well they lodge."

" Yes, yes; the entry into this fair city not long since was a convincing proof of that. There were riches enough displayed to have caused envy in half the world. Why, he would be a rich king who could boast of having the value of this place and its contents in his treasury."

" That may be; for it is well known that the disaffected citizens can send both men and arms to support the cause they shall espouse."

" I know that full well—they have been useful knaves before to-day; but I hope the time for that is past."

" And a quiet reign will be the present one, I sincerely hope; at least, there is now but little prospect of the reverse."

" I think not; we are too secure, and have no longer any open enemies."

" Open enemies there may be none, but there may be more concealed ones than is at all consonant with our wishes. Moreover, France has ever been an enemy when ——"

" Say no more on those matters here; we should have other objects in view now than such a discussion; but to return to these citizens, they are rich and powerful."

" They are—and lodge well; and, moreover, they live well."

"Then they deserve commendation in every respect, since they lead a good life; but they have handsome dames and beautiful daughters."

"Yes; somehow or other, I think that there will be but few places where more beauty can be found than in London."

"In truth no; the citizens are choice in their wives and daughters, and many a fair city dame would dwell elsewhere, but for her birth; but they are admirable maidens, and that's the character in which they appear more charming than any other."

"Some, however, do not lose their charms or their beauty, when they have given up that character for another, as you well wot of."

"Indeed, I do; I know that fact full well. Indeed, there is neither maid nor wife within the city walls that can compare with her."

"No, there are none, I believe; and I shall never rest satisfied till I have won her to my arms;—she must be mine!"

"And doubtless she will be."

Thus the two strangers spoke to one another, the one preserving the character of an attendant upon the other, though they conversed freely.

Notwithstanding the ordinary merchant-like dress of the one, and the slightly inferior habiliments of the other, yet there was an air and gait about them that attracted much attention; there was that about them that could not be disguised, and many an honest citizen looked after them, wondering who they were, while more than one dame looked at them with admiration.

"Who are those strangers, I wonder?" said a little, fat, round body of a mercer; "who are they, I say? They appear to be foreign, and yet what I saw of them, neighbour Watchet, ——"

"I think they don't belong to the good city, neighbour Fanshaw; they have not the gait of quiet honest citizens. I am surprised at their appearance; not even the lord mayor walks in that manner."

"No, nor the aldermen either; but these are strange times, neighbour—strange times, and nobody knows who's who; so we must ever be careful. These men may be foreigners, for all I can tell, and they may be—who knows—who knows but they may be spies? I dare say, there's more there than is meant we should know anything about. Ah, neighbour, neighbour! these are times when—but mum; here's my dame."

"Now, Master Fanshaw, cannot I ever turn my back from the shop but you must be playing the truant? Come, sirrah; marry, who's to be plagued with such a runaway gossip as you?"

"But my good woman——"

"Don't good woman me; marry, an' have I lived all these years, and come to the city to be called a good woman, good dame, or the like?" Oh, no, no, I'll not be good womaned, Master Fanshaw; if you don't know that, I must tell you."

"Well, well, my dear——"

"It isn't well."

"But did you see those two tall, strange-looking men, who just now passed?"

"Indeed I did, Master Fanshaw."

"Well then, they appear to me to be something else than they look."

"Indeed! and what are they in your wisdom? They appear to me to be very proper men; tall and genteel, and that's more than can be said of everybody of my acquaintance."

"In my opinion," said Master Fanshaw, not deigning to notice the allusion, "in my opinion, these men are not merchants, as they would appear to be, but are some political spies; men who have been brought up to peaceful occupations, to trade and commerce, never have so military an air."

"Indeed they do not," said Mistress Fanshaw, with a look of contempt.

"They are spies, and ought to be followed."

"You are a fool, Master Fanshaw; how would you like one of these gallant men to turn round and speak to you—to lay their hands upon you? why—why you'd—"

"Call out to be sure, and have the rascals taken to the guard-house."

"Ha! ha! so you would; but I expect," said Mrs. Fanshaw, with a short laugh, "that before you could be rescued by the guard, they would make me a widow."

"And you would be glad of the opportunity to marry that drunken rascal, Captain, as he calls himself, Captain Withershins; he's no more a captain than I am."

"You dare not call him so before his face; but, captain or no, he's a marvellous, proper man, Master Fanshaw."

Master Fanshaw was violently enraged, and had nearly forgotten his state of vassalage to female usurpation, and inflicted personal chastisement; but he refrained; first, because he would not have been able to maintain his superiority, and secondly, to have acted with severity, though deserved, would have been to have given her the advantage of sympathy; for though a woman be ever so much in the wrong, yet her husband is never right, and deserves all the evils he can meet in public estimation.

Master Fanshaw knew the immense superiority his better half had over him, and, therefore, thought discretion the better part of valour, and said nothing by way of reply.

In the meantime, while this little episode was going on, the two strangers continued to walk onward without noticing any one. There was nothing in their appearance that would have distinguished them from the pains-taking citizen or foreign merchant, for their dress evidently bespoke their civil employment; but there was something in their carriage, a military stateliness, and air of command, which it was quite impossible to conceal.

There seemed, that evening, to be more people about than usual, and that many of them were not entirely citizens; many seemed to come from the vicinity of Blackfriars, and other places of like character, and these persons lounged about; many of them were men who had been engaged in military affairs, and they seemed, with one consent, to have stalked abroad to enjoy the fineness of the evening.

Thus it was, there were many people abroad, though it was an unusual thing after sun-set; and some of the citizens could not do otherwise than notice the occurrence, and many remarks were made concerning it.

Many of these persons followed the strangers, though at a distance; yet it was observed they were following them. Once or twice, indeed, the strangers turned round and gazed upon these moving figures; but they took no further notice than to make a remark or two, and then continued their walk.

"I think the citizens are watchful, to-night," said one of the strangers.

"There seems more than the usual population about," said the other; "what can be the meaning of it all?"

"Something connected with themselves, I'll be sworn; and yet I wonder that the city authorities permit the presence of so many strangers."

"They do, now and then, have a cleaning out of the Augean stable; but there are many who have certainly borne their part in the late wars, and who, having the means of purchasing their clothing and paying for their lodging, are considered as not coming under any peculiar law, and, therefore, they are allowed to remain."

"They are useful-looking men in a breach, but not very ornamental to the city; however, Mars has very little to do with our mission; let Venus shine forth and bless my enterprise."

The strangers had now reached the old church of St. Paul, and there were several individuals collected about the old cross, and a kind of movement took place that seemed to menace the two strangers, who were placed between two knots of men.

"This is very strange," said one to the other; "the light has almost entirely failed us, and these men seem to increase in number."

"Suppose we quicken our pace."

This was immediately done, and the two strangers walked forward with great rapidity, to get out of the throng; but this seemed to be but a signal that had been waited for, when suddenly one man rushed forward and aimed a blow at one of the strangers with a long glittering dagger, saying,—

"Now is the time—the moment has come—and Lancaster for ever!"

"Oh, oh! and is it even thus?" exclaimed King Edward, stepping back a pace or two, for it was he, and as he did so, Hastings stepped forward, and plunged his sword's point into the assassin, exclaiming,—

"Take that, traitor! and may all who raise such a cry in the good city receive the same reward for his pains."

The man fell, with a groan, heavily to the earth, while his dagger flew some feet from him, with a sound that was clear and sharp.

"Curses," mutterd the fallen man; "failed—failed! curses on——"

The man's breath failed him, and his utterance was choked,—in another moment he was a corpse.

There was a pause of a moment or two, and then the strangers were about to move away, and walk up the Cheape, but they were assailed on all sides, by cries of—

"No York! no York! down with the assassins—down with the traitors!"

A score of swords were unsheathed, and a furious rush was made upon the strangers,

whose address and courage, enabled them to sustain this desperate onslaught; but they were compelled to retreat before them; not, however, before there were several wounds given to the assailants, for they were more eager than cautious; and more than one retired with their death-wounds from the fight.

The king and Hastings retreated to the shop of Master Snaffling, the bowyer and at his doorway they made a stand, sheltered on all sides, save one, from attack; and here they were joined by one or two citizens, who seeing them assailed by such numbers, and, judging from their appearance, they were good and respectable citizens, they immediately ran to succour them.

"Guard! guard!" called out the citizens.

"Guard! guard!" exclaimed Snaffling, who, alarmed at the voices outside of his shop, had hastily secured the door, and then rushed up stairs, and looked out of the balcony upon the combatants below, shouting guard, as loud as he could.

This caused much commotion among the assailants, who made a most determined rush upon the few who thus defended themselves so bravely below; but the darkness that prevailed, and the light that came from the bowyer's window, seemed to confuse them; and while it hid the assailed, it exposed the assailants to some desperate thrusts and blows.

It so happened, that the guard was upon the march to set the sentinels for the night, and just at the beginning of the fray, they were at no great distance. Hearing the cries and shouts, they were ordered to march to the spot, and disperse the mob, which they believed was commiting a riot.

In a few moments the cries of "the guard is coming—the guard is coming" were heard on all sides; and there was a desperate and simultaneous rush made upon the king and Hastings; but they were so well protected by the doorway, that none could come to them, save on the points of their swords; and then there was an impediment in the shape of an ornamental projection which the assailants not seeing, threw themselves against it, and were pushed onward by those behind, without deriving any advantage by the mob.

The guard, however, now came up, and in less than two minutes, the whole of the assailants had disappeared, and even the wounded, that were capable of running, were hurried along with the retreating assassins, who were not molested on account of the inutility of doing so, since it was so dark that none could be recognised.

Hastings stepped on one side, and after whispering a few words to the captain, soon drew him on one side, and after a few more words, the men were ordered to clear the streets, and to cause wounded or dead to be removed. The two strangers then proceeded onwards, as if nothing had happened.

"What's this all about?" exclaimed Master Snafflings, to the captain of the guard.

"Oh, some of the rabble of your good city have just attempted the lives of two courtly gentlemen, and they have got the worst of it."

CHAPTER LXV.

The Interview with the Goldsmith.

Hastings and the king, for we have before hinted that the two strangers who entered the city in the garbs of a merchant and attendant, and whose air and mien attracted more than ordinary attention, were the king and his chamberlain, now walked towards Lombard-street, with a quickened pace, and scarce exchanged a word respecting what had passed so recently.

At length, as if wearied by the continued silence, the king said, suddenly turning to Hastings,—

"Methinks it was more than a mere causal rencontre that has taken place; they must have known me."

"That I scarce think possible," said Hastings; "for none knew of your intention to be here."

"That is true," replied the king; "none but yourself knew that I was to be here; and, yet, their cries showed that they were fullwell aware of whom they had before them."

"I know not," said Hastings; "they certainly did cry down with York. And, yet, they were not citizens, they were a rascally mob of traitors, who hide themselves to do mischief, and escape the gallows, the end of them all."

"That is correct enough; but here we are, good Hastings. I long to converse with this incomparable dame. Shall we, think you, carry her off at once? will she be kind?"

"Your majesty has by far the best chance to make way with her, beyond what a subject can hope for, or think of."

"But she will not know who I am," said Edward—"I am a plain merchant."

"That is truer than your majesty thinks for," muttered Hastings to himself.

"What say you, Hastings?" inquired the king. "Did you say ——"

"I said, your majesty, that though she may not know you are the king, yet you are such, and have the air and manners of one; and 'tis that in my opinion that betrayed us to yonder populace, and nothing else."

"Ah, Hastings, I would what you say were true; I should then have more contentment in the prospect; but the women are frail, and should all other considerations fail, I have still an ultimatum they cannot always reject, an argument they are particularly influenced by, more so than any other."

"And what can that be, your majesty?"

"The dazzling prospect of wealth and magnificence—the gaiety and splendour of a court."

"Oh, your majesty has a just notion of the power and influence of such an argument as that, by making it the last. However, I think it will not be required at all."

"Indeed!"

"No; because your majesty's mien and personal appearance is as far beyond other men even as your rank. I do not mean this as flattery, but as some gentle tribute to the failure of others who have sought the dame."

"I think you mean well."

"But were that otherwise, the danger you have this night run to obtain her favours—to obtain even an interview with her ——"

"Hush, Hastings, say no more about that; never let the little episode of to-night escape your lips to any human being. I would have it so."

"Your majesty's wishes are laws."

"'Tis well. Such moments as these are sacred, and do not belong of right to the rank, station, or duties of a king. They are the moments that belong to a man."

"Most assuredly; and many of the happiest moments, too, since they are not encumbered with those badges ambition compels us to wear."

"True—true; but some one approaches."

They separated, and the king again stepped a few paces in advance, and thus they continued to proceed, until they came to Lombard-street, near Cornhill.

There was the goldsmith's shop, carefully secured. Though it showed the appearance of costly articles of plate, yet it was secured by strong iron railings, and a good wire guard on the inside.

"This, then, is Master Shore's," said the king, as he looked round at the shop.

"Yes, this is the house," said Hastings; "and now I must put on this mask, as I would not be known here. If I were it would betray all."

They paused a moment, and when Hastings had made the necessary alteration, he said,—

"I am now ready, if your majesty is disposed to enter."

"Then follow," said the king. "I cannot see if she be here or not."

"You will not see her here at all," said Hastings. "Old Shore takes too much care of the pretty Jane; he knows she's a valuable piece of furniture, and all who see her will covet her, notwithstanding the Ten Commandments."

"He is jealous?"

"Jealous! Yes, he is, indeed—a very dragon for jealousy. But there are means of dragging him away from the beautiful prize."

"Well—we shall see—we shall see what can be done; though the rich citizen may fret and fume about it."

The king now laid his hand upon the door, and entered the shop. Master Shore was there. He was carefully reckoning up a long list of figures in his ledger.

"Is this Master Shore's, the goldsmith?" inquired the king, feigning to be a stranger.

"Yes, it is Master Shore's," said Shore, looking up for a moment.

"Are you Master Shore?"

"I am, good sir."

"Well, then, I have come some distance to see you, Master Shore. I am going to a distant part of the country, but require before I go some plate."

"Sir," said Shore, rising, "will you walk in? I will secure the door, and then we shall not be disturbed by the entrance of any other persons; it's growing late now, and, moreover, I have seen many strange characters about to-night. The streets seem fuller than usual."

"I have noticed the same thing. Can you account for it all?"

"I cannot," said the goldsmith; "though there are always enough of the idle and dissolute, who care not what they do to honest men's goods and gains."

"'Tis a pity, sir, so fair a city should have so foul a speck."

"It should be mended, sir—it should be mended; and these people should all be transported to some place where they want soldiers."

"It doesn't much matter for whom they fight, or aught else."

"If they fall in a good cause, so much the better for the state," said the goldsmith; "if in a bad one, so much the worse for themselves, and the better for the devil."

"Upon my word, a most sound and comfortable doctrine," said the king, laughing, "and, if carried out, would have a most wonderful effect."

"Indeed it would. The worst of it is, these sanctuaries are the receptacles of felons and criminals of all sorts—a mere hot-bed for the raising up of bad and vicious people."

"I see there must be much evil in such a case as this. I have been in many foreign parts, and the same thing is observable. But about your valuables—what have you in the shape of plate and other articles made up?"

"I have some massive and valuable articles," said the goldsmith, turning round, and going to a large strong-looking cupboard or chest; and then taking a bunch of large keys, among which for some time he searched for the key, and having found it, opened the lid, and displayed before the king's eyes some of the most valuable and beautiful articles imaginable.

"Your assortment here is, at all events, most costly, Master Shore."

"It is," said the goldsmith; "not all brought together in an hour; this kind of thing requires time to obtain. Some of that plate once belonged to a very ancient and honourable family."

"And thus their wealth and splendour finds its way to the strong box of the merchant and citizen," said the king.

"Yes," said the merchant; "you see they are sold to ransom some member, or pay the debts of another, and to help them to carry on the strife that has been deluging the country with blood; these are causes which bring greatness to earth, and make the proud low."

"Most true—most true," said Edward, musingly; "and then you see many, through pleasure and vice, will exchange all their ancient jewels and plate for ready cash, so that they may live as they desire, rather than as they should; others to meet fines or give bribes."

The king, during this conversation, looked over many of the articles produced, and took them in his hands, and being desirous to purchase, to some considerable amount, he laid those he chose on one side, saying,—

"This, and that, and those, I will have when we agree about price, presently."

The goldsmith, who was at once persuaded that the supposed merchant had got a large order, or several, from some nobleman, whom the times had deprived of all he had, and whose services gave him the means of replenishing his plate chest, looked upon him with very great respect.

"There," said the king; "I will discharge my debt at once for these, and will send a trusty messenger for them."

"As you please," said Shore; "they shall be well cared for here, and no hurt shall occur,—my house is safe."

The king accordingly saw the plate all safely packed up, and locked in a chest, and then the money was instantly paid.

This at once gained the goldsmith's good will, and he felt persuaded that the merchant was immensely rich, and had, moreover, a vast trade.

"And what news is there of late?—I am a stranger in these parts."

"There is but little doing, I believe. I hope the last battle between the roses has been fought, and that matters are more settled."

"And for the last time?"

"I think so. Warwick is dead, and the prince killed; there's nobody left to disturb the present reign."

"But the present king owed some obligation to the citizens, I believe."

"Why, yes," said the goldsmith smiling; "and, as far as I understand, he's trying to repay them by his attentions to the female part of the community; and it is not every one, seemingly, that takes such things amiss."

"Well," said the king laughing; "but you haven't much to fear; it is said he is married."

"That makes no difference," said the goldsmith; "the king loves his subjects the same as before, but he gives the preference to the females."

"Well, well, you cannot complain of that."

"I cannot truly," said the goldsmith; "but will you walk this way, and drink a glass of wine. I can assure you 'tis good wine; I had it from Burgundy, with some other merchandize."

They entered the parlour, and, having seated themselves, some wine was produced; when they had drunk some, the king said,—

"Sir, 'tis pity you have no mistress to so fair a house, 'twould have given me pleasure to have drunk to her health. However, I think I can fit you with one that's fair and rich, too, that would credit any man."

"Indeed, sir!" replied Shore, "I do not stand in need of your offer, for I am already provided with one. She is, I dare say, alone, and will be glad of your civility. I will send for her."

"You will do me much honour," replied the supposed merchant. "I own, I am well pleased to be able to pay my respects to the wife of a good and worthy citizen."

No more was said, but Master Shore sent for Jane, who, believing it some of her husband's intimates, made no haste; but at length she came, and was much surprised to see so comely and fascinating a merchant as this appeared to be to her.

"This wealthy merchant," said Shore to his wife, "is my most excellent customer, and wishes to do you a civility by drinking your health."

The king gazed on her, and thought she looked even more beautiful than she was before. Her hair was a deep yellow; complexion clear and white; her eyes light and expressive—her features beautifully regular—below the middle height, and her person round, and of faultless symmetry.

Such was Jane Shore, no less celebrated for her beauty and goodness than for her fall, and her subsequent misfortunes and miseries, and her lamentable end.

The king soon recovered from the contemplation of her beauties, which, he could not avoid seeing, was distasteful to her husband, who became suspicious and distrustful the moment his wife's charms became a point of attraction. He complimented Shore, and soon restored his confidence; but after a time Jane understood, from her husband's manner, that he wished her not to remain there very long; and she arose and left the room, not before, however, she had become well pleased with the person and manners of the merchant, whom she considered not only very handsome, but there was something so different in his style of conversation from that of all others she had been used to, and which, indeed, caused Master Shore to appear at a great disadvantage.

As Mrs. Shore had quitted the room, the king's cause for staying was at an end, and as soon as he could, he took his leave of the goldsmith, saying he would see him again, and would probably have some more dealings with him. He arose, and left the house of Master Shore, and then closely followed by Hastings, he made his way westward towards Temple-bar.

"Well, Hastings," said the king, "I must have Mistress Shore, by fair means or foul. It matters not; I think her more beautiful than ever."

CHAPTER LXVI.

The King's Passion.

"And Edward loved Jane as he never yet loved woman."

Hastings and the king made their way back towards the palace, taking care to be as expeditious as they could, lest any of the persons should be lingering about who attacked them once before, and who might do so again with more success than on the previous occasion.

The feelings of the lord chamberlain had been of a character but ill suited to the part he had to enact in the affair. His waiting for Edward, who was conversing with Shore and his wife, was much more calculated to spoil the whole affair than to aid his master.

This, however, he was well aware of, that those who stood in Edward's way, in the pursuit of his ambition or pleasure, must be sacrificed; and this he also knew was always the case with every monarch that reigned, and therefore the king was no worse than his predecessors.

Still there was a galling feeling, that, despite all his efforts to repress it, would arise and cause a tumult of emotion to rise in his breast. Nothing is so hard to conceal and to overcome as a violent passion. However, hard the task, and however his very soul was shaken with the attempt, yet he succeeded, and walked away with the king, but in a silent and a sad humour.

When they reached the palace they entered it by a secret door, and soon after disposed of their disguises; and then retiring to a private apartment, the king flung himself upon a couch, and for some few moments he remained silent, and Hastings awaited his breaking silence before he would speak himself.

This Edward did not do for some time, for he was recalling to his own mind the words and actions of Jane. At length, however, he said,—

"She is beautiful, Hastings."

"She is, your majesty."

"Beautiful beyond any woman I ever saw,—she is perfect—she is symmetry itself, in every feature, in every limb—and her *tout-ensemble* also; with a look and gesture that gives a charm, a reality to all she says and does. She is far beyond what I ever before witnessed."

"Your majesty thinks that common report has not belied her."

"Indeed I do not; but such a lovely flower cannot, must not, shall not be lost in a jealous citizen's house. She must grace our court, and our arms, Hastings; I am resolved upon that."

"Your majesty has had a worse mistress before now," said Hastings, trying to be unconcerned, and laughing.

"In faith, my lord chamberlain, you may say that, for if I had but one, that one would not have been her equal; and, it is God's word, I can't tell the exact number; it would be reckoning up one's sins."

"Sins in which your majesty delights."

"No more—this is no confessional; we must not think of the death of the stag while we are in pursuit: we have leisure to repent when we have done; but now, Hastings, now, we have no such leisure."

"Then what will your majesty attempt about this business?"

"I could send a few score men and have her by force from her suspicious husband, despite his evil looks."

"That would be scarce prudent, and might bring unpleasant consequences."

"Unpleasant consequences!—and wherefore should there be unpleasant consequences? and what avail the complaints of a few churls?"

"We saw the riches of these churls yesterday, your majesty, and know to what they have been applied before, and may be again, were it turn out they believed they had a sufficient reason to do so."

"Well?"

"And, moreover, your majesty must recollect these persons are governed much by the influence of example, and if your majesty were to deprive one man of his wife forcibly, they would all place themselves in that man's situation, and fancy what would be their feelings under such circumstances."

"Very good."

"Well, your majesty, there will be this evil, they will converse over and magnify it; your majesty will be considered a tyrant, and all men of less power will have their hand raised against you. What can we do when fighting against the whole of the commoners? we must be cut to pieces."

"I see—I see," said the king; "'tis a perilous task, and yet—and yet—I scarce know what there is that I am possessed of that I would not give for the quiet possession of her."

"That may be, your majesty; to lose one thing, is almost a sure prelude to another loss, perhaps more important than that."

"So it is."

"Therefore, your majesty, I can see nothing but pacific means that will offer no offence to the people ought to be pursued, or made use of."

"But what can be done?"

"That is a question that will take a little time in resolving."

"Time, Hastings, time; why, time will carry us onward in its current, and we shall be swept away from this theatre of our joys, and our hopes; time will, in its fulness, be no more for us; all we can boast of is, the time present."

"Your majesty used not to urge this matter when you headed armies, and joined in the conflict; you sought honour and ——"

"And a crown."

"And a crown, as your majesty truly observes, and you have it, and long may it remain where it—it now rests."

"But, still I cannot banish the beautiful being from my mind—from my heart; she's a glorious sunbeam in this world of darkness, and of strife. Oh! I never saw her peer."

"And yet your majesty has said the same thing before."

"But never for such a beauty did I feel my heart beat with rapture, hope, and expectation."

"All these feelings may be appeased by the possession of this fair creature, your majesty; but it will require a little caution and patience; these exerted, and all will be as you can wish."

"Very well—very well. What can be done? I must go to the house again."

"To Shore?"

"Yes."

"It will become expensive, your majesty, and he will begin to grow suspicious, and then, no inducement under Heaven will be strong enough to cause him to allow her to appear."

"I noticed that myself," said the king; "he began to be uneasy; but it would be impossible to forego, entirely, the pleasure of seeing her."

"I must see if there are any means other than merely visiting the goldsmith, for that can last but a time or two more."

"Well, well, Hastings, think of it, and let me see the force of your genius in this affair. Have her I must, cost what it will, or what it may."

Thus spoke Edward, who was thoroughly fired by the charms of Jane Shore. It mattered little to him who she was; he loved her, and he would have her; and he would, like David of old, have sacrificed the goldsmith in like manner, as the Jewish monarch did Uriah.

Hastings had now the difficult and disagreeable task of helping another to the mistress he himself, and in vain, sought. What could he do? he could not withdraw—he could not succeed if he did; he had been rejected in all the plenitude of his power and riches, and, therefore, he had no hope whatever.

It was an undignified office, certainly; but these great men think no office, not even a pander's, at all undignified, when that is performed in the behalf of a crowned head; and, wherefore or in what the difference, it is difficult to understand.

But no, he would not draw back; of that he had resolved; and, moreover, he had strong feelings of revenge upon him, and this feeling was increased by rejected love. Moreover, he was fired with ambition; he was the favourite and friend of his sovereign; he was rewarded with his friendship, and he wanted not for countenance and reward.

Yet he must and would continue in the same line he had chalked out, and passion must give way to ambition, to honour, and fidelity to his sovereign; and in this he persevered.

Thrown upon his own resources, angry and capricious, and filled with contradictory humours, after this interview Hastings scarce knew where to go or what to do with himself, and was about to seek some means of passing the evening or the night in some way that would preclude the necessity of thought or reflection.

With this view he was passing through one of the galleries that led to some of the apartments of several of the attendants of the king, when he caught sight, by accident, of Mrs. Blague, of whom we have had occasion to mention.

He was immediately filled with the notion that this woman could procure him an evening's amusement, and thus save him from himself, and he called after her. She, seeing who it was, immediately turned and curtsied to him.

"Ah, Mrs. Blague," said the chamberlain, "I am glad to see you. I don't know what to do with myself this evening."

"Oh, my lord," said Mrs. Blague, "I wonder a man of your lordship's gallantry can ever want for company. There must be some who would be glad of your lordship's society."

While Mrs. Blague was speaking, the thought came across the chamberlain that Mrs. Blague being somewhere in the neighbourhood of Master Shore, would have some knowledge of her or him that might be useful. Thereupon, he determined to question her respecting them.

"You live somewhere in the neighbourhood of Lombard-street, Mrs. Blague?"

"Yes, I do, as your lordship knows, at the old place."

"Do you know Master Shore, the goldsmith, in Lombard-street?" inquired Hastings.

"I do, your lordship."

"He has a very beautiful wife, the daughter of old Wainstead, the mercer?"

"Yes. I know Mrs. Alice—Mistress Jane Shore, too," said Mrs. Blague.

"You do?"

"Yes, your lordship; they know me too, and visit my house often."

"Does she? Then this is fortunate—very fortunate," said Hastings, musingly.

"Indeed, your lordship. What can I do for you, that my acquaintance with Mistress Shore is so very fortunate?"

"I will tell you. But this is a matter that will give occasion to you to exert all your caution and prudence."

"I am not often wanting in either, my lord," said Mrs. Blague.

"In truth, that is a fact. I tell you what it is, Mrs. Blague; you can, I dare say, procure me an interview with Mrs. Shore."

"Yes, yes; that is easy, very easy indeed; for she often comes to my place without any one being with her."

"That is yet more lucky. Now I do not mean to see her myself; but a certain great personage has seen her, and desires opportunities of seeing and conversing with her."

"It can be done."

"'Tis well," said Hastings. "Take this purse, Mrs. Blague. There are a few gold pieces in it, as an earnest of the remainder, when all is successful. Do you think there is any chance of success with her?"

"That depends upon circumstances. Some are easier to overcome than others; and if it be, as I presume you mean, the ——"

"King."

"Oh, yes. Why you will have very little difficulty there, I should say. You will, most probably, find such a dazzling offer too much for even Mistress Jane Shore's virtue to resist."

"Then the king will succeed where I have failed," said Hastings, bitterly.

"And can that be wondered at?" said the wily Mrs. Blague. "Can your lordship not see that where a subject fails a king must overcome?"

"I believe you are right," said the chamberlain; "and yet, were it not so, of two lovers one can but be chosen; it matters not which is rejected. Caprice and fancy are the guides a woman has in her choice."

"These young women, my lord, have no maturity of judgment, and, therefore, you should not be too hard upon them."

"Well, well. Now about our plan. When can we make sure of a meeting at your house with Mistress Jane?"

"That can be done to-morrow night," said Mrs. Blague.

"Indeed! does she come so soon to see you?" inquired the chamberlain, with a look of surprise. "I wish I had known this before."

"Never mind that, my lord; you may, perhaps, render it more profitable and better worth your knowing than at first."

"Tush, woman! you know not what you talk of. But how can you insure me that the king shall not be disappointed of an interview?"

"I can send here one of my boys on a message to your lordship. I will send some lace in a box, and in it you will see a note, with the exact hour at which she will come; or, what will still be better, an intimation that she is at my house, and then your lordship and the other gentleman must make what expedition you can to my place; but come cautiously and quiet."

"Never fear, Mrs. Blague; I will particularly have a regard for that."

"Then it is agreed."

"Agreed."

Hastings then left the palace, satisfied at least he should have the means of proving to he king he had not been idle in his behests.

t

CHAPTER LXVII.

The Invitation to Mrs. Blague's.

"'Tis strange that woman should be woman's greatest foe."

Next morning Hastings saw that Edward had passed his time somewhat uneasily, and he said to him, with a smile,—

"You can guess my malady, Hastings, for I can tell by your eye that you see there is some slight change in me."

Hastings was too old and good a courtier to give a direct reply to this, but said,—

"A disturbed rest, your majesty, will always make itself observable. I am to understand, however, that there has no change taken place suddenly in your feelings towards Jane Shore?"

"None, none, good Hastings. I shall never know rest until I have the beauteous Jane. She must, she shall be mine. I will again see her. I will again go to the goldsmith's shop, and, if I purchase to the amount of my revenue, or pawn my crown jewels, I will frequently visit that place."

"I scarce think that that will be necessary; for, if it were, I fear it would reduce you to such shifts, that could only result in some disagreeable adventure, such as a personal collision with the citizens, which would, indeed, be changing the order of things. It would be a great pity to lose that popularity you have amongst them; moreover, they are your bankers in the hour of need."

"And my creditors in prosperity."

"Surely it is so; and I need hardly add, that it needs not much to prove the necessity that the mutual relations should still be preserved."

"I see all this and acknowledge it; but yet I cannot reconcile all these things and the absence of Mistress Shore. She must—she must be mine, Hastings. Tell me, have you

aught upon this head that can give you consolation and comfort? Tell me, Hastings, can you do this?"

"I think I can."

"Then why, Hastings, did you not say so before, and not husband the cordial and restorative to the very last moment it can be used? Rather apply the surest remedy first, and then it is of the greatest efficacy. But what is it?"

"I have hit upon an old acquaintance, your majesty, that can, I think, be useful to a considerable extent."

"Indeed!"

"Yes, and manage the affair far less expensively than being a continual customer of the goldsmith, which exhausts the finances too much."

"But who is the new acquaintance who is to be useful to me? Don't beat about the bush quite so much, but tell me the whole particulars of it."

"Your majesty has heard or seen one Mrs. Blague, a lace woman, who has some connection with the court?"

"Well, I can understand what you mean, and do think I know something of the dame, and think it just possible that I may have been in her house, too, if it is somewhere near the goldsmith's house, in Lombard-street."

"Your majesty guesses correctly enough. That Mrs. Blague passes for a very worthy and virtuous dame, of lively qualities, and much esteemed by her neighbours, who visit her frequently. Among these visitors are Master Shore and his wife."

"Good."

"Jane frequently visits this dame, and that with her husband's consent; and, being close at hand, she goes often alone, and is therefore easily met with."

"Well," said Edward, "that opens a pleasing prospect and hope of being frequently in the society of this charming woman."

"It does, my liege," said Hastings. "It seems to me that nothing could have been planned better, with a foreknowledge of what was desired, than this lucky accident."

"That is true," said his majesty—"very true, and I am well pleased it is so. And now, Hastings, have you arranged any plan of operation, or how does the case stand?"

"Thus, your majesty," said Hastings. "It is expected that Mistress Shore will meet this Mrs. Blague this very evening; and, should such meeting take place, she will advertise me of it, and then nothing remains but to use what expedition your majesty thinks fit, to reach her house, and be introduced to the lovely dame."

"That I will do right willingly. Be sure to let me know as soon as this messenger comes. Mrs. Blague shall be no loser."

"Of that I have already assured her, and presented her with an earnest, and she will be found conformable to anything that may be desired that shall not cause her ruin."

"Exactly."

Then it was arranged that the king would be in readiness to seek the society of Mrs. Shore, and Hastings should also be in readiness to quit the palace with the king.

* * * * * * *

"So," muttered Hastings to himself, as he passed a splendid apartment in the palace, alone—"so all works well. Yes, all works well for the amour of one, and I shall have the inexpressible satisfaction of helping another to the fruit I would have plucked myself. Oh, inconsistency! And, yet, wherefore should I grieve? She never would have been mine. Edward is fickle in love, and may see some other beauty whom he will love as violently and heedlessly as this. Then, indeed, I may—I may succeed to the king's place in her affections—yes, I may.

"'Tis marvellous, though, I can speak these words 'I may,' without a frenzy rising in my breast—a very whirlwind of passion. But so it is; disappointment cools desire, for love cannot subsist upon rejection and disappointment; it requires to be fed. But, no matter, it may slumber, but it will never go out. The smouldering passion may neither be seen nor felt, and yet it would require but little to recall the feeling to full life and vigour—and so it is with me."

Hastings, notwithstanding these self-assurances, and notwithstanding his great mental efforts, was not able entirely to dispel his love so suddenly and so easily as he endeavoured to reason, and flatter himself that he had subdued his passion for her so far. He was still restless and agitated, nor could he entirely hide these emotions from himself, though he succeeded in doing so in the presence of King Edward.

* * * * * * *

The hours of that day passed heavily and slowly with the king. He looked forward with eagerness to the moment when he should be summoned to seek the society of one he had been so strongly prepossessed with.

Hastings passed also an uncomfortable time, and the hours seemed to fly by him, for he thought the evening came round with far greater expedition than it would have done had he been the principal actor in the affair in hand. But, slow or quick, time does come round, and there can be no stay in such an unnerring and unalterable thing as time. The greatest and most distant events must come in their course; it is inevitable.

The hours glided by in a manner not usual in a palace, and the setting sun was a welcome spectacle to those who gazed upon it. The luminary that gave fruitfulness to the earth sank in a halo of glory, and gilded the rising clouds with all the beauties of the heavens. The sun had set about an hour, and the king was impatient; and Hastings felt uneasy, he knew not why. He was walking up and down an ante-room, with his arms folded, and agitated by many contending emotions and feelings, all of which contended with each other for the mastery. Suddenly an attendant presented himself before the chamberlain, and awaited his speech.

"Well," he said, "what now?"

"There is one without would speak with your lordship."

"Admit him."

The attendant, with a bow, retired, and during the interval of his absence, Hastings muttered between his teeth,—

"So, the time has come; where is my resolution—fled?—No, no, I will be myself. What matters it to me who basks in the sunshine of her smiles and her charms—I cannot. She is nothing to me—nothing, nothing, nothing!"

The door opened, and the attendant ushered one in who had a small box with him. At a sign from Hastings the attendant withdrew, closed the door, and left them alone,

"Whence come you?" inquired Hastings, shortly.

"From one you well wot of, my lord," replied the man; "and I am charged to deliver this into your hands—it is for my Lord Hastings."

"That is correct."

"Then, my lord, look at the contents, and quickly discharge me; despatch in these matters is very necessary."

"What matters, fellow?"

"The matters my mistress sends me upon, I know of no other; and that is her own words."

Hastings opened the box and saw some lace in it; this he barely noticed; but a small note tied with silk, and sealed, was there. He took this, and opening it, read these few words,—

"To my Lord Hastings.

"My lord,—The person you wot of is now at my house, she has but this moment come in. Use what expedition you may. I have arranged all, so that none may interfere with the guest who may come with your lordship.

"Your lordship's servant at command,

"Martha Blague."

Hastings, when he read this note, turned to the man, saying,—

"Tell your mistress that you have given your message to him to whom it was sent, and take this for thy reward."

Hastings, as he spoke, threw the man a piece of silver, and turned away.

"Thanks, my lord, for your nobleness;" but before he could say any more, Hastings, who stayed not to hear his thanks, had left the apartment.

"Now," said the fellow, "there's some sense in coming here, one may pick up a few silver pieces—and here is a good one. Well, I care not how often I come here, though I have to encounter black looks and sudden speeches. My mistress's name, though, seems a very good passport."

The man left the place, while Hastings proceeded straight to the king's room. Edward looked up as he heard the door opened.

"What news, Hastings?—what news have you heard from your accommodating friend?"

"Here is the note, and as it concerns your majesty only, you will perhaps be pleased to peruse it."

"Give it to me," said the king.

Accordingly Hastings handed the important document to the king, who read it, and then crumpling it up, he jumped up, saying,—

"I will go this instant. Come, Hastings, I am waiting to go and see the beauty I have so fondly attached myself to."

"Then I am quite prepared for an instant departure,—there can be nothing to detain us. I am ready—quite ready."

"Then follow me," said Edward.

As he said this he opened a small door in the apartment, and passed out, followed by Hastings, who closed it after him. They descended a small private staircase, and entered a private carriage that was in waiting. Giving instructions where to go to, the king drew up the blinds, and leaning back, awaited in silence the motion of the carriage wheels.

"I never passed such a long day," said the king; "it has appeared as though night would never come—a most tedious day."

"Your majesty feels so interested in the results of the day—that made you wish it gone, and hence it was the more tiresome. Nothing so long and so tiresome as watching the escape of time."

"I think that is quite right, for I have watched it to-day, and have felt as if I never knew a day so long."

"It will now, however, change its character," said Hastings, "and your majesty will soon be able to contrast quick and slow time."

"I shall; for time appears to fly fast when you most desire its stay."

They listened to the various sounds that they heard in their route, and which indicated the several places they arrived at, and when they heard the challenge at the city gates, they knew they had but a short distance to go.

"I wonder," remarked Hastings, "what could have been the cause of that attack your majesty sustained the other morning."

"I had forgotten it," said the king. "I don't know, but I suspect that it was caused by some of the rabble, led on by some agent or outlaws employed for that purpose."

They now passed through Fleet-street and up Ludgate-hill till they came to St. Paul's Churchyard.

"It is very dark," remarked the king, as he looked out of the window.

"Yes, your majesty; it is dark but there are yet many lights beginning to be seen from many of the windows, and sober citizens are going about from place to place without any fear,—true, they carry lanterns mostly."

"Yes, yes, I see," said the king, abstractedly, and then he added,—"you, Hastings, had better remain in the carriage; you will be ready on the instant I want you."

"I can, your majesty. There is one thing I may as well mention."

"What is it?"

"That Mrs. Blague's secret is kept, and those in the house know nothing about it; hence, should your majesty be hurried on to commit any violence, you will raise the inmates upon her alarm, and therefore it would be unavailing."

"I understand; but fear not respecting that. I shall not attempt such a thing; remain, therefore, quiet here until I return."

The chariot stopped within a short distance of the house of Mrs. Blague, and the king got out, leaving Hastings in the chariot to await his return after his interview.

CHAPTER LXVIII.

The Elopement of Jane.

"Virtue slept, and Jane left her husband's home to shame. The smiles she met with hid contempt."

THE time passed disagreeably enough with Hastings, as he sat with impatience awaiting the king's return to the chariot. To wait while another man prosecutes a suit in which you have failed, is not by any means pleasant, and the lord chamberlain felt he was placed in this peculiar situation.

The king, on his part, walked with a light step towards the house of Mrs. Blague, and when he arrived, was admitted by that person herself, who was waiting for him.

She introduced him to Jane under an assumed name, and the whole party were soon engaged in a tete-a-tete, in which Mrs. Blague deserved great credit for her cunning and management, for she knew exactly where both the king would shine and Jane also.

The style of conversation was lively and witty, and in this Jane fully bore out the reputation she had gained, and the king was more and more in love with her, for he saw that she had many qualities that made her more desirable; and he, himself, was no mean master of many things; for, of his time, there were few men better educated, or had equal advantages, or blessed with quicker perceptions and judgment than he. Yes, he could not but admit that, in his court, there were few, if any, who equalled her, and certainly none who were superior to her.

These things inflamed the king's passion to a great height, and, at this juncture, the cunning woman, Mrs. Blague, seeking some pretence, she quitted the room, leaving the king and Mistress Shore together. During this time, the king used his utmost endeavours to make himself agreeable to Jane; but he forebore pressing her too much, lest he should not succeed, and only frighten her, and thus, by acting with precipitancy, destroy the plot. However, he passed some time with her, and when Mrs. Blague returned to the apartment, the king could hardly be prevailed upon to depart, which he did, after making an appointment to meet her there the next night.

* * * * * * * * * *

"Hastings," said the king, "I have seen her, and conversed with her."

"Indeed, your majesty!"

"She's a perfect divinity—an angel, Hastings!" exclaimed the king, throwing himself back in the carriage. "I never saw her equal."

"She is incomparable, I believe, your majesty; the more you know of her the more you desire, and she appears more beautiful and witty each time you are in her society."

"Exactly the case; think of this, Hastings, I have been alone with her and yet I have not declared to her my wishes."

"Indead, your majesty!"

"I cannot understand it, Hastings."

"Nor I."

"I can only attribute it to the influence she exerts by her beauty and excellence."

"She is certainly a paragon—a pattern among women, such as we shall never see again."

"Indeed, that is no more than just; and, I must say, that without her England would become valueless to me."

"But you will see her again? You have not, surely, let so good an opportunity escape your majesty altogether unimproved?"

"Not entirely—not entirely!" said the king. "I have got a promise to meet me to-morrow night, at the same place."

"That is well."

"It is a step gained."

"And wherefore did your majesty not make an approach to the citidal, which you so much desired to take?"

"I did; but it was at too great a distance; my next approach will be somewhat nearer; but I intend going to the goldsmith's to-morrow, and, probably, accompany her to Mrs. Blague's."

"That may produce an explanation at an inopportune moment."

"How do you mean?"

"You may be watched by the jealous goldsmith, and one of the many accidents that happen in these cases may occur; besides, it will not give your majesty a better opportunity of having any conversation with her than you can obtain at Mistress Blague's, and not so good."

"It may be so. I will go to-morrow, Hastings, to the goldsmith's, and see what we can do with him."

"In what respect, your majesty?"

"In faith, Hastings, I can hardly tell; but something may turn up, and then we can, you know, do what may be necessary."

With this, Hastings remained satisfied, and felt convinced the king had some further plan than he chose to divulge.

He could not think or believe that Edward was really inspired with a sincere and lasting passion for this woman; for he had never known him capable of a lasting attachment in this respect, because they were too frequent. He did not think that Edward was torn by many conflicting emotions, and would have hovered about the spot until he could have called her his own, and borne her triumphantly off from her husband's house.

* * * * * * * * *

The next day, Hastings and the king again made their way towards the house of the merchant; they entered his shop, and were cordially met by the goldsmith.

"You sent for your plate," said Shore, "and I hope you have received it all safe."

"Everything is as I wished it, my worthy sir," said the king.

"I am very glad of it, for it was a heavy charge, and one that created a fearful responsibility," said the goldsmith.

"And you are glad you are relieved?"

"I am, very."

"Now, however, I have come about some other matters. I shall require a few more articles I have enumerated in a small list."

"I will attend to it with care."

"I have no doubt."

"I have had much experience in these matters, and, therefore, know well what will do myself credit, and my customers justice."

"The right principles of trade."

"They are, though many say 'twould be impossible to carry on a trade successfully upon that plan; but I have done so, and can say I think I have done better in consequence."

"I am glad that, for once indeed, honesty has proved the best policy."

"It is always in the long run."

"And now about these things?" said the king, with as much of a merchant-like air as he could assume. "Here is the list I have made; see to what of its contents you can help me."

"To the whole," said Shore.

"To the whole?" echoed the king.

"Yes," replied Shore; "to the whole."

"You don't mean that you have all these articles all ready to pack up?"

"Not all."

"Then how will you act?"

"I can get them all ready by midday—to-morrow, if that will do."

"I should require them by that time; but where will you obtain them?"

"I have the means; and I know some merchants that have some of these things by them, and from them I can get them."

"Then to-morrow, let it be."

"At midday?"

"Yes, that will do."

"May I reckon upon your company to dinner with me; 'tis scarcely respectable or right that so much should be done, and yet we should never break bread together."

"Then," said the king, "I will be here, and we will have dinner; and then when we have had a bottle, our acquaintance will terminate."

"So soon?"

"Yes."

"Then I hope we shall each preserve a respectful remembrance of each other, and we may do each other justice, and say, 'he was an honest man.' As a citizen of London, sir, I am more proud of my station and untainted honour even than King Edward can be of his; and long may he rule over these kingdoms."

The king paused, and looked the honest goldsmith in his face, and there seemed to be something that floated in his mind, and made him hesitate a moment or two; but he quickly recovered himself, and then he said,—

"If there are many such subjects as you in the city of London, the city will be the brightest jewel in King Edward's crown."

"There are many such, as I have every reason to believe."

"I honour you, sir, and them," said the king; "but fare you well, till to-morrow noon."

"Farewell," said the goldsmith, extending his hand, which the king grasped—and then turned away and quitted the spot.

Hastings and the king walked some distance in silence. There was something about this interview that did not well sit upon the king's mind, and he seemed as if he was almost ashamed of the plot to destroy the citizen's happiness; but passion subdued these as well as all other considerations, and he would have thought nothing of them at all, but that for the time he had brought himself on a level to the trader, and the language between man and man was much more congenial and understood than when addressed by the subject to a king. However, he soon recovered from this matter, and turning to Hastings, he said,—

"Hastings, I shall go at once to Mrs. Blague's. I would consult her concerning this affair, and if possible shorten the courtship."

"I think it much the best thing that can be done," replied the chamberlain.

With this view they walked to the house of the lace-woman, and was immediately admitted to the private apartment.

Mrs. Blague did not expect such early visitors, and said so.

"I dare say you did not, Mrs. Blague; but I wished to see you to say a few things to you respecting this affair."

"Whatever you please," said Mrs. Blague. "I am at your service in any way in which I can be useful."

"I am sure of that, and I wish to hasten this affair. I wish we could come to some explanation this night."

"Hadn't your majesty better at once declare your feelings to her, and if she reject, declare who you are?"

"I thought I might make you useful in that matter. I will certainly declare to her my feelings, and should she, as I dare say she will, reject me, then you can come to my aid."

"If your majesty will leave the room, I will explain all to her, and then before any time has been given for reflection, you must return to her again."

"That is agreed upon."

"Very well, your majesty; she will be here again, for I have her promise."

"She promised me also."

"Then that is an earnest of success; for it shows she has some kind of regard for you."

"I am content to believe it so."

The king, after some more conversation, left Mrs. Blague's in company with Hastings, and they both made their way back to the palace with as little delay as possible.

"What think you, Hastings, of our plot?" inquired the king, as they entered a private apartment.

"A good plot," your majesty; "a very good plot, and I think you have done the wisest part of all, in attempting to bring it to a conclusion this evening; it is much the best plan."

"I think so too."

They agreed, that at an early hour they would visit Mrs. Blague's, and then learn if any other measures were necessary.

That evening both the king and the lord chamberlain left the palace in the chariot, and again sought the abode of Mistress Blague, with the intention of endeavouring to arrange this affair, and with the hope of doing so successfully.

They came there, and Hastings was once more left in the chariot alone, while the king walked on a few paces, and then entered the house of Mrs. Blague by a private entrance.

"Mistress Blague! has Mistress Jane come?" inquired the king, when he entered.

"No!" replied she; "she has not, but she will be here very shortly. Had she been as anxious as you, she would have been here before this, I am sure."

"Ah, that makes me despair; for, her not doing so, is a proof that she does not feel any of the anxieties I feel."

"She would, did she know the happiness in store for her; but your majesty knows there is much difference in your positions, rank and wealth apart, and she could not therefore do as you do."

"Well, well, you are right—quite right. But who is that?"

This was the entrance of some one in the house, and Mrs. Blague immediately said,—

"That is Mistress Jane."

"I am glad of it,—right glad of it; for I had begun to torment myself with fear, lest she should not come."

There was much conversation, and the king received Jane, as she entered, with so much grace, and with such an air of distinction, that Jane could not but feel she had never seen such a handsome and fascinating man before.

Mrs. Blague, after a little while, left the room, and then the king began his attack upon the virtue of Mistress Shore.

He found her impregnable; and when he came to be rude, she called out for help; and the king, after begging her to consent to his wishes, left the room, when Mrs. Blague entered the apartment, and he left.

Jane related what occurred, and then an explanation took place. Mistress Shore was amazed at what she heard; and for some moments she ceased to speak, but to listen to the discourse of the cunning woman by whom she had been betrayed.

Before there was any time for reflection, the king came back, and throwing himself upon his knees before her, he sought her to listen to his offers.

Whether it was the sight of a king at her feet, the dazzling splendour of a court, or the irresistible nature of his blandishments, is not certain; but she relented, and in the end consented.

The king was overjoyed at his success, and would have carried her off at once; but that she refused to permit, but declared she would send her jewels and things to Mrs. Blague's, and she would follow them.

This was agreed to and the next day the king, accompanied by the lord chamberlain, in the disguise of two merchants, called before the hour at which they had appointed to meet the goldsmith, who was abroad upon the very business he expected to see these merchants.

With them Jane having sent away what she thought she would have, and then she followed with the two presumed merchants, entering the carriage that was in waiting for them; and thus the king gained the prize he sought so eagerly.

CHAPTER LXIX.

Shore's Despair.

"Like unto one madman Shore ran to and fro."

Master Shore was punctual, and, a few moments before the appointed hour at which he was to meet his two good customers and guests, he returned to his own house, and brought with him those things that he had procured at the desire of the strange merchants, whom he now expected to see.

For a few moments he did not notice the absence of his wife; he continued to gaze at the various articles, and to examine them carefully, to ascertain if there were any defects, and to be sure they were the same on second appearance they were at first.

"Yes," he muttered, "these are well worthy of being placed in the choicest collection; metal and make are unexceptionable. Oh, this is the hour at which they were to be here—they have hitherto been punctual, and won't be long."

He turned to some other matters, and made some entries into his account-books, and was lost some minutes in thought, when he suddenly awoke from his reverie, and gave a glance at the time, when he exclaimed,—

"Past the hour! well, they may have had other business to transact, and have been detained longer than they anticipated, and hence their want of punctuality. But where's Jane? I havn't seen her. I will bring her and show her these things, before they have them; she has much taste and judgment; she shall tell me what she thinks of them, and I will seek her myself."

Thus speaking, he went to the apartment of his wife, where he usually found her, and saw she was not there. He paused and mused on the strangeness of the occurrence. I will inquire for her of the housekeeper, and she will be able to tell me where she is—somewhere in the house, I have no doubt; but then I might have to make the rounds of the house as I would a castle, and then find her at the last apartment, and know that I might have entered that as easily at first as at the last."

He at once proceeded to the housekeeper, where he saw that personage engaged in some domestic affair, and at once accosted her by saying,—

"Dame, dame, where is Mistress Shore? I would speak with her—tell me where she is."

"Eh?" said the housekeeper, who was rather deaf.

"Where is Mistress Shore?"

"Oh, ay—take care, indeed. I will take care, fast enough. I always do take care."

"Just so, but tell me where Mistress Shore is," said Shore, speaking very loudly.

"I dare say."

"Where is your mistress—is she anywhere? is she—is she in the house?"

"The house is very well, I am sure; but what do you want with me?"

"Tell me where is Mistress Shore."

"Oh, Mistress Shore?"

"Yes, yes; where is she? I can't find her—I have been over the house, nearly."

"I dare say you couldn't find her, master; she's not to be found in your house, I reckon, just now," said the old housekeeper.

"And why not?" said Shore, feeling uneasy, and yet not knowing what to think, or what the old housekeeper meant.

"Because she's out."

"Out," repeated Shore; "out, did you say?"

"Yes; she went out," said the housekeeper; "and I dare say she'll be some time before she thinks of coming back again."

Shore listened in somewhat an abstracted manner as though he could not comprehend what was said, or that some flashing thought of something too dreadful to utter passed across his brain, and he remained in thought for some moments, and then, as if awakened by some sudden impulse, he turned to the housekeeper, and said,—

"Did you not tell me, but just now, that Mistress Shore had left the house?"

"Yes, I did; and that is the truth," said the housekeeper; "she went out."

"And she knew that I expected guests," said Shore, rather speaking from impulse, and to himself, than to the housekeeper, who, however, not comprehending what was said, remarked,—

"She's gone as you say; but what did you say but now?"

"She knew that I expected guests here, to dine with me, and now 'tis past the hour; and though they have not been here, still she might have been here to receive them for me, if I had been detained—my guests might have been here alone."

"Oh, ay, the guests too," said the housekeeper, nodding her head.

"What, have my guests been?" exclaimed Shore; "speak, you old beldame, speak! and tell me who has been here, and who gone, while I was out, else I'll shake you till you drop."

"Mercy! mercy!" exclaimed the deaf old woman; "save me! save me! he's deranged."

"Tell me, then, has any one been here since I left the house?" cried Shore.

"Yes, yes."

"Who came?"

"The two merchants, who were to have been here now," cried the housekeeper.

"And they are gone?"

"Oh, ay, they are gone."

"Before or after my wife was out?"

"Before she went out."

"And—and—and how soon after did she go?" inquired Shore, hesitatingly; "after they went out?"

"She didn't go out after them at all," said the old woman; "she went out with them—they all went out together—Mistress Shore and the merchants all went out together."

Shore staggered back against the wall, where he leaned a moment or two.

"Gone—gone!" he muttered; "surely—no, it cannot be; and yet she is not here. Where can she be gone to?—gone with my customers; they had but little knowledge of her; they had seen her only while I was here, and could have known nothing of her, more than myself; it is useless to think to question her virtue. Old woman," said he, suddenly turning to the housekeeper, and speaking loud, "tell me, truly, did Mistress Shore go out with these visitants of mine? did she go out to go away with them?"

"Yes," said the housekeeper; "she did—she saw them, and after they had some talk with her, she went with them."

"Curses, curses!" muttered Shore, between his teeth; and he rushed to his sitting-room, to hide his own emotion; but almost unconscious of what he did. He was at first so overpowered by his feelings, that he gave way to a despair almost amounting to madness; and, for some time, he was incapable of coming to any active resolve upon what he had better do, under such an emergency.

He could hardly believe his beautiful Jane could have left him. He thought she might have gone somewhere, upon some other matter; and yet, why she should go out at such a juncture as that, he could not account for.

"This is most unexpected by me," he exclaimed for about the twentieth time.—"Where can she have gone, and why did she go? There was no one with whom she has gone that I could have suspected. These merchants were scarcely men who would have committed such deeds—they are men of substance and wealth. Oh! Heavens! what can be done—where can I go—and whom can I see? Who will tell me anything about my beautiful wife? Oh, God! what a pang of exquisite pain is this! Jane, Jane, Jane! Where are you, my beautiful wife? Oh, God! she has left me.—Yes 'tis too true—too true, she has left me?"

Then another burst of mingled passion and grief; swept across his soul, and displayed the man's strong and hidden passions.

"Why—why," he exclaimed, "could not fate have aimed some more fatal shaft at me than this? Why could she not have destroyed my life or her's? Then, indeed, I had mourned; but it would have been a less pang than that which now scorches my brains. I had died over and over again; dying is but a cessation of pleasure or pain; and who would not encounter such a negative evil, rather than the positive one I now suffer from?—Oh! Jane, Jane, what do I not feel?"

He pressed his hands against his temples, and remained in that posture some minutes; and then suddenly he started up, and looking around him, he said—

"Yes; she cannot have left me! she must have gone—to—to—to—ay; to some place, or other, to visit somewhere, or some one or other of her friends. I must be moving—I will go round to them all. Ay; she might have gone to Simon in the Cheape. She has gone there before, and may be there now; and, perhaps, these merchants, after all, did but go at the same time she went, and walked with her as a kind of protection, till they left her there. Yes, yes; she has gone there; and yet, why she should at such a moment, I cannot at all understand; but it will be a great relief to me to find that she is there. Simon is not the most tractable of men, and I have but little hope of ever making anything of him. But no matter; let me find her, and I shall be careless of him or any one like him."

He now walked very hastily down Lombard-street, towards the house he sought. He saw no one; and Shore looked at everything on his route, but he made the best of his way towards the spot.

"Master Shore, master Shore," said a voice close beside him; but Shore heeded him not who spoke, but pressed onwards with hasty strides.

"Master Shore," said a merchant, who had before spoken, to one who stood near him, "seems in haste this morning."

"And I should say in trouble too," remarked a lean spare man, to whom he had first spoken to, "if I am any judge of countenance?"

"He does seem as if some unwonted occurrence had disturbed him."

"Yes, he is in haste; and perhaps has some heavy calamity hanging over him that we know not of."

"And who is he?"

"Master Shore is a good and substantial citizen enough."

"Indeed!"

"Ay; he is a goldsmith, and one in good repute, and wealthy; he married old Wainstead's daughter, Jane, a very beautiful woman."

"She was not partial to the match, was she?" inquired the other.

"Well, I don't know much about that; the father seemed to desire it."

"It was a good match."

"No doubt, for he was a good and substantial citizen, and I know not what can have disturbed him; he looks very odd, and sees nobody, in my opinion."

"He does not—he does not; but never mind, we can't help it; we will proceed, an it please you," said the latter man.

The two merchants moved onward, and soon forgot Shore, who now arrived at the late mercer's house. Without waiting to look or ascertain if any one was there, he went at once into the shop where he had so often been with Wainstead.

He looked around, as if he expected to see something that should at once have assured him that Jane was present; but instead of this, he met the cold countenance of Simon himself.

"Well," he said, "what now?"

"Is Jane here?" he inquired, in an anxious tone, that he endeavoured to conceal.

"No," said Simon.

"She is—she must be."

"She isn't, and mustn't," said Simon, decisively.

Shore paused a moment, and then, looking Simon steadily in the face, he said, in a stern voice, to him,—

"Simon, I will not be trifled with. Tell me where Mistress Shore is."

"I can't."

"Sirrah, tell me at once where your mistress is, or dread my vengeance."

"I sha'n't," said Simon.

"You will not tell me where she is; then you know?"

"I don't."

"Come, Simon, do not trifle with me now; you said but a moment ago that you wouldn't tell me, and therefore you must know."

"I didn't; and I don't."

"Liar!"

"Pho, pho," said Simon; "I said I shouldn't dread your vengeance, since you don't recollect what you say; and all I have to tell you is, that Mistress Shore hasn't been here to-day."

"This will not do. She must be here; she is here, and I will see her."

"You won't, and you can't."

Shore stamped his foot with rage, and his emotions were too strong for utterance. He looked at Simon with a look of anger; that Simon indeed cared little about, but returned his gaze very steadily and coolly.

"She is here," said Shore, "and I will see her; I will search the house, and ascertain for myself if she be here."

"Oh, no, Master Shore, you will not; you can't go up-stairs—you can't go over the house—and you can't make any search."

"And why not?"

"Because I won't let you."

"You will not let me! I will soon do what I will, despite of you. Because you are in charge of the business, remember you are not master."

So saying, he made an attempt to pass Simon, and to enter the private part of the house, but Simon stepped before him, and pushed him back. Enraged yet more at this, he made an attack upon Simon, and a desperate effort to get into the house; but this only made Simon more enraged, and eventually he pushed him clean out of the house.

CHAPTER LXX.

Shore's search after Jane.

"THERE," said Simon, when he had turned Master Shore out of the shop, "there, don't you come here again with your wills and wonts, thats and shalls—I have a will of my own; and I can thoroughly maintain my own superiority in this place. Mistress Shore here, indeed! You ought to know where she is; I don't, and that's all about it."

Simon returned into the shop, while Shore, who had been thrown down in the fray, now rose, brushing the dust off his cloak, and venting bitter reproaches against Simon; but the latter heard them not, and heeded them not; and Shore himself, immediately after finding he could not make any impression upon Simon, he crossed over to Snafflings' the bowyer, and entering the shop, he found the bowyer engaged in sorting and examining bow-cases.

"Ah, Master Shore," he exclaimed, "Master Shore, these are stirring times, and bows are wanted. There's no weapon like a good bow—better than any other, in the hands of a good archer; for, mind you, he will pick off his man before he gets near him, and therefore runs no danger."

"Master Snafflings."

"Ay, Master Shore, it's true what I say—a good archer, with a good bow, such as I have got here now, will pick off his man at a hundred and fifty yards."

"Well, but ——"

"It is true, though I grant you there ain't many who can do it with certainty; and though I will not run down the use of other weapons, or of their utility when at close quarters, but, without disparaging others, I will say this, that it was our archers who have gained us many a good battle, not to say anything about Poictiers, Agincourt, and Cressy."

"You have a goodly list of battles won by the bow, but that is not what I have come about. I called here, for I have just encountered a heavy domestic affliction."

"Ay—indeed, Master Shore, domestic affliction! Why, I thought you had less to encounter with on that head than any other?"

"Ah, nobody, Master Snafflings, can be sure of anything but misfortune and ill-will."

"Misfortune and ill-will, Master Shore! and who can bear you ill-will?—nobody, of course, Master Shore. You are blest with a beautiful wife, and belong to the first guild, are wealthy, and I know not what besides—what can you desire, Master Shore?"

"Ah, Master Snafflings, I have lost that one item in the sum of happiness that you have enumerated, which I prize most of all."

"Indeed! Master Shore, that's a bad affair,—I am truly sorry to hear it. Has some merchant died, or become insolvent?"

"No, no, that could be borne; but it's my wife, Jane, that I speak of; she has left me, Mr. Snafflings—she has left me. Curses, man.! 'tis enough to cause one's blood to boil through one's veins, and burst them with agony."

"Mistress Shore left you!" exclaimed the bowyer, in surprise. "Master Shore, Master Shore, there's nothing in all England that can compensate a man for such a terrible calamity as that."

"No; no, not in all England, as you say, Snafflings; but—but one's blood cannot endure it. I feel as if I had some burning fluid coursing through my veins. Where is she—where can she have gone to—and with whom? are questions I cannot, with anything like certainty, answer."

"Can you answer them at all, Master Shore?—tell me that."

"But in part."

"Where is she gone?" inquired the bowyer.

"I cannot tell where she is gone," said Shore, "nor is it likely I could."

"And you have no suspicion?"

"None."

"Whom has she gone with?" inquired Snafflings, with a catechistical air.

"She went from my house with two merchants to whom I had sold some valuable merchandizes, and I had been out to obtain elsewhere some other matters they required, and was back at an appointed hour to meet them, as they were to dine with me at that time, and I was to conclude the sales I had made them."

"And they came?"

"While I was out they came, and Mistress Shore left my house with them."

"With them?"

"Yes, with them. Curses on them and theirs! Wherefore came they at all?"

"It is very extraordinary," said Snafflings.

"It is extraordinary!"

"To tell you the truth, and a bit of my mind," said the bowyer, looking carefully round the shop to see no one was near, as he lowered his voice—"to tell you a bit of my mind, if a woman does anything at all amiss, I think the best thing, after all, would be her leaving home entirely; on my honour, I should console myself with the reflection I know the worst, and can make up my mind to the future deprivation of what people say so much."

"Master Snafflings, I am more particular; I want my wife; I cannot tamely see myself robbed of that I loved so well, or valued so highly."

"Well, well," said Snafflings, "you know everybody has their way of thinking, and between us, in private, I have mine; but you think differently now. What did you think first when you found she left the house?"

"I really cannot tell; but thinking she cannot have known the merchants before, I had a strong belief that she had gone to the house of her late father, kept by Simon."

"Ay, ay; I know."

"I inquired of him if he had seen her, and only obtained an impudent negative. And, when I charged him with falsehood, he replied in a yet more insolent style; and when I made a demonstration of looking into the house and making a search myself, he thrust me forcibly out."

"Oh, dear, me! Well, that Simon is a strange man—very strange man."

"So he is; and it entirely confirms the suspicion that she must either be in the house, or else he knows something about her."

"Well, I shouldn't be at all amazed at such an event," said Snafflings.

"What can be done? Do you know anything about those who go in and out of the house?"

"No, I don't; and yet I think I know who does, or who is likely to know something, albeit, I cannot answer for it."

"Nay, we cannot get direct evidence, but indirect may lead to something better. What think you, Master Snafflings?—tell me truly what you think or believe is likely."

"You know that knave of mine, or that used to be—Jacob, I mean?"

"Yes, I recollect him; a very thin man."

"A complete bow-case; bless you, Master Shore, I could span him round."

"Well, well!"

"I think he must know something of it, because he used to know some of the inmates, and may do so now."

"Where is he now?" inquired Shore. "I would go and see him, and endeavour to wring from him some information that may lead me to search in the right quarter."

"You may, you may—and I heartily wish you may. You have my good wishes, Mr. Shore. I am sure I wish you may get what you desire in this affair—I do indeed, Master Shore."

"Where is Jacob?"

"He is at Caxton's."

"What, Caxton, the printer, near the abbey, Westminster?"

"The same."

"I will go there and see him."

"But they will not admit you."

"But he must come out."

"Neither will they allow any one to come in or go out."

"I will try.—I will go at once. I am in great haste, Master Snafflings, so I bid you good day."

"Well, I declare—there he goes. Well, well, he is in a hurry to get his wife back again. I shouldn't, I know, and many a man besides; but what is, is—and what isn't, isn't; and so things are as they are, I suppose."

So saying, the honest bowyer set about his own affairs, having watched Master Shore out of sight, as he hurried in the direction of St. Paul's.

Shore soon passed by the old building that went under that denomination, and then made the best of his way across the fields towards the spot where the old abbey stood, and thereabouts stood the rooms where Caxton lived and had his printing-presses arranged, and whence issued some of the first specimens of that art in England.

It was now past noon some time, and Shore hastened on, hoping to find Jacob, and question him concerning the incomers and outgoers of the house of the late mercer.

"If I found that she had but left her home upon any sudden offence, or upon anything but a guilty errand—if I was once assured of that, if I were but sure and satisfied that she were pure and virtuous, then, indeed, I would restore her to her former place in my breast. But, oh, God! should it be otherwise, should she indeed have been guilty—as circumstances would seem to indicate, then, what a state of misery and wretchedness has she produced? Oh, little, little does she know the result even to herself! she cannot maintain the same advantages over her destroyer that she does now! No, no; the time will come when satiety and—and decaying charms will cause each successive lover to turn his back upon her, and she will wander a poor and hungry wretch, dying without a friendly hand to close her eyes. Loathsomeness, poverty, pain, and anguish, will be the accompaniments of such a death-bed as that she will have to encounter. May curses fall upon the head of him who has done this! may he riot for awhile, and then sink in misery and disgrace; may he suffer all the disgrace man can suffer—all the misery he can feel, and die friendless, unpitied, and forlorn!"

Shore was thus hurried on by his feelings to utter these thoughts almost audibly, as he walked rapidly towards the house of the printer, but before he arrived there his passion then had entire mastery over him, and he utteerd curse on curse, not loud but deep.

By the time he reached the door he was much excited, and, having demanded admission rather hastily, a man came forward to know what it was he wanted.

"You have a man named Jacob here, have you not?"

"Well?" said the porter.

"Shew me where he is; I must speak with him."

"Indeed you cannot."

"I must."

"You must not; no one is admitted here—you cannot come in."

"But I will and must."

Before the man could make any reply, Shore rushed by him, and, as he endeavoured to throw himself in his way, he was thrown down, and Shore passed into the press-room. There was a scene of confusion and alarm here, for no sooner did Jacob see Shore, than he was seized with the belief that he was come to apprehend him for certain rose nobles that were missing, and which had been abstracted by him from his late master the bowyer.

"Jacob," said Shore, "come; I would speak with you, come out."

"You can't stop here—leave the place."

"I must and will see him; come out, Jacob, come out, don't be afraid."

"A—a—afraid!" said Jacob to himself, "w—w—whose afraid? I a—a—ain't; b—b—but I don't like dogs, and I don't like a bigger man than myself."

"You must go out," said the men, of whom there were several; "it can't be helped, you must go."

"I will not, without him."

As Shore spoke he contrived to seize Jacob by the leg as he was crawling under some presses, and, there being some cross pieces, Jacob got considerably scraped before he was pulled out, and then both he and Shore were forced out of the house.

"Now answer me truly," said Shore, "as you value your life."

"Y—ye—yes," stammered Jacob, "but d—d—don't hold me so tight, I can't speak."

"Do you know who is at Master Wainstead's—at the house, I mean, that was his?"

"Yes, I d—d—do."

"Who, then?"

"Simon ——"

"And who else?"

"Nobody, that I know."

"Mind tell the truth, or this moment shall be your last."

"Mercy! mercy! I have told the truth, as far as I know. I know nothing more, if you were to pound me. Let me go—let me go!"

Convinced he could gain no information from the trembling wretch, or that he really knew nothing, he flung him from him, and began to retrace his steps towards London.

He had not gone far, however, before he was overtaken by the faded gallant, who had seen and learnt a little of his interview with Jacob, and thought something might be done.

"Ah," he exclaimed, "whither so fast, good master? that is a cunning rascal you had to deal with."

"Do you know him?"

"I do; there are few men in the City that I do not; and, moreover, ah—ah! I know the way to worm a secret out of such fellows."

"Indeed; and how?"

"It can't be done by shaking them, or you would have had one. But what is it you desire to know? I may be able to serve you, if it is anything requiring caution, courage, and perseverance."

Shore, seized with the idea that the most unlikely means might succeed when the probable had failed, related all about the occurrence.

"Ah, I see; you have been wrong; you ought to have waited and lied close; now let me conduct the affair, and, if she is to be found, I'll know something of her before long; and if she be not in London, I will find where she is—but ah! ah! you must—ah! give me something to carry on the war with, and defray the charges."

Shore took a heavy purse, and gave him some gold, and, when he put the purse up again, the faded gallant, allured by the purse, suddenly struck him on the head, and he fell to the earth. In another moment Shore was rifled, and the faded gallant having secured his purse, he fled rapidly across the fields in the direction of London, rejoicing at the lucky incident, being persuaded that one bird in the hand was worth two in the bush.

CHAPTER LXXI.

Shore's Sickness.

In those times there were but few foot passengers from Westminster to London, the distance was considered great, and the road not at all times safe; and indeed we may see by this case alone that cupidity would easily find a spot where it could let itself have full scope; and in this instance it could be stopped only by the commission of the crime it led to.

The faded gallant never thought of staying by the side of the inanimate body of Shore to see if there were any probable return of life; he made his way with the utmost celerity towards that part of the country which promised him the most protection, and that was the city of London.

Away he went, and the shadows were not far thrown to the south when he arrived at the nearest gate and passed through, he being known pretty well at the city gates. He was not long in seeking some choice locality where he might hide and shine at the same time, spend his plunder and enjoy the produce of crime, as it is said, some men can.

In the meantime, poor Shore lay helpless and insensible. No good Samaritan came by that way and succoured him; he lay there stunned, insensible, and to appearance dead.

The hours passed by, and the sun sunk in the west; the night clouds came floating up, and the sun shone through the heavy masses, exhibiting every variety of tint, from the light orange to the deep blue and red, which shaded off to the most complete black. Tints of green, too, and azure blue diversified the heavens.

It was a glorious thing to see that sunset. It was short but it was glorious and beautiful to see, but there by the roadside lay Shore, unconscious of the beams of the setting sun, or the beauties that were heaped up in the western horizon.

At length, as the last rays were yet lingering over the hills to the west, the sound of voices came along the road, and the sound of horses' feet came from the quarter whence he had come. The jingling of armour and the ringing of the sword against the saddle-bow, and the neighing of horses, all sounded for some time in the distance, and at length the party came up.

It was but a party of three armed men. They rode on horseback, and their strong steeds came along at an ambling pace.

"They will have a fine night for their rounds," said one of the party.

"Yes; but 'tis rather cold," said another.

"We can't pick and choose our weathers and seasons; a trooper mustn't be particular, I reckon."

"And yet a trooper may be able to judge what's comfortable, and tell what's good, and he shall be a good soldier, too."

"There's very few who are used to all that's good and comfortable that's at all fit for active duty in the field."

"There are few who understand what's good and comfortable," persisted the trooper, "better than the citizens of London."

"Granted; the dogs have well-filled purses, and therefore they may well do so."

"Ay; but for citizens they make very good soldiers, and they are seldom loath."

"Yes—yes, they are all brave enough, I will admit that; but they are not regular bred soldiers; men who know their duty, and can bear a shock without shrinking."

"If you make a citizen into a regular soldier he will be as well able to do his duty as another man."

"Granted."

"Then my argument is proved from your own admission; men may be as good and as hardy soldiers as any in England, though they may know what good quarters and good living are; as instance the turbulent citizens of our far-famed city of London."

"You can't come the old soldier over us, Hugh; but you are too cunning for me. I can't tell how you've done it, but you have brought it round to your own liking; that is all well enough, but it ain't satisfactory."

"Well, well; I won't trouble you with any more of that kind of argument; you don't seem to appreciate it at all."

"Hilloa!" said one of the troopers, "what's that a-head, yonder?"

"Where?"

"Just by the bush."

"I don't know till I see; it looks as if some traveller had made too free with the juice of the barley-corn."

"He's happy."

"I doubt if he's in a state to say whether he be or he be not happy from the way in which he is lying."

The party rode up to the spot where Shore was lying, and the one commanding the party said, as he looked at him,—

"Here's been some foul play here; the man's been murdered and rifled. Look at his dress; it's all disordered."

"There has been some rough work. Shall I dismount and see to it?"

"You may."

The trooper dismounted, and gave his horse to his comrade, and then approaching Shore, he looked at him for a moment, and turning him over on his back, he placed his hand on the region of the heart a few moments.

"Does he live?" inquired the other.

"He does; but he is quite insensible, and incapable of motion."

"What's to be done?"

"We can't leave him here."

"That would be to allow him to perish. We can place him behind one of us, and carry him to the city gate."

"We can leave him there—the surgeons will attend to him."

"Do so at once, and we will hasten or trot back to the gate."

The trooper immediately lifted Shore up, and placed him behind his companion; and passing his belt round them both he secured the wounded man to the trooper.

"Now, lads," said the sergeant, "let's set spurs to our cattle, and we will make the best of our way; we shall not be long reaching the city gates, and then our duty is done."

The men put their horses to a sharp trot, and, before it was quite dark, they reached the city gate; and, having answered the challenge, they were at once admitted.

"Ah," said the officer of the guard, "what means this? you have one more with you than you informed me of."

"Ay, but he's a dead 'un," said the trooper, "or next to it, and that goes for nothing, in countrymen, you know."

"Well, well, but how came he in this state?" said the officer, looking at Shore.

"That's what we have all been talking about, and couldn't find it out; but suppose he has been both robbed and ill-treated."

"Where did you find him?"

"By the road side—half of a mile hence—he was quite insensible."

"So he is now. What are you going to do with him?" inquired the officer.

"Leave him here," returned the sergeant.

"Leave him here?"

"Yes."

"You must carry him on."

"On?"

"Yes."

"Where to?"

"Oh, I don't know. I have nothing to do with dead or dying men."

"Well," said the sergeant, "this is the first occasion I have heard of a soldier refusing to give shelter and assistance to a fellow creature; he seems to be a man who can pay, provided he lives; and if one could find out where he resides, there would be no difficulty in getting paid for the trouble; however, we will carry him on to the next guard house."

"No no, let him come in," said the officer; "we will do the best we can for him; but the truth is, my good friend, we have little room; our hospital, here, is nearly full, and many of the cases are infectious; however, one sick man doesn't often catch the complaint of another; in the morning I can hand him over to some of the civil authorities, who may know him."

"Very well," said the soldier, "I am satisfied when I have done my duty; and, if you take charge of him, I have no more to say."

"Let it be so."

Some men were ordered to take Shore from the trooper, and carry him into the hospital, or a temporary place that could be got ready. A leech was sent for to attend to the wounded man.

The ordinary attendant being absent—indeed there was no well organised plan in these cases, at all; whoever happened to be at home or nearest, was sent for—another person came with many grave grimaces.

He was introduced to the patient, and professed there was much danger, that he had a serious contusion on the brain.

The first thing he did was to have Shore's head entirely shornr of his hair; and then he ordered him a variety of messes, which, as he was utterly insensible, he was unable to take, and escaped that part of the infliction.

However, an old woman, who happened to be there, made several attempts to procure re-animation, without effect. Yet she succeeded so far, that his breathing was now loud and distinct, and he lay there rolling about, but unable to see or to speak.

The morning came, and it was evident that he suffered from some other evil, besides the mere blow—fever and delirium seemed to be coming stronger each hour, and he now threw his hands and arms about in a restless and uneasy manner.

Moans and groans escaped his lips, but no articulate sounds; indeed, he seemed to keep his mouth shut, his teeth close, edge to edge, and his lips were black with heat.

The officers in the morning visited him, and inquired of the attendant if there were any hopes of getting him to speak.

"No, no," said the old woman, "I don't know what the leech may say about it, but it seems to me that he has a very serious illness upon him, but it will be long before he's able to speak, save the ravings of madness."

"Then we are not likely to find out who he is?"

"No, we are not, indeed."

"That's very unfortunate—very unlucky—we shall not now get rid of him."

"That you won't."

"Then I must adopt some other method of ascertaining who or what he is."

"He seems to be a citizen."

"Yes, yes; he is a citizen, that his evident, from his appearance."

"And a wealthy one."

"Yes; his garb must have cost a round sum, and it is not made to be showy only—it is good and sober."

"Just so; he will be inquired for, no doubt, before the day is out."

"I hope so; but I will inquire of Snafflings, the bowyer, who lives in the Chepe, and who is coming to-day to see to my men's bows, and see they are all in condition."

"He knows almost everybody, does Master Snaffling—he's everywhere."

"On that I rest my hope; see to him, and I will bring him here as soon as he comes;" and so saying, he left the room.

He had scarcely left the room, before the old nurse, who had been unable to attend to her part of the business, came cautiously up to him, and carefully inserted her hands into his pocket, but she found nothing there to reward her for her trouble. She withdrew them with a disappointed air, and muttered between her teeth, but quite audibly,—

"Whoever's been there before, have made their work of it; however, it's too bad. I am entitled to something for my pains, surely, but whatever comes through a soldier's hands, comes very well sifted indeed; there's no hope of a gleaning after such workmen, much less a harvest; they make quick work of it."

* * * * * * * *

In a short time Master Snafflings came to inspect a number of bows that had been in use some time, and which were still to remain in use if they were fit. He was now in the full height of his glory—not a man so great as he. His words were listened to with reverence by the soldiers who crowded around him, to hear his remarks of bows and archers; for Snafflings was great upon such occasions, and seemed as if he had been made for such moments; he shone in full splendour, and was eloquent.

Suddenly the commanding officer entered the room, and the men immediately made way.

"Good morrow, bowyer. What news to-day? Are you here about the bows?"

"I am, worthy captain; according to your commands here am I."

"'Tis well. Step this way."

"With much pleasure."

"Do you know many of the citizens?"

"Yes; I know many of the citizens of this good city,"

"Can you inform me if any one's missing among them?"

"I know of none."

"We have a wounded man here who was brought in last night."

"Indeed!"

"Yes; and we know not who he is."

"He cannot speak, I suppose?"

"No; he is quite senseless now, and remains perfectly helpless."

"And has he been left in that state all night? Why, if he be a citizen, he deserves better treatment than that."

"He has had proper attention paid him, as far as our means of accommodation suffices. Follow me, and you shall yourself see him. You may be able to tell me who he is."

CHAPTER LXXII.

The Recovery.

The bowyer followed the officer into the room where lay the sick man, and much did he wonder in his own mind why the officer should have taken that method to ascertain who the unfortunate man could be; but he thought he could have no other.

The room was small, and had only an end light, which admitted but a dim radiance into the room; and at first the eyes would hardly enable a person to distinguish objects clearly: but after a few moments objects began to be a little more distinct and clear.

"This is the only place we had to put him," said the officer, "because the infirmary is filled with infectious diseases."

"Good God!" said the bowyer, backing away; "you don't mean to say there are any cases of infectious diseases?"

"Oh! plenty."

" A—a—are they very bad?"

" Very malignant, indeed," said the officer, who began to amuse himself by tantalizing and frightening the worthy citizen, who had a great horror of any infectious disease.

" Well, then, I'd rather not stop."

"Oh! there's no fear—not to a man like you; it's only injurious to those who are nervous, and then they never escape."

" I ain't frightened, you know; but I may carry the infection about me to others; and I would sooner d—d—die myself than be the cause, the innocent cause of any mischief happening to other people; I would, indeed."

" Oh! would you?"

" I would."

" Very good."

" I will go now."

" Not just yet; turn your attention to the wounded man. He may, perhaps, be infectious, for all I know; but citizen should never desert citizen, you know, in the hour of danger."

" Certainly not," said Snafflings; " but a leech is the most proper visitor in these cases. I can do him no good."

" If you can tell who he is," said the officer, "you will do him some good; because we could then send him home."

The officer at the same time brought Master Snafflings close to the bed on which was stretched the unfortunate goldsmith, who moaned loudly, and threw his clenched hands about in the air, sometimes striking and sometimes clutching at the empty air.

" There he is, poor fellow. 'Tis a pity he should be left there alone to die, without his kindred, if he have any; not that I care mnch about these things, but you citizens have a great fancy to die in your beds—have you not?"

" Yes, yes, we certainly do prefer that," said Snafflings; " and that is no wonder, as seeing we are brought up with such notions."

" Do you know him?"

" I think—yes, surely—I do know him somewhere—but he is so altered I can scarce recognise who he is."

" Of course he looks different now to what he did some time since. He's lost his hair, which was cut off by order of the leech."

The patient now turned round in bed, and Snafflings at once recognised his friend Shore; he had seen him in the morning.

" Do you know him?"

" Yes, Heaven help me! It is my neighbour the goldsmith."

" Who?"

" Shore—'tis Master Shore, the goldsmith of Lombard-street. A respectable citizen is Master Shore, I assure you."

" Master Shore," repeated the officer, whistling, " the goldsmith, say you?"

" Yes, it is Master Shore, I can assure you. I only saw him this morning."

" Indeed! Did you know where he was going to when he left you?"

" To Caxton's, the printer, Westminster Abbey."

" Aye; then it was on his road back that he met with the disaster, or on his road thither, I cannot tell which. No doubt he carried a heavy purse with him?"

" Yes, no doubt; he was a wealthy man, and therefore would in general have money about him; and it is the more likely, since he went across the fields upon the heat of the moment."

" Ay, and that purse has been the temptation to commit the deed."

" No doubt. Will you send him home by some of your people?"

" And where to?"

" He dwells in Lombard-street. He should go at once, for he needs immediate assistance."

" He shall be sent; but would it not better, as he requires it, that you should see him safely home, and see that he has proper attention? His family may be alarmed."

" He has but an old housekeeper now, and therefore he must be left to the charge of servants under any circumstances."

" Then there is greater need of your assistance. You will, doubtless, go with him, and see him properly taken care of, and a leech sent for who will be equal to the necessity of the case?"

" Well," said the bowyer; " but the disease—the malignant—the contagious—the—the ——"

" Nothing," said the officer. " Your friend here has as little of anything contagious about him as you in the way of disease. His evil arises from injuries. I tell you he was picked up insensible in the road."

The bowyer recollected that what with his anxiety, he might well, with the blows he had received, become seriously ill, and therefore he said,—

" I will take him home at once. He is no doubt very bad. Will you send some of your men with him? I have none at hand, and time may be of great consequence to him."

" Be it so. He shall be at once conveyed between a double file of men, and you can show them the way to his abode."

" I will," said the bowyer.

In a very short while, Shore was laid upon a sort of palanquin, which was supported by six men of the city-guard, at the head of whom marched the bowyer. There was some curiosity manifested by the citizens at this strange procession. The soldiers moved forward through the city; and with them the bowyer, who looked as if he had the command of the party. Then they made their way through Fleet-street, and thence to Lombard-street; and when they arrived at the house of Shore, they stopped before it, and a great crowd had collected, and Master Snafflings was besieged by one and the other.

" Master Snafflings," said one; " what ails our good neighbour, Master Shore?"

" Good Master Snafflings," said another; " wherefore do these men besiege our neighbour's door?"

" Is Master Shore dead, good Master Snafflings; or has he committed treason, that the guard have surrounded his house?"

" Be quiet, good neighhours, our friend Shore hath a bad accident."

" An accident?"

" Yes."

" And what has he done?"

" Nothing, neighbour," said the impatient bowyer; " it is not at all likely that he would do anything, seeing he is insensible."

" Insensible!"

" Yes—quite."

" Goodness, neighbour, has Master Shore fallen down in a fit—eh?"

" He has been robbed and maltreated, and left all but dead by the way-side."

" Poor Master Shore, it will be a sad blow to his beautiful wife. She will cry her beautiful eyes out. Oh, Master Shore is a happy man to have such a beautiful and witty wife; she is a pattern to all ranks."

" Yes," said another; " there are few women so gifted by nature as she."

" You say right; she is good and beautiful, and it must be a dreadful thing for her to see her husband come home in such a state."

Little did they at that moment think, to what cause the state he was in was owing; little did they think to what a forlorn home he had come to, and the loss he had just suffered; and the welcome he had to receive, was only what himself could give.

Little could they suspect the misery and wretchedness that surrounded him on all sides—a misery all his wealth could not purchase a repression of, for only a short interval.

Yes, they little dreamed of the change that had so far come over the spirit of the scene, and which had rendered wretched a suspicious and hasty man's home, and Shore's home was like to become much worse from the very occurrence taking place, that he, from his own jealousy, constantly went about in fear of. He could not well recover from such a blow as this, and no doubt it would have such an effect upon a man of his temperament, that he would never perfectly recover from it.

It was some minutes before they could get into the shop; for Master Shore had left no one there, save the deaf housekeeper, who was leisurely enough in all concerns, and especially in that of hearing.

At length she came and opened the door and gaped in astonishment, when she saw the number of persons on the outside.

" Oh, sirs," she exclaimed, " you have mistaken my master's house for the guard-house. I pray you not to stay here."

" Come, come, good dame," said the bowyer, stepping forward; " we bring your master home to you, we have him here."

" Have who?"

" Why, your master."

" He didn't say anything about it," said the housekeeper, rather surprised, with a notion that they wanted to leave some wounded person there.

"This is your master," said the bowyer.

"Where?" exclaimed the housekeeper.

"Come," said the bowyer to the soldiers; "come in; we cannot stand here, endeavouring to let an old woman recover her hearing again—come in and follow me. Shut the door though."

So saying, he pushed the old housekeeper on one side, and then they entered the house, they passed by the old woman, who was struck with amazement at this piece of audacity; but then she saw her master, for they lowered him when they had got in the passage.

"Oh!" she exclaimed; "you have got him with you. Oh! what's the matter with him, who has done this thing to him?"

"Master Shore," said Snafflings, "has met with an accident, and has, for all we know, met with his death-blow. We must put him to bed at once, therefore get it ready."

"Come this way," said the housekeeper, who preceded them to her master's sleeping-room, having an instinctive knowledge that it was there they wished to place him.

They placed him on his bed, and then the bowyer said to the archers,—

"Now, good fellows, I must thank you for your assistance; all that can be done has been done, and now we must send for a leech. Return to your quarters, and report to your captain that he is in safe keeping."

The archers departed.

"Now," said Snafflings, "you must send for a leech; for he will require the aid of a skilful one. He has been in this state for several hours, and I think he is very much hurt."

"Alas!" said the housekeeper, "I know no leech. Master Shore never cared for such, and, in relation to himself, he never needed have one. He used to say there was much more danger in taking their drugs, besides expense, than there was in allowing the disease to run its course."

"But this is altogether a case of necessity," replied the bowyer. "Whom does he ever send to in case of any sudden emergency?"

"To whom? indeed, to nobody that ever I knew of. He never had one."

"Then I must seek for some one myself; the man cannot be left to die thus, like a dog, for want of decent care and attention. Yes, yes, he must have a leech."

So saying, he turned from the bed; but before he left the room he returned to say,—

"Now, good dame, let everything be so ordered that nothing be wanted that is usually required in the case of sickness."

Snafflings then left the house in search of a leech, and soon after returned with one, to whom he related all that had occurred.

"Oh!" said the leech, "there is much to apprehend in this case. I expect there will be fever and delirium. We must have care; his head must be shaved, and some blood taken."

The bleeding seemed to have the effect of causing a partial return of the senses, though not of that sense which enables a man to converse, and recognise those that are around him.

Shore, when he was able to speak, raved and tossed about. He called for Jane; he seemed to dream, to think, and to rave only about Jane.

"Jane, where are you? Jane —wife—Mrs. Shore—here, come to me. Come back, my beautiful Jane—come back, and no one shall reproach you. Oh, Jane, do not leave me here to die!"

And thus he would rave for hours at a time. The leech would call and see his patient; but no amendment seemed to take place, and Master Shore was reduced to mere bones. There he lay, with a slow fever burning and consuming life's energies, and his brain disordered.

It was a sickly sight, to see even that man stretched upon the bed of sickness, and no one sitting by his couch to give him the required attendance—the many little tender offices that most men can obtain when laid prostrate on a bed of sickness such as this.

No kind wife was near, to moisten the parched lips, the burning brow. No one was there to give the bitter draught, with fervent hopes of a recovery, that it would do the sufferer good—that, in fact, he would be well again.

The old housekeeper attended upon him, for well she knew that he would have admitted none, and when he was sensible, it would retard his perfect recovery to have another about him.

In spite of all things, however, the goldsmith began to recover, though very slowly, and he was very weak and almost doubled up.

His lank and lean body was wretchedly so when he first sat up. He could scarcely be recognised as the same man who had before been the thrifty goldsmith.

But what were his thoughts when he first came to be conscious of the bereavement he had suffered by the loss of his wife, can be better conceived than described.

CHAPTER LXXIII.

Shore's Convalescence.

SHORE was now recovering from the effect of his late illness. He had recovered; but some weeks had passed over his head, while he was nearly insensible to the care which his old housekeeper had paid, or the attentions of the leech. His recovery was slow and gradual, and the changes appeared to be of such a character that they were rather felt than seen.

His whole person was more attenuated, and careworn, and miserly than before, while there was an appearance of a restless, unsettled state of mind, evinced by the shifty and unsteady motion of his eye, which was ever watching and looking about from side to side, whether he were alone, or in the presence of any of his friends.

His friends, too, were unwilling to inform him of the worst. He was well aware that his wife had left him, but he had yet to learn for whom. His friends had, as yet, preserved that from him; for his love for Jane was so great, that he would endeavour to recall her to a sense of her duty, and take her back again, could she be induced to accept any of his propositions.

It was deemed advisable to say nothing about it, until it should be absolutely necessary and safe to communicate the fact to him.

Master Snafflings was standing at his door, just preparing to walk out and call upon Master Shore, and see how he was getting on. He had not called or heard of him for two whole days.

"It is time I went to the poor man," thought Snafflings to himself. "He had a terrible bereavement; at least he thinks so, though, God help me! I know some people as would run the risk of breaking their necks, provided it would unyoke them; and I am not too happy; but I mustn't think of this when I'm at home."

"Ha! Master Snafflings," said a loud voice behind him; "how fare you this morning? Quite well, eh?"

The bowyer turned round to see who it was that had thus saluted him; for he had been too much occupied with his own thoughts to recognize the voice of him who spoke; for Master Snafflings had had a matrimonial squabble before he got out, which suggested thoughts to his mind that were farther from the fact than the desire.

"Oh, Master Brook! is it you? I am right glad to see you. Why, it is many days since we met."

"A few weeks, Master Snafflings."

"I believe it is. How are you in health now—as hearty as usual, Master Brook? You look well."

"And I am well, Master Snafflings. Give me your hand."

The two citizens shook hands heartily for some minutes, when the new comer said,—

"What news—what news? I have been absent in Yorkshire for some weeks, and now I am as a stranger in my native city."

"I see you want to make believe that you have forgotten you ever were a citizen."

"No, no, Master Snafflings. How are Master Shore and his beautiful wife, Jane? Is he as jealous as ever?"

"What! do you not know that there has been a great calamity there?"

"No. Any one dead?"

"Not exactly that, though something near it; and yet something Master Shore would about prefer, I dare say; not that I would, for if any one would run away with ——"

"Eh?"

"Ah, well! it's a sad thing for Master Shore, at all events."

"Indeed! what is it you speak of? Tell me the tale, will you, Master Suaffling, or must I hear it from anybody else? for if it be generally, or even partially known, I am sure to know of it before long, you see."

"It isn't that I hesitate to tell you, good Master Brook; but I hardly know how to tell it. You, see Master Brook, Master Shore and his wife did not live more happily than many a better matched pair live in these days."

"I see; I know they are somewhat opposed to each other. In all the usual points they ought to assimilate—such as age and temper, inclinations, tastes, and love; in all these things they differed; though I have known many others who have been as opposed, and yet agree."

"Ah!" said the bowyer, "I dare say you have; but beshrew me if I believe it real; it is all hypocrisy—all, Master Brook; but that's neither fish nor flesh. They have, since you left London, parted."

"Parted?"

"Yes."

"Mutually?"

"Why, in some measure, the separation was mutual, because they were both apart. However fair Mistress Jane proved, as many a one before her has proved, as false as fair."

"You don't mean to say that, good Master Snafflings? Why, it is shocking to human nature to think one so beautiful should be so very deceitful."

"But it is so."

"And what did Master Shore say to such a proceeding?"

"Oh, poor man, I hardly know what happened; but he went frantic, sought for her everywhere, but she was to be found nowhere. He was laid up long with a dangerous illness."

"Has anything been heard of Mistress Jane?"

"Oh, it is notorious."

"I mean does Shore know where his frail wife is? Who has she chosen for her paramour in this affair?"

"Can you imagine who?"

"No."

The bowyer looked one way and then another, to see if he were unobserved; when, seeing all was clear, he said, in a tone of voice that much alarmed Master Brook,—

"It is Edward the Fourth who has stolen Mistress Shore."

"The king?"

"Yes."

"Mercy!"

"And admit no strange customers to the presence of your wife, if she be young, handsome, and frail, which last you never discover until it is too late; therefore take heed at first."

"I see, it is good advice; but is Shore aware of who it is that has done him this wrong?"

"I think not; he may suspect; but if he did, I doubt if he now remembers it. I am somehow puzzled to know what to do."

"Inform him of that fact, and then he may make up his mind that his wife will never more think of him. She is by far too well off to think of such a man as Shore, and, moreover, she is too much surrounded by gaieties of all kinds, and costly magnificence, to think of her tarnished fame. A royal lover has charms sufficient to gild even that."

"In truth you speak correctly enough; especially does it so appear to a woman young and beautiful as she was. But I am going to Shore now, and shall see what frame of mind I find him in, and act accordingly; but some one may have been there before me, and informed him of it. I abstained from doing it solely because I would not risk anything serious."

"When you see him give him Master Brook's greeting, and say that I commiserate his misfortune; but she was unworthy of him. He is rich, and may purchase many pleasures that may serve him to win his mind back to, at least, contentment or indifference towards his misfortunes."

"I will, I will, Master Brook. Good-even to you."

"Good-even, Master Snafflings, and may you never have to regret such a loss."

"No surely I never should," soliloquized Snafflings. "If my helpmate was to die, what a happy widower I should make; but that never will be. I'm fixed as fate, and must put up with it."

He now arrived at the goldsmith's house, where he was admitted by the old housekeeper, to whom he said,—

"Well, dame, how is Master Shore to-day—any better?"

"Oh, ay," said the old woman, who was as deaf as ever, "the day is, as you say, very well; but Master Shore wants to speak with you—he's waiting quite impatiently to see you."

"Indeed! good dame, then show me to him, I pray you."

The old woman led the way to the apartment in which Shore was waiting to see, Master Snafflings. She had not heard the last injunction, but did what was desired knowing it to be necessary and desired by the visitor.

"Master Shore," said Snafflings, as he entered the room, "Master Shore, may I give you joy of your complete restoration to health; you can walk out now; you will gather strength from the exercise."

"This has been a severe shock, Master Snafflings; a severe shock; but Heaven be praised! I have got over it so far, and shall now be able to seek her."

"Seek her!"

"Yes."

"Whom?"

"Jane; yes, Master Snafflings, I must seek her, I grieve to confess it; and yet I cannot do otherwise. I cannot live without her, false, shameless, and polluted as she is. I must find her out, and must do something to rescue so much beauty from the depth of misery to which she must ultimately fall into, unless I can save her. Advise me, good Master Snafflings; advise me to do this, and help me to do it."

"I am sorry I cannot, Master Shore; believe me, you had better pursue this matter no further; your honour, and that of your friends will urge your adopting this advice. Forget her—forget her."

"Forget her!" said Shore, in a deep, suppressed voice; "I would I had never seen her; then I should never have had this misery to suffer. I wish I could tear her from my heart though I parted with my life-blood at the time. No, no, Master Snafflings, I cannot forget her."

"Indeed, Master Shore, you must; if not per advice yet per force. I am ill at concealing things—but tell me, do you know where your wife is to be found if you could go to her?"

"No; but I suppose some minion of the court ——"

"You do not know, or have not heard?" said Snafflings, earnestly.

"If I have I have no recollection of it; all is a blank in my mind. There are many things I know to have passed, and that I have heard, and yet the only sure thing I can remember is my loss, and the only one I can think of is her recovery, and restoration to my arms."

"And that will never be," said Snafflings, positively.

"Never be?" said Shore, looking up; "never be, Master Snafflings—never be? is Mistress Jane dead?" said Shore, turning a shade yellower than he was.

"Dead to you, Master Shore."

"And why dead to me?"

"Because she is with one whom you can never hope to withdraw her from. She will never return."

"Never! never!" said Shore.

"No—never."

"Tell me where is she, then, since you know so much?"

"I do know so much," said the bowyer, "but did not like to tell you until I knew you were strong enough to bear the news I have to tell you."

"I am as strong as I shall be. I shall remember better; my constitution is broken up more, and my mind with it, for I dream all night, and think all day. I strive to remember my dreams, lest they may be true. I have dreamt it, Master Snafflings, or I may have been told, but I am sure it has haunted me in my sleep, that Jane was with the king."

"And that is true."

"True!"

"Yes; as true Master Shore as we are mortal men. Depend upon it, you can do no good in that quarter, for Edward is too successful among the fair dames of London."

Shore groaned aloud, and covering his face with his hands for some moments, he shook as though an ague had seized him.

"It is no dream," he murmured; "it is no dream, and yet I had hoped it were otherwise; but are you sure, Master Snafflings, are you sure?"

"I am sure the whole town is rank with it."

"God help me—God help me!" sighed the bereaved man. "I would now I had confined her to her own chamber, under lock and key."

"And who would care to have such a one even under lock and key? Who could place his love on one so frail, or his honour in the keeping of one who could not even guard her own?"

"Oh! Master Snafflings, you knew her not as I knew her. You knew not her beauty

—her loveliness. I can never banish her from my mind; she will be there as long as my body and life hold together. God! I love her yet."

"You must learn to forget her—forget the past—forget what she was, but remember what she is."

"The knowledge of the one is accompanied by the other. The remembrance of the past makes the present more bitter. The present will form a terrible contrast to the past. I would I could forget; but as well might the doomed one escape from madness, as I escape from the damning reflections that follow the contemplation of the past and future. Oh! Snafflings, this has been my severest blow through life. I shall never recover it."

"Try; engage in business; turn your attention to money-making; try anything. You can purchase delights—pleasures. You are rich, Master Shore."

"And even I cared nothing for these things, save for her. My riches have lost all their value for me. When she was here they were invaluable, and the only one thing

more I sought; but they were for her, to deck her dainty form. Alas! I have been too fond and devoted."

"But she never loved you, Master Shore. What can you expect?"

"Constancy to the marriage vow is not so rare a virtue, I presume," said Shore, sharply, "that it would have been too much to expect it in her. Without it woman is valueless—a mere painted toy."

"And being such, you cannot risk life, health, and wealth, for such a thing. You cannot, Master Shore."

"Ah, Master Snafflings, as I said before, you knew her not as I knew her. She had a thousand pretty ways with her—in fact, she was not as other women. Oh, Jane!—Jane!"

Master Snafflings, ill qualified as he was to make any protracted efforts at consolation, was conscious that he had outdone himself upon this occasion, and could do no more. He looked upon the unfortunate goldsmith with eyes of pity, yet he could not but think that he had gone crazed when he heard him give way thus.

"Well, well," he murmured; "I can do no more. You are fit now to take upon yourself the management of your own affairs, and the direction of your own acts; but I can only warn you not to attempt to go near the court. Should you do so, the result would be unsafe to you. King Edward would not mind finding some means of quietly putting any one out of the way that gave him any trouble."

"The man he had most injured!"

"Yes; that would be one of the greatest additional motives that he could find, seeing it would get rid, not only of a troublesome man, but one who might seek reparation. Depend upon it, you would not be safe."

"I know not—I care not," said Shore, in a paroxysm of despair.

"Farewell, then, Master Shore—farewell; and God speed you!"

"Farewell," said Shore, "and may Heaven avert such a calamity from your house as that which will now haunt me until I find the repose of the grave. Farewell, good Master Snafflings; but take this ring in token of my estimation of the good offices I have received at your hands. Farewell!"

So saying, Shore drew off his hand a valuable ring, which he handed to Snafflings, who took it.

"Farewell!" he said, "farewell; and may peace and quietude yet find their way to your breast."

So saying, Master Snafflings left the unhappy goldsmith to the tortures of his own disordered imagination.

Long did the unfortunate and jealous-minded Shore rock himself to and fro on his chair, and look around him from time to time, and recalling every now and then some one trait of his wife's character on lighting upon some one thing that she used, or more particularly fancied, until he became almost distracted in his mind.

"I will go out, I will go out," he murmured; "this is madness—my brain whirls, and I shall lose my senses. Oh, God! what a thing it would be to find myself under the restraint of a madhouse. Oh, Jane, Jane! you cannot know the misfortunes and miseries you have brought on me."

Terrified at his own situation, he rose up, seizing his coat and hat, hurried out of the house, which alarmed the housekeeper, who hobbled after him, exclaiming,—

"He's mad—sure, he's mad! Master Shore—master—he's gone—he's gone; well, if he ain't brought home again, it'll be a mercy. St. Anthony preserve us! 'tis the first time he has been out since his illness, and I'll warrant he's gone to seek Mistress Jane. Ah! well, he'd better leave her alone; she's a loose fish now, and has skated away."

With this pithy remark to herself, she returned along the passage and resumed her domestic duties.

In the meantime, the goldsmith went from place to place, hurrying forward at a rapid rate, having no object and no end to his journey.

Hence, in a few hours, he had thoroughly and entirely fatigued himself. Indeed, it is astonishing how thoroughly tired a human being gets after walking rapidly about for several hours, without cessation or object. Shore did not for some time feel it—those emotions of the mind which hurried him onward, made him insensible to the feeling of fatigue, until his mind became exhausted by its own efforts of thought, and then he was compelled to seek his own home.

Tired with extreme exertion, mental and bodily, he threw himself upon the bed, and then, without feeling any other want than rest, he fell asleep, without speaking to any one.

In this state he remained until early the following morning, when he awoke, recovered in body, but his mental disorder was as great as ever.

"Business," he muttered, "cannot be attended to. It would be a farce to keep open the shop. I'll give it up; I have no heart to seek more gold; and yet there was a time when I loved it more than anything mortal; but now it is mere dross, I care not for it. I cannot live here. I must go elsewhere; time, travel, and change of scene may do me good; but I'll no longer remain a citizen of London, to be looked upon as poor Master Shore, who was bereaved of his wife.

"No, no; I would have done much to have saved her, but, alas! it cannot be done! Master Snafflings spoke truly when he said 'twould be dangerous to attempt to recall her to her duty, for, succeed or not succeed, my life must follow as a forfeit; but she would not be turned, she had too magnificent, too splendid and gorgeous a scene to quit, such as would dazzle any woman, much more one young, beautiful, and, perhaps, vain. No, no; let her live, let her live and enjoy the present, she shall never see me, or know that I have suffered so much; for to do what she has done would argue an utter insensibility to my sufferings, and, therefore, she would smile upon my pangs. I will leave London, I will leave England, and, in a foreign travel, I will endeavour to forget all I once knew."

To the surprise of all, Master Shores's business fell off; indeed, the goldsmith's shop had scarce been opened since his recovery, and even the old housekeeper thought that things were very strange.

Shore, however, was each day effecting some part of his scheme of travel, of conveying away his treasures, and depositing in places of safety, his accumulated hoards of wealth.

Some of this he resolved to take with him, as he would not only require it; but he would still carry on some merchandise in the foreign countries he would visit, and, moreover, it would form an excuse for traversing dominions that otherwise he would scarce pass through in safety.

"My character of a merchant will be an answer to all inquiries. I may prosper; at all events, 'tis all I can do. I must arrange matters with some merchants in this city, to transmit me my treasure, or so much of it as I may, from time to time, require."

These arrangements he from that time began to make. He deposited his treasure with some of the richest merchants, both English and Jews, and this took him some few weeks to perform.

During this time his friends saw but little of him. They believed he was going to decay, and regretted his downfall, not so much for Shore's own sake, as from the cause, it being one which came home to every man's hearth.

At length the shop was shut up, and the citizens would say as they passed the place, and look up at the dismal-looking house—for it had recently become so, as though the very bricks had become aware of the intended desertion, and put on a more gloomy look than before, as if anticipating the peculiar appearance of an empty house,—

"Ha! there was as rich and thriving a trade as any in London; but now it is gone to wreck and ruin. The owner is a distracted man, and goods and valuables are fast fleeting away. How terribly some people's domestic affairs interfere with their business. Had it been my lot, neighbour, I'd have tried to put up with the loss, and consoled myself as well as I could."

"And so would I. Nay, I'd give a handsome sum if any one would permanently deprive me of my domestic dragon."

"And yet she's pretty."

"Ay, so I thought before I married her; but, somehow or other, familiarity breeds contempt. What her face may do, why, her tongue undoes, which was not so during courtship."

"That's very true, and hence it is there is so much change in husbands after marriage."

"Ay, there's changes on both sides. But come on, neighbour, we waste our time in contemplating Master Shore's miseries. All I say is, he is a ruined man, and though she never loved him, and the marriage was ill advised, he didn't deserve to receive his undoing at such hands."

The two worhty citizens, who had been walking by Shore's house, but had paused a moment or so to contemplate it, now resumed their walk on business.

* * * * * * *

It was early one morning, while Master Snafflings was busy in his shop, polishing bows and bow cases, when some one entered the shop. It was, we have said, very early; the shop had not been open many minutes, and the worthy bowyer could not see very well, for it was very dark, and he used a lamp to aid him in his work.

Hearing some one's footsteps, he turned round to see who the new comer was. The manner in which houses were then built, was upon the plan, apparently, of depriving the lower story of all the light they could, and the bowyer shaded his eyes with his hands a moment, before he could tell who it was.

"Master Snafflings."

"Ah! Master Shore, I didn't know you in that dress; you are out betimes this morning."

"I am," said Shore, in a hollow voice.

"Has anything happened—anything the matter?" inquired Snafflings, surprised at the voice and appearance of Shore.

"No, good Master Snafflings—nothing happened that could be prevented. I came thus early to bid you farewell!"

"Farewell?"

"Yes. You have done me some service; and I could not leave London—aye, England, without coming to bid you farewell. I shall see no one else, it would only tear open afresh wounds that I would not have probed, for each time I feel fresh agony, and each time more acutely than the first."

"You going to leave England, Master Shore?" said the bowyer, much amazed. "Surely you need not go to such an extremity as that? Consider the dangers of the voyage, and after that the dangers that are so plenty in foreign countries that beset merchants on every side."

"I have bethought myself of all this," replied Shore; "I have no other means of preserving my existence. I must leave London and England for awhile. I know she is here living in splendour, nay, perhaps, in happiness. I can never preserve my reason. God, what a wrong for a man to suffer, and yet compelled to put up with, and yet not even seek redress for so grievous a wrong."

"Think no more of that subject, Master Shore, and if you must go I'll not say anything to prevent it. I wish you a safe voyage, and a pleasant time of it, and a safe and happy return."

"Ah, about that we'll say nothing. I may or may not. I cannot conceive why I should; but it is all in the hands of fate, Master Snafflings. Farewell!"

"Farewell!" replied Snafflings; and without saying more, Shore turned round, and slowly quitted the bowyer's shop. He left London and proceeded to France, and for some years he was not heard of by any of his friends.

CHAPTER LXXIV.

Jane Shore lives in the Splendour of the Court.

WHAT a different life now dawned upon Jane Shore, while misery and sorrow sat heavy on the head of her husband. All that was fair and magnificent met her view, all that could entrance the senses were at her command, and Edward was so enchanted with his new mistress, that he gave up all other pleasure for that of her society.

Her power over the king was complete, and he, too, one of the most, if not the most amorous monarch that ever sat on the English throne, and proverbially fickle also.

Strange to say that he should thus suddenly become not only fascinated and swayed by so charming a woman, he who of all men had the greatest opportunities and facilities for being inconstant, but that he should be more true in his love for her than any of the high-born court beauties who were considered more likely, from tact and talent, to enchain the erratic fancy of such a monarch. Yet so it was, Jane effected, apparently without art or effort, all that others had in vain endeavoured to achieve by the utmost address.

There were none of the courtiers, even Hastings himself, but who expected that she would share the fate of the king's other mistresses, and he was somewhat surprised when he perceived that the king not only maintained the same appearance of tenderness towards her, but that he really felt it, and he, moreover, gave up his other mistresses, and sought no new ones.

This to the gay courtiers of Edward's court was a matter of surprise, and, after awhile, produced much badinage amongst them, as the king's constancy was a thing they could not understand.

Amid the many predictions of her downfall, Jane continued to tread her even course. She saw the king's love for her was great, nay, that it had no limit; and her power of doing good or evil was also boundless. Jane chose the former.

The disposition of Jane was naturally amiable and tender. She could not bear to look upon misfortune; she could not hear the cry of distress, without affording relief; she could not be implored for mercy without doing something towards soothing the unhappy object of commiseration.

Perhaps, in all this there might have been the thought that her own position was not the securest—that she, too, might topple down from her present power, and stand in need of that aid she dispensed to many.

Perhaps, also, the thought that in the multitude of good deeds her own equivocal position might be gilded—that, in fact, her shameless abandonment of her husband's roof might be hidden from the eyes of men, while only her good deeds might be seen—

that, in fact, the one voice, that of her husband, crying for justice and revenge, should be hushed amidst the tumult of her praises.

Many, if not a due proportion of all of these motives, no doubt, had their weight with her; and we may lay, perhaps, more stress upon the fact, that the feelings that arose at the time had no small share in the scale, the preponderance of which was the ruling motive to acts of charity, goodness, and mercy.

Perhaps Edward, too, was charmed with this constant exercise of discreet power, uniformly on the side which enlists the feelings of the gentle and amiable; and this tended much to bind together those affections she had succeeded in gaining.

It soon became known among the courtiers that Jane Shore was the king's favourite mistress, that he each day showed her more and more affection, that, in short, nothing was wanting that a monarch could bestow, save those rights which would have made her a queen in name, while she was such in fact.

When all this was perceived, Jane was soon besieged by those who had any suit to make, or anything to gain, or who desired to escape the king's anger, or to obtain his favour—all alike sought her.

She was lodged by her royal paramour in the most imperial style. Nothing could be thought of that was not there to minister to her comfort, ease, or pleasure, and every sense had its appropriate gratification.

Jane's first suit to the king was one of mercy; but we will relate it as it occurred.

Hastings, who had never, since his royal master had become possessed of Jane, approached her but with the utmost respect, and had discarded all thoughts of love towards her, as inimical to himself, one morning sent a letter to her by an aged woman. Jane was informed that some one desired to see her, and that she had been driven away more than once, but it had been ascertained that she was the bearer of a letter from Lord Hastings to herself.

"Let me have it," she replied.

"But the old woman will not let it go out of her own possession, and insists, moreover, that she must see you, and she won't go away."

"Cannot you ascertain what is the nature of the errand?" said Jane.

"We have tried, but can get nothing out of her, save tears. She is very urgent to see you."

"Well, then, admit her," said Jane; "we must hear what she may have to say, the more especially as she bears a letter from my Lord of Hastings."

The old woman was accordingly admitted, after a short delay. She appeared to be suffering from some deep grief, for her eyes were red and swollen; but she advanced respectfully towards Jane, and presented Lord Hastings' letter.

"Whom do you bring this from, my good dame?" she inquired.

"From the noble Marquis of Hastings; and he bade me give it into your own hands only."

Jane read the letter. It was to beg her interest in behalf of the old woman's son, whose story would be seen from what the mother would relate; but every word was true, and he could himself vouch for it. Knowing her influence with the king, he had sent the old woman to plead her own cause in person.

"And what is it you desire of me, my good dame?" inquired Jane, kindly; "what I can do for you I will, as much for the noble marquis's sake as for that of justice and mercy."

"Oh, kind and gentle lady! you see before you a bereaved parent—a widow, whose only hope is in her lost and only son."

"Well, good dame, go on."

"I had seven sons, lady, and they have all died in the service of his present majesty, save one."

"Alas! that is a sad loss—a loss hard to bear."

"Yes, lady, it was hard to bear; and the only consolation I had, was, that they died in defence of their king, his present majesty, Edward the fourth."

"Indeed! that was some consolation, if such can exist, for the loss of those so near and dear to you; but it must be a consolation."

"It is, and the only one; but it is of my remaining son that I would beg your interposition and good offices with the king."

"And on what account? What has he been doing? or, perhaps, it is some post he desires?"

"No, lady, no! he has been led astray, and has been found in the company of conspirators. I know not, even, if he be guilty, for they will not let me see him. I have tried, but have been rudely pushed back. If he suffer, then, indeed, I am lone and desolate, and have nothing but beggary before me."

"He supported you then?"

"He did, and so did they, when they lived; but, alas! they are dead, and unless you can avert the doom that now hangs over the head of my last and only son, I shall never more know what happiness is."

Jane was much affected by the old woman's manners and depth of feeling which appeared in her actions and manners. She bade her be of good cheer and to return home, and if all that she had told her were true, she would see her son, or hear from him; she, Jane, would do her best to intercede for her with the king.

"Thanks, generous and kind lady," said the old woman, tears falling fast; "words cannot express my feelings and gratitude for this."

* * * * * * *

Jane, afterwards, related all the particulars to the king, who staid, at her earnest entreaty, the execution of the unfortunate young man, and the circumstances being inquired into, it was discovered that they were all strictly true. The old woman's son was pardoned, and a gratuity given her for the loss she had sustained in the service of the state.

By such actions as these, Jane won golden opinions, and Edward never refused her a favour, which is good proof that those she asked, were such as he could grant, and that she never abused her power, for she never took presents or bribes, as others have done.

Nor was her power bounded by mere acts of mercy and charity towards the poor. Among the courtiers, and on the most important matters, her influence was sought, and often exercised; but never in a bad cause or bad motive.

Such a life as this was sure to bring down upon her the good will of all classes; and none who saw her and conversed with her but were charmed with her affability, and were never known to express any jealousy of the power it was within her sphere to exert over King Edward.

Indeed it was often considered advantageous; for, though the talents of Edward were splendid and showy, yet he was inclined to be cruel and revengeful; but men who have been embroiled in civil war generally are, and the exceptions were not at all numerous in these times.

Contrary to all belief, she long retained the affection of the king, and, whatever intrigues were carried on were done with his sanction or knowledge. Indeed the king would retire to the apartments of Jane to pass away whole hours in conversation and gentle dalliance; nothing could exceed the love and harmony that subsisted between the royal ov er and his gentle mistress.

CHAPTER LXXV.

Jane meets with an Old Lover.

SUMMER and winter had passed, the change of the seasons had marked the annual revolution of the sun, and a second year appeared, and had progressed, and yet Jane Shore held the affections of Edward the Fourth as firmly as she had on the first time they met. In her the monarch found one whom he could love, and on whom he could lavish all his caresses and confidence, without any fear of guile or deceit.

And she, too, during all this time, had not received one check to her happiness. Indeed she appeared to be the happiest being about Edward.

In private it may be presumed that she had moments when recollection would recall the past from memory's cells, but of that no one knew anything, and saw nothing.

If she thought of the past, it might be but to compare it with the present, and then she had nothing to regret. See what a contrast!

Could any comparison be more unfortunate for the goldsmith, her husband, than the parallel between him and her present lover! none on earth—neither personally nor in the home she had, and the palace she now enjoyed.

Shore was jealous, and beyond her age considerably; he was miserly and parsimonious though rich, and he was all in this respect what Edward was not.

Edward, on the other hand, was the highest person in the kingdom, generous to profusion, and loved her fondly, but with the love of a young man.

Could the contrast between the present and past be more complete; nay, the worst was the past; and, being such, was the weakest in effect upon the mind, while the present was all joy and sunshine, and anything that could make life worth living for; this was the present, and, of course, the most impressed upon her mind.

Her sorrows and regrets, therefore, could be but very faint, and very seldom exercised; not that Jane forgot entirely those to whom she had formerly been obliged; they received benefits from an unseen hand, but they knew whence the gift came.

These, and many other traits in her character, endeared her to all who knew her, and, at the same time, those who would have been more forward and willing to detract from her ordinary merits, and traduce her, were disarmed of their weapons, and malice could do no more than point to the one great breach of moral law, which it is more than possible that, had they been fair enough to have had the opportunity, they would have done the same thing.

Because people are good, virtuous, and discreet, it is not to be imagined that they are so much so, that a deviation from these qualities is impossible; far from it—there has never been a sufficient temptation.

However, Jane was universally admitted, on all hands, to be as sensible as she was beautiful, and as gentle as she was kind and commiserate. Jealousy was disarmed of its sting, and detraction of its malignity, and none could be said to bear her any ill-will.

* * * * * * *

One fine morning, as Jane was seated at the window of her own room in the palace; it was one in which there was a charming look out; a prospect could be had of the palace gardens, while beyond the walls, were hills and trees in the distance. A balcony ran beneath it, terminating with some steps that had been placed there on purpose to permit Jane to wander over these gardens at leisure, and also to permit the king to enter her chamber without the necessity of going through the palace at a different point.

Jane was sitting at the window, and her eyes wandered over the beautiful scene beneath, when suddenly a shadow darkened the path; she looked again, but it had vanished.

While she was occupied in imagining a cause for this, the same appearance occurred again. This time she observed the form of a man, enveloped in a cloak, and a slouched hat drawn over his brow, to conceal both form and feature.

Jane knew that it was an unusual thing to see any one in that part of the royal gardens; and, moreover, it was especially at such a time and so attired, and, evidently, desirous of concealing himself.

Pondering what could be the cause of this strange occurrence, she was suddenly startled from her reverie by the entrance of a stranger from the balcony into her apartment.

For a moment he paused and looked at her earnestly, and a struggle seemed to be going on within his breast, caused by some contending emotions, the cause of which she could not know, or even his object in thus entering her apartment.

"What means this intrusion?" at length said Jane, though she felt a strange choking sensation at her throat.

"Intrusion!" said the stranger, in a hollow voice.

"Yes; you are unknown to me, and it would cost you dear if you are found here."

"It may. I do not dispute it; but I shall not regret it. I have spent time enough in getting thus far, and now my errand is done."

"Who are you? I know you not, and why do you come here?"

The stranger threw off his hat and cloak, and at once revealed himself.

"Walter Fane!" exclaimed Jane.

"The same," replied Walter Fane, in the same hollow tone, that spoke of the strong emotion under which he laboured.

Jane continued to gaze upon him with a mixture of pity and sorrow, and she felt some remains of a former feeling, that had since been dormant, because others had taken its place.

"Yes," he said; "I am Walter Fane, and I have but little to thank man that I am yet Walter Fane."

"Indeed!"

"Yes; my life has been sought, my prospects have been destroyed, every hope blighted, and my happiness blasted, never to revive; and yet I live."

"You are yet young, and may expect a long and honourable career."

"I an honourable career! Oh, Jane, Jane! you can know but little of the fire that consumes my very soul, and sears my brain. I can do nothing. I am fit for nothing but to die; and yet I could not even do that without again seeing you."

"It were better you had not done so, Walter; this may bring mischief upon you and me."

"Oh, no! no one is near; Jane, dear Jane, my heart beats as it did of yore; your form has never been erased from my heart, and yet God knows what I have suffered, or what I did suffer when—when I heard——"

"Say no more," said Jane; "what is done cannot be undone; let bygones be bygones, and hasten home."

"No, no, Jane, hear me; I bore your marriage, though it drove me mad. It was a thing that one could not help; others had the disposal of the events which no other did or would control, but my heart was nigh bursting with grief; but when I heard that you had left the house of your husband for the king, a great pang then shot through my heart, for the beautiful and idolized being of my heart had sunk to a greater depth than I could have deemed it at all possible."

"What can all this tend to, Walter?" said Jane; "no good; for if you come here with the intention of upbraiding me, you do me injustice. I heard of your misfortunes, of your imprisonment and danger, and sought to avert it."

"You?"

"Aye, but I met not with the reception I had anticipated. But no more of this; you must go, Walter Fane; you must go."

"I cannot—will not go; look down upon me. Oh, Jane!" he exclaimed, throwing himself upon his knees before her, and taking one of her hands between his own, "how, my love, I fled before those who have sought my life, and only valued my existence that I might one day throw myself at your feet, and beseech you to quit these gay scenes for ever!"

"Hush, hush! Walter Fane, I may not hear this; know you whose place this is?"

"Ah, well—too well; 'tis the royal palace, and the king its owner."

"Do you not know that this may cost you your life?"

"I care not for life or anything else, if it be apart from you. I have passed month after month in concealment of one kind and another, and I have suffered unheard-of misery; but my only hope was in you. The hope of seeing, and one day being with you, cheered me on, and many a danger I encountered with the hope that I should one day be blessed by your smiles; my hopes may be presumptuous and unfounded, but they are what I have said. In some other clime we may live and be happy; a soldier's wife, at least, you may be; I will protect and love you; I cannot offer you a palace, but I can a heart."

"Walter Fane, this is madness; do not let me have cause to grieve for you, for myself; cease this useless conversation—useless, I say—ay, worse than useless, for it is criminal."

"Criminal, Jane!"

"Ay, criminal; it is treason against your king."

"Oh, Heaven! what magic is there in that word to woman's ears; what will not the pomp and magnificence of majesty procure the owner of them! Heaven preserve my brain from reeling under the heavy burthen of thought that now creeps over it."

"Cease—cease—cease!"

"No—no—no, Jane! think not I can see you and feel not all the madness of passion that I once felt, that I now feel, and have never for one moment freed myself of—oh! Jane, Jane!"

"Begone, Walter Fane—oh, begone, before worse comes of it. Say, is there aught that I can do that will aid you—money or employment? Tax my power to aid you, but do not thus cruelly stay here for no other purpose, for none other can be affected than that of causing me to feel that things might have been other than they are."

"Do not think, dear Jane; I will have nothing, take nothing; you, and only you, are all that I ask or care for; do not think I will live but for you."

"How now, traitor! Ah! who have we here?"

The sound of these words caused them both to start, and the next moment the king entered the apartment from the balcony, fury flashing from his eyes, and he was in the act of drawing his sword.

CHAPTER LXXVI.

The King's Promises.

WALTER FANE started to his feet when he heard the words of the king, who now entered the room with his drawn sword, as if with the intention of sacrificing him on the spot, and which, in the anger of the moment, he would undoubtedly have done, but for what followed. Walter Fane moved not from the spot; he was overpowered by various emotions difficult to describe; he could not or would not attempt to escape or defend himself.

"Audacious villain! cannot we prevent the intrusion of such as thou into our most private apartments, traitorously assaulting those within? Take the reward of thy temerity and crime!"

"Sire, your majesty has ever been great and good to me; spare this man's life?"

As she spoke she threw herself upon her knees before the king, and between him and the object of his wrath.

"Jane," said the king, drawing back. "Can this be? Did my eyes deceive me Was not yonder ruffian at your feet? Was he not beseeching you? Was ——"

"All—all is as your majesty says; and yet he knew not what he did. Misfortune—heavy misfortune—has brought him to what he now is; and I fear that much of it will lay heavy on my conscience."

"Come—come, my darling Jane—rise; to see thee a suppliant, that is unusual, and I cannot understand it—my mind misgives me."

"Your majesty has no cause for doubt; Heaven's my witness, I never harboured a thought injurious to your majesty. So good and so generous as you have been to me, it would have been the blackest ingratitude."

"Well, Jane—well, sweet one."

"Spare this young man's life, sire—spare it; else I never shall know ease or happiness more."

"Indeed! Why so warm an interest in this stranger?"

"He was my father's apprentice, and he has done good service to me; he saved me from worse than death—from violence, my good liege."

"Well, Jane, we must not be ungrateful. But I think I remember something of the sort, when we gave an entertainment to our good citizens."

"Yes—yes, your majesty; that was one occasion he perilled his life for me. Then can I feel otherwise than deeply indebted to him?"

"Well, and what would he now?"

"He has been the sport of his enemies ever since—enemies whom he would never have known but for his interference to protect me. Yes, sire, it is needless to mention names; but he has been an inmate of a prison, and doomed to death; and but by the interposition of Heaven alone he has been saved. His prospects are ruined."

"Well, good fellow, we cannot be ungrateful, though our means are less than our subjects' deserts. But, hark ye, come no more here, as you value the life you now have given you."

"My liege," said Walter, dropping on one knee.

"Nay, go thy way; we would hear no more."

"Thanks, your majesty,—do not deem me ungrateful."

"Your majesty has conferred but half a boon," said Jane.

"Ah! what sayest thou? Wouldst thou tax our forbearance yet further? Hast thou feelings stronger than those of gratitude towards this young spark?"

"Impossible, your majesty; but all things flow from your majesty, and I have not the means, without your gracious permission, of even being just, much less grateful."

"What wouldst thou, fair one? Is not life for life a fair repayment? But speak thy mind, I charge thee, so that we may dismiss this gallant."

"It is this, your majesty. His life has been granted him, but the means of keeping it honourably and usefully to himself—to make it even desirable, he has not; he is utterly ruined. Cannot, or will not, your majesty find some honest employment, in which he will honourably serve your majesty, and render life valuable and himself grateful."

"What sayest thou, fellow? Wilt thou serve us truly and faithfully as we grant this prayer?"

"I will do so, your majesty, while life is granted me,—send me where you will, I will faithfully serve you; however distant the clime, I will do it faithfully and willingly. Sire, I thank you."

"You shall have employment in some of our foreign possessions, where your quality and condition will be unknown. You can gain honour and profit."

"Thanks, your majesty—thanks. May I ask one more boon?"

"Oh! what now?"

"Might I take leave of her who has been the cause of so much good fortune to fall upon me?"

The king hesitated, and he gazed steadily and sternly upon him; but Jane interposed, saying,—

"Grant this our last request, your majesty. There can be no danger—it will be the last."

"It shall be the last," muttered the king to himself, and then he added aloud,—

"Even that request will I grant. See, Jane, what hard conditions you exact from us; but this shall be as you desire it; we will not stint or stop at granting thy favours, because 'tis a doing of justice for thee. And yet we cannot help thinking the deed was its own reward, especially as the motive may not have been purely a disinterested one. What sayest thou, fair one?"

"The motive, your majesty, I look not at; but the deed I profited by."

"Ah! so thou didst."

"Moreover, that which followed it—the persecution of this young man—he bore because he had served me. That was not necessary to serve any purpose he could have, your majesty; and, be it remembered, he could not even know that I was acquainted with even a part of his misfortunes; but your majesty's goodness and generosity have relieved me from the obligation under which I laboured."

"Begone, and seek our lodge: and tell those whom you find there to lodge thee for a day or two, until we can provide for thee. Say not another word in our presence, but begone!"

Walter Fane did not dare to dispute this command, which was given in an imperious tone. On the contrary, he bowed low, and, without lifting his eyes even to take a farewell look at Jane,—that Jane whom he was perhaps never to look upon again—he left the apartment as he entered it—by the balcony.

There was a pause of some moments ere either Jane or the king spoke. The latter had withdrawn his eyes from her once or twice, as though he feared to continue to gaze upon her.

"Well," said the king, after waiting for Jane to speak, "how comes it that I found that intruder here?"

"I knew not of his coming, your majesty. I even knew not that he lived."

"How entered he the apartment that none of my people knew aught about it?"

"He concealed himself in the garden; at least, he suddenly came in from the balcony, before I was aware of his intention, and then I knew him not."

"How came he in the garden?"

"That I know not."

"Humph!" said the king.

"Your majesty, I fear, is angry with me; and yet, as I live, I am not deserving of your displeasure. I had not sought this interview. If I had even known it beforehand, I would have prevented it."

"You would, Jane?"

"I would, my liege, as being unprofitable to both, and producing much unhappiness to one. But I am not now sorry for what has happened."

"Ah! what sayest thou?"

"That I regret not that he came here, or that your majesty entered at the time you did."

"Did you fear the spark would have been too pressing in his gratitude?"

"No, your majesty."

"Then why are you satisfied that I came to disturb so quiet a *tete-a-tete* as that which you were enjoying with this young fellow?"

"Because, your majesty, it has relieved me of a heavy debt of gratitude, which I had no means of repaying. He was ruined through me, and became an outcast through me in the world, and suffered from a hopeless passion. Now, however, I have repaired his losses, and returned his obligation; and, for his passion, he must see it is utterly hopeless, and ungrateful on his part to allow it even to exist."

"And are these thy thoughts and feelings, Jane?" inquired Edward.

"Ay, they are, indeed, my generous benefactor and liege."

"Then I will not harbour a thought that injures thee."

"Your majesty will do no less than justice. You think less than becomes yourself. Ingratitude could never live in the breast of one who has had so many proofs of your goodness and munificence."

"Well, well, say no more, sweet Jane, say no more. I believe thee. All this that I have promised shall be done. The young man shall be provided for, and shall take his leave of you."

"Thanks, generous sire."

"But you must not expect to see him again. I shall send him over to Calais or Guienne."

"I would not wish to do so. Having done all that is just, I have no further wish regarding him, save that he should be permanently at a distance."

"I commend your discretion," replied the king.

The subject was then dropped, and the king continued his conversation upon various subjects for some time, until he left the apartment, and proceeded in search of Lord Hastings, his chamberlain, whom he took aside, saying,—

"Hastings, I would speak with you concerning a matter private to myself, in which I have received some vexation."

"Indeed, my liege; I am truly surprised to hear that such is the case, especially in your majesty's private affairs."

"I want your aid, good Hastings."

"My aid is always at your majesty's command when needful."

"And it is needful now."

"Then command me, my liege, and I will cheerfully obey you."

"I know you too well, my lord, to believe otherwise. I have your duty, and your friendship also: and I prize the one equally as I do the other."

"Your majesty is ever gracious. Your good opinion shall never be undeserved," replied Hastings, with a bow at the compliment the king made him.

"I believe it. Do you ever remember a young man of the name of Walter Fane, my lord?"

"Yes; I think the name seems familiar to my ear, though, at this moment, I cannot tell when or where I have heard it, or how I became acquainted with it."

"Do you not recollect a certain disturbance that took place upon our first coming to the throne?"

"There were several, your majesty, not to say battles."

"Exactly; but I allude to one that took place at an entertainment given by us to our good citizens of London, when one of them, Wainstead, the mercer, had some attack made upon himself or family, which was frustrated by a youth, an apprentice, I believe?"

"Yes, yes," said Hastings; "your majesty has entirely recalled the circumstances to my memory. I recollect him now.

"Do you know what has become of him of late?"

"He was thrown into prison, I believe, and condemned to die; but I cannot say whether he be living or dead now, your majesty."

"I can inform you that he lives," said the king.

"Lives, your majesty! in that case it must be through your majesty's goodness, I presume."

"Oh, no, Hastings; but he has broken prison, and eluded the officers of justice; for, I presume, he couldn't be imprisoned without a sufficient cause?"

"No, indeed; that were improbable—if not impossible."

"Nay, he has done more than that; he has intruded himself into the palace—secretly, of course."

"Your majesty ——"

"Peace; hear me out; he has obtained an interview with Jane, and on his knees before her I found him."

"Such insolence deserves death."

"It does, Hastings; and, in the height of my anger, I had nearly dyed my hands in his ignoble blood; but his life was besought of me by Mistress Shore, and I could not refuse the boon."

"Your majesty's clemency, methinks, was not so well bestowed as on some other occasions," said Hastings.

"It is about this I wish to see thee. I wish, Hastings, that you would take this young man in hand. To please Jane, I have promised him employment abroad, and that he shall take his leave of her before he goes."

"Your majesty ——"

"See to it, good Hastings."

"I will; but your majesty amazes me; 'tis the reverse of what I expected. Your majesty's clemency and generosity perfectly astonish me; they are unexampled."

"Yes, yes; I believe they are; but I promised that it should be so, and it must."

"Surely, your majesty ——"

"But I do not intend that he should long enjoy the fruits of his insolence and audacity, for, having found his way once into the palace, there is no knowing when he may do the like."

"Certainly not; your majesty's clemency would be but another inducement to commit the same piece of audacity over again; clemency would be misplaced."

"What I wish you to do for me is this: he must have some one to wait for his coming out, after having seen Mistress Shore, as I have agreed to permit; then, you understand me, Hastings?"

"Yes, your majesty; I understand your majesty; you would have the execution under sentence of which he lay in prison, but which his escape evaded for a time, now put in force?"

"Exactly; the very thing."

"Then I will obtain the services of the public executioner to wait for him outside the apartment, and then he will relapse into the hands of those who are his fitting guardians."

"Truly; but see that all the previous part of the promises I have made be properly fulfilled."

"I will, my liege."

"The interview will take place in my own apartment; there is a private staircase into some of the court-yards—that will be spot."

"All things shall be in readiness, your majesty," said Hastings; and, with this understanding, the king quitted Lord Hastings, who went another way.

CHAPTER LXXVII.

The Farewell, and Murder of Walter Fane.

It may seem strange that a monarch like Edward should engage in so barbarous an act as the murder of a subject, especially when he could guard against any inconvenience that might arise from his life, and more, that he should go through so much duplicity before the deed of blood should be committed; but it must be remembered that he had been solicited by Jane, whom he never yet refused a favour; indeed, she seemed to have so much power over the mind of such a man as Edward, that while he deemed her worthy of his love he could not refuse her anything.

The king's susceptibility of female charms, and even the romance he exhibited in some of the intrigues in which he engaged, would form matter of surprise if laid before the public of these times; but it will be sufficient to allude to his own marriage, which took place privately, actuated alone by a romantic love for a beautiful woman, whom he had in vain solicited upon less honourable terms; and, in doing this, he made the Earl of Warwick, surnamed "The King-maker," once his firm friend, now his declared enemy in arms against him, deeming himself affronted by this marriage taking place while he was negociating at a French court for the hand of a princess, which he obtained, when the news first reached him.

It is not, therefore, a matter of surprise that he should have promised Jane, whom he loved fondly and voluntarily, these favours, or that he should have kept them so far; but the premeditated murder does appear strange.

Perhaps the solution may be found in the fact that King Edward, before he came to the throne, and during his reign, was engaged in a long and cruel civil war, which hardened men's minds to deeds of blood as a mere ordinary, justifiable matter.

To kill a man was but to get rid of an enemy, and the reverse; and hence the violence and impulsiveness of his nature broke loose in acts such as we have noticed. Indeed, Edward was the accuser of his own brother, and procured his condemnation in parliament, where he appeared personally to accuse him. He was condemned, and the only favour shown him was the choice of his mode of death, which was a singular one—for he preferred being drowned in a butt of Malmsey wine.

But of Edward, with regard to Jane, it might be urged for his dallying with the moment of murder, that he did so because Jane, having dismissed her former lover, should never expect to see him again, and, therefore, could have no suspicion of the refined piece of cruelty that the king had invented.

The moment came when Walter Fane was to take his leave of Jane. He had been well taken care of by the Marquis of Hastings, in his own residence, and placed under the care of a domestic in that nobleman's household, and provided with what was necessary, and was afterwards informed by that nobleman that he would have a post assigned him in Calais under the orders of the governor of that place.

Walter was elated with these prospects, but saddened by the knowledge that he was about to quit for ever one whom he loved so dearly and so well.

"Her remembrance," he said to himself, "can never be effaced from my heart; no, it is too deeply engraved ever to be obliterated, save but by the hand of death. But to what purpose is this?—none; and yet it must be and will be. We are not the masters of our thoughts and affections, and mine will be a source of sorrowful regret to my dying day. The king, too, has been good and gracious to me—more so than I could have any way expected. He has permitted me a last farewell; that is more than I could have hoped for. But so it is—wonderful grace in a monarch so formed by nature and circumstances as to be gracious to one and cruel to another."

Thus soliloquised Walter Fane, as he walked, accompanied by a messenger, to take leave of Jane Shore in the apartment of the king.

The messenger was the most villanous-looking man that ever Walter Fane had seen. He could not help looking at the man, whose very clothes seemed to fit him but ill. Indeed, he appeared to have been suddenly thrust into a livery by far too handsome to agree with his dark, brutal-looking face.

"Methinks, friend, you have not been long in that livery," said Walter Fane, as they neared the palace.

"And why?"

"Because you fit it so ill."

"That may be the fault of the clothes," said the man, "since they might have been made to fit me."

"In which case, the failure is as great as the former," said Walter.

The man made no answer, but scowled, and muttered something to himself; and they both walked in silence until they came to the palace.

"Which way are we to go in?" inquired Walter Fane.

"Follow me," said the messenger, and then he turned aside, and entered an avenue of trees.

"Do you know what part I am going to?" inquired Walter.

"To the private apartments of the king," replied the man.

"The private apartments of the king!" said Walter, in some surprise. "You must make a mistake, my good friend; I am not to see the king?"

"That may be true, nevertheless; but I take it you are going to see the king's mistress, in which case you'll go to the place I have orders to take you, or go back again."

There was something so brutally harsh about the man's manner, and the allusion to Jane was so grating to Walter Fane's ears, that he could hardly refrain from striking the man.

"Lead on," he said, and then relapsed into silence.

Walter Fane was disagreeably reminded of Jane's position with the king; she was a mistress—though a royal mistress—and had left the home of her husband to become one. This jarred his feelings.

It is singular how differently we look at the same acts when performed under other circumstances—especially when they affect ourselves.

Had Jane Shore been guilty of the same dereliction of duty, and had flown to the arms of Walter Fane, with what a different view would he have looked upon the offence. The opprobrium that seemed to hover over the act would have been changed to excess of love, and would have flattered his self-love; and thus it is viewed by all men when it is for them that this weakness is shown.

However, Walter Fane had no time to make any such reflections, had he been so inclined, which he certainly was not, for the messenger halted at a small arched passage, and said,—

"This way—up these stairs, and take the gallery to the left; open the first door you see—it will lead into a small lobby, from which opens one more door: it is a double door—open it, and enter; you will there see whom you desire; but be brief—I wait for you below. Again, I say, be brief."

Walter Fane made no reply to this surly injunction of the messenger, but entered the archway fearlessly; and then, endeavouring to recollect the directions as well as he could, he ascended the stairs, crossed the gallery, and entered the lobby, which was very dark.

After pausing a few moments to accustom his eyes to the light, or rather the want of it, he discovered the doorway, and found, as his guide had truly told him, it was a double door.

His heart beat quick, and then, after a moment's pause, to stay the tumult of feeling that was rising in his breast, he pushed open the door, and entered a small, but magnificently furnished, apartment.

The light was not great, but sufficient to dazzle Walter Fane, and he stood bewildered for an instant, and then advanced a few steps before he could see her whom he sought to bid a long and last farewell.

"Walter Fane," said a low, sweet, musical voice.

Walter's heart sprang to his lips, for well he knew those tones; they were Jane's; and yet there was a mixture of kindness and melancholy in its sweetness, that found a response in his own bosom, and in another moment he was at her feet.

"Rise, Walter, rise—it is not fitting for you to be in that posture, or me to permit it."

"Ah! Jane, how much have I not to thank and bless you for."

"Think not of it," said Jane; "but remember, that, as you conduct yourself, so will my good opinion of you increase. I shall hear of you."

"From me?"

"No, not from you, but of you. We must never see each other again. It is well that it should be so. It is useless to inquire why, or to mourn over the past; think of the future and new existence, and remember not the past, save as a motive for exertion and enjoyment of the blessings and honours that I hope may be your's."

This was said in a kind but dignified tone, which awed Walter somewhat—he had not been used to it—it was new; he paused for a few seconds, and then Jane said,—

"You leave England for France?"

"I do."

"Calais, I believe?"

"Yes; you know all about my prospects there, then?"

"He who has bestowed them upon you has informed me what he has done for you, and what awaits you if you persevere in a line of honour and loyalty; and it will be happiness to me to hear you well spoken of."

"Jane," said Walter Fane, in a low and saddened tone, "this is the last time I may ever see you."

"It will; it is better it should be so for us both."

"Be it so; but I cannot help recurring to past times. My mind, in spite of all my efforts, will recall you to me as when you were in your father's house in the Chepe."

"It is madness."

"It may be so; but it is a madness that will cling to my soul to the very last hour of my life. Oh, Jane—Jane! what years of happiness have I not missed—missed did I say?—ay, cheated out of by an adverse fate."

"Know you not that there may be others within hearing. Speak no more on this subject; spare my feelings. If it be any consolation to you, I tell you I am happy—quite happy."

"Jane!"

"Farewell, Walter Fane—farewell, I say, for the last time! It is our last meeting—make it not a sorrowful one. Bid me adieu, and leave me."

As she spoke Jane seemed to tremble, and evidently strove hard against the exhibition of the feelings that were each moment rising stronger in her bosom.

"Farewell, Jane!" said Walter, and the tears came to his eyes—"farewell! May you never be otherwise than happy—it is my sincere prayer. You shall have no cause to blush for the favours I have received through you. I will deserve them. Adieu—for ever!"

He seized her hand—one was spread over her eyes—he pressed it to his heart, and then, suddenly stealing one kiss from her lips, he said,—

"Farewell! oh, farewell for ever!"

"Adieu!" was the only word she uttered, and then, as Walter Fane rushed from the apartment, she sunk back, in the chair she occupied, insensible.

Walter Fane, when he hurried from the room in which he had taken an impulsive farewell of Jane Shore—his eyes were swimming in tears—made for the door that opened from the lobby into the gallery, and had just reached it, when a dark figure darted from behind a projection, and with one blow buried a long and glittering dagger in his back, between the shoulders, till the point of the blade came out through the ribs of the left side.

He sprung up, and threw his arms in the air; but it was his last motion. He fell backwards on the floor.

"There" soliloquized the messenger,—"I never planted a blow better in my life. He didn't make one gasp; it went clean through his heart. 'Twas well done."

CHAPTER LXXVIII.

Shore's Return and Death.

A LAPSE of several years now occurred, which brought no change in the life of Jane Shore; not even in the affections of the monarch, who is so well remembered for his amours.

These were bustling times. Many battles were fought between Englishmen, until Edward the Fourth had no enemies to contend with in his native land; but he now thought it high time to engage his nobility, and the more warlike and turbulent of the nation, in arms against their national enemies in France; from whom, however, they gained little, save what the timidity and meanness of the then reigning prince of that nation chose to submit to; which, however honourable to England, was more discreditable to the French.

Years passed on; many events took place, which it is needless to recount here, since they produced no change in the position and influence of Jane Shore.

Her power with the king was as great as ever it had been, and always exerted for a good cause, and never from a bad motive. She was so gentle and modest in her demeanour that she gained the love and respect of all men.

The courtiers crowded round her, and made her the medium of obtaining the favours of the king; yet so well did she conduct herself, that none envied her power, but were rather disposed to aid or submit to it.

Her beauty was as fresh, and just as great, as at the day when she first plighted her afterwards broken vows to Shore, her husband, at the altar. Her eye was as bright, her smile as thrilling, and her step as elastic and light.

A few years made no alteration in the appearance of Jane; they had rather added to her beauty.

Edward, during the latter course of his reign, became exceedingly tyrannical, and sunk in pleasures of various kinds, yet all this seemed not to impair the love he bore Jane.

Indeed, on one occasion he gave a *fete* to celebrate the birthday of that lady. The city of London rang from one end to the other with shouts of joy at the *fete* that was to be given, though it was not known for what purpose, but the wise men of the city imagined it was to cajole them, into giving more subsidies for another useless French war, a thing always popular.

At the eve of this *fete* there came a knock at Master Snafflings' door; it was a dull, dark night, and the few passengers that went along the Chepe were lighted by the lamps and candles that were placed in the windows of the houses for that purpose—a very inefficient mode of lighting, and not enough to prevent highway robberies of a very daring character being committed.

Master Snafflings listened to the knock; it was dull and timid, and he thought he detected the sound of a suspicious knock, as if it had been one to induce him to open his door, and permit the entrance of robbers, and he forthwith barred the door.

He sat down very quietly, polishing a bow-case, and examining the weapons of the king's archers, to see they were all in good order.

Again came the timid tap-tap at the door, and a faint voice exclaimed,—

"Open the door, good Master Snafflings—an you be alive."

"Mercy on me," exclaimed Master Snafflings; "mercy on me, it must be, and yet—no, it's not a ghost."

Master Snafflings took a huge two-edged sword, and a sharp one it was, which he held aloft in one hand, while with the other he drew the bolts, placing the lamp in such a position that its rays should fall upon whatever object might enter, be it robber, ghost, or goblin; and up he held the sword ready to annihilate any one who came not upon a legitimate errand.

There entered, however, an aged man, one who appeared aged from years or misfortunes; he appeared to halt, as if he were feeble and incapable of much exertion.

"Master Snafflings," said the figure, drawing a tattered cloak closely around his shoulders.

"Yes, that's my name," said Snafflings, bolting the door. "What do you want with me? here I am."

The stranger paused a few moments, and then said,—

"You do not remember me, then?"

Snafflings felt his blood freeze as he gazed upon the emaciated form of the old man, and said,—

"By the holy rood, I know not; but I fear to suspect—I—I—surely—surely it cannot be—eh?"

"It is not many years since we parted," observed the unfortunate. "I am poor now; is that the cause of thy forgetfulness, Master Snafflings?"

"God of Heaven," exclaimed Snafflings, stepping back, and letting the sword fall with a clang that rung through the apartment. It was lucky Snafflings held not the lamp, too, or he would have let that fall also, and then total darkness would have added to the bowyer's confusion. "God of Heaven!" he repeated; "it cannot be; yet surely it is Master ——"

"Shore."

"Eh?"

"Yes; I am the goldsmith, that was, of Lombard-street."

"Merciful Providence! Come in, Master Shore; come in to my room; here—come in; you look ill, very ill."

"I am ill in more ways than one, good Master Snafflings—ill more ways than one."

"Sit down, and say what I can do for you, Master Shore. Believe me, it grieves me to see you so."

And the good bowyer bustled about in a small, well furnished apartment, threw more logs on the fire, and trimmed the lamp, between which and the light from the fire the room was thoroughly warmed and illuminated.

"A cup of wine, Master Snafflings, and some food, if I may yet crave so much at your hands. A man's altered circumstances strangely alter his liberty with his friends."

"Say no more upon that score, Master Shore," said the bowyer. "Say nothing upon that score, though I should be loth to take offence now; but I do not deserve it; such as my house affords you are yet welcome to."

"Thanks, thanks, Master Snafflings. I have suffered much, and hence I am not so well attuned in mind as I ought to be; adversity sits ill upon my shoulders, and shortens one's temper."

"There, Master Shore—there is some wine, and I flatter myself it is good; and all I have in the way of eatables is the remains of a venison pasty."

"Such things have not passed my lips for many a day; it is nearly four-and-twenty hours since I ate."

"In God's name, eat," said the kind-hearted bowyer, pushing the whole of the contents of the dish towards him; "you do look famished."

"I am; and yet my appetite is not good or great. I will eat, for life's sake, but I fear I am too far gone to last many days."

"You know not what food and generous wine may do for you."

"It cannot make me forget the past, Master Snafflings. I cannot forget her. I would not have come back in poverty and hunger to London, where I was known as the rich goldsmith; I would have remained in a foreign country, and there died alone and forgotten—it matters but little to me where the body lies; I would have crawled into any hole, and laid me down to meet the last extremity man can suffer; but I could not die. I must come back here to see her; yes, Master Snafflings—to see her once again."

"For the love of Heaven, let me beg and implore you not to do so. It can do you no good."

"None," said Shore, decisively.

"Then why attempt it?"

"Because I shall then die. My breath then can leave my body."

"This is sheer insanity."

"It may be so, Master Snafflings; but be it so or not, it will urge me to see her. Ah! Master Snafflings, you know not the jealous love which I bore that woman. You know not the strength and endurance of the passion I now feel maddening my brain. Nay, never look scared, man. I do not feel thus upon every subject. I am amenable to reason upon all others."

"Well," said the honest bowyer, "if it hadn't been for your wife, I might have not been quite so much astonished. You see I calmly bear my bereavement."

"You!"

"Yes; my wife's gone."

"Gone! Where? Who deprived you of her? You, too, dishonoured?"

"Oh, dear, no! That would have been an extraordinary instance of insanity. No, no; my good woman was taken from me by death, about two years ago."

"Are you married again?"

"Again!" almost shouted the bowyer, as he nearly jumped off his seat; "do you think I ain't quite satisfied with the experience I have already had. Oh! Master Shore, Master Shore, experience makes fools wise, they say; though I say he is a wise man who is taught by experience. No, no; I have not married again; and, what's more, I'll tell you a word in your ear—I never will."

There was then a pause of some moments, and the bowyer would not disturb the eating of his guest by any remarks, and waited until he had eaten enough, and pushed away his platter.

"Thanks, good Master Snafflings; you have given me what I could not purchase," said Shore.

"And is it so with you, Master Shore? Has misfortune so far become your master?"

"Yes; all, all is gone—wife, goods, and money—all—all—all!"

"You must have had ill-luck."

"Very ill luck—very; added to which, I did not carry my usual habits of carefulness and thoughts about with me; my mind was encumbered by a heavy misfortune. I made many ill bargains, which were followed by worse—some speculations failed, and, to complete my misfortunes, the vessel in which my last valuables were shipped was wrecked by a storm, and then I was penniless."

"And what have you done since?" inquired the bowyer.

"I have begged my way from France, and, by a mercy, got a passage on board a vessel to this country, and here I am a beggar!"

"Well, Master Shore, there are changes in this life; but hope for better things, and go not to the palace."

"Indeed! and wherefore not?"

"Because you may and will fail in your object, which, I suspect, will cost you your life."

"And then my sufferings will cease. Ah, Master Snafflings, I care not for death! I have nothing to fear now—nothing to hope or to expect."

"Then go not near her."

"I cannot restrain myself,—it is the fascination of the serpent, which draws its victim within reach of its fangs. I know it and feel it, but can no more escape my destiny than I could bring down any of the starry host."

"Well, well," said the bowyer, "I can do no more than recommend you not to go to the palace."

"I shall not."

"Then how do you expect to see her?" exclaimed the bowyer.

"I hear there is to be a fete."

"Yes; there will be one."

"Then I will throw myself in the way of the carriage, and endeavour to force myself into her notice; and, should I die in the attempt, I shall be satisfied."

The bowyer would have endeavoured to persuade him not to do so, but he felt it was useless. He did tell him that, in the pageant of to-morrow, Jane would not appear, as she was not thrust forward on such occasions.

The goldsmith had heard that she would be present, and would not be argued out of his belief.

Snafflings gave him a bed in his house that night, and at breakfast in the morning the bowyer became fully aware of the miserable condition of his guest. He was evidently in the last stage of disease; his naturally spare frame was extremely attenuated, his cheeks hollow, and his eyes sunken, and there was a hectic flush on his cheek; otherwise, his appearance was of a sallow hue.

It was piteous to look upon him, and the good bowyer was grieved to see him pull his narrow threadbare cloak around him, and totter from the house with an eagerness that was ill matched by his strength.

There was much bustle in the city that day; and when the procession had passed through the gates of Temple Bar, and was wending its way along the country road that led towards Westminster, Shore, who had hitherto been unable to thrust himself forward, his strength being unequal to the task, now, however, contrived to throw himself in the way of a carriage, in which Jane, with some other ladies, was riding.

He had intended to have made some appeal to her feelings. God knew for what purpose—he did not; certainly it was not for aid. He would have starved rather than have eaten of anything that came from such a source.

Instead of saying aught, he staggered forward, uttered the one word—"Jane!" and then, with a shriek, fell senseless to the earth.

There was an instant commotion, and the carriage was stopped for a moment. The king and Lords Hastings and Howard, who were with him, also paused.

"What is the meaning of this?" exclaimed the king, glancing at the carriage in which Jane and the ladies were riding.

Fortunately for Jane, she saw not what had happened, neither did she hear the exclamation; indeed, she was riding somewhat in private, and none knew that she was there, save some few of the household, from whom Shore had his information. It was not deemed good policy to allow her publicly to appear on state occasions.

"What does this old man mean by lying in the road?"

"As I live, your majesty, 'tis Shore!"

"Who?"

"Shore, the goldsmith, my liege."

Edward appeared startled; but instantly recovering himself, he ordered that Shore should be taken away by some archers, and the carriage driven on, while he himself rode by the side of the carriage, to keep Jane from witnessing what was going on at the same time.

Shore was rudely seized by several archers, sent by Lord Hastings, with orders to convey him to some place of security, intending that he should linger out his days in confinement.

Thrust rudely into a small, damp dungeon, he was left to himself, and for some hours he remained in a state of insensibility.

However, he awoke from this state, and for some time endeavoured to pierce the darkness by which he was surrounded, but it was unavailing.

"Where am I?" he said, in a low voice. "Where am I? Oh, God, I am dying! Will no one aid me with a glass of water? Will no one smooth my dying pillow, or cheer my last moments with one kind word? Oh! Jane, Jane! What unheard-of misery I have endured for your sake! I suffer—ay, what would I not suffer?—if you were now by my side! But, no! alone, and in the darkness of a dungeon, I die. Jane! Jane!"

Shore was right—he was dying; and, when the guard came to give him food, he was found dead, lying on his back.

CHAPTER LXXIX.

Death of Edward the Fourth.

Years rolled rapidly by, and, though they seem long in futurity, and little less in the passing, yet, when past, they seem short indeed. What seems a long life to look forward to, when remembered, seems but a span.

The star which had been in the ascendant now was louring, and the fate of Jane was fast approaching such a consummation as she never could have contemplated, or even her bitterest enemies, if she had any, hope or desire.

She was the happy and distinguished companion of Edward; and, what is strange in such a monarch, his love for her knew no diminution during his whole life. It was one scene of benefits conferred upon herself, or upon those whose will she espoused.

To her credit, though placed in such a position that she might well have been excused for even a few indiscretions, yet history has but preserved the remembrance of one; and that was the leaving of her husband's arms for those of the king.

Otherwise, her life was blameless; and never has any woman been named whose memory is otherwise so spotless.

But, though beloved and admired by all, and though she had caused so much good, and though there were so many who owed so much to her favour, yet there have been none who have met with a fate so utterly undeserved by her actions.

But the times changed, and Edward the Fourth was mortal. He led a gross life, and was seized with a disorder that proved fatal to him.

He was in his forty-second year when he died, having reigned twenty-three. His career was ended; and then the star of Jane Shore was on the decline.

The Marquis of Hastings was the friend and confidant of Edward, and true to him to the last; and, after the connexion between Jane Shore and his sovereign commenced, he had never permitted his love for her to be any stumbling block in the way of his advancement, and his perfect intercourse with his sovereign.

Indeed, it might have been presumed that his love for Jane, once so violent, was now extinguished.

It was, however, only smothered. It lay dormant, but not dead, within him, and when the king was consigned to his long home, he then showed that his love was as enduring as any that man ever felt.

Not only did his love keep through several years, but the beauty and charms of Jane must have suffered no detraction. On the contrary, they were preserved with all the freshness and health of youth; for, when freed from those trammels caused by the royal lover, he (the marquis) offered her that protection which her destitution required.

Shortly after the death of Edward, we see her in the character of mistress to this powerful nobleman, who was the object of suspicion and dislike to the Duke of Gloucester.

This unscrupulous man, afterwards Richard the Third, was jealous of the power of the Marquis of Hastings, at the same time he was desirous to gain him over to his side, which could not be done to the extent that he desired, and, therefore, resolved upon his death at the first convenient opportunity.

The Duke of Gloucester was now protector, which office he had seized, and enjoyed for some time.

The public mind was not prepared for any great change, at least, such an one as that contemplated by Duke Richard.

In the meantime he strengthened all his partizans and weakened his enemies; he seized all the important posts, and the possession of the persons of his nephews—his brother's children.

Hastings was treated with some consideration for a time, but this must have an end, and the duke must determine upon his ruin.

He utterly despaired of making Lord Hastings a participator and a supporter of himself in all his crimes and plans, though he had succeeded in gaining his concurrence to a few, but he was impregnable to all assaults upon his allegiance to the children of his late sovereign.

This was the point, of all others, in which Duke Richard required his aid and concurrence, and his refusal was a signal for his downfall.

Several noblemen were executed, or, we should say, barbarously murdered, at Pomfret Castle, at the instigation of the Duke of Gloucester, though with the consent and concurrence of Hastings, and on the selfsame day a counsel was summoned by the protector at the Tower.

As this portion of English history is essential to our purpose in following the fortunes of the beautiful but unfortunate Jane Shore, we must detail it.

The Marquis of Hastings, not dreaming of any plot against himself, received the message which summoned him to the council table, and at once determined upon attending there.

All who have heard of the Duke of Gloucester know what he was capable of. The most bloody-minded cruelties that could be perpetrated by man, could be perpetrated by him with a smiling face.

It was no indication of safety to any man to know that he was engaged in a pleasant conversation with Gloucester, for he might have determined upon taking his life ere a few more hours had elapsed from that time.

When the council had assembled, there was the Duke of Gloucester in one of the easiest and most jocund humours it was possible to imagine, at least so historians assert.

The counsellors were present, but had not commenced any business, and the duke, turning to the Bishop of Ely, said, in an agreeable tone—

"My Lord Morton, I passed your gardens in Holborn; they seem finely kept, and do you much credit, as I dare say they give you pleasure."

"Yes, your highness," replied Morton, "they do, indeed, afford some amusement, and profit also."

"I should judge as much," said the duke; "for I saw some very fine strawberries there, that made me desire that I were there—in truth, they looked luscious and tempting to the taste."

"Your highness can command them at your pleasure," said the bishop.

"You are complaisant," said the duke, "and I will take it as a favour that you send for some for me."

"With the greatest willingness and pleasure," said the bishop, who immediately called a servant, and said to him—

"Go to my gardens in Holborn. and bring some strawberries for his highness of Gloucester, and see that you use despatch."

The servant bowed, and departed from the place.

Some one now entered the council chamber, and delivered a message to the duke, who thereupon arose, saying,—

"Pardon my absence, lords; but I am called away for a few moments—I will return anon."

The duke left the council chamber and was absent some minutes.

"Do you know," inquired Lord Stanley of the Archbishop of York, "the cause of our coming hither?"

"Not more than the summons of his highness of Gloucester," replied the archbishop. "I presume, however, his highness will enlighten us upon that point."

"No doubt," remarked Hastings, "something unpleasant has suddenly occurred relative to the government of the realm; some unquiet news may have reached him, and we yet in ignorance of it."

"I cannot imagine what quarter it could come from," said Morton.

"Nor I; probably some of the queen's friends are ill-advised enough to draw to a head."

"It is as likely that the Scots may have endeavoured to surprise Berwick, which they yielded to his highness in the last reign."

"That is possible—they are unquiet neighbours; but time will tell us all we desire to know."

"And here comes his highness back again, and in a hurry, if I mistake not."

This was the truth, for the Duke of Gloucester re-entered the council chamber with a quick step and flushed face, and he scowled upon all around him, and paused ere he spoke, as though he were about to burst with passion.

The counsellors looked astonished to see so sudden and remarkable a change come over the duke's face, for they had no suspicions they were in any danger.

"My lords," he said, in a harsh, cracked voice, "tell me, and tell me truly, what those deserve, by way of punishment, for having plotted and planned against my life? I, my lords, who have the cares of the state, and the welfare of the whole empire resting on my shoulders—I, too, who am so nearly allied to the king—what punishment do such merit who have done these things?"

"They merit the punishment of traitors," replied Hastings, who, as well as the others, was surprised.

"But who can have plotted against your highness's life?" inquired the Bishop of Ely, in a calm tone.

"The traitors," replied the Duke of Gloucester, "are the sorceress, my brother's wife, the queen dowager, and Jane Shore, his mistress, with their associates."

"Indeed!"

"Yes; and see to what a state they have reduced me by their devilish incantations and witchcraft."

As he spoke he bared his arm, which was all shrivelled and decayed, and exposed it to them all.

The counsellors, however, were not much astonished at the fact of the misfortune, because they well knew it had been so from his birth, but they were amazed, and that in no slight degree, at the accusation; but nothing was too gross for Richard of Gloucester, or too great an imposture.

Above all present was the Marquis of Hastings thunder-stricken, for he, since Edward's death, as we have already stated, had engaged in an intrigue with Jane, which ended in her becoming his lordship's mistress; he was most especially concerned at the turn things were about to take.

"Certainly, your highness," said the marquis, "if they be guilty of these crimes, they deserve the severest punishment that can be awarded them."

"And do you answer me," exclaimed the protector, "with your ifs and ands? you are the chief shelterer of that witch Shore, and you are yourself a traitor."

"I a traitor!"

"Yes; and I swear by St. Paul that I will not dine until your head be brought to me."

He then struck the table with his hand. It was a signal to armed men, who were stationed at hand for the purpose, to rush in—they did so.

"Seize the traitor!" said Gloucester, and he pointed to Lord Hastings.

A scene of confusion instantly ensued, and the armed men rushed in among them. One of those, through accident or design, aimed a desperate blow with a poll axe at Lord Stanley. That nobleman was well aware of his design, and, with much presence of mind, he immediately slunk under the table, at which a short time before he had sat as a counsellor.

This nobleman thus saved his life, but not without a severe wound in the head, which he received from the pole-axe in the protector's presence, who, probably, would have been better pleased had his head been cleaved in two by the same blow.

Hastings was immediately seized, and, as he was being hurried off, without a word of defence being uttered or asked, Gloucester said,—

"Away with the traitor, to meet a traitor's doom!"

Without permitting a moment's delay, to utter a word, he was taken into a small private court-yard, where there were some timber logs; and one of them was selected for the purpose of the executioner's block.

"You will not murder me thus?" said Hastings, who, although a brave man and a good soldier, liked not the manner of death.

"It is the duke's orders."

"But a priest—surely a confessor will not be denied me?"

"You must be content, my lord, to die suddenly; such are our orders. We dare not disobey. This can be no hardship to a soldier."

"But a soldier, in time of peace, good fellow, would desire to live as other folk, and die as they do."

"We have no time to parley," said the man; "the Duke of Gloucester is no lamb for us to play with. Come, my lord, we are ready, and you must be per force. This is the block."

Hastings saw it would be useless to say more to such men, who had been chosen for such a service by such a man as the Duke of Gloucester. He resigned himself to his fate, and, giving a last look at the blue sky above him, he bore the stroke of the axe with great fortitude, and met his death without uttering another word.

Thus fell the Marquis of Hastings, a man of great ability, a good and brave soldier, and a nobleman of approved fidelity to Edward the Fourth, which attachment he bore to that monarch's children, and hence his death at the hands of the usurper, who could not corrupt him.

It would be needless to enter further into the historical particulars of the age; so much has been touched upon as served to explain the cause and the manner of the downfall of Jane.

Her two most powerful friends and protectors were dead—Edward and Hastings. She was now without friends, and had to seek a return of those favours she had been so liberal and profuse in during the continuance of her prosperity.

Alas, for human-nature! Gladly would we close our tale at this point; but our duty points out to us the path we must pursue, and show the world its own features, however hideous they may be; and the only consolation we hove is the hope that these may be softened, and that the asperities of humanity only want to be seen to be smoothed and amended.

CHAPTER LXXX.

The Citation of Jane.

It cannot be supposed that Gloucester would stop at the enormities he had already committed. No; he hurried on to more, and excused himself to the citizens of London for the suddenness of the execution, by telling them the offences of which each had been accused were only suddenly discovered—a singular motive, truly; but anything served to beguile a multitude.

Men looked on, but were silent; and Gloucester proceeded in his plans. He, to keep up the farce of accusations of witchchaft, ordered Jane to appear before the council, to answer to the charge, and at the same time gave orders that her goods should be seized and confiscated.

This was a sudden and violent change—such as could not have been anticipated by any human being. She was so gentle and so beautiful, so inoffensive and yet so good, that upon her it came like a thunder-clap. Her senses were stunned; and when she was so rudely thrust before the council, she appeared so eminently handsome and gentle, that a murmur of pity ran through the place.

The Duke of Gloucester scowled upon the counsellors; but he showed no other signs of displeasure.

When the question was put to her as to what she could say in answer to such a fearful accusation as that of having, in league with the powers of darkness, endeavoured to charm away the life of the protector,—

"I appeal to that Heaven," she said, "to which I hope to go when life shall cease, to witness my innocence of a crime so foul and so foreign to my nature. I am innocent in word and thought. My life never yet disclosed one act that could be so vilely construed. I say again I am innocent, and may Heaven shield me from the malice of my accusers. I challenge any one proof."

There was a silence of some moments; and then the accusation was proceeded with; but was so bold, so bar of facts, and so destitute of proof, that even that assembly, constituted as it was, could not entertain it, and the duke exclaimed,—

"She may be thankful that the laws of men are more merciful than her case deserves; but she must not escape justice altogether—let her be removed, but not discharged."

Jane Shore was removed in custody; and many who knew the duke's character believed that, when once removed and placed in the solitude of a prison, she would never more be heard of—that he would have her destroyed.

For some reason or other, quite unaccountable, the duke did not order what he might have termed a private execution to further the ends of public justice; or, in other words, she was not murdered.

For some days she languished in uncertainty of mind respecting her fate.

What a change had come over the spirit of the scene. Jane, the courted and beloved of a king—a monarch alike successful in love and war; then the favoured mistress of that monarch's greatest minister—she who had heaped benefits on all, and never one with an unworthy motive, was now the inmate of a miserable dungeon!

Strange and fearful destiny! What would old Wainstead, the mercer, had he lived, have said? Would he not have sunk through the very bowels of the earth? He would have desired to hide his head for very shame sake, at the disgrace that was heaped upon him.

But he was spared all that; he was a tenant of the silent tomb. And Shore, the jealous but injured husband—what would he have said to such a change of fortune—such a fall?—such sufferings would have been all that even he could have desired by way of revenge or justice for the pangs he had suffered.

Yes, even he could not have desired more: she was shorn of all protection and riches, for they had been seized, even to her very household goods; she had nothing left her; and, if she ever escaped from her confinement, she would be compelled to trust to the kindness and humanity of those for whom she had so often interested herself.

Alas! she little thought that there was not one of the many who had been so deeply indebted to her who would have made the smallest effort to prevent her from perishing with hunger. Such is the gratitude of mankind.

Bitter were her thoughts as she lay in prison; and yet she had not much to accuse herself of, save one heavy crime; but even that was somewhat palliated, when we come to consider that her marriage was not one of her own seeking, and that her husband was every way an unsuitable match for her as regarded age and disposition.

However, passing over this, the reflections that rose in her mind were not such as were at all calculated to remove or soften any of the horrors of her situation. Edward was dead, and so was Hastings; and whom had she now to fly to for protection, even supposing she should get clear of her prison?

One morning, as she there sat ruminating upon the past, the present, and the future, she heard the door of her cell open, and on looking up to ascertain the cause of a visit at an unusual hour, she observed an ecclesiastic enter the cell.

For some moments he gazed at her most offensively without speaking, and then he said, in an assumed voice,—

"Jane Shore."

"Yes," said Jane, "that is me. What would you with me?"

"I am come to cite you to appear before the Consistorial Court, for the purpose of answering for your conduct and crimes in respect to the breaches of morality you have caused during your life."

"My former accusation failed," said Jane; "does vengeance seem so sweet to you all that you would not let me escape the censure of even the wicked?"

"Adultery is not so light a crime," said the man, "that we should permit it to be passed without punishment; and if you be found guilty, you will assuredly not escape from the court without spiritual condemnation and punishment."

"Be it so; your duty is done."

The man paused, muttered, and seemed inclined to utter some brutality, but feared to do so.

He turned and left the cell.

Again Jane was left alone to her meditations; not a sound was there to disturb the onward current of her thoughts, which were likely soon enough to become of such a character that, from the consideration of little evils, they would come to ponder on gigantic ones, which were perfectly fearful to contemplate.

"Why should these hard-hearted ecclesiastics," she thought, "go out of their way to disturb me in the unobtrusive privacy of my life? Surely they might find others more guilty,—whose deeds did injury to others, and who never did a good deed at all. Oh, I can see it;—it is merely to curry favour with such men of blood as this Richard of Gloucester, whom I have more than once obliged.

"Ay, even he, although he be the protector now, was a traitor once; moreover, I can predict that a frightful reign of murder and bloodshed will come about; not one of these men, who affect so much purity as to affect horror at my crimes, but will aid and abet him in any wickedness."

This was no more than the truth; the ecclesiastics were found to favour persons who have power in all ages, and the subordinates themselves were frequently those who were called upon to perpetrate enormities.

Some, indeed, there were who would now and then break through the rule of wickedness, and become eminent for their dignity, learning, and virtue; yet these men would undoubtedly have shown the same qualification, if placed in any other position that required the exhibition of such qualities.

Men were amazed and confounded at the murders—that were called executions—that took place, and the coolness and indifference manifested by those who had been the primary cause of them.

So much so were they occupied by the various schemes with which Richard seemed rife, that they often forgot the more immediate evils that pressed upon them, because they happened to be of much less importance.

Even the fate of Jane Shore, whose very beauty seemed a loadstone that drew all sympathies to her, was for a time forgotten.

But there was soon cause enough to excite anew the sympathies of those who had ever felt a regard for her.

With the citizens of London she was an especial favourite; this arose from several causes, one of which was, she came from themselves—they respected her father, who was a worthy man and a good citizen. Again, whatever were Shore's domestic faults or disagreements, yet he was respected as a citizen, and a wealthy one to boot, which of itself was enough to procure respect.

There was a yet more powerful reason; she had on one or two occasions backed the city corporation, and obtained them more than one privilege which they desired, and which they had often striven for in vain.

Now, however, they were again called upon to witness an act of barbarity in the trial of Jane Shore for the crimes of adultery, &c.

It was especially cruel, because there were none living who could demand justice—none living who could say they were injured; and finally the prosecution was arranged and undertaken under the auspices of those who were the greatest law-breakers in the realm, and the most barbarous of men, who never scrupled at the commission of any crime.

The day was drawing nigh when the influence of one so high and powerful as the lord protector, and something more, of the state, was to be exerted to crush one so little likely to interfere with the wild and lawless schemes of ambition of Richard, Duke of Gloucester, as Jane Shore.

True, it may be deemed necessary that he should proceed in the prosecution after he had commenced it, and because he had accused Hastings in conjunction, and caused him to be suddenly executed.

But this precaution was quite and absolutely unnecessary to such a man as the duke, because he never had any care for consistency of conduct, save that which pointed out the way to procure success for his own selfish purposes.

Alas! poor Jane, that the power of a state should be directed against her, whose errors, grave as they were, were but a feather's weight in the influence that was to be exerted against her, or in that of the motives which were the main cause of the prosecution.

She scarcely knew what she had to answer for; none were ever injured by her, nor did the citation say more than grossly allude to the fact of her being the king's and then Hastings's mistress.

To such charges she could not but be sensible that she was doomed to be found guilty, and sentenced to whatever punishment her enemies could by any possibility inflict upon her.

CHAPTER LXXXI.

The Penance.

THE preliminaries of the trial were not unnecessarily long; indeed, she was treated somewhat unceremoniously, and she was placed on her trial, and compelled to plead.

Her beauty and modesty were observable on this occasion, and many there were who pitied her unfortunate condition. She who had done so much good, conferred so many benefits, and whose conduct, when she had it in her power to do otherwise, was blameless, save the one exception of leaving her husband's roof.

These feelings, however, had no influence with the hard-featured, iron-hearted ecclesiastics, who tried and condemned her to do penance in a white sheet, in St. Paul's Cathedral.

Alas! poor Jane, her steps downward had commenced with the death of her royal lover; and then another was taken, and a fearfully deep one, too, when Lord Hastings fell a victim to the usurper, Richard of Gloucester; now, however, her downward course, like the rolling stone, fearfully increased in rapidity as it neared the bottom of the descent.

She heard her condemnation and sentence with a heart filled with a variety of emotions, and she was carried away, if not fainting, at least in a state of such mental bewilderment that she could not be said to be cognizant of what was passing around her.

The shame that was put upon her by this event sat on her countenance; she felt and bent to the blow, but with such a grace, that many felt more indignation towards her persecutors than anger with herself.

She was carried back to her place of confinement to await the execution of her sentence.

It was several hours after she had been thrust back into her cell ere she recovered from the shock she had received, though expected, at her condemnation.

Tears came to her relief, and after a time she exclaimed,—

"Thank Heaven my father does not live to see my shame! It would have been a cruel death to him—a death that I should have felt myself guilty of inflicting upon one who loved me so dearly.

"And yet, to what a state am I reduced, when I am compelled to be thankful that my father is dead. Oh, this is a terrible day!"

She paused, and, after a time, again spoke in sad accents,—

"Oh, Shore! how amply are you avenged for the past, could you but see me suffer. Perhaps I may meet his eyes when I am arrayed in the garb of the repentant sinner. God forbid! and yet what have I to hope, after being exposed to public gaze and contempt? Where go to—where can I hide my head from the faces of those who know me?

"Many are there who will be present who once knew me. Heaven grant me strength to go through the awful ordeal that I have to pass through!"

We will not accompany Jane through all her reflections, which, as may be well imagined, were numerous and most bitter, but proceed to continue our narrative.

* * * * * * *

The morning of the day dawned upon Jane Shore that was to complete her degradation before the eyes of the world.

She was led forth, clad in a white sheet, into St. Paul's church, where she was compelled to stand for some time, subject to the gaze of the multitude, most of whom, however, felt regret and sorrow at the degradation thus unnecessarily heaped upon her, and their countenances assumed a respectful demeanour, which showed how much they sorrowed for and pitied her.

There was a great concourse of people, who had collected on purpose to view one who had been so long the favourite of a monarch—one who had retained his affections when no other could.

Her misfortunes were the motives to pity and sorrow, and they gazed at her with more respect and decorum than was at all usual in mobs.

In truth, the assemblage of people was composed of, in a very large proportion, respectable citizens, and men of substance, who were attracted thither by the fame of the affair, and its connection with other matters that should have been foreign to it.

"Neighbour," said one citizen to another, "methinks I see more in this affair than most men."

"Ay, neighbour, so do I."

"The Duke of Gloster has done this from motives of private spite."

"Or, more likely, to endeavour to persuade the people that he really believes her guilty of witchcraft."

"The only witchery about her," said a third, "was her great beauty, which has been in this case her ruin."

"Ay, the only person she can hurt is herself."

"Jane Shore was ever ready to help those who needed help."

"That's true, neighbour."

"And those men who have sentenced her to this shameful punishment deserve the same themselves, and, moreover, have no care for morality or immorality."

"Not a whit."

"I understand old Shore is dead," said one of the speakers.

"Is he?"

"Yes; he died in great poverty."

"And so is his wife likely to do. There were great faults on both sides."

"Indeed!"

"Yes; he was mean, jealous, and suspicious; but I don't countenance Jane in her desertion of him, only I think she has led such an uniform life of kindness and usefulness to the oppressed, that she did not deserve this."

"No; especially from those who are her accusers, or rather persecutors."

"They are so."

"See, how pale and downcast she looks. Shame, and a sense of her own degradation, seem to weigh heavy upon her."

"Poor thing—poor thing! Those who have placed her here ought to have been here themselves, or in a worse place."

"They do say," added another, "that she bewitched the Protector."

"More likely some one, who shall be nameless, has a kind of connection with him that will last beyond time."

"That's dangerous talk."

"Yes, but deserved and true."

The speakers separated and the crowd moved about.

It will be useless to depict the many faces that gazed upon the unfortunate Jane Shore, whose name and condition, as well as her crimes, were set forth in a kind of document and read to the crowd.

This penance was of the severest character to Jane, whose sensitive mind shrank from the rude gaze of the multitude, and she never once looked up at them during the trying time she had to go through. It was some hours after the ceremony had been gone through, that Jane Shore, thrust from even the shelter of a prison, wandered through the streets of London.

A proclamation had been issued, forbidding any one to aid, or help, or harbour the unfortunate Jane.

Indeed, the severest penalties had been declared against those who should so assist her with either shelter or food, so great was the animosity that seemed to be borne against her by the Duke of Gloucester, who had taken pains, by no means equal to the importance of the occasion, to get her punished for something or other.

People in general greatly pitied her, and felt greatly for her situation, but the sympathy was not active, from the fear of offending the powers that were, and knowing the extraordinary tyranny of the Duke of Gloucester, who, if he were aware of a single instance of disobedience to any proclamation of his, would inflict the most severe and exemplary punishment upon the offender.

Besides this, the friends that Jane had so often obliged by favours now turned their backs upon her.

It was dark, and Jane felt she was a wanderer; she had no home, no place where she could obtain even the shelter of a roof for one night.

This was the first occasion upon which she had experienced the full misery of her situation.

But, oh! how great was the relief from the awful mental agony that she suffered during the exposure that had been inflicted upon her. This was, to her sensitive mind, a worse trial than any she could picture to herself. If she were once again hidden from the rude gaze of the multitude, then she would be comparatively happy.

Oh! no one can tell the pangs of anguish she suffered on that occasion; penitent she was, the tears came down fast and fell upon the white garment by which she was enveloped, and when she was released, a kind of stupor came over her that secured her from that excess of grief which now filled her.

Thus she continued for some hours after she had been released from the hands of her gaoler. She went forth a houseless, harmless wanderer, without friend or hope of any kind.

CHAPTER LXXXII.

Jane's former Friends.

THERE is perhaps no enemy so deadly in his enmity as he who has been greatly obliged at a former period; it seems as though it were necessary that such an one should feel hatred in a stronger degree, than one whose anger is kindled without any previous feelings existing at all, between the two individuals, the hated and the hater. This may be because, in the former instance, those feelings require a greater degree of strength to overcome them than is simply enough to excite our ill feelings; and it is from nearly the same feelings that one experiences a greater amount of ingratitude from a former friend than a recent acquaintance. Be the cause what it may the result is, at least, acknowledged.

This unpalatable truth, Jane Shore, at least, was doomed to experience in a fearful degree.

For some time she knew not where to hide her head; she dared not seek any of her friends; at least any of those with whom she had associated, and those whom she knew years gone by, would not now recollect her.

She had no tie—no one was bound to her by the ties of blood and relationship; even old Simon, who would have sold his soul to have supported her, was gone. He was no longer in the land of the living.

Poor Simon had died of a mixture of old age and a broken heart. His character was singular. Contrarieties he seemed to delight in; but Jane was the only being whom he seemed to delight in. He considered her perfect, and when he found it was not so, then he, poor fellow, first began to give ground to the inroads that age made upon his constitution.

Till that time he seemed to have been of an iron constitution; but the fact was, Simon's spirit had been an impenetrable barrier to the effects of the evils that flesh is heir to; but that once gone, nothing remained to carry on the war against the inroads of nature.

Alas! poor Simon sank into the grave, gloomy and dejected. He would take no notice of any one—would communicate with no one, and sank beneath the accumulated evils that beset him, and died with the name of Jane on his lips, that being the last sound that was heard issuing from them. This little incident proving that his affections were as strong as his manners were singular and sudden.

With him died the only friend that would have done aught for the hapless outcast; he would have toiled to the utmost to have saved her from the miseries that her misfortunes entailed upon her. Ay, he would have died cheerfully in her service, and have regretted that he died only because he could no longer administer to her wants.

Jane thought of this sad event with tears, as she wandered through the streets by night, glad that darkness hid her from the sight of men, for she feared now to encounter the eyes of any human being. She thought they must read her unhappy degradation upon her face.

Oh, how bitter were the few first hours she passed after the recovery from the stunning effects of the shock her mental powers had received.

It was then she became fully and entirely aware of the great change that had taken place. In the darkness of the streets she could give full vent to her feelings, without having the misfortune to attract the attention of heedless curiosity. She could now give way to tears, and she did so to the full.

After wandering about for some time she became exhausted, and sat down in a doorway, there to rest, and ponder upon the misery that had come upon her.

Would she—the gently-nurtured child of a fond father—the favourite of a powerful monarch, even in her wildest dreams, have thought of the bare possibility of such a thing coming to pass?

No, no! she knew that death might come, but nothing else. She never thought of a reversal of the present moments of ease, happiness, and splendour.

Who would, who could have thought that such a malignant fate as that from which she suffered would ever have overtaken her? Certainly she herself was the last to have imagined such a thing possible, because she could not conceive any human being of so malignant a character as he who was the primary cause of her misfortunes.

After some hours spent in grief and thought, she was so much exhausted that nature could hold out no longer, and leaning her head against the door-pillar, she fell into a deep slumber.

How long she slept she knew not. She had not been disturbed during the night, but this was more owing to the darkness of the night, which completely hid her from view, and at that time there were no lamps in London, and the doorways were well adapted for concealing robbers and murderers, of whom there were plenty.

Jane's poverty-stricken and miserable appearance would have been no safety to her, for those who infested the streets were often capable of the greatest acts of brutality; indeed, her escape from violence was more owing to the fact that she was unobserved by any of these wretches.

The guard, too, had not observed her from the same cause, but, when morning broke, and there was light enough to distinguish objects clearly, then, indeed, her danger of interruption was greater.

The sun had scarcely risen above an hour or two, when the guard coming round, halted before the doorway where Jane had been compelled to seek shelter through excessive fatigue.

Seeing a female sleeping there, deathly pale and chilly, he exclaimed,—

"Poor thing—poor thing; she seems beautiful. What on earth could be the cause of her choosing such a resting-place as that?—she is surely living."

"I know not that, an' please you," said an archer.

"Do you doubt?"

"She is pale."

"Yes, she is."

"And I cannot see her breathing," said the archer; "and that, you know, is something like death, if not death itself."

"I will see myself; at all events, she must not remain here—she must be taken to the guard-house."

"She's doing no harm," said the archer.

"But, for humanity sake, she must not be allowed to remain there; she will perish with cold."

"It's a trouble," said the archer.

Not heeding this last argument, the officer stepped into the doorway, and paused for a moment; he was much stricken with the delicacy and beauty of Jane, which shone, despite her sorrows, but, recovering from his surprise, he took her gently by the shoulders, and shook her, saying,—

"Hilloa! hilloa!—awake!"

Jane started up, and glared wildly about her for a moment, utterly unable to understand what had happened.

"She is mad," thought the officer of the guard, but said, "What do you want here? —how came you to sleep here?"

"I was tired, and nature would no longer hold against time and weariness," said Jane, who now recovered herself.

"And why are you not at home?" said the officer.

"I have no home."

"No home!"

"None."

"Good Heaven! what are you, then?" inquired the officer.

"An outcast—a wanderer."

The man paused for some moments; he was not sure he had heard aright. There was something so very different in her tones and manner of speech from the commonalty, that he felt persuaded she belonged to some family of rank, and that some temporary misfortune or incident that he could not fathom, had driven her out, and caused her to become desperate, and perhaps insane.

With these thoughts in his mind, he determined to question her more closely with the view of finding out to whom she belonged, so that he might earn their thanks, and perhaps a reward, by restoring her, and, with that intention, he said,—

"Who are you?"

"Jane Shore."

As Jane spoke these words, she shrank back, and so did the officer.

There was a pause of some moments' duration, during which the officer seemed to be pondering in his own mind upon the propriety of doing something, but, glancing at his companions, he said,—

"I am sorry for you."

Jane was sensible of the kindness and humanity of the man's words, but she knew that he dared not offer her any relief, that her name was a bye word—she was an outcast, and it was dangerous in any one who should assist her even to a crust of bread.

"God of heaven! am I left thus alone in so large a city, where my father was so much respected, where his wealth was so great? Where, alas! is it now—for I cannot claim it—all, all, that was and would be mine is gone, seized, and carried away from me!"

She looked up to heaven, and, as she did so, she gave a start, as her eyes encountered the "Golden Fleece."

Yes, she had slept beneath the doorway of the very house in which she first saw the light, and where she had passed so many of her best days—some of her happiest moments.

Yes, in the darkness of the night she had wandered about from place to place, and, by a strange chance of fortune, she found herself at this place.

"Strange!" she continued. "It seems as if unkind Fortune was determined that she would show me the worst at once; and the best shelter is the doorway of the house in which I was born. God give me strength! And yet wherefore should I seek such aid? No, no; to die is to be happy—to escape from misery and the sharp pangs of hunger. What agony would not death spare me! Oh, Heaven! let me die, let me die!"

She staggered away from a spot where she had so often stood in happier times; she could not endure the many recollections and thoughts that crowded upon her brain; she hastened away as quickly as she could go.

This was necessary; for she felt that there was a dreadful chill come over her. The cold, damp air in which she had slept seemed to have seized upon her frame, and she felt as though her body was scarcely half vivified by the circulation of the blood, and dreadful cramping pains seemed to seize her.

Jane made many efforts to obtain some relief from among those who had known her in better days, and people who had largely benefited by her prosperity; but they, one and all, sheltered themselves under the proclamation that had been issued, threatening pains and penalties against any one who should harbour her or assist her.

Thus she found that she, who had done so many good actions towards others, could not, in the time of distress, find one who could be induced, by a sense of former benefits and obligations, to do one kind act towards her. She was, emphatically, homeless and friendless.

And thus she wandered about the streets, sorrowing and famishing, day after day, till people wondered how it was that she lived.

CHAPTER LXXXIII.

The Miseries of the Outcast.

WHO is that wandering object of misery, clad in tatters and in dirt—whose gait is that of one who is suffering all the evils that flesh is heir to? Who is she, that every one shuns and turns aside to avoid her? Who is she, with haggard look, who gazes with a restless, hollow eye upon the objects that meet her view, at each step she takes, as though she would devour the very stones? Who is that walking, hobbling mass of rags, dirt, and misery?

That was once the favourite of a king—the mistress of a powerful nobleman—but now the wretched outcast, Jane Shore, whose life excited pity, but whose necessities scarce ever produced pity enough to induce those who knew her to offer her the smallest aid.

How great is the change! The beautiful, lovely, laughing girl, whose delicate complexion was the pride of her lovers, but who now was pale, sallow, haggard, and woe-worn.

The delicate roundness and plumpness of her figure had gone, and nothing but projecting bones, hollow eyes, and a famine-worn body remained.

Those only who had seen her waste day after day could have known her; but they, seeing such a gradual though rapid change, knew her by sight.

It was a miracle how she retained any vitality in the wretched-looking body that stalked about—the impersonification of famine; but so it was. She must pick up some refuse garbage that the very dogs in the streets refused; or she must now and then obtain a small portion of food, by way of alms, upon the sly, when no one was nigh, or which sometimes a stranger might, because he knew her not, have bestowed upon her.

From such sources as these she must have drawn her wretched existence, but from no other.

It was strange that Jane should have consented to live at all; it was surprising that she had not ended her miseries and life together; but she did not. She lived on, dragging on one of the most wretched and degraded existences that ever was led by a human being.

Gaunt and famished as was her appearance, she was worse clad, and polluted by the wretched, tattered rags she wore. Dirty and dishevelled her hair—her body becoming contracted and diseased—she presented a most remarkable contrast between what she was at an earlier period.

She wandered about, and slept in doorways and unfrequented places. None knew of her hiding-place, or it is more than likely she might have been sought and relieved in secret, or, perhaps, what was just as probable, murdered!

One day she was, as usual, wandering about. She was more than usually famished; she had not tasted food for thirty hours; and then it was many a month since she had enough for one meal. She stopped opposite a baker's shop, where there was abundance of that bread she was dying for want of.

There she stood, with greedy eyes and famished countenance, watching the bread as though it were something to see food. She dared not beg—knowing well she could be punished if any harsh citizen chose.

Yes, there she stood, watching the motions of the baker as he took the loaves from one shelf to another. Oh, how she looked and longed for some of that bread to satisfy the cravings of hunger; her mouth seemed to move as if in anticipating the pleasures that arose from mastication. But, alas! these were pleasures that seldom fell to her share.

At length, the baker, who had observed her all along, and endeavoured to withdraw his eyes and his thoughts from the starving woman on the outside, could not see her unmoved by pity.

"I can't stand this," he said to himself; "I know the poor being is starving; she must be—but the penalty is too heavy, and I have a family, too."

For some time this recollection seemed to be enough to steel his heart against the famished looks of the desperately wretched woman; but, at length, he muttered,—

"No, I cannot stand it—I must give her something."

Then he went to the door, and looking to the right and left, to see that he was not observed, and taking a loaf off the shelf, he held it towards her, saying,—

"For God's sake, take it and eat it; do not come here again, unless you desire to bring vengeance and ruin upon me."

She seized the loaf, and muttering a few inaudible words for thanks, hurried away with her prize.

Not so fortunate was the baker who had relieved her, for some curious eyes had watched him, and vengeance came down with a terrific swoop upon him, for no other crime than having shewn that he was humane, and could not coldly see a fellow creature suffer all the pangs of starvation when he could avoid it.

That act of humanity has been handed down to posterity, with its accompanying punishment.

Poor Jane wandered about, if possible, getting worse and worse; the horrible extent to which she suffered, no human being can believe.

At length, thinking her end was come, she dragged her body with what little strength that remained, towards the outskirts of the town. It was a difficult matter to crawl along as far as Bishop's-gate—but she did so; her feebleness was so great that she was compelled to halt every few minutes to rest.

She would not die in the streets of London if she could avoid it. No; that was too terrible even to her, lost as she was to most of the feelings that people usually possess upon that subject. But she could not die in the streets, and have her body exposed to those who were her enemies, for them to exult over; or to the sight of those who once knew her; perhaps, it might be she would be mangled by dogs and other animals that used to prowl about.

This was too horrible not even to make Jane Shore, fallen as she was, shudder at the prospect; therefore, it was the reason she crawled away from the haunts of man, to lie down in peace and quietude to die.

Yes; that was the last object she could have, or had; death would be a welcome release from the load of misery she bore; death to her now was no evil—she shrank not from it; indeed, she sought the grim visitant, and welcomed his approach.

The unfortunate woman dragged herself along the road, and listened to the sounds of the birds as they carolled in the air. She thought how happy all nature seemed, and that she alone was miserable and unhappy, she alone suffered degradation and unspeakable wretchedness.

She looked around her, but saw nothing that indicated the least that bore any similitude to her; she was alone in everything.

"What have I done? Oh, what have I done that I should thus be singled out for such a horrid fate? Oh, Heaven! pardon my impatience under such sufferings that have never been equalled in their kind and their duration. Heaven, pardon my sins. I can scarce pray—I have nothing to pray for—I cease to hope—cease to think—in ceasing to live I have the happiest prospect I have had for many years; for then, at least, there is an end to human misery."'

She dragged herself onwards, but at so slow a rate, that it was nearly evening ere she reached a certain portion of Shoreditch, [illegible] then; it was a portion of the northern road, with fields and [illegible] side. Here she was sinking; she could no longer stand; but, from sheer exhaustion, she fell into a kind of swoon beside a small stunted bush or tree, that grew by the side of a ditch.

There the wretched creature lay insensible, with her lower extremities immersed in the muddy fluid, that ran through the water-course.

She lay there for some time, before she was noticed by any human being. At length a carter came up with his team; he stopped as he looked at the bundle of dirty rags, for such the body of the unfortunate Jane appeared.

"Whoa—whoa—whoa!" he shouted to his team; and pushing his hat on one side, he began to scratch his head.

"Why, what have we here?"

"What's the matter?" inquired his companion, who was riding.

"That's more than I know. Come and see, will'ee?"

The other man came up, and peeped at the body, and said,—

"Why, dang it, mon, it's a woman."

"A woman! 'tis more like a bundle of dirty rags."

"Yees, it is; but it's a woman, for all that, inside on 'em."

"What shall we do with un, leave or take her up?"

"She be dead!"

"Yes, I think so."

"Then we will go on, and say nothing about her to any one."

"Yes; but suppose she bean't dead, what then?"

"Well, then, suppose we take her in the cart, and put her down somewhere in town."

"But I don't know who'll take any care on her."

"Not I; but some of the guards must; perhaps they'll put her into some of the convents."

"Ah! that's well thought on. Just get a whisp of straw, so that we can lay hold on her, without any harm."

This being done, they lifted her into the cart they were driving, and then they proceeded towards London at an unabated pace, where they arrived just in time before the gates were shut for the night.

"What are we to do with this body?" inquired the carter of one of the guards, who stood on duty at the gate.

"What body?" inquired the guard.

"Why, a woman's body, to be sure."

"Not your own, then?"

"If thee hadn't been on duty, I'd a given thee a taste of my body, dang thee. We picked up a dead woman coming along the river."

"Where is it?"

"In the cart."

"Let's see it."

"Look, then," said the carter, pointing to it.

"Is she dead?"

"It's very like; she was in a ditch when we found her."

"You must leave her here; we'll send her to the bone-house, if dead; and you must attend to say when and where the body was found."

This was all agreed to, and the body was just about to be consigned to the bone-house, when some one observed signs of life; she had recovered enough to be able to breathe, and swallow very languidly. But a violent fever had seized upon her, and she was carried to a convent, where she was to be taken care of.

It was some months ere she was well enough to speak or crawl about; for some time she resisted all efforts to say who she was; and it was not until she was convalescent, that she consented to say who she was.

"I am Jane Shore," was the reply.

It was magical; they all shrunk from her; but before she left the convent, they gave her a loaf of bread, and enjoined her never to appear before them. She was not seen afterwards.

CHAPTER LXXXIV.

Conclusion.

For some years Jane Shore was not heard of. What had become of her no one knew, and no one cared; but she was supposed to have perished miserably in some obscure place or other, and at length she was forgotten by all, even by her persecutors.

One morning, as the guard was about changing, there was a loud knocking at the door of Master Nicholas Scanner, who was not yet up.

Now, Master Nicholas Scanner was a very popular leech; he had been in the east, and was well skilled in simples and the cure of various disorders.

When, therefore, he heard a knocking at his door, he concluded that some parties desired his service. This, at that early hour, was provoking; he turned in his bed, again and again, quite vexed and angry. Each time he did so he endeavoured to persuade himself into the belief that it was a delusion—the knocking was a mere mockery.

This, however, did not cause any abatement of the fact; the knocking continued just as before, or rather increased, and then came a cessation, which induced the leech to believe that the door had been opened.

In this he was right enough, and the sound of his servant's feet approaching his room testified to the fact; and seeing there was but little hope of any more sleep, he resigned himself to his fate.

"Master! master!"

"Well, what now, Peter?"

"You're wanted, master."

"I dare say. Sure as the sunrise is, that people always want me at an inconvenient hour; as if their maladies were always coming on at a most inconvenient time. Bless my heart, what can people be thinking of?"

"Don't know, master."

"Well, what do they want?"

"They want you, master."

"Confound you! have you no manners, but you must answer me with a quibble? I'll not put up with such behaviour from you, Peter."

"Very well, master; but shall I tell you all I have heard—do you intend to hear my message?"

"Yes, knave; speak it out quickly, or I'll teach thee more haste."

"Well, well, master! there's a woman lying in extremity; and they have sent for you. They say there is no time to lose."

"A woman, eh?"

"Yes."

"Well, then, there's no great harm done, Peter; I'll go to sleep."

"Just as you like; only Master Salter sent up to say that he wished, as an act of humanity, and a favour to him, you would come immediately."

"Oh! Master Salter, eh? and an act of humanity, too! I wonder how two such things came to be coupled together; it ain't a very usual thing with him, at all events, and being something extraordinary, I suppose I must go."

So saying, the leech arose, and, in an ill-humour, dressed himself as quickly as he could.

"Is the messenger below?" inquired the leech.

"Yes, master."

"Then send him up."

Peter immediately departed, and in a few moments returned with the individual who had disturbed the slumbers of Nicholas Scanner.

"Well, knave, who is this woman whom your master desires me to attend to?"

"Please you, sir leech, I don't know; but she is a poor woman. Yes, sir leech, a poor woman—a very poor woman."

"Don't you know what's the matter with her?" inquired the leech.

"Please, sir leech, I think she's dying—yes, dying."

"Very good, then, what was the use of sending for me? Have you no knowledge of what she ails—whether it's a fit—disease—or starvation?"

"Please, sir leech, I think it's all three—it's very like it."

"Thy stupidity entitles thee to the reward of martyrdom," said Nicholas Scanner.

"Please, sir leech, you are very good; but any small coin," said the messenger, with a low reverence as he spoke.

"I'll coin thee! Get thee back, and tell Master Salter that I'll be with him immediately—make haste, or I may be there before you."

The messenger abruptly departed, and made the best of his way home, leaving the leech to follow him to Whitefriars. The leech was not long after him, but stayed only to furnish himself with some medicaments, which he thought might be of use to him in any emergency that might occur.

Master Salter was a lodging-house keeper, and, as such, he had but little compassion for the wants and wishes of other people, save they were such as could offer a consideration in return for services done and performed.

His tenement was situated in the sanctuary of Whitefriars, where all sorts of lawless characters congregated together to escape the doom of the laws, and his lodgers were usually of this class, or rather they were entirely so.

To this place it was that the leech wended his way, and he came just as Peter was explaining to his master as well as he could the message sent by the leech.

"Well, Master Salter; you see I am here in accordance to your summons."

"Yes, Master Nicholas Scanner; I see you are, and I'm right glad to see it, for, I take it, this is a case of real extremity."

"Say you so? Then I am quite willing to lend what aid I may. You knew how far my poor skill will go you may command me."

"I know that, Master Scanner, else I had not sent for you, for this is a poor job. I've a woman at the top of my house here as I believe is dying, or something very near it. If you'll follow me," said Salter, "you'll see her."

They now began ascending a variety of dark, ricketty stairs; they were very steep, and had a number of awkward turns in them. The bannisters were everywhere broken, to some extent, more or less; the stairs creaked and wheezed at every step, and each room seemed occupied by lodgers of some grade or other, and well peopled.

At length, after much trouble and toil, they reached the highest landing; and then the leech, seeing two rooms, said, as he turned to Salter,—

"Which of these rooms?"

"Neither."

"Neither!"

"No; up this ladder."

"You don't mean to say that the woman is up there, merely lying under the tiles?"

"Yes, I do; and a very good place, too. I'll warrant there's many a good Christian, that can pay his way, would be glad of such a place. Bless your simplicity, it's a beautiful place of its sort inside. Just go up, and see, now."

"I will certainly go up," said the leech, "but don't expect it such as even a criminal could put up with."

The leech began ascending a round ladder that led into the loft that had been parted in two, one part on one side, and the other on the other side, to admit of converting it into two apartments.

Entering the one that Master Salter pointed out, he perceived a woman lying on a few planks of boarding.

The room, or loft, was a long one, but there was no fire-place, the bare rafters and tiles were rent to the eye, and the wind came in at every crack. There was a small kind of skylight, through which the only rays of light that came into the room entered.

It was an appalling scene of wretchedness and destitution, no one article of furniture was to be seen, not a table or chair, or stool, bedstead, bed, or any contrivance, or substitute for such.

There was no one article of clothing, save what she had on.

The leech walked up to the unfortunate woman, who lay insensible, and placed his hand upon her heart, where he kept it for some time.

"Does she live?" inquired Salter.

"In saying she does, I am saying the utmost I can; there is a very feeble pulse, very feeble, indeed, barely enough to enable one to recall life, even supposing all things are favourable."

"What do you want?"

"Just set her gently up, and then I will give her some cordial; it will restore her, if aught can do it. It is a costly recipe, one that I learned among the Copts in Egypt, when I sojourned among them."

The lodging-house-keeper did as he was desired by the leech, when he held her head in a proper position, and then dropping out of a phial some portion of its contents between her parted lips, he waited with patience and calmness to see the result.

For this he did not wait long, for a slight tremor ran through her frame, and this was the first sign of returning animation.

"See, she revives," said the leech; "the divine elixir never yet failed in any case that ever I yet used it. I confidently believe it will do in all cases where the restoration of sensibility is at all possible."

"It is a very valuable medicine," said Salter, "and much too good to be wasted upon such as she."

"My friend, I perceive the female who lies here has been of a very different class of society to what she appears to be long; those long, taper fingers never yet did hard work."

"They are dirty enough."

"That may be; misery is but a poor promoter of either wisdom or cleanliness; she is a mass of human misery and squalor."

"You may say that."

"She has seen much misery; but see, she revives."

The unfortunate woman gave a partial turn on the floor, the hardness of which seemed to hurt her, and she said,

"Oh!" and then groaned and shrank from the place, as though she feared a repetition of the pangs she felt.

"Get some wine, good Master Salter."

"Wine, did you say?"

"Yes, wine; and good generous liquid too."

"And who's to pay?"

"Never mind; it must be had, even if you do, or the woman will die."

Master Salter turned very slowly away, to go down the steps, with no good grace; but he went, and the leech called to him as he went to hasten his errand; to this he responded in a kind of grunt and disappeared.

In the meanwhile the wretched being opened her eyes, and gazed around for a few moments, and uttered several audible groans, but spoke not.

The leech propped her up in the best way he was able, and then waited for the re-appearance of the landlord, who soon after came, bringing with him some wine in a small vessel.

"Here," he said, "is wine; 'tis a pity it is to be wasted down such a throat as that. I would sooner have swallowed it myself."

Master Nicholas Scanner took no notice of this speech, but taking the wine in one hand, and kneeling down by the side of the patient, he held her head back and poured some of it down her throat.

For some moments this appeared to produce no effect, but, after a short while, she began to revive and to look about her.

"I am dying," she said; "I am dying."

"Unhappy woman," muttered the leech; "come, come, let us hope you may not be so bad."

"Not so bad," she repeated, in a faint voice; "not so bad; and who bade me hope? Hope! when have I hoped save for death—ha! ha! no hope, no hope for the wretched and the injured; especially the injured; no hope for those that are gone."

"Peace, peace," said the leech; "if it be as you say, such misery will be well exchanged for the quiet of the grave."

"It would," said the dying woman, in a kind of hoarse whisper.

"Then prepare for it."

"Will she die?" inquired Master Salter, with some curiosity. "Won't she get better?"

"No, no. She is too far gone; but you must have some kind of mattrass brought her, and a pillow, that she may lie more at ease—a blanket to cover her, as well. I will wait here while you send them up," said the leech.

"Indeed! you have given yourself more trouble than ever I wished you, Master Nicholas Scanner. I didn't think you'd have been so liberal in your orders; but I shall know another time."

Not, however, disputing the orders, he went down stairs, and gave the orders to a servant to bring them to him at the foot of the ladder, and then he brought them up, and threw them down on the floor, saying,—

"There, Master Scanner, there; for anybody else besides yourself, I wouldn't have taken all this trouble for nothing, as I am a sinner."

Scanner made no reply, but continued to gaze upon her and watch her; but when the mattrass and things were arranged, he aided Salter in placing her upon them, and then he said,—

"You must let her have a little broth, and things of that kind, often, but in small quantities—about noon I will come and see her again."

"Very well. I hope she won't trouble you or me again, after that; this is quite enough for once, I'm sure. Do you think she will live?"

"Probably till noon."

"Eh?"

"Until noon."

"And no longer?"

"No."

There was a short pause, during which the leech continued to gaze upon the woman, but at length turned away, saying,—

"Yes, yes; I will be back again at noon; do as I tell you—there is something in that woman that bespeaks a life of the most abject misery, and yet she was never born to such a life, I feel convinced, from her appearance—but no matter, you cannot understand all this, Master Salter."

"I, truly; no—I don't, and don't want neither. I do understand this, however, that there is a great deal of trouble to be encountered in all this."

"Never mind, never mind!"

"But I do, though. I suppose it's no use doing so, now, at all events; in for a penny in for a pound; but no matter, somebody must pay it."

And, comforted by this assurance, Master Salter attended the leech to the threshold of his door; and, as he was going, said to him,—

"At noon, eh?"

"Yes; by noon."

* * * * * * * * *

Noon was close at hand, and the leech was as good as his word, and true to his appointment, he came to the house of Master Salter, whom he found in the way, regaling himself with a dish of salt fish, and some choice wine; though he was a hard-fisted man, yet he loved himself better than his means, and continued to indulge himself, though all the world starved.

"Well, Master Salter, well, how gets on the poor woman? is she yet living?"

"She was an hour since."

"And now you don't know?"

"Truly do I not. I have been having my dinner, and, as I cannot do two things at once, why I am compelled to neglect the one while I attend to the other."

"And so you attend to the most agreeable."

"Why, as for that, good and learned Master Nicholas Scanner, you know the waste of the human body that I must provide against."

"Yes, yes; I know that very well, and you are doing so most effectually; but to my patient."

"Just let me finish my dinner; will you have a glass of Burgundy? it is right good, I assure you—some of the best."

"I will. I have been up early, and this is noon only, it is true, but I have been up long enough to make it eve, according to ordinary computation, so I will taste thy Burgundy."

"There, sir leech, tell me if thou ever tasted better; and, if thou hast, beshrew me if thou hasn't been at the table of Charles the Bold."

"I have even done that, good Master Salter. I have been at the table of the Prince of Burgundy."

"Oh, what sort of man be he?"

"A hot and fiery one."

"And so I have heard."

"But thanks for thy Burgundy—it is good; but I have no time. I must see my patient, for I am wanted far hence."

"Then I'll be with thee," said Master Salter; "I'll be with thee—come along."

Having duly swallowed the last mouthful, he washed it down with a draught of Burgundy, and then rose to lead the way to the wretched creature's hole.

After having accomplished the ascent of the stairs, they came to the ladder, and this, also, was ascended, and they both entered the loft.

The wretched being lay in the same posture as she was last placed in by the landlord. Master Nicholas Scanner gazed upon her with a doubtful expression, and shook his head, saying,—

"She is sinking fast."

"Who is she, I wonder?" inquired Salter, in a low tone; "perhaps she has some friends who would discharge her debts."

"Woman," said the leech, as he knelt by her side, "I must tell you that you have not long to live. You are, no doubt, aware of that?"

"I am," was the faint reply.

"Have you friends whom you would wish to see?" inquired the leech.

"I have none," she replied, in the same low tone that she spoke in, barely moving her jaws or lips to speak, only her tongue, and that but slowly.

"Have you any relations?"

"None—none!"

"What a wretch, to be sure," said Salter; "no friends, no relatives—oh, shocking!"

"Would you desire the attendance of a priest to comfort you in such a strait? Say so, and you shall have one shortly."

"No, no; they are my persecutors, my enemies, and my accusers, and judge; oh, no—no priests."

"Very well, my good woman; I would do all I could to give you any pleasure or tranquillity at such a moment as this, though I don't think they are of much use to any one."

The unfortunate creature was now seized with her death-pangs, and the leech, by a sudden impulse, said,—

"Tell me who are you? what are you?"

"I am an outcast—I—I—am—Jane Shore. I—I am dying."

"Jane Shore!" exclaimed the leech, starting backwards at the very sound of the name.

"Jane Shore!" echoed Master Salter.

There was a sudden flash of spirit returned to the almost expired body, and she, by a great effort, raised herself upon her elbow, and with an unearthly fire in her eye, and her hollow cheeks seemed flushed for a moment, as she said,—

"Yes; I am the persecuted Jane Shore; I have lived, as God alone can know; the extent of human sufferings and debasement that I have known, no tongue can tell; but it has been such that death is—oh, you cannot tell how sweetly welcome. I have been persecuted; but Heaven has avenged me, for my enemies have all died violent deaths. I have lived to be punished for my errors, and they have died for them; may Heaven accept the atonement of me and of them; I die in peace, but oh, how gladly I welcome death!"

It would seem that this last effort wasted the whole energies; the expiring frame exhausted itself in one bright flash, and all is darkness.

"She is dead," said the leech.

It was so.

* * * * * * *

The last words of Jane were strictly true. She had lived a life of penance; it seemed to have been imposed upon her; she could not escape by death from the horrors by which she was surrounded, until her allotted course was run.

Those who had been the main cause of her miseries, however, died violent deaths; and many of those who had been friends in prosperity, but enemies in adversity, were punished for their misdeeds.

She had lived to see a London mob collect round the house of Mrs. Blague, and burn and pillage her house, and she herself only escaped death by being left insensible in the streets. She afterwards died in poverty and misery.

The tyrannical Duke of Gloucester, afterwards Richard the Third, died in battle at Bosworth field, a death too mild for his deserts.

Antonio Vassa, the dark and wily conspirator, ceased to be of service to the duke when the latter became king, and his services were no longer required or rewarded by his former patron.

Finding such to be the case, Vassa quitted England; sailed to Spain, where he hoped, among the different kings of that country, to find employment for his talents in mischief-making; but here he failed, his impiety bringing him under the censure of the Inquisition, and he was seized and thrown into the dungeon of that fearful body, where he lay some time, but eventually perished by a most miserable and painful death, thus fully realising the prophecy of the brutal governor of the gaol, Sir Godfrey, whom he poisoned.

THE END.

www.ingramcontent.com/pod-product-compliance
Lightning Source LLC
Chambersburg PA
CBHW080819020726
47501CB00009B/2347

* 9 7 8 1 5 3 5 8 0 6 1 1 4 *